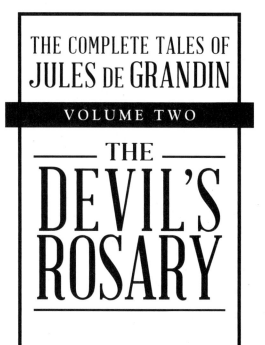

THE COMPLETE TALES OF
JULES DE GRANDIN
VOLUME TWO

— THE —
DEVIL'S ROSARY

SEABURY QUINN

EDITED BY GEORGE A. VANDERBURGH

Night Shade Books
New York

Night Shade books may be purchased in bulk at special discounts for sales promotion, corporate gifts, fund-raising, or educational purposes. Special editions can also be created to specifications. For details, contact the Special Sales Department, Night Shade Books, 307 West 36th Street, 11th Floor, New York, NY 10018 or info@skyhorsepublishing.com.

Night Shade Books® is a registered trademark of Skyhorse Publishing, Inc. ®, a Delaware corporation.

Visit our website at www.nightshadebooks.com.

10 9 8 7 6 5 4 3 2 1

Library of Congress Cataloging-in-Publication Data is available on file.

Print ISBN: 978-1-59780-927-6
Ebook ISBN: 978-1-59780-929-0

Cover illustration by Donato Giancola
Cover design by Claudia Noble

Printed in the United States of America

TABLE OF CONTENTS

^ Cover by Curtis C. Senf
* Cover by Hugh Rankin

THE COMPLETE TALES OF Jules de Grandin is dedicated to the memory of Robert E. Weinberg, who passed away in fall of 2016. Weinberg, who edited the six-volume paperback series of de Grandin stories in the 1970s, also supplied many original issues of *Weird Tales* magazine from his personal collection so that Seabury Quinn's work could be carefully scanned and transcribed digitally. Without his knowledge of the material and his editorial guidance, as well as his passion for Quinn's work over a long period of time (when admirers of the Jules de Grandin stories were often difficult to come by), this series would not have been possible, and we owe him our deepest gratitude and respect.

Introduction

by George A. Vanderburgh and Robert E. Weinberg

WEIRD TALES, THE SELF-DESCRIBED "Unique Magazine," and one of the most influential Golden Age pulp magazines in the first half of the twentieth century, was home to a number of now-well-recognized names, including Robert Bloch, August Derleth, Robert E. Howard, H. P. Lovecraft, Clark Ashton Smith, and Manly Wade Wellman.

But among such stiff competition was another writer, more popular at the time than all of the aforementioned authors, and paid at a higher rate because of it. Over the course of ninety-two stories and a serialized novel, his most endearing character captivated pulp magazine readers for nearly three decades, during which time he received more front cover illustrations accompanying his stories than any of his fellow contributors.

The writer's name was Seabury Quinn, and his character was the French occult detective Jules de Grandin.

Perhaps you've never heard of de Grandin, his indefatigable assistant Dr. Trowbridge, or the fictional town of Harrisonville, New Jersey. Perhaps you've never even heard of Seabury Quinn (or maybe only in passing, as a historical footnote in one of the many essays and reprinted collections of Quinn's now-more-revered contemporaries). Certainly, de Grandin was not the first occult detective—Algernon Blackwood's John Silence, Hodgson's Thomas Carnacki, and Sax Rohmer's Moris Klaw preceded him—nor was he the last, as Wellman's John Thunstone, Margery Lawrence's Miles Pennoyer, and Joseph Payne Brennan's Lucius Leffing all either overlapped with the end of de Grandin's run or followed him. And without doubt de Grandin shares more than a passing resemblance to both Sir Arthur Conan Doyle's Sherlock Holmes (especially with his Dr. Watson-like sidekick) and Agatha Christie's Hercule Poirot.

Indeed, even if you were to seek out a de Grandin story, your options over the years would have been limited. Unlike Lovecraft, Smith, Wellman, Bloch, and other *Weird Tales* contributors, the publication history of the Jules de Grandin tales is spotty at best. In 1966, Arkham House printed roughly 2,000 copies of *The Phantom-Fighter*, a selection of ten early works. In the late 1970s, Popular Library published six paperback volumes of approximately thirty-five assorted tales, but they are now long out of print. In 2001, the specialty press The Battered Silicon Dispatch Box released an oversized, three-volume hardcover set of every de Grandin story (the first time all the stories had been collected), and, while still in production, the set is unavailable to the general trade.

So, given how obscure Quinn and his character might seem today, it's justifiably hard to understand how popular these stories originally were, or how frequently new ones were written. But let the numbers tell the tale: from October 1925 (when the very first de Grandin story was released) to December 1933, a roughly eight-year span, de Grandin stories appeared in an incredible sixty-two of the ninety-six issues that *Weird Tales* published, totaling well-over three-quarters of a million words. Letter after letter to the magazine's editor demanded further adventures from the supernatural detective.

If Quinn loomed large in the mind of pulp readers during the magazine's hey-day, then why has his name fallen on deaf ears since? Aside from the relative unavailability of his work, the truth is that Quinn has been successfully marginalized over the years by many critics, who have often dismissed him as simply a hack writer. The de Grandin stories are routinely criticized as being of little worth, and dismissed as unimportant to the development of weird fiction. A common argument, propped up by suspiciously circular reasoning, concludes that Quinn was not the most popular writer for *Weird Tales*, just the most prolific.

These critics seem troubled that the same audience who read and appreciated the work of Lovecraft, Smith, and Howard could also enjoy the exploits of the French ghostbuster. And while it would be far from the truth to suggest that the literary merits of the de Grandin stories exceed those of some of his contemporaries' tales, Quinn was a much more skillful writer, and the adventures of his occult detective more enjoyable to read, than most critics are willing to acknowledge. In the second half of the twentieth century, as the literary value of some pulp-fiction writers began to be reconsidered, Quinn proved to be the perfect whipping boy for early advocates attempting to destigmatize weird fiction: He was the hack author who churned out formulaic prose for a quick paycheck. Anticipating charges that a literary reassessment of Lovecraft would require reevaluating the entire genre along with him, an arbitrary line was quickly drawn in the sand, and as the standard-bearer of pulp fiction's popularity, the creator of Jules de Grandin found himself on the wrong side of that line.

First and foremost, it must be understood that Quinn wrote to make money, and he was far from the archetypal "starving artist." At the same time that his Jules de Grandin stories were running in *Weird Tales*, he had a similar series of detective stories publishing in *Real Detective Tales*. Quinn was writing two continuing series at once throughout the 1920s, composing approximately twenty-five thousand words a month on a manual typewriter. Maintaining originality under such a grueling schedule would be difficult for any author, and even though the de Grandin stories follow a recognizable formula, Quinn still managed to produce one striking story after another. It should also be noted that the tendency to recycle plots and ideas for different markets was very similar to the writing practices of *Weird Tales*'s other prolific and popular writer, Robert E. Howard, who is often excused for these habits, rather than criticized for them.

Throughout his many adventures, the distinctive French detective changed little. His penchant for amusingly French exclamations was a constant through all ninety-three works, as was his taste for cigars and brandy after (and sometimes before) a hard day's work, and his crime-solving styles and methods remained remarkably consistent. From time to time, some new skill or bit of knowledge was revealed to the reader, but in most other respects the Jules de Grandin of "The Horror on the Links" was the same as the hero of the last story in the series, published twenty-five years later.

> He was a perfect example of the rare French blond type, rather under medium height, but with a military erectness of carriage that made him look several inches taller than he really was. His light-blue eyes were small and exceedingly deep-set, and would have been humorous had it not been for the curiously cold directness of their gaze. With his wide mouth, light mustache waxed at the ends in two perfectly horizontal points, and those twinkling, stock-taking eyes, he reminded me of an alert tomcat.

Thus is de Grandin described by Dr. Trowbridge in the duo's first meeting in 1925. His personal history is dribbled throughout the stories: de Grandin was born and raised in France, attended medical school, became a prominent surgeon, and in the Great War served first as a medical officer, then as a member of the intelligence service. After the war, he traveled the world in the service of French Intelligence. His age is never given, but it's generally assumed that the occult detective is in his early forties.

Samuel Trowbridge, on the other hand, is a typical conservative small-town doctor of the first half of the twentieth century (as described by Quinn, he is a cross between an honest brother of George Bernard Shaw and former Chief Justice of the United States Charles Evans Hughes). Bald and bewhiskered, most—if not all—of his life was spent in the same town. Trowbridge is old-fashioned and somewhat conservative, a member of the Knights Templar, a vestryman in the Episcopal Church, and a staunch Republican.

While the two men are dissimilar in many ways, they are also very much alike. Both are fine doctors and surgeons. Trowbridge might complain from time to time about de Grandin's wild adventures, but he always goes along with them; there is no thought, ever, of leaving de Grandin to fight his battles alone. More than any other trait, though, they are two men with one mission, and perhaps for that reason they remained friends for all of their ninety-three adventures and countless trials.

The majority of Quinn's de Grandin stories take place in or near Harrison-ville, New Jersey, a fictional community that rivals (with its fiends, hauntings, ghouls, werewolves, vampires, voodoo, witchcraft, and zombies) Lovecraft's own Arkham, Massachusetts. For more recent examples of a supernatural-infested community, one need look no further than the modern version of pulp-fiction narratives . . . television. *Buffy the Vampire Slayer*'s Sunnydale, California, and *The Night Strangler*'s Seattle both reflect the structural needs of this type of super-natural narrative.

Early in the series, de Grandin is presented as Trowbridge's temporary house guest, having travelled to the United States to study both medicine and modern police techniques, but Quinn quickly realized that the series was due for a long run and recognized that too much globe-trotting would make the stories unwieldy. A familiar setting would be needed to keep the main focus of each tale on the events themselves. Harrisonville, a medium-sized town outside New York City, was completely imaginary, but served that purpose.

Most of the de Grandin stories feature beautiful girls in peril. Quinn discovered early on that Farnsworth Wright, *Weird Tales*'s editor from 1924 to 1940, believed nude women on the cover sold more copies, so when writing he was careful to always feature a scene that could translate to appropriately salacious artwork. Quinn also realized that his readers wanted adventures with love and romance as central themes, so even his most frightening tales were given happy endings (. . . of a sort).

And yet the de Grandin adventures are set apart from the stories they were published alongside by their often explicit and bloody content. Quinn predated the work of Clive Barker and the splatterpunk writers by approximately fifty years, but, using his medical background, he wrote some truly terrifying horror stories; tales like "The House of Horror" and "The House Where Time Stood Still" feature some of the most hideous descriptions of mutilated humans ever set down on paper. The victims of the mad doctor in "The House of Horror" in particular must rank near the top of the list of medical monstrosities in fiction.

Another element that set Quinn's occult detective apart from others was his pioneering use of modern science in the fight against ancient superstitions.

De Grandin fought vampires, werewolves, and even mummies in his many adventures, but oftentimes relied on the latest technology to save the day. The Frenchman put it best in a conversation with Dr. Trowbridge at the end of "The Blood-Flower":

> "And wasn't there some old legend to the effect that a werewolf could only be killed with a silver bullet?"
>
> "Ah, bah," he replied with a laugh. "What did those old legend-mongers know of the power of modern firearms? . . . When I did shoot that wolfman, my friend, I had something more powerful than superstition in my hand. *Morbleu*, but I did shoot a hole in him large enough for him to have walked through."

Quinn didn't completely abandon the use of holy water, ancient relics, and magical charms to defeat supernatural entities, but he made it clear that de Grandin understood that there was a place for modern technology as well as old folklore when it came to fighting monsters. Nor was de Grandin himself above using violence to fight his enemies. Oftentimes, the French occult investigator served as judge, jury and executioner when dealing with madmen, deranged doctors, and evil masterminds. There was little mercy in his stories for those who used dark forces.

While sex was heavily insinuated but rarely covered explicitly in the pulps, except in the most general of terms, Quinn again was willing to go where few other writers would dare. Sexual slavery, lesbianism, and even incest played roles in his writing over the years, challenging the moral values of the day.

In the end, there's no denying that the de Grandin stories are pulp fiction. Many characters are little more than assorted clichés bundled together. De Grandin is a model hero, a French expert on the occult, and never at a loss when battling the most evil of monsters. Dr. Trowbridge remains the steadfast companion, much in the Dr. Watson tradition, always doubting but inevitably following his friend's advice. Quinn wrote for the masses, and he didn't spend pages describing landscapes when there was always more action unfolding.

The Jules de Grandin stories were written as serial entertainment, with the legitimate expectation that they would not be read back to back. While all of the adventures are good fun, the best way to properly enjoy them is over an extended period of time. Plowing through one story after another will lessen their impact, and greatly cut down on the excitement and fun of reading them. One story a week, which would stretch out this entire five-volume series over two years, might be the perfect amount of time needed to fully enjoy these tales of the occult and the macabre. They might not be great literature, but they don't pretend to be. They're pulp adventures, and even after seventy-five years, the stories read well.

Additionally, though the specific aesthetic values of *Weird Tales* readers were vastly different than those of today's readers, one can see clearly see the continuing allure of these types of supernatural adventures, and the long shadow that they cast over twentieth and early twenty-first century popular culture. Sure, these stories are formulaic, but it is a recipe that continues to be popular to this day. The formula of the occult detective, the protector who stands between us and the monsters of the night, can be seen time and time again in the urban fantasy and paranormal romance categories of commercial fiction, and is prevalent in today's television and movies. Given the ubiquity and contemporary popularity of this type of narrative, it's actually not at all surprising that Seabury Quinn was the most popular contributor to *Weird Tales*.

We are proud to present the first of five volumes reprinting every Jules de Grandin story written by Seabury Quinn. Organized chronologically, as they originally appeared in *Weird Tales* magazine, this is the first time that the collected de Grandin stories have been made available in trade editions.

Each volume has been graced by tremendous artwork from renowned artist Donato Giancola, who has given Quinn's legendary character an irresistible combination of grace, cunning and timelessness. We couldn't have asked for a better way to introduce "the occult Hercule Poirot" to a new generation of readers.

Finally, if Seabury Quinn is watching from above, and closely scrutinizing the shelves of bookstores, he would undoubtedly be pleased as punch, and proud as all get-out, to find his creation, Dr. Jules de Grandin, rising once again in the minds of readers around the world, battling the forces of darkness . . . wherever, whoever, or whatever the nature of their evil might be.

When the Jaws of Darkness Open,
Only Jules de Grandin Stands in Satan's Way!

Robert E. Weinberg
Chicago, Illinois, USA

and

George A. Vanderburgh
Lake Eugenia, Ontario, Canada

23 September 2016

"Loved by Thousands of Readers": The Popularity of Jules de Grandin

by Stefan Dziemianowicz

F ANS OF WEIRD TALES, the groundbreaking pulp fiction magazine that changed the course of modern horror and fantasy fiction in the first half of the twentieth century, regularly debate who was the most popular author published in its pages. Although *Weird Tales* published the work of virtually every weird fiction writer of consequence during that time period—including H. P. Lovecraft, Clark Ashton Smith, Robert E. Howard, Robert Bloch, August Derleth, Ray Bradbury, and Manly Wade Wellman, to name but a few—a compelling case could be made for Seabury Quinn, on the strength of how the magazine's readers regarded his most memorable literary creation, the occult detective Jules de Grandin.

Although less well remembered today than *Weird Tales'* leading luminaries, Quinn racked up honors in the magazine that are mind-boggling even for the era of multi-million-words-per-year pulpsmiths. He published a total of 146 stories in *Weird Tales* over thirty years, an average of more than one story per two issues of the magazine's 279-issue run. Ninety-three of those stories, most of which ran to novella-length, featured Jules de Grandin and his sidekick Dr. Samuel Trowbridge, whose first adventure appeared in the October 1925 issue and whose last appeared in September 1951. That's an average of one Jules de Grandin story per three issues of the magazine. The statistics are even more formidable when you consider that the bulk of the de Grandin stories appeared in *Weird Tales* before 1934. In the years 1926, 1927, 1928, and 1933, Quinn placed seven stories featuring his psychic sleuth in each year's twelve issues. In 1929, he placed nine. In 1930 and 1932 (the year that the sole Jules de Grandin novel, *The Devil's Bride*, was serialized over six consecutive issues) de Grandin made ten appearances apiece. No other author in *Weird Tales* ever came close to duplicating this feat.

Equally impressive is the number of the magazine's covers that the de Grandin stories copped. The second adventure of Jules de Grandin, "The Tenants of Broussac" in the December 1925 issue, was the first to be featured on the cover. Over the next twenty-four years, a Jules de Grandin adventure made the cover an additional thirty-six times—seven of them in the year 1930 alone. And de Grandin stories shared mention on the cover with works by other writers another six times, meaning that nearly half of all of the adventures of Jules de Grandin merited cover honors—yet one more feat that no other *Weird Tales* author could claim.

It's hard to know why any phenomenon catches fire as rapidly as Quinn's tales of Jules de Grandin did in *Weird Tales*, but the author's familiarity to the editor and readers of the magazine up to that point may have played a role. His first fiction sale to *Weird Tales*, the werewolf story "The Phantom Farmhouse," appeared in the October 1923 issue and remained one of the most requested reprint stories for the magazine's duration. Quinn had also contributed a series of thirteen weird crime articles under the series names "Servants of Satan" and "Weird Mysteries," some of whose contents he would later mine for de Grandin's adventures.

Farnsworth Wright, the editor of *Weird Tales* when de Grandin made his debut, appears to have recognized early that Quinn had latched onto a memorable storytelling approach in his fusion of weird fiction and detective fiction. He appended a note to the end of "The Terror on the Links," the first de Grandin story in the October 1925 *Weird Tales*, promising that "further adventures of the little French scientist, de Grandin, will be narrated in 'The Tenants of Broussac,'"—indicating that he had already bought a second story in the series before the magazine's readers had even read the first. He used his editorial paragraphs in the December 1925 issue of the *Weird Tales* letter column, "The Eyrie," to promote the third de Grandin story effusively: "Even Poe never wrote a more gripping tale of terror than Seabury Quinn has penned in 'The Isle of Missing Ships,' which will be printed month after next." And at the end of the fifth de Grandin adventure, "The Dead Hand," published in the May 1926 issue, the magazine posted an ad listing back issues featuring the four preceding de Grandin stories for sale.

The readers responded in kind to Wright's enthusiasm. "The greatest series of stories published in *Weird Tales*, I think, are the Jules de Grandin ones," wrote a reader in the July 1926 "Eyrie." A letter writer in the February 1927 issue concurred: "Jules de Grandin is one of your most interesting and entertaining characters. Sometimes the plots are a little far-fetched, but the story is always told in such style with occasional humor and scientific theories mixed into the mystery, which carry the interest to the last word."

Smart editor that he was, Wright used "The Eyrie" to stoke reader enthusiasm for the magazine and its contributors. In the September 1926 issue, after having asked readers to name their favorite stories published in the magazine to date, he revealed that Quinn led the pack, garnering five of the readers' top-thirty picks. In the February 1927 issue he showed how much he believed that readers valued Quinn's work by offering a signed typescript of the de Grandin tale "The Man Who Cast No Shadow" to "the writer of the most helpful and constructive letter to 'The Eyrie' discussing the stories in this issue." Small wonder, then, that readers were so adulatory in their subsequent praise of Quinn and de Grandin. "Seabury Quinn's stories . . . are without a doubt above all others, and I wish to say that he has the immortal Poe shoved off the map," wrote a reader in April 1927. He was echoed by another letter writer the following month, who wrote that "Jules de Grandin and Seabury Quinn should become synonymous with the immortal Poe."

The fans were not alone in their praise of Jules de Grandin. Quinn's stories also received accolades from colleagues and writers-to-be. Robert E. Howard, the future creator of the sword-and-sorcery legend Conan the Cimmerian, was a *Weird Tales* author for less than a year when he praised the stories in the February 1926 "Eyrie" as "sheer masterpieces," and continued, "The little Frenchman is one of those characters who live in fiction. I look forward with pleasurable anticipation to further meetings with him." Future *Weird Tales* author Henry Kuttner considered Quinn a favorite writer, and over time Quinn and his series were praised by Greye La Spina, Manly Wade Wellman, Ray Bradbury, and other *Weird Tales* stalwarts. It's well known that horror titan H. P. Lovecraft did not think highly of the de Grandin stories, but several of Lovecraft's acolytes praised them in the "Eyrie," among them J. Vernon Shea, Willis Conover, Duane Rimel, and Bernard Austin Dwyer.

Fans of the de Grandin stories were not uncritical. They frequently provided analysis of why de Grandin and his adventures appealed to them. "There is no more inspiring, pleasant, amusing character in fiction than this little French criminologist, always courteous, civil, active, yet with a hard line of viciousness and heartlessness in him," wrote a reader to the April 1928 issue. Another letter-writer in October 1930 gave reasons for the impact of Quinn's tales: "He has a delightfully finished style of writing, most refreshing after the infernal, cut-down, written-to-sell stuff the authors of America have allowed an ignorant public to force on them." Writing in the February 1933 issue, one reader elaborated further on why Quinn's tales of de Grandin hit their mark:

"There never has been one story by him that wasn't dynamic and tense until the last word. Not only does he give a fine narrative, but an extremely plausible explanation also is incorporated in his stories." Other letter writers singled the verisimilitude with which Quinn made esoteric subjects accessible to the layman: "He is meticulously correct without being pedantic and without annoying the lay reader by technical language," wrote a self-proclaimed student of legal medicine in the October 1929 "Eyrie." "Such exactness and the ability to explain medical and legal matters in plain language are far greater assets in an author than most publishers realize."

It's not going too far to suggest that within a few years of his appearance in the magazine, a cult had grown up around Jules de Grandin. Readers smitten by how believable de Grandin seemed as a character wrote to *Weird Tales* asking if he was a person in real life. When more than a few issues of the magazine appeared without a de Grandin story, readers fearful that the series had been discontinued deluged the magazine with letters. "It is a real feat to create a character in fiction so likable, so human, and so fascinating that he immediately makes himself loved by thousands of readers," Wright wrote to allay such concerns in the August 1928 issue, "and this is just what Seabury Quinn has done in creating the temperamental and vivacious Jules de Grandin for your delectation." When de Grandin appeared in only three issues of *Weird Tales* in 1931, Wright had to mollify complaining readers with the explanation that Quinn had been busily writing the novel-length work *The Devil's Bride*, to be serialized in multiple issues of the magazine the following year. Fans even had the audacity to warn Quinn not to write anything *but* de Grandin stories. "Jules de Grandin is just as perfect as he thinks he is (which is saying a lot)," wrote a reader in December 1930. "Tell Seabury Quinn that if he ever writes any other type of story the readers will come en masse and lynch him." Another writer in the July 1935 "Eyrie" was more temperate in explaining why he felt the de Grandin stories outranked Quinn's other fiction: "Seabury Quinn is just another writer when he leaves Harrisonville [the town in which all of de Grandin's adventures took place], but de Grandin puts him at the top of your list."

And yet, as much as readers adored de Grandin and did not want his adventures to end, some were aware of the formulaic quality of many of his adventures and proposed ideas to bring variety to the series. "Can't Seabury Quinn take him and friend Trowbridge out of Harrisonville?" one reader wrote of de Grandin in July 1930. "It would seem that one city is the only spot left where our beloved Jules may spin his webs—and what a demon-infested place to live! Too long has he tarried in a prosaic little city. Let him conquer new worlds. And one suggestion: Just once—in a really, gripping, tragically sad tale I would like to have de Grandin bested—just once. Don't you think it would make him even more human and lovable than he is now?"

Another writer in the February 1931 issue also took issue with de Grandin's invincibility. "Someday, give us a story in which the inimitable Frenchman fails—fails miserably through overlooking some item that he should have known. It might be well, in order that some beautiful girl who usually figures in their adventures may come out of it well and happy, to have Trowbridge discover and correct de Grandin's oversight, thus giving the worthy Trowbridge something to remind de Grandin of in future when the Frenchman gets too cocky."

Whether or not Quinn was receptive to such reader comments, it appears that he did read them. In the May 1929 "Eyrie," a de Grandin fan complained that Quinn's stories "allow the forces of evil almost unlimited modes of self-expression, while restricting the opposite force to use by the hero of such symbols as a holy relic or sprig of some plant, waved under the nose of the particular devil in the case." Quinn responded in the letters section of the July 1929 issue with a sternly worded *two-page* analysis of the last six de Grandin stories published to rebut that reader's claims and concluded, "My traducer has done nothing but make a blanket accusation, without one shred of evidence to support it."

If anyone needed more evidence of the high regard in which *Weird Tales* readers held Quinn's Jules de Grandin stories, the proof was in the reader poll tallies. "The Eyrie" had been in existence in *Weird Tales* since its first issue was published in March 1923, but it wasn't until the end of 1925 that the magazine began encouraging readers to write in and name their favorite story. That this editorial policy coincides with readers becoming openly vocal in their support of the de Grandin stories in "The Eyrie" seems far from coincidental. The reader poll tallies were not exactly scientific. Wright usually reported the top three stories chosen by the readers, sometimes only the number-one pick, and he occasionally diplomatically reported that two, three, or even four stories were in a dead heat for first place. Regardless, more that fifty Jules de Grandin stories made the top three reader picks, and more than thirty placed or tied for first. In the March 1929 issue of *Weird Tales*, the readers went one better. Quinn was one of several top writers for the magazine whose stories the readers urged the magazine to publish in a hardcover collection. They went to so far as to propose a title for the book: *The Phantom Fighter*. Thirty-seven years later, Arkham House, a publisher who regularly mined *Weird Tales* for the contents of its books, brought out the first collection of Jules de Grandin stories under that very title.

In retrospect, Seabury Quinn's tales of Jules de Grandin played a vital role in the development of weird fiction, if largely through their relationship with *Weird Tales* and its readers. The stories were not the best written in the magazine, but they delivered the requisite thrills and chills that readers looked for in *Weird Tales* stories and in the pulps in general. More importantly, perhaps, they appeared in the magazine with a satisfying regularity that made readers look forward to buying and reading the next issue. When the first Jules de Grandin story was published in 1925, *Weird Tales* was a magazine still feeling its way toward the greatness it would eventually come to know. Only the year before it had been rescued from financial insolvency after a disastrous first year of publication. Farnsworth Wright had been in its editor's seat for just twelve months when Jules de Grandin made his debut. Reader response to the de Grandin stories surely seemed a gift to him and the magazine. Exploiting (in the best sense) Quinn's prolificacy, Wright used the popularity of the de Grandin tales to forge a community of loyal readers through "The Eyrie" and keep them engaged with the magazine.

By the 1930s, when de Grandin's presence in the pages of *Weird Tales* began to wane, the magazine had by then mustered the lineup of writers that we associate with its golden age. Quinn was among them, but only infrequently with tales of Jules de Grandin: he had discovered that his non–de Grandin weird tales had begun to frequently rank as high in the reader polls as his tales of the intrepid Frenchman, and the freedom to write outside of the series must have felt liberating. We can only speculate what *Weird Tales'* prospects might have been had the Jules de Grandin series not struck a chord with readers when they did. This five-volume set collecting the complete adventures of Jules de Grandin gives contemporary readers a chance to enjoy stories that were instrumental in helping *Weird Tales* to become the magazine it is revered as today, and to lay the foundations of modern weird fiction.

THE
DEVIL'S
ROSARY

The Black Master

J ULES DE GRANDIN POURED a thimbleful of Boulogne cognac into a wide-mouthed glass and passed the goblet back and forth beneath his nose with a waving motion, inhaling the rich, fruity fumes from the amber fluid. "*Eh bien*, young *Monsieur*," he informed our visitor as he drained the liqueur with a slow, appreciative swallow and set the empty glass on the tabouret with a scarcely suppressed smack of his lips, "this is of interest. Pirate treasure, you do say? *Parbleu—c'est presque irrésistible.* Tell us more, if you please."

Eric Balderson looked from the little Frenchman to me with a half-diffi-dent, deprecating smile. "There really isn't much to tell," he confessed, "and I'm not at all sure I'm not the victim of a pipe-dream, after all. You knew Father pretty well, didn't you, Dr. Trowbridge?" he turned appealingly to me.

"Yes," I answered, "he and I were at Amherst together. He was an extremely levelheaded sort of chap, too, not at all given to daydreaming, and—"

"That's what I'm pinning my faith on," Eric broke in. "Coming from any-one but Dad the story would be too utterly fantastic to—"

"*Mordieu*, yes, *Monsieur*," de Grandin interrupted testily, "we do concede your so excellent *père* was the ultimate word in discretion and sound judgment, but will you, for the love of kindly heaven, have the goodness to tell us all and let us judge for ourselves the value of the communication of which you speak?"

Eric regarded him with the slow grin he inherited from his father, then continued, quite unruffled, "Dad wasn't exactly what you'd call credulous, but he seemed to put considerable stock in the story, judging from his diary. Here it is." From the inside pocket of his dinner-coat he produced a small book bound in red leather and handed it to me. "Read the passages I've marked, will you please, Doctor," he asked. "I'm afraid I'd fill up if I tried to read Dad's writing aloud. He—he hasn't been gone very long, you know."

Adjusting my pince-nez, I hitched a bit nearer the library lamp and looked over the age-yellowed sheets covered with the fine, angular script of my old classmate:

8 Nov. 1898—Old Robinson is going fast. When I called to see him at the Seaman's Snug Harbor this morning I found him considerably weaker than he had been yesterday, though still in full possession of his faculties. There's nothing specifically wrong with the old fellow, save as any worn-out bit of machinery in time gets ready for the scrap-heap. He will probably go out sometime during the night, quite likely in his sleep, a victim of having lived too long.

"Doctor," he said to me when I went into his room this morning, "ye've been mighty good to me, a poor, worn-out old hulk with never a cent to repay all yer kindness; but I've that here which will make yer everlastin' fortune, providin' ye're brave enough to tackle it."

"That's very kind of you, John," I answered, but the old fellow was deadly serious.

"'Tis no laughin' matter, Doctor," he returned as he saw me smile. "'Tis th' truth an' nothin' else I'm tellin' ye—I'd 'a' had a go at it meself if it warn't that seafarin' men don't hold with disturbin' th' bones o' th' dead. But you, bein' a landsman, an' a doctor to boot, would most likely succeed where others have failed. I had it from my gran'ther, sir, an' he was an old man an' I but a lad when he gave it me, so ye can see 'tis no new thing I'm passin' on. Where he got it I don't know, but he guarded it like his eyes an' would never talk about it, not even to me after he'd give it to me."

With that he asked me to go to his ditty-box and take out a packet done up in oiled silk, which he insisted I take as partial compensation for all I'd done for him.

I tried to tell him the home paid my fee regularly, and that he was beholden to me for nothing, but he would not have it; so, to quiet the old man, I took the plan for my "everlastin' fortune" before I left.

9 Nov. 1898—Old John died last night, as I'd predicted, and probably went with the satisfied feeling that he had made a potential millionaire of the struggling country practitioner who tended him in his last illness. I must look into the mysterious packet by which he set such store. Probably it's a chart for locating some long-sunk pirate ship or unburying the loot of Captain Kidd, Blackbeard, or some other old sea-robber. Sailormen a generation ago were full of such yarns, and recounted them so often they actually came to believe them.

10 Nov. '98—I was right in my surmise concerning old John's legacy, though it's rather different from the usual run of buried-treasure maps.

Some day, when I've nothing else to do, I may go down to the old church in Harrisonville and actually have a try at the thing. It would be odd if poor Eric Balderson, struggling country practitioner, became a wealthy man overnight. What would I do first? Would a sealskin dolman for Astrid or a new side-bar buggy for me be the first purchase I'd make? I wonder.

"H'm," I remarked as I put down the book. "And this old seaman's legacy, as your father called it—"

"Is here," Eric interrupted, handing me a square of ancient, crackling vellum on which a message of some kind had been laboriously scratched. The edges of the parchment were badly frayed, as though with much handling, though the indentures might have been the result of hasty tearing in the olden days. At any rate, it was a tattered and thoroughly decrepit sheet from which I read:

in ye name of ye most Holie Trinitie

I, Richard Thompson, being a right synfull manne and near unto mine ende do give greeting and warning to whoso shall rede herefrom. Ye booty which my master whose name no manne did rightly know, but who was surnamed by some ye Black Master and by somme Blackface ye Merciless, lyes hydden in divers places, but ye creame thereof is laid away in ye churchyard of St. Davides hard by Harrisons village. There, by daye and by nite do ye dedde stand guard over it for ye Master sealed its hydinge place both with cement and with a curse which he fondlie sware should be on them & on their children who violated ye sepulchre without his sanction. Yet if any there be who dare defye ye curse (as I should not) of hym who had neither pitie ne mercie ne lovingkindness at all, let hm go unto ye burrieing ground at dedde of nite at ye season of dies natalis invicti & obey ye direction. Further hint I dast not gyvve, for fear of him who lurks beyant ye portales of lyffe to hold to account such of hys servants as preceded him not in dethe. And of your charity, ye who rede this, I do charge and conjure ye that ye make goode and pieous use of ye Master hys treasure and that ye expend such part of ye same as may be fyttinge for masses for ye good estate of Richard Thompson, a synnfull man dieing in terror of his many iniquities & of ye tongueless one who waites himme across ye borderline

When ye star shines from ye tree
Be it as a sign to ye.
Draw ye fourteen cubit line
To ye entrance unto lyfe
Whence across ye graveyard sod
See spotte cursed by man & God.

"It looks like a lot of childish nonsense to me," I remarked with an impatient shrug as I tossed the parchment to de Grandin. "Those old fellows who had keys to buried treasure were everlastingly taking such care to obscure their meaning in a lot of senseless balderdash that no one can tell when they're serious and when they're perpetrating a hoax. If—"

"*Cordieu*," the little Frenchman whispered softly, examining the sheet of frayed vellum with wide eyes, holding it up to the lamplight, then crackling it softly between his fingers. "Is it possible? But yes, it must be—Jules de Grandin could not be mistaken."

"Whatever are you maundering about?" I interrupted impatiently. "The way you're looking at that parchment anyone would think—"

"Whatever anyone would think, he would be far from the truth," de Grandin cut in, regarding us with the fixed, unwinking stare which meant deadly seriousness. "If this plat be a *mauvaise plaisanterie*—how do you call it? the practical joke?—it is a very grim one indeed, for the parchment on which it is engraved is human skin."

"What?" cried Eric and I in chorus.

"Nothing less," de Grandin responded. "Me, I have seen such parchments in the Paris *musée*; I have handled them, I have touched them. I could not be mistaken. Such things were done in the olden days, my friends. I think, perhaps, we should do well to investigate this business. Men do not set down confessions of a sinful life and implore the possible finders of treasure to buy masses for their souls on human hide when they would indulge in pleasantries. No, it is not so."

"But—" I began, when he shut me off with a quick gesture.

"In the churchyard of Saint David's this repentant Monsieur Richard Thompson did say. May I inquire, Friend Trowbridge, if there be such a church in the neighborhood? Assuredly there was once, for does he not say, 'hard by Harrison's village,' and might that not have been the early designation of your present city of Harrisonville?"

"U'm—why, yes, by George!" I exclaimed. "You're right, de Grandin. There *is* a Saint David's church down in the old East End—a Colonial parish, too; one of the first English churches built after the British took Jersey over from the Dutch. Harrisonville was something of a seaport in those days, and there was a bad reef a few miles offshore. I've been told the church was built and endowed with the funds derived from salvaging cargo from ships stranded on the reef. The parish dates back to 1670 or '71, I believe."

"H'm-m." De Grandin extracted a vile-smelling French cigarette from his black-leather case, applied a match to it and puffed furiously a moment, then slowly expelled a twin column of smoke from his nostrils. "And '*dies natalis invicti*' our so scholarly Monsieur Richard wrote as the time for visiting this churchyard. What can that be but the time of Bonhomme Noël—the Christmas season? *Parbleu*, my friends, I think, perhaps, we shall go to that churchyard and acquire a most excellent Christmas gift for ourselves. Tonight is December 22, tomorrow should he near enough for us to begin our quest. We meet here tomorrow night to try our fortune, *n'est-ce-pas?*"

Crazy and harebrained as the scheme sounded, both Eric and I were carried away by the little Frenchman's enthusiasm, and nodded vigorous agreement.

"*Bon*," he cried, "*très bon!* One more drink, my friends, then let us go dream of the golden wheat awaiting our harvesting."

"But see here, Dr. de Grandin," Eric Balderson remarked, "since you've told us what this message is written on this business looks more serious to me. Suppose there's really something in this curse old Thompson speaks of? We won't be doing ourselves much service by ignoring it, will we?"

"Ah bah," returned the little Frenchman above the rim of his half-drained glass. "A curse, you do say. Young *Monsieur*, I can plainly perceive you do not know Jules de Grandin, A worm-eaten fig for the curse! Me, I can curse as hard and as violently as any villainous old sea-robber who ever sank a ship or slit a throat!"

2

THE BLEAK DECEMBER WIND which had been moaning like a disconsolate banshee all afternoon had brought its threatened freight of snow about nine o'clock and the factory- and warehouse-lined thoroughfares of the unfashionable part of town where old Saint David's church stood were noiseless and white as ghost-streets in a dead city when de Grandin, Eric Balderson and I approached the churchyard pentice shortly before twelve the following night. The hurrying flakes had stopped before we left the house, however, and through the wind-driven pluvial clouds the chalk-white winter moon and a few stars shone frostily.

"*Cordieu*, I might have guessed as much!" de Grandin exclaimed in exasperation as he tried the iron grille stopping the entrance to the church's little close and turned away disgustedly. "Locked—locked fast as the gates of hell against escaping sinners, my friends," he announced. "It would seem we must swarm over the walls, and—"

"And get a charge of buckshot in us when the caretaker sees us," Eric interrupted gloomily.

"No fear, *mon vieux*," de Grandin returned with a quick grin. "Me, I have not been idle this day. I did come here to reconnoiter during the afternoon—*morbleu*, but I did affect the devotion at evensong before I stepped outside to survey the terrain!—and many things I discovered. First, this church stands like a lonely outpost in a land whence the expeditionary force has been withdrawn. Around here are not half a dozen families enrolled on the parish register. Were it not for churchly pride and the fact that heavy endowments of the past make it possible to support this chapel as a mission, it would have been closed long ago. There is no resident sexton, no *curé* in residence here. Both functionaries dwell some little distance away. As for the *cimetière*, no interments have been permitted here for close on fifty years. The danger of grave-robbers is *nil*, so also is the danger of our finding a night watchman. Come, let us mount the wall."

It was no difficult feat scaling the six-foot stone barricade surrounding Saint David's little God's Acre, and we were standing ankle-deep in fresh snow within five minutes, bending our heads against the howling midwinter blast and casting about for some starting-point in our search.

Sinking to his knees in the lee of an ancient holly tree, de Grandin drew out his pocket electric torch and scanned the copy of Richard Thompson's cryptic directions. "H'm," he murmured as he flattened the paper against the bare ground beneath the tree's outspread, spiked branches, "what is it the estimable Monsieur Thompson says in his so execrable poetry? 'When the star shines from the tree.' Name of three hundred demented green monkeys, when *does* a star shine from a tree, Friend Trowbridge?"

"Maybe he meant a Christmas tree," I responded with a weak attempt at flippancy, but the little Frenchman was quick to adopt the suggestion.

"*Morbleu*, I think you have right, good friend," he agreed with a nod. "And what tree is more in the spirit of Noël than the holly? Come, let us take inventory."

Slowly, bending his head against the wind, yet thrusting it upward from the fur collar of his greatcoat like a turtle emerging from its shell every few seconds, he proceeded to circle every holly and yew tree in the grounds, observing them first from one angle, then another, going so near that he stood within their shadows, then retreating till he could observe them without withdrawing his chin from his collar. At last:

"*Nom d'un singe vert*, but I think I have it!" he ejaculated. "Come and see."

Joining him, we gazed upward along the line indicated by his pointing finger. There, like a glass ornament attached to the tip of a Yuletide tree, shone and winked a big, bright star—the planet Saturn.

"So far, thus good," he murmured, again consulting the cryptogram. "'Be it as a sign to ye,' says our good Friend Thompson. *Très bien, Monsieur*, we have heeded the sign—now for the summons.

"'Draw ye fourteen cubit line'—about two hundred and fifty-two of your English inches, or, let us say, twenty-one feet," he muttered. "Twenty-one feet, yes; but which way? 'To the entrance unto life.' U'm, what *is* the entrance to life in a burying-ground, *par le mort d'un chat noir*? A-a-ah? Perhaps yes; why not?"

As he glanced quickly this way and that, his eyes had come to rest on a slender stone column, perhaps three feet high, topped by a wide, bowl-like capital. Running through the snow to the monument, de Grandin brushed the clinging flakes from the bowl's lip and played the beam of his flashlight on it. "You see?" he asked with a delighted laugh.

Running in a circle about the weathered stone was the inscription:

SANCTVS, SANCTVS, SANCTVS
Vnleff a man be borne again of VVater &
Ye Holy Spirit he fhall in nowife . . .

The rest of the lettering had withered away with the alternate frosts and thaws of more than two hundred winters.

"Why, of course!" I exclaimed with a nod of understanding. "A baptismal font—'the entrance unto life,' as old Thompson called it."

"My friend," de Grandin assured me solemnly, "there are times when I do not entirely despair of your intellect, but where shall we find that much-cursed spot of which *Monsieur*—"

"Look, look, for God's sake!" croaked Eric Balderson, grasping my arm in his powerful hand till I winced under the pressure. "Look there, Dr. Trowbridge—*it's opening!*"

The moon, momentarily released from a fetter of drifting clouds, shot her silver shafts down to the clutter of century-old monuments in the churchyard, and, twenty feet or so from us, stood one of the old-fashioned boxlike grave-markers of Colonial times. As we looked at it in compliance with Eric's panic-stricken announcement, I saw the stone panel nearest us slowly slide back like a shutter withdrawn by an invisible hand.

"Sa-ha, it lies this way, then?" de Grandin whispered fiercely, his small, white teeth fairly chattering with eagerness. "Let us go, my friends; let us investigate. Name of a cockroach, but this is the *bonne aventure!*

"No, my friend," he pushed me gently back as I started toward the tomb, "Jules de Grandin goes first."

It was not without a shudder of repulsion that I followed my little friend through the narrow opening in the tomb, for the air inside the little enclosure was black and terrible, and solid-looking as if formed of ebony. But there was no chance to draw back, for close behind me, almost as excited as the Frenchman, pressed Eric Balderson.

The boxlike tomb was but the bulkhead above a narrow flight of stone stairs, steep-pitched as a ship's accommodation ladder, I discovered almost as soon as I had crawled inside, and with some maneuvering I managed to turn about in the narrow space and back down the steps.

Twenty steps, each about eight inches high, I counted as I descended to find myself in a narrow, stone-lined passageway which afforded barely room for us to walk in single file.

Marching ahead as imperturbably as though strolling down one of his native boulevards, de Grandin led the way, flashing the ray from his lantern along the smoothly paved passage. At length:

"We are arrived, I think," he announced. "And, unless I am mistaken, as I hope I am, we are in a *cul-de-sac*, as well."

The passage had terminated abruptly in a blank wall, and there was nothing for us to do, apparently, but edge around and retrace our steps. I was about to suggest this when a joyous exclamation from de Grandin halted me.

Feeling along the sandstone barrier, he had sunk to his knees, prodded the stone tentatively in several places, finally come upon a slight indentation, grooved as though to furnish hand-hold.

"Do you hold the light, Friend Trowbridge," he directed as he thrust the ferrule of his ebony cane into the depression and gave a mighty tug. "Ah, *parbleu*, it comes; it comes—we are not yet at the end of our tape!"

Resisting only a moment, the apparently solid block of stone had slipped back almost as easily as a well-oiled trap-door, disclosing an opening some three and a half feet high by twenty inches wide.

"The light, my friend—shine the light past me while I investigate," de Grandin breathed, stooping almost double to pass through the low doorway.

I bent as far forward as I could and shot the beam of light over his head, and lucky for him it was I did so, for even as his head disappeared through the cleft he jerked back with an exclamation of dismay. "Ha, villain, would you so?" he rasped, snatching the keen blade from his sword cane and thrusting it through the aperture with quick, venomous stabs.

At length, having satisfied himself that no further resistance offered beyond the wall, he sank once more to his bended knees and slipped through the hole. A moment later I heard him calling cheerfully, and, stooping quickly, I followed him, with Eric Balderson, making heavy work at jamming his great bulk through the narrow opening, bringing up the rear. De Grandin pointed dramatically at the wall we had just penetrated.

"*Morbleu*, he was thorough, that one," he remarked, inviting our attention to an odd-looking contrivance decorating the stones.

It was a heavy ship's boom, some six feet long, pivoted just above its center to the wall so that it swung back and forth like a gigantic pendulum. Its upper end was secured to a strand of heavily tarred cable, and fitted with a deep notch, while to its lower extremity was securely bolted what appeared to be the fluke from an old-fashioned ship's anchor, weighing at least three stone and filed and ground to an axlike edge. An instant's inspection of the apparatus showed us its simplicity and diabolical ingenuity. It was secured by a brace of wooden triggers in a horizontal position above the little doorway through which we had entered, and the raising of the stone-panel acted to withdraw the keepers till only a fraction of their tips supported the boom. Pressure on the sill of the doorway completed the operation, and sprung the triggers entirely back, permitting the timber with its sharpened iron tip to swing downward across the opening like a gigantic headsman's ax, its knife-sharp blade sweeping an arc across the doorway's top where the head of anyone entering was bound to be. But for the warning furnished by the beam of light preceding him, and the slowness of the machine's operation after a century or more of inactivity, de Grandin would have been as cleanly decapitated by the descending blade as a convict lashed to the cradle of a guillotine.

"But what makes the thing work?" I asked curiously. "I should think that whoever set it in place would have been obliged to spring it when he made his exit. I can't see—"

"S-sst!" the Frenchman cut me off sharply, pointing to the deadly engine.

Distinctly, as we listened, came the sound of tarred hawsers straining over pulley-wheels, and the iron-shod beam began to rise slowly, once more assuming a horizontal position.

I could feel the short hairs at the back of my neck rising in company with the boom as I watched the infernal spectacle, but de Grandin, ever fearless, always curious, wasted no time in speculation. Advancing to the wall, he laid his hand upon the cable, tugging with might and main, but without visible effect on the gradually rising spar. Giving over his effort, he laid his ear to the stones, listened intently a moment, then turned to us with one of his quick, elfish smiles. "He was clever, as well as wicked, the old villain who invented this," he informed us. "Behold, beyond this wall is some sort of a mechanism worked by running water, my friends. When the trigger retaining this death-dealer is released, water is also undoubtlessly permitted to run from a cask or tank attached to the other end of this rope. When the knife-ax has descended and made the unwelcome visitor shorter by a head, the flowing water once more fills the tank, hoists the ax again to its original position, and *pouf!* he are ready to behead the next uninvited guest who arrives. It are clever, yes. I much regret that we have not the time to investigate the mechanism, for I am convinced something similar opens the door through which we entered—perhaps once each year at the season of the ancient Saturnalia—but we did come here to investigate something entirely quite different, eh, Friend Balderson?"

Recalled to our original purpose, we looked about the chamber. It was almost cubical in shape, perhaps sixteen feet long by as many wide, and slightly less in height. Save the devilish engine of destruction at the entrance, the only other fixture was a low coffin-like block of stone against the farther wall.

Examining this, we found it fitted with hand-grips at the sides, and two or three tugs at these heaved the monolith up on end, disclosing a breast-high, narrow doorway into a second chamber, somewhat smaller than the first, and reached by a flight of some five or six stone steps.

Quickly descending these, we found ourselves staring at a long stone sarcophagus, bare of all inscription and ornament, save the grisly emblem of the "Jolly Roger," or piratical skull and thigh-bones, graven on the lid where ordinarily the name-plate would have rested, and a stick of dry, double-forked wood, something like a capital X in shape, which lay transversely across the pirate emblem.

"Ah, what have we here?" inquired de Grandin coolly, approaching the coffin and prying at its lid with his cane-sword.

To my surprise, the top came away with little or no effort on our part, and we stared in fascination at the unfleshed skeleton of a short, thick-set man with enormously long arms and remarkably short, bandy legs.

"Queer," I muttered, gazing at the relic of mortality. "You'd have thought anyone who went to such trouble about his tomb and its safeguards would have been buried in almost regal raiment, yet this fellow seems to have been laid away naked as the day he was born. This coffin has been almost airtight for goodness knows how many years, and there ought to be some evidence of cerements left, even if the flesh has moldered away."

De Grandin's little blue eyes were shining with a sardonic light and his small, even teeth were bared beneath the line of his miniature golden mustache as he regarded me. "Naked, unclothed, without fitting cerements, do you say, Friend Trowbridge?" he asked. Prodding with his sword blade between the skeleton's ribs a moment, he thrust the flashlight into my grip with an impatient gesture and put both hands elbow-deep into the charnel box, rummaging and stirring about in the mass of nondescript material on which the skeleton was couched. "What say you to this, and these—and these?" he demanded.

My eyes fairly started from my face as the electric torch ray fell on the things which rippled and flashed and sparkled between the little Frenchman's white fingers. There were chains of gold encrusted with rubies and diamonds and greenly glowing emeralds; there were crosses set with amethyst and garnet which any mitered prince of the church might have been proud to wear; there were ear- and finger-rings with brilliant settings in such profusion that I could not count them, while about the sides of the coffin were piled great stacks of broad gold pieces minted with the effigy of his most Catholic Majesty of Spain, and little hillocks of unset gems which sparkled and scintillated dazzlingly.

"Regal raiment did you say, Friend Trowbridge?" de Grandin cried, his breath coming fast as he viewed the jewels with ecstasy. "*Cordieu*, where in all the world is there a monarch who takes his last repose on such a royal bed as this?"

"It—it's real!" Balderson breathed unbelievingly. "It wasn't a pipe-dream, after all, then. We're rich, men—*rich!* Oh, Marian, if it only weren't too late!"

De Grandin matter-of-factly scooped up a double handful of unset gems and deposited them in his overcoat pocket. "What use has this old *drôle* for all this wealth?" he demanded. "*Mordieu*, we shall find better use for it than bolstering up dead men's bones! Come, my friends, bear a hand with the treasure; it is high time we were leaving this—Trowbridge, my friend, watch the light!"

Even as he spoke I felt the flashlight slipping from my fingers, for something invisible had struck me a numbing blow across the knuckles. The little lantern fell with a faint musical tinkle into the stone coffin beside the grinning skull and we heard the soft plop as its airless bulb exploded at contact with some article of antique jewelry.

"Matches—strike a light, someone, *pour l'amour de Dieu!*" de Grandin almost shrieked. "It is *nécessaire* that we have light to escape from this so abominable place without having our heads decapitated!"

I felt for my own flashlight, but even as I did so there was a faint hissing sound, the sputter of a safety match against its box, and—the breath of a glowing furnace seemed suddenly to sweep the room as the heavy, oppressive air was filled with dancing sheets of many-colored flames and a furious detonation shook the place. As though seized in some giant fist, I felt myself lifted bodily from the floor and hurled with devastating force against the wall, from which I rebounded and fell forward senseless on the stone-paved floor.

"Trowbridge—Trowbridge, good, kind friend, tell us that you survive!" I heard de Grandin's tremulous voice calling from what seemed a mile or more away as I felt the fiery trickle of brandy between my teeth.

"Eh? Oh, I'm all right—I guess," I replied as I sat up and forced the little Frenchman's hip-flask from my lips. "What in the world happened? Was it—"

"*Morbleu*," laughed my friend, his spirits already recovered, "I thought old Bare-bones in the coffin yonder had returned from hell and brought his everlasting fires with him. We, my friends, are three great fools, but Jules de Grandin is the greatest. When first I entered this altogether detestable tomb, I thought I smelled the faint odor of escaping illuminating-gas, but so great was my curiosity before we forced the coffin, and so monstrous my cupidity afterward, that I dismissed the matter from my mind. Assuredly there passes close by here some main of the city's gas pipes, and there is a so small leak in one of them. The vapor has penetrated the graveyard earth in small quantities and come into this underground chamber. Not strong enough to overpower us, it was none the less in sufficient concentration to explode with one great *boom* when Friend Balderson struck his match. Fortunately for us, the doors behind are open, thus providing expansion chambers for the exploding gas. Otherwise we should have been annihilated altogether entirely.

"Come, the gas has blown away with its own force and we have found Friend Trowbridge's flashlight. *Mordieu*, my ten fingers do itch most infernally to be at the pleasant task of counting this ill-gotten wealth!"

SCRAMBLING OVER THE CEMETERY wall was no light task, since each of us had filled his pockets with Spanish gold and jewels until he scaled almost twice his former weight, and it was necessary for Balderson and de Grandin to boost me to the wall crest, then for de Grandin to push from below while I lent a hand from above to help Balderson up, and finally for the pair of us to drag the little Frenchman up after us.

"Lucky for us the wind has risen and the snow recommenced," de Grandin congratulated as we made our way down the deserted street, walking with a rolling gait, like heavy-laden ships in a high sea; "within an hour the snow inside the cemetery will be so drifted that none will know we visited there tonight. Let us hail a taxi, *mes amis*; I grow weary bearing this great weight of wealth about."

3

"NAME OF A SMALL green rooster," Jules de Grandin exclaimed delightedly, his little blue eyes shining with elation in the light of the library lamp, "we are rich, my friends, rich beyond the wildest dreams of Monte Cristo! Me, I shall have a Parisian *appartement* which shall be the never-ending wonder of all beholders; a villa on the Riviera; a ducal palace in Venice—no less!—and—*grand Dieu*, what is that?"

Above the wailing of the storm-wind, half obliterated by the keening blasts, there came to us from the street outside the scream of a woman in mortal terror: "Help—help—ah, help!" the last desperate appeal so thin and high with panic and horror that we could scarce distinguish it from the skirling of the gale.

"Hold fast—courage—we come! we come!" de Grandin shouted, as he burst through the front door, cleared the snow-swept porch with a single bound and raced hatless into the white-swathed street. "Where are you Madame?" he cried, pausing at the curb and looking expectantly up and down the deserted highway. "Call out, we are here!" For another moment he searched the desolate street with his gaze; then, "Courage!" he cried, vaulting a knee-high drift and rushing toward a dark, huddled object lying in the shifting snow a hundred feet or so away.

Balderson and I hurried after him but he had already raised the woman's lolling head in the crook of his elbow and was preparing to administer stimulant from his ever-ready flask when we arrived.

She was a young girl, somewhere between seventeen and twenty to judge by her face, neither pretty nor ill-favored, but with the clean, clear complexion of a well-brought-up daughter of lower middle-class people. About her flimsy party dress was draped a cloth coat, wholly inadequate to the chill of the night, trimmed with a collar of nondescript fur, and the hat which was pushed back from her blond bobbed hair was the sort to be bought for a few dollars at any department store.

De Grandin bent above her with all the deference he would have shown a duchess in distress. "What was it, *Mademoiselle?*" he asked solicitously. "You did call for assistance—did you fall in the snow? Yes?"

The girl looked at him from big, terrified eyes, swallowed once convulsively, then murmured in a low, hoarse whisper: "His eyes! Those terrible eyes—they—ah, Jesus! Mercy!" In the midst of a pitiful attempt to sign herself with the cross, her body stiffened suddenly, then went limp in the Frenchman's arms; her slender bosom fluttered once, twice, then flattened, and her lower jaw fell slowly downward, as if in a half-stifled yawn. Balderson, layman that he was, mistook her senseless, imbecile expression for a bit of ill-timed horseplay and gave a half-amused titter. De Grandin and I, inured to vigils beside the moribund, recognized the trade mark stamped in those glazed, expressionless eyes and that drooping chin.

"*Ad te, Domine*—" the Frenchman bent his blond head as he muttered the prayer. Then: "Come, my friends, help me take her up. We must bear her in from the storm, then notify the police. Ha, something foul has been abroad this night; it were better for him if he runs not crosswise of the path of Jules de Grandin, *pardieu!*"

Breakfast was a belated meal next morning, for it was well after three o'clock before the coroner's men and police officers had finished their interrogations and taken the poor, maimed clay that once was gay little Kathleen Burke to the morgue for official investigation. The shadow of the tragedy sat with us at table, and none cared to discuss future joyous plans for squandering the pirate treasure. It was de Grandin who waked us from our gloomy reveries with a half-shouted exclamation.

"*Nom d'un nom*—another!" he cried. "Trowbridge, Balderson, my friends, give attention! Hear, this item from *le journal*, if you please:

TWO GIRLS VICTIMS OF FIEND

Early this morning the police were informed of two inexplicable murders in the streets of Harrisonville. Kathleen Burke, 19, of 17 Bonham Place, was returning from a party at a friend's house when Drs. Trowbridge and de Grandin, of 993 Susquehanna Avenue, heard her screaming for help and rushed out to offer assistance, accompanied by Eric Balderson, their house guest. They found the girl in a dying condition, unable to give any account of her assailant further than to mumble something concerning his eyes. The body was taken to the city morgue for an inquest which will be held today.

Rachel Müller, 26, of 445 Essex Avenue, a nurse in the operating-room at Mercy Hospital, was returning to her home after a term of special night duty a few minutes before 3 A.M. when she was set upon from behind by a masked man wearing a fantastic costume which she described to the police as consisting of a tight-fitting coat, loose, baggy pantaloons and high boots, turned down at the top, and a stocking-cap on his head. He seized her by the throat, and she managed to fight free, whereupon he attacked her with a dirk-knife, inflicting several wounds of a serious nature. Officer Timothy Dugan heard the woman's outcries and hurried to her rescue, finding her bleeding profusely and in a serious condition. He administered first aid and rang for an ambulance in which she was removed to Casualty Hospital, where she was unable to give a more detailed description of her attacker. She died at 4:18 this morning. Her assailant escaped. The police, however, claim to be in possession of several reliable clues and an arrest is promised in the near future.

"What say you to that, my friends?" the Frenchman demanded. "Me, I should say we would better consult—"

"Sergeant Costello, sor," Nora McGinnis, my household factotum, announced from the breakfast room door as she stood aside to permit the burly, red-haired Irishman to enter.

"Ah, *bonjour, Sergent*," de Grandin greeted with a quick smile. "Is it that you come to lay the clues to the assassin of those two unfortunate young women before us?"

Detective Sergeant Jeremiah Costello's broad, red face went a shade more rubescent as he regarded the diminutive Frenchman with an affectionate grin. "Sure, Dr. de Grandin, sor, 'tis yerself as knows when we're handin' out th' straight goods an' when we're peddlin' th' bull," he retorted. "Ain't it th' same wid th' johnny darmes in Paree? Sure, it is. Be gorry, if we had so much as one little clue, rayliable or not, we'd be huggin' an' kissin' ourselves all over th' place, so we would. 'Tis fer that very reason, an' no other, I'm after troublin' ye at yer breakfast this marnin'. Wud ye be willin' to listen to th' case, as far as we know it, I dunno?"

"Say on, *mon vieux*," de Grandin returned, his eyes shining and sparkling with the joy of the born manhunter in the chase. "Tell us all that is in your mind, and we may together arrive at some solution. Meantime, may I not make free of Dr. Trowbridge's hospitality to the extent of offering you a cup of coffee?"

"Thanks, sor, don't mind if I do," the detective accepted, "it's mortal cold outside today.

"Now to begin wid, we don't know no more about who committed these here murthers, or, why he done it, than a hog knows about a holiday, an' that's a fact. They tell me at headquarters that th' little Burke gur-rl (God rest her soul!) said something about th' felly's eyes to you before she died, an' Nurse Müller raved about th' same thing, though she was able to give some little bit of dayscription of him, as well. But who th' divil would be goin' around th' streets o' nights murtherin' pore, definseless young women—it's cases like this as makes policemen into nervous wrecks, Dr. de Grandin, sor. Crimes o' passion an' crimes committed fer gain, they're meat an' drink to me, sor—I can understand 'em—but it's th' divil's own job runnin' down a johnny who goes about committin' murthers like this. Sure, 'tis almost always th' sign of a loose screw in his steerin' gear, sor, an' who knows where to look fer 'im? He might be some tough mug, but 'tisn't likely. More apt to be some soft-handed gentleman livin' in a fine neighborhood an' minglin' wid th' best society. There's some queer, goin's on among th' swells, sor, an' that's gospel; but we can't go up to every bur-rd that acts funny at times an' say, 'Come wid me, young felly me lad; it's wanted fer th' murther o' Kathleen Burke an' Rachel Müller ye are,' now can we?"

"Hélas, non," the Frenchman agreed sympathetically. "But have you no clue of any sort to the identity of this foul miscreant?"

"Well, sor, since ye mention it, we have one little thing," the sergeant replied, delving into his inside pocket and bringing forth a folded bit of paper from which he extracted a shred of twisted yarn. "Would this be manin' annything to ye?" he asked as he handed it to de Grandin.

"U'm," the little Frenchman murmured thoughtfully as he examined the object carefully. "Perhaps, I can not say at once. Where did you come by this?"

"'Twas clutched in Nurse Müller's hand as tight as be-damned when they brought her to th' hospital, sor," the detective replied. "We're not sure 'twas from th' murtherer's fancy-dress costume, o' course, but it's better'n nothin' to go on."

"But yes—most certainly," de Grandin agreed as he rose and took the find to the surgery.

For a few minutes he was busily engaged with jeweler's loop and microscope; finally he returned with the shred of yarn partly unraveled at one end. "It would seem," he declared as he returned the evidence to Costello, "that this is of Turkish manufacture, though not recent. It is a high grade of angora wool; the outer scales have smooth edges, which signifies the quality of the fleece. Also, interwoven with the thread is a fine golden wire. I have seen such yarn, the wool cunningly intermixed with golden threads, used for tarboosh tassels of wealthy Moslems. But the style has not prevailed for a hundred years and more. This is either a very old bit of wool, or a cunning simulation of the olden style—I am inclined to think the former. After all, though, this thread tells little more than that the slayer perhaps wore the headgear of a Mohammedan. The nurse described him as wearing a stocking-cap or toboggan, I believe. In her excitement and in the uncertain light of early morning a fez might easily be mistaken for such a piece of headgear."

"Then we're no better off than we were at first?" the Irishman asked disappointedly.

"A little," de Grandin encouraged. "Your search has narrowed somewhat, for you need only include among your suspects those possessing genuine Turkish fezzes a hundred years or more old."

"Yeah," commented Costello gloomily. "An' after we've run all them down, all we haf ter do is go down ter th' seashore an' start countin' th' grains o' sand."

"*Tiens*, my friend, be not so downcast," de Grandin bade. "Like your so magnificent John Paul Jones, we have not yet commenced to fight. Come, *Sergent*, Trowbridge, let us to the morgue. Perhaps we shall discover something there, if the pig-clumsy physicians have not already spoiled matters with their autopsy knives.

"Balderson, *mon brave*, do you remain to guard that which requires watching. You have small stomach for the things Friend Trowbridge and I shall shortly look upon."

SIDE BY SIDE IN the zinc-lined drawers of the city morgue's refrigerator lay the bodies of Kathleen Burke and Rachel Müller. De Grandin bent above the bodies, studying the discolorations on their throats in thoughtful silence. "U'm," he commented, as he turned to me with a quizzical expression, "is there not something these contusions have in common, Friend Trowbridge?"

Leaning forward, I examined the dark, purplish ridges banding both girls' throats. About the thickness of a lead-pencil, they ran about the delicate white skins, four on the left side, one on the right, with a small circular patch of discoloration in the region of the larynx, showing where the strangler had rested the heel of his hand as a fulcrum for his grip. "Why," I began, studying the marks carefully, "er, I can't say that I notice—by George, yes! The center finger of the throttler's hand was amputated at the second joint!"

"*Précisément*," the Frenchman agreed. "And which hand is it, if you please?"

"The right, of course; see how his thumb pressed on the right side of his victim's throats."

"*Exactement*, and—"

"And that narrows Costello's search still more," I interrupted eagerly. "All he has to do now is search for someone with half the second finger of his right hand missing, and—"

"And you do annoy me excessively," de Grandin cut in frigidly. "Your interruptions, they vex, they harass me. If I do not mistake rightly, we have already found him of the missing finger; at least, we have seen him."

I looked at him in open-mouthed amazement. Men afflicted with mysterious sadistic impulses, I knew, might move in normal society for years without being subject to suspicion, but I could recall no one of our acquaintance who possessed the maimed hand which was the killer's trade mark. "You mean—?" I asked blankly.

"Last night, or early this morning, *mon vieux*," he returned. "You, perhaps, were too immediately concerned with dodging exploding gases to take careful note of all we saw in the charnel chamber beneath the ground, but me, I see everything. *The right middle finger of the skeleton we found in the coffin with the treasure was missing at the second joint.*"

"You're joking!" I shot back incredulously.

For answer he pointed silently to the still, dead forms before us. "Are *these* a joke, my friend?" he demanded. "*Cordieu*, if such they be, they are an exceedingly grim jest."

"But for heaven's sake," I demanded, "how could that skeleton leave its tomb and wander about the streets? Anyhow, Nurse Müller declared it was a man who attacked her, not a skeleton. And skeletons haven't eyes, yet poor little Kathleen spoke of her assailant's eyes the first thing when we found her."

He turned his back on my expostulations with a slight shrug and addressed himself to the morgue master. "Have they arrived at the precise causes of death, *Monsieur?*" he asked.

"Yes, sir," the official replied. "The little Burke girl died o' heart failure consequent upon shock. Miss Müller died from loss o' blood an'—"

"Never mind, my friend, it is enough," de Grandin interrupted. "Strangulation was present in both cases, but apparently was not the primary cause of either death. That was all I desired to learn.

"Trowbridge, my friend," he assured me as we parted at the mortuary door, "he practises."

"Practises—who?" I demanded. But de Grandin was already out of earshot, walking down the street at a pace which would have qualified him for entry in a professional pedestrians' race.

4

THE CONSOMMÉ WAS GROWING cold in the tureen, Balderson and I were becoming increasingly aware of our appetites, and Nora McGinnis was on the verge of nervous prostration as visions of her elaborate dinner spoiling on the stove danced before her mind's eye when Jules de Grandin burst through the front door, a film of snowflakes from the raging storm outside decorating his shoulders like the ermine on a judge's gown. "Quick, Friend Trowbridge," he ordered as he drew up his chair to the table, "fill my plate to overflowing. I hunger, I starve, I famish. Not so much as one little crumb of luncheon has passed my lips this day."

"Find out anything?" I asked as I ladled out a liberal portion of smoking chicken broth.

"*Cordieu*, I shall say so, and he who denies it is a most foul liar!" he returned with a grin. "Observe this, if you please."

From his pocket he produced an odd-looking object, something like a fork of dried weed or a root of desiccated ginger, handing it first to me, then to Eric Balderson for inspection.

"All right, I'll bite—what is it?" Eric admitted as the little Frenchman eyed us in turn expectantly.

"*Mandragora officinalis*—mandrake," he replied with another of his quick smiles. "Have you not seen it before?—"

"U'm"—I searched the pockets of my memory a moment—"isn't this the thing we found on the old pirate's coffin last night?"

"Exactly, precisely, quite so!" he replied delightedly, patting his hands together softly as though applauding at a play. "You have it right, good friend; but last night we were too much concerned with saving our silly heads from the swinging ax, with finding gold and gems, and similar useless things to give attention to matters of real importance. Behold, my friends, with this bit of weed-root and these, I shall make one *sacré singe*—a monkey, no less—of that so vile murderer who terrorizes the city and slays inoffensive young women in the right. Certainly." As he finished speaking, he thrust his hand into another pocket and brought forth a dozen small conical objects which he pitched onto the table-cloth with a dramatic gesture.

"Bullets!" Balderson remarked wonderingly. "What—"

"Bullets, no less," de Grandin agreed, taking a pair of the little missiles into his hand and joggling them up and down playfully. "But not such bullets as you or Friend Trowbridge have seen before, I bet me your life. Attend me: These are silver, solid silver, without a trace of alloy. *Eh bien*, but I did have the fiend's own time finding a jeweler who would undertake to duplicate the bullets of my pistol in solid silver on such short notice. But at last, *grâce à Dieu*, I found him, and he fashioned these so pretty things to my order and fitted them into the shells in place of the nickel-plated projectiles. For good measure I ordered him to engrave each one with a cross at its tip, and then, on my way home, I did stop at the church of Saint Bernard and dip them each and every one into the font of *eau bénite*. Now, I damn think, we shall see what we shall see this night."

"What in the world—" I began, but he shut me off with upraised hand.

"The roast, Friend Trowbridge," he implored, "for dear friendship's sake, carve me a liberal portion of the roast and garnish it well with potatoes. Do but permit that I eat my fill, and, when the time arrives, I shall show you such things as to make you call yourself one colossal liar when you recall them to memory!"

Sergeant Costello, thoroughly disgruntled at hours of vigil in the snowy night and completely mystified, was waiting for us beside the entrance to Saint David's churchyard. "Sure, Dr. de Grandin, sor," he announced as he stepped from the shelter of the pentice, blowing on his numbed fingers, "'tis th' divil's own job ye gave me tonight. Me eyes have been skinned like a pair o' onions all th' night long, but niver a bit o' annyone comin' in or out o' th' graveyard have I seen."

"Very good, my friend," de Grandin commented. "You have done most well, but I fear me one will attempt to pass you, and by the inward route, before many minutes have gone. You will kindly await our outcoming, if you please, and we shall be no longer than necessary, I assure you."

Forcing the sliding door of the tombstone, we hastened down the stairway to the burial chamber in de Grandin's wake, sprung the guarding ax at the entrance of the first room and crept into the inner cavern. One glance was sufficient to confirm our suspicions. The stone coffin was empty.

"Was—was it like this when you were here today?" I faltered.

"No," de Grandin answered, "he lay in his bed as calmly as a babe in its cradle, my friend, *but he lay on his side.*"

"On his side? Why, that is impossible! The skeleton was on its back when we came here last night and we didn't move it. How came the change of posture?"

"*Tiens*, who can say?" he replied. "Perhaps he rests better that way. Of a certainty, he had lain long enough on his posterior to have become tired of it. It may be—*sssh!* Lights out. To your quarters!"

Balderson and I rushed to opposite corners of the room, as de Grandin had previously directed, our powerful electric bull's-eye lanterns shut off, but ready to flood the place with light at a second's notice. De Grandin stationed himself squarely in line with the door, his head thrust forward, his knees slightly bent, his entire attitude one of pleased anticipation.

What sixth sense had warned him of approaching danger I know not, for in the absolute quiet of the pitch dark chamber I could hear no sound save the low, short breaths of my two companions and the faint trickle-trickle of water into the tank of the beheading machine which guarded the entrance of the farther room. I was about to speak, when:

Bang! The muffled detonation of a shot fired somewhere above ground sounded startlingly, followed by another and still another; then the rasping, high-pitched cackle of a maniacal laugh, a scraping, shuffling step on the narrow stone stairs, and:

"Lights, *pour l'amour de Dieu*, lights!" de Grandin shrieked as something—some malign, invisible, unutterably wicked *presence* seemed suddenly to fill the chamber, staining the inky darkness still more black with its foul effluvium.

As one man Balderson and I snapped up the shutters of our lanterns, and the converging beams displayed a frightful tableau.

Crouched at the low entrance of the cavern, like a predatory beast with its prey, was a fantastic figure, a broad, squat—almost humpbacked—man arrayed in leathern jerkin, Turkish fez and loose, baggy pantaloons tucked into hip-boots of soft Spanish leather. About his face, mask-like, was bound a black-silk kerchief with two slits for eyes, and through the openings there glowed and glittered a pair of baleful orbs, green-glossed and vitreous, like those of a cat, but fiercer and more implacable than the eyes of any feline.

Over one malformed shoulder, as a miller might carry a sack of meal, the creature bore the body of a girl, a slight, frail slip of femininity with ivory face and curling hair of deepest black, her thin, frilly party dress ripped to tatters, one silver slipper fallen from her silk-sheathed foot, the silver-tissue bandeau which bound her hair dislodged so that it lay half across her face like the bandage over the eyes of a condemned felon.

"*Monsieur le Pirate*," de Grandin greeted in a low, even voice, "you do roam afield late, it seems. We have waited overlong for you."

The mask above the visitant's face fluttered outward with the pressure of breath behind it, and we could trace the movement of jaws beneath the silk, but no word of answer came to the Frenchman's challenge.

"Ah—so? You choose not to talk?" de Grandin queried sarcastically. "Is it perhaps that you prefer deeds to words? *C'est bien!*" With a quick, skipping step he advanced several paces toward the creature, raising his pistol as he moved.

A peal of sardonic, tittering laughter issued from beneath the mask. Callous as a devil, the masked thing dropped the girl's lovely body to the stone floor, snatched at the heavy hanger in his belt and leaped straight for de Grandin's throat.

The Frenchman fired even as his antagonist charged, and the effect of his shot was instantaneous. As though he had run against a barrier of iron, the masked pirate stopped in mid-stride and staggered back an uncertain step, but de Grandin pressed his advantage. "Ha, you did not expect this, *hein?*" he demanded with a smile which was more like a snarl. "You who defy the bullets of policemen and make mock of all human resistance thought you would add one more victim to your list, *n'est-ce-pas, Monsieur*? Perhaps, *Monsieur, le Mort-félon*, you had not thought of Jules de Grandin?"

As he spoke he fired another shot into the cowering wretch, another, and still another until eight silver balls had pierced the cringing thing's breast.

As the final shot went home the fantastical, terrible shape began to change before our eyes. Like the cover of a punctured football the gaudy, archaic costume began to wrinkle and wilt, the golden-tasseled fez toppled forward above the masked face and the black-silk handkerchief itself dropped downward, revealing the unfleshed countenance of a grinning skull.

"Up with him, my friends," de Grandin shouted. "Pitch him into his coffin, clamp down the lid—here, lay the root of mandrake upon it! So! He is in again, and for all time.

"Now, one of you, take up poor *Mademoiselle* and pass her through the door to me.

"Very well, *Sergent*, we come and bring the young lady with us!" he cried as Costello's heavy boots sounded raspingly on the stone steps outside. "Do not attempt to enter—it is death to put your head through the opening!"

A moment later, with the girl's body wrapped in the laprobe, we were driving toward my house, ignoring every speed regulation in the city ordinances.

5

S ERGEANT COSTELLO LOOKED ASKANCE at the rug-wrapped form occupying the rear seat of my car. "Say, Dr. de Grandin, sor," he ventured with another sidewise glance at the lovely body, "hadn't we best be notifyin' th' coroner, an'"—he gulped over the word—"an' gittin' a undertaker fer this here pore young lady?"

"Coroner—undertaker? À *bas les croque-morts!* Your wits are entirely absent harvesting the wool of sheep, *cher sergent*. The only undertaker of which she stands in need is the excellent Nora McGinnis, who shall give her a warm bath to overcome her chill after Friend Trowbridge and I have administered stimulants. Then, unless I mistake much, we shall listen to a most remarkable tale of adventure before we restore her to the arms of her family."

H ALF AN HOUR LATER our fair prize, revived by liberal doses of aromatic ammonia and brandy, thoroughly warmed by a hot sponge and alcohol rub administered by the competent Nora, and with one of de Grandin's vivid flowered-silk dressing-gowns slipped over the sorry remnants of her tattered party costume, sat demurely before our library fire. As she entered the room, Eric Balderson, who had not seen her face before, because of the bandeau which obscured it in the cave, gave a noticeable start, then seemed to shrink back in his corner of the ingle-nook.

Not so Jules de Grandin. Swinging one well-tailored leg across the corner of the library table, he regarded the young lady with a level, unwinking stare till the sustained scrutiny became embarrassing. Finally:

"*Mademoiselle*, you will have the kindness to tell us exactly what has happened to you this night, so far as you can remember," he ordered.

The girl eyed him with a tremulous smile a moment; then, taking a deep breath, launched on her recital like a child speaking a piece in school.

"I'm Marian Warner," she told us. "We live in Tunlaw Street—I think Dr. Trowbridge knows my father, Fabian Warner."

I nodded agreement, and she continued.

"Tonight I went to a Christmas Eve party at Mr. and Mrs. Partridge's. It was a masquerade affair, but I just wore a domino over my evening dress, since we were to unmask at midnight, anyway, and I thought I'd feel more comfortable in 'citizen's clothes' than I would dancing in some sort of elaborate costume.

"There wasn't anything unusual about the party, or about the first part of the evening, that I remember, except, of course, everyone was talking about the mysterious murder of those two poor women.

"They danced a German just before midnight, and I was pretty hot from the running around, so I stepped into the conservatory to slip out of my domino a moment and cool off.

"I'd just taken the gown off when I felt a touch on my arm, and turning round found a man staring into my face. I thought he must be one of the guests, of course, though I couldn't remember having seen him. He wore a jerkin of bright red leather with a wide black belt about his waist, a red fez with gold-and-black tassel, and loose trousers tucked into tall boots. His face was concealed with a black-silk handkerchief instead of a regular mask, and, somehow, there was something menacing and terrifying about him. I think it must have been his eyes, which glittered in the light like those of an animal at night.

"I started back from him, but he edged after me, extending his hand to stroke my arm, and almost fawning on me. He made queer, inarticulate sounds in his throat, too.

"'Go away,' I told him. 'I don't know you and I don't want to. Please leave me alone.' By that time he'd managed to crowd me into a corner, so that my retreat into the house was cut off, and I was getting really frightened.

"'If you don't let me go, I'll scream,' I threatened, and then, before I had a chance to say another word, out shot one of his hands—ugh, they were big and thin and long, like a gorilla's!—and grasped me by the throat.

"I tried to fight him off, and even as I did so there flashed through my mind the description Miss Müller gave of her murderer. Then I knew. I was helpless in the grasp of the killer! That's all I remember till I regained consciousness with Dr. Trowbridge's housekeeper drying me after my bath and you gentlemen standing outside the door, ready to help me downstairs.

"Did they catch him—the murderer?" she added with true feminine curiosity.

"But of course, *Mademoiselle*," de Grandin assured her gravely. "*I* was on his trail. It was impossible he should escape.

"Attend me, my friends," he ordered, slipping from his seat on the table and striding to the center of the room like a lecturer about to begin his discourse. "Last night, when we entered that accursed tomb, I had too many thoughts within my so small brain to give full attention to any one of them. In my hurry I did overlook many important matters. That root of mandrake, by example, I should have suspected its significance, but I did not. Instead, I tossed it away as an unconsidered trifle.

"Mandrake, or mandragora, my friends, was one of the most potent charm-drugs in the ancient pharmacopoeia. With it the barren might be rendered fecund; love forgotten might be reawakened; deep and lasting coma might be induced by it. Does not that Monsieur Shakespeare make Cleopatra say:

'Give me to drink of mandragora,
That I might sleep out this great gap of time
My Antony is away'?

"Most certainly. Moreover, it had another, and less frequent use. Placed upon the grave of one guilty of manifold sins, *it would serve to keep his earthbound spirit from walking.* You perceive the connection.

"When we cast aside that root of mandragora, we did unseal a tomb which was much better left unopened, and did release upon the world a spirit capable of working monstrous evil. Yes. This 'Black Master,' I do know him, Friend Trowbridge.

"When we looked upon the poor relics of those slain women, I noticed at once the peculiarity of the bruises on their throats. '*Parbleu*,' I say to me, 'the skeleton which we saw last night, he had a hand so maimed as to leave a mark like this. Jules de Grandin, we must investigate.'

"'Make it so,' I reply to me in that mental conversation, and so, Friend Trowbridge, when I left you I did repair instantly to that cursed tomb and look about. There, in his coffin of stone, lay the skeleton of the 'Black Master,' but, as I have already been at pains to tell you, on his side, not as we left him lying the night before. '*Mordieu*, this are not good, this are most badly strange,' I inform me. Then I look about and discover the bit of mandrake root, all shriveled and dried, and carelessly tossed to one side where we left it when Friend Trowbridge let fall his light. I—"

"By the way, de Grandin," I put in. "Something hit me a paralyzing blow on the knuckles before I let my flashlight fall; have you any idea what it was?"

He favored me with a momentary frown, then: "But certainly," he responded. "It were a bit of stone from the ceiling. I saw it detach itself and cried a warning to you, even as it fell, but the loss of our light was of such importance that I talked no more about your injury. Now to resume:

"'Can we not now seal him in the tomb with the mandrake once more?' I ask me as I stand beside that coffin today, but better judgment tells me not to attempt it. This old-time sea-devil, he have been able to clothe his bony frame with seeming habiliments of the flesh. He are, to all intents and purposes, once more alive, and twice as wicked as before on account of his long sleep. I shall kill his fantasmal body for good and all before I lock him once and forever in the tomb again.

"'But how shall we slay him so that he be really-truly dead?' I ask me.

"Then, standing beside the coffin of that old, wicked pirate, I think and think deeply. 'How were the were-wolves and witches, the wizards and the war-locks, the bugbears and goblins of ancient times slain in the olden days?' I ask, and the answer comes back, 'With bullets of silver.' Attend me, my friends."

Snatching a red leather volume from the near-by shelf he thumbed quickly through its pages. "Hear what your Monsieur Whittier say in one of his so lovely poems. In the olden times, the garrison of a New England fort was beset by

> . . . a spectral host, defying stroke of
> steel and aim of gun;
> Never yet was ball to slay them in the
> mold of mortals run!
> Midnight came; from out the forest moved
> a dusky mass that soon
> Grew to warriors, plumed and painted,
> grimly marching in the moon.
> "Ghosts or witches," said the captain, "thus
> I foil the Evil One!"
> And *he rammed a silver button from his*
> *doublet down his gun.*

"Very good. I, too, will thus foil the Evil One and his servant who once more walks the earth. I have told you how I had the bullets made to my order this day. I have recounted how I baptized them for the work they were to do this night. Yourselves saw how the counter-charm worked against that servitor of Satan, how it surprised him when it pierced his phantom breast, how it made of him a true corpse, and how the seeming-flesh he had assumed to clothe his bare bones while he worked his evil was made to melt away before the bullets of Jules de Grandin. Now, doubly dead, he lies sealed by the mandrake root within his tomb for evermore.

"Friend Balderson, you have been most courteously quiet this long time. Is there no question you would care to ask?"

"You told Dr. Trowbridge you knew the 'Black Master,'" Eric replied. "Can you tell us something about him—"

"Ah, *parbleu*, but I can!" de Grandin interrupted. "This afternoon, while the excellent jeweler was turning out my bullets, I repaired to the public library and discovered much of that old villain's life and deeds. Who he was nobody seems to know. As to what he was, there is much fairly accurate conjecture.

"A Turk he was by birth, it is generally believed, and a most unsavory follower of the false Prophet. Even in sinful Stamboul his sins were so great that he was deprived of his tongue by way of punishment. Also, he was subjected to another operation not wholly unknown in Eastern countries. This latter, instead of rendering him docile, seemed to make a veritable demon of him. Never would he permit his crews to take prisoners, even for ransom. Sexless himself, he forbade the presence of women—even drabs from Maracaibo and Panama—aboard his ships, save for one purpose. That was torture. Whenever a ship was captured, he fetched the female prisoners aboard, and after compelling them to witness the slaughter of their men folk, with his own hands he put them to death, often crushing life from their throats with his maimed right hand. Does not his history fit squarely with the things we have observed these last two nights? The accounts declare, 'The time and place of his death are uncertain, but it is thought he died somewhere near the present city of Newark and was buried somewhere in Jersey. A vast treasure disappeared with him, and speculation concerning its hiding-place rivals that of the famous buried hoard of Captain Kidd.'

"Now, it is entirely probable that we might add something of great interest to that chronicle, but I do not think we shall, for—"

Absorbed in the Frenchman's animated narrative, Eric Balderson had moved from his shadowed corner into the zone of light cast by the reading-lamp, and as de Grandin was about to finish, Marian Warner interrupted him with a little cry of incredulous delight. "Eric," she called. "Eric Balderson! Oh, my dear, I've wondered and worried so much about you!"

A moment later she had flown across the room, shedding de Grandin's purple lizard-skin slippers as she ran, put both hands on the young man's shoulders, and demanded, "Why did you go away, dear; didn't you kno—"

"Marian!" Eric interrupted hoarsely. "I didn't dare ask your father. I was so wretchedly poor, and there seemed no prospect of my ever getting anywhere— you'd been used to everything, and I thought it would be better for us both if

I just faded out of the picture. But"—he laughed boyishly—"I'm rich, now, dear—one of the richest men in the country, and—"

"Rich or poor, Eric dear, I love you," the girl interrupted as she slipped both arms about his neck and kissed him on the lips.

Jules de Grandin's arms shot out like the blades of a pair of opening shears. With one hand he grasped Sergeant Costello's arm; the other snatched me by the elbow. "Come away, foolish ones," he hissed. "What have we, who left our loves in Avalon long years ago, to do with such as they? *Pardieu*, to them we are a curse, a pest, an abomination; we do incumber the earth!

"Await me here," he ordered as we concluded our march to the consulting-room. "I go, but I return immediately."

In a moment he came tripping down the stairs, a magnificent glowing ruby, nearly as large as a robin's egg, held daintily between his thumb and forefinger. "For their betrothal ring," he announced proudly. "See, it is the finest in my collection."

"Howly Mither, Dr. de Grandin, sor, are ye, a jinny from th' *Arabeen Nights*, to be passin' out jools like that whenever a pair o' young folks gits engaged?" demanded Sergeant Costello, his big blue eyes almost popping from his head in amazement.

"Ah, *mon sergent*," the little Frenchman turned one of his quick, elfish smiles on the big Irishman, "you have as yet seen nothing. Before you leave this house tonight Friend Trowbridge and I shall fill every pocket of your clothes to overflowing with golden coin from old Spain; but e'er we do so, let us remember it is Christmas."

With the certainty of one following a well-worn path, he marched to the medicine closet, extracted a bottle of peach brandy and three glasses, and filled them to the brim.

"To your very good and long-lasting health, my friend," he pledged, raising his glass aloft. "*Joyeux Noël!*"

The Devil-People

1

A BLEAK NORTHEAST WIND, SWEEPING down from the coast of New England and freighted with mingled rain and sleet, howled riotously through the streets as we emerged from Symphony Hall.

"*Cordieu*, Friend Trowbridge," de Grandin exclaimed between chattering teeth as he turned the fur collar of his greatcoat up about his ears and sunk his head between his shoulders, "Monsieur Washington was undoubtlessly a most admirable gentleman in every respect, but of a certainty he chose a most damnable, execrable day on which to be born! Name of a green duck, I am already famished with the cold; come, let us seek shelter, and that with quickness, or I shall expire completely and leave you nothing but the dead corpse of Jules de Grandin for company!"

Grinning at his vehemence, I bent my head to the blast as we buffeted our way against the howling gale, fighting a path over the sleet-swept sidewalks to the glass-and-iron porte cochère of La Pontoufle Dorée.

As we swept through the revolving plate-glass doors a sleek-looking gigolo with greased hair and beady eyes set too close together snatched at our hats and wraps with an avidity which betrayed his Levantine ancestry, and we marched down a narrow, mirror-lined hall lighted with red-shaded electric bulbs. From the dining-room beyond came the low, dolorous moaning of saxophones blended with the blurred monody of indiscriminate conversation and the shrill, piping overtones of women's laughter. On the cleared dancing-floor in the center of the room a file of shapely young women in costumes consisting principally of beads and glittering rhinestones danced hectically, their bare, powdered arms, legs and torsos gleaming in the glare of the spotlight. The close, superheated air reeked with the odor of broken food and the effluvia from women's perfumed gowns and bodies, while the savage, heathen snarl of the jazz band's jungle music throbbed and palpitated like a fever patient's pulses. Soft fronds of particolored silk, sweeping gracefully down from the center of the ceiling, formed a tentlike roof which billowed gracefully with each draft from the doors, and the varicolored lights of the great crystal chandelier gleamed dully through the drifting fog-whorls of tobacco smoke.

"U'm?" de Grandin surveyed the scene from the threshold. "These children of present-day America enjoy more luxury than did their country's father on his birthday at Valley Forge a hundred and fifty-two years ago tonight, Friend Trowbridge," he commented dryly.

"How many in the party, please?" demanded the head waiter. "Only two?" Disdain and hauteur seemed fighting for possession of his hard-shaven face as he eyed us frigidly.

"Two, most certainly," de Grandin replied, then tapped the satin lapel of the functionary's dress coat with an impressive forefinger, "but two with the appetites—and thirsts—of four, *mon garçon.*"

Something like a smile flickered across the cruel, arrogant lips of the servitor as he beckoned to a waiter-captain, who led us to a table near the wall.

"*Voleurs*—robbers, bandits!" the little Frenchman exclaimed as he surveyed the price list of the menu.

"However, it is *nécessaire* that one eats," he added philosophically as he made his choice known to the hovering waiter.

A matronly-looking, buxom woman of uncertain age in a modestly cut evening gown circulated among the guests. Seemingly acquainted with everyone present, she stopped here and there, slapping a masculine back in frank friendship and camaraderie every once in a while, exchanging a quip or word of greeting with the women patrons.

"Hullo, boys," she greeted cordially as she reached our table, "having a good time? Need anything more to brighten the corner where you are?"

"*Madame,*" de Grandin bent forward from the hips in a formal Continental bow, "if you possess the influence in this establishment, you can confer the priceless favor on us by procuring a *soupçon* of *eau-de-vie.* Consider: We are but just in from the outdoor cold and are frozen to the bone on all sides. If—"

"French!" From the delighted expression on the lady's face it was apparent that the discovery of de Grandin's nationality was the one thing needed to make her happiness complete. "I knew it the moment I laid eyes on you," she assured him. "You boys from across the pond simply *must* have your little nip, mustn't you? Fix it? I'll tell the world I can. Leave it to Mamma; she'll see you get a shot that'll start your blood circulatin'. Back in a minute, Frenchy, and, by the way"—she paused, a genial smile on her broad, rather homely face—"how about a little playmate to liven things up? Someone to share the loneliness of a stranger in a strange land? I got just the little lady to do the trick. She's from over the water, too."

"*Mordieu*, my friend, it seems I have put my foot in it up to the elbow," de Grandin deplored with a grimace of comic tragedy. "My request for a drink brings us not only the liquor, but a partner to help consume it, it would seem. Two hundred francs at the least, this will cost us, I fear."

I was about to voice a protest, for supping at a night club was one thing, while consorting with the paid entertainers was something very different; but my remonstrances died half uttered, for the hostess bore down upon us, her face wreathed in smiles, a waiter with a long-necked bottle preceding her and a young woman—dark, pretty and with an air of shy timidity—following docilely in her wake. The girl—she was little more—wore a rich, black fur coat over a black evening gown and swung a small black grosgrain slipper bag from her left wrist.

"Shake hands with Ma'mselle Mutina, Frenchy," the hostess bade. "She's just as lonesome and thirsty as you are. You'll get along like mocha and java, you two."

"*Enchanté, Mademoiselle*," De Grandin assured her as he raised her slender white fingers to his lips and withdrew a chair for her. "You will have a bit of food, some champagne, perhaps, some—" he rattled on with a string of gallant-ries worthy of a professional boulevardier while I watched him in mingled fas-cination and disapproval. This was a facet of the many-sided little Frenchman I had never seen before, and I was not especially pleased with it.

Our table-mate seated herself, letting her opulent coat fall back over her chair and revealing a pair of white, rounded shoulders and arms of sin-gular loveliness. Her eyes rested on the table in timid confusion. As de Grandin monopolized the conversation, I studied her attentively. There was no doubting her charm. Slim, youthful, vibrant she was, yet restrained with a sort of patrician calm. Her skin was not the dead white of the pow-der-filmed performers of the cabaret, nor yet the pink of the athletic wom-an's; rather it seemed to glow with a delicate undertone of tan, like the old ivory of ancient Chinese carvings or the richest of cream. Her face was heart-shaped rather than oval, with almost straight eyebrows of jetty black-ness, a small, straight nose and a low, broad forehead, blue-black hair that lapped smoothly over her tiny ears like folded raven's wings, and delicate, sensitive lips which, I knew instinctively, would have been lusciously red even without the aid of the rouge with which they were tinted. When she raised timid, troubled eyes to de Grandin's face I saw the irises inside the silken frames of curling black lashes were purple as pansy petals. "Humph," I commented mentally, "she's beautiful—entirely too good-looking to be respectable!"

The waiter brought a chicken sandwich and—to my unbounded astonish-ment—a bottle of ginger ale for her, and as she was about to lift a morsel of food to her lips I saw her purple eyes suddenly widen with dread and her cheeks go ash-pale with fright.

"M'sieu'," she whispered, leaning impulsively across the table, "do not look at once, I implore you, but in a moment glance casually at the table at the far corner of the room and tell me if you see anyone there!"

Restraining an impulse to wheel in my chair, I held myself steady a moment, then with elaborate unconcern surveyed the room slowly. At the table indicated by the girl sat four men in dinner clothes. Leanness—the cadaverous emaciation of dissecting-room material—was their outstanding characteristic. Their cheeks were gaunt and hollow, their lips so thin that the outline of the teeth could be marked through them, and every articulation of their skulls could be traced through the tightly stretched. saddle-brown skin of their faces. But a second's study of their death's-head countenances revealed a more sinister feature. Their eyes were obliquely set, like cats', yellow-green and cruel, with long slits for pupils. Changeless in expression they were; set, fixed, inscrutable, pitiless as any panther's—waiting, watching, seeing all, revealing nothing. I shuddered in spite of myself as I forced my gaze to travel casually over the remainder of the room.

De Grandin was speaking in a low, suppressed whisper, and in his little round blue eyes there snapped and sparkled the icy flashes which betrayed excitement. "Mademoiselle," he said, "I see four monkey-faced heathen seated at that table. Hindus they are by their features, perhaps Berbers from Africa, but devil's offspring by their eyes, which are like razors. Do they annoy you? I will order them away, I will pull their crooked noses—pardieu, I shall twist their flap-ears before I boot them from the place if you do but say the word!"

"Oh, no, no!" the girl breathed with a frightened shudder, and I could see it was as if a current of cold horror, something nameless and terrible, flowed from the strange men to her. "Do not appear to notice them, sir, but—Aristide!" she beckoned to a waiter hurrying past with a tray of glasses.

"Yes, Ma'mselle?" the man answered, pausing with a smile beside her chair.

"Those gentlemen in the corner by the orchestra"—she nodded ever so slightly toward the macabre group—"have you ever seen them here before?"

"Gentlemen, Ma'mselle?" the waiter replied with a puzzled frown as he surveyed the table intently. "Surely, you make the joke with Aristide. That table, she are vacant—the only vacant one in the place. It are specially reserved and paid for, but—"

"Never mind," the girl interrupted with a smile, and the man hurried off on his errand.

"You see?" she asked simply.

"Barbe d'une poule bleu, but I do not!" de Grandin asserted. "But—"

"Hush!" she interrupted. "Oh, do not let them think we notice them; it would make them frenzied. When the lights go out for the next number of the show, I shall ask a great favor of you, sir. You are a chivalrous gentleman and will not refuse. I shall take a package from my handbag—see, I trust you perfectly—and pass it to you beneath the table, and you will take it at once to 849 Algonquin Avenue and await me there. Please!" Her warm soft fingers curled themselves about his hand with an appealing pressure. "You will do this for me? You will not fail?—you are not afraid?"

"*Mademoiselle*," he assured her solemnly, returning her handclasp with compound interest, "I shall do it, though forty thousand devils and devilkins bar the way."

As the lights in the big central chandelier dimmed and the spotlight shot its effulgence over the dancing-floor, a petite blonde maiden arrayed in silver trunks, bandeau and slippers pranced out between the rows of tables and began singing in a rasping, nasal voice while she strutted and jiggled through the intricate movements of the Baltimore.

"Come, Friend Trowbridge," ordered de Grandin abruptly, stowing something in his pocket at the same time. "We go, we leave; *allez-vous-en!*"

I followed stumblingly through the comparative darkness of the dining-room, but paused on the threshold for a final backward glance. The zone of spotlight on the dancing-floor made the remainder of the place inky black by contrast, and only the highlights of the table napery, the men's shirt-fronts and the women's arms and shoulders showed indistinctly through the gloom, but it seemed to me the oblique, unchanging eyes of the sinister quartet at the corner table followed us through the dark and shone with sardonic phosphorescence, as the questing eyes of hungry cats spy out the movements of mice among the shadows.

"This is the craziest thing you've ever done," I scolded as our taxi gathered speed over the slippery street. "What do we know about that girl? Nothing, except she's an habitué of a none too reputable night club. She may be a dope peddler for all we know, and this may be just a scheme to have us carry her contraband stuff past the police; or it may be a plan for hold-up and robbery and those devilish-looking men her accomplices. I'd not put any sort of villainy past a gang like that, and—"

De Grandin's slender, mocha-gloved fingers beat a devil's tattoo on the silver knob of his ebony cane as he regarded me with a fixed, unwinking stare of disapproval. "All that you say may be true, my friend," he admitted; "nevertheless, I have a mind to see this business through. Are you with me?"

"Of course, but—"

"There are no buts, *cher ami*. Unless I mistake rightly, we shall see remarkable things before we have done, and I would not miss the sight for half a dozen peaceful nights in bed."

As we rounded a corner and turned into the wide, tree-bordered roadway of Algonquin Avenue another car sped past us through the storm, whirling skidchains snarling savagely against its mudguards.

2

A REAL ESTATE AGENT'S SIGN announced that the substantial brownstone residence which was on Algonquin Avenue was for sale or rent on long-term lease and would be altered to suit the tenant. Otherwise the place was as much like every other house in the block as one grain of rice is like the others in a bag.

Hastening up the short flagstone path leading from the sidewalk, de Grandin mounted the low brownstone stoop, felt uncertainly a moment, located the old-fashioned pull doorbell and gave the brass knob a vigorous yank.

Through the mosaic of brightly stained glass in the front door panel we could descry a light in the hall, but no footsteps came in answer to our summons. "*Morbleu*, this is villainous," the little Frenchman muttered as an especially vicious puff of wind hurled a barrage of sleet into his face. "Are we to stand here till death puts an end to our sufferings? I will not have it!" He struck a resounding blow on the door with the knob of his walking-stick.

As though waiting only the slightest pressure, the unlatched door swung back beneath the impact of his cane, and we found ourselves staring down a long, high-ceiled hall. Under the flickering light of an old-fashioned, prism-fringed gas chandelier we glimpsed the riotous colors of the Oriental rugs with which the place was carpeted, caught a flash of king-blue, rose and rust-red from the sumptuous prayer cloth suspended tapestrywise on the wall, but gave no second glance to the draperies, for at the far end of the passage was that which brought an excited "A-a-ah?" from de Grandin and a gasp of horror from me.

The place was a shambles. Hunched forward like a doll with a broken back, an undersized, dark-skinned man in white drill jacket, batik sarong and yellow turban squatted in a low, blackwood chair and stared endlessly before him into infinity with the glazed, half-pleading, half-expressionless eyes of the newly dead. A smear of red, wider than the palm of a man's hand, and still slowly spreading, disfigured the left breast of his white jacket and told the reason for his death.

Half-way up the stairway which curved from the farther end of the hall another man, similarly attired, had fallen backward, apparently in the act of flight, and lay against the stair-treads like a worn-out tailor's dummy carelessly tossed upon the carpet. His bare brown feet, oddly bent on flaccid ankles, pointed upward; head and hands, lolling downward with an awful awkwardness, were toward us, and I went sick with horror at sight of the open, gasping mouth and set, staring eyes in the reversed face. Under his back-bent chin a terrific wound gaped in his throat like the butcher's mark upon a slaughtered sheep.

"*Grand Dieu!*" de Grandin murmured, surveying the tragic relics a moment: "They were thorough, those assassins."

Darting down the corridor he paused beside the corpses, letting his hand rest on each a moment, then turned away with a shrug. "Dead *comme un mouton*," he observed almost indifferently, "but not long so, my friend. They are still soft and warm. If we could but—*Dieu de Dieu*—another? Oh, villainous! monstrous! infamous!"

Stepping through an arched doorway we had entered a large room to the left of the hall. A carved blackwood divan stood at the apartment's farther end, and a peacock screen immediately behind it. A red-shaded lamp threw its softly diffused light over the place, mellowing, to some extent, the dreadful tableau spread before us. Full length among the gaudy, heaped-up pillows of the divan a woman reclined indolently, one bare, brown arm extended toward us, wrist bent, hand drooping, a long, thin cheroot of black tobacco held listlessly between her red-stained fingers. Small, she was, almost childishly so, her skin golden as sun-ripened fruit, her lips red as though stained with fresh pomegranate juice, and on the loose robe of sheer yellow muslin which was her only garment glowed a redder stain beneath the gentle swell of her left bosom. Death had been kinder to her than to the men, for her large, black-fringed eyes were closed as though in natural sleep, and her lips were softly parted as if she had gently sighed her life away. The illusion of slumber was heightened by the fact that on the henna-stained toes of one slender foot was balanced a red-velvet slipper heavily embroidered with silver thread while its mate had fallen to the floor, as though listlessly kicked off by its wearer.

Treading softly as though passing the sanctuary of a church, the little Frenchman approached the dead woman, felt her soft, rounded arm a moment, then pinched daintily at the cheroot between her dead fingers. "*Parbleu*, yes!" he nodded vigorously. "It was recent, most recent, Friend Trowbridge. The vile miscreants who did this deed of shame had but just gone when we arrived; for see, her flesh still glows with the warmth of life, and the memory of its fire still lingers in this cigar's tobacco. Not more than ten, nor eight, nor scarcely six minutes can have passed since these poor ones were done to death.

"*Eh bien*"—he bent his left hand palm upward, consulting the tiny watch strapped to the under side of his wrist, and turned toward the door with a faint shrug—"anyone can deplore these deaths; it is for Jules de Grandin to avenge them. Come, we must notify the gendarmes and the coroner, then—"

"What about Mademoiselle Mutina?" I asked maliciously. "You promised to wait here for her, you know."

He paused a moment, regarding me intently with his fixed, level stare. "*Précisément*," he assented grimly, "what about her? It remains to be seen. As for my promise—*Mordieu*, when I was a little lad I promised myself I should one day be President of the *République*, but when I grew to a man's estate I found too many important things to do." He swung back the front door, thrust his collar up about his ears with a savage jerk and strode across the low porch into the howling storm.

What warned me to look up I shall never know, for the natural course to have followed would have been that taken by de Grandin and bend my head against the wind; but a subtle something, something so tangible that it was almost physical, seemed to jerk my chin up from my greatcoat collar just in time. From the areaway beneath the porch steps, staring at the retreating Frenchman with a malignancy utterly bestial, was a pair of oblique, yellow-green eyes.

"Look out, de Grandin!" I shrieked, and even as I called I realized the warning was too late, for an arm shot upward, poising a dully gleaming weapon—a dagger of some sort, I thought—for a throw.

Scarcely conscious of my act, I acted. Throwing both feet forward, I slipped on the glassy sleet with which the stone steps were veneered, and catapulted down them like a trunk sweeping down a baggage-chute. My feet landed squarely against the Frenchman's legs, knocking him sprawling, and something whizzed past my ear with a deadly, whirring sound and struck against the flagstone path beyond with a brittle, crackling clash.

Fighting to regain my footing like a cat essaying the ascent of a slate gable, I scrambled helplessly on the sleet-glazed walk, saw de Grandin right himself with an oath and dive head-foremost toward the area where his assailant lurked.

For an instant everything was chaos. I saw de Grandin miss his step and lurch drunkenly over the icy footwalk; saw his brown-skinned assailant spring upon him like a panther on its prey; realized dimly that someone had charged across the narrow yard and sprung to my little friend's aid; then was knocked flat once more by a vicious kick which missed my face only a hair's breadth and almost dislocated my shoulder.

"Catch him, Friend Trowbridge—he flies!" de Grandin shouted, disengaging himself from his rescuer's arms and rushing futilely after his fleeing opponent. Sure-footed as a lynx, the fellow ran over the slippery pavement, crossed the roadway and bolted down the connecting street, disappearing from sight as though swallowed up by the enveloping storm.

"*Merci beaucoup, Monsieur*," de Grandin acknowledged as he turned to his deliverer, "I have not the honor of knowing your name, but my obligation is as great as your help was timely. If you will be so good as to—Trowbridge, my friend, catch him, he swoons!"

"Quick, Friend Trowbridge," the Frenchman ordered, "do you improvise some sort of bandage while I seek conveyance; we must bear him to the house and staunch his wound, else he will bleed to death."

W HILE DE GRANDIN SOUGHT frantically for a taxicab I opened the stranger's clothes and wadded my handkerchief against the ugly knife-wound in his upper arm. Crude and makeshift as the device was, it stopped the flow of blood to some extent, and, while still unconscious, the man did not appear measurably worse off when we arrived at my office some twenty minutes later. While I cut away his shirt sleeve and adjusted a proper pad and bandage, de Grandin was busily telephoning our gruesome discoveries to police headquarters.

A stiff drink of brandy and water forced between his lips brought a semblance of color back to the fainting man's cheeks. He turned his head slowly on the pillow of the examination table and muttered something unintelligible; then, with a start, he rose to a sitting posture and cried: "Mutina, dear love: It is I—Richard! Wait, Mutina, wait a mo—"

As if a curtain had been lifted from before his eyes he saw us and turned from one to the other with an expression of blank bewilderment. "Where—how—" he began dazedly; then: "Oh, I remember, that devil was assaulting you and I rushed in to—"

"To save a total stranger from a most unpleasant predicament, *Monsieur*, for which the stranger greatly thanks you," de Grandin supplied. "And now, if you are feeling somewhat better, will you not be good enough to take another drink—somewhat larger this time, if you please—of this so excellent brandy, then tell us why you call on Mademoiselle Mutina? It so happens that we, too, have much interest in that young lady."

"Who are you?" the youth demanded with sharp suspicion.

"I am Jules de Grandin, doctor of medicine and of the faculty of the Sorbonne, and sometime special agent of the *Sûreté Général*, and this is Dr. Samuel Trowbridge, my very good friend and host," the Frenchman returned with a formal bow. "While saving my life from the miserable, execrable rogue who would have assassinated me, you received an ugly wound, and we brought you here to dress it. And now that social amenities are completed, perhaps you will have the goodness to answer my question concerning Mademoiselle Mutina. Who, may I ask, is she, and what is it you know of her? Believe me, young sir, it is not from idle curiosity, but in the interest of justice, that we ask."

"She is my wife," the young man answered after a moment's thoughtful silence in which he seemed to weigh the advisability of speaking. "I am Richard

Starkweather—perhaps you know my father, Dr. Trowbridge"—he turned to me—"he was president of the old Harrisonville Street Railway before the Public Service took it over."

I nodded. "Yes, I remember him," I replied, "He was two classes ahead of me at Amherst, but we met at alumni gatherings; and—"

"Never mind the reminiscences, Friend Trowbridge," de Grandin interrupted, his logical French mind refusing to be swerved from the matter in hand. "You were about to tell us, *Monsieur*—" He paused significantly, glancing at our patient with raised, quizzical eyebrows.

"I married Mutina in Sabuah Sulu, then again in Manila, but—"

"*Parbleu*—you did marry her twice?" de Grandin demanded incredulously. "How comes it?"

Starkweather took a deep breath, like a man about to dive into a cold stream, then:

"I met Mutina in Sabuah Sulu," he began. "Possibly you gentlemen have read my book, *Malay Pirates as I Knew Them*, and wondered how I became so intimately acquainted with the engaging scoundrels. The fact is, it was all a matter of luck. The Dutch tramp steamer, *Wilhelmina*, on which I was going from Batavia to Manila, put in at Lubuah, and that's how it began. We all went ashore to see the place, which was only a cluster of Chinese *godowns*, a dozen or so European business places and a couple of hotels of sorts. We saw all we wanted of the dried-mud-and-sand town in a couple of hours, but as the ship wasn't pushing out until sometime in the early morning, several of us looked in on a *honky-tonk* which was in full blast at one of the saloons. I don't know what it was they gave me to drink, but it was surely powerful medicine—probably a mixture of crude white rum and *n'gapi*—whatever it was, it affected me as no Western liquor ever did, and I was dead to the world in three drinks. The next thing I remember was waking up the following morning, well after sun-up, to find myself with empty pockets and a dreadful headache, floating out of sight of land in a Chinese *sampan*. I haven't the faintest idea how I got there, though I suspect the other members of the party were too drunk to miss me when they put back for the ship, and the proprietor of the dive, seeing me sprawled out there, improved his opportunity to go through my pockets, then lugged me to the waterfront, dumped me into the first empty boat he found and let me shift for myself. Maybe he cut me adrift; maybe the boat's painter came untied by accident. At any rate, there I was, washed out to sea by the ebbing tide, with no water, no food, and not the slightest idea where I was or how far away the nearest land lay.

"I had barely sense and strength left to set the *sampan's* matting sail before I fell half-conscious into the bottom again, still so sick and weak with liquor that I didn't care particularly whether I ever made land again.

"Just how long I lay there asleep—drugged would be a better term, for that Eastern liquor acts more like opium than alcohol—I haven't the slightest idea. Certainly it was all day; perhaps I slept clear around the clock. When I awoke, the stars were out and the boat was drifting side-on toward a rocky, jagged shore as if she were in a mill-flume.

"I jumped up and snatched the steering paddle, striving with might and main to bring her head around, but I might as well have tried paddling a canoe with a teaspoon. She drove straight for those rocks as if some invisible hand were guiding her to destruction; then, just as I thought I was gone, a big wave caught her squarely under the poop, lifted her over a saw-toothed reef and deposited her on a narrow, sandy shingle almost as gently as if she'd been beached by professional sailors.

"I climbed out as quickly as I could and staggered up the beach, but fell before I'd traversed a quarter-mile. The next thing I knew, it was daylight again and a couple of ugly-looking Malays were standing over me, talking in some outlandish tongue, apparently arguing whether to kill me then or wait a while. I suppose the only thing which saved me was the fact that they'd already been through my pockets and decided that as I had nothing but the tattered clothes I lay in, my live body was more valuable than my wardrobe. Anyhow, they prodded me to my feet with a spear butt and drove me along the beach for almost an hour.

"We finally came to a little horseshoe-shaped cleft in the shore, and just where the sandy shingle met the jungle of *lalang* grass was a village of half a hundred or so white huts clustering about a much larger house. One of my captors pointed toward the bigger building and said something about 'Kapal Besar,' which I assumed to be the name of the village headman.

"He was more than that. He was really a sort of petty sultan, and ruled his little principality with a rod of iron, notwithstanding he was nearly ninety years old and a hopeless paralytic.

"When we got into the village I saw the big house was a sort of combined palace and fortress, for it was surrounded by a high wall of sun-dried brick loopholed for cannon and musketry, and with three or four pieces of ancient ordnance sticking their brass muzzles through the apertures. The wall was topped with an abatis of sharpened bamboo stakes, and a man armed with a Civil War model musket and bayonet stood guard at the gateway through which my finders drove me like a pig on its way to market.

"Inside the encircling wall was a space of smooth sand perhaps ten or twelve feet broad; then a wide, brick-floored piazza roofed over with beams of teak as thick as railway ties laid close together on equally heavy stringers, and from the porch opened any number of doorways into the house.

"My guards led, or drove, me through one of these and down a tiled corridor, while a half-naked boy who popped up out of the darkness like a jack-in-the-box from his case ran on ahead yelling. 'Kapal Besar—hai, *Kapal Tuan!*' at the top of his shrill, nasal voice.

"I was surprised at the size of the room to which I was taken. It was roughly oval in shape, quite fifty feet long by twenty-five or thirty at its greatest width, and paved with alternate black and red tiles. The roof, which rose like a sugar-loaf in the center, was supported on A-beams resting on columns of skinned palm tree boles, and to these were nailed brackets from which swung red-glass bowls filled with coconut-oil with a floating wick burning in each. The result was the place was fairly well illuminated, and I had a good view of the thin, aged man sitting in a chair of carved blackwood at the farther end of the chamber.

"He was a cadaverous old fellow, seemingly almost bloodless, with skin the color of old parchment stretched tight as a drumhead over his skull; thin, pale lips, and a long, straggling white beard sweeping over his tight green jacket. When he looked at me I saw his eyes were light hazel, almost gray, and piercing and direct as those of a hawk. His thin, high-bridged nose reminded me of a hawk's beak, too, and the bony, almost transparent hands which clutched and fingered the silver-mounted bamboo cane in his lap were like a hawk's talons.

"My two guards made profound *salaams*, but I contented myself with the barest nod civility required.

"The old chap looked appraisingly at me while my discoverers harangued him at great length; then, with an impatient motion of his cane, he waved them to silence and began addressing me in Malayan. I didn't know a dozen words of the language, and made signs to him that I couldn't understand, whereupon he switched to an odd slurring sort of Spanish, which I was able to make out with some difficulty.

"Before he'd spoken five minutes I understood my status, and was none too delighted to learn I was regarded as a legitimate piece of sea-salvage—a slave, in plain language. If I had any special talent, I was informed, I'd better be trotting it out for display right off; for, lacking something to recommend me for service in the palace, I would be forthwith shipped off to the yam fields or the groves where the copra was prepared.

"I was at a loss just how to answer the old duffer when I happened to see a sort of guitar lying on the pavement near the door leading to one of the passages which radiated from the audience chamber like wheel-spokes from a hub. Snatching up the instrument, I tuned it quickly, and picking some sort of accompaniment on it, began to sing. I've a pretty fair baritone, and I put more into it that day than I ever did with the college glee club.

"*Juanita, Massa's in de Cold, Cold Ground, Just a Baby's Prayer at Twilight* and *Over There* went big with the old man, but the song that seemed to touch his heart was *John Brown's Body*, and I had to sing the thing from beginning to end at least a dozen times.

"The upshot of it was that I found myself permanently retained as court minstrel, had my torn white duds replaced by a gorgeous red jacket and yellow turban and a brilliantly striped *sarong*, and was assigned one of the best rooms in the palace—which isn't saying much from the standpoint of modern conveniences."

The young man paused a moment, and despite his evident distress a boyish grin spread over his lean, brown countenance. "My big chance came when I'd been there about two months," he continued.

"I prepped at St. John's, and put in a full hitch with the infantry during the war, so the I.D.R. and the manuals of guard duty were as familiar to me as the Scriptures are to a circuit-riding preacher. One day when the disorganized mob old Kapal called his army were slouching through their idea of a guard mount, I snatched his musket from the fellow who acted as top sergeant and showed 'em how to do the thing in proper style. The captain of the guard was sore as a pup, but old Kapal was sitting in the piazza watching the drill, and made 'em take orders from me. In half an hour I had them presenting, porting, ordering and shouldering arms in pretty fair shape, and in two weeks they could do the whole manual, go right by squads and come on right into line as snappily as any outfit you ever saw.

"That settled it. I was made captain-general of the army, wore two swords and a brace of old-fashioned brass-mounted powder and ball revolvers in my waist shawl, and was officially known as Rick-kard Tuan. I taught the soldiers to salute, and the civil population took up the custom. In six months' time I couldn't go for a five-minute stroll without gathering more salutes to the yard than a newly commissioned shavetail in the National Army.

"I'd managed to pick up a working knowledge of the language, and was seeing the people at first-hand, living their lives and almost thinking their thoughts— that's where I got the material for my book. That's how I got Mutina, too.

"One morning after drill Kapal Besar called me into the audience chamber and waved me to a seat. I was the only person on the island privileged to sit in his presence, by the way.

"'My son,' he said, 'I have been thinking much of your future, of late. In you I have found a very pearl among men, and it is my wish that you rear strong sons to take your place in the years to come. Mine, too, mayhap, for I have no men-children to rule after me and there is none I would rather have govern in my stead when it shall have pleased Allah (praised be His glorious name!) to call me hence to Paradise. Therefore, you shall have the choice of my women forthwith.' He clapped his thin old hands in signal as he spoke, and a file of tittering, giggling girls sidled through one of the doors and ranged themselves along the wall.

"Like all Oriental despots, Kapal Besar maintained the *droit du seigneur* rigidly—every woman who pleased him was taken into his seraglio, though the old chap, being close to ninety, and paralyzed from the waist down for nearly twenty years, could be nothing more than nominal husband to them, of course.

"Marriage is simple in Malaya, and divorce simpler. 'Thou art divorced,' is all the husband need say to free himself from an unwanted wife, and the whole thing is finished without courts, lawyers or fees.

"I passed down the line of simpering females, wondering how I was going to sidestep this latest honor royalty had thrust upon me, when I came to Mutina. Mutina signifies 'the Pearl' in Malayan, and this girl hadn't been misnamed. Believe me or not, gentlemen, it was a case of love at first sight, as far as I was concerned.

"She was small, even for a Malay girl—not more than four feet ten, or five feet tall at the most—with smooth, glossy black hair and the tiniest feet and hands I've ever seen. Though she had gone unshod the greater part of her life her feet were slender and high-arched as those of a duchess of the Bourbon court, with long, straight toes and delicate, filbert-shaped nails; and her hands, though used to the heavy work all native women, royal or not, performed, were fine and tapering, and *clean*. She was light-skinned, too, really fairer than I, for her flesh was the color of ivory, while I was deeply sun-burned; and, what attracted me to her more than anything else, I think, her lips and teeth were unstained by betel-nut and there was no smudge or snuff about her nostrils. As she stood there in her prim, modest Malay costume, her eyes modestly cast down and a faint blush staining her face, she was simply ravishing. I felt my heart miss a beat as I paused before her.

"There was a sort of scandalized buzz-buzz of conversation among the women when I turned to Kapal to announce my choice, and the old fellow himself looked surprised for a moment. I thought he was going to renege on his offer, but it developed he thought I'd made an unworthy decision. I'd noticed without thinking of it that the other women kept apart from Mutina, and old Kapal explained the reason in a few terse words. She was, it seemed, *anak gampang*; that is, no one knew who her father was, and such a condition is even more of a social handicap in Malaya than with us. Further, she was suspected of black magical practices, and Kapal went so far as to intimate she had secured the honor of admission to the *zenana* by the use of *guna-guna*, or love potions. Of course, if I wanted her after all he'd said, why, the misfortune was mine—but I was not to complain I hadn't been fairly warned.

"I told him I wanted her if she'd have me, at which he let out a shrill cackle of a laugh, called her to the foot of his throne and spoke so quickly for a minute or so that I couldn't follow him, then waved us all away, saying he wanted to take his siesta."

"I MARCHED FROM THE AUDIENCE chamber to my quarters feeling pretty well satisfied. It really had been a case of love at first sight as far as I was concerned, and I'd made up my mind to pay real courtship to the lovely girl and try to induce her to marry me, for I was determined that, Kapal Besar or no Kapal Besar, I'd not have her as a gift from anyone but herself.

"As I entered my quarters and turned to lay my swords on the couch, I was startled to see a form dart across the threshold and drop crouching to the floor before me.

"It was Mutina. Her little, soft feet had followed me noiselessly down the corridor, and she must have been at my heels when I entered the room.

"'*Kakasih*,' she said as she knelt before me and drew aside her veil, revealing her blushing face, '*laki kakasih amba anghu memuji*—husband, beloved, I adore thee.'

"Gentlemen, did you ever take a drink of rich old sherry and feel its warming glow creep through every vein and nerve in your body? That was the way I felt when I realized what had happened. The rigmarole old Kapal reeled off in the throne-room was a combined divorce-and-marriage ceremony. Mutina was my wife, and—my heart raced like a coasting motor car's engine—with her own soft lips she had declared her love.

"Three weeks later they found Kapal Besar dead in his great carved chair, and fear that I would seize the government almost precipitated a riot, but when I told 'em I wouldn't have the throne as a gift and wanted nothing but a *prau* and crew to take Mutina and me to the Philippines, they darn near forced the crown on me in gratitude.

"Two members of the guard, Hussein and Batjan, with Jobita, Hussein's young wife, asked permission to accompany us, so there was a party of five which set out in the *prau* amid the cheers of the army and the booming of the one of Kapal's brass cannon which could be fired."

Young Starkweather paused in his narrative again, and a sort of puzzled, questioning expression spread over his face. "The day before we left," he went on, "I came into the quarters to get some stuff for the ship and found Mutina backed into a corner, fending off with both hands the ugliest-looking customer I'd ever seen. He was a thin, cadaverous fellow, with slanting, yellow eyes and a face like a walking corpse. I saw in a moment Mutina was deathly afraid of him, and yelled, '*Hei badih iang chelaka!*' which may be freely translated as 'Get to hell out of here, you son of an ill-favored dog!'

"Instead of slinking away as any other native would have done if addressed that way by Rick-kard Tuan, the man just stood there and grinned unpleasantly, if you could call his ugly grimace a grin.

"Sabuah Sulu is a rough place, gentlemen, and rough methods are the rule there. I snatched one of the sabers from my cummerbund and cut at him. The fellow must have been extraordinarily agile; for though I don't see how it happened, I missed him completely, though I'd have sworn my blade cut into his neck. That couldn't have been so, though, for there was no resistance to the steel, and there the man stood, unharmed, after a slash which should have lopped the head clean off his shoulders.

"Mutina seemed more concerned about my safety than the circumstances seemed to warrant, for the intruder was unarmed, while I wore two swords and a pair of pistols, and after he'd slunk away with a final menacing look she threw herself into my arms and wept as if her heart would break. I comforted her as best I could, then ran out to ask the guard who the mysterious man was, but the sentry swore by the teeth and beard of Allah that he had seen no stranger enter or leave the compound that day."

"U'm—a-a-ah?" murmured Jules de Grandin, twisting furiously at the ends of his little golden mustache. "Say on, my friend, this is of the most decided interest."

"We got to Manila without much trouble," Starkweather continued as he shot a wondering look at the little Frenchman. "We passed through the Sulu Sea, landed on southern Luzon and completed the trip overland. We were married with Christian ceremonies by an army chaplain at Manila, and I cabled home for money, then arranged passage for our entire party.

"Coming back to the hotel after making some last-minute sailing arrangements, I thought I noticed the shifty-eyed johnny who annoyed Mutina the day before we left Sabuah Sulu sneaking down the street, and it seemed to me he looked at me with a malicious grin as he ducked around the corner. It couldn't have been the same man, of course, but the resemblance was striking, and so was the coincidence.

"I felt a sort of premonition of evil as I rushed up to our suite, and I was in a perfect frenzy of apprehension when I opened the door and found the rooms empty. Mutina was gone. So were Hussein, Batjan and Jobita. There was no clue to their whereabouts, nothing to tell why or where they'd gone; nothing at all but—this."

From an inside pocket he drew a leather case and extracted a folded sheet of note-paper from it. He passed it to de Grandin, who perused it quickly, nodded once, and handed it to me. A single line of odd, unintelligible characters scrawled across the sheet, but I could make nothing of them till Starkweather translated.

"It's Malayan," he explained. "The same words she first spoke to me: 'Laki kakasih amba anghau memuji—husband, beloved, I adore thee.'

"I was like a crazy man for the next two months. The police did everything possible to find Mutina, and I hired a small army of private detectives, but we never got one trace of any of the three.

"Finally I came home, tried to reconstruct my life as best I could, and wrote my book on the pirates as I had known them.

"Just tonight I learned that Mutina, accompanied by Hussein and Jobita and Batjan, is living in Harrisonville, and that she's an entertainer at La Pantoufle Dorée. I got her address in Algonquin Avenue from one of the club attendants and rushed out there as fast as I could. Just as I entered the yard I saw you scuffling with someone and—believe it or not—I'm sure the man who assaulted you was the one I saw in Sabuah Sulu and later in Manila. I'd recognize those devilish eyes of his anywhere on earth.

"It was good of you gentlemen to bring me here and patch me up instead of sending me to the hospital," he concluded, "but I'm feeling pretty fit again, now, and I must be off. Men, you don't realize, Mutina's in that house, and that slant-eyed devil's hanging around. I've got to go to her right away. I must see Mutina!"

"Then ye'll be after goin' to th' jail, an' nowheres else, I'm thinkin', me boy," a heavy Irish voice announced truculently from the consulting-room door, and Detective Sergeant Jeremiah Costello strode across the threshold.

3

"MUTINA—IN JAIL?" THE YOUNG man faltered unbelievingly.

"Sure, good an' tight, an' where else should she be?" returned the detective with a nod to de Grandin and me. "'Tis sorry I am ter come sneakin' in on yez like this, gentlemen," he apologized, "but th' office sent me up to Algonquin Avenue hotfoot when yer message wuz received, an' after I'd made me arrest I thought I'd best be comin' here ter talk matters over wid yez. Th' bell didn't seem to ring when I pushed th' button, an' it's a cruel cold night outside, so I let meself in, seein' as how yer light waz goin, an' I knew ye'd be up an' ready ter talk."

"Assuredly," de Grandin assented with a nod. "But how comes it that you put Mademoiselle—Madame Mutina under arrest, my friend?"

"Why"—the big Irishman looked wonderingly at the little Frenchman—"what else wuz there ter do, Dr. de Grandin, sor? 'Twas yerself as saw what a howly slaughter-house they'd made o' her place, an' dead men—an' women—don't die widout help. So, when the young woman comes rushin' up ter th' place in a taxi all out o' breath, as ye might say, hot as fire ter be after gittin inside ter meet someone, why, sez I ter meself, 'Ah-ho, me gur-rl, 'tis yerself, an' no one else, as knows sumpin more about these shenanigans than meets th' naked eye, else ye wouldn't be so anxious ter meet someone—wid never a livin' soul save th' pore dead creatures inside th' house ter meet at all, at all.'

"She started some cock-and-bull story about havin' a date wid a gent whose name she didn't know at the house—some foreign man, he were, she said. I'll be bettin' me Sunday boots he wuz a foreigner, too—'twas no Christian American who did those bloody murders, an' ye can be sure o' that, too, savin' yer presence, Dr. de Grandin, sor."

The little Frenchman stroked his tiny wheaten mustache caressingly. "I agree with you, *mon cher*," he assented, "but the young lady's story was not entirely of the gentleman chicken and cow, for it was I whom she was to meet at her house. It was for the purpose of meeting her that Friend Trowbridge and I went there, and found what we discovered. Sergeant Costello, am I a fool?"

"Howly Mither, no!" denied the Irishman. "'If they wuz more fools like you in th' wor-rld, Dr. de Grandin, sor, we'd be after havin' fewer funny houses ter keep th' nitwits in, I'm thinkin'."

"Precisely." de Grandin assented. "But I tell you, *mon brave*, Madame Mutina not only did not commit those killings; she suspected nothing of them. Consider: Is it likely she would have made an assignation with Friend Trowbridge and me had she thought we would find evidences of murder there?"

Costello shook his head.

"*Très bon.* Again: It was twenty-one minutes past eleven when Friend Trowbridge and I left her at La Pontoufle Dorée; it was not later than half-past when we arrived at her house, and the poor ones had not been long dead when we got there—their flesh was warm and there was still heat in the murdered woman's cigar; but they had been dead from ten to fifteen minutes, though not much longer. Nevertheless, if we were with Madame Mutina nine minutes before, she could not have been present at the killing."

"But she might 'a' known sumpin about it," the Irishman persisted.

"I doubt it much. At the night club both Friend Trowbridge and I saw several most unbeautiful men who frightened her greatly. It was at sight of them she entrusted some object to me and begged I go to her home with all speed, there to await her coming. As we drove through the storm on our errand another car passed us with great swiftness. Whether the four unlovely ones rode in it or not, I can not say, but I believe they did. In any event, as we left the house after viewing the murdered bodies, a man closely resembling one of them attacked me from behind, and had it not been for good, brave Friend Trowbridge and this so excellent young man here, Jules de Grandin would now he happy in heaven—I hope.

"As it is"—he seized the pointed tips of his mustache in a sudden fierce grip and twisted them till I thought he would tear the hairs loose—"as it is, I still live, and there is earthly work to do. Come, let us go, let us hasten, let us repair immediately to the jail where I may interview the unfortunate, beautiful Madame Mutina.

"No, my friend," he denied as Starkweather would have risen to accompany us, "it is better that you remain away for a time. Me, I shall undertake that no harm comes to your lady, but for the purposes I have in mind I think it best she sees you not for a time. Be assured, I shall give you leave to greet her at the earliest possible moment."

H IS CHIN THRUST MOODILY into the upturned collar of his greatcoat, the little Frenchman sat beside me in silence as I drove him and Costello toward police headquarters. As we rounded a corner, driving cautiously to avoid skidding over the sleety pavement, he seemed suddenly to arrive at a decision. "Through Tunlaw Street, if you please, good friend," he ordered. "I would stop at the excellent Bacigalupo's for a little minute."

"At Bacigalupo's?" I echoed in amazement. "Why, Mike has been in bed for hours!"

"Then he must arise," was the uncompromising reply. "I would do the business with him."

No light burned in the windows of the tiny flat where Mike Bacigalupo lived above his prosperous fruit stand, but repeated rings at the bell and poundings on the door finally brought a sleepy and none too amiable Italian head from one of the darkened openings, like an irate tortoise peeping from its shell.

"Holà, my friend," de Grandin hailed, "we are come to buy limes. Have the goodness to put ten or a dozen in a bag for us at once."

"Limas?" demanded the Italian in a shocked voice. "You wanta da *lima* at half-pas' fourteen o'clock? You come to hell—I not come down to sell *limas* to Benito Mussolini deesa time o' night. Sapr-r-risti! You mus' t'inka me craze."

For answer de Grandin broke into a flood of rapid, voluble Italian. What he said I do not know, but five minutes later the fruit merchant, shivering with cold inside the folds of a red-flannel bathrobe, appeared at the door and handed him a small paper parcel. More, as we turned away he waved his hand and called, "Arrivederci, amico mio."

I was burning with curiosity as we drove toward headquarters, but long experience with the eccentric little Frenchman had taught me better than to attempt to force his confidence.

It was a frightened and pathetic little figure the police matron ushered into the headquarters room a few minutes later. "M'sieu'," she exclaimed piteously at sight of de Grandin, running forward and holding out both slender ivory hands to him, "you have come to save me from this place?"

"More than that, *ma petit chère*; I have come to save you from those who persecute you, if it please heaven," he replied soberly. "You know not why you are arrested, do you?"

"N-no," she faltered. "I came from the club as quickly as I could, but this man and others seized me as I alighted from my taxi. They would not let me enter my own house or see my faithful friends. Oh, M'sieu', make them let me see Hussein and Batjan and Jobita, please."

"*Ma pauvre*," de Grandin replied, resting his hands gently on her shoulders, "you can not see them ever again. Those of whom we wot—they arrived first."

"D-dead?" the girl stammered half comprehendingly.

He nodded silently as he led her to a seat. Then: "We must see that others do not travel the same path," he added. "You, yourself, may be their next target. You are guilty of no crime, but perhaps it would be safer were you to remain here until—"

As he spoke, never taking his eyes from hers, he rummaged about in his overcoat pocket and suddenly snatched his hand out, crushing one of the limes we had obtained from Bacigalupo between his long, deceptively slender fingers. The pale-gold rind broke beneath his pressure, and a stream of amber juice spurted through the rent, spattering on the girl's bare arm.

"O-o-o-oh—*ai, ai!*" she screamed as the acid liquid touched her flesh, then writhed away from him as though the lime juice had been burning oil.

"*A-hee!*" she gave the shrill, piercing mourning cry of the East as her eyes fastened on the glistening spots of moisture on her forearm, and their round pupils suddenly drew in and shrank to slits like those of a cat coming suddenly out of a darkened room into the light.

"*Bien—très bon!*" de Grandin exclaimed, snatching a silk handkerchief from his cuff and drying her arm. "I am sorry, truly sorry, my poor one; believe me, sooner would Jules de Grandin suffer torture than cause you pain, but it was necessary that I do it. See, it is all well, now."

But it was not all well. Where the gushing lime juice had struck her tender flesh there was a cluster of ugly, red weals on the girl's arm as though her white, soft skin were scalded.

4

FOR A MOMENT THEY faced each other in silence, the alert, blond Frenchman and the magnolia-white Eastern girl, and mutual understanding shone in their eyes.

"How—how did you know?" she faltered.

"I did not know, my little one," de Grandin confessed in a low voice, "but what I learned tonight caused me to suspect. *Hélas*, I was only too right in my surmise!"

He gazed thoughtfully at the prison floor, his narrow chin tightly gripped between his thumb and forefinger, then:

"Are you greatly attached to the Prophet, my child?" he asked. "Would you consent to Christian baptism?"

She looked at him in bewilderment as she replied: "Of course; is not the man of my heart of the Nazarenes? If it so be they go endlessly to be companions of hell-fire, as the Prophet (on whom be peace!) declares in the book of Imran's family, then let Mutina's face be blackened too at the last great day, and let her go to everlasting torment with the man she loves. I ask nothing better in the hereafter than to share his torture, if torture be his portion; but in this life it is written that I must keep far away, else I bring on him the vengeance of—"

"Enough!" de Grandin interrupted almost sternly. "Sergeant, we must release Madame Mutina instantly. Come, I am impatient to take her hence. Trowbridge, my friend, do you engage a clergyman at once and have him at the house without delay. It is of importance that we act with speed."

Mutina had been booked for detention only as a material witness, and it was not difficult for Costello to procure her release. In five minutes they had left for my house in a taxicab while I drove toward Saint Luke's rectory, intent on dragging the Reverend Leon Barley from his bed.

With the clergyman in tow I entered the study an hour later, finding de Grandin, Mutina and Costello talking earnestly, but Starkweather nowhere in sight. "Why, where is—" I began, but the Frenchman's uplifted finger cut my question off half uttered.

"It is better that we name no names at present, Friend Trowbridge," he warned, then to Dr. Barley:

"This young lady has the desire for baptism, *mon père*; you will officiate forthwith? Dr. Trowbridge and I will stand sponsors."

"Why, it's a little unusual," the pastor began, but de Grandin interrupted with a vigorous nod of his head. "*Parbleu*, it is more unusual than you can suppose," he agreed. "It is with the unusual we have to deal tonight my friend, and the ungodly, as well. Come, do us your office and do it quickly, for be assured we have not dragged you from the comfort of your bed for nothing this night."

The Reverend Leon Barley, pious man of God and knowing man of the world, was not the sort of carping stickler for the purity of ecclesiastical rules who casts discredit on the clergy. Though uninformed concerning the ceremony, he realized haste was necessary, and adjusted his stole with the deft quickness learned from service with the A.E.F., and before that in the Philippine insurrection.

Swiftly the beautiful, dignified service proceeded:

"Wilt thou then obediently keep God's holy will and commandments and walk in the same all the days of thy life?" asked Dr. Barley.

"I will, by God's help," murmured Mutina softly.

"Mutina"—Dr. Barley's hand dipped into the Minton salad bowl of water standing on the table and sprinkled a few drops on the girl's bowed head—"I baptize thee in the name of the—"

The solemn pronouncement was drowned in a terrible, blood-chilling scream, for as the sacramental water touched her head Mutina fell forward to the floor and lay there writhing as though in mortal agony.

"Gawd A'mighty!" cried Costello hoarsely. "'Tis th' divil's wor-rk, fer sure!"

"*Sang de Dieu!*" cried Jules de Grandin, bending above the prostrate girl. "Look, Friend Trowbridge, for the love of good God, look!"

Face downward, clawing at the rugs and seemingly convulsed in unsupportable torture, lay Mutina, and the gleaming black hair sleekly parted on her small head *was turning snowy white before our eyes!*

"Great heavens, what is it?" asked the minister unsteadily.

The girl's hysterical movements ceased as de Grandin held a glass of aromatic ammonia and water to her lips, and she whimpered softly as her head rolled weakly in the crook of his elbow.

For a moment he regarded her solicitously; then, as he helped her to a chair, he turned to the clergyman. "It would seem the devil makes much ado about being cheated of a victim," he remarked almost casually. "This poor one was the inheritor of a curse with which she had no more to do than the unborn child with the color of his father's hair. *Eh bien*, I have that upstairs which will do more to revive her body and spirit than all the *eau bénite* in all the world's fonts."

Tiptoeing to the stairs he called: "Richard—Richard, my friend, come down forthwith and see what we have brought!"

There was a pounding of feet on the steps, a glad, wondering cry from the study door, and Richard Starkweather and Mutina, his wife, were locked in each other's arms.

"Come away quickly, my friends," de Grandin ordered in a sharp whisper as he motioned us from the room. "It is a profanation for our eyes to look on their reunion. Anon we must interrupt them, for there is much to be said and much more to be done, but this moment is theirs, and theirs alone."

5

FIVE OF US GATHERED in my drawing-room after dinner the following evening. Sergeant Costello, mellowed with the effects of an excellent meal, several glasses of fifteen-year-old *liqueur Chartreuse* and the fragrant fumes of an Hoyo de Monterey, lolled in the wing chair to the right of the crackling log fire. Richard and Mutina Starkweather, fingers entwined, occupied the lounge before the fireplace, while I sat opposite Costello. In the center, back to the blaze, small blue eyes flashing and dancing with excitement, tiny waxed mustache quivering like the whiskers of an irritable tom-cat, Jules de Grandin stood with his feet well apart, eyeing us in rapid succession. "Observe, my friends," he commanded, thrusting his hand into the inside pocket of his dinner coat and fishing out a newspaper stone proof some four inches by eight inches in size; "is it not the grand surprise I have prepared for our evil-eyed friends?"

With a grandiloquent bow he handed me the paper, bidding me read it aloud. In boldface type the notice announced:

CHEZ LA PONTOUFLE DORÉE
ENGAGEMENT EXTRAORDINARY!
The Sensation of the Year!
La Belle Mutina, former High Priestess of
The Rakshasas
Will Positively Appear at this Club
During the Supper Hour
Tomorrow Night!
La Mutina, Far-famed Malayan Beauty,
Will Perform the Notorious
DANCE OF THE INDONG MUTINA
Disclosing for the First Time
in the Western Hemisphere
The Devilish Rites of the Rakshasas
(Reservations for this extraordinary attraction
will positively not be received
by mail or telephone.)

I glanced at Mutina, sitting demurely beside her husband, then at the exuberant little Frenchman. "All right, what does it mean?" I asked.

"Ah, my friends, what does it not mean?" he replied with a wave of his hand. "Attend me—carefully, if you please:

"Last night at the club, when the good *Madame* took pity on us and lightened our darkness with the lovely presence of Madame Mutina, I was enchanted. When Madame Mutina invited our attention to the pussy-faced evil ones seated at the corner table I was enraged. When we proceeded to Madame Mutina's house and beheld the new-dead stretched so quietly and pitifully there, the spilled blood crying aloud to heaven—and me—for vengeance, *parbleu*, I was greatly interested.

"My friends, the little feet of Jules de Grandin have covered much territory. Where the eternal snow of the northland fly forever before the ceaseless gales, I have been there. Where the sun burns and burns like the fire of the fundamentalists' hell, there have I been. Nowhere, no land, is a stranger to me. And on my many travels I have kept my mind, my eyes and my ears widely open. Ah, I have heard the muted mumblings of the dwellers round Sierra Leone, while the frightened blacks crouch in their cabins and scarce breathe the name of the human leopards for fear of dreadful vengeance. In Haiti I have beheld the unclean rites of *voudois* and witnessed the power of *papaloi* and *mamaloi*. The djinns and efreets of Araby, the *dracus*, werewolves and vampires of Hungary, Russia and Rumania, the *bhuts* of India—I know them all. Also I have been in the Malay Archipelago, and know the *rakshasas*. Certainly.

"Consider, my friends: There is no wonder-tale which affrights mankind after the lights are lit which has not its foundation in present or past fact. The legends of the loves of Zeus with mortal women, his liaisons with Danaë, Io and Europa, they are but ancestral memories of the bad old days when wicked immortals—*incubi*, if you please—worked their evil will on humanity. In the Middle Ages, when faith burned more brightly than at present, men saw more clearly. Recall the story of *Robert le Diable*, scion of Bertha, a human woman, and Bertramo, a foul fiend disguised as a worthy knight. Remember how this misfortunate Robert was the battleground of his mother's gentle nature and his sire's fiendishness; then consider our poor Madame Mutina.

"In Malaya there exists a race of beings since the beginning of the ages, known variously as the people of Antu or Rakshasa. They are inferior fiends, possessing not much of potent magic, for they are heavily admixed with human half-breeds; but at their weakest they are terrible enough. They can in certain instances make themselves invisible, though only to some people. When visible, the Malays say they can be recognized because of their evil eyes, which are yellow-green and sharp as razors. It was such eyes I saw in the villainous faces of the ugly ones who frightened Madame Mutina at the club last night. Even so, I did not connect them with the wicked breed of Rakshasas until we had listened to young Starkweather's story. When he told us of the evil-eyed creatures who persecuted his so lovely wife, and how the sentry at the palace gate declared he had seen no stranger leave, though the scoundrel had fled but a moment before, I remembered how Aristide, the waiter, assured us no one sat at the table where we saw the unlovely four with our own eyes even as he spoke.

"Also, had not the young *Monsieur* told us his lovely lady was *anak gampang*—without known father? But of course. What more reasonable then to suppose her mother had been imposed on by a fiend, even as Bertha of the legend married the foul incubus and was then left without husband at the birth of her daughter? Such things have been.

"Nature, as your American slang has it, is truly grand. She is exceedingly grand, my friends. For every plague with which mankind is visited, good, kind nature provides a remedy, can we but find it. The vampire can not cross running water, and is affrighted of wild garlic blooms. The holy leaves of the holly tree and the young shoots of the ash are terrible to the werewolf. So with the Rakshasa. The fruit and blossom of the lime is to him as molten lead is to us. If he makes an unclean feast of human flesh—of which he is most fond—and disguises it as curried chicken or rice, a drop of lime juice sprinkled on it unmasks it for what it is. A smear of the same juice on his flesh causes him intense anguish, and, while ordinary weapons avail not at all against him—remember how Friend Richard struck one with his saber, yet harmed him not?—a sword or bullet dipped in lime juice kills him to death. Yes.

"Last night, as I thought of these things, I determine on an experiment. *Tiens*, though it worked perfectly, I could have struck myself for that I caused pain to Madame Mutina when I spilled the lime juice on her.

"Now, here we are: Madame Mutina, beautiful as the moon as she lies on the breast of the sea, was part human, part demon. In Mohammed's false religion they have no cure for such as she. 'What to do?' I ask me.

"'Baptize her with water and the spirit,' I answer. 'So doing we shall save her soul alive and separate that which is diabolic from that which is good in her so lovely body.'

"You all beheld what happened when the holy water of sacrament fell upon her head last night. But, *grâce à Dieu*, we have won thus far. She are now all woman. The demon in her departed when her lovely hair turned white.

"Ah, but there was more to the mystery than this. 'Why were those three poor ones done to death? Why did she leave her husband almost at the threshold of the *lune de miel*—how do you say it?—honeymoon?' Those questions I also ask me. There is but one sure way to find out. This morning I talk seriously with her.

"It are needless for me to say she is beautiful—we are men, we have all the excellent eyesight in our eyes. But it is necessary that I report that the he-creatures of the Rakshasas had also found her exceedingly fair. When it was reported that she would be truly married to Friend Richard, not to be a wife in name only to a paralyzed old dodo of a sultan, they were furious. They sent an ambassador to her to say, 'You shall not wed this man.'

"Greatly did she fear these devil-people, but greater than her fear was her love for the gallant gentleman who would take her to wife in the face of all the palace scandal.

"Now, sacred to these unclean Rakshasas is the coconut pearl, the pearl which is truly mother-of-pearl because it contains within an outer shell of lovely nacre an inner core of true pearl, as the coconut shell encloses the white meat. One of these—and they are very rare—our dear Madame Mutina stole from the Rakshasa temple to hold as hostage for the safety of her beloved. That is what she entrusted to me last night when she beheld the evil-eyed ones at the club.

"But though she held the talisman, she still feared the devil-people exceedingly, and when one of them followed her to Manila and threatened death to her beloved if she consorted with him, though it crushed her heart to do so, she fled from her husband, and hid herself securely.

"A woman's love plumbs any depths, however, my friends. Just to be near her wedded lord brought ease to her mangled bosom, and so she followed him to America, and because she dances like a snowflake sporting with the wind and a moonbeam flitting on flowing water, she had no trouble in securing employment at La Pantoufle Dorée.

"The Rakshasas have also traveled overseas. Seeking their sacred token they traced Madame Mutina, and would, perchance, have slain her, even as they murdered her companions, had she not trusted us with the pearl and bidden us bear it away to her house. Knowing where she lived, suspecting, perhaps, that she hid the precious pearl there, the evil ones reached the house before us, slew her friends, and waited for us, but we—Friend Trowbridge and I—put one of them, at least, to flight, while the arrival of Sergeant Costello and his arrest of Madame Mutina prevented their working their will on her. Meantime, I hold the much-sought pearl."

From his jacket pocket he took an object about the size and shape of a hen's egg, a beautiful, opalescent thing which gave off myriad coruscating beams in the rays of the firelight.

"But where do the evil-eyed sons of Satan and his imps hide themselves? Can we find them?" he asked. "Perhaps yes; perhaps no. In any event, it will take much time, and we wish for speed. Therefore we shall resort to a *ruse de guerre*. This morning, after I talked with Madame Mutina I did rush to the office of *le Journal* with a celerity beautiful to behold, and, with the consent of the proprietor of La Pantoufle Dorée, who is an excellent fellow and sells most capital liquor, I inserted the advertisement which Friend Trowbridge has just read.

"*Eh bien*, but the devil-people will surely flock to that cabaret in force tomorrow night. Will they not place reliance in their devilish ability to defy ordinary weapons and attempt to seize the pearl from Madame Mutina as she dances? I shall say they will. But"—he twisted the ends of his mustache savagely—"but they reckon without an unknown host, my friends. You, *cher sergent*, will be there. You, Friend Richard, and you, also, Friend Trowbridge, will be there. As for Jules de Grandin, by the horns, blood and tail of the Devil, he will be there with both feet!

"Ha, *Messieurs les Diables*, tomorrow night we shall show you such a party as you wot not of. Your black blood, which has defied the weapons of men for generations untold, shall flow like springtime freshets when the mounting sun unlocks the icy fetters from the streams!

"And those we do not spoil entirely in the taking, you shall have the pleasure of seating in the electric chair, *mon sergent*," he concluded with a bow to Costello.

6

E VERY TABLE AT LA Pontoufle Dorée was engaged for the supper show the
following night. Here and there the bald head or closely-shaven face of some
regular patron caught the soft lights from the central chandelier, but the vast
majority of the tables were occupied by small, dark, sinister-looking foreigners,
men with oblique eyes and an air of furtive evil which their stylishly cut dinner clothes and sleekly anointed hair could not disguise. Strategically placed,
near every exit, were members of Sergeant Costello's strong-arm squad, looking decidedly uncomfortable in their hired dinner clothes and consuming vast
quantities of the free menu provided by Starkweather's liberal arrangements
with the management with an air of elaborate unconcern. Four patrolmen in
plain clothes lounged near the checkroom counter, eyeing each incoming guest
with shrewd, appraising glances.

Near the dancing-floor, facing each other across a small table, sat de Grandin and Starkweather, while Costello and I made ourselves as inconspicuous
as possible in our places near the swinging doors which screened the main
entrance to the club.

Not many couples whirled and glided on the dancing floor, for the prepon-
derance of men among the patrons was noticeable, and the usual air of well-
bred hilarity which characterized the place was almost entirely lacking.

It was almost half-past eleven when de Grandin gave the signal.

"Now, customers," announced the hostess, advancing to the center of the
floor, "we're in for a real treat. You all know Ma'mselle Mutina; she's danced
here before, but she never did anything like she's going to show tonight. This is
ab-so-lutely the cat's meow, and I don't mean perhaps, either. All set, boys and
girls? Come on, then, give the little lady a big hand!"

Two attendants ran forward, spreading a rich Turkish carpet over the
smoothly waxed boards of the dancing-floor, and as they retreated every light
in the place winked out, leaving the great room in sudden absolute darkness.
Then, like a thrusting sword-blade, a shaft of amethyst light stabbed through
the gloom, centering on the purple velvet curtains beside the orchestra stand.
No sound came from the musicians, and the place was so still I could hear
Costello's heavy breathing where he sat three feet away, and the faint flutter
of a menu-card sounded like the scutter of a wind-blown leaf in a quiet forest
clearing.

Gazing fascinated at the curtains, I saw them move ever so slightly, flutter
a moment, then draw back. Mutina stood revealed.

One little hand on each curtain, she stood like a lovely picture in a frame,
a priceless jewel against a background of opulent purple velvet.

Over her head, covering her snowy hair, was drawn a dark-blue veil, silver-fringed and studded with silver stars, and bound about her brows was a chaplet of gold coin which held the magically glowing, opalescent *indong mutina* against her forehead like the sacred asp on an Egyptian monarch's crown. Her lovely shoulders and bosom were encased in a tight-fitting sleeveless zouave jacket of gold-embroidered cerise satin fringed with gilt hawk-bells. From hips to ankles hung a full, many-plaited skirt of sheerest white muslin which revealed the slim lines of her tapering legs with distracting frankness. About her wrists and ankles were garlands of cunningly fashioned metallic flowers, enameled in natural colors, which clashed their petals together like tiny cymbals, setting up a sweet, musical jingle-jangle each time she moved.

For a moment she poised on slim, henna-stained toes, bending her little head with its jewel of glowing pearl as if in response to an ovation; then, raising her arms full length, she laced her long, supple fingers above her head, pirouetted half-a-dozen times till the flower-bells on her ankles seemed to clap their petals for very joy and her sheer, diaphanous skirt stood stiffly out, whirling round her like a wheel of white. Next, with a quick, dodging motion, she advanced a step or two, retreated, and bent almost double in a profound *salaam* to the audience.

A second of tableau; then with a long, graceful bound she reached the center of the rug spread on the dance floor, turning to the orchestra and snapping her fingers imperatively. A flageolet burst into a strain of rippling, purling minors, a zither hummed and sang accompaniment, a tom-tom seconded with a hollow, thumping rhythm.

"*Hai!*" she cried in gipsy abandon. "*Hai, hai, hai!*"

With a slow, gliding movement she began her dance, hands and feet moving subtly, in perfect harmony. Now she leaned forward till her cerise bodice seemed barely to clear the floor, now she bent back till it seemed she could not retain her balance. Again her little naked feet were motionless on the dark carpet as twin stars reflected in a still pool while her body swayed and rippled from ankle to chin like a cobra rearing upright, and her arms, seemingly boneless, described sinuous, serpentine patterns in the air, her hands bent backward till the fingers almost touched the wrists.

Now pipe and zither were stilled and only the *rhum, rhum, rhum,—rhum-rhum*, of the tom-tom spoke, and her torso throbbed and rippled in the *danse du ventre*.

The music rose suddenly to a shrill crescendo and she began to whirl on her painted toes with a wild fandango movement, her arms straight out from her shoulders as though nailed to an invisible cross, her skirt flickering horizontally about her like some great, white-petaled flower, her little, soft feet making little, soft hissing sounds against the purple carpet as she spun round and round.

Slowly, slowly, her speed decreased. She was like a beautiful top spun at greatest speed, gradually losing its momentum. The music died to a thin, plaintive wail, the pipe whimpering softly, the zither crooning sleepily and the tom-tom's rumble growing fainter and fainter like receding summer thunder.

For a moment she paused, dead-still, only her slim breasts moving as they fought flutteringly for breath. Then, in a high, sweet soprano, she began an old Eastern love song, a languorous, beguiling tune of a people who have made a fine art of lovemaking for uncounted generations.

For thou, beloved, art to me
As a garden;
Even as a garden of rare and beauteous flowers.
Roses bloom upon thy lips,
And the mountain myrtle
In thy eyes.
Thy breasts are even as the lily,
Even as the moonflower
Who unveils her pale face nightly
To the passionate caresses of the moon.
Thy hair is as the tendril of the grape . . .

With slow, gliding steps she retreated toward the archway through which she had come, paused a moment, and held her hands out to the audience, her henna-tipped fingers curled into little, flowerlike cups.

As she halted in her recessional a great shout went up from one of the slant-eyed men nearest the dancing-floor.

In a moment the place was like an unroofed ant-hill.

"Lights!" shouted de Grandin, springing from his seat. "Trowbridge—Costello, guard the door!"

In the sudden welter of bright illumination as every light in the place was snapped on, we saw a circle of the strange people forming and slowly closing on Mutina, more than one of the men stealthily drawing a wicked-looking Malay *kris* from beneath his coat.

Thrusting both hands beneath her star-sown veil the girl brought forth a pair of limes, broke their rinds with frantic haste and sprinkled a circle of the acid, amber juice about her on the floor.

An evil-eyed man who seemed to be the leader of the strangers started backward with a snarl of baffled rage as she completed the circle, and looked wonderingly about him.

"Ha, my ugly-faced friend, you did not expect that, *hein?*" asked Jules de Grandin in high good humor. "Me, I am responsible for it. As a half-breed of your cursed devil-tribe, Madame Mutina could no more have touched a lime than she could have handled a live coal, but with the aid of a Christian priest I have freed her from her curse, and now she does defy you. Meanwhile—"

He got no further. With a yell of fury like the scream of a blood-mad leopard, the razor-eyed creature leaped forward, and at his back pressed a half-score of others of his kind.

"Back to back, *mon brave*," de Grandin commanded Starkweather as he thrust his hand inside his jacket and brought forth an eighteen-inch length of flexible, rubber-bound electric cable tipped with a ball of lead in which a dozen steel spikes had been embedded.

Similarly armed, young Starkweather whirled round, bracing his shoulders to the little Frenchman's back.

Feet well apart, de Grandin and his ally swung their improvised maces, with the regularity of pendulums.

Screams and curses and cries of surprised dismay followed every downstroke of the spiked clubs. The assailants, half their former number, drew back, mouthing obscenities at the pair, then rushed again to the attack.

Mutina was like a thing possessed. Gone was every vestige of Western culture she had picked up during her residence here. She was once more a woman of the never-changing East, an elemental female creature, stark bare of all conventions, glorying in the battle and the savage part her man played in it. Safe inside her barrier of lime juice, she danced up and down in wild elation as de Grandin and Starkweather, slowly advancing across the dance floor, beat a path toward her, smashing arms and ribs and skulls with the merciless flailing of their spiked clubs.

"Bravely struck, O defender of the fatherless!" she screamed. "*Billahi*—by the breath of God, well struck, O peerless warrior!"

"Up an' at 'em boys!" bellowed Costello, seeming to emerge suddenly from the trance of admiration with which he had watched de Grandin and Starkweather battle. "Give 'em th' wor-rks!"

Like terriers leaping on a pitful of rats, Costello's detectives boiled over the dancing-floor. Blackjacks, previously well soaked in lime juice, brass knuckles similarly treated, and here and there a big, raw fist, still wet with its baptism of acid liquid, struck and hammered against brown faces and dashed devastating blows into wicked, slanting yellow eyes.

"BE DAD, Dr. DE Grandin, sor," declared Costello twenty minutes later as he wrung the little Frenchman's slender white hand, "'tis th' broth of a boy ye are, an' no mistake. Never in all me bor-rn days have I seen a better lad wid th' old shillalah. Glory be to Gawd, but ye'd be th' pride o' all th' colleens an' th' despair o' all the boys if ye ever went ter Donnybrook Fair, so ye would, sir!"

"A vintage, *Madame*," de Grandin cried to the stout hostess who hovered near, uncertain whether to bewail the fight which had emptied her establish‑ ment or add her congratulations to Costello's, "a vintage of your rarest, and let it be not less than two quarts. Me, I have serious drinking to do, now that business is finished. Have no fear of the good Sergeant. Have I not heard him say more than once that legging of the boot is more a work of Christian charity than a crime? Certainly.

"To us, my friends," he pronounced when the champagne was brought and our glasses filled with bubbling, pale-yellow liquid. "To stout young Monsieur Starkweather, who fights like a very du Guesclin; to Trowbridge and Costello, than whom no man ever had better friends or better comrades; but most of all, beautiful Mutina, to you. To you, who braved the sorrows of a broken heart and the wrath of the devil-people on earth and the tortures of the False Prophet's everlasting hell hereafter for love of him who is your husband. *Cordieu*, never was toast drunk to a nobler, gentler lady—he who says otherwise is a foul liar!"

He sent the fragile goblet crashing to the floor as the pledge was finished, and turned again to the reunited couple. "Your troubles are like the shadows of him who walks westward in the evening, my friends," he assured them. "For ever and for always they lie behind you. As for the foul Rakshasas—pouf! as young Starkweather and I shattered their evil skulls, their power over you is shattered for all time, even as this—" Snatching the glowing *indong mutina* from the girl's diadem he struck it sharply against the table edge. The iridescent shell cracked, almost as though it had been an egg, and from it dropped the most magnificent pearl I had ever seen. Large as a small marble it was, with a pigeon's-neck luster and deep, opal-like fire-gleams in its depths which held the eyes in fascination as a magic crystal might hold a devotee enthralled. Ignorant as I was of such matters, I knew the thing must be worth at least thirty thousand dollars, perhaps twice that sum.

"To a pearl among women, a pearl among pearls," de Grandin announced, taking Mutina's little hand in his and kissing her painted finger tips, one after the other, then closing them about the lustrous gem. "Take you each other to yourselves, my friends," he bade, "and may the good God bless you and yours for ever and always."

Simply as a child, wholly unmindful of the rest of us, Mutina turned her lips for her husband's caress, and as she did so, I heard her murmur softly: "*Laki kakasih amba kau puji sampei kakol*—best beloved, husband and lover, forever and forever I adore thee!"

The Devil's Rosary

M Y FRIEND JULES DE Grandin was in a seasonably sentimental mood. "It is the springtime, Friend Trowbridge," he reminded as we walked down Tonawanda Avenue. "The horse-chestnuts are in bloom and the black-birds whistle among the branches at St. Cloud; the tables are once more set before the cafés, and—*grand Dieu, la belle creature!*" He cut short his remarks to stare in undisguised admiration at a girl about to enter an old-fashioned horse-drawn victoria at the curb.

Embarrassed, I plucked him by the elbow, intent on drawing him onward, but he snatched his arm away and bounded forward with a cry, even as my fingers touched his sleeve. "Attend her, my friend," he called; "she faints!"

As she seated herself on the taupe cushions of her carriage, the girl reached inside her silver mesh bag, evidently in search of a handkerchief, fumbled a moment among the miscellany of feminine fripperies inside the reticule, then wilted forward as though bludgeoned.

"*Mademoiselle*, you are ill, you are in trouble, you must let us help you!" de Grandin exclaimed as he mounted the vehicle's step. "We are physicians," he added in belated explanation as the elderly coachman turned and favored us with a hostile stare.

The girl was plainly fighting hard for consciousness. Her face had gone death-gray beneath its film of delicate make-up, and her lips trembled and quavered like those of a child about to weep, but she made a brave effort at composure. "I—I'm—all—right—thank—you," she murmured disjointedly. "It's—just—the—heat—" Her protest died half uttered and her eyelids fluttered down as her head fell forward on de Grandin's ready shoulder.

"*Morbleu*, she has swooned!" the little Frenchman whispered. "To Dr. Trowbridge's house—993 Susquehanna Avenue!" he called authoritatively to the coachman. "*Mademoiselle* is indisposed." Turning to the girl he busied himself making her as comfortable as possible as the rubber-tired vehicle rolled smoothly over the asphalt roadway.

She was, as de Grandin had said, a "belle créature." From the top of her velour hat to the pointed tips of her suede pumps she was all in gray, a platinum fox scarf complementing the soft, clinging stuff of her costume, a tiny bouquet of early-spring violets lending the sole touch of color to her ensemble. A single tendril of daffodil-yellow hair escaped from beneath the margin of her close-fitting hat lay across a cheek as creamy-smooth and delicate as a babe's.

"Gently, my friend," de Grandin bade as the carriage stopped before my door. "Take her arm—so. Now, we shall soon have her recovered."

In the surgery he assisted the girl to a chair and mixed a strong dose of aromatic ammonia, then held it to the patient's blanched lips.

"Ah—so, she revives," he commented in a satisfied voice as the delicate, violet-veined lids fluttered uncertainly a moment, then rose slowly, unveiling a pair of wide, frightened purple eyes.

"Oh—" the girl began in a sort of choked whisper, half rising from her seat, but de Grandin put a hand gently on her shoulder and forced her back.

"Make haste slowly, *ma belle petite*," he counseled. "You are still weak from shock and it is not well to tax your strength. If you will be so good as to drink this—" He extended the glass of ammonia toward her with a bow, but she seemed not to see it. Instead, she stared about the room with a dazed, panic-stricken look, her lips trembling, her whole body quaking in a perfect ague of unreasoning terror. Somehow, as I watched, I was reminded of a spectacle I had once witnessed at the zoo when Rajah, a thirty-foot Indian python, had refused food, and the curators, rather than lose a valuable reptile by starvation, overrode their compunctions, and thrust a poor, helpless white rabbit into the monster's glass-walled den.

"I've seen it; I've seen it; *I've seen it!*" She chanted the litany of terror, each repetition higher, more intense, nearer the boundary of hysteria than the one before.

"*Mademoiselle!*" de Grandin's peremptory tone cut her terrified iteration short. "You will please not repeat meaningless nothings to yourself while we stand here like a pair of stone monkeys. What is it you have seen, if you please?"

The unemotional, icy monotone in which he spoke brought the girl from her near-hysteria as a sudden dash of cold water in the face might have done. "This!" she cried in a sort of frenzied desperation as she thrust her hand into the mesh bag pendent from her wrist. For a moment she ransacked its interior with groping fingers; then, gingerly, as though she held something live and venomous, brought forth a tiny object and extended it to him.

"U'm?" he murmured non-committally, taking the thing from her and holding it up to the light as though it were an oddity of nature.

It was somewhat smaller than a hazel-nut, smooth as ivory, and stained a brilliant red. Through its axis was bored a hole, evidently for the purpose of accommodating a cord. Obviously, it was one of a strand of inexpensive beads, though I was at a loss to say of what material it was made. In any event, I could see nothing about the commonplace little trinket to warrant such evident terror as our patient displayed.

Jules de Grandin was apparently struck by the incongruity of cause and effect, too, for he glanced from the little red globule to the girl, then back again, and his narrow, dark eyebrows raised interrogatively. At length: "I do not think I apprehend the connection," he confessed. "This"—he tapped the tiny ball with a well manicured forefinger—"may have deep significance to you, *Mademoiselle*, but to me it appears—"

"Significance?" the girl echoed. "It has! When my mother was drowned in Paris, a ball like this was found clutched in her hand. When my brother died in London, we found one on the counterpane of his bed. Last summer my sister was drowned while swimming at Atlantic Highlands. When they recovered her body, they found one of these terrible beads hidden in her bathing-cap!" She broke off with a retching sob and rested her arm on the surgery table, pillowing her face on it and surrendering herself to a paroxysm of weeping.

"Oh, I'm doomed," she wailed between blanching lips. "There's no help for me, and—I'm too young; I don't want to die!"

"Few people do, *Mademoiselle*," de Grandin remarked dryly. "However, I see no cause of immediate despair. Over an hour has passed since you discovered this evil talisman, and you still live. So much for the past. For the future you may trust in the mercy of heaven and the cleverness of Jules de Grandin. Meantime, if you are sufficiently recovered, we shall do ourselves the honor of escorting you home."

UNDER DE GRANDIN'S ADROIT questioning we learned much of the girl's story during our homeward drive. She was Haroldine Arkright, daughter of James Arkright, a wealthy widower who had lately moved to Harrisonville and leased the Broussard mansion in the fashionable west end. Though only nineteen years old, she had spent so much time abroad that America was more foreign to her than France, Spain or England.

Born in Waterbury, Connecticut, she had lived there during her first twelve years, and her family had been somewhat less than moderately well-to-do. Her father was an engineer, and spent much time abroad. Occasionally, when his remittances were delayed, the family felt the pinch of undisguised poverty. One day her father returned home unexpectedly, apparently in a state of great agitation. There had been mysterious whisperings, much furtive going and coming;

then the family entrained for Boston, going immediately to the Hoosac Tunnel Docks and taking ship for Europe.

She and her sister were put to school in a convent at Rheims, and though they had frequent and affectionate letters from their parents, the communications came from different places each time; so she had the impression her elders led a Bedouin existence.

At the outbreak of the war the girls were taken to a Spanish seminary, where they remained until two years before, when they joined their parents in Paris.

"We'd lived there only a little while," she continued, "when two gendarmes came to our apartment one afternoon and asked for Daddy. One of them whispered something to him and he turned white as a sheet; then, when the other took something from his pocket and showed it, Daddy fell over in a dead faint. It wasn't till several hours later that we children were told. Mother's body had been found floating in the Seine, and one of those horrible little red balls was in her hand. That was the first we ever heard of them.

"Though Daddy was terribly affected by the tragedy, there was something we couldn't understand about his actions. As soon as the *Pompes Funèbres* (the municipal undertakers) had conducted the services, he made arrangements with a solicitor to sell all our furniture, and we moved to London without stopping to pack anything but a few clothes and toilet articles.

"In London we took a little cottage out by Garden City, and we lived—it seemed to me—almost in hiding; but before we'd lived there a year my brother Philip died, and—they found the second of these red beads lying on the cover of his bed.

"Father seemed almost beside himself when Phil died. We left—fled would be a better word—just as we had gone from Paris, without stopping to pack a thing but our clothes. When we arrived in America we lived in a little hotel in downtown New York for a while, then moved to Harrisonville and rented this house furnished.

"Last summer Charlotte went down to the Highlands with a party of friends, and—" she paused again, and de Grandin nodded understandingly.

"Has *Monsieur* your father ever taken you into his confidence?" he asked at length. "Has he, by any chance, told you the origin of these so mysterious little red pellets and—"

"Not till Charlotte drowned," she cut in. "After that he told me that if I ever saw such a ball anywhere—whether worn as an ornament by some person, or among my things, or even lying in the street—I was to come to him at once."

"U'm?" he nodded gravely. "And have you, perhaps, some idea how this might have come into your purse?"

"No. I'm sure it wasn't there when I left home this morning, and it wasn't there when I opened my bag to put my change in after making my purchases at Braunstein's, either. The first I saw of it was when I felt for a handkerchief after getting into the carriage, and—oh, I'm terribly afraid, Dr. de Grandin. I'm too young to die! It's not fair; I'm only nineteen, and I was to have been married this June and—"

"Softly, *ma chère*," he soothed. "Do not distress yourself unnecessarily. Remember, I am with you."

"But what can you do?" she demanded. "I tell you, when one of these beads appears anywhere about a member of our family, it's too late for—"

"*Mademoiselle*," he interrupted, "it is never too late for Jules de Grandin—if he be called in time. In your case we have—" His words were drowned by a sudden angry roar as a sheet of vivid lightning tore across the sky, followed by the bellow of a deafening crash of thunder.

"*Parbleu*, we shall be drenched!" de Grandin cried, eyeing the cloud-hung heavens apprehensively. "Quick, Trowbridge, *mon vieux*, assist Mademoiselle Haroldine to alight. I think we would better hail a taxi and permit the coach-man to return alone with the carriage.

"One moment, if you please, *Mademoiselle*," he ordered as the girl took my outstretched hand; "that little red ball which you did so unaccountably find in your purse, you will let me have it—a little wetting will make it none the less interesting to your father." Without so much as a word of apology, he opened the girl's bag, extracted the sinister red globule and deposited it between the cushions of the carriage seat, then, with the coachman's aid, proceeded to raise the vehicle's collache top.

As the covered carriage rolled rapidly away, he raised his hand, halting a taxicab, and calling sharply to the chauffeur: "Make haste, my friend. Should you arrive at our destination before the storm breaks, there is in my pocket an extra dollar for you."

The driver earned his fee with compound interest, for it seemed to me we transgressed every traffic ordinance on the books in the course of our ride, cutting corners on two wheels, racing madly in the wrong direction through one-way streets, taking more than one chance of fatal collision with passing vehicles.

The floodgates of the clouds were just opening, and great torrents of water were cataracting down when we drew up beneath the Arkright porte-cochère, and de Grandin handed Haroldine from the cab with a ceremonious bow, then turned to pay the taxi-man his well-earned bonus.

"*Mordieu*, our luck holds excellently well—" he began as we turned toward the door, but a blaze of lightning more savage than any we had seen thus far and the roaring detonation of a thunderclap which seemed fairly to split the heavens blotted out the remainder of his sentence.

The girl shrank against me with a frightened little cry as the lightning seared our eyes, and I sympathized with her terror, for it seemed to me the flash must have struck almost at our feet, so nearly simultaneous were fire and thunder, but a wild, half-hysterical laugh from de Grandin brought me round with an astonished exclamation.

The little Frenchman had rushed from the shelter of the mansion's porch and pointed dramatically toward the big stone pillars flanking the entrance to the grounds. There, toppled on its side as though struck fairly by a high-explosive shell, lay the victoria we had ordered to follow us, the horses kicking wildly at their shattered harness, the coachman thrown a clear dozen feet from his vehicle, and the carriage itself reduced to splinters scarcely larger than matchstaves.

Heedless of the drenching rain, we raced across the lawn and halted by the prostrate postilion. Miraculously, the man was not only living, but regaining consciousness as we reached him. "Glory be to God!" he exclaimed piously as we helped him to his feet. "'Tis only by th' mercy o' heaven I'm still a livin' man!"

"*Eh bien*, my friend"—de Grandin gave his little blond mustache a sharp twist as he surveyed the ruined carriage—"perhaps the stupidity of hell may have something to do with it. Look to your horses; they seem scarcely worse off than yourself, but they may be up to mischief if they remain unchaperoned."

Once more beneath the shelter of the porte-cochère, as calmly as though discussing the probability of the storm's abatement, he proposed: "Let us go in, my friends. The horses and coachman will soon be all right. As for the carriage"—he raised his narrow shoulders in a fatalistic shrug—"*Mademoiselle*, I hope *Monsieur* your father carried adequate insurance on it."

2

THE LITTLE FRENCHMAN LAID his hand on the polished brass handle of the big oak door, but the portal held its place unyieldingly, and it was not till the girl had pressed the bell button several times that a butler who looked as if his early training had been acquired while serving as guard in a penitentiary appeared and paid us the compliment of a searching inspection before standing aside to admit us.

"Your father's in the living-room, Miss Haroldine," he answered the girl's quick question, then followed us half-way down the hall, as though reluctant to let us out of sight.

Heavy draperies of mulberry and gold brocade were drawn across the living-room windows, shutting out the lightning flashes and muffling the rumble of the thunder. A fire of resined logs burned cheerfully in the marble-arched fireplace, taking the edge from the early-spring chill; electric lamps under painted shades spilled pools of light on Turkey carpets, mahogany shelves loaded with ranks of morocco-bound volumes and the blurred blues, reds and purples of Oriental porcelains. On the walls the dwarfed perfection of several beautifully executed miniatures showed, and in the far corner of the apartment loomed the magnificence of a massive grand piano.

James Arkright leaped from the overstuffed armchair in which he had been lounging before the fire and whirled to face us as we entered the room, almost, it seemed to me, as though he were expecting an attack. He was a middle-aged man, slender almost to the point of emaciation, with an oddly parchmentlike skin and a long, gaunt face rendered longer by the iron-gray imperial pendant from his chin. His nose was thin and high-bridged, like the beak of a predatory bird, and his ears queer, Panesque appendages, giving his face an odd, impish look. But it was his eyes which riveted our attention most of all. They were of an indeterminate color, neither gray nor hazel, but somewhere between, and darted continually here and there, keeping us constantly in view, yet seeming to watch every corner of the room at the same time. For a moment, as we trooped into the room, he surveyed us in turn with that strange, roving glance, a light of inquiring uncertainty in his eyes fading to a temporary relief as his daughter presented us.

As he resumed his seat before the fire the skirt of his jacket flicked back and I caught a fleeting glimpse of the corrugated stock of a heavy revolver holstered to his belt.

The customary courtesies having been exchanged we lapsed into a silence which stretched and lengthened until I began to feel like a bashful lad seeking an excuse for bidding his sweetheart adieu. I cleared my throat, preparatory to making some inane remark concerning the sudden storm, but de Grandin forestalled me.

"*Monsieur*," he asked as his direct, unwinking stare bored straight into Arkright's oddly watchful eyes, "when was it you were in Tibet, if you please?"

The effect was electric. Our host bounded from his chair as though propelled by an uncoiled spring, and for once his eyes ceased to rove as he regarded the little Frenchman with a gaze of mixed incredulity and horror. His hand slipped beneath his jacket to the butt of the concealed weapon, but:

"Violence is unnecessary, my friend," de Grandin assured him coolly. "We are come to help you, if possible, and besides, I have you covered"—he glanced momentarily at the bulge in his jacket pocket where the muzzle of his tiny Ortgies automatic pressed against the cloth—"and it would be but an instant's work to kill you several times before you could reach your pistol. Very good"—he gave one of his quick, elfish smiles as the other subsided into his chair—"we do make progress.

"You wonder, perhapsly, how comes it I ask that question? Very well. A half-hour or so ago, when *Mademoiselle* your lovely daughter was recovered from her fainting-spell in Dr. Trowbridge's office, she tells us of the sinister red bead she has found in her purse, and of the evil fortune such little balls have been connected with in the past.

"I, *Monsieur*, have traveled a very great much. In darkest Africa, in innermost Asia, where few white men have gone and lived to boast of it, I have been there. Among the head-hunters of Papua, beside the upper, banks of the Amazon, Jules de Grandin has been. *Alors*, is it so strange that I recognize this so mysterious ball for what it is? *Parbleu*, in disguise I have fingered many such in the lamaseries of Tibet!

"*Mademoiselle's* story, it tells me much; but there is much more I would learn from you if I am to be of service. You were once poor. That is no disgrace. You suddenly became rich; that also is no disgrace, nor is the fact that you traveled up and down the world almost constantly after the acquisition of your fortune necessarily confession of wrongdoing. But"—he fixed his eyes challengingly on our host—"but what of the other occurrences? How comes it that *Madame* your wife (God rest her spirit!) was found floating in the Seine with such a red ball clutched in her poor, dead hand?

"Me, I have recognized this ball. It is a bead from the rosary of a Buddhist lama of that devil-ridden gable of the world we call Tibet. How came *Madame* to be grasping it? Who knows?

"When next we see one of these red beads, it is on the occasion of the sudden sad death of the young *Monsieur*, your son.

"Later, when you have fled like one pursued to America and settled in this small city which nestles in the shadow of the great New York, comes the death of your daughter, Mademoiselle Charlotte—and once more the red ball appears.

"This afternoon Mademoiselle Haroldine finds the talisman of impending doom in her purse and forthwith swoons in terror. Dr. Trowbridge and I succor her and are conveying her to you when a storm arises out of a clear sky. We change vehicles and I leave the red bead behind. All goes well until—*pouf!*—a bolt of lightning strikes the carriage in which the holder of this devil's rosary seems to ride, and demolishes it. But horses and coachman are spared. *Cordieu*, it is more than merely strange; it is surprising, it is amazing, it is astonishing! One who does not know what Jules de Grandin knows would think it incomprehensible.

"It is not so. I know what I have seen. In Tibet I have seen those masked devil-dancers cause the rain to fall and the winds to blow and the lightning bolts to strike where they willed. They are worshipers of the demons of the air, my friends, and it was not for nothing the wise old Hebrews named Satan, the rejected of God, the Prince of the Powers of the Air. No.

"Very well. We have here so many elements that we need scarcely guess to know what the answer is. *Monsieur* Arkright, as the roast follows the fish and coffee and cognac follow both, it follows that you once wrested from the lamas of Tibet some secret they wished kept; that by that secret you did obtain much wealth; and that in revenge those old heathen monks of the mountains follow you and yours with implacable hatred. Each time they strike, it would appear, they leave one of these beads from the red rosary of vengeance as sign and seal of their accomplished purpose. Am I not right?" He looked expectantly at our host a moment; then, with a gestured application for permission from Haroldine, produced a French cigarette, set it alight and inhaled its acrid, ill-flavored smoke with gusto.

James Arkright regarded the little Frenchman as a respectable matron might look at the blackmailer threatening to disclose an indiscretion of her youth. With a deep, shuddering sigh he slumped forward in his chair like a man from whom all the resistance has been squeezed with a single titanic pressure. "You're right, Dr. de Grandin," he admitted in a toneless voice, and his eyes no longer seemed to take inventory of everything about him. "I *was* in Tibet; it was there I stole the *Pi Yü* Stone—would God I'd never seen the damned thing!"

"Ah?" murmured de Grandin, emitting a twin column of mordant smoke from his narrow nostrils. "We make progress. Say on, *Monsieur*; I listen with ears like the rabbit's. This *Pi Yü* Stone, it is what?"

Something like diffidence showed in Arkright's face as he replied, "You won't believe me, when I've told you."

De Grandin emitted a final puff of smoke and ground the fire from his cigarette against the bottom of a cloisonné bowl. "*Eh bien, Monsieur*," he answered with an impatient shrug, "it is not the wondrous things men refuse to credit. Tell the ordinary citizen that Mars is sixty million miles from the earth, and he believes you without question. Hang up a sign informing him that a fence is newly painted, and he must needs smear his finger to prove your veracity. Proceed, if you please."

"I was born in Waterbury," Arkright began in a sort of half-fearful, half-stubborn monotone, "and educated as an engineer. My father was a Congregational clergyman, and money was none too plentiful with us; so, when I completed my course at Sheff, I took the first job that offered. They don't pay any too princely salaries to cubs just out of school, you know, and the very necessity of my finding employment right away kept me from making a decent bargain for myself.

"For ten years I sweated for the N.Y., N.H.&H., watching most of my classmates pass me by as though I stood stone-still. Finally I was fed up. I had a wife and three children, and hardly enough money to feed them, let alone give them the things my classmates' families had. So, when I got an offer from a British house to do some work in the Himalayas it looked about as gorgeous to me as the fairy godmother's gifts did to Cinderella. It would get me away from America and the constant reminders of my failure, at any rate.

"The job took me into upper Nepal and I worked at it for close to three years, earning the customary vacation at last. Instead of going down into India, as most of the men did, I pushed up into Tibet with another chap who was keen on research, and a party of six Bhotia bearers. We had no particular goal in mind, but we'd been so fed up on stories of the weird happenings in those mountain lamaseries, we thought we'd go up and have a look—see on our own.

"There was some good shooting on the way, and what few natives we ran into were harmless enough if you kept 'em far enough away to prevent their cooties from climbing aboard you; so we really didn't get much excitement out of the trip, and had about decided it was a bust when we came on a little lamasery perched like an eagle's nest on the edge of an enormous cliff.

"We managed to scramble up the zigzag path to the place, and had some difficulty getting in, but at last the ta-lama agreed we might spend the night there.

"They didn't seem to take any particular notice of us after we'd unslung our packs in the courtyard, and we had the run of the place pretty much to ourselves. Clendenning, my English companion, had knocked about Central Asia for upward of twenty years, and spoke several Chinese dialects as well as Tibetan, but for some reason he'd played dumb when we knocked at the gates and let our head man interpret for us.

"About four o'clock in the afternoon he came to me in a perfect fever of excitement. 'Arkright, old boy,' he whispered, 'this blighted place is simply filthy with gold—raw, virgin gold!'

"'You're spoofing,' I told him; 'these poor old duffers are so God-awful poor they'd crawl a mile on their bare knees and elbows for a handful of copper cash.'

"'*Cash* my hat!' he returned. 'I tell you, they've got great heaps and stacks of gold here; gold enough to make our perishing fortunes ten times over if we could shift to get the blighted stuff away. Come along, I'll show you.'

"He fairly dragged me across the courtyard where our duffle was stored, through a low doorway, and down a passage cut in the solid rock. There wasn't a lama or servant in sight as we made our way through one tunnel after another; I suppose they were so sure we couldn't understand their lingo that they thought it a waste of time to watch us. At any rate, no one offered us any interruption while we clambered down three or four flights of stairs to a sort of cavern which had been artificially enlarged to make a big, vaulted cellar.

"Gentlemen"—Arkright looked from de Grandin to me and back again—"I don't know what it is, but something seems to get into a white man's blood when he goes to the far corners of the world. Men who wouldn't think of stealing a canceled postage stamp at home will loot a Chinese or Indian treasure house clean and never stop to give the moral aspects of their actions a second thought. That's the way it was with Clendenning and me. When we saw those stacks of golden ingots piled up in that cave like firewood around the sides of a New England woodshed, we just went off our heads. Nothing but the fact that the two of us couldn't so much as lift, much less carry, a single one of the bars kept us from making off with the treasure that minute.

"When we saw we couldn't carry any of it off we were almost wild. Scheme after scheme for getting away with the stuff was broached, only to be discarded. Stealth was no go, for we'd be sure to be seen if we tried to lead our bearers down the tunnels; force was out of the question, for the lamas outnumbered us ten to one, and the ugly-looking knives they wore were sufficient warning to us not to get them roused.

"Finally, when we were almost insane with futile planning, Clendenning suggested, 'Come on, let's get out of this cursed place. If we look around a little we may find a cache of jewels—we wouldn't need a derrick to carry off a couple of Imperial quarts of them, at any rate.'

"The underground passages were like a Cretan labyrinth, and we lost our way more than once while we stumbled around with no light but the flicker of Clendenning's electric torch, but after an hour or more of floundering over the damp, slippery stones of the tunnels, we came to a door stopped with a curtain of yak's hide. A fat, shaven-headed lama was sitting beside it, but he was sound asleep and we didn't trouble to waken him.

"Inside was a fair-sized room, partly hollowed out of the living rock, partly natural grotto. Multicolored flags draped from the low ceiling, each emblazoned with prayers or mottoes in Chinese ideographs or painted with effigies of holy saints or gods and goddesses. Big bands of silk cloth festooned down the walls. On each side of the doorway were prayer wheels ready to be spun, and a plate of beaten gold with the signs of the Chinese zodiac was above the lintel. On both sides of the approach to the altar were low, red-lacquered benches for the lamas and the choir. Small lamps with tiny, flickering flames threw their rays on the gold and silver vessels and candlesticks. At the extreme end of the room, veiling the sanctuary, hung a heavy curtain of yellow silk painted with Tibetan inscriptions.

"While we were standing there, wondering what our next move would be, the shuffle of feet and the faint tinkle of bells came to us. 'Quick,' Clendenning ordered, 'we mustn't be caught here!' He ran to the door, but it was too late, for the monk on guard was already awake, and we could see the faint gleam of light from candles borne in procession at the farther end of the corridor.

"What happened next was the turning-point in our lives, gentlemen. Without stopping to think, apparently, Clendenning acted. Snatching the heavy Browning from his belt he hit the guardian monk a terrific blow over the head, dragged him through the doorway and ripped off his robe. 'Here, Arkright, put this on!' he commanded as he lugged the unconscious man's body into a dark corner of the room and concealed himself behind one of the wall draperies.

"I slipped the yellow gown over my clothes and squatted in front of the nearest prayer wheel, spinning the thing like mad.

"I suppose you've already noticed I've a rather Mongolian cast of features?" he asked with a bleak smile.

"*Nom d'un fusil, Monsieur*, let us not discuss personal pulchritude or its lack, if you please!" de Grandin exclaimed testily. "Be so good as to advance with your narrative!"

"It wasn't vanity which prompted the question," Arkright replied. "Even with my beard, I'm sometimes taken for a Chinaman or a half-caste. In those days I was clean-shaven, and both Clendenning and I had had our heads shaved for sanitary reasons before setting out on our trip; so, with the lama's robe pulled up about my neck, in the dim light of the sanctuary I passed very well for one of the brotherhood, and not one of the monks in the procession gave me so much as a second glance.

"The ta-lama—I suppose you'd call him the abbot of the community—led the procession into the temple and halted before the sanctuary curtain. Two subordinate lamas pulled the veil aside, and out of the dim light from the flickering lamps there gradually appeared the great golden statue of Buddha seated in the Golden Lotus. The face of the image was indifferent and calm with only the softest gleam of light animating it, yet despite the repose of the bloated features it seemed to me there was something malignant about the countenance.

"Glancing up under my brows as I turned the prayer wheel, I could see the main idol was flanked on each side by dozens of smaller statues, each, apparently, of solid gold.

The ta-lama struck a great bronze gong with a padded drumstick to attract the Buddha's attention to his prayer; then closed his eyes, placed his hands together before his face and prayed. As his sleeve fell away, I noticed a rosary of red beads, like those I was later to know with such horror, looped about his left wrist.

"The subordinate lamas all bent their foreheads to the floor while their master prayed standing before the face of Buddha. Finally, the abbot lowered his hands, and his followers rose and gathered at the foot of the altar. He opened a small, ovenlike receptacle beneath the calyx of the Golden Lotus and took from it a little golden image which one of his subordinates placed among the ranks of subsidiary Buddhas to the right of the great idol. Then he replaced the golden statuette with another exactly like it, except fashioned of lead, closed the sliding door to the little cavity and turned from the altar. Then, followed by his company, he marched from the chapel, leaving Clendenning and me in possession.

"It didn't take us more than a minute to rush up those altar steps, swing back the curtain and open the door under the Golden Lotus, you may be sure.

"Inside the door was a compartment about the size of a moderately large gas stove's oven, and in it were the little image we had seen the ta-lama put in and half a dozen bars of lead, iron and copper, each the exact dimensions of the golden ingots we'd seen in the treasure chamber.

"I said the bars were lead, copper and iron, but that's a misstatement. All of them *had* been composed of those metals, *but every one was from a quarter to three-fourths solid gold*. Slowly, as a loaf of bread browns by degrees in a bake-oven, these bars of base metal were being transmuted into solid, virgin gold.

"Clendenning and I looked at each other in dumfounded amazement. We knew it couldn't be possible, yet there it was, before our eyes.

"For a moment Clendenning peered into the alchemist's cabinet, then suddenly gave a low whistle. At the extreme back of the 'oven' was a piece of odd-looking substance about the size of a child's fist; something like jade, something like amber, yet differing subtly from each. As Clendenning reached his hand into the compartment to indicate it with his finger the diamond setting of a ring he wore suddenly glowed and sparkled as though lit from within by living fire.

"'For Gawd's sake!' he exclaimed. 'D'ye see what it is, Arkright? It's the Philosopher's Stone, or I'm a Dutchman!'"

"The Philosopher's Stone?" I queried puzzled.

De Grandin made a gesture of impatience, but Arkright's queer, haunted eyes were on me, and he failed to notice the Frenchman's annoyance.

"Yes, Dr. Trowbridge," he replied. "The ancient alchemists thought there was a substance which would convert all base metals into gold by the power of its magical emanations, you know. Nearly all noted magi believed in it, and most of them attempted to make it synthetically. Many of the things we use in everyday life were discovered as by-products while the ancient were seeking to perfect the magic formula. Bötticher stumbled on the method of making Dresden porcelain while searching for the treasure; Roger Bacon evolved the composition of gunpowder in the same way; Gerber discovered the properties of acids, Van Helmont secured the first accurate data on the nature of gases and the famous Dr. Glauber discovered the medicinal salts which bear his name in the course of experiments in search of the Stone.

"Oddly enough, the ancients were on the right track all the while, though, of course, they could not know it; for they were wont to refer to the Stone as a substratum—from the Latin *sub* and *stratus*, of course, signifying something spread under—and hundreds of years later scientists actually discovered the uranium oxide we know as pitchblende, the chief source of radium.

"Clendenning must have realized the queer substance in the altar was possessed of remarkable radioactive properties, for instead of attempting to grasp it in his fingers, as I should have done, he seized two of the altar candlesticks, and holding them like a pair of pincers, lifted the thing bodily from its setting; then, taking great care not to touch it, wrapped and rewrapped it in thin sheets of gold stripped from the altar ornaments. His data were incomplete, of course, but his reasoning, or perhaps his scientifically trained instinct, was accurate. You see, he inferred that since the 'stone' had the property of transmuting base metals with which it came in near contact into gold, gold would in all probability be the one element impervious to its radioactive rays, and consequently the only effective form of insulation. We had seen the ta-lama and his assistants grasp the little image of Buddha so recently transformed from lead to gold with their bare hands, so felt reasonably sure there would be no danger of radium burns from gold recently in contact with the substance, while there might be grave danger if we used anything but gold as wrappings for it.

"Clendenning was for strangling the lama we had stunned when we saw the procession headed toward the chapel, but I persuaded him to tie and gag the fellow and leave him hidden in the shrine; so when we had finished this we crept through the underground passages to the courtyard where our Bhotias were squatting beside the luggage and ordered them to break camp at once.

"The old ta-lama came to bid us a courteous good-bye and refused our offered payment for our entertainment, and we set off on the trail toward Nepal as if the devil were on our heels. He was, though we didn't know it then.

"Our way was mostly downhill, and everything seemed in our favor. We pushed on long after the sun had set, and by ten o'clock were well past the third *tach-davan*, or pass, from the lamasery. When we finally made camp Clendenning could hardly wait for our tent to be pitched before experimenting with our loot.

"Unwrapping the strange substance, we noticed that it glowed in the half-light of the tent with a sort of greenish phosphorescence, which made Clendenning christen it *Pi Yü*, which is Chinese for jade, and by that name we knew it thereafter. We put a pair of pistol bullets inside the wrappings, and lay down for a few hours' sleep with the *Pi Yü* between us. At five the next morning when we routed out the bearers and prepared to get under way, the entire leaden portions of the cartridges had been transmuted to gold and the copper powder-jackets were beginning to take on a decided golden glint. Forcing the shells off, we found the powder with which the cartridges were charged had become pure gold dust. This afforded us some valuable data. Lead was transmuted more quickly than copper, and semi-metallic substances like gunpowder were apparently even more susceptible than pure metals, though the powder's granular form might have sped its transmutation.

"We drove the bearers like slave-masters that day, and they were on the point of open mutiny when evening came. Poor devils, if they'd known what lay behind there'd have been little enough need to urge them on.

"Camp had been made and we had all settled down to a sleep of utter exhaustion when I first heard it. Very faint and far away it was, so faint as to be scarcely recognizable, but growing louder each second—the rumbling whistle of a wind of hurricane velocity shrieking and tearing down the passes.

"I kicked Clendenning awake, and together we made for a cleft in the rocks, yelling to our Bhotias to take cover at the same time. The poor devils were too waterlogged with sleep to realize what we shouted, and before we could give a second warning the thing was among them. Demonical blasts of wind so fierce we could almost see them shrieked and screamed and howled through the camp, each gust seeming to be aimed with dreadful accuracy. They whirled and twisted and tore about, scattering blazing logs like sparks from bursting firecrackers, literally tearing our tents into scraps no larger than a man's hand, picking up beasts and men bodily and hurling them against the cliff-walls till they were battered out of all semblance of their original form. Within five minutes our camp was reduced to such hopeless wreckage as may be seen only in the wake of a tornado, and Clendenning and I were the only living things within a radius of five miles.

"We were about to crawl from our hiding-place when something warned me the danger was not yet past and I grabbed at Clendenning's arm. He pulled away, but left the musette bag in which the *Pi Yü* was packed in my hand. Next moment he walked to the center of the shambles which had been our camp and began looking around in a dazed sort of way. Almost as he came to a halt, a terrific roar sounded and the entire air seemed to burn with the fury of a bursting lightning-bolt. Clendenning was wiped out as though he had never been—torn literally to dust by the unspeakable force of the lightning, and even the rock where he had stood was scarred and blackened as though water-blasted. But the terrible performance didn't stop there. Bolt after bolt of frightful lightning was hurled down like an accurately aimed barrage till every shred of our men, our yaks, our tents and our camp paraphernalia had not only been milled to dust, but completely obliterated.

"How long the artillery-fire from the sky lasted I do not know. To me, as I crouched in the little cave between the rocks, it seemed hours, years, centuries. Actually, I suppose, it kept up for something like five minutes. I think I must have fainted with the horror of it at the last, for the next thing I knew the sun was shining and the air was clear and icy-cold. No one passing could have told from the keenest observation that anything living had occupied our campsite in years. There was no sign or trace—absolutely none—of human or animal occupancy to be found. Only the cracked and lightning-blackened rocks bore witness to the terrible bombardment which had been laid down.

"I wasted precious hours in searching, but not a shred of cloth or flesh, not a lock of hair or a congealed drop of blood remained of my companions.

"The following days were like a nightmare—one of those awful dreams in which the sleeper is forever fleeing and forever pursued by something unnamably horrible. A dozen times a day I'd hear the skirling tempests rushing down the passes behind and scuttle to the nearest hole in the rocks like a panic-stricken rabbit when the falcon's shadow suddenly appears across its path. Sometimes I'd be storm-bound for hours while the wind howled like a troop of demons outside my retreat and the lightning-strokes rattled almost like hailstones on the rubble outside. Sometimes the vengeful tempest would last only a few minutes and I'd be released to fly like a mouse seeking sanctuary from the cat for a few miles before I was driven to cover once more.

"There were several packs of emergency rations in the musette bag, and I made out for drink by chipping off bits of ice from the frozen mountain springs and melting them in my tin cup, but I was a mere rack of bones and tattered hide encased in still more tattered clothes when I finally staggered into an out-post settlement in Nepal and fell babbling like an imbecile into the arms of a *sowar* sentry.

"The lamas' vengeance seemed confined to the territorial limits of Tibet, for I was unmolested during the entire period of my illness and convalescence in the Nepalese village.

"When I was strong enough to travel I was passed down country to my outfit, but I was still so ill and nervous that the company doctor gave me a certificate of physical disability and I was furnished with transportation home.

"I'd procured some scrap metal before embarking on the P. and O. boat, and in the privacy of my cabin I amused myself by testing the powers of the *Pi Yü*. Travel had not altered them, and in three days I had about ten pounds of gold where I'd had half that weight of iron.

"I was bursting with the wonderful news when I reached Waterbury, and could scarcely wait to tell my wife, but as I walked up the street toward my house an ugly, Mongolian-faced man suddenly stepped out from behind a road-side tree and barred my way. He did not utter a syllable but stood immovable in the path before me, regarding me with such a look of concentrated malice and hatred that my breath caught fast in my throat. For perhaps half a minute he glared at me, then raised his left hand and pointed directly at my face. As his sleeve fell back, I caught the gleam of a string of small, red beads looped round his wrist. Next instant he turned away and seemed to walk through an invisible door in the air—one moment I saw him, the next he had disappeared. As I stood staring stupidly at the spot where he had vanished, I felt a terrific blast of ice-cold wind blowing about me, tearing off my hat and sending me staggering against the nearest front-yard fence.

"The wind subsided in a moment, but it had blown away my peace of mind forever. From that instant I knew myself to be a marked man, a man whose only safety lay in flight and concealment.

"My daughter has told you the remainder of the story, how my wife was first to go, and how they found that accursed red bead which is the trade mark of the lamas' blood-vengeance clasped in her hand; how my son was the next victim of those Tibetan devils' revenge, then my daughter Charlotte; now she, too, is marked for destruction. Oh, gentlemen"—his eyes once more roved restlessly about—"if you only knew the inferno of terror and uncertainty I've been through during these terrible years, you'd realize I've paid my debt to those mountain fiends ten times over with compound interest compounded tenfold!'"

Our host ended his narrative almost in a shriek, then settled forward in his chair, chin sunk on breast, hands lying flaccidly in his lap, almost as if the death of which he lived in dread had overtaken him at last.

In the silence of the dimly lit drawing-room the logs burned with a softly hissing crackle; the little ormolu clock on the marble mantel beat off the seconds with hushed, hurrying strokes as though it held its breath and went on tip-toe in fear of something lurking in the shadows. Outside the curtained windows the subsiding storm moaned dismally, like an animal in pain.

Jules de Grandin darted his quick, birdlike glance from the dejected Arkright to his white-lipped daughter, then at me, then back again at Arkright. "Tiens, Monsieur," he remarked, "it would appear you find yourself in what the Americans call one damn-bad fix. Sacré bleu, those ape-faced men of the mountains know how to hate well, and they have the powers of the tempest at their command, while you have nothing but Jules de Grandin.

"No matter; it is enough. I do not think you will be attacked again today. Make yourselves as happy as may be, keep careful watch for more of those damnation red beads, and notify me immediately one of them reappears. Meantime I go to dinner and to consult a friend whose counsel will assuredly show us a way out of our troubles. Mademoiselle, Monsieur, I wish you a very good evening." Bending formally from the hips, he turned on his heel and strode from the drawing-room.

"Do you think there was anything in that cock-and-bull story of Arkright's?" I asked as we walked home through the clear, rain-washed April evening.

"Assuredly," he responded with a nod. "It has altogether the ring of truth, my friend. From what he tells us, the *Pi Yü* Stone which he and his friend stole from the men of the mountain is merely some little-known form of radium, and what do we know of radium, when all is said and done? *Barbe d'un pou*, nothing or less!

"True, we know the terrific and incessant discharge of etheric waves consequent on the disintegration of the radium atoms is so powerful that even such known and powerful forces as electrical energy are completely destroyed by it. In the presence of radium, we know, non-conductors of electricity become conductors, differences of potential cease to exist and electroscopes and Leyden jars fail to retain their charges. But all this is but the barest fraction of the possibilities.

"Consider: Not long ago we believed the atom to be the ultimate particle of matter, and thought all atoms had individuality. An atom of iron, for instance, was to us the smallest particle of iron possible, and differed distinctly from an atom of hydrogen. But with even such little knowledge as we already have of radioactive substances we have learned that all matter is composed of varying charges of electricity. The atom, we now believe, consists of a proton composed of a charge of positive electricity surrounded by a number of electrons, or negative charges, and the number of these electrons determines the nature of the atom. Radium itself, if left to itself, disintegrated into helium, finally into lead. Suppose, however, the process be reversed. Suppose the radioactive emanations of this *Pi Yü* which Monsieur Arkright thieved away from the lamas, so affect the balance of protons and electrons of metals brought close to it as to change their atoms from atoms of zinc, lead or iron to atoms of pure gold. All that would be needed to do it would be a rearrangement of protons and electrons. The hypothesis is simple and believable, though not to be easily explained. You see?"

"No, I don't," I confessed, "but I'm willing to take your word for it. Meantime—"

"Meantime we have the important matter of dinner to consider," he interrupted with a smile as we turned into my front yard. "*Pipe d'un chameau*, I am hungry like a family of famished wolves with all this talk."

3

"Trowbridge, MON VIEUX, THEY are at their devil's work again—have you seen the evening papers?" de Grandin exclaimed as he burst into the office several days later.

"Eh—what?" I demanded, putting aside the copy of Corwin's monograph on Multiple Neuritis and staring at him. "Who are 'they,' and what have 'they' been up to?"

"Who? Name of a little green man, those devils of the mountains, those Tibetan priests, those servants of the *Pi Yü* Stone!" he responded. "Peruse *le journal*, if you please." He thrust a copy of the afternoon paper into my hand, seated himself on the corner of the desk and regarded his brightly polished nails with an air of deep solicitude. I read:

GANGLAND SUSPECTED IN BEAUTY'S DEATH

Police believe it was to put the seal of eternal silence on her rouged lips that pretty Lillian Conover was "taken for a ride" late last night or early this morning. The young woman's body, terribly beaten and almost denuded of clothing, was found lying in one of the bunkers of the Sedgemoor Country Club's golf course near the Albemarle Pike shortly after six o'clock this morning by an employee of the club. From the fact that no blood was found near the body, despite the terrible mauling it had received, police believe the young woman had been "put on the spot" somewhere else, then brought to the deserted links and left there by the slayers or their accomplices.

The Conover girl was known to have been intimate with a number of questionable characters, and had been arrested several times for shoplifting and petty thefts. It is thought she might have learned something of the secrets of a gang of bootleggers or hijackers and threatened to betray them to rival gangsters, necessitating her silencing by the approved methods of gangland.

The body, when found, was clothed in the remnants of a gray ensemble with a gray fox neck-piece and a silver mesh bag was still looped about one of her wrists. In the purse were four ten-dollar bills and some silver, showing conclusively that robbery was not the motive for the crime.

The authorities are checking up the girl's movements on the day before her death, and an arrest is promised within twenty-four hours.

"U'm?" I remarked, laying down the paper.

"U'm?" he mocked. "May the devil's choicest imps fly away with your 'u'ms,' Friend Trowbridge. Come, get the car; we must be off."

"Off where?"

"Beard of a small blue pig, where, indeed, but to the spot where this so unfortunate girl's dead corpse was discovered?" Delay not, we must utilize what little light remains!"

The bunker where poor Lillian Conover's broken body had been found was a banked sand-trap in the golf course about twenty-five yards from the highway. Throngs of morbidly curious sightseers had trampled the smoothly kept fairways all day, brazenly defying the "Private Property—No Trespassing" signs with which the links were posted.

To my surprise, de Grandin showed little annoyance at the multitude of footprints about, but turned at once to the business of surveying the terrain. After half an hour's crawling back and forth across the turf, he rose and dusted his trouser knees with a satisfied sigh.

"*Succès!*" he exclaimed, raising his hand, thumb and forefinger clasped together on something which reflected the last rays of the sinking sun with an ominous red glow. "Behold, *mon ami*, I have found it; it is even as I suspected."

Looking closely, I saw he held a red bead, about the size of a small hazelnut, the exact duplicate of the little globule Haroldine Arkright had discovered in her reticule.

"Well?" I asked.

"*Barbe d'un lièvre*, yes; it is very well, indeed," he assented with a vigorous nod. "I was certain I should find it here, but had I not, I should have been greatly worried. Let us return, good friend; our quest is done."

I knew better than to question him as we drove slowly home; but my ears were open wide for any chance remark he might drop. However, he vouchsafed no comment till we reached home; then he hurried to the study and put an urgent call through to the Arkright mansion. Five minutes later he joined me in the library, a smile of satisfaction on his lips. "It is as I thought," he announced. "Mademoiselle Haroldine went shopping yesterday afternoon and the unfortunate Conover girl picked her pocket in the store. Forty dollars was stolen—forty dollars *and a red bead!*"

"She told you this?" I asked. "Why—"

"*Non, non,*" he shook his head. "She did tell me of the forty dollars, yes; the red bead's loss I already knew. Recall, my friend, how was it the poor dead one was dressed, according to the paper?"

"Er—"

"*Précisément.* Her costume was a cheap copy, a caricature, if you please, of the smart ensemble affected by Mademoiselle Haroldine. Poor creature, she plied her pitiful trade of pocket-picking once too often, removed the contents of Haroldine's purse, including the sign of vengeance which had been put there, *le bon Dieu* knows how, and walked forth to her doom. Those who watched for a gray-clad woman with the fatal red ball seized upon her and called down their winds of destruction, even as they did upon the camp of Monsieur Arkright in the mountains of Tibet long years ago. Yes, it is undoubtlessly so."

"Do you think they'll try again?" I asked. "They've already muffed things twice, and—"

"And, as your proverb has it, the third time is the charm," he cut in. "Yes, my friend, they will doubtlessly try again, and again, until they have worked their will, or been diverted. We must bend our energies toward the latter con-summation."

"But that's impossible!" I returned. "If those lamas are powerful enough to seek their victims out in France, England and this country and kill them, there's not much chance for the Arkrights in flight, and it's hardly likely we'll be able to argue them out of their determination to exact payment for the theft of their—"

"*Zut!*" he interrupted with a smile. "You do talk much but say little, Friend Trowbridge. Me, I think it highly probable we shall convince the fish-faced gentlemen from Tibet they have more to gain by foregoing their vengeance than by collecting their debt."

4

HARRISONVILLE'S NEWEST CITIZEN HAD delayed her debut with truly fem-inine capriciousness, and my vigil at City Hospital had been long and nerve-racking. Half an hour before I had resorted to the Weigand-Martin method of ending the performance, and, shaking with nervous reaction, took the red, wrinkled and astonishingly vocal morsel of humanity from the nurse's hands and laid it in its mother's arms; then, nearer exhaustion than I cared to admit, set out for home and bed.

A rivulet of light trickled under the study door and the murmur of voices mingled with the acrid aroma of de Grandin's cigarette came to me as I let myself in the front door. "*Eh bien*, my friend," the little Frenchman was assert-ing, "I damn realize that he who sups with the devil must have a long spoon; therefore I have requested your so invaluable advice."

"Trowbridge, *mon vieux*," his uncannily sharp ears recognized my tread as I stepped softly into the hall, "may we trespass on your time a moment? It is of interest."

With a sigh of regret for my lost sleep I put my obstetrical kit on a chair and pushed open the study door.

Opposite de Grandin was seated a figure which might have been the origi-nal of the queer little manikins with which Chinese ivory-carvers love to orna-ment their work. Hardly more than five feet tall, his girth was so great that he seemed to overflow the confines of the armchair in which he lounged. His head, almost totally void of hair, was nearly globular in shape, and the smooth, hairless skin seemed stretched drum-tight over the fat with which his skull was generously upholstered. Cheeks plump to the point of puffiness almost forced his oblique eyes shut; yet, though his eyes could scarcely be seen, it required no deep intuition to know that they always saw. Between his broad, flat nose and a succession of chins was set, incongruously a small, sensitive mouth, full-lipped but mobile, and drooping at the corners in a sort of perpetual sad smile.

"Dr. Feng," de Grandin introduced, "this is my very good friend, Dr. Trowbridge. Trowbridge, my friend, this is Dr. Feng Yuin-han, whose wisdom is about to enable us to foil the machinations of those wicked ones who threaten Mademoiselle Haroldine. Proceed, if you please, *cher ami*," he motioned the fat little Chinaman to continue the remark he had cut short to acknowledge the introduction.

"It is rather difficult to explain," the visitor returned in a soft, unaccented voice, "but if we stop to remember that the bird stands midway between the reptile and the mammal we may perhaps understand why it is that the cock's blood is most acceptable to those elemental forces which my unfortunate superstitious countrymen seek to propitiate in their temples. These malignant influences were undoubtedly potent in the days we refer to as the age of reptiles, and it may be the cock's lineal descent from the pterodactyl gives his blood the quality of possessing certain emanations soothing to the tempest spirits. In any event, I think you would be well advised to employ such blood in your protective experiments."

"And the ashes?" de Grandin put in eagerly.

"Those I can procure for you by noon tomorrow. Camphor wood is something of a rarity here, but I can obtain enough for your purpose, I am sure."

"*Bon, très bon!*" the Frenchman exclaimed delightedly. "If those camel-faces will but have the consideration to wait our preparations, I damn think we shall tender them the party of surprise. Yes. *Parbleu*, we shall astonish them!"

SHORTLY AFTER NOON THE following day an asthmatic Ford delivery wagon bearing the picture of a crowing cockerel and the legend

P. GRASSO
Vendita di Pollame Vivi

on its weatherworn leatherette sides drew up before the house, and an Italian youth in badly soiled corduroys and with a permanent expression indicative of some secret sorrow climbed lugubriously from the driver's seat, took a covered two-gallon can, obviously originally intended as a container for Quick's Grade A Lard, from the interior of the vehicle and advanced toward the front porch.

"Docta de Grandin 'ere?" he demanded as Nora McGinnis, my household factotum, answered his ring.

"No, he ain't," the indignant Nora informed him, "an' if he wuz, 'tis at th' back door th' likes o' you should be inquirin' fer 'im!"

The descendant of the Cæsars was in no mood for argument. "You taka dissa bucket an' tella heem I breeg it—Pete Grasso," he returned, thrusting the lard tin into the scandalized housekeeper's hands. "You tella heem I sella da han, I sella da roosta, too, an' I keela heem w'an my customers ask for it; but I no lika for sella da blood. No, *santissimo Dio*, not me! *Perchè il sangue è la vita*—how you say? Da blood, he are da life; I not lika for carry heem aroun'."

"Howly Mither, is it blood ye're afther givin' me ter hold onto?" exclaimed Nora in rising horror. "Ye murtherin' dago, come back 'ere an' take yer divilish—"

But P. Grasso, dealer in live poultry, had cranked his decrepit flivver into a state of agitated life and set off down the street, oblivious of the choice insults which Mrs. McGinnis sent in pursuit of him.

"Sure, Dr. Trowbridge, sor," she confided as she entered the consulting-room, the lard tin held at arm's length, "'tis th' fine gintleman Dr. de Grandin is entirely; but he do be afther doin' some crazy things at times. Wud ye be afther takin' charge o' this mess o' blood fer him? 'Tis meself as wouldn't touch it wid a fifthy-foot pole, so I wouldn't, once I've got it out o' me hands!"

"Well," I laughed as I espied a trim little figure turning into my front yard, "here he comes now. You can tell him your opinion of his practises if you want."

"Ah, Docthor, darlin', ye know I'd niver have th' heart to scold 'im," she confessed with a shamefaced grin. "Sure, he's th'—"

The sudden hysterical cachinnation of the office telephone bell cut through her words, and I turned to the shrilling instrument.

For a moment there was no response to my rather impatient "Hello?"; then dimly, as one entering a darkened room slowly begins to descry objects about him, I made out the hoarse, rale-like rasp of deep-drawn, irregular breathing.

"Hello?" I repeated, more sharply. ·

"Dr. Trowbridge," a low, almost breathless feminine voice whispered over the wire, "this is Haroldine Arkright. Can you come right over with Dr. de Grandin? Right away? Please. It—it's *here!*"

"Right away!" I called back, and wheeled about, almost colliding with the little Frenchman, who had been listening over my shoulder.

"Quick, speed, haste!" he cried, as I related her message. "We must rush, we must hurry, we must fly, my friend! There is not a second to lose!"

As I charged down the hall and across the porch to my waiting car he stopped long enough to seize the lard tin from beside my desk and two bulky paper parcels from a hall chair, then almost trod on my heels, in his haste to enter the motor.

5

"NOT HERE, MONSIEUR, IF you please," de Grandin ordered as he surveyed the living-room where Arkright and his daughter awaited us. "Is there no room without furniture, where we can meet the foeman face to face? I would fight over a flat terrain, if possible."

"There's a vacant bedroom on the next floor," Arkright replied, "but—"

"No buts, if you please; let us ascend at once, immediately, right away!" the Frenchman interrupted. "Oh, make haste, my friends! Your lives depend upon it, I do assure you!"

About the floor of the empty room de Grandin traced a circle of chicken's blood, painting a two-inch-wide ruddy border on the bare boards, and inside the outer circle he drew another, forcing Haroldine and her father within it. Then, with a bit of rag, he wiped a break in the outside line, and opening one of his paper parcels proceeded to scatter a thin layer of soft, white wood-ashes over the boards between the two circles.

"Now, *mon vieux*, if you will assist," he turned to me, ripping open the second package and bringing to light a tin squirt-gun of the sort used to spray insecticide about a room infested with mosquitoes.

Dipping the nozzle of the syringe into the blood-filled lard tin, he worked the plunger back and forth a moment, then handed the contrivance to me. "Do you stand at my left," he commanded, "and should you see footprints in the ashes, spray the fowl's blood through the air above them. Remember, my friend, it is most important that you act with speed."

"Footprints in the ashes—" I began incredulously, wondering if he had lost his senses, but a sudden current of glacial air sweeping through the room chilled me into silence.

"Ah! of the beautiful form is *Mademoiselle*, and who was I to know that cold wind of Tibetan devils would display it even more than this exquisite *robe d'Orient?*" said de Grandin.

Clad in a wondrous something, she explained fright had so numbed her that dressing had been impossible.

"When did you first know they were here?" de Grandin whispered, turning his head momentarily toward the trembling couple inside the inner circle, then darting a watchful glance about the room as though he looked for an invisible enemy to materialize from the air.

"I found the horrible red ball in my bath," Haroldine replied in a low, trembling whisper. "I screamed when I saw it, and Daddy got up to come to me, and there was one of them under his ash-tray; so I telephoned your house right away, and—"

"S-s-st!" the Frenchman's sibilant warning cut her short. "*Garde à vous*, Friend Trowbridge! *Fixe!*" As though drawing a saber from its scabbard he whipped the keen steel sword blade from his walking-stick and swished it whip-like through the air. "The cry is still '*On ne passe pas!*' my friends!"

There was the fluttering of the tiny breeze along the bedroom floor, not like a breeze from outside, but an eery, tentative sort of wind, a wind which trickled lightly over the doorsill, rose to a blast, paused a moment in reconnaissance, then crept forward experimentally, as though testing the strength of our defenses.

A light, pit-pattering noise, as though an invisible mouse were circling the room, sounded from the shadows; then, to my horrified amazement, there appeared the print of a broad, naked foot in the film of ashes de Grandin had spread upon the floor!

Wave on wave of goose-flesh rose on my arms and along my neck as I watched the first print followed by a second, for there was no body above them, no sign nor trace of any alien presence in the place; only, as the keys of a mechanical piano are depressed as the strings respond to the notes of the reeling record, the smooth coating of ashes gave token of the onward march of some invisible thing.

"Quick, my friend, shoot where you see the prints!" de Grandin cried in a shrill, excited voice, and I thrust the plunger of my pump home, sending out a shower of ruddy spray.

As invisible ink takes form when the paper is held before a flame, there was suddenly outlined in the empty air before us the visage of—

"*Sapristi!* 'Tis Yama himself, King of Hell! God of Death! *Holà, mon brave,*" de Grandin called almost jocularly as the vision took form wherever the rain of fowl's blood struck, "it seems we meet face to face, though you expected it not. *Nom d'un porc,* is this the courtesy of your country? You seem not overjoyed to meet me.

"Lower, Friend Trowbridge," he called from the corner of his mouth, keeping wary eyes fixed upon the visitant, "aim for his legs; there is a trick I wish to show him."

Obediently, I aimed the syringe at the footless footprints in the ashes, and a pair of broad, naked feet sprang suddenly into view.

"*Bien,*" the Frenchman commended, then with a sudden forward thrust of his foot engaged the masked Mongolian's ankle in a grapevine twist and sent the fellow sprawling to the floor. The blue and gold horror that was the face of Yama came off, disclosing a leering, slant-eyed lama.

"Now, *Monsieur,*" de Grandin remarked, placing his sword-point against the other's throat directly above the palpitating jugular vein, "I damn think perhaps you will listen to reason, *hein?*"

The felled man gazed malignantly into his conqueror's face, but neither terror nor surrender showed in his sullen eyes.

"*Morbleu,* he is a brave savage, this one," de Grandin muttered, then lapsed into a wailing, singsong speech the like of which I had never heard.

A look of incredulous disbelief, then of interest, finally of amazed delight, spread over the copper-colored features of the fallen man as the little Frenchman progressed. Finally he answered with one or two coughing ejaculations, and at a sign from de Grandin rose to his feet and stood with his hands lifted above his head.

"Monsieur Arkright," the Frenchman called without taking his eyes from his captive, "have the goodness to fetch the *Pi Yü* Stone without delay. I have made a treaty with this emissary of the lamas. If you return his treasure to him at once he will repair forthwith to his lamasery and trouble you and yours no more."

"But what about my wife, and my children these fiends killed?" Arkright expostulated. "Are they to go scot-free? How do I know they'll keep their word? I'm damned if I'll return the *Pi Yü!*"

"You will most certainly be killed if you do not," de Grandin returned coolly. "As to your damnation, I am a sinful man, and do not presume to pronounce judgment on you, though I fear the worst unless you mend your morals. Come, will you return this man his property, or do I release him and bid him do his worst?"

Muttering imprecations, Arkright stepped across the barrier of blood, left the room and returned in a few minutes with a small parcel wrapped in what appeared to be thin plates of gold.

De Grandin took it from his hand and presented it to the Tibetan with a ceremonious bow.

"*Ki lao yeh hsieh ti to lo,*" the yellow man pressed his clasped hands to his breast and bowed nearly double to the Frenchman.

"*Parbleu,* yes, and Dr. Trowbridge, too," my little friend returned, indicating me with a wave of his hand.

The Tibetan bent ceremoniously toward me as de Grandin added, "*Ch'i kan.*"

"What did he say?" I demanded, returning the Asiatic's salute.

"He says, 'The honorable, illustrious sir has my heartfelt thanks,' or words to that effect, and I insist that he say the same of you, my friend," de Grandin returned. "Name of a small green pig, I do desire that he understand there are two honorable men in the room besides himself.

"*En avant, mon brave,*" he motioned the Tibetan toward the door with his sword, then lowered his point with a flourish, saluting the Arkrights with military punctilio.

"Mademoiselle Haroldine," he said, "it is a great pleasure to have served you. May your approaching marriage be a most happy one.

"Monsieur Arkright, I have saved your life, and, though against your will, restored your honor. It is true you have lost your gold, but self-respect is a more precious thing. Next time you desire to steal, permit that I suggest you select a less vengeful victim than a Tibetan brotherhood. *Parbleu,* those savages they have no sense of humor at all! When a man robs them, they take it with the worst possible grace."

"PIPE D'UN CHAMEAU"—JULES DE Grandin brushed an imaginary fleck of dust from the sleeve of his dinner jacket and refilled his liqueur glass—"it has been a most satisfactory day, Friend Trowbridge. Our experiment was one grand, unqualified success; we have restored stolen property to its rightful owners, and I have told that Monsieur Arkright what I think of him."

"U'm," I murmured. "I suppose it's all perfectly clear to you, but I'm still in the dark about it all."

"Perfectly," he agreed with one of his quick, elfin smiles. "Howeverly, that can be remedied. Attend me, if you please:

"When first we interviewed Mademoiselle Haroldine and her father, I smelt the odor of Tibet in this so strange business. Those red beads, they could have come from but one bit of jewelry, and that was the rosary of a Buddhist monk of Tibet. Yes. Now, in the course of my travels in that devil-infested land, I had seen those old lamas do their devil-dances and command the elements to obey their summons and wreak vengeance on their enemies. 'Very well,' I tell me, 'if this be a case of lamas' magic, we must devise magic which will counteract it.'

"'Of course,' I agree with me. 'For every ill there is a remedy. Men living in the lowlands know cures for malaria; those who inhabit the peaks know the cure for mountain fever. They must do so, or they die. Very well, is it not highly probable that the Mongolian people have their own safeguards against these mountain devils? If it were not so, would not Tibet completely dominate all China?'

"'You have right,' I compliment me, 'but whom shall we call on for aid?'

"Thereupon I remember that my old friend, Dr. Feng Yuin-han, whom I have known at the Sorbonne, is at present residing in New York, and it is to him I send my message for assistance. *Parbleu*, when he comes he is as full of wisdom as a college professor attempts to appear! He tells me much in our nighttime interview before you arrive from your work of increasing the population. I learn from him, for instance, that when these old magicians of the mountains practise their devil's art, they automatically limit their powers. Invisible they may become, yes; but while invisible, they may not overstep a pool, puddle or drop of chicken blood. For some strange reason, such blood makes a barrier which they can not pass and across which they can not hurl a missile nor send their destroying winds or devastating lightning-flashes. Further, if chicken blood be cast upon them their invisibility at once melts away, and while they are in the process of becoming visible in such circumstances their physical strength is greatly reduced. One man of normal lustiness would be a match for fifty of them half visible, half unseen because of fresh fowl's blood splashed on them.

"*Voilà* I have my grand strategy of defense already mapped out for me. From the excellent Pierre Grasso I buy much fresh chicken blood, and from Dr. Feng I obtain the ashes of the mystic camphor tree. The blood I spread around in an almost-circle, that our enemy may attack us from one side only, and inside the outer stockade of gore I scatter camphor wood ashes that his footprints may become visible and betray his position to us. Then, inside our outer ramparts, I draw a second complete circle of blood which the enemy can not penetrate at all, so that Monsieur Arkright, but most of all his so charming daughter, may be safe. Then I wait.

"Presently comes the foe. He circles our first line of defense, finds the break I have purposely left, and walks into our trap. In the camphor wood ashes his all-invisible feet leave visible footprints to warn of his approach.

"With your aid, then, I do spray him with the blood as soon as his footprints betray him, and make him visible so that I may slay him at my good convenience. But he are no match for me. *Non*, Jules de Grandin would not call it the sport to kill such as he; it would not be fair. Besides, is there not much to be said on his side? I think so.

"It was the cupidity of Monsieur Arkright and no other thing which brought death upon his wife and children. We have no way of telling that the identical man whom I have overthrown murdered those unfortunate ones, and it is not just to take his life for his fellows' crimes. As for legal justice, what court would listen believingly to our story? *Cordieu*, to relate what we have seen these last few days to the ordinary lawyer would be little better than confessing ourselves mad or infatuated with too much of the so execrable liquor which your prosperous bootleggers supply. Me, I have no wish to be thought a fool.

"Therefore, I say to me, 'It is best that we call this battle a draw. Let us give back to the men of the mountains that which is theirs and take their promise that they will no longer pursue Monsieur Arkright and Mademoiselle Haroldine. Let there be no more beads from the Devil's rosary scattered across their path.'

"Very good. I make the equal bargain with the Tibetan; his property is returned to him and—

"My friend, I suffer!"

"Eh?" I exclaimed, shocked at the tragic face he turned to me.

"*Nom d'un canon*, yes; my glass is empty again!"

The House of Golden Masks

"An' so, Dr. de Grandin, sor," Detective Sergeant Costello concluded with a pitying sidelong glance at his companion, "if there's annything ye can do for th' pore lad,—'tis meself that'll be grateful to ye for doin' it. Faith, if sumpin like this had happened to me whilst I was a-courtin' Maggie, I'd 'a' been a dead corpse from worry in less time than this pore felley's been sufferin'.

"Th' chief won't raise his hand in th' matter wid th' coroner's verdict starin' us in th' face, an' much as I'd like to do sumpin for th' boy, me hands is tied tighter'n th' neck of a sack. But with you, now, 'tis a different matter entirely. Meself, I'm inclined to agree with th' chief an' think th' pore gur-rl's dead as a herring, but if there's sumpin in th' case th' rest of us can't see, sure, 'tis Dr. Jools de Grandin can spot it quicker than a hungry tom-cat smells a rat!"

Jules de Grandin turned his quick, birdlike glance from the big, red-headed Irishman to the slender, white-faced young man seated beside him. "What makes you assume your beloved survives, *Monsieur?*" he asked. "If the jury of the coroner returned a verdict of suicide—"

"But, I tell you, sir, the jury didn't know what they were talking about!"

Young Everett Wilberding rose from his chair and faced the little Frenchman, his knuckles showing white with the intensity of his grip on the table edge. "My Ewell *didn't* commit suicide. She didn't kill herself, neither did Mazie. You *must* believe that, sir!"

Resuming his seat, he fought back to comparative calm as he laced his fingers together nervously. "Last Thursday night Ewell and I were going to a dance out at the country club. My friend, Bill Stimpson, was to take Mazie, Ewell's twin sister. The girls had been out visiting an aunt and uncle at Reynoldstown, and were to meet us at Monmouth Junction, then drive out to the club in Ewell's flivver.

"The girls took their party clothes out to Reynoldstown with them, and were to dress before leaving to meet us. They were due at the Junction at nine o'clock, but Ewell was hardly ever on time, so I thought nothing of it when they failed to show up at half-past. But when ten o'clock came, with no sign of the girls, we began to think they must have had a blow-out or engine trouble. At half-past ten I went to the drug store and 'phoned the girls' uncle at Reynold-stown, only to be told they had left at a quarter past eight—in plenty of time to reach the junction by nine, even if they had bad going. When I heard that I began to worry sure enough. By eleven o'clock I was fit to be tied.

"Bill was getting worried, too, but thought that one of 'em might have been taken ill and that they'd rushed right to Harrisonville without coming through the Junction, so we 'phoned their house here. Their folks didn't know any more than we did.

"We caught the next bus to Harrisonville, and went right up to the Eatons'. When nothing was heard of the girls by four the next morning, Mr. Eaton notified the police."

"U'm?" de Grandin nodded, slowly. "Proceed, if you please, young *Monsieur*."

"The searching parties didn't find a trace of the girls till next day about noon," young Wilberding answered; "then a State Trooper came on Ewell's Ford smashed almost out of shape against a tree half a mile or more from the river, but no sign of blood anywhere around. A little later a couple of hunters found Ewell's party dress, stockings and slippers on the rocks above Shaminee Falls. Mazie—"

"They found th' pore child's body up agin th' grilles leadin' to th' turbine intakes o' Pierce's Mills next day sor," Costello put in softly.

"Yes, they did," Wilberding agreed, "and Mazie was *wearing* her dance frock—what was left of it. Why didn't Ewell jump in the falls with hers on, too, if Mazie did? But *Mazie didn't!*"

Sergeant Costello shook his head sadly. "Th' coroner's jury—" he began, as though reasoning with a stubborn child, but the boy interrupted angrily:

"Oh, damn the coroners jury! See here, sir"—he turned to de Grandin as if for confirmation—"you're a physician and know all about such things. What d'y say to this? Mazie's body was washed through the rapids above Shaminee Falls and was terribly mauled against the rocks as it came down, so badly disfigured that only the remnants of her clothes made identification possible. No one could say definitely whether she'd been wounded before she went into the water or not; but *she wasn't drowned!*"

"Eh, what is it you say?" de Grandin straightened in his chair, his level, unwinking stare boring into the young man's troubled eyes. "Continue, if you please, Monsieur; I am interested."

"I mean just what I say," the other returned. "They didn't find a half-teacup-ful of water in her lungs at the autopsy; besides, this is March, and the water's almost ice-cold—yet they found her *floating* next morning; if—"

"*Barbe d'un chauve canard*, yes!" de Grandin exclaimed. "*Tu parles, mon garçon!* In temperature such as this it would be days—weeks, perhaps—before putrefaction had advanced enough to form sufficient gas to force the body to the surface. But of course, it was the air in her lungs which buoyed her up. *Morbleu*, I think you have right, my friend; undoubtlessly the poor one was dead before she touched the water!"

"Aw, Doc, ye don't mean to say *you're* fallin' for that theory?" Costello protested. "It's true she mightn't 'a' been drowned, but th' coroner said death was due to shock induced by—"

De Grandin waved him aside impatiently, keeping his gaze fixed intently on Everett. "Do you know any reason she might have had for self-destruction, *mon vieux?*" he demanded.

"No, sir—none whatever. She and Bill were secretly married at Hacketstown last Christmas Eve. They'd been keeping it dark till Bill got his promotion—it came through last week, and they were going to tell the world last Sunday. You see, they couldn't have concealed it much longer."

"Ah?" de Grandin's narrow brows elevated slightly. "And they were happy together?"

"Yes, sir! You never saw a spoonier couple in your life. Can you imagine—"

"*Tiens*, my friend," the Frenchman interrupted with one of his quick, elfish grins, "you would be surprised at that which I can imagine. Howeverly, let us consider facts, not imaginings." Rising, he began pacing the floor, ticking off his data on his fingers as he marched. "Let us make a *précis*:

"Here we have two young women, one in love, though married—the other in love and affianced. They fail to keep an appointment; it is not till the day following that their car is discovered, and it is found in such position as to indicate a wreck, yet nowhere near it is sign of injury to its passengers. *Alors*, what do we find? The frock of one of the young ladies, neatly folded beside her shoes, and stockings upon a rock near the Shaminee Falls. In the river, some miles below, next day is found the floating corpse of the other girl—and the circumstances point conclusively that she did not drown. What now? The mishap to the car occurred a half-mile from the river, yet the young women were able to walk to the stream where one of them cast herself in fully clothed; the other is supposed to have disrobed before immersing herself.

"*Non, non*, my friends, the facts, they do not make sense. Women kill themselves for good reasons, for bad reasons, and for no reasons at all, but they do it characteristically. Me, I have seen ropes wherewith despondent females have strangled themselves, and they have wrapped silken scarves about the rough hemp that it might not bruise their tender necks. *Tiens*, would a delicately nurtured girl strip herself to the rude March winds before plunging into the water? I think not."

"So do I," rumbled Costello's heavy voice in agreement. "Th' way you put it, Dr. de Grandin, sor, makes th' case crazier than ever. Faith, there's no sense to it from beginnin' to end. I think we'd better be callin' it a day an' acceptin' th' coroner's decision."

"*Zut!*" de Grandin returned with a smile. "Are you then so poor a poker player, *mon sergent?* Have you not learned the game is never over until the play is done? Me, I shall give this matter my personal attention. I am interested, I am fascinated, I am intrigued.

"To your home, Monsieur Wilberding," he ordered. "When I have some word for you, you will hear from me. Meantime do not despair."

"TROWBRIDGE, MON VIEUX," DE Grandin greeted next morning when I joined him in the dining-groom, "I am perplexed; but yes, I am greatly puzzled; I am mystified. Something has occurred since last night which may put a different face upon all. Consider, if you please: Half an hour ago I received a telephone call from the good Costello. He tells me three more young women have disappeared in a manner so similar to that of Monsieur Wilberding's sweetheart as to make it more than mere coincidence. At the residence of one *Monsieur Mason*, who resides in West Fells, there was held a meeting of the sorority to which his daughter belongs. Many young women attended. Three, Mesdemoiselles Weaver, Damroche and Hornbury, drove out in the car of Mademoiselle Weaver. They left the Mason house sometime after midnight. At six o'clock this morning they had not returned home. Their alarmed parents notified the police, and"—he paused in his restless pacing, halting directly before me as he continued—"a state dragoon discovered the motor in which they rode lying on its side, mired in the swamps beside the Albemarle Road, but of the young women no trace could be found. Figure to yourself, my friend. What do you make of it?"

"Why—" I began, but the shrill stutter of the office 'phone cut my reply in two.

"*Allo?*" de Grandin called into the transmitter. "Yes, Sergeant, it is I—*grand Diable!* Another? You do not tell me so!"

To me be almost shouted as be slammed the receiver back into its hook: "Do you hear, my friend? It is another! Sarah Thompford, an employee of Braunstein *frères'* department store, left her work at half-past five last evening, and has been seen no more. But her hat and cloak were found upon the piers at the waterfront ten little minutes ago. *Nom d'un choufleur,* I am vexed! These disappearances are becoming epidemic. Either the young women of this city have developed a sudden mania for doing away with themselves or some evil person attempts to make a monkey of Jules de Grandin. In either case, my friend, I am aroused. *Mordieu,* we shall see who shall laugh in whose face before this business of the fool is concluded!"

"What are you going to do?" I asked, striving to keep a straight face.

"Do?" he echoed. "Do? *Parbleu*, I shall investigate, I shall examine every clue, I shall leave no stone unturned, but"—he sobered into sudden practicality as Nora McGinnis, my household factotum, entered the dining-room with a tray of golden-brown waffles—"first I shall eat breakfast. One can accomplish little on an empty stomach."

A WIDESPREAD, THOUGH FORTUNATELY MILD, epidemic of influenza kept me busy in office and on my rounds all day. Rainy, fog-bound darkness was approaching as I turned toward home and dinner with a profound sigh of thankfulness that the day's work was done, only to encounter fresh disappointment.

"Trowbridge, Trowbridge, *mon vieux*," an excited voice hailed as I was waiting for the crosstown traffic lights to change and let me pursue my homeward way, "draw to the curb; come with me—I have important matters to communicate!" Swathed from knees to neck in a waterproof leather jacket, his Homburg hat pulled rakishly down over his right eye and a cigarette glowing between his lips, Jules de Grandin stood at the curb, his little blue eyes dancing with excited elation.

"Name of a little blue man!" he swore delightedly as I parked my motor and joined him on the sidewalk; "it is a fortunate chance, this meeting; I was about to telephone the office in hopes you had returned. Attend me, my friend, I have twisted my hand in the tail of something of importance!"

Seizing my elbow with a proprietary grip, he guided me toward the illuminated entrance of a café noted for the excellence of its food and its contempt of the XVIIIth Amendment, chuckling with suppressed delight at every step.

"The young Monsieur Wilberding was undoubtlessly right in his surmises," he confided as we found places at one of the small tables and he gave an order to the waiter. "*Parbleu*, what he lacked in opportunity of observation he made up by the prescience of affection," he continued, "for there can be no doubt that Madame Mazie was the victim of murder. *Regardez-vous*: At the police laboratories, kindly placed at my disposal through the offices of the excellent Sergeant Costello, I examined the tattered remnants of the frock they took from the poor girl's body when they fished her from the river, and I did discover what the coroner, cocksure of his suicide theory, had completely overlooked—a small, so tiny stain. Hardly darker than the original pink of the fabric it was, but sufficient to rouse my suspicions. *Alors*, I proceeded to shred the chiffon and make the benzidine test. You know it? No?

"Very good. A few threads from the stained area of the dress I placed upon a piece of white filter paper; thereafter I compounded a ten percent solution of benzidine in glacial acetic acid and mixed one part of this with ten parts of hydrogen peroxide. Next, with a pipette I proceeded to apply one little, so tiny drop of the solution to the threads of silk, and behold! a faint blue color manifested itself in the stained silken threads and spread out on the white filter paper. *Voilà*, that the stain of my suspicion had been caused by blood was no longer to be doubted!"

"But mightn't this bloodstain have been caused by an injury to Mazie's body as it washed over the falls?" I objected.

"*Ah bah*," he returned. "*You* ask that, Friend Trowbridge? *Pardieu*, I had looked for better sense in your head. Consider the facts: Should you cut your finger, then immediately submerge it in a basin of water, would any trace of blood adhere to it? But no. Conversely, should you incise the skin and permit even one little drop of blood to gather at the wound and to dry there to any extent, the subsequent immersion of the finger in water would not suffice to remove the partly clotted blood altogether. Is it not so?

"*Très bon*. Had a sharp stone cut poor Madame Mazie, it would undoubtlessly have done so after she was dead, in which case there would have been no resultant hemorrhage; but even if a wound had been inflicted while she lived, bethink you of her position—in the rushing water, whirled round and round and over and over, any blood which flowed would instantly have been washed away, leaving no slightest stain on her dress. *Non*, my friend there is but one explanation, and I have found it. Her gown was stained by blood before she was cast into the river. Recall: Did not poor young Monsieur Wilberding inform us the car in which she rode was found a half-mile or more from the river? But certainly. Suppose, then, these girls were waylaid at or near the spot where their car was found, and one or both were done to death. Suppose, again, Madame Mazie's life-blood flowed from her wound and stained her dress while she was in transit toward the river. In that case her dress would have been so stained that even though the foul miscreants who slew her cast her poor, broken body into the water, there would remain stains for Jules de Grandin to find today. Yes, it is so.

"But wait, my friend, there is more to come. Me, I have been most busy this day. I have run up and down and hither and yon like Satan seeking for lost souls. Out on the Albemarle Road, where the unfortunate Mademoiselle Weaver's car was discovered this morning, I repaired when I had completed my researches in the city. Many feet had trampled the earth into the semblance of a pig-coop's floor before I arrived, but *grâce à Dieu*, there still remained that which confirmed my worst suspicions.

"Finding nothing near the spot where the mired car lay, I examined the earth on the other side of the road. There I discovered that which made my hair to rise on end. *Pardieu*, my friend, there is the business of the Fiend himself being done here!

"Leading from the road were three distinct sets of footprints—girl's footprints, made by small, high-heeled shoes. Far apart they were, showing they had been made by running feet, and all stopped abruptly at the same place.

"Back from the roadway, as you doubtless remember, stands a line of trees. It was at these the foot tracks halted, in each instance ending in two little pointed depressions, set quite close together. They were the marks of girls' slippers, my friend, and appeared to have been made as the young women stood on tiptoe.

"'Now,' I ask me, 'why should three young women leave the motor in which they ride, run from the road, halt on their toes beneath these trees, *and leave no footprints thereafter?*'

"'It seems they must have been driven from the road like game in a European preserve at hunting time, then seized by those lying in wait for them among the tree-boughs as they passed beneath,' I reply. 'And you are undoubtlessly correct,' I answer me.

"Nevertheless, to make my assurance sure, I examined all those trees and all the surrounding land with great injury to my dignity and clothing, but my search was not fruitless; for clinging to a tree-bough above one of the girls' toeprints I did find this." From his pocket be produced a tiny skein of light-brown fiber and passed it across the table to me.

"U'm?" I commented as I examined his find. "What is it?"

"Burlap," he returned. "You look puzzled, my friend. So did I when first I found it, but subsequent discoveries explained it—explained it all too well. As I have said, there were no footprints to be found around the trees, save those made by the fleeing girls, but, after much examination on my knees, I found three strange trails leading toward the road, away from those trees. Most carefully, with my nose fairly buried in the earth, I did examine those so queer depressions in the moist ground. Too large for human feet they were, yet not deep enough for an animal large enough to make them. At last I was rewarded by finding a bit of cloth-weave pattern in one of them, and then I knew. They were made by men whose feet had been wrapped in many thicknesses of burlap, like the feet of choleric old gentlemen suffering from gout.

"*Nom d'un renard*, but it was clever, almost clever enough to fool Jules de Grandin, but not quite.

"Feet so wrapped make no sound; they leave little or no track, and what track they do leave is not easily recognized as of human origin by the average Western policeman; furthermore, they leave no scent which may be followed by hounds. However, the miscreants failed in one respect: They forgot Jules de Grandin has traveled the world over on the trail of wickedness, and knows the ways of the East no less than those of the West. In India I have seen such trails left by robbers; today, in this so peaceful State of New Jersey, I recognized the spoor when I saw it. Friend Trowbridge, we are upon the path of villains, assassins, *apaches* who steal women for profit. Yes"—he nodded solemnly—"it is undoubtlessly so."

"But how—" I began, when his suddenly upraised hand cut me short.

Seated in the next booth to that we occupied was a pair of young men who had dined with greater liberality than wisdom. As I started to speak they were joined by a third, scarcely more temperate, who began descanting on the sensational features of a current burlesque show.

"Aw, shut up, how d'ye get that way?" one of the youths demanded scornfully. "Boy, till you've been where Harry and I were last night you ain't been nowhere and you ain't seen nothin'. Say, d'je ever see the *chonkina?*"

"*Dieu de Dieu!*" de Grandin murmured excitedly even as the other young man replied:

"*Chonkina?* What dye mean, *chonkina?*"

"You'd be surprised," his friend assured him. "There's a place out in the country—mighty exclusive place, too—where they'll let you see something to write home about—if you're willing to pay the price."

"I'm game," the other replied. "What say we go there tonight? If they can show me something I never saw before, I'll blow the crowd to the best dinner in town."

"You're on," his companions accepted with a laugh, but:

"Quick, Friend Trowbridge," de Grandin whispered, "do you go straightway to the desk and settle our bill. I follow."

In a moment we stood before the cashier's desk and as I tendered the young woman a bill, the Frenchman suddenly reeled as though in the last stages of drunkenness and began staggering across the room toward the booth where the three sportively inclined youths sat. As he drew abreast of them he gave a drunken lurch and half fell across their table, regaining his balance with the greatest difficulty and pouring forth a flood of profuse apologies.

A few moments later he joined me on the street, all traces of intoxication vanished, but feverish excitement shining in his small blue eyes.

"*C'est glorieux!*" he assured me with a chuckle. "Those three empty-headed young rakes will lead us to our quarry, or I am more mistaken than I think. In my pretended drunkenness, I fell among them and took time to memorize their faces. Also, I heard them make a definite appointment for their trip tonight. Trowbridge, my friend, we shall be there. Do you return home with all speed, bring the pistols, the flashlight and the horn-handled knife which you will find in my dressing-case, and meet me at police headquarters at precisely a quarter of midnight. I should be glad to accompany you, but there is a very great much for me to accomplish between now and then, and I fear there will be little sleep for Jules de Grandin this night. *Allez,* my friend, we have no time to waste!"

D E GRANDIN HAD EVIDENTLY perfected his arrangements by the time I reached headquarters; for a police car was waiting, and we drove in silence, with dimmed lights, through the chill March rain to a lonely point not far from the country club's golf links, where, at a signal from the little Frenchman, we came to a halt.

"Now, Friend Trowbridge," he admonished, "we must trust to our own heels, for I have no desire to let our quarry know we approach. Softly, if you please, and say anything you have to say in the lowest of whispers."

Quietly as an Indian stalking a deer he led the way across the rolling turf of the links, pausing now and again to listen attentively, at length bringing up under a clump of mournful weeping willows bordering the Albemarle Road. "Here we rest till they arrive," he announced softly, seating himself on the comparatively dry ground beneath a tree and leaning his back against its trunk. "Name of a name, but I should enjoy a cigarette; but"—he raised a shoulder in a resigned shrug—"we must have the self-restraint, even as in the days when we faced the *sale boche* in the trenches. Yes."

Time passed slowly while we maintained our silent vigil, and I was on the point of open rebellion when a warning ejaculation in my ear and the quick clasp of de Grandin's hand on my elbow told me something was toward.

Looking through the branches of our shelter, I beheld a long, black motor slipping noiselessly as a shadow down the road, saw it come to a momentary halt beside a copse of laurels some twenty yards away, saw three stealthy figures emerge from the bushes and parley a moment with the chauffeur, then enter the tonneau.

"Ha, they are cautious, these birds of evil," the Frenchman muttered as be leaped from the shadows of the willows and raised an imperative hand beckoningly.

It was with difficulty I repressed an exclamation of surprise and dismay as a dozen shadowy figures emerged, phantomlike, from the shrubbery bordering the highway.

"Are you there, *mon lieutenant?*" de Grandin called, and I was relieved as an answering hail responded and I realized we were surrounded by a cordon of State Troopers in command of a young but exceedingly businesslike-looking lieutenant.

Motorcycles—two of them equipped with sidecars—were wheeled from their covert in the bushes, and in another moment we were proceeding swiftly and silently in the wake of the vanishing limousine, de Grandin and I occupying the none too commodious "bathtubs" attached to the troopers' cycles.

It was a long chase our quarry led us and had our machines been less powerful and less expertly managed we should have been distanced more than once, but the automobile which can throw dust in the faces of the racing-cycles on which New Jersey mounts its highway patrols has not been built, and we were within easy hail of our game as they drew up before the gateway of a high-walled, deserted-looking country estate.

"Now, my lieutenant," de Grandin asked, "you thoroughly understand the plans?"

"I think so, sir," the young officer returned as he gathered his force about him with a wave of his hand.

Briefly, as the Frenchman checked off our proposed campaign, the lieutenant outlined the work to his men. "Surround the place," he ordered, "and lie low. Don't let anyone see you, and don't challenge anyone going in, but—nobody comes out without permission. Get me?"

As the troopers assented, he asked, "All set?"

There was a rattle of locks as the constables swung their vicious little carbines up to "'spection arms," and each man felt the butt of the service revolver and the riot stick swinging at his belt.

"All right, take cover. If you get a signal from the house, rush it. If no signal comes, close in anyhow at the end of two hours. I've got a search warrant here"—he patted his blouse pocket—"and we won't stand any monkey business from the folks inside. Dr. de Grandin's going in to reconnoiter; he'll give the signal to charge with his flashlight, or by firing his pistol when he's ready, but—"

"But you will advance, even though my signal fails," de Grandin interrupted grimly.

"Right-o," the other agreed. "Two hours from now—three o'clock—is zero. Here, men, compare your watches with mine; we don't want to go into action in ragged formation."

Two husky young troopers bent their backs and boosted de Grandin and me to the rim of the eight-foot brick wall surrounding the grounds. In a moment we had dropped silently to the yard beyond and de Grandin sent back a whispered signal.

Flattening ourselves to the ground we proceeded on hands and knees toward the house, taking advantage of every shrub and bush dotting the grounds, stealing forward in little rushes, then pausing beneath some friendly evergreen to glance cautiously about, listening for any sign or sound of activity from the big, darkened house.

"I'm afraid you've brought us out on a fool's errand, old chap," I whispered. "If we find anything more heinous than bootlegging here I'll be surprised but—"

"S-s-sh!" his hissing admonition silenced me. "To the right, my friend, look to the right and tell me what it is you see."

Obediently, I glanced away from the house, searching the deserted park for some sign of life. There, close to the ground, shone a faint glimmer of light. The glow was stationary, for we watched it for upward of ten minutes before the Frenchman ordered, "Let us investigate, Friend Trowbridge. It may betoken something we should know."

Swerving our course toward the dim beacon, we moved cautiously forward, and as we approached I grew more and more puzzled. The illumination appeared to rise from the ground, and, as we drew near, it was intercepted for an instant by something which passed between it and us. Again and yet again the glow was obscured with methodical regularity. For a moment I thought it might be some signal system warning the inmate's of the house of our approach, but as we crawled still nearer my heart began to beat more rapidly, for I realized the light shone from an old-fashioned oil lantern standing on the ground and the momentary interruptions were due to shovelfuls of earth being thrown up from a fairly deep excavation. Presently there was a pause in the digging operations and two objects appeared above the surface about three feet apart—the hands of a man in the act of stretching himself. Assuming he were of average height, the trench in which he stood would be some five feet deep, judging by the distance his hands protruded above its lip.

Circling warily about the workman and his work we were able to get a fairly clear view. The hole was some two feet wide by six feet long, and, as I had already estimated, something like five feet deep.

"What sort of trench usually has those dimensions?" The question crashed through my mind like an unexpected bolt of thunder, and the answer sent tiny ripples of chills through my cheeks and up my arms.

De Grandin's thought had paralleled mine, for he whispered, "It seems, Friend Trowbridge, that they prepare sepulture for someone. For us, by example? *Cordieu*, if it be so, I can promise them we shall go to it like kings of old, with more than one of them to bear us company in the land of shadows!"

Our course brought the grave-digger into view as we crept about him, and a fiercer, more bloodthirsty scoundrel I had never before had the misfortune to encounter. Taller than the average man by several inches he was, with enormously wide shoulders and long, dangling arms like those of a gorilla. His face was almost black, though plainly not that of a Negro, and his cheeks and chin were adorned by a bristling black beard which glistened in the lantern light with some sort of greasy dressing. Upon his head was a turban of tightly twisted woolen cloth.

"U'm?" de Grandin murmured quizzically. "A Patan, by the looks of him, Friend Trowbridge, and I think no more of him for it. In upper India they have a saying, 'Trust a serpent or a tiger, but trust a Patan never,' and the maxim is approved by centuries of unfortunate experience with gentlemen like the one we see yonder.

"Come, let us make haste for the house. It may be we shall arrive in time to cheat this almost-finished grave of its intended tenant."

Wriggling snakelike through the rain-drenched grounds, our progress rendered silent by the soft turf, we made a wide detour round the dark-faced grave-digger and approached the big, forbidding mansion through whose close-barred windows no ray of light appeared.

The place seemed in condition to defy a siege as we circled it warily, vainly seeking some means of ingress. At length, when we were on the point of owning defeat and rejoining the troopers, de Grandin came to a halt before an unbarred window letting into a cellar. Unbuttoning his leather topcoat, he produced a folded sheet of flypaper and applied the sticky stuff to the grimy windowpane, smoothed it flat, then struck sharply with his elbow. The window shattered beneath the impact, but the adhesive paper held the pieces firm, and there was no telltale clatter of broken glass as the pane smashed. "One learns more tricks than one when he associates with *les apaches*," he explained with a grin as he withdrew the flypaper and glass together, laid them on the grass and inserted his hand through the opening, undoing the window-catch. A moment later we had dropped to the cellar and de Grandin was flashing his electric torch inquiringly about.

It was a sort of lumber room into which we had dropped. Bits of discarded furniture, an old rug or two and a pile of miscellaneous junk occupied the place. The stout door at the farther end was secured by an old-fashioned lock, and the first twist of de Grandin's skeleton key sprung the bolt.

Beyond lay a long, dusty corridor from which a number of doors opened, but from which no stairway ascended. "U'm?" muttered the Frenchman. "There seems no way of telling where the stairs lie save by looking for them, Friend Trowbridge." Advancing at random, he inserted his key in the nearest lock and, after a moment's tentative twisting, was rewarded by the sound of a sharp click as the keeper shot back.

No ray of moonlight filtered through the windows, for they were stopped with heavy wooden shutters. As we paused irresolute, wondering if we had walked into a *cul-de-sac*, a faint, whimpering cry attracted our attention. "*Un petit chat!*" Grandin exclaimed softly. "A poor little pussy-cat; he has been locked in by mistake, no doubt, and ha! *Dieu de Dieu de Dieu de Dieu, regardez, mon ami!* Do you, too, behold it?"

The beam of his questing flashlight swept through the darkness, searching for the feline, but it was no cat the ray flashed on. It was a girl.

She lay on a rough, bedlike contrivance with a net of heavily knotted, coarse rope stretched across its frame where the mattress should have been, and was drawn to fullest compass in the form of a St. Andrew's cross; for leathern thongs knotted to each finger and toe strained tautly, holding hands and feet immovably toward the posts which stood at the four corners of the bed of torment. The knots were cruelly drawn, and even in the momentary flash of the light we saw the thongs were of rawhide, tied and stretched wet, but now dry and pulling the tortured girl's toes and fingers with a fury like that of a rack. Already the flesh about fingers and toe-nails was puffy and impurpled with engorged blood cut off by the vicious cinctures of the tightening strings.

The torment of the constantly shortening thongs and the cruel pressure of the rope-knots on which she lay were enough to drive the girl to madness, but an ultimate refinement had been added to her agony; for the bed on which she stretched was a full eight inches shorter than her height, so that her head hung over the end without support, and she was obliged to hold it up by continued flexion of the neck muscles or let it hang downward, either posture being unendurable for more than a fraction of a minute.

"O Lord," she moaned weakly between swollen lips which had been gashed and bitten till the blood showed on them in ruddy froth, "O dear Lord, take me—take me quickly—I can't stand this; I can't—oh, oh,—o-o-oh!" The prayerful exclamation ended in a half-whispered sob and her anguished head fell limply back and swung pendulously from side to side as consciousness left her.

"*Ohé; la pauvre créature!*" De Grandin leaped forward, unsheathing his knife as he sprang. Thrusting the flashlight into my hand, he slashed the cords from her hands and feet, cutting through each group of five strings with a single slash of his razor-sharp knife, and the thongs hummed and sang like broken banjo strings as they came apart beneath his steel.

As de Grandin worked I took note of the swooning girl. She was slight, almost to the point of emaciation, her ribs and the processes of her wrists and ankles showing whitely against the flesh. For costume she wore a wisp of printed cotton twisted bandeauwise about her bosom, a pair of soiled and torn white-cotton bloomers which terminated in tattered ruffles at her ankles and were held in place at the waist by a gayly dyed cotton scarf secured by a sort of four-in-hand knot in front. A close-wrapped bandanna kerchief swathed her head from brow to nape, covering hair and ears alike, and from the handkerchief's rim almost to the pink of her upper lip a gilded metal mask obscured her features, leaving only mouth, nose-tip and chin visible.

As de Grandin lifted her from the bed-frame and rested her lolling head against his shoulder, he tugged at the mask, but so firmly was it bound that it resisted his effort.

Again he pulled, more sharply this time, and, as he did so, we noticed a movement at the side of her head beneath the handkerchief-turban. Snatching off the headgear, the Frenchman fumbled for the mask cords, then started back with a low cry of horror and dismay. The mask was not tied, but *wired to her flesh*, two punctures having been made in each ear, one in the lobe, the other in the pinna, and through the raw wounds fine golden wires had been thrust and twisted into loops, so that removal of the mask would necessitate clipping the wire or tearing the tender, doubly pierced ears.

"Oh, the villains, the assassins, the ninety-thousand-times-damned beasts!" de Grandin gritted through his teeth, desisting in his effort to take off the metallic mask. "If ever Satan walked the earth in human guise, I think he lodges within this accursed kennel of hellhounds, Friend Trowbridge, and, *cordieu*, though the monster have as many gullets as the fabled hydra, I shall slit them all for this night's business!"

What more he would have said I do not know, for the fainting girl rolled her head and moaned feebly as she lay in his arms, and he was instantly all solicitude. "Drink this, *ma pauvre*," he commanded, drawing a silver flask from his pocket and pressing it to her pale lips.

She swallowed a bit of the fiery brandy, choked and gasped a little, then lay back against his arm with a weak sigh.

Again he applied the restorative; then: "Who are you, *ma petite?*" he asked gently. "Speak bravely; we are friends."

She shuddered convulsively and whimpered weakly again; then, so faint we could scarcely catch the syllables, "Ewell Eaton," she whispered.

"*Cordieu*, I did know it!" de Grandin exclaimed delightedly. "*Gloire à Dieu*, we have found you, *ma petite!*

"The door, Friend Trowbridge—do you stand guard at the portal lest we be surprised. Here,"—he snatched a pistol from his pocket and thrust it into my hand—"hesitate not to use it, should occasion arise!"

I took station at the entrance of the torture chamber while de Grandin set about making the half-conscious girl as comfortable as possible. I could hear the murmur of their voices in soft conversation as he worked frantically at her swollen feet and hands, rubbing them with brandy from his flask and massaging her wrists and ankles in an effort to restore circulation, but what they said I could not understand.

I was on the point of leaving my post to join them, for the likelihood of our being interrupted seemed remote, when it happened. Without so much as a warning creak from without, the door smashed suddenly back on its hinges, flooring me as the kick of a mule might have done, and three men rushed pell-mell into the room. I saw de Grandin snatch frantically at his pistol, heard Ewell Eaton scream despairingly, and half-rose to my feet, weak and giddy with the devastating blow I had received, but determined to use my pistol to best advantage. One of the intruders turned savagely on me, brought the staff of a long, spearlike weapon he carried down upon my head, and caught me a smashing kick on the side of the head as I fell.

"TROWBRIDGE, MY FRIEND, ARE you living—do you survive?" Jules de Grandin's anxious whisper cut through the darkness surrounding me.

I was lying on my back, wrists and ankles firmly bound, a bump like a goose-egg on my head where the spear-butt had hit me. Through the grimy window of our cellar prison a star or two winked mockingly; otherwise the place was dark as a cave. How long we had lain there I had no way of telling. For all I knew the troopers might have raided the place, arrested the inmates and gone, leaving us in our dungeon. A dozen questions blazed through my mind like lightning-flashes across a summer night as I strove to roll over and ease the pressure of the knots on my crossed wrists.

"Trowbridge, *mon vieux*, do you live, are you awake, can you hear?" the Frenchman's murmured query came through the darkness again.

"De Grandin—where are you?" I asked, raising my head, the better to locate his voice.

"*Parbleu*, here I lie, trussed like a capon ready for the spit!" he returned. "They are prodigal with their rope, those assassins. Nevertheless, I think we shall make apes of them all. Roll toward me if you can, my friend, and lie with your hands toward me. *Grâce à Dieu*, neither age nor overeating has dulled my teeth. Come, make haste!"

Followed a slow, dragging sound, punctuated with muttered profanities in mingled French and English as he hitched himself laboriously across the rough cement floor in my direction.

In a few moments I felt the stiffly waxed hairs of his mustache against my wrists and the tightening of my bonds as his small, sharp teeth sank into the cords, severing strand after strand.

Sooner than I had hoped, my hands were free, and after a few seconds, during which I wrung my fingers to restore circulation, I unfastened the ropes binding my feet, then released de Grandin.

"*Morbleu*, at any rate we can move about, even if those *sacré* rogues deprived us of our weapons," the Frenchman muttered as he strode up and down our prison. "At least one thing is accomplished—Mademoiselle Ewell is relieved of her torture. Before they beat me unconscious I heard her told tomorrow she would be strangled, but as the Spaniards so sagely remark, 'tomorrow is another day,' and I trust we shall have increased hell's population by that time.

"Have you a match, by any kind of chance?" he added, turning to me.

Searching my pockets, I found a packet of paper matches and passed them over. Striking one, he held it torchwise above his head, surveying our prison. It was a small, cement-floored room, its single window heavily barred and its only article of furniture a large, sheet-iron-sheathed furnace, evidently the building's auxiliary heating-plant. The door was of stout pine planks, nailed and doweled together so strongly as to defy anything less than a battering-ram; and secured with a modern burglar-proof lock. Plainly, there was no chance of escape that way.

"U'm?" murmured de Grandin, surveying the old hot-air furnace speculatively. "U'm-m-m? It may be we shall find use for this, if my boyhood's agility has not failed me, Friend Trowbridge."

"Use for that furnace?" I asked incredulously.

"*Mais oui*, why not?" he returned. "Let us see."

He jerked the heater's cast-iron door open, thrusting a match inside and looking carefully up the wide, galvanized flues leading to the upper floors. "It is a chance," he announced, "but the good God knows we take an equal one waiting here. *Au revoir*, my friend, either I return to liberate us or we say good morning in heaven."

Next instant he had turned his back to the furnace, grasped the iron door-frame at each side, thrust his head and shoulders through the opening and begun worming himself upward toward the flue-mouth.

A faint scraping sounded inside the heater's interior, then silence broken only by the occasional soft thud of a bit of dislodged soot.

I paced the dungeon in a perfect fever of apprehension. Though de Grandin was slight as a girl, and almost as supple as an eel, I was certain I had seen the last of him, for he would surely be hopelessly caught in the great, dusty pipes, or, if not that, discovered by some of the villainous inmates of the place when he attempted to force himself through a register. His plan of escape was suicide, nothing less.

Click! The strong, jimmy-proof lock snapped back. I braced myself for the reappearance of our jailers, but the Frenchman's delighted chuckle reassured me.

"*Mordieu*, it was not even so difficult as I had feared," he announced. "The pipes were large enough to permit my passage without great trouble, and the registers—God be thanked!—were not screwed to the floor. I had but to lift the first I came to from its frame and emerge like a jack-in-the-box from his case. Yes. Come, let us ascend. There is rheumatism, and other unpleasant things, to be contracted in this cursed cellar."

Stepping as softly as possible, we traversed a long, unlighted corridor, ascended two flights of winding stairs and came to an upper hallway letting into a large room furnished in a garish East Indian manner and decorated with a number of mediæval sets of mail and a stand of antique arms.

The Frenchman looked about, seeking cover, but there was nothing behind which an underfed cat could hide, much less a man. Finally: "I have it!" he declared, "*Parbleu, c'est joli!*"

Striding across the room he examined the nearest suit of armor and turned to me with a chuckle. "Into it, *mon ami*," he commanded. "Quick!"

With de Grandin's help I donned the beavered helmet and adjusted the gorget, cuirass, brassards, cuisses and jambs, finding them a rather snug fit. In five minutes I was completely garbed, and the Frenchman, laughing softly and cursing delightedly; was clambering into another set of mail. When we stood erect against the wall no one who had not seen us put on the armor could have told us from the empty suits of mail which stood at regular intervals about the wall.

From the stand of arms de Grandin selected a keen, long-bladed misericorde, and gazed upon it lovingly. Nor had he armed himself a moment too soon, for even as he straightened back against the wall and lowered the visor of his helmet there came the scuffle of feet from the corridor outside and a bearded, muscular man in Oriental garb dragged a half-fainting girl into the room. She was scantily clad in a Hindu version of a Parisian night club costume.

"By Vishnu, you shall!" the man snarled, grasping the girl's slender throat between his blunt fingers and squeezing until she gasped for breath. "Dance you must and dance you shall—as the Master has ordered—or I choke the breath from your nostrils! Shame? What have *you* to do with shame, O creature? Daughter of a thousand iniquities, tomorrow there shall be *two* stretched upon the 'bed of roses' in the cellar!"

"*Eh bien*, my friend, you may be right," de Grandin remarked, "but I damn think you shall not be present to see it."

The fellow toppled over without so much as a groan as the Frenchman, with the precise skill of a practised surgeon, drove his dagger home where skull and spine met.

"Silence, little orange-pip!" the Frenchman ordered as the girl opened her lips to scream. "Go below to your appointed place and do as you are bidden. The time comes quickly when you shall be liberated and we shall drag such of these sow-suckled sons of pigs as remain alive to prison. Quick, none must suspect that help approaches!"

The girl ran quickly from the room, her soft, bare feet making no sound on the thick carpets of the hall, and de Grandin walked slowly to the door. In a moment he returned, lugging a suit of armor in his arms. Standing it in the place against the wall he had vacated, he repeated the trip, filling my space with a second empty suit, then motioning me to follow.

"Those sets of mail I did bring were from the balcony at the stairhead," he explained softly. "In their places we shall stand and see what passes below. Perhaps it is that we shall have occasion to take parts in the play before all is done."

STIFF AND STILL AS the lifeless ornaments we impersonated, we stood at attention at the stairway's top. Below us lay the main drawing-room of the house, a sort of low stage or dais erected at its farther end, a crescent formation of folding-chairs, each occupied by a man in evening clothes, standing in the main body of the room.

"Ah, it seems all is ready for the play," the Frenchman murmured softly through the visor-bars of his helmet. "Did you overhear the tale the little Mademoiselle Ewell told me in the torture chamber, my friend?"

"No."

"*Mordieu*, it was a story to make a man's hair erect itself! This is a house of evil, the abode of *esclavage*, no less, Friend Trowbridge. Here stolen girls are brought and broken for a life of degradation, even as wild animals from the jungle are trained for a career in the arena. The master of this odious cesspool is a Hindu, as are his ten retainers, and well they know their beastly trade, for he was a dealer in women in India before the British *Raj* put him in prison, and his underlings have all been *corah-bundars*—punishment-servants—in Indian harems before he hired them for this service. *Parbleu*, from what we saw of the poor one in the cellars, I should say their technique has improved since they left their native land!

"The headquarters of this organization is in Spain—I have heard of it before—but there are branches in almost every country. These evil ones work on commission, and when the girls they steal have been sufficiently broken in spirit they are delivered, like so many cattle, and their price paid by dive-keepers in South America, Africa or China—wherever women command high prices and no questions are asked.

"Hitherto the slavers have taken their victims where they found them—poor shop-girls, friendless waifs, or those already on the road to living death. This is a new scheme. Only well-favored girls of good breeding are stolen and brought here for breaking, and every luckless victim is cruelly beaten, stripped and reclothed in the degrading uniform of the place within half an hour of her arrival.

"*Mordieu*, but their tactics are clever! All faces obscured by masks which can not be removed, all hair covered by exactly similar turbans, all clothing exactly alike—twin sisters might be here together, yet never recognize each other, for the poor ones are forbidden to address so much as a word to each other—Mademoiselle Ewell was stretched on the bed of torture for no greater fault than breaking this rule."

"But this is horrible!" I interrupted. "This is unbelievable—"

"Who says it?" he demanded fiercely. "Have we not seen with our own eyes? Have we not Mademoiselle Ewell's story for testimony? Do I not know how her sister, poor Madame Mazie, came in the river? Assuredly! Attend me: The fiends who took her prisoner quickly discovered the poor child's condition, and they thereupon deliberately beat out her brains and cast her murdered body into the water, thinking the river would wash away the evidence of their crime.

"Did not that execrable slave-master whom I slew command the other girl to dance—what did it mean?" He paused a moment, then continued in a sibilant whisper:

"This, *pardieu!* Even as we send the young conscripts to Algeria to toughen them for military service, so these poor ones are given their baptism into a life of infamy by being forced to dance before half-drunken brutes to the music of the whip's crack. *Nom d'une pipe*, I damn think we shall see some dancing of the sort they little suspect before we are done—no more, the master comes!"

As de Grandin broke off, I noticed a sudden focusing of attention by the company below.

Stepping daintily as a tango dancer, a man emerged through the arch behind the dais at the drawing-room's farther end. He was in full Indian court dress: a purple satin tunic, high at the neck and reaching half-way to his knees, fastened at the front with a row of sapphire buttons and heavily fringed with silver at the bottom; trousers of white satin, baggy at the knee, skin-tight at the ankle, slippers of red Morocco on his feet. An enormous turban of peach-bloom silk, studded with brilliants and surmounted by a vivid green aigrette was on his head, while round his neck dangled a triple row of pearls, its lowest loop hanging almost to the bright yellow sash which bound his waist as tightly as a corset. One long, brown hand toyed negligently with the necklace, while the other stroked his black, sweeping mustache caressingly.

"Gentlemen," be announced in a languid Oxonian drawl, "if you are ready, we shall proceed to make whoopee, as you so quaintly express it in your vernacular." He turned and beckoned through the archway, and as the light struck his profile I recognized him as the leader of the party which had surprised us in the torture chamber.

De Grandin identified him at the same time, for I heard him muttering through the bars of his visor: "Ha, toad, viper, worm! Strut while you may; comes soon the time when Jules de Grandin shall show you the posture you will not change in a hurry!"

Through the archway stepped a tall, angular woman, her face masked by a black cloth domino, a small round samisen, or Japanese banjo, in her hand. Saluting the company with a profound obeisance, she dropped to her knees and picked a short, jerky note or two on her crude instrument.

The master of ceremonies clapped his hands sharply, and four girls came running out on the stage. They wore brilliant kimonos, red and blue and white, beautifully embroidered with birds and flowers, and on their feet were white-cotton *tabi* or foot-mittens with a separate "thumb" to accommodate the great toe, and *zori*, or light straw sandals. Golden masks covered the upper part of their faces, and their hair was hidden by voluminous glossy-black wigs arranged in elaborate Japanese coiffures and thickly studded with ornamental hairpins. On their brightly rouged lips were fixed, unnatural smiles.

Running to the very edge of the platform, with exaggeratedly short steps, they slipped their sandals off and dropped to their knees, lowering their foreheads to the floor in greeting to the guests; then, rising, drew up in rank before the musician, tittering with a loud, forced affectation of coy gayety and hiding their faces behind the flowing sleeves of their kimonos, as though in mock-modesty.

Again the master clapped his hands, the musician began a titillating tune on her banjo, and the dance was on. More like a series of postures than a dance it was, ritualistically slow and accompanied by much waving of hands and fluttering of fans.

The master of ceremonies began crooning a low, singsong tune in time with the plink-plink of the banjo. "*Chonkina-chonkina*," he chanted; then with a slapping clap of his hands:

"*Hoi!*"

Dance and music came to a frozen stop. The four girls held the posture they had when the call came, assuming the strained, unreal appearance of a motion picture when the film catches in the projecting reel.

For a moment there was a breathless silence, then a delighted roar from the audience; for the fourth girl, caught with one foot and hand upraised, could not maintain the pose. Vainly she strove to remain stone still, but despite her efforts her lifted foot descended ever so slightly.

A guttural command from the show-master, and she paid the forfeit, unfastening her girdle and dropping it to the floor.

A wave of red mantled her throat and face to the very rim of her golden mask as she submitted, but the forced, unnatural smile never left her painted lips as the music and dance began afresh at the master's signal.

"*Hoi!*" Again the strident call, again the frozen dance, again a girl lost and discarded a garment.

On and on the bestial performance went, interminably, it seemed to me, but actually only a few minutes were required for the poor, bewildered girls, half fainting with shame and fear of torture, to lose call after call until at last they danced only in their cotton *tabi*, and even these were discarded before the audience would cry enough and the master release them from their ordeal.

Gathering up their fallen clothes, sobbing through lips which still fought valiantly to retain their constrained smiles, the poor creatures advanced once more to the platform's edge, once more knelt and touched their brows to the floor, then ran from the stage, only the fear of punishment holding their little baked feet to the short, sliding steps of their artificial run rather than a mad dash for sanctuary from the burning gaze and obscene calls of the onlookers.

"*Dieu de Dieu*," de Grandin fumed, "will not the troopers ever come? Must more of this shameless business go on?"

A moment later the showman was speaking again: "Let us now give undivided attention to the next number of our program," he was announcing suavely.

Something white hurtled through the archway behind him, and a girl clothed only in strings of glittering rhinestones about throat, wrists, waist and ankles was fairly flung out upon the stage, where she cowered in a perfect palsy of terror. Her hands were fettered behind her by a six-inch chain attached to heavy golden bracelets, and an odd contrivance, something like a bit, was fastened between her lips by a harness fitted over her head, making articulate outcry impossible. Behind her, strutting with all the majesty of a turkey-cock, came a man in the costume of a South American *vaquero*—loose, baggy trousers, wide, nail-studded belt, patent leather boots and broad-brimmed, low-crowned bat of black felt. In his hand was a coiled whip of woven leather thongs—the bull-whip of the Argentine pampas.

"God and the devil!" swore de Grandin, his teeth fairly chattering in rage. "I know it; it is the whipping dance—he will beat her to insensibility—I have seen such shows in Buenos Aires, Friend Trowbridge, but may Satan toast me in his fires if I witness it again. Come, my friend, it is time we taught these swine a lesson. Do you stand firm and beat back any who attempt to pass. Me, I go into action!"

Like some ponderous engine of olden times he strode forward, the joints of his armor creaking with unwonted use.

For a moment guests and servants were demoralized by the apparition descending the stairs, for it was as if a chair or sofa had suddenly come to life and taken the field against them.

"Here, wash all thish, wash all thish?" demanded a maudlin young man with drunken truculence as he swaggered forward to bar the Frenchman's way, reaching for his hip pocket as he spoke.

De Grandin drew back his left arm, doubled his iron-clad fingers into a ball and dashed his mailed fist into the fellow's face.

The drunken rake went down with a scream, spewing blood and teeth from his crushed mouth.

"Awai, a bhut!" cried one of the servants in terror, and another took up the cry: "A bhut! a bhut!"

Two of the men seized long-shafted halberds from an ornamental stand of arms and advanced on the little Frenchman, one on each side.

Clang! The iron points of their weapons rang against his visor-bars, but the fine-tempered, hand-wrought steel that had withstood thrust of lance and glaive and flying cloth-yard arrow when Henry of England led his hosts to victory at Agincourt held firm, and de Grandin hardly wavered in his stride.

Then, with halberd and knife and wicked, razor-edged scimitar, they were on him like a pack of hounds seeking to drag down a stag.

De Grandin strode forward, striking left and right with mailed fists, crushing a nose here, battering a mouth there, or smashing jaw-bones with the iron-shod knuckles of his flailing hands.

My breath came fast and faster as I watched the struggle, but suddenly I gave a shout of warning. Two of the Hindus had snatched a silken curtain from a doorway and rushed de Grandin from behind. In an instant the fluttering drapery fell over his head, shutting out sight and cumbering his arms in its clinging folds. In another moment he lay on his back, half a dozen screaming Indians pinioning his arms and legs.

I rushed forward to his rescue, but my movement was a moment too late. From the front door and the back there came a sudden, mighty clamor. The thud of gun-butts and riot sticks on the panels and hoarse commands to open in the law's name announced the troopers had arrived at last.

Crash! The front door splintered inward and four determined men in the livery of the State Constabulary rushed into the hall.

A moment the Hindus stood at bay; then, with waving swords and brandishing pikes they charged the officers.

They were ten to four, but odds were not with numbers, for even as they sprang to the attack there sounded the murderous *r-r-r-rat-tat-tat* of an automatic rifle, and the rank of yelling savages wavered like growing wheat before a gust of summer wind, then went down screaming, while the acrid, bitter fumes of smokeless powder stung our nostrils.

"N OM D'UN PORC, MON *lieutenant*, you came not a moment too soon to complete a perfect night's work," de Grandin complimented as we prepared to set out for home. "Ten tiny seconds more and you should have found nothing but the deceased corpse of Jules de Grandin to rescue, I fear."

From the secret closets of the house the girls' clothing had been rescued, wire-clippers in willing hands had cut away the degrading golden masks from the captives' faces, and Ewell Eaton, the three sorority sisters and the poor little shop-girl whose disappearances had caused such consternation to their families were ready to ride back to Harrisonville, two in the troopers' side-cars, the rest in hastily improvised saddles behind the constables on their motorcycles.

"We did make monkeys out of 'em, at that," the young officer grinned. "It was worth the price of admission to see those guys in their dress suits trying to bluff us off, then whining like spanked kids when I told 'em it would be six months in the work-house for theirs. Gosh, won't the papers make hash of *their* reputations before this business is over?"

"Undoubtlessly," de Grandin assented. "It is to be deplored that we may not lawfully make hash of their so foul bodies, as well. Me, I should enormously enjoy dissecting them without previous anesthesia. However, in the meantime—"

He drew the young officer aside with a confidential hand upon his elbow, and a brief, whispered colloquy followed. Two minutes later he rejoined me, a satisfied twinkle in his eye, the scent of raw, new whisky on his breath.

"*Barbe d'un chameau*, he is a most discerning young man, that one," he confided, as he wiped his lips with a lavender-bordered silk handkerchief.

The Corpse-Master

T HE AMBULANCE-GONG INSISTENCE OF my night bell brought me up standing from a stuporlike sleep, and as I switched the vestibule light on and unbarred the door, "Are you the doctor?" asked a breathless voice. A disheveled youth half fell through the doorway and clawed my sleeve desperately. "Quick quick, Doctor! It's my uncle, Colonel Evans. He's dying. I think he tried to kill himself—"

"All right," I agreed, turning to sprint upstairs. "What sort of wound has he?—or was it poison?"

"It's his throat, sir. He tried to cut it. Please, hurry, Doctor!"

I took the last four steps at a bound, snatched some clothes from the bedside chair and charged down again, pulling on my garments like a fireman answering a night alarm. "Now, which way—" I began, but:

"*Tiens*," a querulous voice broke in as Jules de Grandin came downstairs, seeming to miss half the treads in his haste, "Let him tell us where to go as we go there, my old one! It is that we should make the haste. A cut throat does not wait patiently."

"This is Dr. de Grandin," I told the young man. "He will be of great assistance—"

"*Mais oui*," the little Frenchman agreed, "and the Trump of Judgment will serve excellently as an alarm clock if we delay our going long enough. Make haste, my friend!"

"Down two blocks and over one," our caller directed as we got under way, "376 Albion Road. My uncle went to bed about ten o'clock, according to the servants, and none of them heard him moving about since. I got home just a few minutes ago, and found him lying in the bathroom when I went to wash my teeth. He lay beside the tub with a razor in his hand, and blood was all over the place. It was awful!"

"Undoubtlessly," de Grandin murmured from his place on the rear seat. "What did you do then, young Monsieur?"

"Snatched a roll of gauze from the medicine cabinet and staunched the wound as well as I could, then called Dockery the gardener to hold it in place while I raced round to see you. I remembered seeing your sign sometime before."

We drew up to the Evans house as he concluded his recital, and rushed through the door and up the stairs together. "In there," our companion directed, pointing to a door from which there gushed a stream of light into the darkened hall.

A man in bathrobe and slippers knelt above a recumbent form stretched full-length on the white tiles of the bathroom. One glance at the supine figure and both de Grandin and I turned away, I with a deprecating shake of my head, the Frenchman with a fatalistic shrug.

"He has no need of us, that poor one," he informed the young man. "Ten minutes ago, perhaps yes; now"—another shrug—"the undertaker and the clergyman, perhaps the police—"

"The police? Surely, Doctor, this is suicide—"

"Do you say so?" de Grandin interrupted sharply. "Trowbridge, my friend, consider this, if you please." Deftly he raised the dead man's thin white beard and pointed to the deeply incised slash across the throat. "Does that mean nothing?"

"Why—er—"

"Perfectly. Wipe your pince-nez before you look a second time, and tell me that you see the cut runs diagonally from right to left."

"Why, so it does, but—"

"But Monsieur the deceased was right-handed—look how the razor lies beneath his right hand. Now, if you will raise your hand to your own throat and draw the index finger across it as if it were a knife, you will note the course is slightly out of horizontal—somewhat diagonal—slanting downward from left to right. Is it not so?"

I nodded as I completed the gesture.

"Très bien. When one is bent on suicide he screws his courage to the sticking point, then, if he has chosen a cut throat as means of exit, he usually stands before a mirror, cuts deeply and quickly with his knife, and makes a downward-slanting slash. But as he sees the blood and feels the pain his resolution weakens, and the gash becomes more and more shallow. At the end it trails away to little more than a skin-scratch. It is not so in this case; at its end the wound is deeper than at the beginning.

"Again, this poor one would almost certainly have stood before the mirror to do away with himself. Had he done so he would have fallen crosswise of the room, perhaps; more likely not. One with a severed throat does not die quickly.

He thrashes about like a fowl recently decapitated, and writes the story of his struggle plainly on his surroundings. What have we here? Do you—does anyone—think it likely that a man would slit his gullet, then lie down peacefully to bleed his life away, as this one appears to have done? *Non, non;* it is not *en caractère!*

"Consider further"—he pointed with dramatic suddenness to the dead man's bald head—"if we desire further proof, observe him!"

Plainly marked there was a welt of bruised flesh on the hairless scalp, the mark of some blunt instrument.

"He might have struck his head as he fell," I hazarded, and he grinned in derision.

"*Ah bah,* I tell you he was stunned unconscious by some miscreant, then dragged or carried to this room and slaughtered like a pole-axed beef. Without the telltale mark of the butcher's bludgeon there is ground for suspicion in the quietude of his position, in the neat manner the razor lies beneath his hand instead of being firmly grasped or flung away, but with this bruise before us there is but one answer. He has been done to death; he has been butchered; he was murdered."

"WILL YE BE SEEIN' Sergeant Costello?" Nora McGinnis appeared like a phantom at the drawing room door as de Grandin and I were having coffee next evening after dinner. "He says—"

"Invite him to come in and say it for himself, *ma petite,*" Jules de Grandin answered with a smile of welcome at the big red-headed man who loomed behind the trim figure of my household factotum. "Is it about the Evans killing you would talk with us?" he added as the detective accepted a cigar and demitasse.

"There's two of 'em, now, sir," Costello answered gloomily. "Mulligan, who pounds a beat in th' Eighth Ward, just 'phoned in there's a murder dressed up like a suicide at th' Rangers' Club in Fremont Street."

"*Pardieu,* another?" asked de Grandin. "How do you know the latest one is not true suicide?"

"Well, sir, here's th' pitch: When th' feller from th' club comes runnin' out to say that Mr. Wolkof's shot himself, Mulligan goes in and takes a look around. He finds him layin' on his back with a little hole in his forehead an' th' back blown out o' his head, an', bein' th' wise lad, he adds up two an' two and makes it come out four. He'd used a Colt .45, this Wolkof feller, an' it was layin' half-way in his hand, restin' on his half-closed fingers, ye might say. That didn't look too kosher. A feller who's been shot through the forehead is more likely to freeze tight to th' gun than otherwise. Certain'y he don't just hold it easy-like. Besides, it was an old fashioned black-powder gun, sir, what they call a low-velocity weapon, and if it had been fired close against the dead man's fore-head it should 'a' left a good-sized smudge o' powder-stain. There wasn't any."

"One commends the excellent Mulligan for his reasoning," de Grandin commented. "He found this Monsieur Wolkof lying on his back with a hole drilled through his head, no powder-brand upon his brow where the projectile entered, and the presumably suicidal weapon lying loosely in his hand. One thing more: It may not be conclusive, but it would be helpful to know if there were any powder-stains upon the dead man's pistol-hand."

"As far's I know there weren't, sir," answered Costello. "Mulligan said he took partic'lar notice of his hands, too. But ye're yet to hear th' cream o' th' joke. Th' pistol was in Mr. Wolkof's open right hand, an' all th' club attendants swear he was left-handed—writin', feedin' himself an' shavin' with his left hand exclusively. Now, I ask ye, Dr. de Grandin, would a man all steamed up to blow his brains out be takin' th' trouble to break a lifetime habit of left-handed-ness when he's so much more important things to think about? It seems to me that—"

"Ye're wanted on th' 'phone, Sergeant," announced Nora from the door-way. "Will ye be takin' it in here, or usin' th' hall instrument?"

"Hullo? Costello speakin'," he challenged. "If its' about th' Wolkof case, I'm goin' right over—glory be to God! No! Och, th' murderin' blackguard!"

"Gentlemen," he faced us, fury in his ruddy face and blazing blue eyes, "it's another one. A little girl, this time. They've kilt a tiny, wee baby while we sat here like three damn' fools and talked! They've took her body to th' morgue—"

"Then, *nom d'un charneau*, why are we remaining here?" de Grandin inter-rupted. "Come, *mes amis*, it is to hasten. Let us go all quickly!"

WITH MY HORN TOOTING almost continuously, and Costello waving aside crossing policemen, we rushed to the city mortuary. Parnell, the coroner's physician, fussed over a tray of instruments, Coroner Martin bustled about in a perfect fever of eagerness to begin his official duties; two plainclothes men conferred in muted whispers in the outer office.

Death in the raw is never pretty, as doctors, soldiers and embalmers know only too well. When it is accompanied by violence it wears a still less lovely aspect, and when the victim is a child the sight is almost heart-breaking. Bruised and battered almost beyond human semblance, her baby-fine hair matted with mixed blood and cerebral matter, little Hazel Clark lay before us, the queer, unnatural angle of her right wrist denoting a Colles' fracture; a subclavicular dislocation of the left shoulder was apparent by the projection of the bone beneath the clavicle, and the vault of her small skull had been literally beaten in. She was completely "broken" as ever medieval malefactor was when bound upon the wheel of torture for the ministrations of the executioner.

For a moment de Grandin bent above the battered little corpse, viewing it intently with the skilled, knowing eye of a pathologist, then, so lightly that they scarcely displaced a hair of her head, his fingers moved quickly over her, pausing now and again to prod gently, then sweeping onward in their investigative course. "*Tiens*, he was a gorilla for strength, that one," he announced, "and a veritable gorilla for savagery, as well. What is there to tell me of the case, *mes amis?*" he called to the plainclothes men.

Such meager data as they had they gave him quickly. She was three and a half years old, the idol of her lately widowed father, and had neither brothers nor sisters. That afternoon her father had given her a quarter as reward for having gone a whole week without meriting a scolding, and shortly after dinner she had set out for the corner drug store to purchase an ice cream cone with part of her righteously acquired wealth. Attendants at the pharmacy remembered she had left the place immediately and set out for home; a neighbor had seen her proceeding up the street, the cone grasped tightly in her hand as she sampled it with ecstatic little licks. Two minutes later, from a spot where the privet hedge of a vacant house shadowed the pavement, residents of the block had heard a scream, but squealing children were no novelty in the neighborhood, and the cry was not repeated. It was not till her father came looking for her that they recalled it.

From the drug store Mr. Clark traced Hazel's homeward course, and was passing the deserted house when he noticed a stain on the sidewalk. A lighted match showed the discoloration was a spot of blood some four inches across, and with panic premonition tearing at his heart he pushed through the hedge to unmowed lawn of the vacant residence. Match after match he struck while he called "Hazel! Hazel!" but there was no response, and he saw nothing till he was about to return to the street. Then, in a weed-choked rosebed, almost hidden by the foliage, he saw the gleam of her pink pinafore. His cries aroused the neighborhood, and the police were notified.

House-to-house inquiry by detectives finally elicited the information that a "short, stoop-shouldered man" had been seen walking hurriedly away a moment after the child's scream was heard. Further description of the suspect was unavailable.

"*Pardieu*," de Grandin stroked his small mustache thoughtfully as the plainclothes men concluded, "it seems we have to search the haystack for an almost microscopic needle, *n'est-ce-pas?* There are considerable numbers of small men with stooping shoulders. The task will be a hard one."

"Hard, hell!" one of the detectives rejoined in disgust. "We got no more chance o' findin' that bird than a pig has o' wearin' vest-pockets."

"Do you say so?" the Frenchman demanded, fixing an uncompromising cat-stare on the speaker. "*Alors*, my friend, prepare to meet a fully tailored porker before you are greatly older. Have you forgotten in the excitement that I am in the case?"

"Sergeant, sir," a uniformed patrolman hurried into the mortuary, "they found th' weapon used on th' Clark girl. It's a winder-sash weight. They're testin' it for fingerprints at headquarters now."

"Humph," Costello commented. "Anything on it?"

"Yes, sir. Th' killer must 'a' handled it after he dragged her body into th' bushes, for there's marks o' bloody fingers on it plain as day."

"O.K., I'll be right up," Costello replied. "Take over, Jacobs," he ordered one of the plainclothes men. "I'll call ye if they find out anything, Dr. de Grandin. So long!"

The Sergeant delayed his report, and next morning after dinner the Frenchman suggested, "Would it not be well to interview the girl's father? I should appreciate it if you will accompany and introduce me."

"He's in the drawing room," the maid told us as we knocked gently on the Clark door. "He's been there ever since they brought her home, sir. Just sitting beside her and—" she broke off as her throat filled with sobs. "If you could take his mind off of his trouble it would be a Godsend. If he'd only cry, or sumpin—"

"Grief is a hot, consuming fire, Madame," the little Frenchman whispered, "and only tears can quell it. The dry-eyed mourner is the one most likely to collapse."

Coroner Martin had done his work as a mortician with consummate artistry. Under his deft hands all signs of the brutality that struck the child down had been effaced. Clothed in a short light-pink dress she lay peacefully in her casket, one soft pink cheek against the tufted silken pillow sewn with artificial forget-me-nots, a little bisque doll, dressed in a frock the exact duplicate of her own, resting in the crook of her left elbow. Beside the casket, a smile sadder than any grimace of woe on his thin, ascetic features, sat Mortimer Clark.

As we tiptoed into the darkened room we heard him murmur, "Time for shut-eye town, daughter. Daddy'll tell you a story." For a moment he looked expectantly into the still childish face on the pillow before him, as if waiting an answer. The little gilt clock on the mantel ticked with a sort of whispering haste, far down the block a neighbor's dog howled dismally; a light breeze bustled through the opened windows, fluttering the white-scrim curtains and setting the orange flames of the tall candles at the casket's head and foot to flickering.

It was weird, this stricken man's vigil beside his dead, it was ghastly to hear him addressing her as if she could hear and reply. As the story of the old woman and her pig progressed I felt a kind of terrified tension about my heart. ". . . the cat began to kill the rat, the rat began to gnaw the rope, the rope began to hang the butcher—"

"*Grand Dieu,*" de Grandin whispered as he plucked me by he elbow, "let us not look at it, Friend Trowbridge—it is a profanation for our eyes to see, our ears to hear what goes on here. *Sang de Saint Pierre,* I, Jules de Grandin swear that I shall find the one who caused this thing to be, and when I find him, though he take refuge beneath the very throne of God, I'll drag him forth and cast him screaming into hell. God do so to me, and more also, if I do not!" Tears were coursing down his cheeks, and he let them flow unabashed.

"You don't want to talk to him, then?" I whispered as we neared the front door.

"I do not, neither do I wish to tell indecent stories to the priest as he elevates the Host. The one would be no greater sacrilege than the other, but—ah?" he broke off, staring at a small framed parchment hanging on the wall. "Tell me, my friend," he demanded, "what is it that you see there?"

"Why, it's a certificate of membership in the Rangers' Club. Clark was in the Army Air Force, and—"

"*Très bien,*" he broke in. "Thank you. Our ideas sometimes lead us to see what we wish when in reality it is not there; that is why I sought the testimony of disinterested eyes."

"What in the world has Clark's membership in the Rangers got to do with—"

"*Zut!*" he waved me to silence. "I think, I cogitate, I concentrate, my old one. Monsieur Evans—Monsieur Wolkof, now Monsieur Clark—all are members of that club. *C'est très étrange.* Me, I shall interview the steward of that club, my friend. Perhaps his words may throw more light on these so despicable doings than all the clumsy, well-meant investigations of our friend Costello. Come, let us go away. Tomorrow will do as well as today, for the miscreant who fancies himself secure is in no hurry to decamp, despite the nonsense talked of the guilty who flee when no man pursueth."

WE FOUND COSTELLO WAITING for us when we reached home. A very worried-looking Costello he was, too. "We've checked th' fingerprints on th' sash-weight, sir," he announced almost truculently.

"Bon," the Frenchman replied carelessly. "Is it that they are of someone you can identify?"

"I'll say they are," the sergeant returned shortly. "They're Gyp Carson's—th' meanest killer th' force ever had to deal with."

"Ah," de Grandin shook off his air of preoccupation with visible effort, "it is for you to find this Monsieur Gyp, my friend. You have perhaps some inkling of his present whereabouts?"

The sergeant's laugh was almost an hysterical cackle. "That we have, sir, that we have! They burnt—you know, electrocuted—him last month in

Trenton for th' murder of a milk-wagon driver durin' a hold-up. By rights he should be in Mount Olivet Cemetery this minute, an' by th' same token he should 'a' been there when the little Clark girl was kilt last night."

"A-a-ah?" de Grandin twisted his wheat-blond mustache furiously. "It seems this case contains the possibilities, my friend. Tomorrow morning, if you please, we shall go to the cemetery and investigate the grave of Monsieur Gyp. Perhaps we shall find something there. If we find nothing we shall have found the most valuable information we can have."

"If we find nothing—" the big Irishman looked at him in bewilderment. "All right, sir. I've seen some funny things since I been runnin' round with you, but if you're tellin' me—"

"*Tenez*, my friend, I tell you nothing; nothing at all. I too seek information. Let us wait until the morning, then see what testimony pick and shovel will give."

A SUPERINTENDENT AND TWO WORKMEN waited for us at the grave when we arrived at the cemetery next morning. The grave lay in the newer, less expensive portion of the burying ground where perpetual care was not so conscientiously maintained as in the better sections. Scrub grass fought for a foothold in the clayey soil, and the mound had already begun to fall in. Incongruously, a monument bearing the effigy of a weeping angel leaned over the grave-head, while a footstone with the inscription OUR DARLING guarded its lower end.

The superintendent glanced over Costello's papers, stowed them in an inner pocket and nodded to the Polish laborers. "Git goin'," he ordered tersely, "an' make it snappy."

The diggers' picks and spades bored deep and deeper in the hard-packed, sun-baked earth. At last the hollow sound of steel on wood warned us their quest was drawing to a close. A pair of strong web straps was let down and made fast to the rough chestnut box in which the casket rested, and the men strained at the thongs to bring their weird freight to the surface. Two pick-handles were laid across the violated grave and on them the box rested. With a wrench the superintendent undid the screws that held the clay-stained lid in place and laid it aside. Within we saw the casket, a cheap, square-ended affair covered with shoddy grey broadcloth, the tinny imitation-silver name plate and crucifix on its lid already showing a dull brown-blue discoloration.

"*Maintenant!*" murmured de Grandin breathlessly as the superintendent began unlatching the fastenings that held the upper portion of the casket lid. Then, as the last catch snapped back and the cover came away:

"*Feu noir de l'enfer!*"

"Good heavens!" I exclaimed.

"For th' love o' God!" Costello's amazed antiphon sounded at my elbow.

The cheap sateen pillow of the casket showed a depression like the pillow of a bed recently vacated, and the poorly made upholstery of its bottom displayed a wide furrow, as though flattened by some weight imposed on it for a considerable time, but sign or trace of human body there was none. The case was empty as it left the factory.

"Glory be to God!" Costello muttered hoarsely, staring at the empty casket as though loath to believe his own eyes. "An' this is broad daylight," he added in a kind of wondering afterthought.

"*Précisément*," de Grandin's acid answer came back like a whipcrack. "This is diagnostic, my friend. Had we found something here it might have meant one thing or another. Here we find nothing; nothing at all. What does it mean?"

"*I* know what it means!" the look of superstitious fear on Costello's broad red face gave way to one of furious anger. "It means there's been some monkey-business goin' on—who had this burying?" he turned savagely on the superintendent.

"Donally," the other returned, "but don't blame me for it. I just work here."

"Huh, Donally, eh? We'll see what Mr. Donally has to say about this, an' he'd better have plenty to say, too, if he don't want to collect himself from th' corners o' a four-acre lot."

Donally Funeral Parlors were new but by no means prosperous looking. Situated in a small side street in the poor section of town, their only pretension to elegance was the brightly-gleaming gold sign on their window:

JOSEPH DONALLY
Funeral Director & Embalmer
Sexton St. Rose's R.C. Church

"See here, young feller me lad," Costello began without preliminary as he stamped unceremoniously into the small, dark room that constituted Mr. Donally's office and reception foyer, "come clean, an' come clean in a hurry. Was Gyp Carson dead when you had his funeral?"

"If he wasn't we sure played one awful dirty trick on him," the mortician replied. "What'd ye think would happen to you if they set you in that piece o' furniture down at Trenton an' turned the juice on? What d'ye mean, 'was he dead'?"

"I mean just what I say, wise guy. I've just come from Mount Olivet an' looked into his coffin, an' if there's hide or hair of a corpse in it I'll eat it, so I will! "

"*What's that?* You say th' casket was empty?"

"As your head."

"Well, I'll be—" Mr. Donally began, but Costello forestalled him:

"You sure will, an' all beat up, too, if you don't spill th' low-down. Come clean, now, or do I have to sock ye in th' jaw an' lock ye up in th' bargain?"

"Whatcher tryin' to put over?" Mr. Donally demanded. "Think I faked up a stall funeral? Look't here, if you don't believe me." From a pigeon hole of his desk he produced a sheaf of papers, thumbed through them, and handed Costello a packet fastened with a rubber band.

Everything was in order. The death certificate, signed by the prison physician, showed the cause of death as cardiac arrest by fibrillar contraction induced by three shocks of an alternating current of electricity of 7½ amperes at a pressure of 2,000 volts.

"I didn't have much time," Donally volunteered. "The prison doctors had made a full post, an' his old woman was one o' them old-fashioned folks that don't believe in embalmin', so there was nothin' to do but rush him to th' graveyard an' plant him. Not so bad for me, though, at that. I sold 'em a casket an' burial suit an' twenty-five limousines for th' funeral, an' got a cut on th' monument, too."

De Grandin eyed him speculatively. "Have you any reason to believe attempts at resuscitation were made?" he asked.

"Huh? Resuscitate *that*? Didn't I just tell you they'd made a full autopsy on him at the prison? Didn't miss a damn thing, either. You might as well to try resuscitatin' a lump o' hamburger as bring back a feller which had had that done to him."

"Quite so," de Grandin nodded. "I did but ask. Now—"

"Now we don't know no more than we did an hour ago," the sergeant supplied. "I might 'a' thought this guy was in cahoots with Gyp's folks, but th' prison records show he was dead, an' th' doctors down at Trenton don't certify nobody's dead if there's a flicker o' eyelash left in him. Looks as if we've got to find some gink with a fad for grave-robbin', don't it, Dr. de Grandin?

"But say"—a sudden gleam of inspiration overspread his face, "suppose someone had dug him up an' taken an impression of his fingerprints, then had rubber gloves made with th' prints on th' outside o' th' fingers? Wouldn't it be a horse on th' force for him to go around murderin' people, an' leave his weapons lyin' round promiscuous-like, so's we'd be sure to find what we thought was his prints, only to discover they'd been made by a gunman who'd been burnt a month or more before?"

"*Tiens*, my friend, your supposition has at least the foundation of reason beneath it," de Grandin conceded. "Do you make search for one who might have done the thing you suspect. Me, I have certain searching of my own to do. Anon we shall confer, and together we shall surely lay this so vile miscreant by the heels."

"Ah, but it has been a lovely day," he assured me with twinkling eyes as he contemplated the glowing end of his cigar that evening after dinner. "Yes, *pardieu*, an exceedingly lovely day! This morning when I went from that Monsieur Donally's shop my head whirled like that of an unaccustomed voyager stricken by sea-sickness. Only miserable uncertainty confronted me on every side. Now"—he blew a cone of fragrant smoke from his lips and watched it spiral slowly toward the ceiling—"now I know much, and that I do not actually know I damn surmise. I think I see the end of this so tortuous trail, Friend Trowbridge."

"How's that?" I encouraged, watching him from the corners of my eyes.

"How? *Cordieu*, I shall tell you! When Friend Costello told us of the murder of Monsieur Wolkof—that second murder which was made to appear suicide—and mentioned he met death at the Ranger's Club, I suddenly recalled that Colonel Evans, whose death we had so recently deplored, was also a member of that club. It struck me at the time there might be something more than mere coincidence in it; but when that pitiful Monsieur Clark also proved to be a member, *nom d'un asperge*, coincidence ceased to be coincidence and became moral certainty.

"'Now,' I ask me, 'what lies behind this business of the monkey? Is it not strange two members of the Rangers' Club should have been slain so near together, and in such similar circumstances, and a third should have been visited with a calamity worse than death?'

"'You have said it, *mon garçon*,' I tell me. 'It is indubitably as you say. Come, let us interview the steward of that club, and see what he shall say.'

"*Nom d'un pipe*, what did he not tell? From him I learn much more than he said. I learn, by example, that Messieurs Evans, Wolkof and Clark had long been friends; that they had all been members of the club's grievance committee; that they were called on some five years ago to recommend expulsion of a Monsieur Wallagin—*mon Dieu*, what a name!

"'So far, so fine,' I tell me. 'But what of this Monsieur-with-the-Funny-Name? Who and what is he, and what has he done to be flung out of the club?'

"I made careful inquiry and found much. He has been an explorer of considerable note and has written some monographs which showed he understood the use of his eyes. *Hélas*, he knew also how to use wits, as many of his fellow members learned to their sorrow when they played cards with him. Furthermore, he had a most unpleasant stock of stories which he gloried to tell—stories of his doings in the far places which did not recommend him to the company of self-respecting gentlemen. And so he was removed from the club's rolls, and vowed he would get level with Messieurs Evans, Clark and Wolkof if it took him fifty years to do so.

"Five years have passed since then, and Monsieur Wallagin seems to have prospered exceedingly. He has a large house in the suburbs where no one but himself and one servant—always a Chinese—lives, but the neighbors tell strange stories of the parties he holds, parties at which pretty ladies in strange attire appear, and once or twice strange-looking men as well.

"*Eh bien*, why should this rouse my suspicions? I do not know, unless it be that my nose scents the odor of the rodent farther than the average. At any rate, out to the house of Monsieur Wallagin I go, and at its gate I wait like a tramp in the hope of charity.

"My vigil is not unrewarded. But no. Before I have stood there an hour I behold one forcibly ejected from the house by a gross person who reminds me most unpleasantly of a pig. It is a small and elderly Chinese man, and he has suffered greatly in his *amour propre*. I join him in his walk to town, and sympathize with him in his misfortune.

"My friend"—his earnestness seemed out of all proportion to the simple statement—"he had been forcibly dismissed for putting salt in the food which he cooked for Monsieur Wallagin's guests."

"For salting their food?" I asked.

"One wonders why, indeed, Friend Trowbridge. Consider, if you please. Monsieur Wallagin has several guests, and feeds them thin gruel made of wheat or barley, and bread in which no salt is used. Nothing more. He personally tastes of it before it is presented to them, that he may make sure it is unsalted."

"Perhaps they're on some sort of special diet," I hazarded as he waited for my comment. "They're not obliged to stay and eat unseasoned food, are they?"

"I do not know," he answered soberly. "I greatly fear they are, but we shall know before so very long. If what I damn suspect is true we shall see devilment beside which the worst produced by ancient Rome was mild. If I am wrong—*alors*, it is that I am wrong. I think I hear the good Costello coming; let us go with him."

Evening had brought little surcease from the heat, and perspiration streamed down Costello's face and mine as we drove toward Morrisdale, but de Grandin seemed in a chill of excitement, his little round blue eyes were alight with dancing elf-fires, his small white teeth fairly chattering with nervous excitation as he leant across the back of the seat, urging me to greater speed.

The house near which we parked was a massive stone affair, standing back from the road in a jungle of greenery, and seemed to me principally remarkable for the fact that it had neither front nor rear porches, but rose sheer-walled as a prison from its foundations.

Led by the Frenchman we made cautious way to the house, creeping to the only window showing a gleam of light and fastening our eyes to the narrow crack beneath its not-quite-drawn blind.

"Monsieur Wallagin acquired a new cook this afternoon," de Grandin whispered. "I made it my especial business to see him and bribe him heavily to smuggle a tiny bit of beef into the soup he prepares for tonight. If he has been faithful in his treachery we may see something, if not—*pah*, my friends, what is it we have here?"

We looked into a room which must have been several degrees hotter than the stoke-hole of a steamer, for the window was shut tightly and a great log fire blazed on the wide hearth of the fireplace almost opposite our point of vantage. Its walls were smooth-dressed stone, the floor was paved with tile. Lolling on a sort of divan made of heaped up cushions sat the master of the house, a monstrous bulk of a man with enormous paunch, great fat-upholstered shoulders between which perched a hairless head like an owl's in its feathers, and eyes as cold and grey as twin inlays of burnished agate.

About his shoulders draped a robe of Paisley pattern, belted at the loins but open to the waist, displaying his obese abdomen as he squatted like an evil parody of Mi-lei-Fo, China's Laughing Buddha.

As we fixed our eyes to the gap under the curtain he beat his hands together, and as at a signal the door at the room's farther end swung open to admit a file of women. All three were young and comely, and each a perfect foil for the others. First came a tall and statuesque brunette with flowing unbound black hair, sharp-hewn patrician features and a majesty of carriage like a youthful queen's. The second was a petite blonde, fairylike in form and elfin in face, and behind her was a red-haired girl, plumply rounded as a little pullet. Last of all there came an undersized, stoop-shouldered man who bore what seemed an earthen vessel like a New England bean-pot and two short lengths of willow sticks.

"Jeeze!" breathed Costello. "Lookit him, Dr. de Grandin; 'tis Gyp Carson himself!"

"Silence!" the Frenchman whispered fiercely. "Observe, my friends; did I not say we should see something? *Regardez-vous!*"

At a signal from the seated man the women ranged themselves before him, arms uplifted, heads bent submissively, and the undersized man dropped down tailor-fashion in a corner of the room, nursing the clay pot between his crossed knees and poising his sticks over it.

The obese master of the revels struck his hands together again, and at their impact the man on the floor began to beat a rataplan upon his crock.

The women started a slow rigadoon, sliding their bare feet sidewise, stopping to stamp out a grotesque rhythm, then pirouetting languidly and taking up the sliding, sidling step again. Their arms were stretched straight out, as if they had been crucified against the air, and as they danced they shook and twitched their shoulders with a motion reminiscent of the Negroid shimmy of the early 1920s. Each wore a shift of silken netlike fabric that covered her from shoulder to instep, sleeveless and unbelted, and as they danced the garments clung in rippling, half-revealing, half-concealing folds about them.

They moved with a peculiar lack of verve, like marionettes actuated by unseen strings, sleep-walkers, or persons in hypnosis; only the drummer seemed to take an interest in his task. His hands shook as he plied his drumsticks, his shoulders jerked and twitched and writhed hysterically, and though his eyes were closed and his face masklike, it seemed instinct with avid longing, with prurient expectancy.

"*Las aisselles*—their axillae, Friend Trowbridge, observe them with care, if you please!" de Grandin breathed in my ear.

Sudden recognition came to me. With the raising of their hands in the performance of the dance the women exposed their armpits, and under each left arm I saw the mark of a deep wound, bloodless despite its depth, and closed with the familiar "baseball stitch."

No surgeon leaves a wound like that, it was the mark of the embalmer's bistoury made in cutting through the superficial tissue to raise the axillary artery for his injection.

"Good God!" I choked. The languidness of their movements . . . their pallor . . . their closed eyes . . . their fixed, unsmiling faces . . . now the unmistakable stigmata of embalming process! These were no living women, they were—

De Grandin's fingers clutched my elbow fiercely. "Observe, my friend," he ordered softly. "Now we shall see if my plan carried or miscarried."

Shuffling into the room, as unconcerned as if he served coffee after a formal meal, came a Chinese bearing a tray on which were four small soup bowls and a plate of dry bread. He set the tray on the floor before the fat man and turned away, paying no attention to the dancing figures and the drummer squatting in the corner.

An indolent motion of the master's hand and the slaves fell on their provender like famished beasts at feeding time, drinking greedily from the coarse china bowls, wolfing down the unbuttered bread almost unchewed.

Such a look of dawning realization as spread over the four countenances as they drained the broth I have seen sometimes when half-conscious patients were revived with powerful restoratives. The man was first to show it, surging from his crouching position and turning his closed eyes this way and that, like a caged thing seeking escape from its prison. But before he could do more than wheel drunkenly in his tracks realization seemed to strike the women, too. There was a swirl of fluttering draperies, the soft thud of soft feet on the tiled floor of the room, and all rushed pell-mell to the door.

The sharp clutch of de Grandin's hand roused me. "Quick, Friend Trowbridge," he commanded. "To the cemetery; to the cemetery with all haste! *Nom d'un sale chameau*, we have yet to see the end of this!"

"Which cemetery?" I asked as we stumbled toward my parked car.

"*N'importe*," he returned. "At Shadow Lawn or Mount Olivet we shall see that which will make us call ourselves three shameless liars!"

Mount Olivet was nearest of the three municipalities of the dead adjacent to Harrisonville, and toward it we made top speed. The driveway gates had closed at sunset, but the small gates each side the main entrance were still unlatched, and we raced through them and to the humble tomb we had seen violated that morning.

"Say, Dr. de Grandin," panted Costello as he strove to keep pace with the agile little Frenchman, "just what's th' big idea? I know ye've some good reason, but—"

"Take cover!" interrupted the other. "Behold, my friends, he comes!"

Shuffling drunkenly, stumbling over mounded tops of sodded graves, a slouching figure came careening toward us, veered off as it neared the Carson grave and dropped to its knees beside it. A moment later it was scrabbling at the clay and gravel which had been disturbed by the grave-diggers that morning, seeking desperately to burrow its way into the sepulcher.

"Me God!" Costello breathed as he rose unsteadily. I could see the tiny globules of fear-sweat standing on his forehead, but his inbred sense of duty overmastered his fright. "Gyp Carson, I arrest you—" he laid a hand on the burrowing creature's shoulder, and it was as if he touched a soap bubble. There was a frightened mouselike squeak, then a despairing groan, and the figure under his hand collapsed in a crumpled heap. When de Grandin and I reached them the pale, drawn face of a corpse grinned at us sardonically in the beam of Costello's flashlight.

"Dr.—de—Grandin, Dr.—Trowbridge—for th' love o' God give me a drink o' sumpin!" begged the big Irishman, clutching the diminutive Frenchman's shoulder as a frightened child might clutch its mother's skirts.

"Courage, my old one," de Grandin patted the detective's hand, "we have work before us tonight, remember. Tomorrow they will bury this poor one. The law has had its will of him; now let his body rest in peace. Tonight—*sacré nom*, the dead must tend the dead; it is with the living we have business. *En avant* to Wallagin's, Friend Trowbridge!"

"YOUR SOLUTION OF THE case was sane," he told Costello as we set out for the house we'd left a little while before, "but there are times when very sanity proves the falseness of a conclusion. That someone had unearthed the body of Gyp Carson to copy his fingerprints seemed most reasonable, but today I obtained information which led me up another road. A most unpleasant road, *parbleu!* I have already told you something of the history of the Wallagin person; how he was dismissed from the Rangers' Club, and how he vowed a horrid vengeance on those voting his expulsion. That was of interest. I sought still further. I found that he resided long in Haiti, and that there he mingled with the *Culte de Morts*. We laugh at such things here, but in Haiti, that dark stepdaughter of mysterious Africa's dark mysteries, they are no laughing matter. No. In Port-au-Prince and in the backlands of the jungle they will tell you of the *zombie*—who is neither ghost nor yet a living person resurrected, but only the spiritless corpse ravished from its grave, endowed with pseudo-life by black magic and made to serve the whim of the magician who has animated it. Sometimes wicked persons steal a corpse to make it commit crime while they stay far from the scene, thus furnishing themselves unbreakable alibis. More often they rob graves to secure slaves who labor ceaselessly for them at no wages at all. Yes, it is so; with my own eyes I have seen it.

"But there are certain limits which no sorcery can transcend. The poor dead *zombie* must be fed, for if he is not he cannot serve his so execrable master. But he must be fed only certain things. If he taste salt or meat, though but the tiniest *soupçon* of either be concealed in a great quantity of food, he at once realizes he is dead, and goes back to his grave, nor can the strongest magic of his owner stay him from returning for one little second. Furthermore, when he goes back he is dead forever after. He cannot be raised from the grave a second time, for Death which has been cheated for so long asserts itself, and the putrefaction which was stayed during the *zombie's* period of servitude takes place all quickly, so the *zombie* dead six months, if it returns to its grave and so much as touches its hand to the earth, becomes at once like any other six-months-dead corpse—a mass of putrescence pleasant neither to the eye nor nose, but preferable to the dead-alive thing it was a moment before.

"Consider then: The steward of the Rangers' Club related dreadful tales this Monsieur Wallagin had told all boastfully—how he had learned to be a *zombie*-maker, a corpse-master, in Haiti; how the mysteries of *Papa Nebo, Gouédé Mazacca* and *Gouédé Oussou*, those dread oracles of the dead, were opened books to him.

"'Ah-ha, Monsieur Wallagin,' I say, 'I damn suspect you have been up to business of the monkey here in this so pleasant State of New Jersey. You have, it seems, brought here the mysteries of Haiti, and with them you wreak vengeance on those you hate, *n'est-ce-pas?*'

"Thereafter I go to his house, meet the little discharged Chinese man, and talk with him. For why was he discharged with violence? Because, by blue, *he had put salt in the soup of the guests whom Monsieur Wallagin entertains.*

"'Four guests he has, you say?' I remark. 'I had not heard he had so many.'

"'*Nom d'un nom,* yes,' the excellent *Chinois* tells me. 'There are one man and three so lovely women in that house, and all seem walking in their sleep. At night he has the women dance while the man makes music with the drum.

Sometimes he sends the man out, but what to do I do not know. At night, also, he feeds them bread and soup with neither salt nor meat, food not fit for a mangy dog to lap.'

"'Oh, excellent old man of China, oh, paragon of all Celestials,' I reply, 'behold, I give you money. Now, come with me and we shall hire another cook for your late master, and we shall bribe him well to smuggle meat into the soup he makes for those strange guests. Salt the monster might detect when he tastes the soup before it are served, but a little, tiny bit of beef-meat, *non*. Nevertheless, it will serve excellently for my purposes.'

"*Voilà*, my friends, there is the explanation of tonight's so dreadful scenes."

"But what are we to do?" I asked. "You can't arrest this Wallagin. No court on earth would try him on such charges as you make."

"Do *you* believe it, Friend Costello?" de Grandin asked the detective.

"Sure, I do, sir. Ain't I seen it with me own two eyes?"

"And what should be this one's punishment?"

"Och, Dr. de Grandin, are you kiddin'? What would we do if we saw a poison snake on th' sidewalk, an' us with a jolly bit o' blackthorn in our hands?"

"*Précisément*, I think we understand each other perfectly, *mon vieux*." He thrust his slender, womanishly small hand out and lost it in the depths of the detective's great fist.

"Would you be good enough to wait for us here, Friend Trowbridge?" he asked as we came to a halt before the house. "There is a trifle of unfinished business to attend to and—the night is fine, the view exquisite. I think that you would greatly enjoy it for a little while, my old and rare friend."

IT MIGHT HAVE BEEN a quarter-hour later when they rejoined me. "What—" I began, but the perfectly expressionless expression on de Grandin's face arrested my question.

"*Hélas*, my friend, it was unfortunate," he told me. "The good Costello was about to arrest him, and he turned to flee. Straight up the long, steep stairs he fled, and at the topmost one, *parbleu*, he missed his footing and came tumbling down! I greatly fear—indeed, I know his neck was broken in the fall. Is it not so, *mon sergent*?" he turned to Costello for confirmation. "Did he not fall downstairs?"

"That he did, sir. Twice. The first time didn't quite finish him."

Trespassing Souls

1

MID-AUGUST WAS ON US and Harrisonville sweltered under the merciless combination of heat and humidity as only communities in the North Atlantic States can suffer in such conditions. Jules de Grandin and I rocked listlessly back and forth in our willow chairs, too much exhausted for further conversation, unhappily aware that the clock had struck midnight half an hour before, but knowing bed meant only a continuation of discomfort and unwilling to make even the little effort involved in ascending the stairs and disrobing.

"*Morbleu*, Friend Trowbridge," the little Frenchman murmured sleepily, "this day, it is infernal, no less. Were those three old Hebrews transported here, I damn think they would beseech us to take them back to the comforting coolness of Nebuchadnezzar's fiery furnace! If—"

The muffled drum-roll of my office telephone bell sounded a sleepy interruption to his comment, and I rose wearily to respond to the summons.

"Yes," I answered as a frightened voice pronounced my name questioningly over the wire, "this is Dr. Trowbridge."

"This is Aubrey Sattalea," the caller told me. "Can you come over to 1346 Pavonia Avenue right away, please? My wife is very ill—heat prostration, I'm afraid. If she doesn't get help soon, I fear—"

"All right," I interrupted, making a note of the address and reaching for my hat, "fill a hot-water bottle and put it at her feet, and if you've any whisky that's fit to drink, give her a little in water and repeat the dose every few minutes. I'll be right along."

In the surgery I procured a small flask of brandy, some strychnine and digitalis, two sterile syringes, alcohol and cotton sponges, then shoved a bottle of quinine tincture into the bag as an added precaution.

"Better run along to bed, old chap," I advised de Grandin as I opened the front door. "I've been called to attend a woman with heat prostration, and mayn't be back till morning. Just my luck to have the car laid up for repairs when there's no possibility of getting a taxi," I added gloomily, turning to descend the front steps.

The Frenchman rose languidly and retrieved his wide-brimmed Panama from the porch floor. "Me, I suffer so poignantly, it is of no moment where I am miserable," he confided. "Permit me to come, too, my friend. I can be equally unhappy walking beside you in the street or working beside you in the sickroom."

THE SATTALEA COTTAGE WAS a pretty example of the Colonial bungalow type-modified Dutch architecture with a low porch covered by an extension of the sloping roof and all rooms on the ground floor. Set well back from the double row of plane-trees bordering the avenue's sidewalks, its level lawn was bisected by a path of sunken flagstones leading to the three low steps of the veranda. Lights showed behind the French windows letting into a bedroom at the right end of the porch, and the gentle flutter of pongee curtains and the soft whining of an electric fan told us the activities of the household were centered there. Without the formality of knocking we stepped through the open window into the room where Vivian Sattalea lay breathing so lightly her slender bosom scarce seemed to move at all.

She lay upon the bed, uncovered by sheet or blanket, only the fashionably abbreviated green-voile nightrobe veiling her lissome body from the air. Her soft, copper-gold hair, worn in a shoulder bob, lay damply about her small head on the pillow, And her delicate, clean-cut features had the smooth, bloodless semi-transparence of a face cunningly molded in wax.

"La pauvre!" de Grandin murmured as I introduced myself to the frightened young man who hovered, hot-water bottle in hand, beside the unconscious woman, "La belle, pauvre enfant! Quick, Friend Trowbridge, her plight is worse than we supposed; haste is imperative!"

As I undid the fastenings of my emergency kit he advanced to the bed, took the girl's wrist between his fingers and fixed his eyes intently on the dial of the diminutive watch strapped to the underside of her left wrist. "Seventy"—he counted slowly, staring at the little timepiece—"non, sixty-seven—sixty—"

Abruptly he dropped her hand and bent down till his slim, sensitive nostrils were but an inch or so from the girl's gently parted lips.

"Sacré bleu, Monsieur, may I ask where you obtained the liquor with which you have stimulated your wife?" he demanded, staring with a sort of incredulous horror at Sattalea.

The young husband's cheeks reddened. "Why—er—er," he began, but de Grandin cut him short with an impatient gesture.

"No need," he snapped, rising and regarding us with blazing eyes. "*C'est la prohibition, pardieu!* When this poor one was overcome by heat, it was Dr. Trowbridge's order that you give her alcohol to sustain her, is it not so?"

"Yes, but—"

"'But' be everlastingly consigned to the flames of hell! The only stimulant which you could find was of the bootleg kind, is it not true?"

"Yes, sir," the young man admitted, "Dr. Trowbridge told me to give her whisky in broken doses, if I had it. I didn't, but I got a quart of gin a couple of weeks ago, and—"

"Name of a thousand small blue devils!" de Grandin half shrieked. "Stand not there like a paralyzed bullfrog and offer excuses. Hasten to the kitchen and bring mustard and hot water, quickly. In addition to heat prostration, this poor child lies poisoned to the point of death with wooden alcohol. Already her pulse has almost vanished. Quick, my friend; rush, fly; even now it may be too late!"

Our preparations were made with feverish haste, but the little Frenchman's worst predictions were fulfilled. Even as I bent to administer the mixture of mustard and water which should empty the fainting woman's system of the deadly wood alcohol, her breast fluttered convulsively, her pale lids drew halfway open, disclosing eyes so far rolled back that neither pupil nor iris was visible, and her blanched, bloodless lips fell flaccidly apart as her chin dropped toward the curve of her throat and the fatuous, insensible expression of the newly dead spread over her pallid countenance like a blight across a stricken flower.

"*Hélas*, it is finished!" de Grandin rasped in a furious whisper. "Let those who sponsor such laws as those which make poisonous liquor available accept responsibility for this poor one's death!"

He was still swearing volubly in mingled French and English as we walked down the flagstone pathway from the house, and in the blindness of his fury all but collided with an undersized, stoop-shouldered man who paused speculatively on the sidewalk a moment then turned in at the entrance to the yard and sauntered toward the cottage.

"*Pardonnez-moi, Monsieur*," de Grandin apologized, stepping quickly aside, for the other made no move to avoid collision, "it is that I am greatly overwrought, and failed to—

"*Morbleu*, Friend Trowbridge, the ill-mannered *canaille* has not the grace to acknowledge my amends. It is not to be borne!" He wheeled in his tracks, took an angry step after the other, then stiffened abruptly to a halt and paused irresolute a second, like a bird-dog coming to a "point." With an imperative, half-furtive gesture he bade me follow, and stepped silently over the grass in the wake of the discourteous stranger.

Silently we ascended the path and crept up the porch steps, tiptoeing across the veranda to the open window letting into the room of death. The

Frenchman's raised finger signaled me to halt just beyond the line of light shining through the midnight darkness, and we paused in breathless silence as a soft, suave voice inside addressed the stricken husband.

"Good evening, sir," we heard the stranger say, "you seem in trouble. Perhaps I can assist you?"

A heart-wrenching, strangling sob from young Sattalea was the only answer.

"Things are seldom as bad as they seem," the other pursued, his words, pronounced in a sort of silky monotone, carrying distinctly, despite the fact that he spoke with a slight lisp. "When ignorant quacks have failed, there are always others to whom you can turn, you know."

Another sob from the prostrated husband was his sole reply.

"For instance, now," the visitor murmured, almost as though speaking to himself, "two witless charlatans just told you that your love is dead—so she is, if you wish to accept *their* verdict, but—"

"*Monsieur,*" de Grandin stepped across the window-sill and fixed his level, unwinking stare on the intruder, "I do not know what game it is you play; but I make no doubt you seek an unfair advantage of this poor young man. It were better for you that you went your way in peace, and that immediately; else—"

"Indeed?" the other surveyed him with a sort of amused contempt. "Don't you think it's *you* who'd best be on his way? You've already broken his heart with your inability to tell the difference between life and death. Must you add insults to injury?"

De Grandin gasped in a sort of unbelieving horror as he grasped the import of the stranger's accusation. On the bed before us, her pale features somewhat composed by the little Frenchman's deft hands, lay the corpse of the woman we had seen die an hour before; after thirty years of general practise and a full term of hospital duty, I knew the signs of death as I knew the symptoms of chicken-pox, and de Grandin had vast experience in the hospitals of Paris, the military lazarets of the War and infirmaries throughout the world; yet this interloper told us to our faces we were mistaken.

Yet, despite the fellow's impudence, I could not help a sudden twinge of doubt. He was unquestionably impressive, though not pleasantly so. Shorter, even, than the diminutive de Grandin, his height was further curtailed by the habitual stoop of his shoulders; indeed, there was about him the suggestion of a hunched back, though closer inspection showed no actual deformity. His face, narrow, pointed and unnaturally long of chin, was pale as the under side of a crawling reptile, and despite the sultriness of the night showed no more evidence of perspiration than if his skin possessed no sweat-glands. Clothed all in black he was from the tips of his dull-kid shoes to the wide-brimmed felt hat upon his sleek, black hair, and from his stooping shoulders there hung a knee-length cape of thin black silk which gave him the look of a hovering, unclean carrion bird which waited opportunity to swoop down and revel in an obscene feast. But his eyes attracted and repelled me more than anything. They were dark, not black, but of an indeterminate, slate-like shade, and glowed brightly in his toad-belly-white face like corpse lights flickering through the eye-holes of a death mask.

His thin, bloodless lips parted in a sardonic smile which was more than half snarl as he turned his cloaked shoulder on de Grandin, addressing young Sattalea directly. "Do you want to take the word of these ignoramuses," he asked "or will you take my assurance that she is not dead, but sleeping!"

A look of agonized hope flamed up in Sattalea's face a moment. "You mean—" he choked, and the other's soft rejoinder cut his incredulous question in two:

"Of course; it is but the work of a moment to call the wandering spirit to its tenant. May I try?"

"Do not heed him, my friend!" de Grandin cried. "Trust him not, I implore you! I know not what vile chicanery he purposes to practise, but—"

"Be still, you!" Sattalea commanded. "The man is right. You've had your chance, and the best you did was tell me my poor darling is dead. Give him a chance. Oh,"—he stretched imploring hands to the sinister stranger—"I'll give my soul, if you will—"

"*Monsieur*, for the love of the good God, think what it is you say!" de Grandin's shouted injunction drowned out the desperate man's wild offer. "Let this blood brother of Iscariot work his evil if you must; but offer not your soul for sale or barter as you hope one day to stand in spiritual communion with her who was your earthly love!"

The trembling, eager husband ignored the Frenchman's admonition. "Do what you will," he begged. "I'll give you anything you ask!"

The stranger chuckled softly to himself, threw back the corners of his sable cloak as though fluttering unclean wings preparatory to flight, and leaned above the dead woman, pressing lightly on her folded eyelids with long, bony fingers which seemed never to have known the warmth of human blood in their veins. His pale, thin lips writhed and twisted over his gleaming animal-like teeth as he mouthed an incantation in some tongue I could not understand. Yet as he raised his voice in slight emphasis once or twice I saw de Grandin's slim nostrils tighten with quickly indrawn breath, as though he caught a half-familiar syllable in the mutterings.

The stranger's odd, nondescript eyes seemed fairly starting from their shallow sockets as he focused a gaze of demoniacal concentration on the still, dead face before him, and over and over again he droned his formula, so that even I caught the constant repetition of some word or name like *Sathanas—Barran-Sathanas* and *Yod-Sathanas*.

I saw de Grandin mop his forehead as he shook his head impatiently, clearing his eyes of the perspiration which trickled downward from his brow, and take a short half-step forward with extended hand, but next moment both he and I stood stone-still in our places, for, as a crumb of cochineal dropped into a glass of milk incarnadines the white fluid, so a faintest flush of pink seemed creeping and spreading slowly in the dead woman's face. Higher and higher, like the strained shadow of a blush, the wave of color mounted, touched the pallid lips and cheeks, imparted a dim but unmistakable glow of life to the soft curving throat and delicate, cleft chin. A flutter, scarcely more than the merest hinted flicker of motion, animated the blue-veined lids, and a sudden spasmodic palpitation rippled through the corpse's breast.

"It is not good—no good can come of it—" de Grandin began, but Sattalea cut him short.

"You may go!" he shouted, glaring at the little Frenchman across the resurrected body of his wife. "I don't want to see you—either of you again. You damned quacks, you—"

De Grandin stiffened and his face went almost as pale as the mysterious stranger's under the insult, but he controlled himself with an almost superhuman effort. "Monsieur," he answered with frigid courtesy, "I congratulate you on your seeming good fortune. Pray God you need not call on us again!"

With a bow of punctilious formality he turned on his heel to leave the house, but the stranger sent a parting shaft of spiteful laughter flying after him. "No fear of that," he promised. "Hereafter I shall minister to this house, and—"

"The Devil can quote Scripture for his evil ends," the Frenchman interrupted sharply. "I make no doubt his servants sometimes simulate the holy miracles for purposes as sinister. Some day, perhaps, Monsieur, we shall match our powers."

2

"FOR HEAVEN'S SAKE," I asked in bewilderment as we walked slowly through the tree-leafed avenue, "what was it we saw back there? I'll stake my professional reputation we saw that woman die; yet that queer-looking fellow seemed to have no more trouble reviving her than a hypnotist has in waking his subject."

The little Frenchman removed his red-banded Panama and fanned himself with its wide brim. "Le bon Dieu only knows," he confessed. "Me, I do not like it. Undoubtlessly, the woman died—we saw her. Unquestionably, she was revived, we saw that, too; but how? The grip of death is too strong to be lightly loosed, and though I could not understand all the words he said, I most distinctly heard him pronounce the ancient Devil Worshipers' term for Satan not once, but many times. I greatly fear, my friend—*cordieu*, have the care!" he broke off, leaping forward and flinging himself bodily on a short, stout man in clerical garb, hurling him backward to the sidewalk.

Walking with bowed head and mumbling lips the priest had descended from the curb into the path of a hurrying, noiseless motor-car, and but for the Frenchman's timely intervention must inevitably have been run down.

"*Mille pardons*," de Grandin apologized as he assisted the astonished cleric to his feet, "I am sorry to have startled you, but I think no damage has been done, whereas, had I not acted in time—"

"Say no more," the clergyman interrupted in a rich, Irish brogue. "'Tis glad I am to be able to curse ye for your roughness, sir. Sure, 'tis time I was payin' more attention to me feet, anyhow. It's the Lord Himself, no less, provides protection for such as I. You, now, sir, were the instrument of heaven, and I'm not so sure I didn't see an emissary from the other place not long ago."

"Indeed?" returned de Grandin. "I greatly doubt he could have prevailed against you, Father."

"Sure, and he did not," the other replied, "but I was after thinkin' of him as I walked along, and 'twas for that reason I so nearly stepped to me own destruction a moment hence. One o' me parishioners down the street here was called to heaven a little time ago, and I got there almost too late to complete anointin' her. As I was comin' from the house, who should be strollin' up the steps, as bold as brass, but the very divil himself, or at least one o' his most trusted agents.

"'Good evenin', Father,' says he to me, as civil as ye please.

"'Good evenin' to ye, sir,' I replies.

"'Are ye, by anny chance, comin' from a house o' death?' he wants to know.

"'I am that,' I answers, 'and, if I'm not bein' too bold, what affair is it of yours?'

"'Are ye sure the pore woman is dead?' he demands, fixin' me with a pair o' eyes that niver changed expression anny more than a snake's.

"'Dead, is it?' says I. 'How ye know 'tis a woman who lies in her last sleep in yonder house I've no idea, and I don't propose to inquire, but if ye're wantin' to know whether or not she's dead, I can tell ye she is. Sure, 'tis meself that's been ministerin' to the dead and dyin' for close to fifty years, and when the time comes that I can't recognize those the hand o' the Lord has touched, I'll be wearin' me vestments for the last long time, so I will.'

"'Oh, but,' he answers, cool as anny cucumber, 'I think perhaps she's still alive; perhaps she's not dead, but sleepin'. I shall endeavor to awake her.' And with that he makes to push past me into the house.

"'Ye *will* not,' I tells him, barrin' his way. 'I've no idea what sort o' play-actin' ye're up to, young felly, but this I tell ye, Bernardine McGuffy lies dead in that house, and her soul (God rist it!) has gone where neither you nor anny mortal man can reach it. Stand away from that door, or I'll forget I'm a man o' peace and take me knuckles from the side o' your face, so I will.'

"With that he turns away, sirs, but I'm tellin' ye I've niver before seen a human face which more resembled the popular conception o' the Prince o' Darkness than his did that minute, with his long chin, his pale, corpse cheeks and the wicked, changeless expression in his starin', snaky eyes. I—"

"*Pardieu*, do you say it?" de Grandin interpreted excitedly. "Tell me, *Monsieur l'Abbé*, did your so mysterious stranger dress all in black, with a silken cloak draping from his shoulders?"

"Indeed and he did!" the priest replied. "When first I saw him he was standin' and starin' at the house where poor Bernardine died as though debatin' with himself whether or not to enter it, and it was the long black cloak o' him—like the wings o' some dirty buzzard who did but wait his time to flap up to the window o' the room o' death—which first made me mind him particularly."

"U'm? and this was when, if you please?"

"An hour ago, I'd say. I was delayed on me way home by two sick calls—not that I had to make 'em, ye understand, but there I was in the neighborhood, and the pore children were sufferin' with the heat, as were their mother, also. What use are us old fellies who are childless for the sake o' God if not to minister to all His sufferin' little ones?"

"Precisely," de Grandin agreed, raising his hat formally as he turned to leave. To me he murmured as we pursued our homeward way:

"Is it not redolent of the odor of fish, Friend Trowbridge? Half an hour before Madame Sattalea dies this cloaked man appears at another house hard on the tracks of the angel of death, and would have forced entrance had not the sturdy Irish priest barred his way. And did you also note the evil one used the same words to the good father that he addressed to the poor young Sattalea before he worked his devilish arts upon the dead woman—'She is not dead, but sleeping'? *Cordieu*, I think perhaps I spoke more truly than I knew when I remarked the devil can quote Scripture for his purposes. I can not see far into this matter, but nothing I have seen so far looks good."

A tall, rather good-looking young man with prematurely gray hair and the restrained though by no means cheerless manner of his profession rose from one of the rockers on my front porch as de Grandin and I approached the house. "Good evening, Dr. Trowbridge," he greeted. "Old Mr. Eichelberger passed away a while ago, and the boss asked me to run over and get you to give us a certificate. There's not much doing tonight, and I figured you'd probably be awake anyhow; I shouldn't have minded if you couldn't have seen me, though—I'd as lief be driving around as sitting in the office on a night like this."

"Oh, good evening, McCrea," I answered, recognizing the chief assistant to Coroner Martin, who is also the city's leading funeral director. "Yes, I'll sign the certificate for you. Dr. Renshaw helped me in the case, and was actually in attendance this evening, but I've been formally in charge, so the registrar will take my certificate, I suppose. We gave up hope for the poor old gentleman yesterday afternoon; can't do much with interstitial nephritis when the patient's over seventy, you know."

"No, sir," the young mortician agreed, accepting a cigarette from de Grandin's proffered case.

As I returned from the office with the filled-in death certificate, the two of them were deeply immersed in shop talk. "Yes, sir," McCrea was telling de Grandin, "we certainly run up against some queer things in our business. Take what happened this evening, for instance: Mr. and Mrs. Martin had gone out to see some friends, and Johnson, the regular night man, was out on a call, so I was alone in the office. A chap I knew when I was studying at Renouard's called me up from Hackettstown, and I'd just run off when I noticed a shadow falling across the desk. I tell you, sir, I almost jumped out of my chair when I glanced up and saw the darndest-looking individual you ever saw not three feet away and smiling at me like a pussy-cat saying good evening to a canary. The screen door to the office was latched, though not locked, and anybody coming in would have been obliged to rattle the handle, you'd have thought, but there this fellow was, almost down my throat, and I hadn't heard so much as a footstep till I saw him.

"He was an undersized little pipsqueak, bony as a shad and pale as a clown, with a funny-looking black cape, something like those trick overcoats the dukes wear in the European movies, hanging from his shoulders. Can you tie that— wearing a cape on a night like this?"

"A-a-ah?" de Grandin's interjection was so low I could scarcely hear it, but so sharp it seemed to cut through the sultry summer darkness like a razor. "Say on, my friend; I am all attention."

"Humph. I shouldn't be much surprised if there's somebody missing when they call the roll at the Secaucus asylum tomorrow morning, sir. What d'ye think this funny-looking chap wanted?"

"*Cordieu*, I can damn imagine," de Grandin murmured, "but I would prefer that you tell me!"

"No, sir, you don't," the other replied with a chuckle. "You could sit there and guess for a month o' Sundays, but you'd never suspect what he was up to. Listen:

"'Good evening, sir,' he said, grinning at me all the time as if he'd enjoy biting a hunk out of my neck; 'are you interested in money?'

"'Now, what's this, a touch or a stock salesman working overtime?' I asked myself as I looked him over. 'Sure, I am,' I answered. 'Know anyone who isn't?'

"With that he reaches down into his pocket and fishes out a roll of bills— most of 'em yellow, too—big enough to make a hippopotamus take two bites, and sort o' ruffled 'em through his fingers, as a professional gambler might play with the cards before commencing to shuffle. 'I have need of a woman's corpse in my scientific work,' he told me, still ruffling the loose ends of the bills against his thumb. 'If you have such an one here, and it is as yet unembalmed, I will pay you any amount you ask for it.'

"He stopped and stared hard at me with those queer eyes of his, and I could feel the hairs on the back of my neck beginning to stand up like those on a tom-cat's tail when he sees a bulldog coming toward him. Positively, Dr. de Grandin, the fellow had me almost groggy, just looking at me, and the harder I tried to look away the harder I seemed to have to stare at him.

"'Money, much, much money,' he kept repeating in a kind o' solemn sing-song whisper. 'Money to buy liquor, fine clothes, motor-cars, the favors of beautiful women—all these shall be yours if you will let me have a woman's corpse. See, I will give you—'

"'You and who else?' I yelled, jumping up and reaching into the drawer where we keep a pistol for emergencies. 'Get to hell out o' here before I fix you so's they'll have to hold an inquest on you!'

"I reckon I sort o' flew off the handle, sir, for he was a harmless sort of nut, after all, but that funny get-up of his and the soft, sneaky way he had of speaking, and those devilish, unchanging eyes of his all together just about got my goat. Honestly, I believe I'd have let him have a bullet just for luck in another minute."

"And what time was this, if you please?" the Frenchman demanded sharply.

"Almost exactly twelve o'clock, sir. I can place it by the fact that the door had hardly shut on the lunatic when the call to take charge of Mr. Eichelberger's remains came over the 'phone, and, of course, I entered the time up on the arrangement card. The boss came in a minute or so later and said he'd take the call himself while I came over here to get the death certificate."

"Ah?" de Grandin breathed. Then, in a more natural tone he added: "You are doubtlessly right, my friend. Some poor one has made good his escape from the asylum, and wanders about under the delusion that he is a great scientist. Let us hope he startles no more members of your noble calling with his offers of princely bribes."

"Not much fear of that," the young man returned with a chuckle as he turned to descend the porch steps. "I think I put the fear o' God into him when I flashed that gun. He may be crazy, but I don't think he has any special craving to stop a bullet."

"Trowbridge, *mon vieux*," de Grandin almost wailed as the young embalmer entered his motor and drove off, "I shall go wild, *caduc*—crazy like a hatter. Behold the facts: This same damnation man in black goes first to an *entrepreneur des pompes funèbres* and attempts to buy a corpse; next he appears before the house where a woman lies newly dead, and would have forced an entrance. Foiled there, he crops up as if by unclean magic at the very door of Monsieur Sattalea's house almost before we have composed poor, dead Madame Sattalea's limbs. *Mordieu*, it is wicked, it is iniquitous, it is most devilishly depraved, no less! Like a carrion crow, scenting the corpse-odor from afar, he comes unerringly to the place of death, and always he asks for a female cadaver. Twice repulsed, at the third trial he meets success. What in the name of three thousand little blue devilkins does it portend?"

"If we hadn't seen that uncanny show at Sattalea's I'd say McCrea was right, and the fellow's an escaped lunatic," I answered, "but—"

"Ah *hélas*, we have always that fearful 'but' making mock of us," he rejoined. "When first I saw this Monsieur of the Black Cloak I liked his looks little. To one who has battled with the powers of evil as I have, there is a certain family resemblance among all those who connive with devilishness, my friend. Therefore, when I did behold that colorless, cadaverish face of his silhouetted against the evening air, I determined to follow him quietly into the Sattalea house and see what he would do. *Dieu de Dieu*, we did observe a very great plenty. I was wondering about him and the means he might conceivably have employed to bring about Madame Sattalea's seeming revivement when we met the good *curé* and learned from him of the Black One's attempt to break into another dead woman's house; now, *parbleu*, after hearing Monsieur McCrea's story, I am greatly afraid! What it is I fear I do not know. I am like a timid little boy who ventures into the darkened nursery; all about me are monstrous, dreadful things the nature of which I can not descry. I put forth my hand, there is nothing there; but always in the darkness, just beyond the reach of my groping fingers, leers and gibbers the undefined shadow of something terrible and formless. *Cordieu*, my friend, we must make a light and view this terror of the darkness face to face! It shall not play hide-and-go-seek with us. No!"

3

A MILD EPIDEMIC OF SUMMER grippe kept me fully occupied for the succeeding two weeks, and de Grandin was left largely to his own devices. Whether he sought the key to the mystery of the man in black, and under what particular door-mat he looked for it I do not know, for the little Frenchman could be as secretive at some times as he was loquacious at others, and I had no wish to excite his acid comments by bringing the matter up unasked.

One Friday afternoon when August was slowly burning out with its own intensity, we were strolling leisurely toward the City Club, intent on a light luncheon to be followed by a round of golf at the Sedgemoor links when our attention was called to a little boy. Sturdy and straight as a young live-oak he was, his bright, fair hair innocent of covering, his smooth, fair skin tanned to the rich hue of ripened fruit, the sort of lad to give every middle-aged bachelor a twinge of regret and make him wonder if his freedom had been worth while, after all. I smiled involuntarily as my eyes rested on him, but the smile froze on my lips as I noticed the expression of abject misery and fright on his little, sunburned face.

De Grandin noted the lad's affrighted look, too, and paused in quick sympathy. "*Holà*, my little cabbage," he greeted, his small blue eyes taking in every detail of the obviously terrified child, "what is it troubles you? Surely affairs can not be so dreadful?"

The lad looked at him with the trustful gaze all children instinctively bestowed on one they felt to be their friend, and his red, babyish lips trembled pitifully as great tears welled up in his eyes. "I dropped the rice, sir," he answered simply. "Mother sent me to the grocery for it, 'cause they forgot to send it with the rest of the order, and I dropped it. The—the bag broke, and I couldn't gather it up, though I tried ever so hard, and—she'll beat me! She beats me every day, now."

"*Tiens*, is it so?" the Frenchman replied. "Be of courage. I shall give you the price of another sack of rice and your excellent *mère* shall be none the wiser."

"But she told me to hurry," the little chap protested, "and if I'm late I'll be whipped anyway."

"But this is infamous!" Sudden rage flamed in de Grandin's small round eyes. "Come, we shall accompany you. I shall explain all to your *maman*, and all shall be well."

With all the confidence in the world the little boy slipped his small, brown fist into de Grandin's slim white hand and together we walked down the street and turned into the smoothly clipped front yard of—the Sattalea cottage.

Someone was playing the piano softly as we ascended the porch steps, the haunting, eery notes of Saint Saens' *Danse Macabre* falling lightly on our ears as we crossed the porch. Fearfully, on tiptoe, the lad led us toward an open French window, then paused timorously. "If *he's* with her I'll surely catch it!" he whispered, hanging back that we might precede him into the house. "He holds me while she beats me, and laughs when I cry!"

De Grandin caught his breath sharply at the little boy's announcement, and his small face was stern as he stepped softly into the semi-darkened drawing-room. Seated on the bancal before a baby grand piano, her body swaying gently with the rhythm of the music, was a woman—Vivian Sattalea. As I glanced at her delicate, clean-cut features framed in their aureole of rose-gold hair, the carmine of her parted lips blushing vividly against the milky whiteness of her face, I could not help feeling she had undergone some fundamental change since last I saw her. True, on the former occasion she had lain at the very door of death, whereas now she seemed in abundant health, but there was something more than the difference between sickness and health in her changed countenance. Despite her desperate condition when I saw her before, there had been a look of innate delicacy and refinement in the cameo-clear outline of her face. Today there was something theatrical—professional—in her beauty. The ruddy blondness and expert arrangement of her hair, the sophisticated look in her violet eyes, the lines about her full, too-red lips were those of the woman who lives by the exploitation of her charms. And in the flare of her nostrils, the odd tightness of the flesh above her cheek-bones and the hungry curves about her petulant, yearning mouth there was betrayed a burning greed for primal atavistic emotion scarcely to be slaked though every depth of passion be plumbed to the nadir.

Even as we halted at the window, undecided how best to announce our advent, the woman abruptly ceased playing and clutched at the keyboard before her with suddenly convulsed, clenching fingers, the long, polished nails fairly clawing at the polished ivory keys like the unsheathed talons of a feline. And as her hands clenched shut she leaned backward, turning her vivid, parted lips up in a voluptuous smile. From the shadow of the piano another shadow drifted quickly, halted beside the woman and bent downward swiftly to seize her in frenzied embrace.

I gasped in amazement. Holding Vivian Sattalea's cheeks between his hands, kissing her ripe, scarlet lips, was the man in black, the mysterious stranger who had called her errant soul back from God only knew what mystic space the night de Grandin and I pronounced her dead.

"*Cordieu*," I heard the Frenchman murmur, "*c'est une affaire amoureuse!*"

"Your pardon, sir and *madame*," he apologized after a discreet pause, "I would not for the world disturb your innocent pastime, but on the street I did meet *Madame's* little son, and—"

"That sneaking brat!" the woman rasped, freeing herself from her lover's embrace and rising to face de Grandin with furious, flaming cheeks. "I'll teach him to spy on me and drag strangers to the house to—"

"Excuse, please, *Madame*, you will do nothing whatever at all concerning the little man," de Grandin denied in a level, almost toneless voice. "When first we did encounter him in the street he told us he greatly feared a beating at your hands, and I took it on myself to guarantee him immunity. I would not have it said I have failed him."

"We'll see about that!" She took a swift step toward the cowering child, the cold fire of murderous hate gleaming in her eyes, but de Grandin interrupted.

"*Madame*," he reminded, "you forget what it is I have said." Quick as a striking snake his hand shot out, grasping her wrist in a paralyzing grip and halting her in mid-stride.

"Oh!" she sobbed as his steely fingers bit cruelly into her yielding flesh. "Pontou," she turned to the black-clothed man, "will you let this insolent—"

De Grandin released her, but kept his body between her and the frightened child as he regarded the livid-faced man with cold, menacing eyes. "*Monsieur*," he promised, clipping his words with metallic hardness, "should you care to resent any affront you may conceive *Madame* has suffered, I am at your service at any time and place you wish to name."

A moment he waited, his slender body braced for the assault he fully expected, then, as the other made no move, turned a contemptuous shoulder on the woman and her companion.

"Come, *mon brave*," and he took the little boy's hand in his; "let us go. These, they are unworthy to share the company of men like us. Come away. Friend Trowbridge and I shall feed you bonbons and chocolate till you are most gloriously ill, then nurse you back to health again. We shall take you to see the animals at the zoo; we shall—"

"But see here, de Grandin," I expostulated as I followed him to the street, "you can't do this. It's against the law, and—"

"My friend," he assured me, "I have already done it. As for the law, if it would be respected it must be respectable. Any statute which compels a little man like this to live with such an unnatural parent is beneath all honest men's contempt."

H E WAS AS GOOD as his word. Little Aubrey Sattalea spent a glamorous afternoon with us at the zoological garden, stuffed himself to capacity with unwholesome sweetmeats and ate a dinner fit for a longshoreman that night.

The Frenchman was deep in the relation of a highly original version of the story of Cinderella as we sat on the veranda after dinner when quick, angry steps sounded on the front path. "Where's that Frenchman, de Grandin?" a furious voice demanded as Aubrey Sattalea, senior, mounted the porch, his face working with rage. "Where's the man who came to my house and stole my little boy—"

"Here, at your very good service, *Monsieur*," de Grandin announced, rising from his chair and bowing formally, but holding his supple body poised to resist any attack the other made. "As for stealing your fine little man, I pride myself upon it. They shall no longer torture him, though you and a thousand others seek to drag him back."

"What d'ye mean?" Sattalea demanded, advancing menacingly on the diminutive Frenchman.

"Come and see," de Grandin responded, backing slowly toward the hall. As Sattalea followed him into the house, he halted suddenly, snapped on the electric light and thrust his hand down the front of the child's white-linen blouse, ripping the garment open and turning it down to display the lad's slim, straight back. Sattalea and I gave simultaneous gasps of astonished horror. From shoulder to waist the child's back was a mess of crisscrossed, livid wales, the unmistakable signs of recent cruel beatings with a whip or small cane.

"Did *you* do this?" the Frenchman demanded, taking a threatening half step toward the visitor. "*Parbleu*, if you did, though you be twenty times his father, I shall beat you insensible!"

"Good Lord!" the horrified parent exclaimed. "Who—what—"

"Mother did it, Daddy," the little boy broke in sobbingly. "Since that night when she was so ill, that funny-looking man's been coming to the house every day and she's changed so. She says she doesn't love me any more and she beats me for almost nothing—I didn't mean to look in that day he kissed her—honestly, I didn't—but she said I was spying on them and the two of them beat me till—"

"Aubrey! What are you saying?" his father cried.

"*Morbleu*, no more than all the neighbors know, *Monsieur*," de Grandin returned impassively. "This afternoon, when Friend Trowbridge and I had returned from our outing with your son, I took some magazines, which I pretended to sell, and my most persuasive manner to the back doors of the houses of your block. In one small hour's conversation with the domestic servants of the neighborhood I found that you alone are unaware of what goes on in your home."

Sattalea faced the Frenchman with a look of incredulous horror; then, as the import of de Grandin's words sank home, an expression of hopeless desolation spread over his face. "That explains it!" he sobbed. "She *has* changed since that night she di— you gentlemen gave her up for dead! She's grown more beautiful every day, but—but she's not my Vivian, not the girl I married. Sometimes I've felt as though some stranger had come to take her place, and—"

"*Monsieur*, I think it not unlikely," de Grandin spoke softly as he laid his hand on the man's shoulder with an almost fatherly gesture. "Believe me, I can appreciate your trouble. It were best that we did not make mock of Providence, my friend. It is better that we leave bad enough alone, lest it become worse. Alas, the olden days of happiness are gone forever; but we can at least repair the greater wrong before it has gone too far. Will you help me make your home a fit place for your little son to dwell, *Monsieur?*"

"Yes," Sattalea agreed. "I'll do anything you say. Sometimes I think it would have been better if Vivian really had died. She's a changed woman. She used to be so sweet, so gentle, so loving, now she's a very devil incarnate, she's—"

"Let us not waste time," de Grandin interrupted. "Tonight you will inform *Madame* your wife that you must leave town on business early in the morning. When all preparations are made for your seeming trip, you will come here, and remain hidden until I give the word. Then, *parbleu*, we shall show this species of a rat who would buy dead women's bodies who holds the stronger cards—whose magic is more potent—may the Devil, his master, roast me if we do not so!"

4

SHORTLY BEFORE NOON THE following day a taxicab deposited Aubrey Sattalea and several pieces of luggage at my front door, and after seeing the guest secreted in an upstairs room de Grandin excused himself, saying he had several important missions to execute. "Remember, my friend," he warned the visitor, "you are not to leave the house for any reason less urgent than fire, and you will refrain from so much as showing yourself at the window until I say otherwise. The secrecy of your whereabouts is greatly important, I assure you."

Dinner was about to be served when he returned, his little eyes shining with elated excitement. "See, my friends, he ordered as we finished dessert, is it not a pretty thing which I obtained in New York this afternoon?" From his jacket pocket he drew a small case which he snapped open, displaying a tiny, shining instrument bedded in folds of cotton wool.

It was a glass-and-nickel syringe of twenty-five minim size, with a short heavy slip-on needle attached. The piston was of ground glass, set on a metal plunger which led through a cap. On this plunger, instead of the usual metal set-screw, was a tiny, trigger-like, safety lever which locked the piston so that the syringe could be carried full without danger of spilling its contents.

"H'm, I've never seen one quite like it," I admitted, examining the instrument with interest.

"Probably not," the Frenchman returned as he snapped the safety-catch on and off, testing its perfect response to the lightest pressure of his finger. "They are not widely known. For the average physician they are an unnecessary luxury, yet there are times when they are invaluable. In psychiatric work, for instance. The doctor who attends the mad often has need of a syringe which can carry quick unconsciousness, even as the soldier and gendarme has need of his pistol, and when he must draw and use his instrument at one there is no time to stop and fill it. *Voilà*, it is then this little tool becomes most handy, for it can be filled and carried about like a gun, rendered ready for action by the touch of the finger, and there has meantime been no danger of the drug it carries being lost. *C'est adroit, n'est-ce-pas?*"

"But what need have you for it?" I asked. "I don't understand—"

"But of course not," he agreed with a vigorous nod. "But if you will be so good as to wait a few hours—ah, I shall show you a tremendously clever trick, my friends. Meantime, I am wearied. I shall sleep four hours by the alarm clock; then, if you please, we shall perform our duty. Until then—"

Rising, he bowed formally to us in turn and ascended to his bedroom.

Midnight had sounded on the tall clock in the hall and twelve deep, vibrant strokes had echoed from the great gong in the courthouse tower before de Grandin rejoined us, refreshed by his four-hour nap and a cold shower. "Come, my friends," he ordered, filling his new syringe with a twenty per cent solution of cannabis indica and thrusting it handily into his jacket pocket, "it is time we repaired to the rendezvous."

"Where?" Sattalea and I demanded in chorus.

"Wait and see," he returned enigmatically. "Quick, Friend Trowbridge, the car, if you please."

Under his direction I drove to within a hundred feet or so of the Sattalea cottage, then parked the motor at the curb. Together we dismounted and stole softly toward the house.

All was quiet within the dwelling; not a light showed through the long, unshuttered windows, but de Grandin led the way unerringly across the porch, through the drawing-room and down the hall to the white-enameled door of the principal bedroom. There he paused, and in the flash of his pocket electric torch I saw his small, heart-shaped face twitching with excitement. "Are we ready?" he demanded, his narrow, black brows arched interrogatively.

I nodded, and he turned sharply, bearing his weight against the white panels of the door and forcing them inward. Next instant, de Grandin in the lead, Sattalea and I at his elbows, we entered the darkened room.

For a moment I saw nothing but the vague outlines of furniture, only dimly picked out by the moonlight filtering through the Venetian blinds which hung before the window, but as I paused, striving to accustom my eyes to the quarter-light, I made out the hazy, indistinct shape of something human, so still it seemed inanimate, yet somehow instinct with life and viciousness.

"*Permettez-moi*," de Grandin exclaimed, feeling quickly along the wall for the electric switch, pressing the button and flooding the chamber with light. Beyond the bed, clad in pajamas and dressing-gown, crouched the white-faced, stoop-shouldered man who had proved such a mystery to us, his thin, evil features drawn in a snarling grimace of startled fury. Backed against the wall at the bedstead's head, rigid in an attitude of mingled fear and defiance, stood Vivian Sattalea. Her slim, white body showed statuesquely through the silken tissue of her nightrobe, her supple, rounded limbs and torso rather emphasized than concealed by the diaphanous garment. Her arms were extended straight down beside her, her hands pressing the wall against which she leaned till the flesh around the long, brightly polished nails showed little half-moons of white. Her red, passionate mouth was twisted in an animal-snarl of rage, and out of her purple eyes looked something which had never belonged to the woman Aubrey Sattalea married five years before—some evil trespasser in possession, some depraved interloper holding high holiday behind the windows of her soul.

"Vivian!" Sattalea looked in agonized disbelief from the crouching, slinking intruder to his wife, and his honest, commonplace young face seemed fairly to crumble with the devastation of overwhelming disillusion. "Oh, Vivi, how could you—and I loved you so!"

"Well, you silly, fatuous fool!" the woman's voice was thin and wire-edged as she spoke, and that evil, half-seen something seemed dodging back and forth in her wide-open eyes like a criminal lunatic playing hide-and-seek at the barred windows of his cell. "What did you think—did you expect me to put up with *you?* You—"

"Silence!" de Grandin's command, sharp as a whip-crack, cut through her tirade. "The time for speech is past. It is time to act!"

Agilely as a leopard he leaped across the bed, his left hand seizing the crouching, corpse-faced man by the collar of his gown and forcing him backward on the couch. There was a short, fierce struggle, the flash of something bright in the electric light, then a muffled, strangling cry as de Grandin sank the needle of his hypodermic in the other's arm, released the safety-catch and shot the plunger downward.

"Stop—stop, you're killing him!" the woman shrieked, leaping like an infuriated cat from her retreat against the wall and flinging herself on de Grandin, clawing at his face, gnashing at him with her teeth like a tigress fighting for her mate.

The Frenchman thrust his half-conscious antagonist from him with a vigorous shove of his foot, seized the woman's right wrist in his left hand and jerked her forward, so that she lay prone across the bed. As she writhed and twisted in his grip, he shot the hypodermic needle into her rounded arm and forced the piston down, emptying the last dregs of the powerful hypnotic drug into her veins. I saw the white skin around the needle-point swell like an oversized blister as the sense-stealing hashish flooded into her system, saw her red mouth close convulsively, as though she swallowed with an effort, then watched fascinated as her taut, lithe muscles went slowly limp, her lips fell senselessly apart and her eyes slowly closed, the lids fighting fiercely to stay open, and murderous, insatiable hatred looking from her face as long as a flicker of her eyes remained unveiled by the lowering lids.

"Quick, my friends!" de Grandin ordered as her body went flaccid in complete anesthesia. "We must hasten; the drug will not control for long, and we must attack while the barrier of their physical consciousness is down."

Under his directions we laid Vivian Sattalea and her paramour on the bedroom floor, and while Sattalea and I crossed their hands and feet after the manner of memorial effigies on mediæval tombs the Frenchman extracted four waxen candles from the inner pocket of his jacket, placed one at the head and another at the foot of each unconscious form.

Stooping quickly he traced a six-pointed figure in chalk on the bedroom rug, then snapped off the electric light and set the four candles aflame. "Do not step beyond the lines, my friends," he warned, pushing Sattalea and me inside the design he had drawn; "there will soon be that outside which no mortal can look on unprotected and live!"

As the candle flames burned brightly in the hot, still room, I noticed a subtle, indefinable odor, strangely similar to ecclesiastical incense yet differing from it in some way I could not define. There was something soporific about it, and I felt my lids go heavy as I inhaled, but was brought back to attentive consciousness by de Grandin's words. Bending ceremonially to the east, the south, finally to the west, with a sort of jerky genuflection, he had begun a low, sing-song chant. The words he used I could not understand, for they were in some outlandish tongue, but constantly, like the recurrence of the name of Deity in a litany, I caught the surname Amalik, and mingled with it that of Suliman ebn Dhoud and other Arabic and Hebrew titles till the half-dark room seemed fairly redolent with the chanted Oriental titles.

"Look, look, *for God's sake, look!*" rasped Aubrey Sattalea in my ear, seizing my arm in a panic-strengthened grip and pointing toward the northwest corner of the room.

I looked, and caught my breath in a terrified sob.

Rearing nearly to the ceiling of the chamber, so indistinct that it was more like the fleeting, uncertain vision of an object behind us seen from the corner of the eye, there was a monstrous, fear-begetting form. When I gazed directly at it there was nothing but shadow to be seen, but the moment my eyes were partly averted it took sudden substance out of nothing, and its shape was like that of a mighty, black-robed man, and, despite the white beard which fell nearly to the hem of its garment, the being seemed not old as we are wont to consider men, but rather strong with the strength which mighty age gives to giant trees and hills and other things which endure forever. And from the being's shadowy face looked forth a pair of terrifying, deep-set eyes which glowed like incandescent metal, and between its upraised, mighty hands there gleamed the wide blade of a sword which seemed to flicker with a cold, blue, phosphorescent light. Over all my body I could feel the rising of horripilation. The hairs upon my head and the shorter hairs of my hands and arms seemed rising stiffly, as though an electrical current ran through me, and despite my utmost efforts my teeth rattled together in the cachinnation of a chill; for the air about us had become suddenly gelid with that intense, numbing cold which means utter absence of vital heat.

"By the Three Known and One Unknown Elements; by the awful word whispered in the ears of the two Khirams by Shelomoh, the Temple-Builder"— de Grandin made the threefold signs of Apprentice, Fellowcraft and Master with flashing quickness—"by the mastery of Eternal Good over Evil, and by the righteousness of Him who planned the Universe, I bind you to my bidding, O Azra'il, dread Psychopompos and Bearer of the Sword!" De Grandin's voice, usually a light tenor, had deepened to a powerful baritone as he pronounced the awful words of evocation. "Come to my aid, O Powers of Light and of Darkness," he chanted. "To me are ye bound by the words of Power and Might, nor may ye depart hence till my will be done!"

A light wind, colder, if possible, than the freezing air of the room, seemed to emanate from the dreadful form in the darkened corner, making the candle flames flicker and the shadows flit and dance in arabesques across the walls and ceiling of the room. The unconscious man upon the floor moved slightly and groaned as though in nightmare, and the woman beside him shuddered as if the chilling wind had pierced even the barriers of her unconsciousness.

"Speak out, seducer of the dead, destroyer of the living!" de Grandin commanded, fixing his burning gaze on the groaning man. "I command you, declare to us your true name and nature!"

"Pontou," the voice issuing from the supine, drug-bound man was faint as an echo of a whisper, but in that silent room it sounded like a shout.

"Pontou is my name, my birthplace Brittany."

"And what did you there, Pontou?"

"I was clerk to Gilles de Laval, Sire de Retz, Marèchal of France, Chamberlain to His Majesty, the King, and cousin to the mighty Duke of Brittany.

"Aie, but there were brave doings in the château at Marchecoul when the Sire de Retz dwelt there! The castle chapel was gorgeous with painted windows and cloth of gold, the sacred vessels encrusted with gems, and churchly music sounded as the mass was celebrated thrice daily, but at night there was a different sort of mass, for with me as deacon and Henriet as subdeacon, before the desecrated altar of the Galilean Gilles de Retz celebrated la messe noire, and from the throats of little children we drew the 'red milk' wherewith to fill our chalices in honor of Barran-Sathanas, our Lord and Master. Aie, 'twas sweet to hear the helpless little ones plead for mercy as we bound them on the iron grille before the sanctuary, and sweeter still to hear their strangled moans as Henriet and I, or sometimes the great Gilles de Retz himself, passed the keen-edged knife across their upturned throats; but sweetest of all it was to quaff the beakers of fresh lifeblood, still warm from their veins and toss their quivering hearts into the brazier which burned so brightly before the throne of Barran-Sathanas!"

De Grandin's small, white teeth were chattering, but he forced another question:

"Accursed of heaven, when came your career to an end? Speak, by the powers that bind you, I command it!"

"In 1440," the answer came falteringly. "'Twas then Pierre de l'Hôpital came to Nantes with his power of men-at-arms and took us into custody. *Aie*, but the mean little folk who never dared look us in the face before flocked to the courtroom to testify how we had ravished away their brats from the cradle and sometimes from the breast, and made them sacrifices to our Lord and Master, the Prince of Evil!

"Our doom was sealed or ever we stood before the bench of justice, and in all the crowded hall there was none to look on me with pity save only Lizette, the notary's daughter, whom I had taken to the castle and initiated into our mysteries and taught to love the 'red milk' even as I did.

"Five days our trial lasted, and À *mort*—to death, the court condemned us.

"They bore us to the meadow of Bissc beyond the gates of Nantes, and hanged us by the neck. Henriet turned craven at the end, and made his sniveling peace with God, but the Sire De Retz and I stood steadfast to our master, Barran-Sathanas, and our souls went forth unshriven and unrepentant.

"My soul was earthbound, and for weeks I haunted the scenes I knew in life. The fourth month from my execution a butcher died, and as his spirit left his body I found that I could enter in. That very night, as his corpse awaited burial I draped it round me as a man may don a cloak, and went to Rouen, where later I was joined by my light o' love, Lizette. We lived there twenty years, haunting cabarets, filching purses, cutting throats when money was not otherwise to be obtained.

"At length Lizette died, and I was left alone, and though I knew her spirit hovered near me, I could not teach her how to find the flesh to clothe herself. When my second body died, I entered into the cadaver of a headsman, and plied my trade of blood for nearly thirty years, yet always did I seek some way to seize a body for Lizette. The learning I absorbed with Gilles de Retz I added to by going to the East and studying under masters of black magic, but though I nearly succeeded several times, there was always something missing from the charm which was to open the gates to my love-light's spirit into human flesh.

"Ten years ago, in Northern Africa, I came upon the missing words of the incantation, and practised it successfully, but only to have my triumph ravished from me, for the body we used was so weakened by disease that it could not stand the strains we put upon it, and once again Lizette's spirit was discarnate.

"In this city I have searched the homes of the dying in quest of a body suitable to our purposes, and found one when Vivian Sattalea gave up her fleshly garb two weeks ago.

"*Aie*, what pleasures we have known, once more treading the good green earth together. What sins we have committed, what joy we took in torturing the brat the cuckold husband sired and thought my Lizette still mothered! In the dead of night we have broken into churches, defiled the holy elements and—"

"Enough—*parbleu*, too much!" de Grandin shouted. "Pontou, condemned of man, accursed of God, rejected by that very Devil to whom of old you bowed the knee, I charge and enjoin you, by the might, power and majesty of that God whom you have so dishonored, depart hence from this earthly body you have stolen, and enter not into flesh again. And you, Lizette, wanton mistress of a villainous paramour, depart you likewise to that place where spirits such as yours abide, and trouble not the living or the dead again with your uncleanly presence. Begone! *In nomine Domini*, be off, and come not hither any more again!"

As he concluded there sounded a dual groan from the bodies stretched before us on the floor, and from the left breast of the man and from the woman's left bosom there rose what looked like little jets of slowly escaping steam. The twin columns rose slowly, steadily, spreading out and thinning like vapor from a kettle-spout coming in contact with cold air, and as they swirled and twisted they merged and coalesced and clung together for an instant. Then the hovering, indistinct shape in the corner seemed suddenly to swoop downward, enveloped them in its ghostly folds as a drooping cloth might have done, and a soft, swishing noise sounded, as of a gentle wind soughing through bare tree-limbs. That was all. The candle lights winged out as if an extinguisher had pressed on them, and the warm, sultry air of August replaced the frigid cold which had chilled us to the marrow.

"It is finished—all is done, de Grandin's matter-of-fact announcement sounded through the darkness. "Will you be good enough to examine Madame Sattalea, Friend Trowbridge?"

I knelt beside the woman as he snapped on the lights, putting my fingers to her wrist. "Why," I exclaimed in bewilderment, "she's dead, de Grandin!"

"*Précisément*," he agreed with an almost casual nod, "and has been since that evening two weeks ago when you and I pronounced her so. It was but the spirit of the wicked Lizette which animated and defiled her poor, dead flesh. If you will be so good as to sign a certificate of death, I shall prepare for the disposal of this—" he touched the body of the man disdainfully with the polished toe of his dress shoe.

"*Monsieur*," he turned to Sattalea, a look of sympathy on his face, "it were best that you said farewell to *Madame*, your wife, quickly. I go to call Monsieur Martin and bespeak his professional services for her."

"Oh, Vivian, Vivian," young Sattalea sobbed, dropping to his knees and pressing his lips to his wife's lifeless mouth, "if only I could forget these last two weeks—if only I hadn't let him desecrate your dead body with that—"

"*Monsieur*—attention—look at me!" de Grandin cried sharply.

For a moment he stared fixedly into Sattalea's eyes, then slowly put his hands to the other's forehead, stroked his brow gently, and:

"You will forget all that is past—you will not remember your wife's seeming interval of life since the night Friend Trowbridge and I pronounced her dead. Your wife has died of heat-stroke, we have attempted to save her, and have failed—there has been no invasion of her flesh by foul things from beyond, you have no recollection of Pontou, or of anything he has said or done—do you understand? Sleep, now, and awaken in half an hour, not sooner."

A dazed look in Sattalea's eyes and a faint, almost imperceptible nod of his head was the only answer.

"*Très bon!*" de Grandin exclaimed. "Quick, Friend Trowbridge, help me place her on the bed. She must not be found thus when he awakens!"

Working with feverish haste, we clothed the dead man's body in his black garments, bundled him into the tonneau of my car and drove slowly toward the river. At a darkened highway bridge we halted, and after looking about to make sure we were not observed, dropped the corpse into the dark waters. "Tomorrow or next day the police will find him," de Grandin remarked. "Identification will not be difficult, for the young McCrea will testify of his visit to Monsieur Martin's and his attempt to buy a corpse—the coroner's jury will decide a harmless lunatic fell overboard while wandering through the town and came to his death by misadventure. Yes. It is much better so."

"But see here," I demanded as we turned homeward, "what was all that rigmarole that dead man told us? It isn't possible such a monster as that Gilles de Retz ever lived, or—"

"It is unfortunately all too true," de Grandin interrupted. "The judicial archives of the ancient Duchy of Brittany bear witness of the arrest, trial and execution of one of the greatest nobles of France, Gilles de Laval, Sire de Retz and marshal of the King's armies, at a specially convoked ecclesiastical court at Nantes in 1440. Together with two servants, Pontou and Henriet, he was hanged and burned for murder of more than a hundred little children and young girls, and for indisputably proven sorcery and devil-worship. Yes.

"As for the possibility of Pontou's spirit being earthbound, it is quite in line with what we know of evilly disposed souls. By reason of his intense wickedness and his vicious habits, he could not leave the earthly atmosphere, but must perforce hover about the sort of scenes which had pleased him in life. You remember how he was in turn a robber and a public executioner? Good.

"When we were called to attend Madame Sattalea and this so villainous Pontou first appeared on the scene, I was greatly puzzled. The magical formula he mouthed above the corpse of the poor dead lady I could not understand, for he spoke too quickly, but certain words I recognized, and knew them for the sign-words by which the necromancers of old called back the spirits of the dead. That was my first clue to how matters stood.

"When Monsieur McCrea told us of Pontou's attempt to buy a corpse, and the good *curé's* story of his effort to force entrance to a house of death coincided, I knew this evil man must have some special reason for desiring the body of a woman, and a woman only.

"When we met the little lad and went to Monsieur Sattalea's and there beheld the love scene between his wife and the evil black-clothed one, I was certain he had called the evil spirit of some woman long dead to inhabit the body of poor Madame Vivian that he might have companionship of his own wicked kind, and when she called him by name—Pontou—I did remember at once that the evilest of the servants of that blasphemous monster, Gilles de Retz had been so named, and realized something like the story confessed to us tonight might have happened.

"Therefore, I made my plans. The air about us is filled with all sorts of invisible beings, my friend. Some are good, some are very evil indeed, and some are neither one nor the other. Wise old King Solomon was given dominion over them as one of the few mortals who could be trusted not to abuse so great a power. To marshal them to his assistance he did devise certain cabalistic words, and he who knows the ancient Hebrew formulæ can call the invisible ones into visibility, but the risk is great, for the evil ones may come with those who are good, and work great injury. Nevertheless, I determined to make the experiment. By calling aloud the words of Solomon's incantations I provided us with strong spiritual allies, which should force the rebellious spirit of Pontou to speak, whether he willed it or not. Too, when I had so bound Pontou's spirit to answer my inquiries, I had him at a disadvantage—I could also call it forth from the body it had usurped. And once it was clear of that body the ghostly allies I had summoned made short work of it."

"But that dreadful half-seen thing which stood in the corner," I persisted. "What was it? I couldn't see it clearly; indeed, the more closely I looked at it, the vaguer it seemed, but when I looked away I thought I descried a tall, terrible old man with flashing red eyes and a naked sword between his hands. Was it—"

"Pontou the wicked one, who by his necromantic sorcery more than once escaped the bounds of death, had long cheated Azra'il, the Death Angel," he replied. "The ancient lore is full of stories of the psychopompos, or spirit-leader; who takes the severed soul from the new-dead body and conducts it through the frontiers of the spirit world. Perhaps it was none other than Death's own angel who stood among the shadows and waited patiently for the spirits which long had cheated him, my friend. I myself do remember the whispered gossip which went the rounds of St. Petersburg some twenty years and more ago. I was studying in the Imperial Hospital at the time, and servants of the Winter Palace whispered a strange story of a little duchess who accidentally ate some oysters intended for the Tsar, and fell fainting to the floor, and how her little cousin awoke screaming in the night to say a tall, bearded figure had come into their room, then trodden silently into the poisoned child's apartments. Next instant, while still the frightened children's screams rang out, the poisoned little one gave up her soul. I do not know, but—"

"But that's absurd," I cut in. "All this talk of death angels is a lot of old wives' balderdash, de Grandin, you know as well as I. What we call death is nothing but a physiological fact—the breaking-down of the human mechanism for one reason or another. As to the spiritual phases of it, of course, I'm not prepared to say, but—"

"Of course not," he agreed. "We know so little of the spirit world that he who would expound it stamps himself a fool thereby.

"But this I say without fear of denial, my friend, there is one sort of spirit who is no mystery, and with him I would hold immediate communion. In the lower left-hand drawer of your office desk reposes a bottle of Three-Star cognac, distilled in *la belle France* long years before Monsieur Volstead's blighting legislation was thought of. This moment it is full. *Parbleu*, if I do not decrease its contents by half before I am an hour older may every fiend of lowest hell fly off with me!"

The Silver Countess

My dear Trowbridge [the letter ran] If you will be good enough to bring your friend Dr. de Grandin, of whom I've had some favorable reports, out to Lyman's Landing, I think I can present him with a problem worthy of his best talents. More I do not care to write at this time, but I may add that whatever fee he may think proper in the premises will be promptly paid by

Yours cordially,
WALKER SWEARINGEN.

JULES DE GRANDIN LIT a cigarette with slow deliberation, dropped a second lump of sugar in his coffee, and watched the small resultant bubbles rise in the cup as though they were a hitherto unnoted piece of physical phenomena. "The Monsieur Swearingen who writes so cautiously of the case he would present me, then concludes his note as if my performance were to be by royal command, who is he, if you please?"

"We were in college together," I explained. "Swearingen was a shy sort of lad, and I rather took him under my wing during our freshman year. He went into some sort of brokerage concern when he graduated, and we've met only casually since—alumni dinners and that sort of thing. I understand he's piled a monstrous stack of money up, and—well, I'm afraid that's about all I can tell you. I don't really know him very well, you see. There's not much question he thinks the case important, though; I don't believe he's trying to be deliberately mysterious, more likely he thinks the matter too urgent to be set out in writing and prefers to wait for a personal interview."

"U'm? He is wealthy, this one?"

"Very. Unless he's lost his money in unlucky speculation he must be worth at least a million, possibly two."

"*Tiens*, in that case I think we should accept his kind invitation, and unless I greatly miss my guess, he shall be less wealthy when he has paid my fee. I do not greatly fancy his letter; one would think he seeks to hire a mountebank; but there is probably no way in which his self-esteem can be reduced save by collection of a large price. *Alors*, I shall deflate his pocketbook. Will you advise him that we come without delay, and shall expect a handsome fee for doing so?"

Lyman's Landing, Walter Swearingen's summer place, stood on a wide, almost level promontory jutting out into the Passaic. Smooth lawns lay round the house, a tall, carefully tended hornbeam hedge separated the grounds from the highway, and a line of graceful weeping willows formed a lush green background for the red-brick homestead. Painted wicker chairs sat on the lawns, to one side of the house was a rose garden riotous with color; farther away an oblong swimming pool was partially screened by a hedge of arbor-vitae, and a quartette of youngsters played mixed doubles on a grass tennis court.

As we drove toward the house my glance fell on a young girl lounging in a gaily-striped canvas hammock. She wore the regulation "sunworshipper's" outfit—a bright bandanna scarf bound round her bosom like a brassière, a pair of much-abbreviated linen shorts, rope-soled espadrilles, and, as far as I could discern, no more. As we drew abreast of her she kicked off one of her sandals and brushed a hand across the sole of her foot, as if to flick away a pebble that had worked into the shoe as she played.

I heard de Grandin breathe a sharp exclamation and felt the dig of his sharp elbow in my side. "Did you observe, my friend?" he asked in an urgent whisper. "Did you perceive what I did?"

"Could I help it?" I retorted. "Don't you think that little hussy wanted us to? She could hardly have worn less in the bathtub, and she's so elementally sex-conscious she can't let even a pair of middle-aged men drive past without taking off part of—"

"*Larmes d'un poisson!*" he interrupted with a chuckle. "The man who knows anatomy as he knows the inside of his pocket frets at sight of a small naked foot! It was not that I meant, my friend, but no matter. Perhaps it is of no importance; at any rate, you would not understand."

"What d'ye mean?" I countered, nettled as much by his bantering manner as his words. "I understand quite well. I saw five shameless pink toes—"

"*Parbleu*, did you, indeed? Perhaps I did not see what I saw, after all. No matter; we are arrived, and I should greatly like to confer with Monsieur Swearingen concerning this matter which he cannot put on paper, and for which he is prepared to pay so handsomely."

THE THIRTY PLACID, PROSPEROUS years that had passed since our college days had been kind to Walter Swearingen. In addition to wealth he had acquired poise and embonpoint, a heavy, deliberate style of speech, a Vandyke beard, and an odd, irritating manner of seeming to pay half attention to what was said to him and treating the remarks of anyone not primarily interested in money with the grave mock-courtesy an affable adult shows a child's prattle.

"Glad to welcome you to Lyman's Landing, Dr. de Grandin," he acknowledged my introduction. "Er, ah"—he smiled somewhat self-consciously—"there are certain phases of the case that make me think you're better able to handle it than the ordinary type of detective—"

"Monsieur," de Grandin began, and his little blue eyes flashed ominously, but Swearingen characteristically took no notice of the attempted interruption.

"The county police and state constabulary are quite out of the question, of course. To be quite frank, I'm not prepared to say just what *is* behind it all; it has some aspects of a silly childish prank, some similarity to a possible case of kleptomania, and in other ways it like an old fashioned ghost story. I leave its proper labeling to you. U'm,"—he consulted a memorandum—"last Thursday night several of my guests were disturbed by someone in their rooms. None of them actually saw the intruder, but next morning it was found a number of valueless or nearly valueless articles had been stolen. Then—"

"And the missing articles were what, if you please, Monsieur?" This time our host could not ignore the query.

"H'm," he favored the small Frenchman with an annoyed stare, "Miss Brooks—Elizabeth Brooks, my daughter Margery's chum—lost an Episcopal prayer book; Elsie Stephens, another friend, who is a Roman Catholic, missed an inexpensive string of beads; Mr. Massey, one of the young men guests, lost a pocket Testament, and my daughter could not find a small book of devotional poems which had been on her desk. I fancy none of the young people is greatly distressed at his loss, but such things are disturbing, you understand.

"Friday night John Rodman, another guest, had a most disconcerting experience. Sometime between midnight and daybreak he woke in a state of profuse perspiration, as he thought, and feeling extraordinarily weak. It was only by the greatest effort he was able to light his bedlamp and discover that his pyjamas and bedclothes were literally drenched with blood from a small superficial wound in his left breast. We called a physician, and the boy's no worse for his experience, but it caused considerable comment, as you may well imagine. It's impossible he should have wounded himself, for there was no weapon in his room capable of making the incision from which he'd bled—his razors were in the adjoining bathroom, and there were no bloodstains on the floor, so the supposition he had walked in his sleep, cut himself, and then gone back to bed may be ruled out. Besides, the wound was small and almost circular in shape, as if made with an awl or some such small, sharp instrument.

"It was after this unfortunate accident that I wrote Dr. Trowbridge. Last night, however, Mr. Rodman's experience was repeated, the wound being in the left side of his throat this time. Rodman's a fine young chap and wouldn't do anything to embarrass me—he told me of the second wounding privately this morning. Now it's up to us to find out who's behind this nonsense. I realize it may sound like a tempest in a teapot to you, but I'm prepared to pay—"

"*Eh bien*, Monsieur, let us postpone the talk of payment till a later time, if you please," de Grandin put in. "I cannot say how large or small my fee should be until I know what I am called upon to do, and have done it. Meantime, if you will tell me if the beads which Mademoiselle Stephens lost were merely ornamental trinkets or a rosary, it will be of interest."

"Er, yes, I believe such beads are called rosaries," Swearingen returned, evidently annoyed at such a trivial technicality. "Now, if you've any further questions, or suggestions—" He paused expectantly.

De Grandin took his narrow chin between his thumb and forefinger, gazing thoughtfully at the floor. "Is there a guest who has not complained of loss?"

"Oh, yes, we've ten house guests; only those I've mentioned have been annoyed."

"U'm. Perhaps you will be good enough to show us the house, Monsieur. It is well to know the terrain over which one fights."

We made a brief survey of the establishment. It was a big, rambling building with wide halls, broad staircases and large rooms, unremarkable in any way save for the lavish manner in which it had been furnished, and offering no secret nooks or crannies for nighttime lurkers.

"This is the art gallery," our host announced as he pushed open a wide door in the rear of the first floor. "It's the biggest room in the place, and—what the devil!" he paused at the entrance, a frown of mixed perplexity and anger gathering on his face. "By George, this thing is ceasing to be a joke!"

We had only to follow the line of his angry glance to see its cause. Against the farther wall hung an ornate gilt frame, some four feet high by three wide. To the inner edges of the gilded moulding a narrow border of painted canvas adhered, but the picture which the frame had enclosed had obviously been cut away with a less than razor-sharp blade, since ravelled bits of mutilated fabric roughened the lips of the cut.

"This is outrageous, infamous!" stormed Swearingen, striding across the gallery and glaring at the violated frame. "By George, if I can find out who did this I'll prosecute, guest or no guest!"

"And what was the picture which was ravished away?" de Grandin asked.

"It was a picture of the Virgin Mary—'The Virgin of Eckartsau,' they called it—it cost me a thousand dollars, and—"

"*Tenez*, Monsieur, it can not have gone far. Distinctive pictures of the Blessèd Virgin identify themselves; the thief can not easily dispose of it, and the police will have small trouble tracing it and putting reputable dealers on guard."

"Yes, yes, of course; but this is most confoundedly mystifying. My dear man, d'ye realize everything stolen since this business started is of a religious nature?"

De Grandin's answering stare was as expressionless as that of a china doll. "I had begun to suspect it, Monsieur," he replied. "Now this—*Cordieu*, Friend Trowbridge, give attention. Do you observe it?"

With what seemed unjustified excitement he dashed across the wide room to a piece of sculpture, and as he looked at it the tips of his trim, waxed mustache twitched like the whiskers of an eager tom-cat scenting a well-fatted mouse.

It was the top portion of a medieval altar tomb, the effigy of a recumbent woman executed in what appeared to be Carrara marble lying on an oblong plinth about the chamfered edge of which ran an inscription in Romanesque capitals. The figure wore the habit of a Benedictine nun, a leather belt and knotted girdle circling the slender waist, the hands folded demurely across the breast beneath the scapular. The head, however, instead of being coiffed in a nun's bonnet and wimple was crowned with luxuriant long hair, parted in the middle and braided in two long plaits which fell forward over the shoulders and extended nearly to the knees, and on the brow was set a narrow diademlike coronet ornamented with a row of ingeniously carved strawberry leaves. It was a beautiful face the old-time sculptor had wrought, the features delicate, regular and classical, but with an intangible something about them which went beyond mere beauty, something nearly akin to life, something which seemed subtly to respond to the gaze of the beholder.

But it was not on the lovely carven features de Grandin's fascinated gaze rested. His eyes sped swiftly from the slender, curving throat, the gently swelling bosom and delicately rounded knees to the sandaled feet peeping beneath the hem of the monastic gown. Like those of most pietistic figures of its period the effigy's pedal extremities were represented uncovered save for the parchment soles and narrow crossed straps of *religieuse* sandals. With the fidelity characteristic of the elder craftsmen the carver had shown the feet prolapsed, as was natural when the extensor muscles had lengthened in cadaveric flaccidity, but the seat of death had obscured none of their beauty. The heels were narrow and the insteps high, the toes were long, slender and fingerlike, terminating in delicately tapering ends tipped with filbert-shaped nails.

"You see?" he pointed to the nearer foot, almost, but not quite touching it with his fingertip.

"Eh?" I queried, puzzled; then, "By Jove, yes!"

Slender as patrician hands, beautifully formed as they were, the statue's feet were anomalies. Each possessed an extra toe inserted between the long, aquiline fourth digit and the little toe.

"Odd that he should have made such a slip; he was so faithful to detail every other way," I commented.

"U'm, one wonders," he murmured. "Me, I should not be astonished if his faithfulness persisted even here." He shook his head as if to clear his vision, then bent beside the plinth on which the statue lay, deciphering the inscription incised in the stone.

Although the effigy was perfect in every way, the letters of the epitaph had been defaced in several places, so we could not read the legend in its entirety. The part still legible presented considerably more of a puzzle than a key to the lady's identity:

> HIC JACET ELEANOR—A COMITISSA ARGENT . . .
> QVAE OBUT ANNO CHRISTI MCCX . . .
> CVJVS MISEREATVR DEVS

"Humph," I muttered, "evidently this statue once decorated the tomb of a Countess Eleanor somebody who died sometime in the thirteenth century, but—"

"*Regardez-vous*, my friend!" de Grandin's excited comment broke through my stumbling translation. "Observe this, if you please."

Inscribed on the extreme lower edge of the plinth, faint as though scratched with a stylus, was the cryptic notation:

> MAL. III, I

"What make you of it?" he demanded.

"H'm," I hazarded, "the sculptor's signature, perhaps?"

"*Le bon Dieu* knows, not I," he admitted. "I do not think the sculptor would have signed his work thus—he would have used a chisel and his letters would have been more regularly formed. However, one guess is as good as another at this time.

"What have you to tell us of her?" he asked Swearingen who stood before his mutilated painting, oblivious of our inspection of the marble.

"Eh? Oh, that? I don't know much about it. Picked it up at a junk shop in Newark last month. Gloomy sort o' thing. I wouldn't ha' bought it if the face hadn't struck me as being rather pretty. It can't be very valuable. The dealer let me have it for fifty dollars, and I believe I could have had it for half that if

I'd held out. He seemed anxious to get rid of it. Confounded nuisance it is, too. The boys are always flocking in here looking at it—I caught young Rodman kissing it once, and—"

"*Fanons d'un têtard*, do you tell me so?" the Frenchman almost shouted. "Quick, Monsieur, give me the name of that so generous junkman who parted with this bit of almost priceless *virtu* so cheaply—right away, immediately, at once!"

"Eh, what's the hurry?" our host asked. "I don't think—"

"Precisely, exactly, quite so; I am aware of it, *but I do*. The name and address, quickly, if you please. And while we are about it, when was it the young Rodman embraced this—this statue?"

"H'm, last Friday, I believe, but—"

"*Morbleu*, the work was swift! Come, Monsieur, I wait the dealer's name."

"Adolph Yellen, Dealer in Antique Furniture, Bric-à-Brac and Objets d'art," was the legend printed on the rather soiled billhead Swearingen produced in response to de Grandin's insistence.

W E REACHED THE DINGY little shop in Polk Street just as the proprietor was about to fasten the gratings before his windows for the night.

"*Holà, mon ami*," de Grandin called as he leaped from the car and approached the stoop-shouldered, bearded shopman, "you are Monsieur Yellen, I make no doubt? If so, I would that you tell us about a certain statue—a piece of carven marble representing a reclining lady—which you sold Monsieur Swearingen of Lyman's Landing last month."

The little antique dealer regarded him through the astonishingly thick lenses of his horn-rimmed spectacles a moment, then raised his shoulders in a racial shrug. "I do not know nuttings habout her," he returned. "I get her at a auction sale ven der lawyers sell Meestair Pumphrey's things. All I know, I'm gladt to be rid from her—she vas onlucky."

"I hope you're not thinking of buying the piece, sir," interrupted a scholarly-looking young man who had been talking with Mr. Yellen when we arrived. "Mr. Yellen is quite right, it is an unlucky bit of *virtu*, and—"

"Ah, it is that you know something, then?" the Frenchman cut in. "*Bon*, say on, Monsieur, I listen."

"No-o, I can't say I know anything definite about the statue," the young man confessed with a diffident smile, "but I admit a strong antipathy to it. I'm Jacob Silverstein, Rabbi of the Beth Israel Congregation, and it may be simply our traditional theological distaste for graven images that leads me to dislike this woman's effigy, but I must confess the thing affected me unpleasantly from the moment I first saw it. I tried to dissuade Adolph from selling it, and asked him to present it to some museum, or, better still, break it up and throw the pieces in the river, but—"

"One moment, *Monsieur le Rabbin*, is there some reason you should so dislike this piece of lifeless stone. If so, I am interested, if not, *parbleu*, I shall listen to what you say also."

The young Hebrew regarded de Grandin speculatively, as though debating his answer. "You heard Mr. Yellen say the image was unlucky. He bought it, as he told you, at the auction of the late Horace Pumphrey's effects. Mr. Pumphrey was a wealthy eccentric who collected artistic oddities, and this altar tomb was the last thing he bought. Within a month of its acquisition he began to manifest unmistakable symptoms of insanity, and would have been put in restraint if he had not died by falling from a second storey window of his house. There was some gossip about suicide, but the final verdict was death by misadventure.

"The first time I saw the statue in Mr. Yellen's shop it produced a most unpleasant sensation; rather like that one experiences when looking into a cage of snakes at the zoo—you may know you're in no danger, but the ancient human horror of serpents rouses your unconscious fears. After that I avoided it as much as possible, but once or twice I was obliged to pass it and—it was doubtless a trick of the light falling on the figure's features—it seemed to me the thing smiled with a sort of malicious contempt as I went by."

The rabbi paused, a faint flush mounting to his dark, hard-shaven cheeks. "Perhaps I'm unduly prejudiced, but I've always attributed Sydney's trouble to some malign influence cast by that statue. At the time he bought the image Mr. Yellen had a young man named Sydney Weitzer in his employ, a youth he'd known practically all his life, and one of the most honest and industrious boys I've ever seen. Two months after that statue was brought into the shop Mr. Yellen was obliged to discharge him for stealing—caught him red-handed in theft. A few nights later the police arrested him as he attempted to burglarize the store."

"U'm?" de Grandin nodded sympathetically. "Were your losses great, Monsieur Yellen?"

"Ha, dot boy, he vas a *schlemihl!* Vot you t'ink he stold? Books—religious books—old Bibles, prayer books, a missal from Italy vid halluf der pages missink, a worthless old rosary and a vooden statue from a saint. Er lot of dem I vouldn't gaff you terventy dollars for!"

"Am I to understand that he confined himself to stealing worthless religious objects?"

Mr. Yellen lifted an expressive shoulder. "Dey vas all I had. I don't buy moch religious stoffot goes by der richer dealers, but vunce in a vile I get some vid a job-lot of t'ings. Efferyt'ing of der kind in der shop that *schlemihl* stole. Vot he did vid dem Gott only knows. Nobody vid sense vould haff paid him money for dem. Oh, vell,"—he waved his hand in a gesture of finality—"vot can you eggspeck from a crazy feller, anyhow?"

"Crazy—"

"Unfortunately, yes," Rabbi Silverstein broke in. "When Sydney came to trial for attempted burglary his only explanation was to say, 'She made me do it—I had to go to her.' He could not or would not explain who 'she' was, but begged so piteously to be allowed to return to her that the magistrate committed him for observation. Later he was sent to an asylum."

On Jules de Grandin's face there was the absorbed, puzzled look of one attempting to recall a verse or tune that eludes memory. "This is most odd, Monsieur. You think—"

The rabbi smiled deprecatingly. "It's prejudice, no doubt, but I do associate that statue with Mr. Pumphrey's death and Sydney's otherwise inexplicable aberration. The regiment with which I served as chaplain passed through Valence en route to Italy, and made a short halt there. While going through the town I heard a story which might almost apply here. Not far from the city there is the ruin of an old *château fort*, and the country people tell a gruesome legend of a woman called the 'Silver Countess' who—"

"*Mord d'un chat! vie d'un coq!*" de Grandin cried. "But that is it! Since first I saw her lying there so sweetly innocent in six-toed sleep I've wondered what the keynote to this melody of mystery can be. Now, thanks to you, *Monsieur le Rabbin*, I have it! *Adieu*, you have been of the greatest help. Friend Trowbridge, we must hasten back to Lyman's Landing. It is imperative." He bowed courteously to the Jewish gentlemen and fairly dragged me to the waiting car.

"Past a book shop, my friend," he told me. "We must consult a Bible, right away, at once, immediately, and all too well I realize we shall find none at Monsieur Swearingen's."

I drove slowly through the downtown section and finally located a small secondhand book store. De Grandin hurried in and came back in a moment with a small black volume in his hand. "Attend me, my old one," he ordered, "what is the final book of the Old Testament?"

"H'm," I ransacked memory for forgotten Sunday School teachings, "Malachi, isn't it?"

"*Bravo!* And how would you designate the first verse of the third chapter of that book if you wrote it." He thrust a pencil and notebook at me.

After a moment's thought I scribbled "Mal. iii, 1," and returned the book to him.

"*Précisément!*" he exulted. "Now, concentrate. Where have you seen precisely that citation recently—within the last six hours?"

"U'm" I knit my brows. "Why, that's what we saw scratched on the plinth of that statue—"

"But yes, of course; certainly! Now, see this. That verse commences: '*Behold, I will send my messenger.*' What does it mean?"

"Nothing, as far as I'm concerned," I confessed. "It doesn't make sense."

"Perhaps not, perhaps so," he replied thoughtfully. "But of this I am sure: The lady of the six toes who lies at Monsieur Swearingen's is undoubtlessly the 'Silver Countess' of whom *Monsieur le Rabbin* spoke. Does not her epitaph proclaim, '*Hic Jacet Eleanora comitissa,*' which is to say, 'Here lies the Countess Eleanor'? Yes, of course. And though the terminal of the next word is broken we have left the letters a-r-g-e-n-t, which undoubtlessly might be completed as argentum, signifying silver in the Latin, *n'est-ce-pas?*"

"I dare say," I conceded, "but who the devil was this Silver Countess, and what was it she did?"

"That I do not certainly remember," he admitted ruefully. "One little head is far too small to hold the multitude of legends about wicked ladies of the past. However, at the earliest chance I shall ask my friend Dr. Jacoby of the *Musée Metropolitan*. That man knows every bit of scandal in the world, provided the events took place not later than the fifteenth century!"

THE LONG SUMMER TWILIGHT had deepened into dusk by the time we reached Lyman's Landing, and the wide, tree-shaded lawn was like a picture executed in silver and onyx mosaics. "My word," I exclaimed enthusiastically, "it's beautiful, isn't it? Like a bit of fairyland."

"Ha, fairyland, yes," he agreed. "Like fairyland where pixies lure mortals to their doom and Morgaine la Fée queens it over her court of succubi."

We had barely time to change for dinner before the meal was announced, and course followed heavy course, red and white, dry and sweet wines accompanying the food, and cognac bland as May and potent as December complementing coffee, which was served on the terrace.

If the events of the afternoon had worried him de Grandin gave no evidence of it. He ate like a teamster, drank like a sailor, and, judging from the peals of laughter which came from the young people surrounding him, jested like a second Rabelais throughout the meal. But he excused himself when they urged him to join them in an after-dinner swim, and locked himself in Swearingen's study, where he put through a number of urgent telephone calls.

"Little fools," grumbled Swearingen as the youngsters raced toward the pool. "Someone's bound to get hurt jumping in that frog-pond after dark. I'd have the thing filled in, only Margery puts up such a—"

"Mr. Swearingen, oh, Mr. Swearingen!" the hail came from the pool. "Look what we found." A young man came running, followed by the other bathers. Holding it above his head, lest it trail against the lawn, he held a strip of canvas, cracked from rough handling and spoiled by water, but unmistakably a painting, the missing *Virgin of Eckartsau.* "I dived right into it," the boy exclaimed breathlessly. "Fred Boerum hopped in ahead of me, and kicked the water up, and this thing must have come loose from the bottom where it lay and floated up—I stuck my face right into it when I went off the springboard."

"Who the devil put it there?" demanded Swearingen. "When I missed that picture this morning I thought perhaps we had a thief in the crowd; now I think we've been entertaining a lunatic. No one in his right mind would cut a picture from its frame and sink it in the pool. That sort of thing just isn't done."

"You may have right, Monsieur," de Grandin stepped from the house and examined the salvaged painting critically. "However, it appears to have been done here. Tell me, is it possible to drain the pool?"

"Yes, we can cut off the intake and open the drain—"

"Then I suggest we do so instantly. Who knows what more may lie concealed in it?"

In a few minutes the last drop went gushing down the pool's waste pipe, and the rays of half a dozen electric torches played upon the shining tiles. Ten minutes' inspection failed to produce anything more than a few waterlogged leaves, but de Grandin was not satisfied. Dropping to the shallow end of the bath, he began a methodical circuit of the tank, stopping now and then to thrust his fingers under the sill just beneath the coping. At last, as he reached the deep end, he called jubilantly, "To me, Friend Trowbridge; I have found them."

He held three little water-soaked books up for inspection. Their bindings were warped and peeling, their pages mere pulpy ruins, but the gilt letters still adhering to their backs proclaimed them the Book of Common Prayer, the New Testament and "Elegant Extracts of Devotional Poetry." As he regained the ground the Frenchman thrust his hand into his pocket and drew out a small, beautifully carved coral rosary.

"They were securely wedged beneath the ledge," he explained. "Had we not drained the bath there is small doubt they would have lain there till the water had completely destroyed them. *Eh bien*, it is fortunate the young people decided to go swimming this evening."

"But who could have done it?—Who would play a silly, senseless prank like that?" the guests chorused.

No sign of guilt appeared on any face, but every one looked at his neighbor with suspicion. "*Tiens*," de Grandin broke the awkward silence, "we waste time here, my friends. Why do you not repair to the veranda and turn on the radio? It is a superb night for *le jazz, n'est-ce pas?*"

I WAS ON THE POINT of disrobing when he tapped at my door. "Do not retire yet, my friend," he whispered. "We have work to do."

"Work—"

"Precisely. It is her next move. We have called 'check,' but not 'checkmate.' You will take your station in the art gallery, if you please, and stop whoever tries to enter there, or having entered, tries to leave. Me, I shall patrol the corridors, for I have a feeling there will be strange things abroad tonight. Come, the house is silent; let us go."

The wide, low-ceilinged gallery was ghostly-dark, only an occasional beam of moonlight entering the tall leaded windows as the trees outside shifted their boughs in the light breeze. The dim forms of the glassed-in cases filled with bric-à-brac, the shadowy outlines of framed pictures on the walls, and the wraithlike gleam of marbles through the darkness gave the place a curiously haunted air, and I shivered slightly in spite of myself as my vigil lengthened from quarter-hours to halves, and from halves to hours. Somewhere in the main hall a big clock struck three slow deliberate notes, seconded by the staccato triple beat of smaller timepieces; an owl hooted in the willows, and a freshening early morning breeze stirred the trees, momentarily unveiling the windows and letting in long oblique shafts of moonlight. I settled deeper in my chair, muttering a complaint at the task de Grandin had set me. "Foolishness," I mumbled. "Who ever heard of putting a death-watch over a piece of statuary? Silliest thing I ever heard—" Insensibly, I nodded and my tired eyes blinked slowly shut.

How long I napped I do not know. It might have been half an hour, though the chances are it was less. At any rate, I started tensely into full wakefulness with the feeling something near me moved with soft inimical stealth. I looked apprehensively about, noting the ordered rows of glass-doored cases, the pictures, the pallid marble of the statues—ah! I half rose from my seat, my fingers tense on the chair arms as my glance fell on the corner where the funerary statue of the Silver Countess lay. The marble image seemed to have grown, to have risen from its marble bed, to be in slow, deliberate motion. There was a half-seen vision of a pair of carmine lips, of large, intent dark eyes, a curving throat of tawny cream—a mist of white, fine linen.

"Who's there?" I challenged, leaping up and grasping the length of rubber-coated telephone cable de Grandin had handed me as a weapon. "Stand where you are, or—" my fingers felt along the wall, seeking the electric switch—

A gurgling, contemptuous titter, a flouncing of white draperies, the creaking of a window-hinge answered me. Next instant the light flooded on, and I blinked about the empty room.

"Trowbridge, Trowbridge, *mon vieux*, are you within—are you awake?" de Grandin's anxious hail sounded from the hall, and the door behind me swung open. "What has happened—is all well—did you see anything?"

"No—yes—I don't know!" I answered in a single breath. "I must have dropped off and dreamed—when I turned the lights on the place was empty. It *must* have been a dream."

"And did you dream the tight-shut window open?" He pointed to the swinging casement. "And—*grand Dieu des artichauts!*—and this?" He bent above the supine statue of the Countess, his lips drawn back in a sardonic grin. I joined him, glanced once at the marble figure, and fell back with a gasp. The statue's stony, carven lips were smeared with fresh red blood.

"Good heavens!" I exclaimed. "What—"

"What, indeed?" he assented. "Attend me, Friend Trowbridge. 'There is much and very potent evil in this house. Tonight, before I took up my patrol, I smeared the floor before the young Monsieur Rodman's door with talcum powder, that anyone who passed the threshold might surely leave his foot-tracks on the carpet of the hall. When I came back that way I found them—found them plainly marked upon the carpet, and let myself into his room. And what did I find there? Attend me while I tell you. I found him weltering in blood, by blue! Another wound had been pierced in his throat, and yet another in his breast above the heart. I bandaged him forthwith, for he was bleeding freely, then came to tell you of my find. Behold, I find you blinking like in owl at midday, and the casement window open, then this"—he pointed to the statue's gory mouth—"to mock at my precautions.

"Furthermore, my watchful, alert friend, as I rushed through the hall to tell you what I had found, I saw a form, a white form like that of *Madame la Comtesse* about to enter this room. Come, let us go up."

"But—" I expostulated.

"No buts, if you will be so kind. Let us observe those footprints."

On the carpet of the upper hall, beginning at Rodman's door and growing fainter as they receded, was a perfectly defined set of footprints. Someone walking barefoot had stepped into the film of toilet powder and tracked the white dust on the red broadloom. Dropping to my knees I looked at them, looked again, and shook my head in incredulity. The tracks were short and narrow—woman's footprints—and each was of a six-toed foot.

"What—who?" I began, but he silenced me with a bleak smile.

"*Madame la Comtesse* who lies downstairs with blood-stained mouth, has feet which might have made such tracks."

"But that's absurd—impossible! A stone image can't walk. It's against the course of nature—"

"And it is natural that an image should drink blood?" he asked with sarcastic mildness. "No matter. Let us not argue. There is still another explanation. Let us see about it."

Leading me down the corridor he came to pause before a white-enameled door, listened intently at the keyhole a moment, then crept into the room.

By the early-morning greyness we descried a rumpled evening dress thrown carelessly across a chair, a pair of silver sandals on the floor, and draped across another chair a pair of laced-edge crepe panties and a wisp of bandeau.

He laid his finger to his lips and dropped to hands and knees to crawl toward the bedstead, and I did likewise, feeling extraordinarily foolish, but all thought of the ridiculous figure I made vanished as he paused beside the bed and pointed to the sleeper. She wore a filmy night dress of Philippine cotton, and neither sheet nor blanket lay over her. It was with difficulty I stifled a gasp as my gaze came to rest upon her feet. Along their plantar region was a thin film of white powder—talcum powder—and on each there grew an extra toe; not a rudimentary, deformed digit, but one as perfectly shaped as its companions, joining the instep between the bases of the fourth and little toes.

Once more the little Frenchman signaled my attention; then, bending above the sleeping girl, played his flashlight across her face. Her lips were crimson with fresh blood, and at each corner of her mouth a little half-dried trickle of it drooled.

"*Voyez-vous, mon vieux*, are you convinced?" he asked in a low voice.

I made a silencing gesture, but he shrugged his shoulders indifferently. "No need for caution," he returned. "Observe her respiration."

I listened for a moment, then nodded agreement. Her inhalations gradually became faster and deeper, then slowly ebbed to shallowness and hesitancy—a perfect Cheyne-Stokes cycle. Unquestionably she lay in a light coma.

"What does it mean?" I asked as he piloted me toward the door.

"*Parbleu*, I damn think it explains the cryptic writing on that statue's base," he murmured. "Does it not say, '*Behold, I will send my messenger*'? And have we not just gazed upon her messenger in person? I should say damn yes."

"But—"

"*Ah bah*, let us not stand here like two gossiping fishwives. Come with me and I shall show you something more."

"DO YOU NOT THINK it rather cold in here?" he asked as we reentered the art gallery.

"Cold?"

"*Mais oui*, have I not said so?"

"It's rather cool," I admitted, "but what that has to do—"

"Be good enough to place your hand upon the brow of *Madame la Comtesse*," he ordered.

Wondering, I rested my fingertips on the smooth marble features, but drew them away with a sharp exclamation. The lifeless stone was warm as fevered human flesh, velvet-soft and slightly humid to the hand, as if it had been living cuticle.

From the farther wall de Grandin reached down an eleventh century mace, an uncouth weapon consisting of a shaft of forged iron terminating in a metal sphere almost as large as a coconut and studded with angular iron teeth. The thing, designed to crush through tough plate armor and batter mail-protected skulls to splinters, was fully two stone in weight, and seemed grotesquely cumbersome in the little Frenchman's dainty hands, but he swung it to his shoulder as a woodsman might bear his axe as he marched toward the statue.

"Whatever—" I began, but he shook his head.

"I shall complete the work the liberated peasants left unfinished," he paused beside the effigy and raised his ponderous weapon. "*Madame la Comtesse*, your reign is at an end. No longer will you send your messengers before you; no more will guiltless ones go forth to garner nourishment for your vileness!" He swung the iron weapon in a wide arc.

"Good heavens, man, don't! Stop it!" I cried, seizing the iron bludgeon's shaft and deflecting the blow he was about to deliver.

He turned on me, his face almost livid. "You, too, my friend?" he asked, a sort of wondering pity in his tone.

"It seems like sacrilege," I protested. "She's too beautiful—see, anyone would think she knows what you're about and asks mercy!"

It was true. Although the marble lids lay placidly above the eyes the whole look of the face seemed subtly altered, and about the sweet, full-lipped mouth was an expression of pleading, almost as though the image were about to speak and beg the furious little man to stay his hand.

"*Cordieu*, you have it right, my friend," he agreed, "and thus do I requite her pleadings! Mercy, *ha*? Such mercy as she has shown others shall be hers!" The iron weapon thudded full upon the bloodstained marble lips.

Blow after shattering blow he struck; chip after chip of marble fell away. The classically lovely face was but a horrid featureless parody of its former self, devoid of lifelikeness as a dead thing far gone in putrefaction. The fragile hands that crossed demurely on the quiet breast were hewn to fragments; the exquisite six-toed feet were beaten from their tapering ankles and smashed to rubble, and still he swung the desecrating mace, hewing, crashing, splintering, obliterating every semblance to humanity in the statue, leaving only hideous desolation where the lovely simulacrum had lain a few minutes before.

At last he rested from his vandalism and leaned upon the helve of his weapon. "*Adieu, Madame la Comtesse*," he panted, "*adieu pour ce monde et pour l'autre*."

He dabbed his forehead with a lavender-bordered white silk handkerchief. "*Parbleu*, it was no child's-play, that; that damnation statue was tougher than the devil's own conscience. Yes, one requires time to catch one's breath."

"Why'd you do it?" I asked reproachfully. "It was one of the most beautiful pieces of statuary I ever saw, and the idea of your venting your rage on it because that little she-devil upstairs—"

"*Zut!*" he shut me off. "Speak not so of the innocent instrument, my friend. Would you destroy the pen because some character-assassin uses it to write a scurrilous letter? Consider this, if you please." He retrieved a scrap of marble from the floor, a finger from one of the smashed hands, and thrust it at me. "Examine it; closely, *mon vieux*."

I held the pitiful relic up to the light, and nearly dropped it in amazement. "Wh—why, it can't be!" I stammered.

"Nevertheless, it is," he assured me. "With your own eyes you see it; can you deny it with your lips?"

Running through the texture of the ruptured stone, as though soaked into its grain, was a ruddy stain tinting the broken, rough-edged fragment almost to the hue of living flesh, and offering a warm, moist feel to my hand.

"But how—"

"How, indeed, my friend? You saw the stain of warm, new blood on her lips, and on her cheeks you felt the warmth of pseudo-life. Even in her stony veins you see the vital fluid. Is it not so?"

"Oh, I suppose so; but—"

"No buts, my friend; come now and see a further wonder; one I am sure has come to pass."

Dreading some fresh horror I followed him to the telephone and waited while he dialed a number. "*Allo*," he challenged finally, "is this the State Asylum for the Criminal Insane? Bon. I am Dr. Jules de Grandin, and ask concerning one of your inmates; one Sydney Weitzer. Yes, if you will be good enough." To me he ordered, "Take up the adjoining 'phone, my friend; I would that you should hear the message I receive."

"Hello," a voice came faintly after we had waited a few minutes, "this is Dr. Butterforth. I've had charge of Weitzer the past few hours. He's been unusually violent, and we had to strap him up about half an hour ago."

"Ah?" de Grandin breathed. "And now?"

"Damn queer," the other replied. "About ten minutes ago he stopped raving and came out of the delirium like a person waking from a dream. Didn't know where he was or who we were, or what it's all about. Almost had a fit when he found out he was here—couldn't remember being arrested for burglary or anything leading up to his commitment. It's too soon yet to start bragging, but I'm hanged if I don't think the poor kid's regained his sanity. Damnedest thing I ever saw."

"Precisely, you speak truer than you know, my friend," de Grandin returned as he hung up. To me he observed simply, "You see?"

"I'll be shot if I do," I denied. "I'm glad the poor boy's on the mend, but I can't see a connection—"

"Perhaps I can explain it to you," he promised, "but not now." He patted back a yawn and rose. "At present I am very tired. I shall feel better after sleep, a shower and breakfast. When I am rested I shall tell you everything I can. Till then, *à bientôt, cher ami*."

H E DID NOT RISE till after luncheon, and Swearingen was on the verge of apoplexy while he ate an unhurried brunch, but finally he finished and joined us in the library. "It is but fitting what you see together, seeing what is pertinent, and understanding what you see," he told us as he lit a cigarette.

"Let us, for example, take Mademoiselle Hatchot, whom I saw for the first time as we approached your house, Monsieur Swearingen. She was lying in a hammock, and as we passed by she slipped her shoe off, permitting us a glimpse of her so lovely foot. The glimpse was but a wink's-time long, but long enough for me to see she had six toes.

"Now, in my travels I have learned that among all primitive peoples, and among those not so primitive, who still retain traditions of olden days, the possession of an extra toe or finger is regarded as more than a mere physical freak. Those having extra digits are thought to be peculiarly sensitive to either good or evil influence. Though angels may more readily commune with them the same holds true of demons, even the Arch Fiend himself. You may remember that Dulac the great English painter, in recognition of this once-widespread belief, depicted both Circe and Salome with six toes on each foot.

"What your case was I did not know, Monsieur, for you had wisely failed to set on paper that which, had it reached other eyes than ours, might have made you a laughing-stock; but that you had a problem of more than ordinary interest I suspected, so I said to me, 'I shall bear in mind this lady of the six toes; she are undoubtlessly connected with the problem of this house.'

"Then you told me of apparently trifling thefts, and of the odd manner in which a young-man guest had been hurt. Then you show us the statue of *Madame la Comtesse*. I gaze upon her loveliness—and she was very lovely, too— and what is it I see? Six toes on both her feet, *parbleu!* This is most strange; it pulls the long arm of coincidence clear out of joint. Here are two women, one of flesh, one of stone, and each of them has two more toes than usual.

"You tell me that the young men of your party are intrigued by the statue; that one of them has kissed her on the lips, and that he is the same one who has sustained mysterious woundings in the night whereby he has lost blood.

"The olden legends are perhaps but fairy tales to frighten children, yet when great clouds of smoke arise we may look for at least a little fire, and old legends are but the embalmed remains of ancient fact. From earliest times we have stories of men who wrought their ruin by embracing images of evil association, or otherwise acting the lover toward them. These things I think about while I try in vain to decipher the meaning of the inscription on the base of the monument.

"When we go to Monsieur Yellen the antique dealer's to ask about the statue's antecedents we meet a young rabbi, who tells us of a tale he heard in Drôme concerning one known as 'The Silver Countess.' That is sufficient to prime my memory, for I remember hearing tales of that same lady, and I remember the cryptogram of the inscription, 'Mal. iii, 1,' concerning which Friend Trowbridge and I have argued. To test the soundness of my theory I procure a small Bible and have Friend Trowbridge write down the Scriptural inscription which I read. He writes exactly as I have anticipated, and in the Bible I find the first verse of the third chapter of the Book of Malachi begins, '*Behold, I will send my messenger.*—' It is a small thing, but enough. I am on the right trail, though my memory of the Silver Countess is still hazy.

"At once I call my good friend Professor Jacoby by telephone, and what he tells me makes my blood to run like ice water. In the olden days when such things were there lived a woman called the Countess Eleanor, sometimes called the Silver One, or Silver Countess. Her beauty was so great that no man could look in her face without becoming subject to her will. Her skin was like new milk, her lips were like old wine, her hair was like the moonlight—hence her sobriquet—and her soul was blacker than a raven bathed in ink.

"At fourteen she was married to a prowessed knight and went to live with him in his château near Valence, and presently he went away to fight the Turks for the faith that was in him. The Countess did not go with him. She stayed at home, and when he carne back unexpectedly and rushed to greet her in her bower he found her in the embrace of an incubus—a demon lover with whom she had long consorted by stealth.

"*Tiens*, there is no fool like a strong man in love, my friends. Instead of killing her forthwith, he took her to his bosom and forgave her, then went away to fight the infidel again.

"Among the hangers-on at the château was a talented young sculptor to whom the Silver Countess sat for her funerary monument, and when it had been finished she placed the statue in the château chapel where the moon's rays fell on it. There she would go to it, and lay her warm lips on its cold stone mouth, her pulsing, warm bosom against its chilly marble breast. It was not right, it was unholy; but she was lady and mistress of the castle. What could her servants do?

"All soon horror came to the castle. One by one her servants failed and pined away, though no man knew their malady, and when at last there were none to keep watch on her the Countess Eleanor made high holiday with imps and satyrs, incubi and devils, and all the mighty company not yet made fast in hell.

"It could not last. In those days the Church frowned on such practices, and made her frown effective. At a specially convened tribunal the Countess

Eleanor was put upon her trial for witchcraft and diabolism, convicted and sentenced to be hanged and burned like any common witch.

"The night before her execution she interviewed the sculptor of her statue. Next morning, when her sinful body had been burned to ashes and the ashes cast into the Rhine the young sculptor could not be found, but nightly ghostly revels were observed in the château. One by one the holy relics vanished from the chapel, by degrees the other monuments—those duly blessed with bell and book and candle—were defaced; at last the only image perfect and unblemished was that of Countess Eleanor, keeping lonely vigil in the *chapelle mortuaire*.

"Upon a night a hideous thing with blazing eyes and long and matted hair, clothed in motley rags and howling like a beast, attacked a peasant ploughman at the fall of dusk hard by the castle. The peasant defended himself lustily, and his assailant, sorely smitten, made to run away, but the ploughman followed hard, and tracked him to the château chapel, where he and some companions who had joined the chase came on the vanished sculptor lying prone upon the statute of the wicked countess, his lips pressed to hers, and on his mouth and on her stone lips was a smear of blood. The wretch had opened his own veins, sucked forth his blood, then with his mouth all reeking pressed it to the image of the woman he adored in death.

"*Eh bien*, there were ways of making those who did not wish to speak tell all they knew in those old days, my friends. Under torment he confessed that he had made a compact with his leman to steal the blessèd objects from the chapel, since her sinful spirit could not abide their nearness; and thereafter to rend and slay those whom he met and bear their blood in his mouth to her cold, sculptured lips for her refreshment.

"In my country we have a proverb concerning history: '*Plus ça change plus c'est la même chose*—the more it changes the more it is the same.' So it was with Countess Eleanor, it seems. In 1358 when the Jacques revolted, the castle was stormed and taken, but for some reason her tomb was left inviolate. Again, in 1793, when every vestige of kingcraft was swept from France, a guard of Republican soldiers was sent to the château to demolish it, but save to deface the epitaph upon the tomb the *citoyens* did no hurt to the beautiful and evil effigy.

"For years the ruins bore an evil name. No traveler who knew the road would venture near them after dark, but sometimes strange wayfarers took shelter there, and death or madness was their portion.

"The last known chapter of the tragic history was in the war of France's betrayal in 1871. In autumn of that year a foraging party of Uhlans was benighted near the castle and took shelter in the ancient chapel, the only portion of the building still under even partial roof.

"Next morning a company of *francs-tireurs* found them—three dead, the other dying. The dying man related how at midnight he had wakened with the pain of a sword-cut in his side, and seen his corporal lapping flowing blood from the severed throat of a comrade, then, with his dripping mouth, kissing and caressing a statue which lay stark and white in the midnight moonlight. With his pistol he had shot his officer, and the attitude of the man's body bore witness that his tale was true; for across the marble statue lay the dead, his bloody lips fast-hung to those of Countess Eleanor.

"When I had learned these things I knew why old Monsieur Pumphrey went mad directly he had bought that statue; I understood why the poor Jewish young man went crazy and stripped his master's shop of every holy thing, and why thereafter he sought to break and enter the shop. He whom the Silver Countess enthrals she first makes mad, then criminal. He must commit abominations, then seal the contract of his iniquity with a bloody kiss.

"Then it occurs to me this six-toed young lady also has a part in all this business—she and the young Monsieur Rodman who has been seen kissing that abominable statue. I make a survey of the facts. It does not appear that the Countess Eleanor ever partook of female blood; always it was that of a man which was put to her lips. Young Rodman has caressed her, it is possible— indeed, it are quite probable—that he is one of her conquests. But the nature of his woundings seems to negative his having taken his own blood to her. Who, then, has been the go-between, the messenger? Why not the six-toed girl? Is it not logical to think there is *rapport* between the six-toed living woman and the six-toed effigy of the beauteous witch? Why not, *en vérité*?

"Very well. Last night I set a trap. When I found Mademoiselle Hatchot's footprints in the hall I knew young Rodman had been visited by her, and rushed into his room without ceremony. It was well I did so, for he was sorely wounded and bleeding much. I made repairs on him and hurried to the gallery below where I found fresh blood—the blood of the young Rodman, *parbleu!*—upon the statue's lips. It are a sign and seal of evil service rendered by her helpless servant. '*Behold, I will send my messenger*,' was her parting gibe at humanity, carved on her tomb by that poor one whose soul she later stole away with her so evil loveliness.

"'*Madame la Comtesse*,' I tell her, 'I damn believe you have sent your last messenger. I, Jules de Grandin, have found you!' Yes.

"*Alors*, to Mademoiselle Hatchot's chamber I repair and on her little six-toed feet I find the marks of powder I have spread before young Rodman's door; but more important, on her lips I find the trace of the new blood which she has carried to that naughty one who lies all still and cold below. 'It is sufficient evidence,' I tell me. 'At once, immediately, right away, I shall do the needful.' And so I did.

"Against Friend Trowbridge's protests I smash that *sacré* statue like a potter's vessel. Beneath the hammering of my mace she are completely smashed, abolished, ruined, *pardieu!*

"Immediately I call the hospital where the young Weitzer are confined, and find that at the moment of that statue's smashing he regained his sanity. The final link was fitted into the chain. Your so strange case is settled, Monsieur Swearingen."

"What about the Hatchot girl?" asked Swearingen.

"What about the telephone through which you send a message, whether good or bad? She is wholly innocent. By chance she wears twelve toes instead of ten, and by that chance she became servant to a creature of extreme wickedness. Her mental state while in the service of her evil mistress was like that of one in anaesthesia. She knew not what she did, she can remember nothing. Friend Trowbridge can vouch that she lay in a light coma when we inspected her—"

"D'ye expect me to believe this damn nonsense?" Swearingen scoffed.

De Grandin lifted his shoulders in the sort of shrug no one but a Frenchman who wishes to indicate complete dissociation from a matter can give. "What you believe or disbelieve is of no moment to me, Monsieur. Me, I have disposed of the case according to your request.

"Tomorrow, or the next day, or perhaps the next day after that, you will receive my bill for services."

The House without a Mirror

M Y FRIEND JULES DE Grandin was in one of his gayest moods. Reclining against the plank seat of the john-boat he gazed with twinkling, bright blue eyes at the cloudless Carolina sky, tweaked the tips of his diminutive blond mustache till the waxed hairs thrust out to right and left of his small, thin-lipped mouth as sharply as a pair of twin fish-hooks, and gave vent to his own private translation of a currently popular song:

> "*Oui, nous n'avons plus de bananes;*
> *Nous n'avons plus de bananes aujourd'hui!*"

he caroled merrily.

"Say, looka yere, boss," protested our colored factotum from the boat's stern, "does yo' all want ter shoot enny o' dem birds, youh's best be cuttin' out dat music. Dese yere reed-birds is pow'ful skittish, wid so many no'then gemmen comin' dhown yere an' bangin' away all ober de place wid deir pump-guns, an—"

"*Là, là, mon brave,*" the little Frenchman interrupted, "of what importance is it whether we kill ten dozen or none at all of the small ones? Me, I had as soon return to Monsieur Gregory's lodge with empty bag as stagger homeward with a load of little feathered corpses. Have not these, God's little ones, a good right to live? Why should we slay them when our bellies are well filled with other things?"

The Negro boy regarded him in hang-jawed amazement. That anyone, especially a "gemman" from the fabulous "no'th," should feel compunction at slaughtering the reed-birds swarming among the wild rice was something beyond his comprehension. With an inarticulate grunt he thrust his ten-foot pole into the black mud bottom of the swamp canal and drove the punt toward a low-lying island at the farther end of the lagoon-like opening in the waterway.

"Does yo' all crave ter eat now?" he asked. "Ef yuh does, dis yere lan' is as dry as enny 'round yere, an—"

"But of course," de Grandin assented, reaching for the well-filled luncheon hamper our host had provided. "I am well-nigh perished with hunger, and if Monsieur Gregory has furnished brandy as well as food—*Mordieu*, may the hairs of his head each become a waxen taper to light his way to glory when he dies!"

The hamper was quickly unpacked and we sat cross-legged on a slight eminence to discuss assorted sandwiches, steaming coffee from vacuum bottles and some fine old cognac from a generously proportioned flask.

A faint rustling in the short grass at de Grandin's elbow drew my attention momentarily from my half-eaten sandwich. "Look out!" I cried sharply.

"Lawd Gawd, boss, don' move!" the colored boy added in a horrified tone.

Creeping unnoticed through the short, sun-dried vegetation with which the island was covered, a huge brown moccasin had approached within a foot of the little Frenchman and paused, head uplifted, yellow, forked tongue flickering lambently from venom-filled mouth.

We sat in frozen stillness. A move from the Negro or me might easily have irritated the reptile into striking blindly; the slightest stirring by de Grandin would certainly have invited immediate disaster. I could hear the colored guide's breath rasping fearfully through his flaring nostrils; the pounding of my own heart sounded in my ears. I ran my tongue lightly over suddenly parched lips, noting, with that strange ability for minute inventory we develop at such times, that the membrane seemed rough as sandpaper.

Actually, I suppose, we held our statue-still pose less than a minute. To me it seemed a century. I felt the pupils of my eyes narrowing and ceasing to function as if I had just emerged from a darkened room into brilliant sunlight, and the hand which half raised the sandwich to my lips was growing heavy as a leaden fist when sudden diversion came.

Like a beam of light shot through a moonless night something whizzed through the still afternoon air from a thicket of scrub trees some thirty feet behind us; there was a sharp, clipping sound, almost like a pair of scissors snipping shut, and the deadly reptile's head struck the ground with a smacking impact. Next instant the foul creature's blotched body writhed upward, coiling and wriggling about a three-foot shaft of slender, flexible wood like the serpent round Mercury's caduceus. A feather-tipped arrow had cleft the snake through the neck an inch or less behind its ugly, wedged-shaped head, and pinned it to the earth.

"Thank you, friend," de Grandin cried, turning toward the direction from which the rescuing shaft had sped. "I know not who you are, but I am most greatly in your debt, for—"

He broke off, his lips refusing to frame another word, his small, round eyes staring unbelievingly at the visage which peered at us between the leaves.

The Negro boy followed the Frenchman's glance, emitted a single shrill, terrified yell, turned a half somersault backward, regaining his feet with the agility of a cat and scurrying down the mud-flat where our boat lay beached. "Lawdy Gawdy," he moaned, "hit's de *ha'nt*; hit's de swamp ha'nt, sho's yuh bo'n! Lawd Gawd, lemme git erway fr'm heah! Please, suh, Gawd, sabe me, sabe dis pore nigger fr'm de ha'nt!"

He reached our punt, clambered aboard and shoved off, thrusting his pole against the lagoon bottom and driving the light craft across the water with a speed like that of a racing motorboat. Ere de Grandin or I could more than frame a furious shout he rounded the curve of a dense growth of wild rice and disappeared as completely as though dissolved into the atmosphere.

The Frenchman turned to me with a grimace. "*Cordieu*," he remarked, "we would seem to be between the devil and the sea, Friend Trowbridge. Did you, by any chance, see what I saw a moment hence?"

"Ye-es; I think so," I assented. "If you saw something so dreadful no nightmare ever equaled it—"

"*Zut!*" he laughed. "Let us not be ungrateful. Ugly the face is, I concede; but its owner did us at least one good turn." He pointed to the still-writhing snake, pinned fast to the earth by the sharp-tipped arrow. "Come, let us seek the ugly one. Though he be the devil's own twin for ugliness, he is no less deserving of our thanks. Perhaps he will show further amiability and point out an exit from this doubly damned morass of mud and serpents."

Treading cautiously, lest we step upon another snake, we advanced to the clump of scrub trees whence the repulsive face had peered. Several times de Grandin hailed the unseen monster whose arrow had saved his life, but no answer came from the softly rustling bushes. At length we pushed our way among the shrubs, and reached the covert where our unknown friend had been concealed. Nothing rewarded our search, though we passed entirely through the coppice several times.

I was about ready to drop upon the nearest rotting log for a moment's rest when de Grandin's shrill cry hailed me. "*Regardez-vous*," he commanded, pointing to the black, greasy mud which sloped into the stagnant water.

Clearly outlined in the mire as though engraved with a sculptor's tool was the imprint of a tiny, mocassined foot, so small it could have been made only by a child or a daintily formed woman.

"Well—" I began, then paused for lack of further comment.

"Well, indeed, good friend," de Grandin assented with a vigorous nod. "Do not you understand its significance?"

"U'm—can't say I do," I confessed.

"*Ah bah*, you are stupid!" he shot back. "Consider: There is no sign of a boat having been beached here; there is nothing to which a boat could have been tied within ten feet of the water's edge. We have searched the island, we know we are alone here. What then? How came the possessor of this so lovely foot here, and *how did she leave?*"

"Hanged if I know," I returned.

"Agreed," he acquiesced, "but is it not fair to assume that she waded through yonder water to that strip of land? I think so. Let us test it."

We stepped into the foul marsh-water, felt the mud sucking at our boots, then realized that the bottom was firm enough to hold us. Tentatively, step by cautious step, we forded the forty-foot channel, finding it nowhere more than waist-deep, and, bedraggled, mud-caked and thoroughly uncomfortable, finally clambered up the loamy bank of the low peninsula which jutted into the marsh-lake opposite the island of our adventure.

"*Tiens*, it seems I was right, as usual, Friend Trowbridge," the Frenchman announced as we floundered up the bank to solid ground. Again, limned in the soft, moist earth, was a tiny, slender footprint, followed by others leading toward the rank-growing woods.

"I may be wrong," he admitted, surveying the trail, "but unless I am more mistaken than I think, we have but to follow our noses and these shapely tracks to extricate ourselves. Come; *allez vous en!*"

Simple as the program sounded, it was difficult of accomplishment. The guiding footprints trailed off and lost themselves among the dead, crackling leaves with which the wood was paved, and the thick-set trees and thicker undergrowth disclosed nothing like a path. Beating the hampering bushes aside with our guns, staggering and crashing through thorny thickets by main strength and direct assault, we forced our way, turning aside from time to time as the land became spongy with seeping bogwater or an arm of the green, stagnant swamp barred our advance. We progressed slowly, striving to attain open country before darkness overtook us, but before we realized it twilight fell and we were obliged to admit ourselves hopelessly lost.

"No use, old chap," I advised. "The more we struggle, the deeper in we get; with night coming on our chances of being mired in the swamp are a hundred to one. Best make camp and wait for daylight. We can build a fire and—"

"May Satan bake me in his oven if we do!" de Grandin interrupted. "Are we the Babes in the Woods that we should lie down here and wait for death and the kindly ministrations of the robin-redbreasts! Come away, my friend; we shall assuredly win through!"

He returned to the assault with redoubled vigor, beat his way some twenty yards farther through the underbrush, then gave a loud, joyous hail.

"See what is arrived, Friend Trowbridge!" he called. "*Cordieu*, did I not promise we should find it?"

Heavy-footed, staggering with fatigue, I dragged myself to where he stood, and stared in amazement at the barrier barring our path.

Ten feet away stood an ancient wall, gray with weather and lichen-spotted with age. Here and there patches of the stucco with which it had originally been dressed had peeled away, exposing the core of antique firebrick.

"Right or left?" de Grandin asked, drawing a coin from his pocket. "Heads we proceed right; tails, left." He spun the silver disk in the air and caught it between his palms. "*Bon*, we go right," he announced, shouldering his gun and turning on his heel to follow the wall.

A few minutes' walk brought us to a break in the barrier where four massive posts of roughly dressed stone stood sentry. There should have been gates between them, but only ancient hand-wrought hinges, almost eaten away with rust, remained. Graven in the nearest pillar was an escutcheon on which had been carved some sort of armorial device, but the moss of many decades had smothered the crest so that its form was indistinguishable.

Beyond the yawning gateway stood a tiny, box-like gatekeeper's lodge, like the wall, constructed of brick faced with stucco. Tiles had scuffed from its antiquated roof, the panes of old, green bottle-glass were smashed from its leaded casements; the massive door of age-discolored oak leaned outward drunkenly, its sole support, a single lower hinge with joints long since solidified with rust.

Before us stretched the avenue, a mere unkept, overgrown trail straggling between two rows of honey locusts. Alternating shafts of moonlight and shadow barred its course like stripes upon a convict's clothes. Nothing moved among the trees, not even a moth or a bird belated in its homeward flight. Despite myself, I shivered as I gazed on the desolation of this place of bygone splendor. It was as if the ghosts of ten generations of long-dead gentlefolk rose up and bade us stay our trespassing steps.

"*Eh bien*, it is not cheerful," de Grandin admitted with a somewhat rueful grin, "but there is the promise of four walls and at least the remnant of a roof beyond. Let us see what we shall see, Friend Trowbridge."

We passed between the empty gate-pillars and strode up the driveway, traversing perhaps a hundred yards before we saw the house—a low, age-ravaged building of rough gray stone set in the midst of a level, untended grass plot and circled by a fourteen-foot moat filled with green, stagnant water in which floated a few despondent-looking lily pads. The avenue continued to a crumbling causeway, broke abruptly at the moat's lip, then took up its course to the grilled entrance of the house. Two tumbledown pillars reared astride the driveway at the farther side of the break, and swung between them, amazingly, was a mediæval drawbridge of stout oaken planks held up by strands of strong, almost new Manila hawser.

"*Grand diable,*" the Frenchman murmured wonderingly, "a *château fort*—here! How comes it?"

"I don't know," I responded, "but here it is, and it's in tolerable repair—what's more, someone lives in it. See, there's a light behind that window."

He looked, then nodded briefly. "My friend," he assured me, "I damnation think we shall eat and sleep within walls tonight.

"*Allo,*" he shouted through cupped hands, "*holà, là-haut*; we hunger, we thirst, we are lost; we are miserable!"

Twice more he hailed the silent house before lights stirred behind the narrow windows piercing its walls. Finally the iron grille guarding the door swung slowly outward and an elderly, stoop-shouldered man shuffled out, an old-fashioned bull's-eye lantern dangling in his left hand, a modern and efficient-looking repeating rifle cradled in the crook of his right elbow.

"Who calls?" he asked, peering through the darkness and pausing to flash his smoky lantern in our direction. "Who is it?"

"*Mordieu,* two weary, wayworn travelers, no more," de Grandin answered. "All afternoon we have battled with this *sacré* woodland, and lost ourselves most thoroughly. We are tired, *Monsieur*, we are enervated, and the magnitude of our hunger is matched only by that of our thirst."

"Where are you from?" the other challenged, placing his lamp on the ground and surveying us suspiciously.

"From the hunting-lodge of Monsieur Wardman Gregory. In a fortuneless moment we accepted his invitation to come South and hunt the detestable little birds which frequent these morasses. This afternoon our seventy-times-damned traitor of a guide fled from us, leaving us to perish in a wilderness infested by snakes and devil-faced monsters of the woods. Surely, you will not deny us shelter?"

"If you're Gregory's guests it's all right," the other returned, "but if you come from *him*—you needn't look for mercy if I find it out."

"*Monsieur,*" de Grandin assured him, "half of what you say is intelligible, the other half is meaningless. The 'him' of whom you speak is a total stranger to us; but our hunger and fatigue is a real and present thing. Permit that we enter, if you please."

The master of the house eyed us suspiciously a second time; then he turned from his inspection and drew back the ratchet which held the hawser-drum. Creakingly, the drawbridge descended and bumped into place against its stone sill. "Come over," the old man called, taking up his gun and holding it in readiness, "but remember, the first false move you make means a bullet."

"*Parbleu,* he is churlish, this one," de Grandin whispered as we strode across the echoing planks.

Arrived beyond the moat, we assisted our unwilling host to rewind the ropes operating the bridge, and in compliance with a gesture containing more of suspicion than courtesy preceded him to the house.

THE BUILDING'S GRAY, BARE rooms were in keeping with its gray, dilapidated exterior; age and lack of care had more than softened the antique furnishings, it had reduced them to a dead level of tonelessness, without accent, making the big, stone-paved hall in which they stood seem empty and monotonous.

Our host put down his lantern and gun, then called abruptly: "Minerva— Poseidon—we have guests, prepare some food, make haste!"

Through a swinging door connecting with a rear apartment an ancient, wrinkled little yellow woman sidled, paused at the threshold and looked about her uncertainly. "Did yuh say we all has *guests*, Marse Jawge?" she asked incredulously.

"Yes," replied her master, "they've been traveling all day, too. Shake up something to eat, quickly."

"Yas, suh," she returned and scuttled back to her kitchen like a frightened rabbit scurrying into its burrow.

She reappeared in a few minutes, followed by an aged and intensely black little man, each of them bearing a tray on which were slices of cold roast fowl, fresh white bread, preserved fruits, coffee and decanters of red, home-made wine. These they set on the massive table occupying the center of the room, and spread fresh napkins of coarse but carefully bleached linen, then stood waiting attentively.

A certain fumbling ineptness in their movements made me glance sharply at them a second time. Realization was slow in coming, but when it burst upon me I could hardly repress an exclamation. Both the aged servants were stone-blind; only the familiarity of long association enabled them to move about the room with the freedom of those possessing vision. I glanced hastily at de Grandin, and noted that his narrow, expressive face was alight with curiosity as he beheld the expressionless, sightless eyes of the servants.

Our host accompanied us to table and poured a cup of coffee and a glass of wine for himself as soon as we began our attack on the more substantial portions of the menu. He was a man well advanced in years, thin-faced, lean and sunburned almost to the point of desiccation. Time had not dealt gently with him; his long, high-cheeked face, rendered longer by the drooping gray mustache and imperial he affected, seemed to have been beaten into angularity by merciless hammer-blows of unkind fortune. His lips were thin, almost colorless and exceedingly bitter in expression; his deep-set, dark eyes glowed and smoldered with a light of perpetual anger mingled with habitual distrust. He wore a suit of coarse linen crash, poorly tailored but spotlessly clean; his white-cotton shirt had seen better days, though not recently, for its wristbands were frayed and tattered: at the edges, though it, too, was immaculate as though fresh from the laundress's hands.

Ravenous from his fast and the exhausting exercise of the afternoon de Grandin did voracious justice to the meal, but though his mouth was too full for articulate speech, his little, round blue eyes looked eloquent curiosity as they roved round the big, stone-floored hall, rested on the ancient, moldering tapestries and the dull Flemish oak furniture, and finally took minute inventory of our host.

The other noted the little Frenchman's wondering eyes and smiled with a sort of mournful pride. "The house dates from Jean Ribault's unfortunate attempt to colonize the coast," he informed us. "Georges Ducharme, an ancestor of mine, accompanied one of the unsuccessful expeditions to the New World, and when the colonists rose against their leaders at Port Royal, he and a few companions beat a path through the wilderness and finally settled here. This place was old when the foundations of Jamestown were laid. For almost four hundred years the Ducharmes have lived here, serving neither French king nor English, Federal Government nor Confederate States—they are and have always been a law unto themselves, accountable to none but their own consciences and God, sirs."

"U'm?" de Grandin cleared his mouth of roast pheasant and bread with a prodigious swallow, then helped himself to a generous stoup of home-made wine. "And you are the last of the Ducharmes, *Monsieur?*"

Quick suspicion was reborn in the other's dark, deep-set eyes as he regarded the Frenchman. For a moment he paused as a man may pause for breath before diving into a chilling stream; then, "Yes," he answered shortly. "I am the last of an ancient line. With me the house of Ducharme ceases to exist."

De Grandin tweaked the waxed ends of his tiny blond mustache after the manner of a well-fed tom-cat combing his whiskers. "Tell me, Monsieur Ducharme," he demanded as he chose a cigarette from his case with deliberate care and set it alight in the flame of one of the tall candles flickering on the table, "you have, presumably, passed the better part of your life here; of a certainty you are familiar with the neighborhood and its traditions. Have you, by any fortunate chance, heard of a certain monstrosity, a thing of infinite hideousness of appearance, which traverses the trackless wastes of these swamps? Today at noon I was all but exterminated by a venomous serpent, but a timely arrow—*an arrow*, mind you—shot from a near-by thicket, saved my life. Immediately I would have given thanks to the unknown archer who delivered me from the reptile, but when I turned to make acknowledgment, I beheld a face so vilely ugly, so exceedingly hideous, that it startled me to silence. *Eh bien*, it did more than that to our superstitious Negro guide. He shrieked something about a specter which haunts the swampland and fled incontinently, leaving us to face the wilderness alone—may seven foul fiends torment his spirit unceasingly in the world to come!

"Thereafter we did search for some trace of the ill-favored one, but nothing could we find save only a few footprints—*parbleu*, such footprints as a princess might have boasted to possess!" He bunched his slender fingers at his lips and wafted an ecstatic kiss toward the vaulted stone ceiling.

Ducharme made a queer, choking noise in his throat. "You—you found footprints! You—traced—them—here?" he asked in an odd, dry voice, rising and gripping his chair till the tendons showed in lines of high, white relief against the backs of his straining hands.

"By no means," de Grandin answered. "Though we did struggle like flies upon the *papier des mouches* to extricate ourselves from this detestable morass, we found neither sign nor trace of human thing until we were stopped by the wall which girdles your estate, for which last the good God be devoutly thanked!"

Ducharme bent a long, questioning look on the little Frenchman, then shrugged his shoulders. "No matter," he murmured as though speaking to himself; "if you're *his* messengers I'll know it soon enough, and I'll know how to deal with you."

Aloud he announced: "You are probably tired after the day's exertions. If you've quite finished your repast, we may as well retire—we sleep early at Ducharme Hall."

Beside the newel-post of the wide, broad-stepped staircase curving upward from the hall stood a small oaken table bearing several home-dipped candles in standards of antique silver. Taking one of these, our host lit it from the candelabrum on the dining-table, handed it to me, then repeated the process and supplied de Grandin with a taper. "I'll show you to your room," he offered with a courteous bow.

We trooped up the stairs, turned down a narrow, stone-paved corridor and, at Ducharme's invitation, entered a high-celled, stone-floored chamber lighted by a single narrow window with leaded panes of ancient greenish glass and furnished with a four-post canopied bed, a massive chest of deep-carven oak and two straight-backed cathedral chairs which would have brought their weight in gold at a Madison Avenue antique dealer's.

"I'll have Poseidon wait on you in the morning," our host promised. "In spite of his natural handicaps he makes an excellent valet." What seemed to me a cruel smile flickered across the thin, pale lips beneath his drooping mustache as he concluded the announcement, bowed politely and backed from the room, drawing the door soundlessly shut behind him.

For a moment I stood in the center of the little, narrow room, striving to make a survey of our surroundings by the light of our tallow dips; then, moved by a sudden impulse, I ran on tiptoe to the door, seized its ancient, hand-wrought handle and pulled with all my might. Firm as though nailed to its easing, it resisted my strongest effort. As I gave over the attempt to force the panels open and turned in panic to de Grandin I thought I heard the muted echo of a low, malicious chuckle in the darkened corridor outside.

"I say, de Grandin," I whispered, "do you realize we're caught here like flies in a spider-web?"

"Very probably," he replied, smothering a yawn. "What of it? If they slit our throats while we sleep we shall at least have the advantage of a few minutes' repose before bidding Saint Peter *bonjour*. Come, let us sleep."

But despite his assumed indifference I noticed that he placed one of the great carved chairs before the door in such manner that anyone entering the apartment would do so at imminent peril of barked shins, perhaps of a broken leg, and that he removed only his boots and jacket and lay down with his vicious little automatic pistol ready to his hand.

"TROWBRIDGE, MON VIEUX, AWAKE, arise and behold!" de Grandin's sharp whisper cut through my morning sleep. The early October day was well advanced, for a patch of warm golden sunlight lay in a prism-mottled field on the stone pavement of the room, little half-moons of opalescent coloring marking the curved lenses of the green bottle-glass of the casement through which the beams came. Gazing with fixed intensity at some object below, the little Frenchman stood at the half-opened window and motioned me to join him."

As I stepped across the chilled paving-blocks of the bedroom floor the high sweet notes of the polonaise from *Mignon* floated up to us, the singer taking the quadruple trills with the easy grace of a swallow skimming over sunlit water, never faltering in the vocal calisthenics which give pause to many a professional musician. "Wha—who—" I stammered wonderingly as I reached his side. "I thought Ducharme said—"

"S-s-st!" He cut me off. "Remark her; *c'est belle, n'est-ce-pas?*"

Just beyond the drawbridge, full in the rich flood of early-morning sunlight stood a girl, slim, straight and virginal as a hazel wand, her head thrown back, a perfect torrent of clear, wine-rich soprano melody issuing from her throat. Only the rippling cascade of her abundant, wavy auburn hair told her sex, for from feet to throat she was arrayed like a boy—small, sturdy woodsman's moccasins laced calf-high about her straight, slender legs, riding-breeches of brown corduroy belted about her slight waist by a wide girdle of soft brown leather, an olive-drab flannel shirt of military pattern, rolled elbow-high at the sleeves and open at the collar encasing her spare torso. Her back was to us as she trilled her joyous aubade to the rising sun, and I noticed that a leather baldric was swung across her left shoulder, a quiver of arrows with unstrung bow thrust among them laced to the wide suede strap.

Hands as white and delicately formed as any I had ever seen fluttered graciously in rhythm to the music as she poured her very heart out in song; as she ended on a high, true note, she wove her fingers together in a very ecstasy of self-engendered emotion, stood in lovely tableau a moment, then set off toward the forest with a swinging, graceful stride which told of long days spent in walking beneath the open sky with limbs unhampered by traveling-skirts and feet unfettered by modish shoes.

"De Grandin," I exclaimed, "can it be—is it possible—those little, mocassined feet, those arrows—can *she* be the archer who killed the snake yester—"

"You do forget the face we saw," he interrupted in a bleak, monotonous voice.

"But couldn't she—isn't it possible she wore a dreadful mask for some reason—"

"One wonders," he returned before I could complete my argument. "One also wonders who she is and what she does here."

"Yes, Ducharme distinctly told us he was the only one—"

"*Ah bah*," he cut in. "That Monsieur Ducharme, I think he flatters himself he fools us, Friend Trowbridge. Meanwhile—*allo?* Who calls?"

A soft, timid knock sounded on our door, followed by a second rap, then, after a discreet interval, a third.

"Hit's Poseidon, suh," the old Negro's voice answered quaveringly. "Marse Jawge, he done tol' me ter come up yere an' valet y'all dis mo'nin'. Is yuh ready fo' yo' baffs an' shaves, suhs? Ah done got de watah yere fo' yuh."

"By all means, enter, my excellent one," de Grandin replied, crossing to the door and flinging it back. With a start I noticed that it swung inward without resistance.

The old blind servant shuffled into the room, a towel and two old-fashioned razors in one hand, a porcelain basin clutched beneath his elbow and a pewter pitcher of steaming water in the other hand. "Ah'll shave yuh first, den drag in de baff, if yuh please, suh," he announced, turning his sightless eyes toward the corridor where a long, tin bathtub rested in readiness.

"*Bien non, mon brave*," de Grandin denied, "I shall shave myself, as I have done each day since my sixteenth year. Bring me the mirror, if you please."

"Mirruh, suh?" the servant queried. "Dey ain't no sech thing in de house, suh. Minervy an' me, we don' need nuffin like hit, an' Marse Jawge, he manage ter git erlong wid me ter shave him. Mis' Clarimonde, she ain't nebber seen 'er—oh, Lawdy, suh, please, *please*, suh, don' nebber tell Marse Jawge Ah said nuffin erbout—"

"*Tiens*, my friend," the Frenchman reassured, "fear nothing. The best of us sometimes make slips of the tongue. Your lapse from duty shall be safe in my keeping. Meanwhile, however excellently you may barber your master, I fear I must dispense with your services. Trowbridge, my friend, lend me your glasses, if you please."

"My glasses?" I repeated, in surprise. "What—"

"But certainly. Must one draw diagrams before you understand? Is Jules de Grandin a fool, or has he sense? Observe." Taking my spectacles from the carved chest, he fixed them to the back of one of the tall chairs, draping his jacket behind the lenses to make a dark background. Thus equipped he proceeded to regard his image in the primitive mirror while he spread the lather thickly over cheeks and chin, then scraped it off with the exquisitely sharp blade of the perfectly balanced English razor the blind servant handed him.

"*Très bon*," he announced with a satisfied smile. "Behold, I am my own valet this morning, nor has my complexion suffered so much as one little scratch. This old one here, he seems too innocent to practise any wrong on us, but—he who goes to dinner with the devil should take with him a long spoon. Me, I do not care to take unnecessary chances."

Following de Grandin's example, I shaved myself with the aid of my glasses-mirror, and one after the other we laved ourselves in the tubs of luke-warm water the ancient servitor dragged in from the hall.

"If y'all is ready, suhs," the Negro announced as we completed our toilets, "Ah'll 'scort yuh to de dinin'-room. Marse Jawge is waitin' yo' pleasure below."

"Ah, good morning, gentlemen," Ducharme greeted as we joined him in the main hall. "I trust you enjoyed a good night's rest?"

The Frenchman eyed him critically. "I have had worse," he replied. "However, the sense of security obtained by well-bolted doors is not greatly heightened by knowledge that the locks operate from the further side, *Monsieur*.

A faint flush mounted our host's thin cheeks at de Grandin's thrust, but he chose to ignore it. "Minerva!" he cried sharply, turning toward the kitchen. "The gentlemen are down; bring in some breakfast."

The old, blind Negress emerged from her quarters with the promptness of a cuckoo coming from its cell as the clock strikes the hour, and placed great bowls of steaming cornmeal mush before us. Idly, I noticed that the pitcher for the milk accompanying the mush was of unglazed pottery and the pot in which the steaming coffee was served was of tarnished, dull-finished silver.

With a rather impatient gesture, Ducharme motioned us to eat and excused himself from joining us by saying he had breakfasted an hour or so before.

De Grandin's little eyes scarcely left our host's face as he ate ravenously, but though he seemed on the point of putting some question point-blank more than once, he evidently thought better of it, and held his peace.

"It's impossible for me to get a guide for you this morning, gentlemen," Ducharme apologized as we finished breakfast, "and it's hardly practicable for me to accompany you myself. However, if you'll be good enough to remain another day, I think—perhaps—I may be able to find someone to take you back to Gregory's. Provided, of course, you really wish to go there." Something like a sneer crossed his lips as he concluded, and de Grandin was on his feet instantly, his small face livid with rage.

"*Monsieur*," he protested, his little eyes snapping ominously, "on more than one occasion you have been good enough to intimate we are impostors. I have heard much of your vaunted Southern hospitality in the past, but the sample you display leaves much to be desired. If you will be so good as to stand aside we shall give ourselves the pleasure of shaking your dust from our feet forthwith. Meantime, since you have small liking for the post of social host, permit that we compensate you for our entertainment." His face still white with fury, he thrust his hand into his pocket, withdrew a roll of bills and tossed several on the table. "I trust that is sufficient," he added cuttingly. "Count it; if you desire more, more shall be forthcoming."

Ducharme had risen with de Grandin. As the Frenchman finished his tirade, he stepped quickly to the corner and snatched up his rifle. "If either of you attempts to leave this house before I give permission," he announced in a low, menacing voice, "so help me God, I'll blow his head off!" With a quick backward step he reached the door, slipped through it and banged it shut behind him.

"Are you going to stand this?" I demanded angrily, turning to de Grandin. "The man's mad—mad as a hatter. We'll be murdered before sunset if we don't get away!"

"I think not so," he returned, resuming his seat and lighting a cigarette. "As for killing us, he will need more speed than he showed just now. I had him covered from my pocket before he took up his gun, and could have stopped his words with a bullet any time I was so minded, but—I did not care to. There are things which interest me about this place, Friend Trowbridge, and I desire to remain until my curiosity is satisfied."

"But his insinuations—his insulting doubt—" I began.

"*Tiens*, it *was* well done was it not?" he interrupted with a self-satisfied smile. "*Barbe d'un chameau*, I play-acted so well I did almost deceive myself!"

"Then you weren't really angry—"

"Jules de Grandin is quick to anger, my friend, if the provocation be sufficient, but never has he bitten off his nose through desire to revenge himself upon his face. No. Another time I might have resented his boorishness. This morning I desire to remain more greatly than I wish to leave; but should I disclose my real desires he would undoubtlessly insist upon our going. *Alors*, I make the monkey business. To make our welcome doubly sure I deceive Monsieur Ducharme to think that leaving is our primary desire. *C'est très simple, n'est-ce-pas?*"

"I suppose so," I admitted, "but what earthly reason have you for wanting to stay in this confounded place?"

"One wonders," he returned enigmatically, blowing a twin cloud of smoke from his nostrils.

"One certainly does," I agreed angrily. "I, for one—"

He tossed his cigarette into his porringer and rose abruptly. "Is it of significance to you, my friend, that this *sacré* house contains not only not a single mirror, but not so much as one polished surface in which one may by any chance behold himself with the exception of the spectacles which adorn your kindly nose this minute? Or that the servants here are blind?" he added as I shook my head doubtfully. "Or that Monsieur Ducharme has deliberately attempted to mislead us into thinking that he, we and the two blind ones are the only tenants of the place?"

"It is mystifying," I agreed, "but I can't seem to fit the facts into any kind of pattern. Probably they're just coincidences, and—"

"Coincidence is the name we give to that we can not otherwise explain," he interrupted. "Me, I have arrived already at a theory, though much still remains obscure. At dinner tonight I shall let fly a random shot; who knows what it may bring down?"

DUCHARME KEPT OUT OF sight the remainder of the day, and it was not till well after dark we saw him again. We were just concluding our evening meal when he let himself in, a more amiable expression on his sour face than I had seen before.

"Dr. de Grandin, Dr. Trowbridge," he greeted as he placed his rifle in an angle of the wall and drew a chair up to the table, "I have to tender you my humblest apologies. My life has been a bitter one, gentlemen; and I live in daily dread of something I can not explain. However, if I tell you it is sufficient to make me suspicious of every stranger who comes near the house, you may understand something of the lack of courtesy I have shown you. I did doubt your word, sirs, and I renew my apologies for doing so. This morning, after warning you to stay indoors, I went to Gregory's—it's less than a three hours' trip, if you know the way—and made certain of your identity. Tomorrow, if you wish, I shall be happy to guide you to your friends."

The Frenchman bent along, speculative stare upon our host. At length: "You are satisfied from Monsieur Gregory's report that we are indeed physicians?" he asked.

"Of course—"

"Suppose I add further information. Would it interest you to know that I hold degrees from Vienna and the Sorbonne, that I have done much surgical work for the University of Paris, and that in the days after the Armistice I was among those who helped restore to pre-war appearance the faces of those noble heroes whose features had been burned away by Hunnish *flammenwerfer?*" He pronounced the last words with slow, impressive deliberation, his level, unwinking gaze fixed firmly on the dark, sullen eyes of our host.

Quick, incredulous fury flamed in the other's face. "You spying scoundrel—you damned sneak!" he cried, leaping from his chair and making for his rifle.

"Slowly!" De Grandin, too, was on his feet, his small, round eyes blazing with implacable purpose, his little, deadly pistol aimed unwaveringly at Ducharme's breast. "Greatly as I should regret it," he warned, "I shall kill you if you make one further move, *Monsieur*."

The other wavered, for there was no doubting de Grandin's sincerity.

"Ah, that is better," he remarked as Ducharme halted, then returned slowly to his seat. "Now we shall talk sense.

"A moment since, *Monsieur*," he continued as Ducharme dropped heavily into his chair and sank his face in his hands, "I did avail myself of what the Americans call the bluff. Consider, I am clever; the wool can not successfully be drawn across my eyes, and so I suspected what I now know for the truth. Yesterday an arrow saved my life; anon we found small footprints in the mud; last night when we arrived here we met with scant welcome from you, and inside the house we found you waited on by blinded servants. This morning, when I ask for a mirror that I may shave myself, your servant tells there is not one in all the house, and on sober thought I recall that I have seen no single polished surface wherein a man may behold his own image. Why is it? If strangers are unwelcome, if there be no mirrors here, if the servants be blind—is there not something hideous within these walls, something of which you know, but which you desire to be kept most secret? Again, you are not beautiful, but you would not necessarily be averse to regarding your reflection in a mirror. What then? Is it not, perhaps, I think, that you greatly desire that the ugly one—whoever it be—not only not be seen, but shall not see itself? It are highly probable.

"This morning I have seen a so lovely young girl attired for *le footing*, who sings divinely in the early sunlight. But I have not seen her face. No. However, she wears upon her back a bow and quiverful of arrows—and an arrow such as those saved me from the serpent yesterday, one little moment before we beheld the face of awful ugliness.

"Two and two invariably make four, *Monsieur*. You have said there is no other person but yourself and your servants in the house; but even as you doubted me, so I have doubted you. Indeed, from what I have seen, I know you have been untruthful; but I think you are so because of some great reason. And so I tell you of my work in restoring the wrecked faces of the soldiers of France.

"But I am no idle boaster. No. What I say is true. Call in the unfortunate young lady; I shall examine her minutely, and if it are humanly possible I shall remold her features to comeliness. If you do not consent you are a heartless, inhuman monster. Besides," he added matter-of-factly, "if you refuse I shall kill you and perform the operation anyway."

Ducharme gazed unbelievingly at him. "You really think you can do it?" he demanded.

"Have I not said it?"

"But, if you fail—"

"Jules de Grandin does not fail, *Monsieur*."

"Minerva!" Ducharme called. "Ask Miss Clarimonde to come here at once, please."

The old blind woman's slipshod footsteps sounded along the tiled floor of a back passage for a moment, then faded away as she slowly climbed a hidden flight of stairs.

For something like five minutes we sat silently. Once or twice Ducharme swallowed nervously, de Grandin's slim, white fingers drummed a noiseless, devil's tattoo on the table, I fidgeted nervously in my chair, removed my glasses and polished them, returned them to my nose, then snatched them off and fell to wiping them again. At length the light tap-tap of slippered feet sounded on the stairs and we rose together as a tall, graceful figure emerged from the stairway shadow into the aura of light thrown out by the candles.

"My daughter, gentlemen—Clarimonde, Dr. de Grandin; Dr. Trowbridge," Mr. Ducharme introduced in a voice gone thin and treble with nervousness. From the corner of my eye I could see him watching us in a sort of agony, awaiting the horror we were bound to show as the girl's face became visible.

I saw de Grandin's narrow, pointed chin jut forward as he set his jaw against the shock of the hideous countenance, then watched the indomitable will within him force his face into the semblance of an urbane smile as he stepped forward gallantly and raised the girl's slim, white hand to his lips.

The figure which stepped slowly, reluctantly, into the dull luminance of the candles was the oddest patch-work of grotesquerie I had ever seen. From feet to throat she was perfectly made as a sculptured Hebe, slim, straight, supple with the pliancy of youth and abundant health. Shoes of white satin and stockings of sheerest white silk complemented a straight, plain frock of oyster-white which assuredly had come from nowhere but Vienna or the Rue de la Paix; a Manila shawl, yellowed with years and heavily fringed, lay scarfwise over her ivory shoulders and arms; about her throat was clasped a single tight-fitting strand of large, lustrous pearls.

The sea-gems were the line of demarcation. It was as if by some sorcery of obscene surgery the lovely girl's head had been sheared off by a guillotine three inches above the clavicle and replaced by the foulest specimen from the stored-up monstrosities of a medical museum. The skin about the throat was craped and wrinkled like a toad's, and of the color of a tan boot on which black dressing has inadvertently been rubbed, then ineffectually removed. Above, the chin was firm and pointed, tapering downward from the ears in good lines, but the mouth extended a full five inches across the face, sweeping in a curving diagonal from left to right like a musical turn mark, one corner lifted in a perpetual travesty of a grin, the other sagging in a constant snarl. Between the spaces where the brows should have been the glabella was so enlarged that a protuberance almost like a horn stood out from the forehead, while the eyes, fine hazel, flecked with brown, were horrifically cocked at divergent angles so that it was impossible for her to gaze at an object directly before her without turning her head slightly to the side. The nose was long and curved, exaggeratedly high-bridged and slit down the outer side of each flaring nostril as the mouth of a hairlipped person is cleft. Like the throat, the entire face was integumented in coarse, loosely wrinkled skin of soiled brown, and, to make the contrast more shockingly incongruous, a mass of gleaming auburn hair, fine and scintillant as spun rose-gold, lay loosely coiled in a Grecian coronal above the repulsive countenance.

Had the loathsomeness been unrelieved by contrasting comeliness, the effect would have been less shocking; as it was, the hideous face inlaid between the perfect body and glowing, ruddy-diadem of hair was like the sacrilegious mutilation of a sacred picture—as though the oval of the Sistine Virgin's face were cut from the canvas and the sardonic, grinning features of a Punchinello thrust through the aperture.

To his everlasting credit, de Grandin did not flinch. Debonair as though at any social gathering, he bowed the monstrous creature to a chair and launched a continuous flow of conversation. All the while I could see his eyes returning again and again to the hideous countenance across the table, his keen surgeon's mind surveying the grotesque features and weighing his chances of success against the almost foregone certainty of failure.

THE ORDEAL LASTED SOMETHING like half an hour, and my nerves had stretched to the snapping point when sudden diversion came.

With a wild, frantic movement the girl leaped up, oversetting her chair, and faced us, her misdirected eyes rolling with a horrible ludicrousness in their sockets, tears of shame and self-pity welling from them and coursing down the sides of her grotesque face. Her wide, cavernous mouth opened obliquely and she gave scream after scream of shrill, tortured anguish. "I know; I know!" she cried frenziedly. "Don't think you've fooled me by taking all the mirrors from the house, Father! Remember, I go about the woods at will, and *there are pools of quiet water in the woods!* I know I'm hideous; I know I'm so repulsive that even the servants who wait on us must be blind! I've seen my face reflected in the moat and the swamp; I saw the horror in your eyes when you first looked at me, Dr. de Grandin; I noticed how Dr. Trowbridge couldn't bear even to glance at me just now without a shudder! Oh, God of mercy, why haven't I had courage to kill myself before?—Why did I live till I met strangers and saw them turn from me with loathing? Why—"

"*Mademoiselle*, be still!" de Grandin's sharp, incisive command cut through her hysterical words and stung her to silence. "You lament unnecessarily," he continued as she turned her goggling toad-eyes toward him. "*Monsieur*, your father, bids you come to us for a specific purpose; namely, that I inspect your countenance and give him my opinion as a surgeon concerning the possibility of cure. Attend me: I tell you I can so reshape your features that you shall be completely beautiful; you shall grace the salons of Washington, of New York, of Paris, and you shall have young men to do you honor and lay their kisses thick upon your hands and lips, and breathe their tales of love into your ears; you—"

A shriek of wild, incredulous laughter silenced him. "I? I have admirers—lovers? Dear God—the bitterness of the mockery! I am doomed to spend my life among the snakes and toads, the bats and salamanders of the swamps, a thing as hideous as the ugliest of them, cut off from all my kind, and—"

"Your fate may be a worse one, unless I can prevent it," Ducharme broke in with an odd, dry croaking voice.

We turned on him by common consent as he rasped his direful prophecy. His long, goat-like face was working spasmodically; I could see the tendons of his thin neck contracting as he swallowed nervously, and the sad, bitter lips beneath the drooping gray mustache twisted into a smile that was more than half a snarl as he gazed at de Grandin and his daughter in turn.

"You wondered why I greeted you with suspicion when you came asking food and shelter last night, gentlemen?" he asserted rather than asked, looking from the Frenchman to me. "This is why:

"As I told you last night, the Ducharmes have lived here since long before the first English colony was planted in Virginia. Although our plantation has been all but eaten up by the swamps, the family wealth holds out, and I am what is counted a rich man, even in these days of swollen fortunes. It was the custom of our family for generations to send their women to a convent at Rheims for education; the young men were sent to Oxford or Cambridge, Paris or Vienna, occasionally to Louvain or Heidelberg, and their training was completed by the grand tour.

"I followed the family tradition and studied at the Sorbonne when my undergraduate work at Oxford was completed. It was while I lived in Paris I met Inocencia. She was an *Argentina*—a native of the Argentine, a dancer in a cabaret, and as lovely a creature as ever set a man's blood afire. All the students were mad about her, but Ruiz, a fellow-countryman of hers, and I were the most favored of her coterie of suitors.

"Leandro Ruiz was a medical student, the son of an enormously wealthy cattleman, who took to surgery from an innate love of blood and suffering rather than from any wish to serve humanity or earn a livelihood, for he already had more money than he could ever spend, and as for humanitarianism, the devil himself had more of it.

"One night as I sat studying, there came a terrified rapping at my door, and Inocencia fell, rather than ran, into my rooms. She had struggled through the raging sleet-storm from Montmartre, and Ruiz was hot behind her. He had accosted her as she left the café, and demanded that she come forthwith and consort with him—there never was an honorable thought in the scoundrel's mind, and what he could not buy he was accustomed to take by force.

"I had barely time to lock and bar the door when Ruiz and three hired bullies came clamoring up the stairs and battered on the panels like werewolves shut out from their prey. Ha, I left my mark on him that night! As he stooped down to bawl obscenities through the keyhole I thrust, a sword-cane through the lock and blinded him in one eye. Despite his wound he hung around the door nearly all night, and it was not till two gendarmes threatened him and his companions with arrest for public disturbance that they slunk away.

"Next morning Inocencia and I arranged to be married, and as soon as the formalities of French-law could be complied with, we were wed and made a tour of Europe for our honeymoon. When we returned to Paris we heard Ruiz had contracted pneumonia the night he raged outside my quarters in the sleet, and had died and been buried in St. Sulpice. Ha, you may be sure we shed no tears at the news!

"I was nearly thirty, Inocencia barely twenty, when we married. It was not till ten years later that Clarimonde was born, and when at last we had a child to crown our union we thought our cup of joy was surely overflowing. God!" He paused, poured himself a goblet of wine and drained it to the bottom before continuing:

"No hired *bonne* was good enough to take our darling out; Inocencia herself accompanied her on every outing and filled the afternoons with recitals of the thousand cunning things our baby did and said while toddling in the park.

"One day they did not return. I was frantic and set the entire gendarmerie by the ears to search for them. Nowhere could we find a trace till finally my wife's dead body, partly decomposed, but still identifiable, was rescued from the Seine. Police investigation disclosed she had been murdered—her throat severed and her heart cut out, but not before a hundred and more disfiguring wounds had been inflicted with a knife.

"My baby's fate was still unknown, and I lived for weeks and months in a frenzy of mingled despair and hope till—" Again he paused; once more he filled and drained a wine-glass. Then: "At last my fears were set at rest. At daylight one morning the thin, pitiful wailing of a little frightened child sounded at my door, and when the *concierge* went to investigate she found Clarimonde lying there in a basket. Clarimonde, my Clarimonde, her mother's sole remaining souvenir, dressed in the baby garments she had worn the day she vanished, positively identified by the little, heart-shaped birthmark on the under side of her left arm, but, my God, how altered! Her face, gentlemen, was as you see it now, a dreadful, disfigured, mutilated mask of horror, warped and carved and twisted almost out of human semblance, save as the most grotesque caricature resembles the thing it parodies. And with her was a letter, a letter from Leandro Ruiz. The fiend had caused the report of his death to be given us, and bided his time through all the years, always studying and experimenting in plastic surgery that he might one day carry out his terrible revenge, watching Inocencia and Clarimonde when they least suspected it, familiarizing himself with their habits and ways so that he might best set his *apaches* on them and kidnap them when the time was ripe for his devil's vengeance. After dishonoring and torturing Inocencia, he killed her slowly—cut her heart from her living breast before he slashed her throat. The next three months he spent carefully disfiguring the features of our baby, adding horror on horror to the poor, helpless face as though he were a sculptor working out the details of a statue with slow, painstaking care. At last, when even he could think of nothing more to add to the devastation he had made, he laid the poor, mutilated mite on my doorstep with a note describing his acts, and containing the promise that all his life and all his boundless wealth would be devoted to making his revenge complete.

"You wonder how he could do more? Gentlemen, you can not think how vile humanity can be until you've known Leandro Ruiz. Listen: When Clarimonde reaches her twenty-first year, he said he would come for her. If death had taken him meanwhile, he would leave a sum of money to pay those who carried out his will. He, or his hirelings, would come for her, and though she hid behind locked doors and armed men, they would ravish her away, cut out her tongue to render her incapable of speech, *then exhibit her for hire in a freak show*—make my poor, disfigured baby girl the object of yokels' gawking curiosity throughout the towns and provinces of Europe and South America!

"I fled from Paris as Lot fled from Sodom, and brought my poor, maimed child to Ducharme Hall. Here I secured Minerva and Poseidon for servants, because both were blind and could not let fall any remarks which would make

Clarimonde realize her deformity. I secured blind teachers and tutors; she is as well educated as any seminary graduate; every luxury that money could buy has been given her, but never has there been a mirror in Ducharme Hall, or anything which could serve as a mirror, since we came here from Paris.

"Now, gentlemen, perhaps you understand the grounds for my suspicions? Clarimonde was twenty-one this month."

Jules de Grandin twisted the fine, blond hairs of his diminutive mustache until they stood out in twin needle-points each side of his mouth, and fixed a level, unwinking stare upon our host. "*Monsieur*," he said, "a moment hence I was all for going to the North; I would have argued to the death against a moment's delay which kept me from performing the necessary work to restore Mademoiselle Clarimonde's features to their pristine loveliness. Now, *parbleu*, five men and ten little boys could not drag me from this spot. We shall wait here, *Monsieur*, we shall stay here, rooted as firmly as the tallest oak in yonder forest, until this Monsieur Ruiz and his corps of assassins appear. Then"—he twisted the ends of his mustache still more fiercely, and the lightning-flashes in his little, round eyes were cold as arctic ice and hot as volcanic fire—"then, by damn, I think those seventy-six-thousand-times accursed miscreants shall find that he who would step into the hornet's nest would be advised to wear heavy boots. Yes; I have said it."

FROM THAT NIGHT DUCHARME Hall was more like a castle under siege than ever. In terror of abduction Clarimonde no longer roamed the woods, and Mr. Ducharme, de Grandin or I was always on lookout for any strangers who might appear inside the walled park. A week, ten days passed quietly, and we resumed our plans for returning North, where the deformed girl's face could receive expert surgical treatment.

"I shall give Mademoiselle Clarimonde my undivided attention until all is accomplished," de Grandin told me as we lay in bed one evening while the October wind soughed and moaned through the locust-trees bordering the avenue and a pack of tempest-driven storm clouds harried the moon like hounds pursuing a fleeing doe. "With your permission I shall leave your house and take up residence in the hospital, Friend Trowbridge, and neither day nor night shall I be beyond call of the patient. I shall—

"*Attendez, voilà les assassins!*" Faintly as the scuffing of a dried twig against the house, there came the gentle sound of something scratching against the rubble-stone of the wall.

For a moment the Frenchman lay rigid; then with bewildering quickness he leaped from the bed, bundled the sheets and pillows together in simulation of a person covered with bedclothes, and snatched down one of the heavy silken cords binding back the draperies which hung in mildewed festoons, between the mahogany posts. "Silence!" he cautioned, tiptoeing across the chamber and taking his station beside the open casement. "No noise, my friend, but if it is possible, do you creep forward and peer out, then tell me what it is you see."

Cautiously, I followed his instructions, rested my chin upon the wide stone window-sill and cast a hurried glance down the wall.

Agilely as a cat, a man encased in close-fitting black jersey and tights was scaling the side of the house by aid of a hooked ladder similar to those firemen use. Behind him came a companion, similarly costumed and equipped, and even as I watched them I could not but marvel at the almost total silence in which they swarmed up the rough stones.

I whispered my discovery to de Grandin, and saw him nod once understandingly. "*Voleurs de nuit*—professional burglars," he pronounced. "He chose expert helpers, this one. Let us await them."

A moment later there was a soft, rubbing sound as a long steel hook, well wrapped in tire-tape, crept like a living thing across the window-sill, and was followed in a moment by a slender and none too clean set of fingers which reached exploringly through the casement.

In another instant a head covered by a tight-fitting black jersey cowl loomed over the sill, the masked eyes peered searchingly about the candlelit room; then, apparently satisfied that someone occupied the bed and slept soundly, the intruder crept agilely across the sill, landed on the stone floor with a soft thud and cleared the space between bed and window in a single feline leap.

There was the glint of candlelight on sharpened steel and a fiendish-looking stiletto flashed downward in a murderous arc and buried itself to the hilt in the pillow which lay muffled in the blankets where I had lain two minutes before.

Like a terrier pouncing on a rat de Grandin leaped on the assassin's shoulders. While awaiting the intruder's advent he had looped the strong curtain cord into a running noose, and as he landed on the other's back, driving his face down among the bedding and effectively smothering outcry, he slipped the strangling string about the burglar's throat, drew it tight with a single dexterous jerk, then crossed its ends and pulled them as one might pull the draw-string of a sack. "Ha, good *Monsieur le Meurtrier*," he whispered exultantly, "I serve you a dish for which you have small belly, *n'est-ce-pas?* Eat your fill, my friend, do not stint yourself, Jules de Grandin has plentiful supply of such food for you!

"So!" He straightened quickly and whipped the cord from his captive's throat. "I damnation think you will give us small trouble for some time, my friend. Attention, Friend Trowbridge, the other comes!"

Once more he took his place beside the window, once more he cast his strangling cord as a masked head protruded into the room. In a moment two black-clad, unconscious forms lay side by side upon the bed.

"Haste, my friend, *dépêchez vous*," he ordered, beginning to disrobe our prisoners as he spoke. "I do dislike to ruin Monsieur Ducharme's bedding, but we must work with what we have. Tear strips from the sheets and bind these unregenerate sons of pigs fast. There is no time to lose; a moment hence and we must don their disguises and perform that which they set out to do."

We worked feverishly, tying the two desperadoes in strip after strip of linen ripped from the sheets, gagging them, blindfolding them; finally, as an added precaution, lashing their hands and feet to the head—and footposts of the bed. Then, shedding our pajamas, we struggled into the tightfitting jerseys the prisoners had worn. The stocking-like garments were clammily wet and chilled me to the marrow as I drew them on, but the Frenchman gave me no time for complaint. "*Allons, en route*, make haste!" he ordered.

Leaving the unconscious thugs to such meditations as they might have upon regaining consciousness, we hastened to Ducharme's chamber.

"Fear not, it is I," de Grandin called as he beat imperatively on our host's door. "In our chamber repose two villains who gained entrance by means of scaling ladders—from the feel of their clothes, which we now wear, I should say they swam your moat. We go now to lower the drawbridge and let the master villain in. Do you be ready to receive him!"

"*Holà!*" he called a moment later as we let ourselves out the front door and lowered the drawbridge. "Come forth, all is prepared!"

Two men emerged from the darkness beyond the moat in answer to his hail, one a tall, stoop-shouldered fellow arrayed in ill-fitting and obviously new clothes, the other small, frail-looking, and enveloped from neck to high-heeled boots in a dark mackintosh or raincoat of some sort which hung about his spare figure like the cloak of a conspirator in a melodramatic opera. There was something infinitely wicked in the slouching truculent swagger of the big, stoop-shouldered bully, something which suggested brute strength, brute courage and brute ferocity; but there was something infinitely more sinister in the mincing, precise walk of his smaller companion, who advanced with an odd sort of gait, placing one foot precisely before the other like a tango dancer performing to the rhythm of inaudible music.

"Judas Iscariot and Company," de Grandin whispered to me as the queerly assorted couple set foot on the drawbridge; then with an imperative wave of his hand he beckoned them toward the house and set off up the driveway at a rapid walk. "We must not let them get close enough to suspect," he whispered, quickening his pace. "All cats are gray in the dark, and we much resemble their friends at a distance, but it is better that we take no chances."

Once or twice the other two called to us, demanding to know if we had encountered resistance, but de Grandin's only answer was another gesture, urging them to haste, and we were still some ten feet in the lead when we reached the door, swung it open and slipped into the house, awaiting the others' advent.

The candles burned with a flickering, uncertain light, scarcely more than staining the darkness flooding the big stone hall as the two men trailed us through the door. By the table, the candlelight falling full upon her mutilated face, stood Clarimonde Ducharme, her hideously distorted eyes rolling pathetically in their elongated sockets as she turned her head from side to side in an effort to get a better view of the intruders.

A shrill, cackling laugh burst from the smaller man. "Look at that; Henri," he bade, catching his breath with an odd, sucking sound. "Look at that. That's *my* work; isn't it a masterpiece?"

Mockingly, he snatched the wide-brimmed soft black-felt hat from his head, laid it over his heart, then swept it to the floor as he bowed profoundly to the girl. "*Señorita hermosa, yo beso sus manos!*" he declared, then burst into another cackle of cachinnating laughter. As he removed his headgear I observed he was bald as an egg, thickly wrinkled, and wore a monocle of dark glass in his right eye.

His companion growled an inarticulate comment, then turned toward us with an expectant look. "Now?" he asked. "Shall I do it now and get it over?"

"*Si, como no?*—certainly, why not?" the smaller man lisped. "They've served their purpose, have they not?"

"Right," the big man returned. "They did the job, and dead men tell no tales—"

There was murderous menace in every movement of his big body as he swaggered toward de Grandin. "Come, little duckie," he bade mockingly in *gamin* French, "come and be killed. We can't have you running loose and babbling tales of what you've seen tonight the first time you get your hide full of *vin ordinaire.* Say your prayers, if you know any; you've precious little time to do it. Come, duckie—" As he advanced he thrust his hand beneath his ill-fitting jacket and drew a knife of fearsome proportions, whetting it softly against the heel of his hand, smiling to himself as though anticipating a rare bit of sport.

De Grandin gave ground before the other's onslaught. Two or three backward running steps he took, increasing the distance between them, then paused.

With a flick of his left hand he swept the disguising hood from his features and smiled almost tenderly at the astonished bully. "*Monsieur,*" he announced softly, "it sometimes happens that the weasel discovers the duck he hunts to be an eagle in disguise. So it would seem tonight. You have three seconds to live; make the most of them. *Un—deux—trois!*" The spiteful, whip-like report of pistol sounded sharp punctuation to his third count, and the bravo stumbled back a step, an expression of amazement on his coarse face, a tiny bruised-looking circle almost precisely bisecting the line of heavy, black brows which met above his nose.

"Wha—what?" the smaller villain began in a strangled, frightened scream, wheeling on de Grandin and snatching at a weapon beneath his cloak.

But George Ducharme leaped out of the darkness like a lion avenging the slaughter of its mate and bore him, screaming madly, to the floor. "At last, Leandro Ruiz—at last!" he shouted exultantly, fastening his fingers on the other's thin, corded neck and pressing his thumb into the sallow, flaccid flesh. "At last I've got you! You killed my wife, you deformed my baby, you've made me live in a hell of fear for eighteen years; but now I've got you—*I've got you!*"

"*Eh bien*, have a care, *Monsieur*, you are unduly rough!" de Grandin protested, tapping Ducharme's shoulder gently, "Be careful I implore you!"

"What?" George Ducharme cried angrily, looking up at the diminutive Frenchman, but retaining his strangling hold on his foeman's throat. "D'ye mean I'm not to treat this dog as he deserves?"

The other's narrow shoulders rose nearly level with his ears in an eloquent shrug. "I did but caution you, my friend," he answered mildly. "When one is very angry one easily forgets one's strength. Be careful, or you kill him too swiftly.

"Come, Friend Trowbridge, the night is fine outside. Let us admire the view."

The prisoners in the bedroom were only too glad to take their departure without stopping to inquire concerning their late employer. From remarks they dropped while we hunted clothing to replace the conspicuous black tights of which we had relieved them, I gathered they had distrusted Ruiz's good faith, and insisted on payment in advance. That Monsieur Ruiz had left, leaving no address, and consequently would not be in position to extort return of his fee with the aid of the gigantic Henri was the best possible news we could have given them, and they took speedy farewell of us.

THE FOLLOWING DAY DE Grandin and I set out for the North, accompanied by the Ducharmes. Clarimonde traveled closely veiled, and we occupied a drawing-room suite on the B. & O. fast train which bore us from Washington to Harrisonville. The first night in New Jersey was spent at my house, Clarimonde keeping closely to her room, lest Nora McGinnis, my faithful but garrulous Irish household factotum, behold her mutilated features and spread news of them along the kitchen-door telegraph line.

A suite of rooms at Mercy Hospital was engaged the following day, and true to his promise, de Grandin took up residence in the institution, eating sleeping and passing his entire time within half a minute's walk of his patient.

What passed in the private operating-room Ducharme's money made possible for his daughter's case I did not know, for the press of my own neglected practise kept me busy through most of the daylight hours, and de Grandin performed his work unassisted except by three special nurses who, like him, spent their entire time on duty in the special suite secured for Clarimonde.

Nearly three months passed before my office telephone shrilled one bright Sunday morning and de Grandin's excited voice informed me he was about to remove the bandages from his charge. Ten minutes later, out of breath, with haste, I stood in the comfortably furnished sitting-room of Clarimonde's suite, and stared fascinated at the little Frenchman who posed and postured beside his patient like a lecturer about to begin his discourse.

"My friends," he announced, sweeping the circle composed of Ducharme, the nurses and me with twinkling eyes, "this is one of the supreme moments of my life. Should my workmanship be successful, I shall proceed forthwith to get most vilely, piggishly intoxicated. If I have failed"—he paused dramatically, then drew a small, silver-mounted automatic pistol from his pocket and laid it on the table beside him—"if I have failed, Friend Trowbridge, I beseech you, write in the death certificate that, my suicide was induced by a broken heart. *Allons.*"

With a pair of surgical scissors he slit the outermost layer of bandages about the girl's face and began unwinding the white gauze with slow, deliberate movements.

"*A-a-ah!*" The long-drawn exclamation came unbidden from all of us in chorus.

The wrinkled, blotched, leather-like skin which had covered the girl's face had, by some alchemy employed by de Grandin, been bleached to an incredibly beautiful shade of light, suntanned *écru*, smooth as country cream and iridescent as an alloy of gold and platinum. Above a high, straight brow of creamy whiteness her soft auburn hair was loosely dressed in a gleaming diadem of sunstained metallic luster. But it was the strange, exotic molding of her features which brought our hearts into our eyes as we looked. Her high, straight forehead continued down into her perfectly formed nose without the slightest indication of a curve—like the cameo-fine formation of the most beautiful faces found on recovered artistic treasures of ancient Greece. With consummate skill the Frenchman had made the enlargement of her eyes an ally in his work, for while he had somewhat decreased the length of the cuts with which Ruiz had mutilated the girl's eyes, he had left the openings larger than normal and raised them slightly at the outer corners, imparting to the face which would have otherwise been somewhat too severe in its utter classicism a charming hint of Oriental piquancy. The mouth was still somewhat large, but perfect in its outline, and the lips were thin, beautifully molded lines of more than usual redness, in repose presenting an expression of singular sweetness, retracting only slightly when she smiled, giving her face an expression of languid, faint amusement which was as provocative in its appeal as the far-famed smile of Mona Lisa.

"My God—Clarimonde, you're *beautiful!*" Ducharme cried brokenly, and stumbled across the floor to drop kneeling before his daughter, burying his face in her lap and sobbing hysterically.

"*Pipe d'une souris!*" de Grandin pocketed his pistol and bent above his patient. "Jules de Grandin and none other shall have the first kiss from these so beautiful lips!" He placed a resounding salute upon the girl's scarlet mouth, then turned toward the adjoining room.

"Behind that door," he announced, "I have secreted several pints of the hospital's finest medicinal brandy, Friend Trowbridge. See to it, if you please, that I am not disturbed until I say otherwise. For the next four and twenty hours Jules de Grandin shall be delightfully engaged in acquiring the noblest case of delirium tremens the institution's staff has ever treated!"

Children of Ubasti

JULES DE GRANDIN REGARDED the big red-headed man entering the break-fast room with a quick, affectionate smile. "Is it truly thou, *mon sergent?*" he asked. "I have joy in this meeting!"

Detective Sergeant Jeremiah Costello grinned somewhat ruefully as he seated himself and accepted a cup of steaming, well-creamed coffee. "It's me, all right, sir," he admitted, "an' in a peck o' trouble, as I usually am when I come botherin' you an' Dr. Trowbridge at your breakfast."

"Ah, I am glad—I mean I grieve—no, *pardieu*, I mean I sorrow at your trou-ble, but rejoice at your visit!" the little Frenchman returned. "What is it causes you unhappiness?"

The big Irishman emptied his cup at a gigantic gulp and wrinkled his fore-head like a puzzled mastiff. "I dunno," he confessed. "Maybe it's not a case at all, an' then again, maybe it is. Have you been readin' the newspaper accounts of the accident that kilt young Tom Cableson last night?"

De Grandin spread a bit of butter on his broiled weakfish and watched it dissolve. "You refer to the mishap which occurred on the Albemarle Pike—the unfortunate young man who died when he collided with a tree and thrust his face through his windshield?"

"That's what they say, sir."

"Eh? 'They say?' Who are they?"

"The coroner's jury, when they returned a verdict of death by misadven-ture. Strictly speaking, it wasn't any of my business, but bein' on the homicide squad I thought I'd just drop round to the morgue and have a look at the body, an' when I'd seen it I came over here hot-foot."

"And what was it you saw that roused your suspicions, *mon vieux?*"

"Well, sir, I've seen lots of bodies of folks killed in motor accidents, but never one quite like young Cableson's. The only wound on him was a big, jag-ged gash in the throat—just one, d'ye mind—an' some funny-lookin' scratches on his neck—" He paused apologetically, as if debating the wisdom of continuing.

"*Cordieu*, is it a game of patience we play here?" de Grandin demanded testily. "Get on with thy story, great stupid one, or I must twist your neck!"

I laughed outright at this threat of the sparrow to chastise the turkey cock, and even Costello's gravity gave way to a grin, but he sobered quickly as he answered. "Well, sir, I did part of me hitch in China, you know, and once one of our men was picked up by some bandits. When we finally come to him we found they'd hung him up like a steer for th' slaughter—cut his throat an' left him danglin' by th' heels from a tree-limb. There wasn't a tin-cupful o' blood left in his pore carcass.

"That's th' way young Cableson looked to me—all empty-like, if you get what I mean."

"*Parfaitement*. And—"

"Yes, sir, I was comin' to that. I went round to th' police garage where his car was, and looked it over most partic'lar. That's th' funny part o' th' joke, but I didn't see nothin' to laugh at. There wasn't half a pint o' blood spilled on that car, not on th' hood nor instrument board, nor upholstery, an' th' windshield which was supposed to have ripped his throat open when he crashed through it, that was clean as th' palm o' my hand, too. Besides that, sir—did ye ever see a man that had been mauled by a big cat?"

"A cat? How do you mean—"

"Lions an' tigers, an' th' like o' that, sir. Once in th' Chinese upcountry I seen th' body of a woman who'd been kilt by a tiger, one o' them big blue beasts they have there. There was something about young Cableson that reminded me of—"

"*Mort d'un rat rouge*, do you say so? This poor one's injuries were like those of that Chinese woman?"

"Pre-*cise*-ly, sir. That's why I'm here. You see, I figure if he had died natural-like, as th' result o' that accident, his car should 'a' been wringin' wet with blood, an' his clothes drippin' with it. But, like I was sayin'—"

"*Parbleu*, you *have* said it!" de Grandin exclaimed almost delightedly. "Come, let us go at once." He swallowed the remaining morsel of his fish, drained his coffee cup and rose. "This case, he has the smell of herring on him, *mon sergent*."

"Await me, if you please," he called from the hall as he thrust his arms into his topcoat sleeves. "I shall return in ample time for Madame Heacoat's *soirée*, my friend, but at present I am burnt with curiosity to see this poor, unfortunate young man who died of a cut throat, yet bled no blood. *A bientôt*."

A LITTLE AFTER EIGHT O'CLOCK that night he came into my bedroom, resplendent in full evening dress. "Consider me, Friend Trowbridge," he commanded. "Behold and admire. Am I not superb, magnificent? Shall I not be the pride of all the ladies and the despair of the men?" He pirouetted like a dancer for my admiration.

To do him justice, he was a sight to command a second look. About his neck hung the insignia of the Legion of Honor; a row of miniature medals including the French and Belgian war crosses, the *Médaille Militaire* and the Italian Medal for Valor decorated the left breast of his faultless evening coat; his little wheat-blond mustache was waxed to needle sharpness and his sleek blond hair was brushed and brilliantined until it fitted flat against his shapely little head like a skullcap.

"Humpf," I commented, "if you behave as well as you look I suppose you'll not disgrace me."

"O, *la, la!*" He grinned delightedly as he patted the gardenia in his lapel with gentle, approving fingers. "Come, let us go. I would arrive at Madame Heacoat's before all the punch is drunk, if you please." He flung his long, military-cut evening cape about him with the air of a comic-opera conspirator, picked up his lustrous top hat and silver-headed ebony cane and strode debonairly toward the door.

"Just a moment," I called as the desk 'phone gave a short, chattering ring.

"Hullo, Trowbridge, Donovan speaking," came a heavy voice across the wire as I picked up the instrument. "Can you bring that funny little Frog friend of yours over to City Hospital tonight? I've got a brand new variety of nut in the psychopathic ward—a young girl sane as you or I—well, anyhow, apparently as sane as you, except for an odd fixation. I think she'd interest de Grandin—"

"Sorry," I denied. "We're just going to a shindig at Mrs. Heacoat's. It'll be a frightful bore, most likely, but they're valuable patients, and—"

"Aw, rats," Dr. Donovan interrupted. "If I had as much money as you I'd tell all the tea-pourin' old ladies to go fry an egg. Come on over. This nut is good, I tell you. Put your toad-eater on the 'phone, maybe he'll listen to reason, even if you won't."

"*Hélas*, but I am desolated!" the Frenchman declared as Donovan delivered his invitation. "At present Friend Trowbridge and I go to make the great whoopee at Madame Heacoat's. Later in the evening, if you please, we shall avail ourselves of your hospitality. You have whisky there, yes? *Bon.* Anon, my friend, we shall discuss it and the young woman with the *idée fixe.*"

M RS. HEACOAT'S WAS THE first formal affair of the autumn, and most of the élite of our little city were present, the men still showing the floridness of golf course and mountain trail, sun-tan, painfully acquired at fashionable beaches, lying in velvet veneer on the women's arms and shoulders.

Famous lion-huntress that she was, Mrs. Heacoat had managed to impound a considerable array of exotic notables for her home-town guests to gape at, and I noted with amusement how her large, pale eyes lit up with elation at sight of Jules de Grandin. The little Frenchman, quick to understand the situation, played his rôle artistically. "Madame," he bent above our hostess's plump hand with more than usual ceremony, "believe me, I am deeply flattered by the honor you have conferred on me."

What would have been a simper in anyone less distinguished than Mrs. Watson Heacoat spread over the much massaged and carefully lifted features of Harrisonville's social arbiter. "So sweet of you to come, Dr. de Grandin. Do you know Monsieur Arif? Arif Pasha, Dr. Jules de Grandin—Dr. Trowbridge."

The slender, sallow-skinned young man whom she presented had the small regular features, sleek black hair and dark, slumbrous eyes typical of a night club band leader, or a waiter in a fashionable café. He bowed jerkily from the hips in continental fashion and murmured a polite greeting in stilted English. "You, I take it, are a stranger like myself in strange company?" he asked de Grandin as we moved aside for a trio of newcomers.

Further conversation developed he was attached to the Turkish consulate in New York, that he had met Mrs. Heacoat in England the previous summer, and that he would be exceedingly glad when he might bid his hostess good night.

"*Tiens*, they stare so, these Americans," he complained. "Now, in London or Paris—"

"Monsoor and Modom Bera!" announced the butler, his impressive, full-throated English voice cutting through the staccato of chatter as the booming of the surf sounds through the strains of a seaside resort band.

We turned casually to view the newcomers, then kept our eyes at gaze; they were easily the most interesting people in the room. Madame Bera walked a half-pace before her husband, tall, exquisite, exotic as an orchid blooming in a New England garden. Tawny hair combed close to a small head framed a broad white brow, and under fine dark brown brows looked out the most remarkable eyes I had ever seen. Widely separated, their roundness gave them an illusion of immensity which seemed to diminish her face, and their color was a baffling shade of greenish amber, contrasting oddly with her leonine hair and warm, maize-tan complexion. From cheek to cheek her face was wide, tapering to a pointed chin, and her nostrils flared slightly, like those of an alert feline scenting hidden danger. Her evening dress, cut rather higher than the prevailing mode, encased her large, supple figure with glove tightness from breast to waist, then flared outward to an uneven hem that almost swept the floor. Beneath the edge of her sand-colored chiffon gown her feet, in sandals of gold kid, appeared absurdly small for her height as she crossed the room with a lithe, easy stride that seemed positively pantherine in its effortless grace.

Older by a score of years than his consort, Monsieur Bera yet had something of the same feline ease of movement that characterized her. Like hers, his face was wide from cheek to cheek, pointed at the chin and with unusually wide nostrils. Unlike his wife's, his eyes were rather long than round, inclined to be oblique, and half closed, as if to shade them from the glitter of the electric lights. Fast-thinning grey hair was combed back from his brow in an effort to conceal his spreading bald spot, and his wide mouth was adorned by a waxed mustache of the kind affected by Prussian officers in pre-Nazi days. Through the lens of a rimless monocle fixed in his right eye he seemed to view the assemblage with a sardonic contempt.

"*Ye Allah!*" the young Turk who stood between de Grandin and me sank his fingers into our elbows. "*Bism' allah ar-rahman ar-rahim!* Do you see them? They look as if they were of *that people!*"

"Eh, you say what?" whispered Jules de Grandin sharply.

"It is no matter, sir; you would not understand."

"*Pardonnez-moi*, Monsieur, I understand you very well, indeed. Some little time ago I had to go to Tunis to make investigation of a threatened uprising of the tribesmen. Disguised as a *Père Blanc*—and other things—I mingled with the natives. It was vile—I had to shave off my mustaches!—but it was instructive. I learned much. I learned, by example, of the djinn that haunt the ruins of Carthage, and of the strange ones who reside in tombs; a weird and dreadful folk without a name—at any rate, without a name which can be mentioned."

Arif Pasha looked at Jules de Grandin fearfully. "You have seen them?" he asked in a low breath.

"I have heard much of them, and their stigmata has been described to me. Come, let us seek an introduction to *la belle* Bera."

"Allah forbid," the young Turk denied, walking hastily away.

The lady proved gracious as she was beautiful. Viewed closely, her strange eyes were stranger still, for they had a trick of contracting their pupils in the light, bringing out the full beauty of their fine irises, and expanding in shadow till they seemed black as night. Too, I noted when she smiled her slow wide smile, all four canine teeth seemed overprominent and sharp. This, perhaps, accounted for the startling contrast between her crimson lips and her perfect dentition. Her hands were unusual, too. Small and fine they were, with supple, slender fingers but unusually wide palms, and the nails, shaped to a point and brightly varnished, curved oddly downward over the fingertips; had they been longer or less carefully tended they would have suggested talons. Her voice was a rich heavy contralto, and when she spoke slow hesitant English there was an odd purring undertone beneath her words.

The odd characteristics which seemed somehow exotically attractive in his wife were intensified in Monsieur Bera. The over-prominent teeth which lent a kind of piquant charm to her smile were a deformity in his dun-lipped mouth; the overhanging nails that made her long fingers seem longer still were definitely claw-like on his hands, and the odd trick of contracting and expanding his pupils in changing lights gave his narrow eyes a furtive look unpleasantly reminiscent of the eyes of a dope-fiend or a cruel, treacherous cat.

"Madame, I am interested," de Grandin admitted with the frankness only he could employ without seeming discourteous. "Your name intrigues me. It is not French, yet I heard you introduced as Monsieur and Madame—"

The lady smiled languidly, showing pearly teeth and crimson lips effectively. "We are Tunisians," she answered. "Both my husband and I come from North Africa."

"Ah, then I am indeed fortunate," he smiled delightedly. "Is it by some great fortune you reside in this city? If so I should greatly esteem permission to call—"

I heard no summons, but Madame Bera evidently did, for with another smile and friendly nod she left us to join Mrs. Heacoat.

"Beard of a small blue man!" de Grandin grinned wryly as we rejoined the young Turk, "it seems that Jules de Grandin loses his appeal for the sex. Was ever the chilled shoulder more effectively presented than by *la charmante* Bera?

"Come, *mes amis*," he linked his hands through our elbows and drew us toward the farther room, "women may smile, or women may frown, but champagne punch is always pleasant to the taste."

We sampled several kinds of punch and sandwiches and small sweet cakes, then made our adieux to our hostess. Outside, as Arif Pasha was about to enter his taxi, de Grandin tapped him lightly on the shoulder. "If we should hear more of them, I can find you, my friend?" he asked cryptically.

The young Turk nodded. "I shall be ready if you call," he promised.

"WOULD YOU GUYS LIKE a spot o' proletarian whisky to take the taste of all that champagne out o' your mouths?" asked Dr. Donovan as we joined him in his office at the hospital.

"A thousand thanks," de Grandin answered. "Champagne is good, but whisky, as your saying puts it so drolly, hits the spot. By all means, let us indulge.

"You are not drinking?" he asked as Donovan poured a generous portion for him, and a like one for me.

"Nope, not on duty. Might give some o' my nuts bad ideas," the other grinned. "However, bottoms up, you fellers, then let's take a gander at my newest curio.

"It was early this morning, half-past four or so, when a state constabulary patrol found her wandering around the woods west of Mooreston with nothing but a nightdress on. They questioned her, but could get nowhere. Most of the time she didn't speak at all, and when she did it was only to slobber some sort o' meaningless gibberish. According to Hoyle they should have taken her to the State Hospital for observation, but they're pretty full over there, and prefer to handle only regularly committed cases, so the troopers brought her here and turned her over to the city police.

"Frankly, the case has my goat. Familiar with dementia præcox, are you, Doctor?" he turned questioningly to de Grandin.

"Quite," the Frenchman answered. "I have seen many poor ones suffering from it. Usually it occurs between the ages of fifteen and thirty-five, though most cases I have observed were in the early thirties. Wherever I have seen it the disease was characterized by states of excitement accompanied by delusions of aural or visual type. Most patients believed they were persecuted, or had been through some harrowing experience—occasionally they posed, gesticulated and grimaced."

"Just so," agreed Donovan. "You've got it down pat, Doctor. I thought I had, too, but I'm not so sure now. What would be your diagnosis if a patient displayed every sign of ataxic aphasia, couldn't utter a single intelligent word, then fell into a stupor lasting eight hours or so and woke up with a case of the horrors? This girl's about twenty-three, and absolutely perfect physically. What's more, her reflexes are all right—knee-jerks normal, very sensitive to pain, and all that, but—" He looked inquiringly at de Grandin.

"From your statement I should suggest dementia præcox. It is well known that such dements frequently fall into comatose sleeps in which they suffer nightmares, and on awaking are so mentally confused they cannot distinguish between the phantoms of their dreams and their waking surroundings."

"Precisely. Well, I had a talk with this child and heard her story, then gave her a big dose of codeine in milk. She slept three hours and woke up seemingly as normal as you or I, but I'm damned if she didn't repeat the same story, chapter and verse, that she gave me when she first came out of her stupor. I'd say she's sane as a judge if it weren't for this delusion she persists in. Want to come up now and have a look at her?"

Donovan's patient lay on the neat white-iron hospital cot, staring with wide frightened eyes at the little observation-grille in the unlocked door of her cell. Even the conventional high-necked, long-sleeved muslin bed-gown furnished by the hospital could not hide her frail prettiness. With her pale smooth skin, light short hair and big violet eyes in which lay a look of perpetual terror, she was like a little frightened child, and a wave of sympathy swept over me as we entered her room. That de Grandin felt the same I could tell by the kindly smile he gave her as he drew a chair to her bedside and seated himself. He took her thin blue-veined hand in his and patted it gently before placing his fingers on her pulse.

"I've brought a couple of gentlemen to see you, Annie," Dr. Donovan announced as the little Frenchman gazed intently at the tiny gold watch strapped to the underside of his wrist, comparing its sweep second hand with the girl's pulsation. "Dr. de Grandin is a famous French detective as well as a physician; he'll be glad to hear your story; maybe he can do something about it."

A tortured look swept across the girl's thin face as he finished. "You think I'm crazy," she accused, half rising from her pillow. "I know you do, and you've brought these men here to examine me so you can put me in a madhouse for always. Oh, it's dreadful—I'm not insane, I tell you; I'm as sane as you are, if you'd only listen—"

"Now, Annie, don't excite yourself," Donovan soothed. "You know I wouldn't do anything like that; I'm your friend—"

"My name's not Annie, and you're *not* my friend. Nobody is. You think I'm crazy—all you doctors think everyone who gets into your clutches must be crazy, and you'll send me to a madhouse, and I'll really *go* crazy there!"

"Now, Annie—"

"My name's not Annie, I tell you. Why do you keep calling me that?"

Donovan cast a quick wink at me, then turned a serious face to the girl. "I thought your name was Annie. I must have been mistaken. What is it?"

"I've told you it's Trula, Trula Petersen. I used to live in Paterson, but lost my place there and couldn't get anything to do, so I came to Harrisonville looking for work, and—"

"Very good, Friend Donovan," de Grandin announced, relinquishing the girl's wrist, but retaining her fingers in his, "when first this young lady came here she could not tell her name. Now she can. *Bon*, we make the progress. Her heart action is strong and good. I think perhaps we shall make much more progress. Now, Mademoiselle," he gave the girl one of his quick friendly smiles, "if you will be so good as to detail your adventures from the start we shall listen with the close attention. Believe me, we are friends, and nothing you say shall be taken as a proof of madness."

The girl's smile was a pitiful, small echo of his own. "I do believe you, sir," she returned, "and I'll tell you everything, for I know I can trust you.

"When the Clareborne Silk Mills closed down in Paterson I lost my place as timekeeper. Most of the other mills were laying off employees, and there wasn't much chance of another situation there. I'm an orphan with no relatives, and I had to get some sort of work at once, for I didn't have more than fifty dollars in the bank. After trying several places with no luck I came to Harrisonville where nobody knew me and registered at a domestic servants' agency. It was better to be a housemaid than starve, I thought.

"The very day I registered, a Mrs. d'Afrique came looking for a maid, and picked two other girls and me as possibilities. She looked us all over, asked a lot of questions about our families, where we were born, and that sort of thing, then chose me because she said she preferred a maid without relatives or friends, who wouldn't be wanting to run out every evening. Her car was waiting outside, and I had no baggage except my suitcase, so I went along with her."

"U'm?" de Grandin murmured. "And she did take you where?"

"I don't know."

"*Hein?* How do you say?"

"I don't know, sir. It was a big foreign car with a closed body, and she had me sit in the tonneau with her instead of up front with the chauffeur. When we'd started I noticed for the first time that the windows were of frosted glass, and I couldn't see where we went. We must have gone a long way, though, for the car seemed traveling very fast, and there were no traffic stops. When we finally stopped we were under a porte-cochère, and we entered the house directly from the car, so I couldn't get any idea of surroundings."

"*Dites!* Surely, in the days that followed you could look about?"

A look of terror flared in the girl's eyes and her pale lips writhed in a grimace of fear. "The days that followed!" she repeated in a thin scream; "it's the days that followed that brought me *here!*"

"Ah? Do you say so?"

"*Now* we're gettin' it!" Donovan whispered in my ear with a low chuckle. "Go ahead and ask her, de Grandin; you tell him, Annie. This is goin' to be good."

His voice was too low for de Grandin and the girl to catch his words, but his tone and laugh were obvious. "Oh!" the patient wailed, wrenching her hand from de Grandin's and putting it to her eyes. "Oh, how cruel! You're all making fun of me!"

"Be silent, *imbécile*," de Grandin turned on Donovan savagely. "*Parbleu*, cleaning the roadways would be more fitting work for you than treating the infirm of mind! Do not attend him, Mademoiselle." He repossessed himself of the girl's hand and smoothed it gently. "Proceed with your narrative. I shall listen, and perhaps believe."

For a moment the little patient shook as with an ague, and I could see her grip on his fingers tighten. "Please, *please* believe me, Doctor," she begged. "It's really the truth I'm telling. They wanted—they wanted to—"

"Did they so, *pardieu?*" de Grandin replied. "Very good, Mademoiselle, you escaped them. No one shall hurt you now, nor shall you be persecuted. Jules de Grandin promises it. Now to proceed."

"I was frightened," she confessed, "terribly frightened from the moment I got into the car with Mrs. d'Afrique and realized I couldn't look out. I thought of screaming and trying to jump out, but I was out of work and hungry; besides, she was a big woman and could have overpowered me without trouble.

"When we got to the house I was still more terrified, and Mrs. d'Afrique seemed to notice it, for she smiled and took me by the arm. Her hands were strong as a man's—stronger!—and when I tried to draw away she held me tighter and sort of chuckled deep down in her throat—like a big cat purring when it's caught a mouse. She half led, half shoved me down a long hall that was almost bare of furniture, through a door and down a flight of steps that led to the basement. Next thing I knew she'd pushed me bodily into a little room no bigger than this, and locked the door.

"The door was solid planking, and the only window was a little barred opening almost at the ceiling, which I couldn't reach to look through, even when I pushed the bed over and stood on it.

"I don't know how long I was in that place. At first I thought the window let outdoors, but the light seemed the same strength all the time, so I suppose it really looked out into the main basement and what I thought weak sunlight was really reflected from an electric bulb somewhere. At any rate, I determined to fight for my freedom the first chance I had, for I'd read stories of white slavers who kidnaped girls, and I was sure I'd fallen into the hands of some such gang. If I only had!

"How they timed it I don't know, but they never opened that door except when I was sleeping. I'd lie awake for hours, pretending to be asleep, so that someone would open the door and give me a chance to die fighting; but nothing ever happened. Then the moment I grew so tired I really fell asleep the door would be opened, my soiled dishes taken out and a fresh supply of food brought in. They didn't starve me, I'll say that. There was always some sort of meat—veal or young pork, I thought—and bread and vegetables and a big vacuum bottle of coffee and another of chilled milk. If I hadn't been so terribly frightened I might have enjoyed it, for I'd been hungry for a long time.

"One night I woke up with a start. At least, I suppose it was night, though there was really no way of telling. There were voices outside my door, the first I'd heard since I came there. 'Please, please let me go,' a girl was pleading sobbingly. 'I've never done anything to you, and I'll do anything—*anything* you ask if you'll only let me go!'

"Whoever it was she spoke to answered in a soft, gentle, purring sort of voice, 'Do not be afraid, we seek only to have a little sport with you; then you are free.'

"It was a man's voice, I could tell that, and I could hear the girl sobbing and pleading in terror till he took her upstairs and closed the basement door.

"I didn't know what to think. Till then I'd thought I was the only prisoner in the house, now I knew there was at least one more. 'What were they doing to her—what would they do to me when my turn came?' I kept asking myself. I'd read about the white-slave stockades of Chicago where young girls were 'broken in' by professional rapists, and when I heard the sound of several people running back and forth in the room right above me I went absolutely sick with terror. It seemed to me that several people were running about in tennis shoes or bare feet, and then there was a scream, then more running, and more screams. Then everything was still, so still that I could hear my heart beating as I lay there. I kept listening for them to bring her back; but they never did. At last I fell asleep."

De Grandin tweaked the waxed ends of his little blond mustache. "This Madame d'Afrique, what did she look like, *ma pauvre?*"

"She was a big woman—tall, that is, sir, with lots of blond hair and queer-looking brown-green eyes and odd, long nails that turned down over her finger-tips, like claws. She—"

"Name of an intoxicated pig, they are undoubtlessly one and the same! Why did I not recognize it at once?" de Grandin exclaimed. "Say on, my child. Tell all; I wait with interest."

The girl swallowed convulsively and gave her other hand into his keeping. "Hold me, Doctor, hold me tight," she begged. "I'm afraid; terribly afraid, even now.

"I knew something dreadful was going to happen when he finally came for me, but I hadn't thought how terrible it would be. I was sound asleep when I felt someone shaking me by the shoulder and heard a voice say, 'Get up. We're going to let you go—if you can.'

"I tried to ask questions, to get him to wait till I put on some clothes, but he fairly dragged me, just as I was, from the bed. When I got upstairs I found myself in a big bare room brightly lighted by a ceiling chandelier, and with only a few articles of furniture in it—one or two big chairs, several small footstools, and a big couch set diagonally across one corner. It was night. I could see the rain beating on the window and hear the wind blowing. In the sudden unaccustomed light I saw a tall old man with scant white hair and a big white mustache held me by the shoulder. He wore a sort of short bathrobe of some dark-colored cloth and his feet were bare. Then I saw the woman, Mrs. d'Afrique. She was in a sort of short nightgown that reached only to her knees, and like the man she, too, was barefooted. The man shoved me into the middle of the room, and all the time the woman stood there smiling and eyeing me hungrily.

"'My wife and I sometimes play a little game with our guests,' the old man told me. 'We turn out the lights and enjoy a little romp of tag. If the guest can get away in the darkness she is free to go; if she can not—' He stopped and smiled at me—the cruellest smile I've ever seen.

"Wh—what happens if she can not?' I faltered.

"He put his hand out and stroked my bare arm. 'Very nice,' he murmured, 'nice and tender, eh?' The woman nodded and licked her red lips with the tip of her red tongue, while her queer green eyes seemed positively shining as she looked at me.

"'If the guest can not get away,' the man answered with a dreadful low laugh, then he looked at the woman again. 'You have eaten well since you came here,' he went on, apparently forgetting what he'd started to say. 'How did you like the meat we served?'

"I nodded. I didn't know what to say. Then: 'Why, it was very nice,' I whispered, fearing to anger him if I kept silent.

"'Ye-es, very nice,' he agreed with another laugh. 'Very nice, indeed. That meat, dear, tender young lady—that meat was the guests who couldn't get away!'

"I closed my eyes and thought hard. This couldn't be true, I told myself. This was just some dreadful dream. They might be going to maul and beat me— even kill me, perhaps—to satisfy their sadistic lust, but to kill and *eat* me—no, such things just couldn't happen in New Jersey today!

"It was a lucky thing for me I'd closed my eyes, for while I stood there swaying with nauseated horror I heard a faint click. Instantly I opened my eyes to find the light had been shut off and I was standing alone in the center of the great room.

"How'd you know you were alone if the light had been shut off?" demanded Donovan. "You say the room was pitch-dark."

The girl never turned her head. Her terrified eyes remained steadily, pleadingly, on de Grandin's face as she whispered:

"By *their* eyes!"

"The woman stood at one end of the room, the man had moved to the other, though I'd heard no sound, and in the darkness I could see their eyes, like the phosphorescent orbs of wild jungle-beasts at night.

"The steady, green-gleaming eyes came slowly nearer and nearer, sometimes moving in a straight line, sometimes circling in the darkness, but never turning from me for an instant. I was being stalked like a mouse by hungry cats—the creatures could see in the dark!

"I said a moment ago it was fortunate for me I'd closed my eyes. That's all that saved me. if they'd been open when the lights went out I'd have been completely blinded by the sudden darkness, but as it was, when I opened them the room was just a little lighter than the absolute darkness of closed eyes. The result was I could see their bodies like moving blotches of shadow slightly heavier than that of the rest of the room, and could even make out the shapes of some of the furniture. I could distinguish the dull-grey of the rain-washed window, too.

"As I turned in terror from one creeping shadow-thing to the other the woman let out a low, dreadful cry like the gradually-growing miaul of a hunting cat, only deeper and louder. The man answered it, and it seemed there was an undertone of terrible, half-human laughter in the horrible caterwaul.

"It seemed to me that all the forces of hell were let loose in that great dark room. I heard myself screaming, praying, shrieking curses and obscenities

I'd never realized I even knew, and answering me came the wild, inhuman screeches of the green-eyed things that hunted me.

"Scarcely knowing what I did I snatched up a heavy footstool and hurled it at the nearer pair of eyes. They say a woman can't throw straight, but my shot took effect. I saw the blurred outline of a body double up with an agonized howl and go crashing to the floor, where it flopped and contorted like a fish jerked from the water.

"With a shrill, ear-splitting scream the other form dashed at me, and I dropped to my knees just in time to avoid a thrashing blow it aimed at me—I felt my nightdress rip to tatters as the long sharp nails slashed through it.

"I rolled over and over across the floor with that she-devil leaping and springing after me. I snatched another hassock as I rolled, and flung it behind me. It tripped her, and for a moment she went to her knees, but her short dress offered no hindrance to her movement, and she was up and after me, howling and screaming like a beast, in another second.

"I'd managed to roll near the window, and as I came in contact with another stool I grasped it and hurled it with all my might at the panes. They shattered outward with a crash, and I dived through the opening. The ground was scarcely six feet below, and the rain had softened it so it broke my fall almost like a mattress. An instant after I'd landed on the rain-soaked lawn I was on my feet and running as no woman ever ran before."

"Yes, and then—?" de Grandin prompted.

The girl shook her slim, muslin-clad shoulders and shuddered in the ague of a nervous chill. "That's all there is to tell, sir," she stated simply. "The next thing I knew I was in this bed and Dr. Donovan was asking me about myself."

"That's letter-perfect," Donovan commented. "Exactly the way she told it twice before. What's your verdict, gentlemen?"

I shook my head pityingly. It was all too sadly evident the poor girl had been through some terrifying experience and that her nerves were badly shaken, but her story was so preposterous—clearly this was a case of delusional insanity. "I'm afraid," I began, and got no farther, for de Grandin's sharp comment forestalled me.

"The verdict, *mon cher* Donovan? What can it be but that she speaks the truth? But certainly, of course!"

"You mean—" I began, and once again he shut me off.

"By damn-it, I mean that the beauteous Madame Bera and her so detestably ugly spouse have overreached themselves. There is no doubt that they and the d'Afriques are one and the same couple. Why should they not choose that name as a *nom de ruse*; are they not from Tunis, and is Tunis not in Africa? But yes."

"Holy smoke!" gasped Donovan. "D'ye mean you actually believe this bunk?"

"*Mais certainement*," de Grandin answered. "So firmly do I believe it I am willing to stand sponsor for this young lady immediately if you will release her on parole to accompany Friend Trowbridge and me."

"Well, I'm a monkey's uncle, I sure am," declared Dr. Donovan. "Maybe I should have another room swept out for you an' Trowbridge." He sobered at the grim face de Grandin turned on him. "O.K. if that's the way you want it, de Grandin. It's your responsibility, you know. Want to go with these gentlemen, Annie?" He regarded the girl with a questioning smile.

"Yes! I'll go anywhere with him, he trusts me," she returned; then, as an afterthought, "And my name's not Annie."

"All right, Annie, get your clothes on," Donovan grinned back. "We'll be waitin' for you in the office."

As soon as we had reached the office de Grandin rushed to the telephone. "I would that you give this message to Sergeant Costello immediately when he arrives," he called when his call to police headquarters had been put through. "Request that he obtain the address given by Monsieur and Madame d'Afrique when they went to secure domestic help from Osgood's Employment Agency, and that he ascertain, if possible, the names and addresses of all young women who entered their employ from the agency. Have him take steps to locate them at once, if he can.

"*Très bon*," he nodded as Trula Petersen made her appearance dressed in some makeshift odds and ends of clothing found for her by the nurses. "You are not *chic*, my little one, but in the morning we can get you other clothes, and meantime you will sleep more comfortably in an unbarred room. Yes, let us go."

A little after four o'clock next afternoon Costello called on us. "I got some o' th' dope you're wantin', Dr. de Grandin," he announced. "Th' de Africays hired four girls from Osgood's about a week apart; but didn't seem to find any of 'em satisfactory. Kept comin' back for more."

"Ah? And these young women are now where, if you please?"

"None of 'em's been located as yet sir. It happens they was all strangers in town, at least, none of 'em had folks here, an' all was livin' in furnished rooms when they was hired. None of 'em's reported back to her roomin' house or applied to Osgood's for reëmployment. We'll look around a bit more, if you say so, but I doubt we'll find out much. They're mostly fly-by-nights, these girls, you know."

"I fear that what you say is literally true," de Grandin answered soberly. "They have flown by night, yes flown beyond all mortal calling, if my fears are as well grounded as I have reason to believe.

"And the address of Monsieur and Madame Ber—d'Afrique? Did you ascertain it from the agency?"

"Sure, we did. It's 762 Orient Boulevard."

"Good. I shall go there and—"

"Needn't be troublin' yourself, sir. I've been there already."

"*Ah bah*; I fear that you have spoiled it all. I did not wish them to suspect we knew. Now, I much fear—"

"You needn't; 762 Orient Boulevard's a vacant lot."

"Hell and ten thousand furies! Do you tell me so?"

"I sure do. But I got something solid for us to sink our teeth into. I think I've uncovered a lead on th' Cableson case."

"Indeed?"

"Well, it ain't much, but it's more'n we knew before. He wasn't alone when he died; least wise, he wasn't alone a few minutes before. I ran across a pair o' young fellers that saw him takin' a lady into his coupé on th' Albermarle Pike just a little way outside Mooreston late th' night before he was found dead with his car jammed up against a tree."

"*Chapeau d'un bouc vert*, is it so? Have you a description of the lady of mystery?"

"Kind of, yes, sir. She was big and blond, an' wrapped in some sort o' cloak, but didn't wear a hat. That's how they know she was a blonde, they saw her hair in th' light o' th' car's lamps."

The little Frenchman turned from the policeman to our guest. "My child," he told her, "the good God has been most kind to you. He has delivered those who harried you like a brute beast into the hands of Jules de Grandin."

"What are you going to do?" I asked, wondering.

"Do?" His waxed mustaches quivered like the whiskers of an irritable tomcat. "Do? *Parbleau*, should one slap the face of Providence? *Mille nons*. Me, I shall serve them as they deserve, no less. May Satan fry me in a saucepan with a garnish of mushrooms if I do not so!"

A moment later he was thumbing through the telephone directory. "Ah, Madame Heacoat," he announced when the lady finally answered his call, "I am unhappy, I am miserable; I am altogether desolate. At your charming soirée I met the so delightful Monsieur and Madame Bera, and we discovered many friends in common. Of the goodness of their hearts they invited me to call, but *hélas* I have misplaced my memorandum of their address. Can you—ah, *merci bien; merci bien une mille fois*—a thousand thanks, Madame!

"My friends," he turned on us as he laid down the 'phone, "we have them in a snare. They are the clever ones, but Jules de Grandin is more clever. They dwell near Mooreston; their house abuts upon the Albermarle Pike. To find them will be a small task.

"Trowbridge, my old and rare, I pray you have the capable Nora McGinnis, that queen among cooks, prepare us a noble dinner this night. There is much to be done, and I would do it on a well-fed stomach. Meantime I shall call that Monsieur Arif and request his presence this evening. It was he who first roused my suspicions; he deserves to be here at the finish."

A LITTLE BEFORE DINNER A special messenger from Ridgeway's Hardware Store arrived with a long parcel wrapped in corrugated paper which de Grandin seized and bore to his room. For half an hour or more he was engaged in some secret business there, emerging with a grin of satisfaction on his face as the gong sounded for the evening meal.

He took command at table, keeping up a running fire of conversation, most of it witty, all of it inconsequential. Stories of student days at the Sorbonne, droll tales of the War, anecdotes of travel in the far places of the world—anything but the slightest reference to the mystery of Monsieur and Madame Bera he rattled off like a wound-up gramophone.

Finally, when coffee was served in the drawing room, he lighted a cigar, stretched his slender patent-leather-shod feet to the blazing logs and regarded Trula Petersen and me in turn with his quick, birdlike glance. "You trust me, *ma petite?*" he asked the girl.

"Oh, yes."

"*Très bon.* We shall put that trust to the test before long." He smiled whimsically, then:

"You have never hunted the tiger in India, one assumes?"

"Sir? No! I've never been anywhere except Norway where I was born, and this country, where I've lived since I was ten."

"Then it seems I must enlighten you. In India, when they would bring the stripèd one within gunshot, they tether a so small and helpless kid to a stake. The tiger scents a meal, approaches the small goat; the hunter, gun in hand, squeezes the trigger and—*voilà*, there is a tigerskin rug for some pretty lady's boudoir. It is all most simple."

"I—I don't think I understand, sir," the girl faltered, but there was a telltale widening of her eyes and a constriction of the muscles of her throat as she spoke.

"Very well. It seems I must explain in detail. Anon our good friend Arif Pasha comes, and with him comes the good Sergeant Costello. When all is ready you are to assume the same costume you wore when they brought you to the hospital, and over it you will put on warm wrappings. Thereafter Friend Trowbridge drives us to the house of Monsieur Bera, and you will descend, clad as you were when you fled. You will stagger across the lawn, calling pitifully for help. Unless I am much more mistaken than I think one or both of them will sally forth to see who cries for help in the night. Then—"

"O-o-o-oh, *no!*" the girl wailed in a stifled voice. "I couldn't! I wouldn't go there for all the money in the world—"

"It is no question of money, my small one. It is that you do it for the sake of humanity. Consider: Did you not tell me you woke one night to hear the odious Bera leading another girl to torture and death? Did not you thereafter hear the stamping of feet which fled and feet which pursued, and the agonized scream of one who was caught?"

The girl nodded durably.

"Suppose I tell you four girls were hired by these beast-people from the same agency whence you went into their service. That much we know; it is a matter of police record. It is also a matter of record that none of them, save you, was ever seen again. How many other unfortunate ones went the same sad road is a matter of conjecture, but unless you are willing to do this thing for me there is a chance that those we seek may escape. They may move to some other place and play their infernal games of hide-and-seek-in-the-dark with only the good God knows how many other poor ones.

"Attend me further, little pretty one: The night you escape by what was no less than a miracle a young man named Thomas Cableson—a youth of good family and position—young, attractive, in love; with everything to live for, drove his coupé through Mooreston along the Albermarle Pike. A short distance from Mooreston he was accosted by a woman—a big, blond woman *who sought for something in the roadside woods.*

"In the kindness of his heart he offered her a ride to Harrisonville. Next morning he was found dead in his motor. Apparently he had collided with a roadside tree, for his windshield was smashed to fragments, and through the broken glass his head protruded. But nowhere was there any blood. Neither on the car nor on his clothing was there any stain, yet he had bled to death. Also, I who am at once a physician and an observer of facts, examined his poor, severed throat. Such tears as marred his flesh might have been made by teeth, perhaps by claws; but by splintered glass, never. What happened in that young man's car we cannot know for certain, but we can surmise much. We can surmise, by example, that a thing that dotes on human flesh and blood had been thwarted of its prey and hunted for it in those roadside woods. We can surmise that when the young man, thinking her alone upon the highroad, offered her a ride, she saw an opportunity. Into his car she went, and when they were come to a lonely spot she set upon him. There was a sudden shrill, inhuman scream, the glare of beast-eyes in the dark, the stifling weight of a body hurled on unsuspecting shoulders, and the rending of shrinking flesh by bestial teeth and claws. The car is stopped, then started; it is run against a tree; a head, already almost severed from its body, is thrust through the broken windshield, and—the nameless horror which wears woman's shape returns to its den, its lips red from the feast, its gorge replenished."

"De Grandin!" I expostulated. "You're raving. Such things can't be!"

"Ha, can they not, *parbleu?*" he tweaked the ends of his diminutive mustache, gazing pensively at the fire a moment, then:

"Regard me, my friend. Listen, pay attention: Where, if you please, is Tunis?"

"In northwest Africa."

"*Précisément.* And Egypt is where, if you please?"

"In Africa, of course, but—"

"No buts, if you please. Both lie on the same dark continent, that darksome mother of dark mysteries whose veil no man has ever completely lifted. Now, regard me: In lower Egypt, near Zagazig, are the great ruins of Tell Besta. They mark the site of the ancient, wicked city of Bubastis, own sister of Sodom and Gomorrah of accursèd memory. It was there, in the days of the third Rameses, thirteen hundred years before the birth of Christ, that men and women worshiped the cat-headed one, she who was called Ubasti, sometimes known as Bast. Yes. With phallic emblems and obscenities that would shock present-day Montmartre, they worshipped her. Today her temples lie in ruins, and only the hardest stones of her many monuments endure.

"But there are things much more enduring than granite and brass. The olden legends tell us of a race apart, a race descended from the loins of this cat-headed one of Bubastis, who shared her evil feline nature even though they wore the guise of women, or, less often, men.

"The fellaheen of Egypt are poor, wretchedly poor, and what the bare necessities of living do not snatch from them the tax-collector does; yet not for all the English gold that clings and jingles at Shepard's Hotel in Cairo could one bribe a fella to venture into the ruins of Tell Besta after sunset. No, it is a fact; I myself have seen it.

"For why? Because, by blue, that cursèd spot is ghoul-haunted. Do not laugh; it is no laughing matter; it is so.

"The ancient gods are dust, and dust are all their worshippers, but their memories and their evil lives after them. The fellaheen will tell you of strange, terrible things which dwell amid the ruins of Bubastis; things formed like human creatures, but which are, as your own so magnificent Monsieur Poe has stated,

'. . . neither man nor woman,
. . . neither brute nor human
They are ghouls!'

"Yes, certainly. Like a man's or woman's, their faces are, so too are their bodies to some extent; but they see in the dark, like her from whom they are whelped, they wear long nails to seize their prey and have beast-teeth to tear it, and the flesh and blood of living men—or dead, if live be not available—they make their food and drink.

"Not only at Tell Besta are they found, for they are quick to multiply, and their numbers have spread. In the ruined tombs of all North Africa they make their lairs, awaiting the unwary traveler. Mostly they are nocturnal, but they have been known to spring on the lone voyager by day. The Arabs hate and fear them also, and speak of them by indirection. 'That people,' they call them, nor does one who has traveled in North Africa need ask a second time what the term connotes.

"Very well, then. When our friend Arif Pasha first showed fright, like a restive horse in the presence of hidden danger, at sight of those we know as Monsieur and Madame Bera, I was astonished. Such things might be in darker Africa, perhaps in Persia, or Asiatic Turkey, but in America—New Jersey—*non!*

"However, Jules de Grandin has the open mind. I made it a duty to meet this so strange couple, to observe their queer catlike eyes, to note the odd, claw-like nails of their hands, but most of all to watch their white, gleaming teeth and hear the soft, purring intonation of their words.

"'These are queer folk, Jules de Grandin,' I say to me. 'They are not like others.'

"That very night we visited the City Hospital and listened to our little Trula tell her fearsome story. What she had to say of those who hired her and would have hunted her to death convinced me of much I should otherwise not have believed.

"Then came Sergeant Costello's report of the four girls hired by this Madame d'Afrique, whom we now know to be also Madame Bera—girls who went but did not return. Then comes the information of the strange woman who rode with the young Cableson the night he met his death.

"'Jules de Grandin,' I tell me, 'your dear America, the place in which you have decided to remain, is invaded. The very neighborhood of good Friend Trowbridge's house, where you are to reside until you find yourself a house of your own, is peopled by strange night-seeing things.'

"'It is, *hélas*, as you have said, Jules de Grandin,' I reply.

"'Very well, then, Jules de Grandin,' I ask me, 'what are we to do about it?'

"'*Mordieu*,' I answer me, 'we shall exterminate the invaders. Of course.'

"'*Bravo*, it are agreed.'

"Now, all is prepared. Mademoiselle Trula, my little pretty one, my small half orange, I need your help. Will you not do this thing for me?"

"I—I'm terribly afraid," the girl stammered, "but I—I'll do it, sir."

"Bravely spoken, my pigeon. Have no fear. Your guardian angel is with you. Jules de Grandin will also be there.

"Come. Let us make ready, the doorbell sounds."

A RIF PASHA AND COSTELLO waited on the porch, and de Grandin gave a hand to each. "I haven't any more idea what th' pitch is than what th' King o' Siam had for breakfast this mornin'," Costello confessed with a grin when introductions had been made, "but I'm bankin' on you to pay off, Dr. de Grandin."

"I hope your confidence is not misplaced, my friend," the Frenchman answered. "I hope to show you that which killed the poor young Cableson before we're many hours older."

"What's that?" asked the detective. "Did you say 'that,' sir. Wasn't it a person, then? Sure, after all our bother, you're not goin' to tell me it was an accident after all?"

De Grandin shrugged. "Let us not quibble over pronouns, my old one. Wait till you have seen, then say if it be man or woman, beast or fiend from hell."

Led by de Grandin as ceremoniously as though he were escorting her to the dance floor, Trula Petersen ascended the stairs to don the ragged bedgown she wore the night she fled for life through the shattered window. She returned in a few moments, her pale childish face suffused with blushes as she sought to cover the inadequate attire by wrapping de Grandin's fur-lined overcoat more tightly about her slim form. Above the fleece-lined bedroom slippers on her feet I caught a glimpse of slender bare ankle, and mentally revolted against the Frenchman's penchant for realism which would send her virtually unclothed into the cold autumn night.

But there was no time to voice my protest, for de Grandin followed close behind her with the corrugated cardboard carton he had received from Ridgeway's in his arms. "Behold, my friends," he ordered jubilantly displaying its contents—four magazine shotguns—"are these not lovely? *Pardieu*, with them we are equipped for any contingency!"

The guns were twelve-gauge models of the unsportsmanlike "pump" variety, and the barrels had been cut off with a hack-saw close to the wood, shortening them by almost half their length.

"What's th' armament for, sir?" inquired Costello, examining the weapon de Grandin handed him. "Is it a riot we're goin' out to quell?"

The little Frenchman's only answer was a grin as he handed guns to Arif Pasha and me, retaining the fourth one for himself. "You will drive, Friend Trowbridge?" he asked.

Obediently, I slipped into a leather windbreaker and led the way to the garage. A minute later we were on the road to Mooreston.

He had evidently made a reconnaissance that afternoon, for he directed me unerringly to a large greystone structure on the outskirts of the suburb. On the north was the dense patch of second-growth pine through which the autumn wind soughed mournfully. To east and west lay fallow fields, evidently reservations awaiting the surveyor's stake and the enthusiastic cultivation of glib-tongued real estate salesmen. The house itself faced south on the Pike, on the farther side of which lay the grove of oak and chestnut into which Trula had escaped.

"Quiet, my friends, *pour l'amour d'un rat mort!*" de Grandin begged. "Stop the motor, Friend Trowbridge. *Attendez, mes braves. Allons au feu!*

"Now, my little lovely one!" With such courtesy as he might have shown in assisting a marchioness to shed her cloak, he lifted the overcoat from Trula Petersen's shivering shoulders, bent quickly and plucked the wool-lined slippers from her feet, then lifted her in his arms and bore her across the roadway intervening between us and the lawn, that gravel might not bruise her unshod soles. "Quick, toward the house, *petite!*" he ordered. "Stagger, play the drunken one—cry out!"

The girl clung trembling to him a moment, but he shook her off and thrust her almost roughly toward the house.

There was no simulation in the terror she showed as she ran unsteadily across the frost-burnt lawn, nor was the deadly fear that sounded in her wailing, thin-edged cry a matter of acting. "Help, help—please help me!" she screamed.

"*Excellent; très excellent*," applauded from his covert behind a rhododendron bush. "Make ready, *mes amis*, I damn think they come!"

A momentary flash of light showed on the dark background of the house as he spoke, and something a bare shade darker than the surrounding darkness detached itself from the building and sped with pitiless quickness toward the tottering, half-swooning girl.

Trula saw it even as we did, and wheeled in her tracks with a shriek of sheer mortal terror. "Save me, save me, it's he!" she cried wildly.

Half a dozen frenzied, flying steps she took, crashed blindly into a stunted cedar, and fell sprawling on the frosty grass.

A wild, triumphant yell, a noise half human, half bestial, came from her pursuer. With a single long leap it was on its quarry.

"*Mordieu, Monsieur le Démon*, we are well met!" de Grandin announced, rising from his ambush and leveling his sawed-off shotgun.

The leaping form seemed to pause in midair, to retrieve itself in the midst of its spring like a surprised cat. For an instant it turned its eyes on de Grandin, and they gleamed against the darkness like twin spheres of phosphorus. Next instant it pounced.

There was a sharp click, but no answering bellow of the gun. The cartridge had misfired.

"*Secours*, Friend Trowbridge; *je suis perdu!*" the little Frenchman cried as he went down beneath an avalanche of flailing arms and legs. And as he fought off his assailant I saw the flare of gleaming green eyes, the flash of cruel strong teeth, and heard the snarling beastlike growl of the thing tearing at his throat.

Nearer than the other two, I leaped to my friend's rescue, but as I moved a second shadowy form seemed to materialize from nothingness beside me, a battle-cry of feline rage shrilled deafeningly in my cars, and a clawing, screaming fury launched itself upon me.

I felt the tough oiled leather of my windbreaker rip to shreds beneath the scoring talons that struck at me, looked for an instant into round, infuriated phosphorescent eyes, then went down helpless under furious assault.

"There is no power nor might nor majesty save in Allah, the Merciful, the Compassionate!" Arif Pasha chanted close beside me. "In the glorious name of Allah I take refuge from Shaitan, the stoned and rejected!" A charge of BB shot sufficient to have felled a bear tore through the clawing thing above me, there was a sharp snapping of metal, and a second blaze of searing light as the riot gun roared again.

The ear-piercing scream of my assailant diminished to a growl, and the growl sank to a low, piteous moan as the form above me went limp, rolled from my chest and lay twitching on the frosted earth.

I fought unsteadily to my knees and went faint at the warm stickiness that smeared the front of my jerkin. No need to tell a doctor the feel of blood; he learns it soon enough in his grim trade.

Costello was battering with his gunstock at the infernal thing that clung to de Grandin, not daring to fire for fear of hitting the struggling Frenchman.

"Thanks, friend," the little fellow panted, wriggling from beneath his adversary and jumping nimbly to his feet. "Your help was very welcome, even though I had already slit his gizzard with this—" He raised the murderous double-edged hunting knife with which he had been systematically slashing his opponent from the moment they grappled.

"Good Lord o' Moses!" Costello gasped as de Grandin's flashlight played on the two forms quivering on the grass. "'Tis Mr. an' Mrs. Bera! Who'd 'a' thought swell folks like them would—"

"Folks? *Parbleu*, my friend, I damnation think you call them out of their proper name!" de Grandin interrupted sharply. "Look at this, if you please, and this, also!"

Savagely he tore the black-silk negligee in which the woman had been clothed, displaying her naked torso to his light. From clavicle to pubis the body was covered with coarse yellowish hair, curled and kinky as a bushman's wool, and where the breasts should have been was scarcely a perceptible swelling. Instead, protruding through the woolly covering was a double row of mammillae, unhuman as the dugs of a multiparous beast.

"For the suckling of her whelps, had she borne any, which the good God forbid," he explained in a low voice. He turned the shot-riddled body over. Like the front, the back was encased in yellowish short hair, beginning just below the line of the scapulae and extending well down the thighs.

A quick examination of the male showed similar pelage, but in its case the hair was coarser, and an ugly dirty grey shade. Beneath the wool on its front side we found twin rows of rudimentary teats, the secondary sexual characteristics of a member of the multiparæ.

"You see?" he asked simply.

"No, I'm damned if I do," I denied as the others held silence. "These are dreadful malformations, and their brains were probably as far from normal as their bodies, but—"

"Ah *bah*," he interrupted. "Here is no abnormality, my friend. These creatures are true to type. Have I not already rehearsed their history? From the tumuli of Africa they come, for there they were pursued with gun and dog like the beast-things they are. In this new land where their kind is unknown they did assume the garb and manners of man. With razor or depilatories they stripped off the hair from their arms and legs, and other places where it would have been noticeable. Then they lived the life of the community outwardly. Treasure from ravished tombs gave them much money; they had been educated like human beings in the schools conducted by well-meaning but thickheaded American missionaries, and all was prepared for their invasion. America is tolerant—too tolerant—of foreigners. More than due allowance is made for their strangeness by those who seek to make them feel at home, and unsuspected, unmolested, these vile ones plied their dreadful trade of death among us. Had the she-thing not capitulated to her appetite for blood when she slew young Cableson, they might have gone for years without the danger of suspicion. As it was"—he raised his shoulders in a shrug—"their inborn savageness and Jules de Grandin wrought their undoing. Yes, certainly; of course.

"Come, our work is finished. Let us go."

The Curse of the House of Phipps

JULES DE GRANDIN DREW a final long puff from his cigarette, ground its butt against the bottom of the ash tray and emitted a tapering cone of smoke from his pursed lips, regarding our visitor with narrowed eyes. "And your *gran'père*, also, Monsieur?" he asked.

"Yes, sir; and my great-great-grandfather, and his father. Not a man of my branch of the family since old Joshua Phipps has lived to see his children. Joshua fell dead across the threshold of his wife's room ten minutes after she became a mother. Elijah, the son whom Joshua never saw, died in the last assault on Cornwallis's works at Yorktown. News travelled slowly those days, but when the company returned to Massachusetts they told his widow of their captain's death. All agreed he was shot through the lungs a little after ten in the morning. Half an hour earlier his wife had given birth to a son. That son died at Buena Vista the same day his son was born, and that son, my great-grandfather, was shot in the draft riots in New York during the Civil War. His twin children, a son and daughter, were born the same night. My grandfather died at San Juan Hill with Teddy Roosevelt the same day my father was born. I was born June 6, 1918—"

"*Mordieu*, the day that your so glorious Marines met the *boche* at Château-Thierry—"

"Precisely, sir. I was born a little after noon. My father went down shortly after one o'clock, full o' machine gun bullets as a pudding is of plums.

"Call it superstition, coincidence—anything you like—but I can't shake off the thought of it—"

"*Parfaitement*," the little Frenchman agreed. "The remembrance of these so strange deaths has bored into your inner consciousness like a maggot in a cheese. You are—how do you say in American? *Sans bouc*—goatless?"

"Exactly," the other smiled wanly. "If it were something I could sink my hands in—something tangible that I could shoot or stick a bayonet into—I'd stand up to it and say, 'You be damned!' but it's not. The men of my family—except old Joshua, perhaps—seem to have been pretty decent fellows. They fought their country's battles; they paid their debts; they were good to their wives, but—there it is. The birth of a child is the death warrant of every Phipps descended from Joshua of the Massachusetts Bay Colony, and I don't mind admitting that it's got my goat. I've been more than ordinarily successful in my work—I'm an architect, you know—I've several good commissions right now, but I just can't seem to get my mind on 'em. I've as much to live for as most men—work, achievement, possibly a woman's love and children; but there's this constant threat eating into me like a canker-worm, walking at my elbow, lying down to sleep with me and rising with me in the morning. I can't shake it any more than I can my skin. It hangs on like Sinbad's Old Man of the Sea. I've consulted half a dozen of these so-called occultists, even went to a clairvoyant and a couple of mediums."

He gave a short, hard laugh. "Did they help? Like hell! They all say, 'Fear nothing; evil from without cannot prevail against the good within!' or some such fiddle-faddle. I'm not after fairy-tale comfort, Dr. de Grandin; I want some assurance of safety, if it's to be had.

"Once I tried a psychoanalyst. He wasn't much better than the other quacks. Used a lot of learnèd-sounding double-talk about relative subconsciousness, fear complexes and inhibitions, then assured me it was all in my mind—but you can damned well bet he couldn't explain why all my male ancestors died as soon as they became fathers, and he didn't attempt it. Now"—the young man looked almost challengingly into de Grandin's thoughtful eyes—"they tell me you've an open mind. You don't slop over about the spirits of the departed, but you don't pooh-pooh any intimation of the supernatural. The mediums and occultists I've been to were a lot of ignorant charlatans. The psychoanalyst didn't seem to grasp the idea that there's something more than the merely natural behind all this—he waved aside everything that couldn't be recorded on one of his instruments or hadn't been catalogued by Freud. I believe that you can help if anybody can. If you can't do something for me, God have mercy. His mercy didn't seem to help my ancestors much."

"I appreciate your confidence and frankness, Monsieur," de Grandin answered. "Also, I concur in the pious wish that you may have the assistance of Deity. It may be true, as you say, that heaven's mercy did little or nothing for your ancestors, but then in olden days Providence was not assisted by Jules de Grandin. Today the case is different.

"Suppose, now, we commence at the commencement, if you please. You have, perhaps, some intimation concerning the untimely taking-off of your forebears? You have heard some plausible reason why your so distinguished ancestor *Monsieur Josué* found death's grinning countenance where he thought to look upon the features of his first-born?"

"Yes!" young Phipps answered tersely, a slight flush mounting to his face. "You'll probably call it a lot o' nonsense, but I'm convinced it's—it's a family curse!"

"U'm?" de Grandin thoughtfully selected a long black cigar from the humidor, bit its end and struck a match. "You interest me, Monsieur. Who cursed your family, and why, if you please?"

"Here," Phipps drew a small brown-leather volume from his pocket and thrust it into the Frenchman's hand, "you'll find the history of it there. Obediah, Joshua's younger brother, wrote it in his diary way back in 1755. Start reading there; I've checked the pertinent entries in red," he indicated a dog-eared page of ancient, porous paper closely barred with fine writing in faded logwood ink. "Obediah's comments may seem melodramatic in the cold light of the twentieth century; but when we remember how Joshua fell strangled with blood at the entrance of his wife's chamber, and how his son and his son's sons died without seeing their children, it doesn't seem so overdrawn, after all. Something else: Every man jack of 'em died in such a way that his mouth was smeared with blood. Oh, the old curse has been carried out to the letter, whether by coincidence or not!"

"U'm?" de Grandin repeated noncommittally, taking the slender book in his hand and examining its binding curiously.

It was a cap octavo volume, bound in beautifully tanned leather carved with scrolls, *oeils-de-boeuf* and similar ornaments dear to eighteenth century bookbinders. Across the back was stamped in gold:

> OBEDIAH PHIPPS
> HYS JOURNALL

"Friend Trowbridge," de Grandin rushed quickly through the book's yellowed leaves, then passed it to me, "have the kindness to read us what old Monsieur Obediah set down in the long ago. Me, I understand the barbarities of your language passably, but I think we shall get the fuller effect by hearing you read aloud. I should make sad hash of the old one's entries. Read on, my friend, like Monsieur Balaam's ass, I am all ears."

Adjusting my pince-nez I moved nearer the desk lamp, glanced hastily at the indicated page, then, bending closer, for the once-black ink had faded to pale sepia with the passage of two hundred years, I read:

3d. Sep. 1775—This day came the trained band from fighting with the French; Joshua my brother looking mighty fine and soldier-like in his scarlet coat and the long sword which swung from his baldric. With them are come a parcel of prisoners of war, holden at the King his Majesty's pleasure.

Mostly children and young folk they be, and though they are idolaters and not of our Christian faith, I find it in my heart to pity their hard lot, for from this day they must be bearers of burdens, hewers of wood and drawers of water, bound to menial service to our people that the Commonwealth's substance be not eaten up in keeping them in idleness.

What is it I say? Obediah, it is well you are for Harvard College and the law, for the sternness of the soldier's trade or the fiery Gospel of the Lord of Hosts are things too hard for thee, meseemeth. And yet, while none shall hear me murmur openly against the fate of these poor wretches, I pity them with all my soul.

One among them rouses my compassion most. A lissome chit of girl, she, with nut-brown hair and eyes as grey as the sea, and such a yearning in her pale, frightened child-face as might wring compassion from a stone. I hear tell she will be put on the block on Wednesday next, though it is understood that Brother Joshua shall have her for his household drudge in part requital of his valiant work against the Frenchmen and the Indians. If this be so, God pity the poor wench, for Joshua is a hard man and passionate, never sparing of himself or others, and prodigal with fist and whip to urge his servants unto greater diligence.

"*Eh bien*, Monsieur," remarked de Grandin as I sought the next marked sage in the diary, "it seems this Monsieur Joshua of yours was the very devil of a fellow."

"Huh, you haven't got to first base yet," Phipps answered with a grimness of expression that belied the lightness of his words.

I found the second red-checked passage and began:

29th Sep. 1755 —Have pity, gentle Saviour, for I, the meanest of thy creatures and a sinful man, harbor thoughts of blood and death against mine own kin. On Lord's Day I visited my brother, and as I made to enter at the kitchen did behold Marguerite DuPont, the Popish serving wench, bearing water from the well. A brace of heavy buckets, oaken-staved and bound with brass, she staggered under, and their weight was like to bear her down, had not I hastened to her succor.

A look of passing wonder she gave me as I took the bucket-yoke from off her shoulders and placed it on mine own, and, "*Merci beaucoup, M'sieu*", she whispered, with the words dropping me a curtsey as though she were a free woman and mine equal in station.

Her hands are red and rough with toil, but small and finely made, and in die greyness of her eyes dwells that to make a man's heart beat the faster. Perchance she is a witch, like most of the idolaters, as Parson did expound at meeting that same morning. Howbeit, she is very fair to look on, nor do I take shame to myself for that I took her burden on me.

"C'est le sabbat, n'est-ce-pas, M'sieu'?" she asks me as I set the buckets down beside the doorstep, and when I nodded she looked at me so sadly I was like to weep for very pity.

Then from the bodice of her gown she drew a tiny cross-shaped thing, a bit of sinful vanity shaped like the cross whereon our Lord suffered for the vileness of mankind, and would have raised the symbol to her lips.

"What means this heathenry, ye Papist slut?" bellows Brother Joshua, bursting from the house-door like a watchdog from his kennel at scent of a marauder. "What means this demonry in a Christian man's house?" with which he struck the fond thing from her hand and caught her such a cuff upon the ear that down she fell beside it.

The lass picked up the cross and would have hid it in her dress again, but Joshua was quicker, and ground it under heel, well-nigh crushing her frail hand therewith.

She sprang up like a pantheress, her mild eyes all aflame, and defied him to his face.

"Thou harlot's brat, I'll learn ye to act so to your betters!" raged he, and struck her on the mouth with his clenched hand, so that the blood flowed down her chin and onto her kirtle.

"Nay, brother," I opposed, "entreat her not thus spitefully. 'Tis Lord's Day, and she, of all the townsfolk, labours. 'Remember the Sabbath Day to keep it holy . . . thou and thy manservant and thy maidservant . . .' As for her vanity, bethink you that her faith, mistaken though it be, is dear to her as ours is to us."

"Now, as the Lord liveth," swore Brother Joshua, "meseemeth thou art half a Papist thyself, Obediah. Whence comes this sudden courage to champion the Popish bitch? The Sabbath Day, quotha? at knoweth she of sabbaths, save those wherein the witches and warlocks make merry? Rest and meditation on the Sabbath are for the Lord's elect, not such as she. Now go thy ways, and quickly, lest I forget thou art my brother, and do thee injury."

Lord Christ, forgive! In that wild moment I could have slain him where he stood, nor had a thought of guilt for doing it. In will, if not in act, I am another Cain!

2d. Nov. '55, the next marked entry read.

At college, hard at work upon the middle voice of Greek, yet making sorry business of it.

Mea culpa,—I have sinned. Into my heart hath crept a lustful and unhallowed love for Marguerite DuPont, the kitchen-drudge.

What boots it is she be a bondmaid and a servant of the Antichrist? What matter though she be joined to her idols like Ephraim of old? Surely, though we approach God through Jesus Christ, our Lord and Saviour, or through His maid-mother Mary, the goal we seek is still the same, however different be our roads. And yet I may not tell her of my love; I dare not clip her in mine arms and whisper 'dearmeats to her. She is my brother's thing and chattel, bound even as his blackamoors and Indians are bound, though by the letter of the law she is a war-captive and subject to release on ransom or exchange. Woe me, that I have loved a Hagar in the tents of Abraham!

"Name of a small blue man, Friend Trowbridge," de Grandin tweaked the ends of his diminutive mustache, "I think I sniff the odour of romance here. Read on, I pray. I burn, I itch, I am consumed with curiosity."

"9th June, '56," I read, turning to the next marked entry.

O Lord Christ, fill me plenteously with Thy love, for love of woman never shall be mine! This day sennite Marguerite gave birth to a man-child. She holds her peace right stubbornly, though many of the goodwives, and even Parson himself, have urged her to declare her partner in iniquity that he may stand his trial with her for adultery. Anon, when she is taken from her bed, she must make recompense for her sin, and if her paramour be not discovered, must bear the scarlet symbol of concupiscence alone upon her bosom to her life's end.

Brother Joshua shows strange kindness for one so stern and upright. The child is cared for by his orders, and he has even visited the wretched mother in the outhouse where she lies. Forgive me, brother, I did wrong thee when I said thy heart was flint.

The child is dark, unlike its mother, and well favoured withal. 'Tis pity it must go through life as *filius nullius*, according to the lawmen's phrase.

5th Dec. '56, the next entry was headed.

My brother builds a house without the town. Foundations are already digged, and soon the chimneys will be raised. The idea likes me much, for when the building is completed he will take Marguerite and the child there, and she shall thus have respite from the townsfolk's jeers.

11th Dec. '56—My brother's charity is interpreted. 'Twas passing strange that he who would have rayed a flea for hide and tallow should have spent his substance on a bond-woman's brat. Her bastard? Nay, his own! The child she bore was his, and he who calls himself a man of war and valiant battler for the Lord, has taken refuge from his shame behind a woman's petticoat, and left her lonely to bear calumny, while she for very loyalty to her child's sire forbore to name him to the elders, however much they pressed her to declare her paramour.

25th Dec. 1756—O Marguerite, my Marguerite, how fondly have I loved thee! I had e'en thought of asking thee for wife and giving my name to thy brat, but now it is too late—have pity, Heaven!—too late!

Marguerite is no more, and on my brother's brow is graved indelibly the brand of Cain. From Cujo his blackamoor slave I have the tale, and though I may not denounce him, for I have but my own word, sith word of slave may not be taken in the court against the master, I here and now brand him a murderer. Joshua my brother, *Thou art the man!*

Together with his black slaves and his Indians, as precious a crew of cut-throats as ever hanged in chains, my brother went to his new house to lay the hearth, and with him went the child and Marguerite. In the darkness of the night they heard her singing to the babe as she gave suck, a wanton song wherewith the Popists greet the Christmas-tide, "*Venite adoremus.*"

"What means this heathenry within a half-built Christian house?" asks Brother Joshua, and catches her a smart cuff on the ear so that the child fell down upon the floor, and as it set up a wailing he spurned it with his foot. Thereat my Marguerite rose up and snatched a dagger from her dress and wounded him full sore, for she was like a she-bear when it sees its cub threatened.

"By Abraham and Isaac, and by the Joshua whose name I bear, I'll lay the hearthstone of my house according to the ancient rites!" my brother swears. "My house shall have to guard it that which none other in the colony can boast!"

And then they digged a great hole in the earth before the fireplace, and laid her bound therein, and rolled the hearth-slab forward to cement it over her.

So when she knew her end was come, and all hope fled, she cursed him in the English tongue she scarce could frame to form aright.

"Wo to thee, soiler of the innocent and hider of thy shame," she told him. "The wrath of God be on thy head and countenance, and on thy sons and thy sons' sons from generation unto generation. May thou and thy descendants drink blood in the day thy first-born is delivered. May thou and thy seed never look upon the faces of thy children or on thy wives in motherhood, and may this curse endure while hatred lasts!"

What more she would have said they know not, for even Joshua paled before her maledictions, and gave the signal for the stone to be put in its place.

De Grandin was leaning forward, his little round blue eyes fixed on me in a set, unwinking stare as I turned to the next entry. Young Phipps, too, sat rigidly, and it seemed to me the very air of my peaceful study was pregnant with the presence of those tragic actors in the old New England tragedy.

"3rd. Mar. '58," I read. "Joshua this day intermarried with Martha Partridge."

The next item was the last in the book, and seemed much later than the others, for the ink retained some semblance of its original blackness.

25th Dec. 1758—The curse has fallen. This night Martha my brother's wife, who hath been gravid, was delivered of a son whom they will call Elijah. Joshua sate before the fire in his great chair, gazing into the flames and on the hearth-stone which hides the evidence of the filthy act he wrought two little years agone, and thinking the Lord God only knows what thoughts. Did you see Marguerite's pale face in the flames, brother; did the wind in the chimney recall her pleading voice as you waited the midwife's summons to ascend the stairs?

Anon they came and said he had a son, and straightaway he rose up and went to look on him. But at the entrance of the chamber he fell down like Sisera of old when Jael smote him. And in that moment salt and bitterness were in his mouth, for from his lips gushed forth a bloody spate that dyed his beard and stained the oaken planking of the floor. He never saw the features of his lawful first-born son.

Have pity, Jesu!

It was dead-still in the study as I closed the little book. The soft hiss of a pine log in the fireplace sounded through the shadows, and the hooting of a motor horn outside came to us like a doleful period to the tale of futile love and stark tragedy.

"It sounds fantastic to me," I commented as I returned the book to young Phipps. "I remember the Arcadians were expatriated by the New England colonists during King George's War—Longfellow tells the story in *Evangeline*—but I never heard the poor devils were made virtual slaves by the New Englanders, or that they—"

"Many unpleasant things concerning our histories we forget easily, my friend," de Grandin reminded with a slightly sarcastic smile. "Your Monsieur Whittier the realist takes up the tale where Monsieur Longfellow the romanticist leaves off. However,"—he raised his shoulders in a shrug—"why hold resentment? The crimes the ancestors committed against New France was nobly atoned for by their descendants. Did not your soldiers from New England pour out virile young blood like water in two vast transfusions—twice in one generation, by blue! when *la belle France* bled white with the *sale boche's* bayonet wounds? At Cantigny and Château-Thierry and in the Argonne and on the beaches of Normandy they died all gloriously, while the descendants of those very Arcadians rested comfortably at home, enjoying the protection of Britain's arm, making no move to help the land whence they had sprang—*parbleu*, I damn think they had sprung too far!"

"But that other," I protested. "Burying a live woman under a hearthstone—why, it's incredible. They might have done such things in heathen times, but—"

"*Hélas*, Friend Trowbridge, your ecclesiastical learning is little better than your knowledge of history," de Grandin cut in. "Those old ones, Christian as well as pagan, laid the foundations of their houses, forts and even churches in blood. Yes.

"Saint Columba, founder of the abbey of Inona, inhumed one of his monks named Oran alive beneath the walls because he feared the demons of the earth might tear the holy structure down unless appeased by human sacrifice. Later historians have endeavored to sugar-coat the facts—later writers have revised the tale of *Chaperone Rouge* to make the little girl and her *gran'mère* come forth alive from the wolf's belly, also.

"Again, no later than 1885, was found another evidence of such deeds done by Christians. That year the parish church of Holsworthy, in north Devonshire, England, was restored. In the southwest angle-wall the workmen found a human skeleton interred; its mouth—and nose-places were stopped with mortar. The evidence was plain; it was a live-burial designed to make the walls stand firm because of human sacrifice to the earth-demons. Once more: In tearing down an ancient house in Lincolnshire the workmen found a baby's skeleton beneath the hearth. Yes, my friends, such things were done, doubtlessly, in olden days, and our Monsieur Joshua was but reviving a dead-but-not-forgotten custom of the past when he declared he'd lay the hearthstone of his house according to the ancient rites."

"H'm," I reflected, "it hardly seems possible such bigotry could have obtained so late, though. Just think, the Revolutionary War began only fifteen years later, yet here was a man so intolerant that—"

"*Eh bien*, again you do forget, my friend," the little Frenchman chuckled. "Your war of revolution had been fought and won, also your second war with England, and our so glorious Revolution was a *fait accompli* while yet the Catholics burned Protestant and Jew with fine impartiality. It was not till the year that Andrew Jackson held New Orleans from the British—1814—that the last *auto da fé* had been held in Spain. And not till 1829 were Catholics granted civil rights in England. Until that time they could not vote or hold a public office—yet the legislation to enfranchise them met with violent, bloody opposition.

The soldiers had to be called out to put down 'anti-Papist' mobs. But we indulge in reminiscence unduly. It is with Monsieur Phipps' problem we must deal.

"Tell me," he turned to the visitor, "is this house of blood and sorrow where your wicked ancestor met death still standing, and if so, where?"

"Yes," Phipps replied. "I've never been there, but it's still owned by the family, though it's been unoccupied for twenty-five years or more. I'm told it's in remarkably good condition. It stands just outside the present city of Woolwich, Massachusetts."

De Grandin drummed thoughtfully on the desk top. "I think it would be well for us to go there, my friend."

"What, out to that old ruin, now?"

"*Précisément.* When water is polluted one seeks the source of the stream. It seems to me the fountainhead of the doom resting on your menfolk may be that unhallowed grave where Marguerite DuPont lies buried without benefit of clergy or the tribute of a single tear, save such as your great-uncle Obediah may have shed for her in secret."

"CAB, SIR? TAXI? TAKE you to the best hotel in town," a lean, lank Yankee youth challenged as we alighted from the B. & M. train and lugged our handbags from the Woolwich station.

"*Holà, mon brave,*" de Grandin challenged in his turn, "you know the country hereabouts, I doubt not—and the old landmarks, yes?"

"Ought to," the other answered with a grin, "been here all my life."

"*Très bon.* You are the man we seek, and none other. Can you deliver us in good condition at the old Phipps homestead—you know that place?"

An expression of blank amazement came to the Jehu's lean, weather-stained face. The Frenchman's request, it appeared, was comparable to that of a tourist in Naples asking to be driven to the rim of Vesuvius' crater.

"D'ye mean ye want to go there?"

"Assuredly. It stands and may be readied, *n'est-ce-pas?*"

"Oh, yeah, you can *git* there a' right, but—"

"But getting back is something else again, one is to understand? No matter. Do you transport us thither. We shall take responsibility for getting back."

The youth led us to a dilapidated Ford which seemed in the last stages of paralysis agitans and took almost as much coaxing as a balky mule to get under way.

For half an hour we drove through wide well-kept streets and along a smooth highway, finally headed up a rutted clay road to the cedar-pillared entrance of a weed-choked park. "This is as far's I go," our driver announced as he brought the limping vehicle to a halt.

"But no, it is that we desire assistance with the luggage," de Grandin protested, only to meet with a determined shake of the head.

"Not me, Mister. I contracted to bring ye here, an' I done it, but nothin' was said about my goin' into that place, an' I ain't a-goin'—"

"Eh, what is it you tell me?" de Grandin tweaked the ends of his mustache. "Is it a place of evil reputation?"

"*Is* it? Say, brother, you couldn't get th' State Militia to camp there overnight. 'Course, I don't believe in ghosts or nothin' like that, but—"

"*Mais certainement*, so much is evident," de Grandin's features creased in one of his quick elfin smiles, "but you would not test your disbelief too strongly, is it not? Very well, we thank you for the transportation. As to that in which you disbelieve so staunchly, we shall endeavor to cope with it unaided, and with the burden of our luggage, also."

The old Phipps mansion was, as Edwin Phipps had told us, in remarkably good repair for its age and the neglect it had suffered during the past quarter-century. The door that pierced the centre of the building was of adz-cut timber, roughly smoothed with a jack-plane and hung on massive "Holy Lord" hinges of hand-wrought iron. It seemed strong enough to withstand a siege supported by anything less than modern artillery.

Edwin produced a key of hammered brass massive enough to have locked the Bastille, fitted it to the iron-rimmed keyhole and shot back the bolts. Hardly conscious that I did so, I wondered that the lock should work so smoothly after years of disuse.

"*Entrez*," de Grandin stood aside and waved us forward; "the great adventure is begun, my friends."

The room we entered was like the setting of a stage. Obviously it was originally intended as both entrance-hall and living room, possibly as dining room as well. Lofty and paneled in some sort of age-darkened wood, with a fireplace large enough to drive a limousine through, it gave that impression of immensity and chill one gets in going through a Continental cathedral. A broad staircase, balustraded in hand-wrought oak, ran to a gallery whence three doors, one to the right, two to the left, gave off. There were also doors letting through the right wall of the hall, but none to the left. At the stairway's foot, by way of newel post, stood a massive bronze cannon, muzzle down, evidently the spoil of some raid led by old Joshua against the French, for engraved on its breech were the Bourbon arms and a regal crown surmounting a flourishing capital *L*. In the centre of the hall was a great table of Flemish oak; several straight-backed chairs, faded and mouldering with age, stood sentry against the walls. Before the monstrous fireplace, almost on the hearthstone, yawned a massive armchair upholstered in tattered Spanish leather. I wondered if this could be the "great chair" in which old Joshua sat when the midwife came to call him to his son, and to the doom pronounced on him and his by Marguerite DuPont.

De Grandin glanced about the place and shook his shoulders as if a chill more bitter than that of the December day had pierced his fur-lined greatcoat. "*Pour l'amour d'un bouc*, a little fire would help this place immensely," he murmured. "Phipps, my friend, do you dispose our belongings as seems good to you. Trowbridge, *mon vieux*, by your leave you and I will sally forth in search of fuel for yonder fireplace."

We had included a pair of Boy Scout axes in our outfit, and in a few minutes cut a plentiful supply of dry wood from the fallen trees in the grove behind the house.

"How is it with your nose, my friend?" he asked as we stacked our forage by the rear door—the very door where Obediah Phipps had taken Marguerite DuPont's burden on his shoulders.

"My nose?" I looked inquiringly at him.

"*Précisément*. Your nose, your proboscis; the thing with which you smell."

"I hadn't noticed anything wrong—"

"So? Did you detect a strange smell in the house?"

"H'm. There's that mingling of dust and dry leather, mildew and decay you always smell in old houses, particularly those that have been shut up a long—"

"*Mais non*, it was not that. I can not quite place it, and I am puzzled. It is a sort of blending of the odours of naphtha and linseed oil—"

"About the only place you're likely to smell that would be a printshop. Printer's ink is made of—"

"*Mordieu!*" he slapped me on the shoulder. "*Tu parles, mon vieux! L'imprimerie*—the printing-office, yes! The place where they spread ink containing linseed oil and naphtha and the good God knows what else on the type, then wash it off with benzine. Why should there be a smell like that in this old house, I ask to know?" He eyed me fiercely, almost accusingly.

"Haven't the slightest idea. I hadn't noticed it. Perhaps your nose played tricks on you. These old houses are as full of strange smells as—"

"As my poor head shall be of maggots until the mystery is solved," he supplied. "No matter; we can give it our attention in the morning. Meanwhile we have our work to do, and me, I am most vilely hungry.

"*Mille pardons*, little one," he murmured almost humbly as he crossed the wide slate hearthstone to lay logs in the fireplace, "we do not tread upon your grave with wanton feet."

DINNER WAS A SIMPLE meal: Fried eggs and bacon and potatoes washed down with strong boiled coffee, tinned biscuit thickly spread with Camembert and a bottle of Saint Estephe which de Grandin had insisted on bringing. Camp cots were set up on the freestone floor of the great hall, and we rolled ourselves in several thicknesses of blankets before ten o'clock had sounded on de Grandin's little travelling timepiece. "*Bonne nuit, mes braves*," the little Frenchman murmured sleepily. "Let us sleep like the clear conscience; we have much to do tomorrow."

The fire had died down to a sullen smouldering embers, and shadows once more held dominion in the great cold hall when I awakened with a start. Had I been dreaming, or had there been a Presence bending over me? I wondered as I opened sleepy eyes and looked about. Whatever it had been, it had not been hostile, I knew. Just for a moment I had sensed something, something white and misty, bending above me, a pleasant, comforting something like a mother soothing her child in the night—smooth, calming hands passing lightly over my features, a gentle murmuring voice, a faintly familiar scent breathed through the darkness.

"Trowbridge, *mon ami*," de Grandin's whisper came, "did you see—did you feel it?"

"Ye-es, I think so—" I began, but stopped abruptly at the sound from Edwin Phipps's cot.

"*Ug—ou!*" Half exclamation, half frightened, strangling cry it was, and in the quarter-light we saw him rear upright in his blankets, wrestling with a thing invisible to us.

"It—something tried to choke me!" he gasped as de Grandin and I rushed to his aid. "I was asleep and dreamed someone—a woman, I think—bent over me, stroking my cheeks and forehead, then suddenly it—whatever it was— seemed to change, to go as savage as a lunatic, and grasped me by the throat. Lord, I thought I was a dead pigeon!"

He rose from his cot, accepted a sip of brandy from de Grandin's flask, and felt his neck gingerly. "'Spect it was a dream," he murmured with a shamefaced grin, "but 'such stuff as dreams are made on' is mighty solid hereabouts if it were."

I was about to make some soothing commonplace remark when de Grandin's minatory hiss and upraised finger cut me short. Distinctly through the outside darkness came the echo of a shot, a second one, and a woman's wailing, terrified scream, both curiously faint and far-away seeming.

We waited tensely a moment, then, as the woman's cry repeated, de Grandin snatched up his coat and tiptoed to the front door. As he flung it open the muffled quality of the sounds was explained. While we slept before the fire a sleet-storm had come up, and though there was but little wind the icy dribble fell with a hiss almost menacing as that of a snake.

An indistinct form blundered through the sleet-stabbed dark; it was not well-defined—a sort of something mantled in light-colored draperies weaving to and fro as if it lacked the sense of sight, or followed a zigzagging trail. Now and again it stopped with raised arms, then bowed above the ice-glazed ground and criss-crossed back and forth, clashing into shrubs, caroming from tree to bush to broken garden ornament. "What is it?" I asked uneasily. There was that about the lurching form which made me unwilling to see it at close quarters.

"*Parbleu*, it is a woman!" Jules de Grandin exclaimed, and even as he answered came the faint, exhausted hail:

"Help! Help; please help me!"

Together the Frenchman and I dashed into the storm, seized the half-fainting girl and dragged her to the shelter of the house.

"Thanks!" she gasped as we brought her into the hall. "I think I'd have been done for in another moment. If—you—hadn't—" her voice broke, and she slumped down, an inert wet huddle on the freestone floor.

"*Grand Dieu*, Friend Trowbridge, see; it is that she is wounded!" cried de Grandin as he bent to raise her. "*Assistez-moi, s'il vous plaît.*"

On the left sleeve of her suede trench coat showed a spot of angry red, and as I helped him take away the garment I saw the leather was pierced by two small holes, one at the rear of the sleeve, the other at the front. Obviously, a bullet-wound.

Working quickly, we removed her overcoat and Fair Isle sports vest, then washed and bandaged the wound as best we could. For lack of better styptic we made a pack of boric acid powder, of which we fortunately had a small can, and crushed aspirin tablets, thus approximating Senn's first-aid dressing. For bandages we requisitioned three clean handkerchiefs from de Grandin's dressing-case, and tore a towel lengthwise to knot it round her neck for a sling.

"How comes it, Mademoiselle, that you flee wounded through the storm?" de Grandin asked as he lowered the glass of brandy-and-water from her lips. "What *sacré bête* has done this monstrous thing?"

The girl gave him a smile that was half grin, and wrinkled her nose at him. "I only wish I knew," she answered. "If I could get him up my alley—" She broke off with a wince of pain, then took command of herself again.

"Joe Darnley and I were driving home from Branchmoore when this storm came down on us like a circus tent collapsing. Something went wrong with the gadget that works the jiggermacrank just as we came to the lane leading here. The storm had got us all confused, and neither of us knew just where we were, so while he got out to tinker with the thingununy in the engine I took the flash and looked for landmarks. Just as he got the doololly fixed and we were ready to start, another car came rushing down the road—no lights, either!—and someone in it shouted for us to get the hell out o' there. Guess we didn't move fast enough, for they started shooting, and I felt something like a blow from a fist, then a hornet-sting, on my left arm. It hurts like fury, too!" She made a little face, then turned to de Grandin with a brave effort at a smile.

"Joe Darnley's a swine. The contemptible thing stepped on the gas and left me there, wounded and lost. I screamed for help and started to run—not in any special direction; just run, that's all. Presently I saw your light and—here I am." She gave the Frenchman another friendly smile, then seemed to stiffen with sudden frightened realization.

"I say, this is the old Phipps house, isn't it? Who—who are you? I thought this place was deserted—I've always heard it was haunted by—" She broke off with another effort at a smile, but it was not highly successful.

"*Eh bien*," de Grandin chuckled, "the story is a long one, Mademoiselle. However, we are here quite lawfully, I assure you. *Permittez-moi*. This is Monsieur Edwin Phipps, one of the owners of the property; this is Dr. Samuel Trowbridge, of Harrisonville, New Jersey. I am Jules de Grandin of Paris and elsewhere, and all of us are at your service."

She nodded in frank friendliness. "It's no mere figure of speech when I say I'm glad to meet you. My name's DuPont—Marguerite DuPont, of Woolwich, Massachusetts. I'm assistant at the public library, and very much in debt to you gentlemen for services rendered."

"Good gracious!" I exclaimed.

"Marguerite DuPont!" young Phipps repeated in a sort of awed whisper.

"*Sacré nom d'un fromage bleu!*" swore Jules de Grandin.

She looked at us with puzzled resentment. "What's the matter? DuPont's a good name, isn't it?"

"Good?" de Grandin echoed. "O, *la la!* It is an excellent-good name, indeed!" Then:

"Your pardon, Mademoiselle. The name DuPont is intimately connected with the tragedy of this old house, and with the bloody doom that dogs the family that owns it. Tomorrow, or the next day, or the next day after that, when you are feeling stronger, we shall explain in detail. Now, if you please, you shall lie down and rest, and we shall take especial pains that no harm comes to one of your name in this place, of all others."

After some good-natured argument we agreed the girl should occupy Phipps's cot, for the identity of the charming guest's name with that of the author of the family curse seemed to have unnerved the youngster, and he declared sleep impossible.

Nevertheless, we all dropped off after a time, de Grandin once more rolled in his blankets like an Indian, I lying on my cot and watching the flames of the replenished fire, the girl sleeping lightly as a child, her cheek pillowed on her uninjured hand; Phipps hunched in his ancestor's great chair before the fireplace.

I T WAS MARGUERITE'S SCREAM that wakened me. Bolt upright, wide awake as if sleep had not visited my lids, I looked about the great dark hall. Phipps still sat in the great armchair before the dying fire, de Grandin, apparently, slept undisturbed in his blankets; Marguerite DuPont sat erect in bed, lips parted to emit another scream.

A creak on the wide oaken stairs diverted my attention from the frightened girl. Slowly, seeming more to float than walk, a tall, white shrouded figure came toward us.

"*Conjuro te, sceleratissime, abire ad tuum locum!*" the sonorous Latin words of exorcism rang through the high-ceiled hall as de Grandin, now thoroughly awake, hurled them at the ceremented figure bearing down on us.

He paused a moment, as though testing the efficacy of the spell, and from the fluttering folds of the advancing specter's winding-sheet there came a peal of wild, derisive laughter.

I caught my breath in dismay, for the laughter seemed completely infernal, mad as a cachinnating echo from a madhouse, sounding the death-knell of sanity, but Jules de Grandin advanced on the apparition. "Ha, so *Monsieur le Fantôme*, you are not to be deterred by words? You try to make one *sacré singe* of Jules de Grandin? Perhaps you have an appetite for this?"

The speed with which he snatched the little Belgian automatic from his pocket was incredible, and the shots followed in such quick succession that they seemed like a single prolonged report.

The mocking laughter stopped abruptly as a tuned-out radio, and the sheeted thing swayed for a moment then fell head-foremost down the wide stairway.

"Good heavens!" I gasped. "I—I thought it was a—a—"

"*Un fantôme?*" de Grandin supplied with a half amused, half hysterical laugh. "Me, I think that that was the intention of the masquerade, and I damnation think they set their stage poorly. In the first dullness of awakening I also was deceived, but I heard a stair creak underneath his foot, and ghosts do not cause creaky boards to squeak. *Alors*, I turned from exorcism to execution, and"—he indicated the sheet-swathed form—"it seems I made a real ghost where there was a make-believe before. I have skill at that, my friend. Oh, yes."

Bending over the white cheesecloth-wrapped figure he drew the cerements aside. The man beneath was naked to the waist and wore a pair of corduroy trousers tucked into Army-surplus combat boots. Six bullet-wounds, as blue as bruises and hardly bleeding at all, were pitted in his left breast in a space that could be covered by a man's hand. From the corners of his mouth twin threads of blood trickled, indicting pleural haemorrhage.

"Why, it's Claude Phipps!" the DuPont girl gasped in an awe-struck voice. Frightened almost senseless when she thought she saw a ghost, she showed only a sort of fascinated curiosity at sight of the dead body.

"Eh, what is it you say, Mademoiselle—Phipps?" de Grandin queried sharply.

"Yes, sir. Claude Phipps. He's always been a wild sort, never seemed to keep a job, but just a little while ago he started making money. Big money, too. Everybody thought he played the races. Maybe so. I wouldn't know. His family's lived in Woolwich since I don't know when, and last year he and Marcia Hopkins were married and built a lovely home over at Mallowfield. But now—"

"But now, indeed, Mademoiselle," de Grandin cut in. "One wonders. There is more here than we see. This childish masquerade of ghosts; the warning you and your unvalorous escort received, your wounding—

"Down, my friends! *Ventre à terre!* Keep from the light!" Matching his command with performance, he flattened himself to the floor and the rest of us followed instant suit.

Nor were we a second too quick. The thunderous roar of sawed-off shotguns bellowed even as we dropped, and a shower of slugs whistled over us.

The Frenchman's little pistol barked a shrewish rejoinder, and Edwin Phipps, revolver in hand, wriggled across the floor, firing rapidly. Somebody screamed in the dark and the crash of rending wood was followed by a hurtling body striking the hall floor with a thud. The ensuing silence was almost deafening; then a whimper from the fallen man before us and a piteous groan from the balcony told us the battle was ended with all casualties on the other side.

By the light of our electric torches we examined our late foemen. The man who fell from the balcony when the balustrade gave way had shattered his left tibia and fractured his left clavicle. The man above was shot through the right shoulder and left thigh, neither wound being serious except for profuse haemorrhage.

For a few minutes, with improvised bandages and splints, de Grandin and I worked feverishly. We were rigging a crude Spanish windlass to staunch the bleeding from our late enemy's leg when Marguerite called shrilly: "Fire! The house is burning!"

"My God!" our patient begged hoarsely. "Get us out o' here, quick! There's two drums o' benzine in th' cellar, an'—Quick, Mister. There's a car hid in th' woodshed!"

No second warning was necessary. We piled the wounded men on cots and rushed them from the house, found the Cadillac concealed in the crumbling woodshed and set the motor going. Five minutes later, with Marguerite for pilot, we started down the road for Woolwich.

We did not take our departure too soon. The house, entirely of wood save for its chimneys and hall-paving, was burning like an English village balefire on Guy Fawkes Day before we reached the highway. Before we'd travelled half a mile there came a muted detonation and showers of sparks and burning brands shot into the sleet-stabbed December night.

"That would be *le pétrole*," murmured Jules de Grandin sadly. "It seems our task is somewhat delayed by this night's business."

"How's that?" I asked.

"It is that we must wait until the embers of that wicked house have cooled—a week, perhaps—before we draw the fires of the old grudge," he replied enigmatically.

THE STORY THAT THE wounded men told the police surgeon to whom we turned them over was not particularly novel. Claude Phipps, ne'er-do-well descendant of the proud old family, had grown to manhood with all the vices and few, if any, of the virtues of his ancestors. His widowed mother had sufficient money to send him to art school, but not enough to support him as a dilettante, and his attempts to support himself were abortive. He was one of those who could be trained but not taught; though he could copy almost anything with photographic fidelity he had no more ability to compose a picture than his brush or palette or mahl-stick. Enraged at failure and on the brink of actual starvation, he took up engraving as a trade and had no difficulty in earning high wages, but his passion for expensive living and his frustrated snobbery made a prosperous craftsman's life distasteful. Since boyhood he had consorted with petty criminals, race touts, petty gamblers and the like, and when one of these introduced him to an ex-convict who had been a counterfeiter the result was predictable as the outcome of a motion picture mystery. He became the chief engraver of the ring, the two men we had captured were his plant-printer and assistant; the former convict and his associates distributed the product.

The evil legends of the old Phipps homestead and the fact that it had been untenanted for years provided them a cheap and relatively safe headquarters, and their plant was set up in the cellar, while the sleeping rooms upstairs provided them with a *pied-à-terre*. Once or twice neighbours had attempted half-hearted investigation of strange lights and sounds observed there after dark, but the ghost-outfit with which the unbidden tenants had provided themselves, accompanied by appropriately eerie shrieks and demoniacal laughter, discouraged amateur detectives.

Recently, however, Treasury operatives had been becoming uncomfortably inquisitive, and "the boss" had ordered operations discontinued when one last lot of spurious bills had been printed. It was with the fear of the Secret Service in their minds that Claude and his assistants had discovered Marguerite and her escort apparently reconnoitering the approaches of the house and fired on them.

The two survivors were for shooting us at once when our presence was discovered, for they had no doubt we were Treasury operatives, but Claude prevailed on them to let him try his spectral masquerade before resorting to firearms.

"U'm," de Grandin murmured thoughtfully as the wounded man concluded his recital. "This Monsieur Claude of yours, he lived at Mallowfield, did he not? Will you be good enough to furnish us his address?"

As soon as our business with the police was concluded he rushed from the station house and hailed a taxicab. "To 823 Founders' Road, Mallowfield," he ordered, and all the way through the long drive he seemed almost like a victim of acute chorea.

A light burned in the upper front room of the pretty little suburban villa before which the taximan deposited us, and through a rear window showed another gleam of lamplight. A large closed car was parked at the curb, and as we passed it I espied the device of a Mercury's caduceus on its license plate, thus proclaiming its owner a member of the medical fraternity.

No answer came to de Grandin's sharp ring at the doorbell, and he gave a second imperative summons before a light quick step sounded beyond the white-enamelled panels. A pleasant-faced woman in hospital white opened the door and regarded us with a half-welcoming, half-inquiring smile. "Yes?" she asked.

"Madame Phipps? She is here—she may be seen?" de Grandin asked, and for once his self-assurance seemed to have deserted him.

The nurse laughed outright. "She's here, but I don't think you can see her just now. She had a little son—her first—two hours ago."

"Sacré nom! Le sort—the ancient curse—it still holds!" he exclaimed. "I knew it, I was certain; I was positive we should find this, but I had to prove it! Consider: Monsieur Claude the worthless, I shot him some two hours ago; he died with blood upon his mouth, and almost in that same moment his wife became the mother of his firstborn. This is no business of the monkey with which we deal, mon ami; mille nons; it is a matter of the utmost gravity. But certainly." He nodded solemnly.

"Nonsense!" I broke in. "It's just coincidence, a gruesome one, I'll grant you, but—well, I still say it's just coincidence."

"You may have right," he agreed sombrely. "But men have died with blood upon their mouths by such coincidences as this since 1758. Unless we can—"

"Can what?" I prompted as we retraced our steps toward the waiting taxi.

"No matter. Hereafter we must deal in deeds, not words, Friend Trowbridge."

IT WAS ALMOST A week before the fire-ravaged ruins of the old house cooled sufficiently to permit us to rummage among charred timbers and fallen bricks. The great central chimney stood like the lone survivor of a burned forest among the blackened wreckage. The heat-blasted paving of the hall, supported by the arches of the vaulted cellar, remained intact, as did the mighty fireplace with its arch of fieldstone; otherwise the house was but a rubble of burned joists and fallen brick.

The little Frenchman had been busily engaged during the intervening time, making visits here and there, interviewing this one and that, accumulating stray bits of information from any source which offered, particularly interviewing the French Canadian priest who served the Catholic parish within the confines of which the ancient house had stood.

Beginning with a call of perfunctory politeness to inquire concerning her wound, Edwin Phipps had spent more and more time in Marguerite DuPont's company. What they talked of as they sat before the pleasant open fire of her cottage while he assisted her with tea things, lighted her cigarette and otherwise made his two hale hands do duty for her injured member I do not know, but that their brief acquaintanceship was ripening into something stronger was evidenced by the glances and covert smiles they exchanged—silent messages intended to deceive de Grandin and me, but plainly read as hornbook type.

I was not greatly surprised when Edwin drove Marguerite up to the site of the old house late in the forenoon of the day appointed by de Grandin for "*la grande experience.*"

Beside the little Frenchman, with stole adjusted and service book open, stood Father Cloutier of the Church of Our Lady of Perpetual Help. Near the cleric, viewing the scene with a mixture of professional dignity and wondering expectation, stood Ricardo Paulo, sexton of the church and funeral director, and near him was an open casket with the white silk of its tufted lining shining in the bright December sunshine.

From a roll of burlap de Grandin produced a short, strong crowbar, inserted its wedge-end between the slate hearthstone and the pavement, and threw his weight upon the lever. "Quick, Friend Trowbridge, lend me your bulk," he panted, bearing heavily upon the bar. "I lack the weight to budge it, me!"

I joined him, bore down on the crowbar, and wrenched the iron sidewise at the same time. The great slab came away from its anchorage, tilted obliquely a moment, then rolled back.

Before us lay a stone-walled crypt some two and a half feet deep by four feet wide, more than six feet long, floored with a bed of sand. I am not certain just what I expected; a skeleton, perhaps; perhaps a desiccated lich, kiln-dried from long immurement in a crypt before the great fireplace.

A girl, young slim and delicate, lay on the sand that floored the catacomb. From linen cap to heavy brogans decorated with brass knuckles she was carefully arrayed as if clad to attend a town meeting of old Woolwich. True, her wrists were bound together with a rawhide thong, but the fingers of her hands lay placidly together as though folded in prayer, and her face was calm and peaceful as the faces of few who die "naturally" in bed are.

But what amazed me most was the startling resemblance between the dead girl and Marguerite DuPont who even now came timidly to look upon the features that had lain beneath the stone of sacrifice for almost two hundred years.

"A-a-ah!" de Grandin let his breath out slowly between his teeth. "*La pauvre, la pauvre belle créature!* Now, *Monsieur le Curé*, is the time—"

Something—a wisp of vapour generated by the burning of the house and confined in a cranny of the hearth-grave, perhaps—wafted from the martyred French girl's tomb and floated lightly in the chill midwinter air. Next instant Edwin Phipps had fallen to the pavement, clawing at his neck and making uncouth gurgling noises. About him, as if his clothing were steeped in warm water, hung a steamlike wraith of fume, and at the comers of his mouth appeared twin tiny stains of blood, as though a vessel in his throat had ruptured.

"No—no; you shall not have him! He's mine; *mine*, I tell you!" the cry seemed wrung from Marguerite DuPont who, on her knees beside the fallen man, was fighting frantically to drive the hovering vapour off, beating at it with her hands as if it were a swarm of summer gnats.

"To prayers, Friend Priest! *Pour l'amour d'un canard*, be about your work all quickly!" De Grandin waved imperatively to the mortician and his assistants.

"*Enter not into judgment with Thy servant, o Lord; for in Thy sight shall no man he justified, unless through Thee he find pardon . . .*" Father Cloutier intoned.

Quickly, but with astonishingly dextrous gentleness, the funeral assistants lifted the girl's body from its crypt and placed it in the waiting casket. There was a sharp click, and the casket lid was latched.

Like steam dissolving in the morning chill the baleful vapour hanging round young Phipps began to disappear. In a moment it was gone, and he lay panting, his head pillowed in the crook of Marguerite's uninjured arm, while with her handkerchief she wiped the blood away from his mouth.

"*Eternal rest grant unto her, O Lord, and let perpetual light shine upon her . . .*"

De Grandin's sudden laugh broke through the priest's cantillation. "*Barbe d'un ver de terre, c'est drole ça*—but it is funny, that, my friends! Me, I knew all; I have made much inquiry of late, yet never did I foresee that which has transpired. Jules de Grandin, thou great *stupide*, the good jest is on thee!

"Observe them, if you please, Friend Trowbridge," he nodded with delight toward Phipps and Marguerite. "Is it not one excellent-good joke?"

I looked at him in wonder. Edwin was recovering under Marguerite's ministrations, and as he opened his eyes and murmured something she bent and kissed him on the mouth.

"What's so damn funny?" I asked.

"Forgive my seeming irreverence," he begged as we set out for the cemetery to witness the interment of poor Marguerite DuPont's body, "but as I said before, I knew much that is withheld from you, and might have foreseen that which has occurred had I not been one great muttonhead. Attend me, if you please:

"You have expressed surprise that Mademoiselle Marguerite shows such a strong resemblance to her whom we have but a moment since raised from her unconsecrated grave. *Parbleu*, it would be strange if it were otherwise. The one is great-great-granddaughter of the other, no less! Consider: When first the young Monsieur Phipps advised us of this so mysterious doom that overhangs his family I was greatly interested. If, as the olden Obediah recounted in his journal, poor Marguerite DuPont lay buried underneath the evil hearthstone of that wicked house, I thought perhaps the memory of an ancient grudge—resentment which held fast like death—was focused there, for where the misused body lay, I thought, there would be found the well-spring of the malediction which has dogged the house of Phipps. Therefore, I told me, we must go there, untomb the body of unfortunate one and give it Christian burial. A fervent Catholic she had lived, such, presumably, she died, though there was no priest to shrive her soul or read the burial service over her. These omissions, I told me, must be remedied, and then perhaps she should have peace and the bane of her old curse might be unloosed. You see the logic of my reasoning? *Bien.*

"So to that old and very wicked house we went and on the very night of our arrival comes Mademoiselle Marguerite the second praying shelter from the storm and those miscreants who have wounded her.

"Anon there comes that Monsieur Claude intent on frightening us away, but I am not deceived and shoot him dead as a herring. He dies, and in that same hour his son is born. Thus by accident or design the old doom falls on him.

"What I did not know at the time was that the lady we had rescued was a lineal descendant of that Marguerite DuPont whose body we have come to accord Christian burial. Remember how it is recorded that she bore a son to wicked old Monsieur Joshua. That son assumed his mother's name, since craven cowardice had caused his father to disown him.

"At first the scandal of his birth hung on him like a dirty cloak, but those were stirring times, the freedom of a people trembled in the balance, and men were measured more by deeds than by paternity. From out the crucible of war came Joshua DuPont a hero, and later he became a leading citizen of Woolwich. His progeny retained his virtues, and the family which he founded now ranks with that from which he sprang. DuPont is now an honoured name in Woolwich.

"This much I learned by discreet inquiry; what I could not know, because my eyes were everywhere but where they should have been, was that the hatred of the ancestors offered no bar to the love of their descendants, *Parbleu*, that Monsieur Cupid, he shoots his arrows where he damn pleases, and none may say him nay!

"Today, when the last gasp of dying hatred would have overwhelmed Friend Edwin, Mademoiselle Marguerite does battle with her ancestress for the life of him she loves and—how is it the Latin poet sings?—*Amor omnia vincit*—love conquers all, including family curses. Yes. I am very happy, me." He drew a handkerchief from his cuff and dabbed at his eyes.

HALF AN HOUR AGO de Grandin and I returned from the pretty home Edwin and Marguerite Phipps have built in Harrisonville. This afternoon their first-born son, Edwin de Grandin Phipps, *aetatis* six months and five days, was christened with all the ceremony ordained by the Book of Common Prayer, with Jules de Grandin and me for godfathers. There was much to eat and more to drink attendant on the function, and I regret to say my little friend returned in a condition far removed from that approved by the good ladies of the W.C.T.U.

Seated on the bed, one patent leather shoe removed, he gazed with mournful concentration at the mauve-silk sock thus exposed. "I wonder if she sometimes thinks of me," he murmured. "Does she dream within the quiet of her cloister of the days we wandered hand in hand beside the River Loire?"

"Who?" I demanded, and he looked up like a man awakened from a dream.

"My friend," he answered solemnly, "*Je suis ivre comme un porc*—me, I am drunk like a pig!"

The Drums of Damballah

I

"AND SO, GOOD FRIENDS, I bid you Happy New Year." Jules de Grandin replaced his demitasse on the Indian mahogany tabouret beside his easy chair and turned his quick, elfin smile from Detective Sergeant Costello to me.

"Thanks, old chap," I returned, taking the humidor which Costello had been eyeing wistfully ever since we adjourned to the drawing-room for coffee and passing it toward him.

The big Irishman selected one of the long, red-and-gold belted Habanas and fondled it between his thick, capable fingers. "Sure, Dr. de Grandin, sor," he muttered, "'tis meself that wishes th' same to you, an' many more of 'em, too."

"*Eh bien*, my friend," de Grandin bit a morsel of pink peppermint wafer and held it daintily between his teeth as he sipped a second draft of the strong black coffee, "you do not appear in harmony with the season. Tell me, are you not happy at the New Year?"

"Yeah," Costello returned as he struck a match and set his cigar alight, "I got lots o' cause to be happy right now, sor. Happy like it wuz me own wake I'm goin' to. To tell ye th' truth, sor," he added, turning serious blue eyes on the little Frenchman, "'tis Jerry Costello that'll be lucky if he ain't back in uniform, poundin' a beat before th' New Year's a month old."

"*Parbleu*, do you tell me?" de Grandin demanded, his smile vanishing. "How comes it?"

Costello puffed moodily at his cigar. "There's been hell poppin' around the City Hall for th' last couple o' weeks," he returned, "an' they've got to make a example o' someone, so I reckon old Jerry Costello's elected."

"Eh, you are in trouble? Tell me, my friend; I am clever, I can surely help you."

The big detective gazed moodily at the fire. "I only wish ye could, sor," he answered slowly, "but I'm afraid ye can't. There's been more devilment goin' on in town th' last two weeks than I ever seen in a year before, an' there ain't no reason for any of it. I just can't make head nor tail of it, an' th' mayor an' th' newspapers is ravin' their heads off about police inefficiency. Lookit this, for example: Here's young Mr. Sherwood, just th' slip of a lad he is, right out o' divinity school. First thing he does when he gits ordained is to open a little chapel over in th' East End, workin' night an' day amongst th' poor folks. He gits th' men to lay off th' gin an' razors, an' even bulls some of 'em into going to work instead o' layin' around all day an' lettin' their women support 'em. That's th' kind o' lad he wuz; fine an' good enough to be a priest—God forgive me for sayin' it! An' what happens? Why, just last week they find him in th' little two-by-four room he used for a study wid his head all bashed in an' his Bible torn to shred an' th' pieces layin' all around th' place.

"All right, sor, that's th' first, but it ain't th' last. That same night th' little Boswell gur-rl—as pritty a bit o' wee babyhood as ye ever seen—she disappears. Th' nurse has her out in th' park, ye understand, an' is hurryin' home, for it's turnin' dark, an' right while she's passin' th' soldiers' monument, out pops someone an' swipes her over th' head so hard she's laid up for three days wid concussion o' the brain.

"We searched high an' low for th' little one; but never hide nor hair o' her do we find. Rewards are posted, an' th' papers is full of it; but no one steps up to claim th' money. 'Twarn't no ordinary kidnapin', either, for whoever stole her tried his level best to kill th' nurse at th' time, an' would 'a done it, too, if she hadn't been one o' them old fashioned gur-rls wid long hair piled on top o' her head, so's th' coil of it broke th' force o' the blackjack he hit her wid.

"An' lissen here, sor: 'Twas on th' same night some dirty bums breaks into St. Rose's Church an' steals a crucifix from one o' th' altars—bad cess to 'em!

"Now, crimes is like 'most everything else: they don't happen just because, sor. There's got to be some motive back of 'em. That's what's makin' a monkey out o' me in these cases. Nobody had anything agin th' pore young preacher. He didn't have a relative, much less an enemy in th' world, as far as we could find out, an' as for money, if he'd 'a' had two nickels to jingle together, he'd 'a' been out givin' one of 'em to some worthless, no-account darky to buy food or coal oil, or sumpin' like that. It couldn't 'a' been an enemy that kilt him, an' it couldn't 'a' been robbery yet there he wuz, cold an' still, wid his head mashed in like a busted punkin an' his Bible all torn to scraps."

"Ah?" de Grandin sat forward in his chair, his little, round eyes narrowed to slits as he gazed intently at the big policeman. "Say on, my friend; I think, perhaps, I see some sense to these so senseless crimes, after all."

Costello gave him an astonished look as he continued: "We might set pore Mr. Sherwood's murder down to some crazy man, sor, and we might think Baby Boswell was just kidnapt by someone who wuz holdin' her for ransom, waitin' till her parents gits even more discouraged before he puts in his bid for money; but who th' divil would want to burglarize a church? An' why didn't they break open th' pore box while they wuz about it, 'stead o' stealin' just one little brass crucifix? I tell ye, sor, there ain't no reason to none of it; an' I can't make head nor tail—"

"Yo're wanted on th' tellyphone, Dr. Trowbridge, sor," announced Nora McGinnis, my household factotum, thrusting her head through the draw- ing-room door and casting a momentary glance of unqualified approval toward the towering bulk of Sergeant Costello.

"Dr. Trowbridge?" an agitated voice called in response to my curt "Hello?"

"Can you come over to Mrs. Sherbourne's at once, please? One of the guests has fainted, and—"

"All right," I cut in, hanging up the receiver, "I'll be right over.

"Want to come?" I called to de Grandin and Costello. "There's a fainting woman over at Sherbourne's, and they seem to need a licensed practitioner to administer aromatic ammonia. Come along, Sergeant; a drive in the air may cheer you up."

THE OLD YEAR WAS dying hard as we drove toward the Sherbourne mansion. A howling wind, straight from the bay, tore through the deserted streets, flinging sheets of razor-sharp sleet against the windshield and overlaying the pavement with a veneer of gleaming, glass-smooth ice. Though our destination was a scant quarter-mile away, we were upward of half an hour covering the course, and I swore softly as I descended from the car, feeling certain that the young woman had long since recovered from her swoon and we had had our freezing drive for nothing.

My apprehensions proved unfounded, however, for a frightened hostess met us in the hall and conducted us to the upper room where her unconscious guest lay upon the snowy counterpane, an eiderdown quilt thrown lightly over her and a badly demoralized maid struggling ineffectually to force a hastily-mixed dose of aromatic spirit between her blanched lips.

"We've tried everything," Mrs. Sherbourne twittered nervously as de Gran- din and I entered the room; "aromatic spirit and sal volatile don't seem the least good, and—"

"When did the young *mademoiselle* swoon, and where, if you please?" de Grandin cut in softly, slipping out of his fur-lined greatcoat and taking the unconscious girl's thin, lath-like wrist between his fingers.

"Just before we called you," our hostess replied. "She seemed in the highest spirits all evening, singing, playing the old-fashioned games, dancing—oh, she was having an awfully good time. Just a little while ago, when Bobby Eldridge wanted someone to do the tango with him, she was the first to volunteer. The music had hardly started when she fell over in a heap, and we can't bring her to. It wasn't till all the home-made remedies had failed that I called you, Dr. Trowbridge," she added apologetically.

"U'm," de Grandin consulted his watch, comparing its ticks with the girl's pulsation. "She has eaten unwisely this evening, perhaps?"

"No. She hasn't eaten anything. That's the queer part of it. Everyone was eating and—I'm sorry to say—drinking considerably, too. We have to serve liquor to keep the young people satisfied since prohibition, you know. But Adelaide didn't touch a thing. I asked her if she were unwell, and she assured me she wasn't, but—"

"Precisely, *Madame*," de Grandin dropped the girl's wrist and rose with a business-like gesture. "If you will be so good as to leave us alone a moment, I think we shall revive Mademoiselle Adelaide without great difficulty." To me he whispered as our hostess withdrew:

"I think it is another case of foolish pursuit of the slender figure, Friend Trowbridge. This poor one seems half starved, to me, and—*barbe d'un chat*, what is this?" As he broke off he seized my hand and guided it to the unconscious girl's solar plexus.

Beneath the flimsy chiffon of her party frock I felt the hard, unyielding stiffness of a—corset.

"*Morbleu*," de Grandin chuckled. "Not content with starving herself to the thinness of an eel, the poor foolish one must needs encase herself in a corset so tight her breath can not find room to fill her lungs. Come, let us extricate her."

Deftly as though he had served as lady's maid all his life, he undid the fastenings of the girl's frock, laid back the silken folds and leaned above her to unloose the corset-hooks which bound her torso; but:

"*Sacré nom d'un poisson aveugle*, what in damnation's name have we here?" he demanded sharply. From hips to breast the girl was tightly bound in a corselet of some coarse, fibrous substance, irritant as the hair shirt of a Carmelite nun, and sewn upon the scarifying garment was a crazy patchwork of red, black and checkered cloth, not arranged in orderly or symmetrical design, but seemingly dropped at random, then fastened where it fell.

"S-o-o-o?" the little Frenchman let his breath out slowly between his teeth. "What connection has this one with this devilish business of the monkey which has so puzzled our good friend—

"Quick, my friend," he ordered, turning sharply to me, "bring up the good Costello, at once, right away, immediately. Do not delay; it is important."

Bewildered, I descended the stairs, hailed the sergeant from my waiting car and led him to the room where de Grandin waited.

"*Très bon*," the little Frenchman nodded as we entered. "Do you stand by the door, *cher sergent*; display your badge prominently. Now, Friend Trowbridge, let us to work!"

Drawing a tiny gold-handled pocket-knife from his waistcoat, he slit the queer-looking corset lengthwise and drew it from the girl's slim body, inviting my attention to the network of deep, angry scratches inflicted by the raw fiber on her tender white skin as he did so. "Now—" he put a wide-mouthed vial of smelling-salts to her nostrils, waited till her lids fluttered slightly, then seized the half filled glass of aromatic spirit and held it to her mouth.

The girl half choked as the restorative passed her lips, then put a thin, blue-veined hand up, pushing the glass from her. "I"—she stammered sleepily—"where am—oh, I must have fainted. Did anyone—you *mustn't* undo my dress—you *mustn't*, I tell you! I won't have—"

"*Mademoiselle*," de Grandin's usually suave voice grated unpleasantly as he cut through her hysterical words, "your gown has already been unloosed. This gentleman"—he indicated Costello with a nod—"is of the police. I have summoned him, and here he remains until you have given satisfactory answers to my questions. Upon your replies depends whether he leaves this house alone or—" He paused significantly, and the girl's dark hazel eyes widened in terror.

"Wha—what do you want?" she faltered.

"Await us in the hall, if you please, my sergeant," de Grandin bade; then, as the door closed behind the big policeman: "First of all, you will please tell us how comes it that you wear this so odious thing." He touched the patchwork-covered corset with the tip of his forefinger, gingerly, as though it had been a venomous reptile.

"It—it was a bet, a silly, foolish wager," she returned. "I wore it tonight just to prove I could stand the irritation a whole evening." She paused looking questioningly at the Frenchman's stern-set face to note the effect of her explanation; then, with sudden vehemence: "You've got to believe me," she almost screamed. "It's the truth, the truth, *the truth!*"

"It is a lie, and a very clumsy one, in the bargain," de Grandin shot back. "Come, Mademoiselle, the truth, if you please; we are not to be trifled with."

The girl gazed back defiantly. She was thin as almost fleshless bones could make her, yet gracefully built, and her long, oval face had that tantalizing pale olive complexion which in certain types of woman proclaims abundant health as surely as florid coloring does in others. Her deep hazel eyes, tragic with terror, turned questioningly toward the window, then the door beyond which Costello waited, and finally came to rest on de Grandin's glowing blue orbs. "I—won't—tell—" she began with deliberate emphasis; then, "Oh!" The interruption was half cry, half gasp, and came simultaneously with the crashing clatter of broken glass.

Shattered to a dozen fragments, one of the small panes of the bedroom window fell inward on the margin of hardwood floor bordering the Persian rug, and the girl wilted forward as though pushed from behind, then slid back with a slow, twisting motion, one hand fluttering upward toward her breast like a wounded white bird vainly trying to regain its nest.

Two inches below and slightly to the right of the gentle swell of her left bosom the hard, polished haft of a dagger protruded, and on the flimsy chiffon of her frock there spread with terrifying rapidity a ruddy, telltale stain. She was dead before we could ease her back upon the pillows.

"On guard, *Sergent,* close the doors, permit none to enter and none to leave!" de Grandin shouted, leaping to the window and tearing open the sash. "Call the station, have a cordon of police thrown round the house—another murder has been done, but by the beard of a bullfrog, the guilty one shall not escape!"

The big Irishman took charge with characteristic efficiency. Under his energetic guidance the guests and servants were gathered in the main drawing-room; within five minutes a siren shrieked its strident warning and a police car deposited a squad of uniformed men at the Sherbourne door. Assisted by powerful hand-searchlights brought from the station house, we scoured every inch of the grounds surrounding the mansion, and while a police stenographer stood by with pencil and notebook, Costello interrogated one after another of the horrified merrymakers. Half an hour's work convinced us we were up a blind alley. Not a hint or track of footprint showed on the hard-frozen sleet covering the lawn and encasing the tall poplar tree which stood beside the window through which the deadly missile had been hurled; not a guest at the party, nor a servant in the house, had left the building for a moment since de Grandin's shouted warning rang through the night; nowhere was there even the shadow of a clue at which the finger of suspicion could be pointed.

"Well, I'm damned; I sure am!" Costello ruefully admitted as he completed the investigation and prepared to notify Coroner Martin. "This looks like another one o' them cases wid no reason a-tall for happenin', Dr. de Grandin, sor. Ye can see for yerself how it is, now. Why should anyone want to murder that pore young gur-rl like that, an—" He lapsed into moody silence, drumming silently on the polished top of the telephone table as be waited for central to make his connection with the coroner.

"H'm, one wonders," de Grandin murmured, half to Costello, half to himself, as he snapped the mechanism of his pocket lighter and thrust the tip of an evil-smelling French cigarette into the cone of blue flame. But from the dancing lights in his small round eyes and the quick, imitable manner in which the ends of his carefully waxed blond mustache twitched, I knew he had already formulated a theory and bided his time to put it into words. "Come, Friend Trowbridge," he urged, tugging at my elbow. "There is nothing more we can accomplish here; besides, I greatly desire drink. Let us go."

2

"TIENS, MY FRIEND, IT seems the old year died in a welter of blood last night," de Grandin remarked the following morning as he pushed back his coffee cup and lighted an after-breakfast cigarette. "Regard this in the morning's news, if you please." He passed a copy of the *Journal* across the table, indicating the article occupying the right-hand column of the front page. Taking the paper, I read:

TORTURERS KILL GUARD IN ROBBERY
Novice Yeggs Slash Watchman
to Learn Safe Combination
He Did Not Know

The body of William Lucas, 50-year-old night watchman at the Eagle Laundry, 596 Primrose Street, was found early this morning on the company's loading platform. He had been tortured to death because he would not reveal the combination of the firm's safe. The safe had not been opened.

When found, the body had a slash on each hand, one on the sole and instep of each foot, another across the throat under the chin, and a deep knife wound in the back. In a vacant lot behind the laundry detectives found a stained paper bag containing a brace and bit, a glass cutter, a wire cutter, a metal trimmed stiletto sheath and a pair of low shoes.

The attempted safe robbery was so wholly the work of novices that police were able to reconstruct the crime in its entirety. The murderers, police said, left a multitude of clues. At least two men entered the building in Primrose Street before the last truck was parked in the sheds at nine o'clock last night. The robbers evidently knew that heavy collections were made by drivers on their final routes and that the money could not be banked until after the holiday, hence there would be a substantial amount in the office safe.

The yeggmen laid out their kit of cheap tools some time after midnight, took off their shoes and tiptoed after the watchman as he made his rounds. They found him in the rear of the building as he was punching the clock in the dynamo room, and forced him to accompany them to the office, where the torture began.

While one of the burglars tortured and questioned Lucas in vain the other turned to the safe and tampered with it. The lifted handles bear the impress of red-stained fingers.

Some time during the torture Lucas died. The coroner's physician will say today whether he died as a result of the slash in his throat, the wound in his back, or whether he bled to death from the many smaller wounds inflicted on different parts of his body.

The murderers dumped the body into a laundry basket and dragged it through the building to the landing platform. A trail of stains led the police along the way. On the loading platform, where the body was abandoned, one of the thugs left a most incriminating clue. The floor bore the mark of a large foot with long, prehensile toes, clearly outlined in crimson. This print definitely establishes the fact that there were at least two robbers, as the low shoes found in the bundle with the burglars' tools were too small to fit the footmark. They must have belonged to the other robber, who also tiptoed in stockinged or bare feet after the unfortunate watchman.

Lucas, police said, was tortured to reveal something he did not know. The combination of the safe had not been entrusted to him.

"Why," I exclaimed, "that's villainous! The idea of torturing that poor fellow! It—"

"Sure, Dr. Trowbridge, sor, 'tis bad enough, th' blessed saints know but 'tis sumpin' we can sink our teeth into, at any rate," announced Costello's heavy voice from the doorway. "'Scuse me for sneakin' in on ye like this, gentlemen," he apologized, "but it's crool cold outside this mornin' an' I thought as how ye wouldn't mind if I let meself in unannounced like, seein' th' door wuz unlocked annyhow."

"*Bien non*, by no means," de Grandin assured him, motioning to a chair. "Tell me, my friend, is this press account accurate?"

The detective nodded over the rim of the cup of steaming coffee I had poured him. "Yes, sor," he returned. "I wuz in charge at th' laundry, an' checked th' facts up wid th' reporters before they shot their stuff in. They're right this time—for a wonder. Praise be, we've got clear sailin' in a case at last. None o' yer mysterious, no-motive crimes here, sor. Just a case o' plain petermen's wor-rk, an' done be amatoors, in th' bargain. It looks open-an'-shut to me."

He fumbled in his pocket a moment, producing two narrow slips of paper. "I got a couple o' subpoenas from th' coroner for you gentlemen," he announced, handing us the summonses to appear at the inquest on the death of Adelaide Truman, "but if ye'd like to run over to th' Eagle Laundry an' look th' place over before ye tell what ye know to Coroner Martin, I'd be happy to take ye. I've got a police car waitin' outside."

"By all means," de Grandin assented eagerly. "This latest case of yours, my friend, it is a bit too obvious. It is altogether possible that someone makes the practical joke at our expense."

THE DEAD NIGHT WATCHMAN was not a pretty sight. However inexperienced they might have been as burglars, his assassins had done their murdering with the finesse of veterans. To me the only question was whether the unfortunate man died from the gaping slash across his throat or the deep incision which pierced his back just under the vertebral extremity of his left scapula. Either would have been almost instantly fatal.

De Grandin gave the body little more than passing notice. Instead he has-tened to the office where the atrocity had been committed, and cast a fierce, searching glance about, rushed to the single window and sent the shade sailing upward with a jerk of the cord, finally dropped to his knees and began exam-ining the floor with the nervous intensity of a terrier seeking the scent of a vanished rat.

I watched him in amazement a moment, then turned to rejoin Costello, but his sudden elated exclamation brought me to a halt. "*Voilà!*" he cried, springing to his feet. "*Triomphe*; I have found it; it is here! *Pardieu*, did I not say so? Assur-edly. Behold, my friend, what the good Costello and his fellows failed to see, and would not have recognized, had they done so, was not hidden from Jules de Grandin. By no means. *Regardez-vous!*"

In the palm of his outstretched hand lay a tiny cruciform thing, two burnt matches bound together in the form of a cross with a wisp of scarlet silk.

"Well?" I demanded, for the little man's shining eyes, quivering nostrils and excited manner indicated he placed great importance on his find.

"Well?" he echoed. "*Non*, my friend, you are mistaken; it is not well, or rather it is very well, indeed, for I now begin to understand much. Very damn much, indeed. This so detestable thing"—he indicated the crossed matches in his palm—"it is the key to much which I began dimly to per-ceive last night when Friend Costello strung together his so strange series of seemingly meaningless and unrelated crimes. Certainly. I now think, at least I believe—"

"All ready, gentlemen?" Sergeant Costello called. "We'll be gittin' over to th' coroner's, if ye're all done. Th' boys are finished wid th' fingerprints an' mea-surements, an' they'll be comin' from th' morgue for th' pore felly out yonder before long."

DE GRANDIN SAT WRAPPED in moody silence as the big police car bore us toward the coroner's. Once or twice he made as though to speak, but appeared to think better of it, and leaned back in his seat with tightly compressed lips and knitted, thoughtful brows. At last:

"What d'ye think of it all, Dr. de Grandin, sor?" Costello asked tentatively. "Have ye formed any theory yet?"

"U'm," de Grandin struck a match, carefully shielding its orange flame with his cupped hands as he set his cigarette alight, then expelled a double column of smoke from his nostrils. "I shall not be greatly astonished, *mon vieux*, if the man who slew Mademoiselle Truman last night and the miscreant who did the unfortunate Lucas to death shortly afterward prove one and the same. Yes, I am almost convinced of it, already, though a careful search of the poor dead ones' antecedents must be made before we can be certain."

"Arrah!" Costello looked his incredulity. "D'ye mean th' felly that murdered th' pore gur-rl an' tried to rob th' laundry wuz th' same?"

"*Précisément.* Furthermore, I am disinclined to believe that any robbery was intended at the Eagle Laundry. Rather, I think, it was a carefully calculated murder—an execution, if you please—which took place there. The bloody hand-prints on the safe door, the new and wholly inadequate burglars' tools so left that the police could not help but find them, the very obviousness of it all—it was the camouflage they made, my friend. *Mordieu*, at this very moment the miscreants lie snugly hidden and laugh most execrably at our backs. Have a care, villains, Jules de Grandin has entered the case, and you shall damn laugh on the other side of your mouths before all is done!" He struck his knee with his clenched fist, then continued more quietly: "There is much more to this case than you have seen, my Sergeant. By example, there is that patchwork corset, and the two burned matches—"

"A corset—two burnt matches!" Costello's tone indicated rapidly waning confidence in de Grandin's sanity.

"Exactly, precisely; quite so. In addition there is the murder of the innocent young clergyman, the stealing away of a helpless little baby, and much more devilment, which as yet we have not seen. Sergeant, my friend, these crimes without reason, as you call them, are crimes with the best—or worst—reason in the world, and this latest killing which you so stubbornly persist in thinking part of an unsuccessful burglary, it too is a link in the chain. These things are but the tail-tip of the serpent. This monstrous body we have yet to glimpse."

"Glory be to God!" ejaculated Costello with more force than piety as he bit off an impressive mouthful of chewing tobacco and set to masticating it in methodical silence.

3

I SAW BUT LITTLE MORE of Jules de Grandin that day. As soon as his brief testimony before the coroner had been concluded he excused himself and disappeared on some mysterious errand. Dinner was long over and I was preparing to turn in for some much-needed sleep when his quick step sounded in the hall and a moment later he burst into the study, eyes gleaming, mustache fairly on end with excitement. "*Mort dun bouc vert!*" he exclaimed as he dropped into a chair and seized a cigar from the humidor; "this day I have run back and forth and to and fro like a hound on the trail of a stag, my friend! Yes, I have been most active."

"Find out anything?" I asked.

"Assuredly yes. More than I had hoped; much more," he declared. "Attend me: The poor Mademoiselle Truman whose so tragic death we witnessed, she was not born here. No, she was a native of Martinique. Her parents, Americans, lived in Fort de France, and she was but the merest babe when Pelée erupted so terribly in 1902, killing nearly every living being in the capital. Both her father and mother perished in the catastrophe, but she was rescued through the heroism of a native *bonne* who fled inland and found such shelter as none but she and her kind could. For the next five years the child dwelt as a native peasant among the blacks, speaking Creole, wearing native clothes, nourished by native food and—*worshiping native gods.*

"Do you know Martinique, my friend? It is most beautiful; lovely as the island where Circe dwelt to change men into swine before destroying them utterly. A curse lies on those lovely islands of the Antilles, my friend, the curse of human bondage and blood drawn by the slave-driver's lash. Wherever Europe colonized and brought black slaves from Africa she brought also the deadly poison of the jungle Obeah. In North America it was not so. Your Negroes grew up beside the whites, a pleasant, loyal, glad-hearted race; but in the islands of the Caribbean they interbred with the savage Indians and grew into fiends incarnate. Yes. Consider how they rose against their masters, exterminating man and woman and tender, helpless babe; how they marched on the European settlements with the bodies of white infants impaled upon their pikes for standards, and slew and slaughtered—till even their insatiable blood-lust was slaked.

"Very well. That they had just cause for revolt no one can deny. It is not pleasant, even for a savage, to be stolen from his home and made to serve as slave in distant lands, and the sting of the whip is no less painful to a black back than to a white one; but the dreadful aspects of their revolts, the implacable savagery with which they killed and tortured, that is something needing explanation. Nor is the explanation far to seek. Beside their bonfires, far back amid the hills, they practised weird rites and made petition to strange and awful gods—dread, bestial gods out of darkest Africa, more savage still than the savages who groveled at their altars. It was from these black and blood-dewed altars that the insurgent slaves drew inspiration for their atrocities.

"Nor is that dread religion—*Vôdunu, Obeah,* or by whatever savage name it may be called—dead by any means. Today the Marines of your country fight ceaselessly to put it down in Haiti; the weak-spined Spanish government, and after it the forces of the Republic, have been powerless to stamp it out from the Cuban uplands; the Danish West Indies and the Dutch colonies turned their faces and declared there was no such thing as voodoo in their midst; and France has had no better luck in Martinique. No. The white man governs there; he can never hope to rule.

"Now, the aborigines of Martinique were known as the Caribs. A terrible folk they were—and are. Your very English word 'cannibal' comes from them, since *cariba* was what Columbus' sailors said when referring to the abominations of the Caribs when they returned to Spain. There are those who say that the Caribs were rooted out in the war waged on them by the French in 1658. It is, *hélas*, not so. They fled back to the hills, and there they mated with the blacks, producing a race tenfold more terrible than either of its parents. These are those who keen the voodoo chant before black altars in the uplands, who burn the signal fires at night, and, upon occasion, make sacrifices of black goats, or white goats without horns, to their deities. They keep the flame of hatred for the white man undying, and it was because of that the native nurse-woman risked her life to save poor little Baby Adelaide from the volcano.

"Ha, I see your question forming. 'Why,' you ask 'should she have risked her life to bear away the offspring of her master; why should she so carefully rear that little girl child when the holocaust of Pelée's eruption was done?' Ah, my friend, subtle revenge is sweet to the half-breed Carib as to the white man. That a child of the dominant and hated *blancs* should be reared as a Carib, taught their language, imbued with their thoughts, finally trained and initiated into their abominable religion and made to serve as priestess at their dreadful sacrificial rites—ah, that, indeed, would be a fit requital for all the woes her ancestors had undergone at the white man's hands. Yes.

"And so it was. For five years—the formative period of her life—poor Mademoiselle Adelaide lives as a Creole. When she was at last so steeped in savage lore that never, while life should last, could she throw away the influence, the 'faithful nurse' returned to Fort de France with her story of having rescued and nurtured the orphaned child of her employers. Relatives in America were located by colonial authorities and the little girl brought here—and with her came her faithful *bonne*, her foster-mother, old Black Toinette of the Caribs."

He rose abruptly, took half a turn across the study floor, then stopped and faced me almost threateningly.

"*And Toinette was a mamaloi of the voodooists!*" he fairly hissed.

"Well?" I demanded, as be continued to stand staring fixedly at me.

"'Well' be everlastingly burned in the lowest subcellar of hell!" he flared back. "It is not well. It is most damnably otherwise, my friend.

"Mademoiselle Adelaide was never allowed to forget that whatever gods she might pay outward homage to, the *real* gods, the great gods, were Damballah, Legba and Ayida-Wedo. When she was but a little child she astonished her Sunday School teacher by making such an assertion in answer to a catechism question, and when she was a grown young woman, eighteen years of age, her aunt, with whom she lived, surprised her and her aged nurse fantastically dressed and making worship to an obscene thing carved in the likeness of a serpent. The old woman was instantly dismissed; though, in gratitude for her services, she was given a pension; but poor Mademoiselle Adelaide's aunt tells me her niece paid many secret visits to old Toinette's dwelling, and what went on behind the closed doors of that house can better be conjectured than described, I fear.

"Now, attend me: Those who have traveled in Haiti have often been struck by certain oddnesses of dress, sometimes exhibited by the peasant women, dresses sewn over with crazy-quilt patterns, not beautiful, but most bizarre. Such patchwork is worn as penance, sometimes sewn to a corset of irritative substance, as by example, the fiber of certain species of gourds. When so worn it is at once an evidence of penance and purification, like the hair-shirts of certain monastic orders in mediæval times. Now, undoubtlessly, for some reason old Toinette ordered Mademoiselle Adelaide to wear that damnable garment of voodoo penance last night. Remember, the old nurse never for an instant lost her dominance over the poor child. No. The constant irritation of the sharp-pronged corset against her tender skin induced a fainting fit. I, who have traveled much and observed much, at once recognized the thing for what it was, and bade her tell us how it came that she wore it. She refused, but one who watched her through the window feared she was about to speak, and stopped her mouth with blood."

"Well," I cut in, "if this is so, why not go round to this old woman's house and arrest her? She can be made to talk, I suppose."

"Ah bah," he returned. "Do you think I have not considered that? You do me small courtesy, my friend. To the old one's house I went posthaste, only to find that she and her son—a hulking brute with arms as long as those of any ape—had decamped sometime during the night and none knows where they went."

He paused a moment, drawing at his cigar with short quick puffs; then: "How high would you say the lowest limb of the tree which grows beside Madame Sherbourne's house is from the ground—the tree from which an evilly disposed one might easily have hurled a dagger and slain Mademoiselle Adelaide?"

"H'm," I made a hasty mental calculation. "All of fifteen feet, I'd say. It's absurd to think anyone climbed it, de Grandin; he couldn't have reached the lowest limb without a ladder, for the trunk was literally glazed with ice, and no one could have swarmed up it. Nothing but an ape could have climbed that tree, thrown a knife and scuttled down again before the police came, at least not without leaving some trace, and—"

"Precisely, exactly, entirely so," he agreed, nodding vigorously. "*Tu parles, mon vieux*—you have said it. No one but an ape—or an ape-man. Did you examine the bloody footprint at the laundry where the ill-fated Lucas met his death?"

"Why, no; but—"

"Of course not; but I did. It might almost have been made by a gorilla, so great and long-toed was it. Only one accustomed to going barefoot, and much accustomed to using his toes in climbing, could have made that track. It took but a single glance to tell me that the maker of that footprint has arms of most extraordinary length. Such an one could have leaped the distance from the earth to catch that tree-limb, and climbed the icy trunk without great trouble. Such an one it was, undoubtlessly, who watched outside to see that Mademoiselle Adelaide made no betrayal, and who did the needful when he feared she was about to break beneath my questioning. Yes. Certainly."

"But see here," I expostulated. "Aren't you going pretty far in your assumptions? Because a man has an abnormally long foot is no sign he has unusually long arms like this hypothetical ape-man of yours."

"Do you say so?" he demanded sarcastically. "The great Alphonse Bertillon says otherwise. It was he who fathered the science of anthropometry—the science of measuring man—and it is one of his cardinal rules that the length of a man's foot from calyx to great toe-tip is the exact distance between the inner bend of his elbow and his radius. Here, let us test it!"

Reaching suddenly he snatched off one of my house slippers, and grasping my ankle bent my right foot upward to the inner side of my left arm. Dubiously I fitted the heel against the inner bend of my elbow, then stared in incredulous amazement. It was as he said. No rule could have measured my arm from wrist to elbow more accurately than my own foot!

"You see?" he asked with one of his quick smiles. The *Sûreté Général* long since adopted the Bertillon system, and the *Sûreté Général* makes no mistakes.

"Very well; to proceed with my day's discoveries: Having unearthed the poor *mademoiselle's* unhappy history, I turned my attention to the unfortunate Monsieur Lucas. Here, again, the trail of Africa's step-daughters lay across my path. In his younger days Lucas had been an American soldier, and served with distinction against the Spaniards in '98. Remaining in Cuba after peace was declared, he married a native woman and moved inland. There he became involved in certain of the less savory native mysteries, and served a term in prison. He moved to Haiti without the formality of divorcing his Cuban wife and found another companion for his joys and sorrows. *Tiens*, I greatly fear the latter far outweighed the former. His wife, an unlettered peasant woman, was but a step removed from savagery. She initiated him into the voodoo religion, and once more he worshiped in the *Houmfor* or voodoo mystery-house.

"Anon he tired of life in Haiti and come to this country. *But so did others.* My friend, in this very city of Harrisonville, New Jersey, there is a well-organized chapter of votaries of the Snake-Goddess. What they purpose doing I do not know for sure; that it portends no good I am most abominably certain. Lucas, homesick for the days in the Caribbean, perhaps, perhaps for some other reason, sought out these voodooists, and was recognized by some of them. He attended one or more of their meetings, and was there either branded as a traitor, or refused to countenance such inimical schemes as they broached. In any event, he was considered more valuable dead than alive, nor were they slow to carry out his death sentence. Everything points that way—the multiple wounds, the torture before the *coup-de-grâce*, most of all the two crossed matches which we found. They are a sign well recognized wherever voodoo is dominant. On one occasion, as I well know, the sight of such a silly, inconsequential object in the Palace at Port-au-Prince so frightened the president of Haiti that he remained indoors for two whole days! It was a bit of bravado, leaving those matches beside the body of their victim, but then they could not know that anyone here would recognize them; they could not know that Jules de Grandin would enter the case. No.

"Undoubtlessly the murder of the poor young clergyman was another link in this sinister chain. He labored lovingly among his dusky flock; they loved him. More, they trusted him. Beyond question some of them had heard the voodoo hell-broth brewing in their midst and had consulted him. He knew too much. He is dead.

"*Alors—*"

The sharp, cachinnating chatter of the telephone bell cut through his low, earnest words. "*Allo?*" he called irritably, snatching up the instrument. "Ah, Sergeant, yes. What? Do you say it? But certainly; right away; immediately; at once.

"Friend Trowbridge," he turned to me, his eyes flashing with anticipation, "it has come. That was the good Costello. He asks that we go to him at once."

"What did he say?" I asked.

"'Dr. de Grandin, sor,'" the little Frenchman's imitation of the big Irishman's excited brogue was a masterpiece of mimicry, "hell's broke loose over in Paradise Street. Th' blacks are shootin' th' night full o' holes an' two o' me men is hit hard, a'ready. We're nadin' a couple good doctors in a hurry, an' we 'specially nade a fela as can be handy wid the guns. Come a'runnin', sor, if yo' plaze."

4

GREATLY TO MY RELIEF, there was no longer need of "a felly who could be handy wid th' guns" when we arrived at that dingy thoroughfare ironically labeled Paradise Street by the city fathers. Reserves from half a dozen precincts and police headquarters, armed with riot paraphernalia had drawn a cordon round the affected area, and riot guns, tear-gas bombs and automatic rifles had cowed the recalcitrant blacks by the time I drew up at the outer of line of policemen and made our errand known. De Grandin was furious as a hen under a hydrant when he saw the last patrol wagon of arrested rioters drive off. With a pair of heavy French army revolvers bolstered to the cartridge belts which crossed his womanishly narrow waist, he marched and countermarched along the sidewalk, glaring into the darkness as though challenging some disturber of the peace to try conclusions with him.

"Dam' funny thing, this," Costello remarked as he joined us. "I know these here boys, an', speakin' generally, they're an orderly enough lot o' fellies. 'Course, they shoot craps now an' agin, an' git filled up wid gin an' go off on a rampage, 'specially of a Saturday night; but they ain't never give us no serious trouble before.

"Tonight, though, they just broke out like a rash. Kelley, from Number Four, wuz poundin' his beat down the lower part o' th' street, when be noticed a strange smoke sort o' scuttlin' down th' walk, an' not likin' th' felly's looks, started after 'im. Ye know how it is, Dr. de Grandin, for ye've mingled wid th' Paris police yerself. It's just natural for boys, dogs an' policemen to chase anything that runs from 'em, so when this here dinge started to run, so did Kelley.

"Th' felly slips into a doorway, wid Kelley right behind him, when *zingo!* there comes a charge o' buckshot an' Kelley goes down wid enough lead in 'im to sink a ship.

"He sounds his whistle before he goes out, though, an' a couple o' th' boys come a-runnin', an' I'm damned if th' whole street ain't full o' bullets in less time than ye can rightly say, 'Jack Robinson,' sor. Th' riot call goes out, an' we wound 'em up in pretty good shape, but three o' th' boys is hit bad, Kelley especially. He'll not pound a beat for many a long day, I'm thinkin'."

"H'm," de Grandin took his narrow chin between his thumb and forefinger and gazed thoughtfully at the snow-covered pavement, "did Monsieur Kelley, by any happy chance, describe the man he pursued before he was so villainously assaulted?"

"Only partly, sor. 'Twas a shortish sort o' felly, wid extra-ordinary long arms, accordin' to Kelley, an'—

"A thousand maledictions! I did know it!" de Grandin shouted. "It is the ape-man, Friend Trowbridge; the one who slew Mademoiselle Adelaide, and poor Lucas, the watchman; undoubtlessly the one who killed the clergyman, as well. *Nom d'un chameau*, we must find him! He and his twenty-times accursed dam are the keys of this whole so odious business or Jules de Grandin is a perjured liar!"

"WOULD YE BE AFTER givin' me an' a couple o' th' boys a lift, Dr. Trowbridge, sor?" Costello asked as de Grandin and I prepared to depart. "Th' doin's here is about over; an' I'd like to git back an' report before I hit th' hay."

With Costello behind me, and two uniformed men standing on the running board, I set out for police headquarters, choosing the wide, unfrequented roadway of Tuscarora Avenue in preference to the busier thoroughfares. Although it was not late the darkened avenue had a curiously deserted aspect as I drove slowly beneath the bare-limbed trees, and the sudden appearance of a hatless man, waving his arms excitedly, stung my startled nerves almost like the detonation of a shot in the quiet night.

"Police!" the stranger cried. "Is that a police car?"

"Well, sor, it is an' it ain't," Costello responded, "There's a load o' bulls ridin' in it; but ye couldn't rightly call it a departmental vehicle. What's on yer mind? I see yer hat ain't."

"My daughter," the other answered, almost sobbing, "My daughter Marrien—she's disappeared!"

"Ouch, has she now?" the detective soothed. "Sure, that's too bad. How long's she been gone—a week maybe?"

"No—no; now, just a few minutes ago!"

"Arrah, sor, how d'ye know she ain't gone to th' movies, or visitin' a friend, or sumpin'? Don't ye go gittin'—"

"Be quiet!" the distraught man cut in. "I'm Josephus Thorndyke; I think you know me; by name, at least."

We did. Everybody knew the president of the First National Bank of Harrisonville and director of half the city's financial enterprises. Costello's bantering manner dropped from him like a cloak as he jumped from the car. "Tell us about it, sor," he urged deferentially.

"She was complaining of a headache," Thorndyke replied, "and went to her room half an hour or so ago. I went up to ask if I could do anything, and found her door locked. She never did that—never. I knocked and got no answer. I went away, but came back in ten minutes and found her door still locked, though the light was burning. I had a pass the key, and when I couldn't get an answer I let myself in. Before I could unlock the door, I had to push key out; her door was locked on the inside—get that."

"I'm listenin'," Costello assured him. "Go on, sor."

"Her room was empty. She'd undressed, but hadn't changed her clothes— the window was open, and her room was empty. I ran down the back stairs and asked the cook, who'd been in the kitchen all the time, if Miss Marrien had gone through. She hadn't. Then I ran outside and looked on the ground, fearing she might have been seized with faintness and fallen from the window. It's a thirty-foot drop to the ground, and if she'd fallen she'd have been killed or so badly injured that she couldn't have moved, but there was no sign of her outside. I know she didn't come down the front stairs, for I was reading in the hall, and I've searched the house from top to bottom; but she's not there. There's not a piece of her clothing missing; but she's gone—vanished!"

"U'm, an' did ye call th' precinct, sor?"

"Yes, yes; they told me all the men were out on riot duty, and they'd send someone over in the morning. In the morning! Good God! Do you realize my child's gone—faded into the night, apparently? And they talk of sending someone round tomorrow!"

"Sure, it's lucky ye saw us when ye did," Costello muttered. Then: "This is right in your line, Dr. de Grandin; will ye be after goin' in wid me an' takin' a look around?"

"Assuredly, by all means, yes," the Frenchman agreed. "Lead on, my old one; I follow close behind."

THE TALL, HATCHET-FACED MAN with the mane of iron-gray hair who had accosted us seemed to take a fresh grip on his self-control as he led the way toward the house. "It may seem queer that I should be so positive about my daughter's not having changed her clothes," he suggested as we filed up the path toward the oblong of orange light which marked the mansion's open door, "but the fact is Marrien and I are nearer to each other than the average father and daughter. Her mother died when she was a wee baby—only three years old—and I've tried to be both father and mother to her since. There isn't a dress or hat, hardly a pair of gloves or hose, in her whole wardrobe that I don't know by sight, for she consulted me before buying anything. I've studied women's magazines and fashion books and even trailed round to dressmakers salons with her in order to keep posted on such things and be able to discuss clothes intelligently with her. She's the speaking image of her sainted mother when I married her thirty years ago, and—she's all I've got to love in the world; all I have to think of or live for!

"Now you understand," he added simply, as he led us to the white-enameled door of a spacious bedroom on the second floor and stood courteously aside to let us enter.

We glanced quickly about the apartment. The scent of gardenias lay heavy in the air; a crimson Spanish shawl, embroidered in brilliant silk, which trailed across the back of a carved Italian chair, was redolent with the perfume. A cheval-glass in a gilded frame reflected the ivory walls and the ormolu dressing-table set with ivory and gold toilet articles. Above the ivory-tiled fireplace where piled beech logs snapped and crackled cheerfully on polished brass firedogs, there hung a magnificent life-sized copy of Rossetti's *Beata Beatrix*, the closed eyes and parted, yearning lips of the figure suggesting, somehow, the motherless girl's vague, half-understood longings. On the bed's white counterpane lay a long-skirted evening gown of rose tulle and satin; a pair of tiny silver-kid sandals lay beneath an ivory slipper chair, one standing on its sole, the other lying on its side, as though discarded in extremist haste. A pair of moonlight-gray gossamer silk stockings lay crumpled wrong side out beside the shoes. It was a lovely, girl-woman's room, as expressive of its owner as a Sargent portrait; but empty now, and desolate as a body from which the soul has fled.

Unconsciously, instinctively, de Grandin bowed quickly from the hips in his quaint foreign manner as he entered this atmosphere supercharged with femininity; then, with Gallic practicality, he began a swift appraisal of the place.

The window was open a few inches from the bottom—a cat would have had difficulty in creeping through the opening—and, as Thorndyke had told us, there was no other exit from the room, save the door by which we entered, for the adjoining bath was without window, light and air coming from a skylight with adjustable sideslats that pierced the ceiling. "U'm; you are positive the door was locked on the inside when you made entrance, *Monsieur?*" de Grandin asked turning to the distraught father.

"Of course I am. I had to push the key—"

"Be gob, there's a drain-pipe runnin' down th' house widin three feet o' th' windy," Costello interrupted, drawing back from his inspection of the outside walls, "but it's crusted wid ice a quarter-inch thick. 'Twould take a sailor to slip down it an' a gorilla or sumpin' to climb it, I'm thinkin'."

"Ha?" de Grandin paused in his stride across the room and joined the detective at the window. "Let me see—quickly. Yes, you have right, my friend; the most athletic of young women could not have negotiated that descent. Yet—" He paused in silent thought a moment, then shrugged his shoulders impatiently. "Let us proceed," he ordered.

We searched the house from cellar to ridgepole, questioned the servants, confirmed Thorndyke's assertion that the back stairs could not be descended without the user being seen from the kitchen. At length, with such lame assurances as we could give the prostrated father, we prepared to leave.

"You have, perhaps, a picture of Mademoiselle Marrien for the *Sûreté's* information?" de Grandin asked as we paused by the drawing-room door.

"Yes; here's one," Thorndyke replied, taking a silver-framed portrait from a console table and extending it to the Frenchman. "Be careful of it; it's the only—"

"A-a-ah?" the sharp, rising note of de Grandin's exclamation cut short the caution.

"Good heavens!" I ejaculated.

"Mother o' Moses; would ye look a' that?" Costello added.

As mirrored likeness counterfeits the beholder, or twin resembles twin, the photograph of Marrien Thorndyke simulated the fine-cup, delicate features of Adelaide Truman, whose tragic death we had witnessed not twenty-four hours earlier.

Moving nearer the light to examine the picture, de Grandin paused in midstride, his sensitive nostrils contracting as he glanced sharply at a corsage bouquet of pale-lavender orchids, occupying a silver vase on a side table. Cautiously, as though approaching some living thing of uncertain temper, he lowered his nose toward the fragile, fluted-edged blossoms, then drew back abruptly. "These flowers, *Monsieur*; they came from where, and when, if you please?" he demanded, regarding Thorndyke with one of his fixed, unwinking stares.

Our host smiled sadly. "We don't know," he returned. "Some unknown admirer sent them to Marrien this evening; they came just before dinner. Queer thing; there was no card or message with them, and nobody saw the messenger who delivered them. The bell rang, and when Parnell answered it, there was an unmarked flower-box waiting in the vestibule, but no sign of any messenger. That struck me as especially odd; those chaps usually hang around in hope of a tip."

The little Frenchman's shrewd eyes had lost their direct, challenging look. He was staring abstractedly toward the drawing-room wall with the expression of one attempting to recall a forgotten bar of music or a half-remembered line of verse. "It is," he muttered to himself, "it is—*parbleu*, but certainly!" Of Thorndyke he demanded:

"You say *Mademoiselle* your daughter went to her chamber complaining of *mal de tête* shortly after dinner?"

"Yes; as a matter of fact we hadn't quite finished when she excused herself. It struck me as strange at the time, too, for she hardly ever suffers with headache. I think—"

"*Précisément, Monsieur*; so do I. I think this whole business has the odor of deceased fish on it. Sergeant,"—he turned to Costello—"your suggestion concerning the difficulty of ascending that drain-pipe was well made."

"How's that, sor? D'ye mean—"

"I mean the yokel finding a rib buried here, a vertebra interred there, and a clavicle hidden elsewhere in the earth would say, 'Behold, I have found some bones,' while the skilled anatomist finding the same things would declare, "Here we have various parts of a skeleton. My friends"—he swept us with a quick, challenging stare—"we are come to the door of a most exceedingly dark closet in which there rattles a monstrous skeleton. No matter, Jules de Grandin is here; he will turn the light upon it; he will expose the loathsome thing. *Parbleu*, he will drag it forth and dismember it piece by piece, or may the devil serve him as mincemeat pie at next Thanksgiving dinner!

"*Bon soir, Monsieur,*" he bowed to Thorndyke, "I know not the location of your vanished daughter; but I can damnation guess the sort of place where she lies hidden.

"Come, my friends," he motioned Costello and me before him, "there are thoughts to think, plans to make, and afterward, deeds to do. Let us be about them."

ONCE MORE IN MY study, he fell to pacing the floor with long, silent strides, soft-footed and impatient as a prisoned panther. "*Cordieu,*" he murmured; and, "*Morbleu,* they were clever, those ones. They used the psychology in baiting their trap. Yes."

"What the dickens are you talking about?" I demanded.

"Of Mademoiselle Marrien and her orchids," he replied, pausing in his restless walk. "Consider, my friend: When Monsieur Thorndyke gave us his daughter's picture and I moved to examine it beneath the light, my nose was assailed by a so faint, but reminiscent odor. I looked about for its source. Such a smell I have found upon the lips of those drugged that their houses might be robbed—once, even, I discerned it on certain fowls which had been stolen without making outcry. This was in Guiana. I recognized that smell, but at first I could not call it by name. Then I perceived the orchids, and bent to smell them. It was there. I am 'warm,' as the children say when they play their hide-away game. I ask to know concerning the bouquet. What do I learn? That they have come all mysteriously for Mademoiselle Marrien, none knows whence, or by whom brought. Thereupon I see everything, all quickly, like a flash in the dark. Being a woman, Mademoiselle Marrien can not help but thrust her nose into those flowers, even though she knows that orchids possess no perfume. It is a woman's instinctive act. Very good. The ones who sent those orchids traded on this certainty, and dusted the petals of those flowers with a powder made from the seeds of the *Datura stramonium.* These seeds are rich in atropine and scopolamine. Taken internally, in sufficient quantity, they cause headache, giddiness, nausea, unconsciousness, finally death. Inhaled in the form of powder, they adhere to the mucous membrane of the nose and throat, and within a short time cause violent headache, even unconsciousness, perhaps. That is sufficient for the miscreants' purposes. They would not slay Mademoiselle Marrien—yet. No. Beside roadway she must tread, the path into the grave would be a thoroughfare of joy."

"You're raving!" I assured him. "Granting your fantastic theory, how did Marrien Thorndyke manage to evaporate from her room and leave the door locked on the inside?"

For a long moment he stared at me; then: "How does the fledgling, which can not fly, manage to leave its nest when the serpent goes ravening among the tree-tops?" he returned as he pivoted on his heel and departed for bed.

5

IT WAS SOMETHING AFTER five o'clock next evening when my office telephone rang. "Trowbridge, *mon vieux*, come at once, immediately, this instant!" de Grandin's excited voice commanded. "She is found, I have located her!"

"She? Who?"

"Who but Mademoiselle Marrien, *par l'amour d'un bouc?*" he returned. "Come, I await you at police headquarters."

Quickly as possible I made my way to City Hall, wondering, meanwhile, what lay behind the little Frenchman's excited announcement. All day he had been off on some mysterious business of his own, a note beside my plate informing me he could not wait for breakfast, and would not return "until I do arrive."

In the guardroom at headquarters I found him, smoking furiously, talking excitedly, gesturing strenuously; obviously in his element. Beside him were Sergeant Costello, four plainclothes men and a dozen uniformed patrolmen, armed with an imposing assortment of gas bombs, riot guns and automatic rifles.

"*Bienvenu, mon brave!*" he greeted. "But now, I was telling the good Costello of my cleverness. Wait, you too shall hear: All day I have haunted the neighborhood of Paradise Street, searching, looking, seeking a sign. But an hour since I chanced to spy a *conjun* store, and—"

"A *what?*" I asked.

"A *conjun* shop—a place where charms are sold. By example, they had there powdered bones of black cats; they are esteemed most excellent for neutralizing an enemy's curse. They had also preserved bat wings, love potions, medicines warranted to make an uncongenial wife or husband betake himself elsewhere with greatest celerity—all manner of such things they had.

"I engaged the proprietor in talk. I talked of many things, and all the while I looked about me. The street was well paved and cleanly swept before the shop, there was not patch of muddy earth about the neighborhood, yet the fellow's boots and trouser-knees, even his hands, were stained with new, fresh clay. '*Parbleu*,' I say to me, 'this will bear investigating!'

"Forth from that shop I went, and walked quickly up the alley which runs behind it. The rear of the yard was fenced, but, *grâce a Dieu*, the fence contained a knothole, and to it I did glue my eye. Nor was my patience unrewarded. No. Anon I saw the dusky dispenser of charms come from his back door and scuttle across his *paved* back yard, entering a tiny shed of rough boards which stood near the rear of his lot. There was no chance for his feet to become muddied that way, my friend.

"I wait for him to emerge. My watch counts fifteen minutes, but still he does not come. 'Has he died in there?' I ask me. At last it is no longer to be endured. All silently I leap the fence and cross the yard, then peer into the little house.

Pardieu, what do I see? A hole, my friend: a great, gaping hole, like the open top of a newly digged well, and leading into it there is a ladder. Nothing less.

"Into that hole I lower myself, and when I reach the bottom I find the end is not yet. No; by no means. From the hole there runs a tunnel through the earth, and Monsieur the Black Man, whom I have followed, is nowhere to be seen. 'Very well,' I tell me, 'where he has gone, I, too, may go.' And so I do.

"That tunnel, my friend, it leads me across the street to the cellar of an old, long-disused house, a house whose doors have been boarded up and which has apparently been so long unused that even the newest of the many 'FOR SALE' signs which decorate its façade is quite illegible.

"*Tiens*, I look into that cellar, but I do not long remain to see what is there, for to be surprised in that place is to bid a swift *adieu* to life, and I have no desire to die. But in the little while I squat there like a toad-frog I hear and see so much that I can guess much more.

"I do not wait, not I; instead I come here with all speed and gather reinforcements. *Voilà*.

"Sergeant, the sun has set, already there is that beginning to commence which needs our early intervention. Friend Trowbridge and I will go first—it is a matter for no gossip where doctors go—do you and several of your men come shortly afterward, and guard the exits to the old, dark house. Anon, let the machine-gunners come, and take position all round the premises. When I whistle, or you hear a shot, come, and come quickly, for there will be great need of you."

"WE ARE ARRIVED, MY friend," he whispered as he led the way up a particularly malodorous alley and paused before a rickety board fence. "Come, let us mount."

We scaled the creaking barrier and dropped as quietly as possible to a brick-paved yard scarcely larger than an areaway. Guided entirely by memory, for we dared not show a light, de Grandin led the way to a wooden outhouse, paused a moment then began to descend a flimsy ladder reaching down a ten-foot hole in the earth.

For some distance we crept along a narrow, clay-floored tunnel, and finally came to a halt as the faint, reflected glow of a wavering light reached us. And with the light came the unmistakable acrid odor of crowded, sweating humanity, raw, pungent gin and another faint, indefinable stench, foul, nauseating, somehow menacing, as though, itself unrecognized, it knocked upon the long-forgotten door of a dim ancestral memory—and fear.

Inch by cautious inch we crept forward until at last we looked through a jagged opening into a low-ceiled, brick-walled cellar, illuminated by the smoke-dimmed rays of a single swinging oil lantern.

About the room in crescent-formation were ranged, four or five deep, eighty or more men and women. They differed from each other in both kind and degree, heavy-featured, black-skinned full-bloods crouching cheek by jowl with mulattoes, coarsely clothed laborers huddled beside dandified, oily-haired "sheiks," working-women herded in with modishly dressed she-fops of the dance halls and restaurants. Only in the singleness of purpose, the fixed intentness of their concentrated stares, did they seem held together by any sort of bond.

At the far side of the cellar was erected a grotesque parody of an altar. On it were saucers containing meal, salt and whole grains of corn, a bottle of square-face gin, a roughly carved simulacrum of a half-coiled snake, several tin cups, a machete honed to a razor edge and, turned upside down, a heavy, beaten brass crucifix. With a start I recalled Costello's story of the ravished church and the cross which had so strangely disappeared.

But I had no time for reflection, for my attention was quickly drawn to the group before the altar; two men and a woman squatting cross-legged before wide-topped kettle-drums, an aged and unbelievably wrinkled Negress arrayed in gaudy, tarnished finery resembling the make-up of a gipsy fortune-teller, and a young white woman, nude save for the short kilt of scarlet cloth belted about her waist, the turban of a bandanna tied round her head and the inane, frivolous bands of crimson ribbon, which circled her wrists and ankles.

She was squatted tailor-fashion facing the drums, and swayed slightly from the hips as the musicians kept up a constant thrumming rumble—a sort of sustained, endlessly long-drawn note—by beating lightly and with incredible quickness on the parchment drumheads with the padded drumsticks. There was something curiously unlifelike in the way her hands were folded in her scarlet lap, a sort of tired listlessness wholly out of keeping with the strained, taut look on her face.

The aged Negress was whispering to her with cracked, toothless sibilance, and, though I could not catch the words, I knew she urged some act which the girl stubbornly refused, for time and again the old hag wheedled, argued, cajoled, and as often the girl shook her head slightly but doggedly, as though her nerves and body were almost worn to the point of yielding, but her spirit struggled doggedly on.

But each time the crone repeated her request the drummers increased the volume of their racket ever so little, and, it seemed to me, the very persistence of sustained vibration was wearing the girl's resistance down. Certainly she was already in a state bordering on hypnosis, or else bound fast in the thrall of some potent drug; every line of her flaccid, unresisting body, the droop of her bare white shoulders, the very passivity with which she crouched upon the chill, bare earth proclaimed it.

At length the tempo of the drums increased and the volume of the rumble rose till it shook back low yet deafening echoes from the walls. The girl gave one final stubborn headshake, then nodded slowly, indifferently, as though too tired to hold her chin up for another instant. Her head sank forward, as though she napped, and her sloping shoulders drooped still further. The concentrated thought of the circling audience, the ceaselessly repeated importunities of the hag and the never-ending rumble of the drums had worn down her resistance; her psychic strength was broken, and she was but a mute and helpless tool, a helpless, mindless instrument without conscience or volition.

A quick, sharp order from the aged hag, who now assumed the rôle of priest-ess or mistress of ceremonies, and the girl rose slowly to her feet, put forth her hand and lifted the hinged top of a small square box reposing underneath the altar. As she turned her profile toward us I felt my heart stand still, for she was the counterpart of Adelaide Truman, the girl from Martinique. More, she was the original of the picture Thorndyke showed us, the missing Marrien!

A frightened squawk sounded as her groping hands explored the opened box. Next instant she straightened to her fullest height, two game cocks, one black, the other red, held firmly by the feet in her outstretched hands. For a moment she swayed, like a reed shaken in the wind, then, with a sinuous, side-stepping, sliding motion, described a narrow circle before the altar.

From its place before the reversed cross the ancient Negress snatched the machete, the blade flashed once, twice, in the lantern light, and the fowls beat the air tumultuously with their wings as their heads fell to the earthen floor.

And now the girl whirled and pirouetted frenziedly, the flapping rooster in her hands showering her with blood from their severed necks, so that her white shoulders and breast, even her cheeks and lips, were red as the flaunting cloth of her scanty costume.

The old high priestess snatched the dying cockerels from her hierophant's hands and held their spurting necks above a tin cup, pressing on their breasts and sides to force the flow of blood as one might press a leather water-bot-tle. When the last drop of blood was emptied in the cup, the gin bottle was uncorked and its fiery contents mingled with the chickens' gore.

Then followed a sort of impious travesty of communion. From hand to hand the reeking cup was passed, men and women sucking at it eagerly, slopping its ruddy contents on their clothes, smearing their faces with the sanguine mixture.

The drink drove them to frenzy. White eyes rolled madly, jaws dropped, lips slavered, as they swayed drunkenly from side to side. "Coq blanc, le coq blanc—the white cock!" they screamed. A young girl half rose from her seat on the floor, clutched her dress with both hands and ripped the garment down the front, exposing her bronze bosom, then fell to the floor again, rolling over and over, gibbering inarticulately, foaming at the mouth like a rabid she-dog. The drums roared and thundered, men howled and shouted hoarsely, women screamed or groaned in a perfect ecstasy of neuro-religious fervor—the bestial, unreasoning hysteria which sent the Sudanese fanatics fearlessly into Kitchener's shrapnel barrages at Khartoum. "*Coq blanc—coq blanc*," the cry rose insistently.

The blood-spattered girl ceased her rhythmic whirling a moment and reached once more into the covered box. Again she straightened before the lines of frantic blacks, and in her up-stretched hands she held displayed for all to see a trembling white rooster—the *coq blanc* for which they clamored.

Once more the machete flashed in the lantern light, and the poor bird struggled convulsively in its death spasm between her upraised hands, its blood douching her hair, brow and cheeks as she turned her face to bathe it in the gory cataract.

A pause fell on the crowd as she flung the cockerel's corpse contemptuously behind her—and wheeled about until her outstretched finger tips all but touched the altar's edge. So stiff it was that the labored nasal breathing of the audience rasped gratingly as we lay in our covert, wondering what new obscenity was next.

The drums halted their sullen muttering and the withered hag began a high-pitched, singsong chant of invocation.

From a door at the farther side of the cellar shambled the vilest thing I had ever seen in human form. Short, hardly more than five feet tall, he was, but with a depth of chest and breadth of shoulder like those of a gorilla. Like a giant ape's too, were his abnormally long-toed feet and his monstrous arms, which hung so far below his knees that it seemed he might have touched his knuckles to the earth; yet he scarcely stooped an inch to do so. Slope-headed, great-mouthed, half beast, half human he seemed as he advanced with a rolling gait and paused before the altar, then, bending quickly, dragged forth a heavy wooden chest bound round with iron reinforcement. I did not need de Grandin's nudge to call attention to the dozen or more augur-holes piercing the top and ends of the box; I saw them at first glance, and in the same moment my nostrils caught the strengthened odor of that stench which had first appalled me as we crept along the tunnel.

The drums began again, and with their rhythmic mutter came the muted moaning of the audience, a sound half fearful, half eloquent of adoration, but wholly terrifying.

The girl before the altar crouched and genuflected, her head bowed low, her arms uplifted, as though she were a postulant bending to receive the veil which makes her sacrosanct from the world and undisseverable bride of the Church. And from the iron-bound chest the hideous ape-man dragged forth a squirming, white-bellied snake, a loathsome, five-inch-thick reptile with wicked, wedge-shaped head and villainous, unwinking eyes, *and laid it like a garland round the girl's uncovered shoulders!*

Sluggishly, as though but partially aroused from a torpor, the monstrous reptile coiled its length—it was all of fifteen feet—about the bare arms of its holder, slid its twining bulk about her breast and torso, its tail encircling her slender waist, its head protruding underneath her left arm and swinging pendulously from side to side as its evil, changeless eyes glared viciously in the lantern light and its forked tea-colored tongue flickered lambently.

So heavy was the serpent's weight the girl was forced to plant her naked feet apart as she smoothed the dull, gleaming scales with her taper finger tips and massaged the white-armored throat gently as slowly, slowly, she forced the horrid face upward, turned it toward her face and—my stomach retched at the sight—*kissed it on the mouth!*

The throng of worshipers went wild. Men and women clung together in strangling embraces and rolled and wallowed on the floor. Some rose erect and tossed their arms aloft, screaming peals of triumphant laughter or unmentionable obscenities. "She has kissed the Queen! She kisses the Queen! The prophecy is fulfilled!" I heard one votary shout, and, mingled with the drums' unceasing roar came cries of "*Ybo, lé, lé; Ybo, c'est l'heure de sang—*"

I almost screamed aloud as de Grandin's elbow struck me in the ribs. The ape-man had left the room, returning with a burlap sack flung across his shoulder, a sack in which something tiny moved and struggled and whimpered with the still, small voice of a little child in fear and pain. He tossed the sack upon the floor and, grinning horribly, turned toward the girl, handling the noisome reptile with the skill of an adept as he uncoiled it from her white body and placed it, wound into a writhing knot, upon the altar by the desecrated cross.

Into the girl's hands he put the gleaming, razor-edged machete, then turned once more to the struggling, whimpering something in the sack.

"*Le bouc, le bouc sans cornes—le bouc blanc sans cornes*—the goat without horns—the white goat without horns!" howled the congregation frenziedly. "*Le blanc sans cornes—*"

"My friend," de Grandin whispered, "I damn think the time is come!"

A crashing double report shattered the atmosphere as his heavy army revolvers bellowed almost in unison. There was a scream from the region of the altar, a yell of apprehension from the congregation, and the sharp tinkle of broken glass as a bullet smashed the chimney of the lantern illuminating the place, plunging us into instant impenetrable darkness.

Sharp as acid, piercing as a knife-thrust, de Grandin's shrill whistle sounded through the dark, followed by the deafening roar of his pistols as he fired point-blank into the milling mass of humanity in the darkened cellar.

A crash like all the thunders of heaven let loose at once roared over us, followed by the tramping of heavy-soled boots on the empty floors of the old house, then the pounding of hurrying feet upon the cellar stairs. Costello, with unerring efficiency, had hurled two hand grenades at the outer door of the house, then charged through the opening thus created, taking no chances of delay while his men battered down the stout oak panels.

"Are ye there, Dr. de Grandin, sor?" he shouted as half a dozen powerful bull's-eye lanterns lighted the place. "Are ye all right, sor?"

A choking, rasping gurgle beside me answered. Turning sharply I saw the little Frenchman struggling frantically in the coils of the monster snake. With reptilian instinct the thing had crawled from the altar when darkness came, and made for the tunneled exit, encountering de Grandin in its course, and wrapping itself about him.

I snatched the machete from the altar and aimed a blow at the creature's head, but:

"The tail, Friend Trowbridge, strike off its tail!" he gasped.

The keen steel sheared through the reptile's tail, leaving eight inches of it wrapped about a ceiling beam, and with a writhing crash the great, gray-spotted tubular body unloosed its hold upon the Frenchman's trunk and slipped twisting to the earth like a monstrous spring released from its tension.

Half consciously, half instinctively, I realized the wisdom of de Grandin's advice. Had I lopped off the serpent's head, muscular contraction would have tightened its coils about him, and he would inevitably have been crushed to pulp. By striking off its tail I had deprived it of its grip on the ceiling beam, which it used as a fulcrum for its hold, and thereby rendered it impotent to tighten itself about his body.

The little Frenchman's execution had been terrible. Four of the snake-worshipers lay stark and dead upon the floor, four more were nursing dreadful wounds, and the rest were huddled together in abject terror and made no resistance as Costello's men applied the handcuffs.

In a crumpled heap before the altar lay Marrien Thorndyke, her eyes fast closed, her respiration so light I had to listen a second time at her blood-smeared breast before I could detect the faintest murmur of her heart.

"An overcoat for her, Friend Costello, if you please, or she will surely take pneumonia," de Grandin ordered. "Wrap her warmly and bear her to the hospital. By damn, I greatly fear her nerves have had a shock from which they will not soon recover, but she is in better case than if we had not arrived in time. At the worst she will recover from her illness and live; had we not found her, I greatly fear there would not have remained enough for l'entrepreneur des pompes funèbres to bury."

"The entrepreneur des pompes funèbres—the undertaker?" I demanded. "Do you mean she would have been killed?"

"No less," he returned shortly, then:

"*Holà*, my little cabbage, is it hide-and-go-seek you play in there?" he cried as from the rough sack he lifted a tiny morsel of pink, baby flesh and folded it against his bosom. "Ha, my little goatling," he chuckled, "it is better that I find you thus than that you serve as 'the goat without horns' for these abominations. Attend me, Sergeant. Wrap this one warmly and see that she is given milk to drink, then bid Monsieur and Madame Boswell come to police headquarters to see what they shall see. Name of a cannon, but I think the sight of this one will surely stop their eyes from weeping!"

"Now"—he turned to survey the cellar with a fierce glance as he reached again for his heavy pistols—"where is that misbegotten *sacré bête*, that ape in half-human shape? Is it possible I missed him with my first shot."

It was not. Stretched on his back, his short, bandy legs and long, monkey-like arms twisted grotesquely, lay the ape-man, a gaping wound in his temple telling eloquently of the accuracy of de Grandin's marksmanship. The creature's shattered head was pillowed in the lap of the aged hag, who bent above him, dropping tears upon his ugly countenance and wailing, "*A-hé, a-hé, mon beau, mon beau brave fils; mort, mort; mort!*"

De Grandin looked uncertainly at the weeping crone a moment, then removed his hat. "Mourn for your Caliban, Sycorax," he bade, not ungently, and, turning to Costello:

"Leave her a little while with her dead before you make her arrested, my friend," he begged. "Ill-favored as an ape he was, and wicked as the foul fiend's own self, but he was her son, and to a mother every son is dear, and beautiful, though he be ugly as a pig and vicious as a scorpion.

"*Précisément, exactement*, quite so," the Frenchman agreed with a serious nod of his head.

6

"NO, NO, MY FRIEND," Jules de Grandin shook his head in vigorous denial, "it was but the ability to recognize what I did behold which enabled me to lead us to the snake-worshipers' den. When Sergeant Costello mentioned the ravishing away of the blessed cross from the church was when I first began to suspect what now we know to be the facts. Consider, if you please—" he checked the items off upon his fingers:

"First comes the murder of the excellent young clergyman, a murder without motive, it appears, and most cruelly executed. That meant little; a madman might have done it.

"Then we have the stealing of little Baby Boswell; by itself that, too, meant little; again a maniac might be to blame.

"Next comes the stealing of a part of the sanctified furniture from the altar. Once more our hypothetical crazy man may be responsible; but would the same lunatic commit all three crimes, or would three separate madmen decide to act so near together? Possibly, but not likely.

"Considered separately, these are but three motiveless crimes; viewed as connected links in a chain of misdemeanors, they begin to show some central underlying motivation. 'Let us suppose,' I say to me, 'the same man have done all these things—he have slain Monsieur Sherwood who is influential for good among the blacks; he have stolen away a baby girl; he have desecrated the sanctuary of a church. What sort of people do so?'

"All quickly I think; all quickly I remember. In voodoo-ridden Haiti, during the reign of the tyrant Antoine-Simone, he and his daughter Célestine, who were reputed to be grande mamaloi of the island—a sort of female pope of the voodooists—those two did actually succeed in hoodwinking Monseigneur the Archbishop of Haiti to bless and almost bury in consecrated ground the carcass of a slaughtered he-goat which they had substituted for the corpse of one of the palace suite. What they desired of the cadaver of a stinking goat which had been blessed with bell, book and candle only God, the Devil and they knew, but the fact remains they wanted it, and but for a fortunate accident would have succeeded in obtaining it.

"This I recalled when the good Costello told of the ravishment of the church, and so I thought, perhaps, I saw one tiny, small gleam of light amid the darkness of these many so strange crimes.

"Then like a confirmation of my theory comes the discovery of the patchwork corset—pure voodoo, that—upon the body of a white girl. 'Ha,' I say to me, 'here are a new angle of this devil's business.'

"Her murder follows quickly; a murder obviously committed to stop her mouth with blood. We search for the killer; but nowhere can we find him. Only the apes of Tarzan could have gained a vantage-point to hurl the fatal knife, then effect escape from immediately beneath our noses.

"Comes then the killing of Monsieur Lucas, the watchman. When I see his dead corpse all mutilated I tell me, 'This is no ordinary killing; this is the ritual murder of some most vile secret society.' And even as I come to that conclusion what do I find but the two burnt matches which mean that voodoo vengeance has been wreaked upon a backslider. Voilà! The mystery is a mystery no more. And the so long footprint marked in blood at the murder-scene—there is the track of my ape-man, the one who could have murdered Mademoiselle Adelaide because of his peculiar ability to climb that ice-encrusted tree beside the room where we interviewed her. Yes, the same one have undoubtlessly done both murders.

"All quickly I investigate her unhappy past, and likewise that of the murdered watchman. I have told you what I found. Undoubtlessly this old nurse of the murdered girl, this old Toinette, is a voodoo mamaloi, or high priestess; she have settled here, she have made many unfortunate Negroes her dupes; aided by the ape-man, she have planned the supreme revenge upon the white oppressor—she has raised up a white girl to serve the snake-goddess of Obeah, to perform the sacrifice not of a goat, as is done at ordinary ceremonies, but of 'the goat without horns'—a human infant, and a white one, at that. Thus is explained the kidnaping of little Baby Boswell.

"'Jules de Grandin,' I tell me, 'we must work fast if we are to circumvent this abominable abomination.'

"Then comes the riot when the police are defied with guns, an occurrence without parallel, the good Costello declared. It are most significant. I recall that the bloody massacre which drove the French from Haiti was plotted round a voodoo watch-fire on August 14, 1791, by rebellious slaves led by one Doukman, a voodoo *papaloi*, or priest. Impossible as it seems, a disordered brain had conceived the possibility of waging war against the law here in New Jersey, America. Only alcohol, drugs or religious frenzy, perhaps a mixture of them all, could nurture such an insane plan.

"Quickly on the riot's heels comes the abduction of Mademoiselle Marrien. I see her remarkable resemblance to the dead Mademoiselle Adelaide; I observe the headache-producing powder on the mysteriously delivered orchids; once more the trail of voodoo cunning lies across my path. Her room was inaccessible to any but an ape; yet she is gone. Ha, but there is an ape-man dodging back and forth between all the happenings in this so mysterious chain of circumstances; once more I think I see his handiwork. Yes, it is unquestionably so.

"'These wicked ones, they will not be denied their triumph,' I tell me. 'Having deprived themselves of the priestess they so carefully trained from childhood, they steal another, as like her in appearance as possible, and by means of drugs and drums, and *le bon Dieu* only knows what sort of foul magic, they break her will in pieces and force her to serve in place of her they slew.

"I seek a likely place for them to congregate; by great good luck and more than ordinary intelligence, I find it. Forthwith I come to Friend Costello for reinforcements. The rest we know."

"But see here, de Grandin," I asked, "in the voodoo temple tonight you said something about Marrien Thorndyke being in peril of her life. Would the same thing have applied to Adelaide Truman? D'ye think old Toinette would have risked her life in the Martinique earthquake to save the child, only to have her slaughtered in the end?"

"*Mais certainement,*" he assented. "Does not the shepherd repeatedly risk his life for his flock, only that they may at last be driven to the shambles?"

"But she was a priestess, a being regarded almost as divine," I insisted. "Surely they would not have harmed her after electing her to celebrate their rites. Why—"

"Why, of a certitude, they would," he interrupted. "The sacrifice of the priest or priestess, even of the god's own proxy, is no strange thing in many religions. The priest of Dionysus at Potmice was sacrificed following the performance of his priestly office; the Phrygian priests of Attis were of old destroyed when they had done serving their god; a man impersonating Osiris, Sun God of Egypt, was first worshiped with all fervor, then ruthlessly slain in commemoration of the murder of Osiris by Set; and among the ancient Aztecs, Chicomecohuatl, the Corn Goddess, was likewise impersonated by a beauteous maiden who afterward was butchered and flayed in public. Yes, there is nothing strange in the slaughter of a venerated priestess by her worshipers, my friend."

"Well, annyway, Dr. de Grandin, sor, ye sure ran th' murtherin' divils down an' settled that ape-felly's hash in tidy order," Costello interrupted. "Good thing ye did, too. He sure deserved killin', but we'd never 'a' convinced a jury he kilt pore little Miss Truman or even the Eagle Laundry's watchman, Lucas."

"*Eh bien*, my friend," de Grandin cast one of his quick, elfin smiles at the big Irishman, "all that which ends well ends satisfactorily, as Monsieur Shakespeare remarks. The motiveless, meaningless crimes which threatened your tranquility will trouble you no more; neither will the criminals.

"Trowbridge, Costello, good friends"—he filled three glasses with amber cognac and passed us each a bumper—"let us leave off this business as we began it; I bid you Happy New Year."

The Dust of Egypt

IT WAS AN ODD couple Nora McGinnis ushered into my drawing room that snowy February night. The man was good-looking, extraordinarily so, with fine, regular features crowned by a mass of dark hair, broad forehead and deep, greenish-hazel eyes set well apart beneath brows of almost startling blackness. His chest was deep and well developed, and his wide, square shoulders told of strength and stamina beyond the usual. Yet he was scarcely more than five feet tall, and the trousers of his well-tailored dinner suit hung baggily on limbs shriveled to mere skeletal proportions. His right knee bent awkwardly at a fixed, unchanging angle which made his walk little more than a lurching, painful hobble, and the patent leather oxfords on his feet were almost boyish in their smallness. Obviously, poliomyelitis had ravaged his once splendid body hideously, leaving a man half-perfect, half-pitiable wreck.

The woman, apparently almost of an age with her companion—somewhere near twenty-five, I judged—was in everything but deformity his perfect feminine counterpart. Close as a skullcap of black satin her manishly shingled, jetty hair lay against her small, well-shaped head; her features were so small and regular as to be almost insignificant by reason of their very symmetry; her walk was one of those smooth, undulant gaits which announce a nervous balance and muscular co-ordination not often found in this neurotic age. A sleeveless evening frock of black net and satin fell in graceful folds almost to her narrow, high-arched insteps, and the tiny emerald buttons decorating her black-satin pumps were matched by the emerald studs set in the lobes of her small ears and, oddly, by the greenish lights in her black-fringed hazel eyes. She was devoid of makeup, save the vivid scarlet of her lips.

I examined the two small oblongs of cardboard Nora had handed me before admitting the visitors. "Mr. Monteith?" I asked tentatively.

"I am he," the young man answered with a quick smile which lighted his somber, brooding countenance with a peculiar charm, "and this is my sister, Louella." He paused a moment, as though embarrassed, then:

"We've been told you have a friend, a Dr. de Grandin, who occasionally interests himself in matters which have, or seem to have, a supernatural aspect. If you would be good enough to tell us how we might get in touch with him—"

"*Avec beaucoup de félicité!*" Jules de Grandin interrupted with a laugh. "Stretch forth your hand, and touch, *mon ami*; I am he whom you seek!"

"Ah?" young Monteith stared at the little Frenchman, scarcely knowing how to acknowledge the unusual introduction. "Ah—"

"*Précisément,*" de Grandin assented as he waved the callers to a seat upon the fireside lounge. "We are very well met, I think; this had promised to be a dull evening. Now, regarding this seemingly so supernatural matter concerning which you would consult Jules de Grandin—" he raised his narrow, black brows till they described twin Saracenic arches and paused expectantly.

Young Monteith ran his hand over his smoothly brushed black hair and directed a look almost of appeal at the little Frenchman. "I hardly know how to begin," he confessed, then cast a puzzled glance about the room, as though seeking inspiration from the Dresden figurines on the mantelpiece.

"Why not at the beginning?" de Grandin suggested pleasantly as he drew out his slim gold cigarette case, courteously proffered it to the visitors, then held his pocket lighter for them to set the tobacco alight.

"The case concerns my uncle—our uncle's—death," Mr. Monteith replied as he expelled a cloud of fragrant gray smoke from his nostrils. "It may have been natural enough—the death certificate read heart failure, and there were no legal complications—but both my sister and I are puzzled, and if you can spare the time to investigate it, we'd—here," he broke off, drawing a thin packet of papers from his inside pocket, "this is a copy of Uncle Absalom's will; we might as well start with it as anything."

The little Frenchman took the sheets of foolscap with their authenticating red seals and held them to the light.

"In the Name of God, Amen," he read: "I, Absalom Barnstable"—Barn-sta-ble, mon Dieu, what a name!—"being of sound and disposing mind and memory and in full bodily vigor, yet being certain of the near approach of unescapable and inevitable doom, do hereby make, publish and declare this, my last will and testament, hereby revoking any and all other will or wills by me at any time heretofore made.

"First—I commend my spirit to the keeping of God my Savior, and my body to be buried in my plot in Vale Cemetery.

"Second—"

"You can skip the second, third and fourth paragraphs," Mr. Monteith interrupted; "the fifth is the only one bearing further on our problem."

"Very well," de Grandin turned the page and continued: "Fifth— And it is my will and desire that my said nephew and niece, David and Louella Monteith, aforesaid, do take up residence in my house near Harrisonville, New Jersey, as soon as they shall be apprized of the provisions hereof, and shall there remain in residence for the full term of six months, and at the end of that time, *unless intervening occurrences shall have prompted them to take such action earlier,* or unless it shall have become physically impossible so to do, they shall remove from the said house the mummy of the Priest Sepa and see it safely transported overseas and buried in the sands of the Egyptian desert; and I do especially make the faithful carrying-out of these injunctions conditions precedent to their succession to the residuum of my estate."

De Grandin finished reading and glanced from the brother to the sister with his odd, unwinking stare.

"We are the residuary legatees of Uncle Absalom's estate," David Monteith explained. "It amounts to something like $300,000."

"*Parbleu*, for half that sum I should undertake the interment of all the shriveled mummies in the necropolis of Thebes!" the Frenchman returned. "But where is the *outré* feature of your case, my friends? True, your estimable uncle seems to have been peculiar, but eccentricity is the privilege of age and wealth. Why should you not make yourselves comfortable in his late dwelling for half a year, then bury the so long dead Egyptian gentleman with fitting honors and thereafter enjoy yourselves in any manner seeming good to you?"

It was the girl who answered. "Dr. de Grandin," she asked in a charmingly modulated contralto voice, "didn't you notice the odd phraseology in the opening paragraph of Uncle Absalom's will? If he had said 'being certain of the near approach of unescapable and inevitable death' we should have paid little attention to it, for he was past eighty years old, and even though he seemed strong and active as a man of sixty, death couldn't have been so far away in the natural course of things; but he didn't say, 'death,' he said, 'unescapable and inevitable *doom*'."

"*Exactement*," de Grandin agreed calmly, but the sudden light which shone in his little round blue eyes betrayed awaking interest. "*Précisément, Mademoiselle*; what then?"

"I'm certain that horrible old mummy he mentions in his will had something to do with it," she shot back in a low, almost breathless voice. "Show him the transcription, David," she ordered, turning to her brother.

Mr. Monteith produced a second paper from his pocket. "Louella found this in an old escritoire in the library the day before Uncle Absalom died," he explained. "She meant to ask him about it, but never got the chance. It may shed some light on the case—to you. It only makes it more mysterious to us."

"Transcription of the Tablet found in the Tomb of Sepa the Priest," de Grandin read:

"Sepa, servant and priest of Aset, the All-Mother, Who Is and Was and Is to Be, to whoso looks hereon, greeting and admonition:

"Impious stranger, who has defiled the sanctuary of my sepulcher, be thou accursed. Be thy uprisings and thy down-lyings accursed; accursed be thy goings-out and thy returnings; cursed be thou in labor and in rest; may thy nights be filled with terrifying visions and thy days with travail and with pain, and may the wrath of Aset, who Was and Is and Is to Be, be on thee and on thy house for all time. May thy body be the prey to kites and jackals and thy soul endure the torture of the Gods. Unburied shalt thou die, and bodiless and accursed shalt thou wander in Amenti forever and forever, and be this malediction on thee and on thy house until such time as my relics be once again interred in the sands of Khem. I have said."

"*Eh bien*, he cursed a vicious curse, this one," the Frenchman remarked as he concluded. "And what is this we have here?"

Pasted to the bottom of the sheet bearing the translation of the old curse was a newspaper cutting bearing a London dateline:

London, Nov. 16.—The strange death of Richard Bethell, son of Lord Westbury, today revived the legend of the curse of death that hovers over those who disturb the graves of the ancient lords of Egypt.

His death is the tenth among the leaders of Lord Carnarvon's expedition to the Valley of the Kings in Egypt, which uncovered the tomb of King Tutankhamen.

Bethell, who was secretary to Howard Carter, leader of the expedition, was found dead in bed in the aristocratic Bath Club. Physicians are at a loss as to what caused his end.

"U'm?" de Grandin put the paper down and regarded the visitors once more with his direct, level stare. "And what of your late uncle?" he demanded. "Tell me what you can of his life; more particularly of his death."

Again it was the girl who answered. "Uncle Absalom was educated for the Unitarian ministry," she began, "but he never accepted the vocation. About the time he was to take up his ministerial work he met a young lady in New Bedford, Massachusetts, and fell violently in love with her. Yankee clippers still traded with the Orient and Near East in those days, and Miss Goodrich's father, who was a ship-owner, offered Uncle Absalom a share in the business if he would give up his clerical career. He shipped as supercargo on the *Polly Hatton* at his future father-in-law's suggestion, and in the course of a three-year cruise touched at Alexandria, Egypt.

"He seems to have had plenty of time to go inland exploring, for he made a trip up the Nile and with a party of Arabs broke into a tomb somewhere near Luxor and brought back several mummies, some papyri and some funerary statues. It was comparatively easy to get such things out of Egypt in those days, so Uncle had little difficulty in bringing his finds—or would you call them loot?—away. Oddly enough, they proved the foundation of his fortune.

"Unknown to Uncle Absalom and the master of the ship, Mr. Goodrich had died of smallpox while the *Polly Hatton* was on her cruise, and when they came to appraise his estate he was found to be practically bankrupt. Harriet, his daughter, married a wealthy young ship-chandler, and was the mother of two children when her 'fiancé' finally returned to New Bedford.

"But the mummies Uncle Absalom had found proved rather valuable ones. Egyptology was just beginning to be the important science it is today, and the papyri found in the mummy-cases gave a great deal of valuable information the officials of the British Museum had only guessed at before. They paid Uncle £200—a great deal of money in those days—for his finds, and made him a liberal offer for any further antiquities he might bring them.

"When Uncle Absalom returned to New England to find his expected bride already a wife and mother, his entire nature seemed to change almost overnight. The quiet, bookish divinity student was transformed into a desperate adventurer. The Civil War had been over five years, and the country was beginning to drift into the period of hard times which ended in the panic of 1873. Plenty of young men who'd served in the Union army and navy were out of work, and Uncle Absalom had no trouble recruiting a company of followers without respect either for danger or decency, provided there was money to be had for their work.

"Poor Uncle Absalom! I'm afraid everything he did during the next twenty years or so wouldn't bear too close scrutiny! The returns from his first venture in grave robbery had proved so good that he went into it as a business.

"Even though most of them were Mohammedans and didn't believe in the old gods, the Egyptians didn't take kindly to foreigners despoiling the ancient tombs, and Uncle and his men encountered resistance more than once; but the men who had fought with Grant and Sherman and Farragut weren't the kind to be stopped by unorganized Arabs, or even by the newly organized gendarmerie of Egypt. They robbed and plundered systematically, taking their loot to a sort of buccaneers' cache they'd established at a desert oasis, and when they'd accumulated enough spoil to make it worth while, they'd take it out in an armed caravan, sometimes striking for the Red Sea, sometimes going boldly to the Mediterranean and woe betide whoever tried to stop them!

"Of course, both the English and the French went through the motions of combating this wholesale grave robbery, but both countries had more important things to attend to, and Uncle's men helped them subdue rebellious natives more than once; so many of his crimes were winked at officially. Also, the great museums of London, Paris, Berlin and St. Petersburg were glad to buy whatever he had for sale, and often bid against each other for his wares; so he grew rich and, in a way, respected. The curators of those museums weren't so very different from people over here," she added with a smile. "When I was in school in Washington it was common gossip that the senators and congressmen who championed prohibition most eloquently in the halls of Congress were the bootleggers' best customers in private life.

"What had started as a purely commercial enterprise with the additional element of adventure to help him forget the way he had been jilted at length became a real passion with Uncle Absalom. He learned to decipher the Egyptian hieroglyphics, for he'd been a first-rate Greek scholar in college and Boussard's discovery of the Rosetta Stone in 1799 had furnished the key to the old written language, you know. Long before he retired from his dangerous profession Uncle was rated as one of the foremost authorities on both ancient and modern Egypt, and two universities and the British government made him handsome offers for his services when he finally gave up tomb-robbing as a vocation.

"On his retirement he made a number of gifts to the Egyptian departments of the museums which had been his best customers, but the cream of his finds he retained for his private collection and kept them in his house near Harrisonville.

"I don't suppose you ever even heard of him, Dr. Trowbridge?" she turned her odd, rather melancholy smile on me. "He's lived just outside town for almost ten years, but when we came to visit him the taxi driver had never heard of 'Journey's End,' where he lived, and we had a great deal of trouble finding him. You see, he had hardly been outside his own grounds once since settling here, and most of his things, including staple groceries, he bought from a mail order house in Chicago. I don't believe half-a-dozen people in the whole city knew him, or even knew of him.

"David and I came to visit him last month in response to an urgent invitation. He intimated he intended making us his heirs, and as we're orphans and were his only living relatives, it seemed no more than human charity to accede to his request.

"He was a wonderful-looking old man, courteous, gentle and very learned. He did everything possible to make us welcome, and we should have been very happy at 'Journey's End' if it hadn't been for an air of—well—uncanniness, which seemed to permeate the whole place. Somehow, both David and I seemed to feel alien presences there. We'd be reading in the library, or sitting at table, or, perhaps, just going about our affairs in the house, when suddenly we'd have that strange, eerie feeling of someone staring fixedly at the backs of our heads. When we'd turn suddenly—as we always did at first—there'd be no one there, of course; but the feeling was always there, and instead of wearing off it became stronger and stronger. Since Uncle's death I've noticed it more than David has, though.

"Uncle Absalom never mentioned it, and, of course, neither did we—except to each other—but I'm sure he felt it too, for there was a furtive, almost fearful, look in his eyes all the time, and the queer, haunted expression seemed to grow on him, just during the little time of our visit. It was only ten days before his death when he made his will, and you remember how he speaks of 'unescapable and inevitable *doom*'—instead of 'death'—in the opening paragraph.

"Now, I realize all this is not enough to excuse our belief in anything super-natural being involved in Uncle Absalom's death; that is, not enough to con-vince a disinterested third party who hadn't felt the queer, terrifying atmosphere of 'Journey's End' and seen the took of hopeless fear grow into an expression of almost resignation in Uncle Absalom's face," she admitted, "and I'm not sure you'll see anything so very unusual in what occurred the night he died. David will have to tell you about that; curiously enough, though everyone else in the house was awake, I slept through it all, and have no first-hand knowledge of anything."

"I compliment you, *Mademoiselle*," de Grandin declared with one of his characteristically courteous bows. "You tell your story most exceedingly well. Already I am convinced. I shall most gladly undertake the case.

"Now, young *Monsieur*," he addressed the crippled boy, "add what you can to the so graphic narrative *Mademoiselle* your sister has detailed. I listen; I am all attention."

DAVID MONTEITH TOOK UP the story. "Uncle Absalom died shortly after New Year's—the ninth of January, to be exact," he began. "He and Louella had gone to bed about ten o'clock, but I stayed up in the library reading. It's—pardon the personal reference—it's rather difficult for me to dress and undress, and sometimes I sit up rather late, just to defer the trouble of going to bed. So—"

"It hurts him," his sister interrupted, her eyes welling with tears. "Some-times he suffers terribly, and—"

"Louella, dear, don't!" the boy cut in. "As I was saying, gentlemen, I sat up late that night, and fell asleep over my book. I woke with a start and found the night, which had been clear and sharp earlier, had become stormy and bit-ter cold. A perfect gale was blowing, and soft, clinging snowflakes were being dashed against the window-panes with such force that they struck the glass with an audible impact.

"Just what wakened me I can't say with certainty. I thought at first it was the shrieking of the wind, but, looking back, I'm not so sure; for, blending with the recollection of the dream I'd been having when I woke, was a sound, or combination of sounds—"

"*Mille pardons, Monsieur,* but what of this dream?" de Grandin interrupted. "Such stuff as dreams are made on are oftentimes of greatest importance in cases like this."

"Why," David Monteith colored slightly, "it was a silly hodgepodge I'd been dreaming, sir; it couldn't possibly have any bearing on what happened later. I dreamed I heard two people, a man and a woman, come up the stairs from Uncle Absalom's museum, which was on the ground floor, and pass the library on their way to Uncle's room. And in the absurd way dreams have of making things appear, I thought I could look right through the solid wall and see them, the way you do in those illusional scenes they sometimes have in the theater. They were both dressed in ancient Egyptian costume, and were speaking together in some outlandish language. I'd been reading Munzinger's *Ostafrikanische Studien* when I fell asleep; I expect that accounts for the dream."

"U'm; possibly," de Grandin conceded. "What then, if you please?"

"Well, as I said, when I woke I thought I heard a sort of soft, but very clear, chiming sound, something like sleigh-bells heard a long way off, yet different, somehow, and with it what I took to be a woman's voice singing softly.

"I leaned back in my chair, half asleep still, wondering if some dream image hadn't carried over into my semiconsciousness, when there came a new sound, totally unlike the others.

"It was my Uncle Absalom's voice, not very loud, but terribly earnest, arguing with, or pleading with someone. Gradually, as I sat there listening, his words became louder, he almost shouted, then broke off with a sort of scream which seemed to die half-uttered, as though his mouth had suddenly been stopped or his throat grasped in a strangling hold.

"I lifted myself out of my chair and hurried toward the upper story as well as I could, but the stairway leading to the third floor was some twenty feet down the corridor and the stairs were steep and winding; so, with my handicap, I couldn't make very good time.

"While I was still half-climbing, half-crawling up the stairs, I beard a woman's scream, 'Howly Mither, 'tis th' banshee!' and recognized Maggie Gourlay, my uncle's cook and housekeeper. She and her husband, Tom, were his only servants, and shared all the household duties between them.

"When I finally reached the landing above, Maggie stood at the far end of the hall, her teeth fairly chattering, her eyes bulging with terror.

"'Ouch, Misther David, 'tis all over wid Misther Absalom, God rist 'im!' she hailed me as I came up. ''Tis meself just seen the banshee woman lave 'is room. Don't go nigh, Misther David; she may be waitin' fer others o' th' family.'

"'Nonsense,' I panted. 'Didn't you hear my uncle call? Come here; we must see what he wants.'

"'Wurra, wurra, 'tis nothin' but a praste an' an undertaker he'll be nadin' now, sor!' she answered, without coming a step nearer.

"I couldn't wait for the superstitious old fool to get over her hysteria, for my uncle might be seriously ill, I thought; so I rapped sharply on his door, then, receiving no answer, pushed my way into his room.

"Uncle Absalom lay on his bed, the covers thrown back, one foot hanging just off the floor, as though he had been in the act of rising. His arms were folded over his breast, his fingers locked together, clasping a pillow tightly against his chest and face.

"I switched on the light and removed the pillow; then I knew. I'd never seen a newly dead man before, but I needed no one to tell me my uncle was dead. I think we recognize death instinctively, just as a child recognizes and hates a snake without having been told reptiles are deadly. My uncle's jaw had sagged and his tongue had fallen forward and outward, as though he were making an inane grimace, and there was a bright, transparent film over his still opened eyes.

"I turned back his pajama jacket to feel his heart, and then it was I noticed the mark. It was just to the right of his left breast, a sort of deep purple, like a discolored bruise or a St. Andrew's birthmark, less than an inch high, and faintly raised, like the wale left by a whiplash. Here"—the young man leaned forward, took a slender gold pencil from his pocket and drew a design on the margin of his uncle's will—"it was like this:"

"*Mordieu*, do you say it?" de Grandin exclaimed in a low, tense voice. "*Barbe dun singe, c'est le plus étrange!*"

"Something else I noticed, though at the time it made little impression on me," Monteith continued: "There was a distinct odor of spice or incense—almost the odor you find in a Catholic church after services—in the room. It wasn't till considerably later, when I began rearranging my recollections, that I recalled it.

"Once I'd made sure Uncle Absalom was dead, Maggie and Tom seemed to have no more fear. They came into the room, helped me arrange his body, then assisted me down the hall to find Louella. She'd slept through it all, and I had to hammer on her door to waken her."

"You, *Monsieur?*" de Grandin asked. "Did not the servants knock?"

"Why"—the young man seemed to catch his breath as sudden recollection struck him—"why no; they didn't.

"D'ye know, Dr. de Grandin," he leaned toward the little Frenchman in his earnestness, "I believe they kept behind me purposely. At the time I thought nothing of it, but since you asked me about who knocked on Louella's door, I distinctly remember Tom held me under one arm and Maggie under the other, but both walked a little behind me, and both stood back when we halted at my sister's room."

"U'm?" de Grandin murmured. "And then what, if you please?"

"When Louella finally woke and let us in, she seemed so sleepy I had to shake her to make her understand what had happened. At first she just looked uncomprehendingly at me and kept repeating whatever I said to her in a dreamy singsong voice."

"U'm?" de Grandin murmured again. "And—"

"By George, yes! Now I think of it, there was that same scent of incense in her room, too. I'm positive it wasn't in the hall or anywhere else; just in Uncle's room and hers."

"*Tiens*, at any rate, it was the odor of sanctity you smelled," the French-man returned with a chuckle. "Now, concerning this so strange mark you found upon *Monsieur* your uncle's breast. Was it—"

"I was coming to that," Monteith interrupted. "As soon as we could we got in touch with the nearest physician, Dr. Canby. He came about an hour later, examined Uncle Absalom's body, and gave a certificate of death by heart failure.

"I asked him about the mark and wanted to know if, in his opinion, it had any significance. He just looked at me and asked, 'What mark?'

"We argued about it for a while, and both of us lost our tempers a little, I think. Finally, distasteful as it was, I went into Uncle's room, unbuttoned his sleeping-jacket and pointed to his breast."

"Yes, and then?" de Grandin demanded, leaning toward the narrator, his little eyes fairly aglow with anticipation.

"Nothing," Monteith returned in dull, anticlimactic voice. "There was nothing there. The mark had disappeared."

"A-a-ah?" de Grandin let his breath out slowly between his teeth as he leaned back in his chair.

"But, Dave, are you *sure* you saw that mark on Uncle's flesh?" the girl asked gently. "In the excitement and the poor light, mightn't you have imagined—"

"No," the young man answered positively. "I'm certain it was there when I found Uncle Absalom, and just as certain it had disappeared when I looked the second time."

"*Mais oui, Mademoiselle*," de Grandin put in. "Monsieur your brother is undoubtlessly right. This business, it promises interest. Dr. Trowbridge and I shall do ourselves the honor of calling on you tomorrow or as soon thereafter as may be."

WE SAT LONG BEFORE the fire after David and Louella Monteith had gone. The Frenchman smoked cigarette after cigarette in moody silence, staring at the leaping flames in the fireplace as fixedly as a crystal-gazer seeking inspiration from his globe. At length:

"Friend Trowbridge, it is most remarkable, is it not?" he demanded abruptly.

"What?" I answered.

"That sign, that stigma on Monsieur the Grave-Robber's breast."

"Why, yes," I agreed. "It is odd it should have showed a few moments after death, then disappeared. I wonder, after all, if the girl was right. Young David might have imagined it, and—"

"*Non*," he cut in. "The disappearance is the least mystifying phenomenon of all. It is of its form I speak. Did not you recognize it?"

"Why, no. It looked something like the conventionalized outline of a boot to me, but—"

"Ah bah," he exclaimed, "that sign, my friend, was the ideograph standing for the Goddess Aset, or, as she is better known to us, Isis, whom the Egyptians of old knew as the All-Mother. She Who Was and Is and Is to Be. It was she whom the priest Sepa, who so violently cursed the despoilers of his tomb, served, you will remember."

"Well—"

"Exactly, precisely, quite so; I damn think we shall see interesting things before he have done with this matter, friend."

Early next morning he set off to visit the old priest in charge of the local Greek Orthodox Church. I stopped by the rectory something after four o'clock in the afternoon and together we set out to visit the Monteiths.

2

"JOURNEY'S END," THE QUAINT old Georgian house where Absalom Barnstable had spent the closing uneventful decade of his adventurous life and finally met mysterious death, was three stories high, flat-roofed, not particularly beautiful, and unexpectedly comfortable. Built of time-mellowed red brick with slightly discolored facings of white stone, it stood a dozen yards or so back from the Albemarle Pike, in the sparsely settled country lying ten miles east of Harrisonville. An iron railing, ornamented with faces, javelins and twining garlands, after the fashion of the late eighties, divided the front yard from the road, and on each side of the door, which was approached by three white-stone steps, grew a small privet tree neatly clipped and trimmed into a pyramid of dull, rich green.

The entire ground floor, with the exception of kitchen, pantry and furnace room, was given over to a museum for housing the late owner's antiquities. Partitions separating the big, high-ceiled rooms had been knocked out, and the major part of the story made into one great storehouse of curios—brightly painted mummy-cases, glass-fronted cabinets containing bits of ancient *vertu*, and tall, mahogany wardrobes, each furnished with secure locks, storing such relics as were not for open display.

The second story contained a large, old-fashioned formal drawing-room, a library with walls lined from baseboard to molding with book-laden shelves, and an open fireplace of almost baronial proportions, a dining-room vast as a banquet hall, and two guest-bedrooms, each with private bath. Sleeping-quarters for the family and servants and two large lumber rooms occupied the top floor.

Old Tom Gourlay, butler and majordomo of the establishment, met us at the gate and helped us with our luggage when we arrived at the house shortly before six in the evening. Behind him, in the lower entranceway, waited his wife, Maggie, looking very demure in her black bombazine dress and white apron, but an expression of lurking suspicion—a certain grimness about her lips and hardness in her eyes—made me glance sharply at her a second time as we followed her husband up the wide stairway to the library where our host and hostess waited.

The Frenchman noted the woman's odd air of constraint, too, for he whispered as we ascended, "She will bear watching, that one, Friend Trowbridge."

Dinner was served shortly after our arrival, and despite de Grandin's efforts at small talk the meal proved a gloomy one, for we caught ourselves looking furtively at each other from under lowered lids, and though the old butler maintained his air of well-bred, stoical calm, on more than one occasion I caught a glimpse of Maggie Gourlay standing at the serving-pantry door, her queer, hard gaze fixed intently on Louella Monteith's sleek, bowed head.

Shortly after coffee had been served in the library de Grandin excused himself and, motioning me to accompany him, stole silently down the stairs. "The surest defense lies in attack, my friend," he explained as he led the way toward the kitchen. Then, as we entered the big, steamy room without preliminary knock, he demanded:

"Tell me, my friends, what was it you observed the night your unfortunate employer met his end?"

The servants started as though he had flung an accusation at them. Old Tom opened his lips, licked them lightly with the tip of his tongue, then closed them again and averted his eyes, like a sullen schoolboy chided by his teacher.

Not so his wife. An angry, challenging light shone in her Celtic blue eyes as she answered: "Why don't ye ask her about it, sor? She'll be better able ter tell ye than Tom or me, good Christians that we be."

"*Dites*," de Grandin pursed his lips, "is it an accusation that you make, my old one?"

"I'm making no accusations, an' I'm sayin nothin' agin nobody," the woman returned sullenly, "leastwise, not widin hearin' distance of ears as miss nothin'. See here, sor,"—she softened, as women always did when Jules de Grandin regarded them with that elfish, provocative smile of his—"ye're from th' other side; have ye ever been to Ireland—do ye know annything o' her fairy lore?"

"Ah-ho," de Grandin let his breath out with a half-chuckle, "the winds blows that way, *hein?* Yes, my excellent one, I have been to your so beautiful island, and I know much of her traditions. What is it you have seen which reminds you of the old sod?"

The woman hesitated, casting a half-defiant, half-fearful glance at the ceiling above her; then, confidentially:' "What sort o' folk is it as can't call a name three times runnin' or eat three helpin's o' food at wan meal, or drink three sups o' drink?" she demanded with a sort of subdued ferocity.

The Frenchman met her earnest, searching stare with a level, unwinking look. "Fairy folk, and witches, and ghosts of the departed who masquerade as living men," he answered glibly, as though reciting a lesson learned by rote. "Also those who have sold themselves to the Evil One, or they who have any manner of traffic with the Powers of Darkness—"

"True for ye, sor," she interrupted with a satisfied nod. "Ye're a gentleman, an' non o' these learned fools who laugh at th' old-time truths an' call 'em superstition. Then listen:

"When first they came here, th' crippled Misther David an' she who calls herself his sister, I wuz mightily afeared o' th' green eyes of her, an' of her pale, bloodless face an' her smilin' red lips, so thin an' cruel, wid th' white teeth flashin' so close behint 'em, so I sets a trap fer her. Whenever she wanted me, I pretended not to hear her call th' first time, nor th' second. Did she call twice? She did, sor. Did she call th' charmed third time? *Niver!*

"An', 'Tom,' sez I to me old man, 'do you be watchin' how she eats an' drinks at the table while ye're servin' th' dinners,' an' to make sure he wuzn't fooled be th' wicked, false beauty of her pale face, I climbs th' stairs an' watches her from th' servin-panthry door myself. More than wanst I watched her, sor, but niver, as God an' th' blessed St. Patrick hear me spake, did I see her put th' third piece o' meat or bread in her mouth, nor did she ever take a third cup o' wine, though Tom at me express orders would fill her glass no more than half full, so she'd have all th' chanct a Christian woman needed ter ask for a third helpin' o' th' crater."

"U'm?" de Grandin tweaked the tightly waxed ends of his diminutive blond mustache. "And what else, if you please? The night your master died, by example—"

"Jest so, sor," she broke in eagerly. "'Twas afther we'd heard old Misther Abs'lom cry out in mortal anguish an' whilst Misther Davy—poor lad!—wuz clumpin' an' clompin' up th' stairs from th' lib'ry below, we seen it come out from his room. All scairt an' terror-shook as we wuz, I hollered out that 'twas th' banshee that walked th' house be night, but 'twarn't, sor. 'Twuz her—or *it*—sor, as howly St. Bridget hears me say it, 'twas her!

"Sure, an' I seen her come sneakin' from out his door, wid her cruel, red lips parted in a divil's laugh an' her terrible green eyes shootin' fire at me through th' dark, freezin' me where I stood.

"Down th' hall she went, sor, so quiet-like ye'd have swore she floated, for niver mortal woman stepped so softly, an' when she turned th' corner o' th' corridor, I knew we'd seen an evil thing that night; a witch-woman from Kylena-granagh Hill, arrayed in th' likeness o' pore Misther Abs'lom's blood-kin. Then it wuz me lips wuz loosened, an' I called aloud ter Misther Davy to beware—fer who knew but that she looked fer more o' th' masther's blood to destroy, havin' already kilt th' old man dead wid her magic power."

"I DECLARE, I'M SO SLEEPY I can scarcely keep my eyelids up!" Louella Monteith told us a few minutes after we rejoined her and her brother in the library upstairs. "I've not stirred from the house today, but I haven't been so drowsy since—" she broke off abruptly, her eyes widening with something like horror.

"Yes, *Mademoiselle?*" de Grandin prompted softly.

"Since the night Uncle Absalom died," she answered. "I was terribly drowsy from right after dinner that evening, too, and slept like a log from the moment I went to bed—remember what trouble David had to waken me when he and the servants came to my room, to tell me—"

"*Précisément*," de Grandin agreed. "By all means, *Mademoiselle*, do not let us keep you from your needed rest. Dr. Trowbridge and I are here to help, not to make nuisances of ourselves."

"You won't mind?" she asked gratefully as she rose to leave. "Good-night, gentlemen; good-night, Davy, dear; don't sit up too late, please."

Midnight sounded on the tall clock in the hall, still we talked and smoked in the library. David Monteith was widely read and widely traveled, and his flow of conversation was as interesting as it was varied in subject-matter. We were discussing some comic idiosyncrasies of Parisian *concierges* and taxi-drivers when de Grandin halted the talk with upraised hand.

Quickly as a cat and as silently, he stole to the door, motioning over his shoulder for me to shut off the library lights. A moment he stood silent in the doorway of the darkened room, then crept down the hall toward the stairs leading to the museum below.

Ten minutes or so later he rejoined us with a shamefaced smile. "Jules de Grandin grows old and nervous, I fear," he admitted with a humorous lift of his eyebrows. "He starts at shadows and hears ghostly footsteps in the creaking of old floor-boards. My friends, it is late. My vote is that we retire: Do you agree?"

"NON, MY FRIEND, IT may not be," he denied as I prepared to disrobe shortly after we had bid our host good-night. "Remove the shoes, by all means; otherwise remain clothed. I fear we shall have small sleep this night."

"But," I protested, "I thought you were so sleepy. You said—"

"Assuredly," he agreed with a nod as he replaced his evening shoes with a pair of soft-soled slippers, "and the mother who would still her little one's fear declares she hears nothing when she is most certain she hears a burglar prying at the window-latch. Attend me, my friend:

"While you, Monsieur Monteith and I talked all pleasantly in the library I did descry the soft, so silent step of someone creeping down the stairs. At once I bid you shut off the light, that I might not stand out in silhouette against its glow and thus betray myself; then I did reconnoiter.

"All quietly down the stairway Mademoiselle Louella did steal, and to one of those great, fast-locked cabinets she went unerringly, though the museum was dark as Pluto's own subcellar.

"Today she told me she knew not where the keys of those locked cases were—that her late uncle had them in a secret place and that she knew it not—but with a key she did unlock that cabinet door, and though that key was one of many on a ring, she made no difficulty finding it in the dark, or in fitting it to the lock. No.

"Anon she turned back, and on her arms and in her hands were many things; objects I could not certainly identify, but seeming to be articles of clothing and ornaments—grave-loot from the old ones' tombs, I doubt not, and worth a kingly ransom for their great antiquity, whatever their intrinsic worth might be."

"But why did you pretend you'd seen nothing?" I demanded. "Do you suspect—"

"I suspect nothing; I know nothing," he rejoined. "I declared my mission fruitless that the young *monsieur* might not have new perplexities added to those he already has. What sort of business Mademoiselle Louella makes—or proposes to make—I do not know. At any rate, her actions were most strange, and we shall be advised to sit with one eye and one ear fast-glued to our keyhole throughout the night."

3

WRAPPING MYSELF IN A dressing-gown, I dropped into one of the deep wing chairs flanking the bedroom fireplace and lighted a cigar.

Jules de Grandin paced the length of the chamber, lighted a cigarette and flung it aside after two or three puffs, drew something from the pocket of his lounge-robe and examined it, replaced it, finally seated himself on the extreme edge of the easy-chair across the hearth and seemed to freeze statue-still.

Once or twice I essayed a remark, but his quickly lifted hand cut me short each time. His attitude was one of intent listening for some expected sound, and I found myself thinking again how suggestive of a feline the fellow little was. With his round, blue eyes widened by the intentness of his attention, the sharp, needle-fine ends of his waxed mustache fairly quivering with nervous tautness and his delicate, narrow nostrils now and again expanding as though he would discover the presence of that for which he waited by virtue of his sense of smell, he was for all the world like a tensed, expectant, but infinitely patient tom-cat stationed at the entrance of a promising rathole.

Time crept by with weighted feet. I yawned, stretched myself, tossed away my cigar, and fell into a doze.

"Trowbridge, *mon vieux*, arouse!" de Grandin's sibilant whisper cut through my nap. "Awake, my friend—listen!"

In the room above us, the chamber where crippled David Monteith slept, there sounded the indistinct murmur of a voice—a woman's voice—and blending with it like a cunningly played accompaniment to a soloist's recitation was the faint, musical chiming of a bell. Yet it was not like any bell I had ever heard; rather it was like a staff of chimes with a single, tri-toned note, or a major note with two undertones pitched differently.

"Sounds like—" I began.

"*Zut!* Be quiet—come!" commanded Jules de Grandin.

Silently as a panther stalking through the jungle, he led the way into the corridor and up the stairs. Before the door of David's room he paused, raising his hand in an arresting, minatory gesture.

The voice behind the panels was that of Louella Monteith, yet strangely different from it; deeper, more reverberant than the girl's usual contralto. The words she spoke were in a language strange to me, but reminiscent, somehow, of such few phrases of Hebrew as I had learned when as a young hospital intern I'd ridden an ambulance through the crowded foreign sections of the city. And blending with the cold, passionless monotone of the woman's voice was a second one, a man's voice, quivering with passion, accusatory, low and vindictive as a serpent's hiss.

With a quick movement of his left hand de Grandin thrust the door back and advanced across the threshold, the tableau thus revealed struck me numb with blank amazement.

Although no light burned, the scene was clear-cut as though enacted in brilliant moonlight, for a silvery, radiant luminance without apparent source seemed to permeate the atmosphere of an Egyptian room.

Crouched on a couch, his eyes wide with grisly, unbelieving horror, was David Monteith. Kneeling on the drugget in an attitude half of adoration, half cringing servility, was a man clothed only in a loin-cloth. His shaven head accented his lean, cruel features. One of his long, bony hands was extended, pointing fiercely at young Monteith, and it seemed to me the pointed hand was like an aimed weapon, serving to direct the unabating flood of invective the kneeling creature hurled toward the man upon the bed.

But it was the woman that stood in regal, awful majesty in the midst of the moon-like effulgence who caught and riveted my attention. Louella Monteith it was, but a changed, transmuted version of the girl we knew. Upon her head was the crown of Isis—the vulture cap with beaten gold and blue-enamel wings and the vulture's head with gem-set eyes, above it two upright horns between which shone the red gold disk of the full moon, beneath them the uræus, emblem of Osiris.

About her neck lay a broad collar of hammered gold thick-set with emeralds and carnelian, and round her wrists were bands of gold and gleaming, blue enamel in which were studded emeralds and coral. Her bosom was bare, but high beneath her breasts was clasped a belt of blue and gold from which cascaded a diaphanous garment of web-fine linen gathered in scores of tiny, narrow pleats and fringed about the hem with a border of sparkling gems which hung an inch or less above the narrow, arching insteps of her white and tiny feet. In one hand she held a gold and crystal instrument fashioned like a cross with an elongated loop at its top, while in the other she bore a three-lashed golden scourge, the emblem of Egyptian royalty.

All this I noted in a sort of wondering daze, but it was the glaring, implacable eyes of her which held me rooted to the spot. Like the eyes of a tigress, or a leopardess, they were, and glowed with a horrid, inward light, as though illumined from behind by the phosphorescent luminance of an all-consuming, heatless flame.

Even as we halted spellbound she raised her golden scourge and aimed it at the man upon the bed, while the crouching thing at her feet gave vent to a wild, demoniac cachinnation—a triumphant laugh of hatred appeased and vengeance satisfied. A low, weak moan came from David Monteith, a groan of abysmal agony, as though his tortured soul were being ravished from his tormented flesh and tore his crippled body into tatters as it was dragged forth.

I started forward with a cry of horror, but Jules de Grandin was before me. "Accursed of God!" he shouted, and his voice was harsh and strident as a battle-cry. "Fallen foes of the Lord Jehovah; upstarts against the power of the most High; *in nomine Domini, conjuro te, scleratissime, abire ad tuum locum!* Hence, loathed remnants of a false and futile faith; in the name of Him who overcame ye, I command it!"

For a moment—or an eternity, I know not which—there was dead, frozen silence in that weirdly lighted room. Every actor in the drama stood sculptured-still, like a figure on a graven monument, and only the frantic pulsation of my heart sounded in my ears.

The Frenchman thrust his right hand into the pocket of his lounge-robe and brought forth something—a tiny golden reliquary, a little thing of gold and modest, purple amethyst so small a man might hide it in the hollow of his hand—and letting it slip through his fingers swung it by a slender golden chain, waving it slowly to and fro in the air as though it were a censer. "By the power of the one who cast ye out, O Aset, Aset of olden Egypt, by the memory of Cyrillus of Alexandria, I conjure ye," he chanted slowly. "Behold the thing which I have brought from out the Land of Khem, even that which the holy one of old upraised against ye and against your power; behold, and be afraid!" He swung the little golden cross ceremonially before him and advanced into the room.

The groveling man-shape cut short its horrid laughter, and with jaws still agape, half-rose, half-crawled across the floor, its lean and claw-like hands upraised as if to ward away some stream of invincible power which flowed from out the bit of gold de Grandin held.

Jabbering half-formed words in an outlandish tongue, words I could not understand, but which were clearly an appeal, the thing retreated as de Grandin pursued inexorably.

I held my breath in horror, then almost screamed aloud as the Frenchman and his adversary reached the room's boundary, for the hunted creature *passed directly through the wall*, as though brick and mortar had no substance!

The little Frenchman turned from his quarry and approached the form of Isis, which seemed to stand irresolute beside the bed. Only, it was no longer a goddess we beheld, but a woman. True, she was still beautiful and queenly in her trappings of barbaric splendor, but the odd and moonlike light no longer shone around her, nor was there an aura of dread and fearsomeness about her, and the awful, flowing eyes which filled my soul with fear were now recognizable for what they were—the likeness of staring, vengeful eyes *drawn in luminous paint upon her lowered lids!*

"To your chamber, *Mademoiselle*, I command it!" de Grandin ordered in a low, authoritative voice. Then, to me:

"Look to Monsieur David, Friend Trowbridge. You will find him suffering from shock, but not greatly hurt otherwise, I think."

Quickly, I ministered to the fainting man upon the bed, forced water mixed with brandy down his throat, pressed a vial of sal volatile to his nostrils and bathed his wrists and temples. He rallied slightly, gasped once or twice, then lapsed into a heavy, natural sleep. When at last he lay quietly on his pillow I opened his pajama jacket to listen to his heart, and on the flesh of his left breast, faint, but still recognizable for what it was, lay a tiny, reddish stigma, thus:

I hurried to de Grandin to tell him of my find, and met him tiptoeing from Louella Monteith's room. "Softly, my friend," he warned with upraised finger; "she sleeps."

"WHERE'S DAVID?" LOUELLA MONTEITH asked as she joined de Grandin and me at breakfast the following morning. "He's usually an early riser—I hope he's not ill today?" She turned to ascend the stairs to her brother's chamber, but de Grandin put forth a detaining hand.

"Your brother had rather a trying night, *Mademoiselle*," he said. "Dr. Trowbridge has given him an opiate; it will be some time before he wakes."

"Oh"—the concern in her eyes was very real—"don't tell me the poor boy's had another of his spells! He suffers so! Usually he calls me if he's ill in the night, and I do what I can to help him; but last night I didn't hear a thing. I slept so soundly, too. Do you—"

She brightened as a consoling thought seemed to come to her. "Of course," she smiled. "Why should he have called me when we had two physicians in the house? I'm sure you did everything possible for him, gentlemen."

"Precisely; we did, *Mademoiselle*," Jules de Grandin returned noncommittally as he gave his undivided attention to the well-filled plate of bacon and eggs before him.

"NO! I TELL YOU; I'll never willingly look at that she-devil again, so long as I live!" David Monteith almost shouted in response to de Grandin's suggestion. "Talk all you will of her being my sister; I tell you she's the vilest most unholy thing unhanged. Oh God, why doesn't the law recognize witchcraft today? How I'd enjoy denouncing her, and seeing her tied to the stake!" He leaned back on his pillow, exhausted by the vehemence of his emotion, but his deep-set, greenish hazel eyes glowed with fury as he looked from one of us to the other. Then:

"She killed Uncle Absalom, too. I know it. Now I understand what old Maggie Gourlay meant when she warned me against the banshee. It was Louella—my sister! She killed our uncle, and she almost finished me last night. I tell you—"

"And *I* tell *you*, Monsieur David, that you talk like an uncommonly silly fool!" de Grandin broke in sharply. "Hear me, if you please—or if you do not please, for that matter. Attend me, listen, pay attention, forget your chuckle-headedness! You talk of witch-burning, and, *parbleu*, you do well to do so, for you assuredly show the shallow-emptiness of head which so characterized those old ones who sent innocent women to the flames!

"*Non*, listen to me," he bade sharply as the other would have spoken. "You will hear me through, if I must knock you senseless and bind you to the bed in order to keep you quiet!

"Your story of your uncle's death did greatly interest me when first you told it. That old Sepa, the Priest of Aset, or Isis, as we call her nowadays, had any personal part in it I did not seriously consider; but that the constant, continuous, subconscious *thought* of that old one's curse had much to do with it I was very certain. Consider, my friend, you know how half-a-dozen people, thinking together, can sometimes influence one in a company? You have seen it demonstrated? Good. So it was in this case, only more so; much more so. For generations the dwellers in Egypt bowed the knee to Aset, the All-Mother, she whom they worshiped as She Who Was and Is and Is to Be. Now, whether such a personality as hers ever existed or not is beside the question; let but enough persons loose thoughts of her, and they have created a thought-image of such strength that only *le bon Dieu* knows its limitations.

"So with the vengeance of the dead. For more generations than you have hairs upon your head the Egyptians believed implicitly that he who broke the rest of the entombed dead laid himself open to direst vengeance. And to strengthen this belief, those who were buried were wont to place a curse-stone in their tombs, denouncing the disturbers of their long rest in such language as old Sepa directed against your late uncle. Yes, it is so.

"Your late lamented kinsman spent much time among the ancient tombs. It was inevitable he should have absorbed some sort of half-agnostic belief in the potency of the old ones' curses. That sort of thing grows on one.

"Anon, having retired, he sets himself to translating the various tablets and papyri he had collected. At length he comes upon the curse-stone from old Sepa's grave.

"Now, we do not realize when the *Uncinaria americana* infects our systems with its eggs, but anon we suffer drowsiness, anemia and dropsy. We have no desire to do anything but sit about and sleep—we have the disease known as hookworm, for the eggs have germinated. So it was with old Sepa's curse. *Monsieur* your uncle wrought out the translation of the curse-stone, and paid little heed to what he read—at first. But all the same the idea of a dreadful doom awaiting him who invaded that wicked old one's tomb was firmly lodged in his subconscious mind, and there it germinated, and grew into a monstrous thing, even as the hookworm's eggs grow in the body of their victim. And when your uncle read of the young Englishman's death, and how he was the tenth to die of those who opened Tutankhamen's tomb, such doubts as he might have had disappeared utterly. He did resign himself to death by Sepa's vengeance.

"Your sister, being sensitive to thought-influence, at length became infected, too. It was as if your uncle, all unknowingly, transferred his fearful thoughts to her subconscious mind, much as a hypnotist imposes his thought and will upon his subject. Your sister is tall, stately, beautiful. She had the peculiar greenish eyes which go with mysticism. What more natural than that your uncle should have conceived the Goddess Aset as in your sister's image, and, so conceiving, impregnated your sister with his thought. All unknowingly, she was to him, and to herself, the very incarnation of that olden one—that probably non-existent one—whose wrath had been called down on *Monsieur* your kinsman by the curse-stone found in Sepa's grave.

"Very good. Upon the night in which your uncle died your sister did arise, descend the stairs into the museum, and there equip herself with the garments once worn by some Egyptian priestess. Consider, now: She did not consciously know what was in those cabinets below, she knew not which keys fitted the locks, she did not know how the ancient priestesses arrayed themselves, for she had no knowledge of archeology, yet she went unerringly to the proper case, chose the proper trappings, and donned them in the proper manner. Why? *Because Your uncle's thought guided her!*

"All this she did at the urge of her subconscious mind. Her conscious mind, by which she recognized external things, was fast asleep meanwhile. Yet so deftly did her dream-commanded mind order the disguise that she even went so far as to trace the likeness of open, staring eyes upon her lids with phosphorescent paint.

"And then, arrayed as Aset, she did repair to your uncle's room, and with her went the thought-concept of another one, the thought-induced and thought-begotten likeness of the long-dead Sepa.

"With ancient ritual she read aloud your uncle's doom, the doom he had decreed upon himself by his persistent thought, and he—poor man!—believing that his doom was sealed, did die for very fright.

"Now, concerning yourself: Like her, you knew of the curse; like her you had read of the death of the young Englishman who violated the tomb of Tut-ankhamen. Very well. Subconsciously you feared the curse which Sepa had put upon your uncle and your uncle's kin hovered over you. Although you strove to shake it off, the thought would not die, for the more you dismissed it from your conscious mind, the deeper it penetrated into your subconscious, there to fester like a septic splinter in one's finger. Yes.

"Last night was the crucial time. Once more *Mademoiselle* your sister donned Aset's unholy livery; once more she did pronounce the doom of Sepa upon your uncle's kin—and, *parbleu*, she did almost succeed in doing it! Friend Trowbridge and I were not a second too soon, I damn think."

"But the mark—the mark on Uncle Absalom's breast, and which Dr. Trow-bridge said appeared on mine too; what of that?" young Monteith persisted.

"Perhaps you have not seen it, but I have," de Grandin returned: "a hyp-notist can, by his bare mental command, cause the blood to leave his subject's arm, and make the member become white and cold as death. So with the death-sign on your uncle's breast, and yours. It was but the stigma of a mental order—a thought made physically manifest."

"But what did you do—what did you use?" Monteith demanded. "I saw you drive the ghost of Sepa from the room with something. What was it?"

"To understand, you must know the history of Isis," de Grandin answered. "Her cult was one of the most powerful of all the ancient world. Despite the sternest opposition she had her votaries in both Greece and Rome, and she was the last of the old gods to be expelled from Egypt, for notwithstanding the Christianizing of the land and the great strength of the Alexandrian Church, her shrine at Philae continued to draw worshipers until the sixth century of our era.

"Now, while Christianity still struggled with the remnant of the olden faiths there lived in Alexandria a certain priest named Cyril, a very holy man, who by virtue of his piety wrought many miracles. Also, when more than once the women of his congregation declared themselves spellbound by the ancient Goddess Aset, he was wont to cast the spell from off them by the use of a certain sacred amulet, a little cross of gold supposed to hold a tiny remnant of the True Cross within itself. This very sacred reliquary is in the present custody of the *Papa* of the Greek Orthodox Church in Harrisonville. Often have I heard the old man speak of it.

"Accordingly, when we came here to 'Journey's End' to try conclusions with the ancient gods of Egypt, I begged the use of that same relic from its custodian and brought it with me.

"And, as I have said, thoughts have power. It was the thought of Priest Sepa's ancient curse which worked the death of your uncle and all but caused your own; yet here was a little, so small piece of gold which also carried the concentrated thought of centuries. Adored as a caster-out-of spells by generations of pious Christians, once regarded as efficacious against the same old goddess by whom your house was so beset, it was ideally suited to my purpose. I did fight thought with counter-thought; against the evil thought-concepts of Aset and of Sepa her priest I set the defensive thought-power of Cyril, the Alexandrian monk, who once cast Aset forth from out the bodies of his bewitched parishioners. The tiny relic in my hand focused, so to speak, the thoughts which negatived the harmful power of Aset and her followers, and—Aset and her ghostly worshiper are gone. If—"

"I—don't—believe—a—word—of—it!" Monteith interrupted slowly. "You're saying all this to shield Louella. She's bad—wicked clear through, and I don't ever want to see her again. I—"

"*Monsieur!*" de Grandin's voice was sharp-edged as a razor. "Look at this!"

Once more he drew the little golden cross of Cyril from his pocket, holding it before the young man's eyes. As young Monteith gazed wonderingly at it, the Frenchman continued in a low, earnest voice: "You will hear and obey. You will sleep for half an hour, at which time you will awake, completely forgetting all which occurred last night, remembering only that the thing which menaced your family and household has forever departed. Sleep. Sleep and forget. I command it!

"And that, my friend, is that," he announced matter-of-factly as Monteith's eyelids lowered in compliance with his order.

"Now what?" I asked.

"I think we would better burn the mummy of Priest Sepa and the translation of his curse-stone," he responded. "The uncle's will absolved his legatees from burying the mummy if it became physically impossible—I propose rendering it so. Come, let us cremate the old one,"

Together we dismembered the desiccated corpse of the Egyptian, casting the pieces on the glowing coals of the furnace, where they burned with sharp, fierce spurts of flame and quickly turned to light, gray ashes which wafted, upward through the draft of the firebox.

"What about the uncanny feeling Louella complained of, de Grandin?" I asked as we pursued our grisly task. "You know, she said she felt as though someone were staring at her from behind?"

"*Mais oui*," he chuckled as he fed a mummified forearm to the flames. "I shall say she had good cause to feel so. Did not the excellent Maggie and her husband stare her out of countenance from the rear, always seeking to see her take a third helping of food or wine? *Parbleu*, Mademoiselle Louella desired the boyish figure, therefore she eats sparingly, therefore she is tried and condemned by the so excellent Irish couple on the charge of being a fairy! *C'est drôle, n'est-ce-pas?*"

When we returned to the upper floor, David Monteith was up and disposing of an excellent breakfast.

"Good old Lou," we heard him tell his sister, "of course I wasn't ill last night. I slept like a top—overslept, in fact; aren't I an hour late to breakfast?" He smiled and patted his sister's hand reassuringly.

"Ah, *parbleu*, Jules de Grandin, you are clever!" the little Frenchman murmured delightedly. "You have removed all danger from these young people and assured their happiness by exorcizing the devil of bad memories. Yes. Come with me, Jules de Grandin; I shall take you to the library and give you a magnificent-great drink of whisky."

The Brain-Thief

"TIENS, MONSIEUR, YOU AMAZE me, you astound me; I am astonished, I assure you. Say on, if you please; I am entirely attentive." Jules de Grandin's voice, vibrant with interest, came to me as I closed the front door and walked down the hall toward my consulting room.

"Holà, Friend Trowbridge," he hailed as his quick ear caught my step outside, "come here, if you please; there is something I would have you hear, if you can spare the time."

The tall young man, prematurely gray at the temples, seated opposite de Grandin rose as I entered the study and greeted me with an air of restraint.

"Oh, how d'ye do?" I growled grudgingly, then turned my back on the visitor as I looked inquiringly at de Grandin. If there was one person more than another whom I did not desire my roof to shelter, it was Christopher Norton. I'd known the cub since his first second of life, had tended him for measles, whooping-cough and chickenpox, had seen him safely through adolescence, and was among the first to wish him luck when he married Isabel Littlewood. Now, like every decent man in the city, I had no desire to see any of him, except his back, and that at as great a distance as possible. "If you'll excuse me—" I began, turning toward the door.

"Parbleu, that is exactly what I shall not!" de Grandin denied. "I know what you think, my friend; I know what everyone thinks, but I shall make you and all of them change your minds; yes, by damn, I swear it! Come, good friend, be reasonable. Sit and listen to the story I have heard, suspending your judgment meantime.

"Say it again, young Monsieur," he ordered the visitor. "Relate your so pitiful tale from the beginning, that Dr. Trowbridge may know as much as I."

There was such a look of distress on young Norton's face as he looked half-pleadingly, half-fearfully at me that, had he been anything but the thoroughgoing scoundrel he was, I could have found it in my heart to be sorry for him. "It seems Isabel and I have been divorced," he began, almost tentatively. "I—I suppose I wasn't as good to her as I might have been—"

"You *suppose*, you confounded young whelp!" I burst out. "You *know* you treated that girl as no decent man would treat a dog! You know perfectly well you broke her heart and every promise you made her at the altar—you smashed her life and betrayed her confidence and the confidence of every misguided friend who trusted you—" I choked with anger, and wheeled furiously on de Grandin. "Listen to me," I ordered. "I don't know what this good-for-nothing young reprobate has been telling you, but I tell you whatever he's said is a pack of lies—lies from beginning to end. I've known him all his life—helped him begin breathing thirty years ago by slapping his two-seconds-old posterior with a wet towel—and I've known the girl he married all her life, too. He and she were born within a city block of each other, less than a month apart. Their parents were friends, they went to school together and played together, and were boy and girl sweethearts. When they finally married, all us old fools who'd watched them grow from childhood swarmed round and gave them our blessing. Then, by George, before they'd been married a year, this young jackanapes showed himself in his true colors. He abused her, beat her, finally deserted her and ran off with his best friends wife. If that's the sort of story you've listened to, I'm surprised—"

"*Cordieu*, surprised you most assuredly shall be, my friend, but not as you think," de Grandin interrupted. "Be good enough to seize your tongue-tip between thumb and forefinger while the young *Monsieur* concludes his story."

"I don't expect you to believe me, sir," young Norton began again; "I don't know I'd believe such a story if it were told me—but it's true, all the same. As far as I can remember, the last time I saw Isabel was this morning when I left for the office. We'd had a little misunderstanding—nothing serious, but enough to put us both in a huff—and I stopped at Caminelli's and bought some roses as a peace-offering on my way home tonight.

"I fairly ran the last half-block to the house, and didn't wait for the maid to let me in. It was when I got in the hall I first noticed changes. Most of the old furniture was gone, and what remained was standing in different places. I thought, 'She's been doing a lot of house-cleaning since this morning,' but that was all. I was too anxious to find her and make up, you see.

"I called, 'Isabel, Isabel!' once or twice, but no one answered. Then I ran upstairs."

He paused, looking pleadingly at me, and the half-puzzled, half-frightened look which had been on his face throughout his recital deepened.

"There was a nurse—a nurse in hospital uniform leaving the room as I ran down the upper hall," he continued slowly. "She looked at me and smiled, and said, 'Why, how nice of you to bring the flowers, Mr. Norton. I'm sure they'll be delighted.'

"That 'they' didn't mean anything to me then, but a moment later it did. On the bed, with a little, new baby cuddled in the curve of her elbow, lay Betty Baintree! Try and realize that, Dr. Trowbridge; Betty, Jack Baintree's wife, whom I'd last seen at the Colony Country Club dance last Thursday night, was lying in bed in my house, a young baby in her arms!

"She greeted me familiarly, 'Why, Kit, dear,' she said 'I didn't expect you so soon. Thanks for the flowers, honey.' Then: 'Come kiss baby; she's been restless for her daddy the last half-hour.'

"It was then she seemed to notice the look of blank amazement on my face for the first time. 'Kit, boy, whatever is the matter?' she asked. 'Don't you—'

"'Wha—what are you doing here, Betty?' I managed to gasp. 'Isabel—where is she?'

"'Isabel?' she echoed incredulously. 'What's got into you, dear—what makes you look so strangely? Haven't you any greeting for your wife and baby?'

"'My—wife—and—baby?' I stammered. 'But—'

"I don't know just what happened next, sir. I've a confused recollection of staggering from that accursed room, stumbling down the stairs and meeting the nurse, who looked at me as though she'd seen a ghost, then tottering toward the door and running, hatless and coatless, to my mother's house in Auburndale Avenue. I ran up the steps, tried the door and found it locked. Then I almost beat in the panels with my fists. A strange maid, not old Sadie, answered my frantic summons and looked at me as though she suspected my reason. The family occupying the house was named Bronson, she told me. They'd lived there for the past two years—'since shortly after the widow Norton's death.'

"'Am I mad, or is this all some horrible nightmare?' I asked myself as I turned once more toward my home, or rather toward the house which had been my home this morning.

"It wasn't a dream, as I assured myself when I returned and found Betty crying hysterically in bed with the nurse trying to comfort her and looking poisoned daggers at me as I came in the door.

"I got my hat and coat and wandered about town looking for someone I knew—someone who might offer me a ray of comforting light to guide me through the terrible fog into which I seemed to have plunged. Half a block from home I met Dr. Raymond, of the Presbyterian Church, whom I'd known since I was a lad in his Sunday School's infant class. I spoke to him, tried to stop him, but he passed me without a sign of recognition. Either he cut me dead or failed to see me, as though I'd been a disembodied spirit.

"Finally, I managed to locate Freddy Myers. He and I were in high school and college together, and had always been good friends. He let me in, but that was about all. Not a word of greeting, save a chilly 'How do you do?' Not a smile, not even a handshake did he offer me, and he remained standing after

I'd come into the hall and made no move to take my hat and coat or invite me to be seated.

"I put the proposition squarely up to him; told him what I'd just been through, and asked him for God's sake to tell me where Isabel was. The news of my mother's death two years before was shock enough, but Isabel's disappearance—Betty Baintree in my house, and the baby—I was like an earthman suddenly set down on the moon.

"For a while Fred listened to me as he might have listened to the ravings of a drunken man; then he asked me if I were trying to kid him. When I assured him I was sincere in my questions, he grew angry and told me, just as you have, Dr. Trowbridge, how I'd abused Isabel, how my disgraceful amours with other women had finally forced her to divorce me, and how I was ostracized by every decent man who'd known me in the old days. Finally, he ordered me out and told me he'd punch my face if I ever spoke to him again.

"I don't know what to think, sir. Freddy's abuse was so genuine, his anger so manifestly sincere and his scorn so patently righteous that I knew it couldn't all be some ghastly practical joke of which I was the victim. Besides, there was the strange maid in Mother's house and the news of Mother's death—*that* couldn't have been arranged, even if Isabel and Betty and Freddy had joined in a conspiracy to punish me for the burst of nasty temper I showed this morning.

"For a little while I thought I'd gone crazy and all the astonishing things which seemed to have happened were only the vagaries of a lunatic. Indeed, sir, I'm not sure I'm sane, even yet—I hope to God I'm not! But what am I to do? Can't anybody explain the situation to me? Suppose you found yourself in my place, sir." He turned appealing, haunted eyes on me.

"Then I remembered hearing someone tell of the wonderful things Dr. de Grandin did," he concluded. "I'd been told he'd corrected maladjusted destinies as though by magic sometimes; so I've come here as a last resort.

"You're my last hope, Dr. de Grandin," he finished tragically. "I don't know, except by inference and such reconstruction of events as I can make from the crazy, meaningless things I've seen and heard tonight, what's happened, but one thing seems certain: For the last two years time has stood still for me. There's been a slice of two years carved right out of my memory, and all the terrible things which have occurred during that period are a sealed book to me. Can't you do something for me, sir? If you can't, for God's sake, send me to a lunatic asylum. I don't know just what sins I've committed, but even though I've committed them unconsciously, the uncertainty of it all is driving me to madness and an asylum seems the only refuge left."

Jules de Grandin brushed the tightly waxed ends of his small blond mustache with the tip of a well-manicured forefinger. "I think we need not consider the padded cell as yet, my friend," he encouraged. "At present I am inclined to prescribe a stiff dose of Dr. Trowbridge's best brandy for you—and a like potion for myself.

"And now, *Monsieur*," he continued as he drained the final drop of cognac from his goblet, "I would suggest that you take the medicine I shall prepare, then go to bed—Friend Trowbridge has a spare chamber for your accommodation."

For a few moments he busied himself in the surgery, returning with a beaker of grayish, cloudy liquid, which young Norton tossed off at a gulp.

T EN MINUTES LATER, WITH my unwelcome guest soundly sleeping in my spare bedroom de Grandin took up a pencil and pad of note-paper and turned to me. "Tell me, *mon vieux*," he ordered, "all you can of this so unfortunate young man's domestic tragedy."

"Humph," I retorted, still smarting at the generous use he had made of my hospitality, "there's precious little to tell. Kit Norton is a rotter from the backbone out; there's not an ounce of decency in his whole makeup. The girl he married was one of the finest young women in the city, absolutely above reproach in every way, and they seemed ideally happy for a little time; then, without a moment's warning, his whole nature seemed to change. He became an utter sot, found fault with everything she did and blamed her for his business reverses—he had plenty of 'em, too, for he began to neglect his real estate office at the same time he began neglecting his wife—and it wasn't long before his affairs with other women became the scandal of the town. The climax came when he and Betty Baintree eloped.

"Norton and Frank Baintree had been inseparable friends from boyhood. Frank married Betty a short time after Kit and Isabel were married, and the couples continued the friendship. When Kit and Betty ran off, of course, the lid blew off the whole rotten mess. It was then we all realized Kit's contemptible conduct toward Isabel was all part of a deliberately planned scheme to force her to divorce him—and the proof of it was that Betty had acted toward Frank just as Kit had acted toward Isabel for about the same period. There's no doubt of it, the brazen pair had conspired to force a divorce so they could be free to marry, and when their plans failed to work, they had the effrontery to elope, leaving identical notes with their deserted partners. It's an unsavory business from start to finish, de Grandin, and I wish you hadn't gotten mixed up in it, for—"

"*Non*, let us not be too hasty, Friend Trowbridge," the little Frenchman interrupted. "See, you have already given me much of importance to think of. Had not Madame Betty's conduct been identical with that of Monsieur Christopher, I might have seen a reason for it all; as it is—*eh bien*, I know not quite what to think. Such cases, however, are not altogether unknown. Once before I have seen something like this. A certain tradesman in Lyons—a draper, he was—left his home for the shop one morning, and was heard from no more. Five years passed, and he was thought dead by all who knew him, when *pouf!* where should he be found but living in Marseilles, happy and respectable as could be, with another wife and a family of fine, healthy children? In Lyons he had been a draper; in Marseilles he was a bricklayer—a trade, by the way, for which he had no apparent ability in his former life. Maurice Simon, his name was, but in Marseilles he knew himself only as Jean Dufour. Every test was made to prove him a malingerer, but it seemed established beyond all reasonable doubt that the unfortunate man was actually suffering a split consciousness—all memory of his former life in Lyons was completely obliterated from his mind, and his wife and children were utter strangers to him. Reproaches and argument alike left him unmoved. 'I am Jean Dufour, bricklayer, of Marseilles,' he repeated stubbornly. At last they managed to convince him of his identity. The realization of what he had done, how he had wrecked two women's lives and the lives of his children, drove him mad. He died raving in a hospital for the insane."

"But that can't possibly be the case here," I expostulated. "We know—"

"*Pardonnez-moi*, we know nothing; even less," de Grandin denied. "Come, let us go."

"Go?" I echoed. "Go where?"

"To interview Madame Betty, of course," he returned coolly. "I may be wrong, but unless I am more mistaken than I think, we may find interesting developments at her home."

Grumbling, but with my curiosity piqued, I rose to accompany him to the pretty little cottage where Kit Norton had taken his bride three years before.

"It is most strange," he muttered as we passed through the quiet streets. "It seems hardly likely the poor Monsieur Christopher should have suffered the same fate. And yet—" he broke off musingly.

"What's that?" I asked sharply, annoyed at his persistent sympathy for young Norton.

"I did but think aloud," he returned. "The unfortunate gentleman of Lyons, of whom I spoke earlier in the evening—his aberration was an oddly tangled one. Investigations by the police showed that several days before he deserted his family and set out for Marseilles, he had an altercation with a certain fortune-telling man from the East; indeed, he had gone so far as to tweak his nose, and the Oriental had pronounced a curse of forgetfulness on him."

As we paused before the cottage gate a long roadster, driven as though contending for a racing-trophy, dashed past us and stopped at the curb with a screeching of sharply applied brakes. A moment later its occupant leaped out and ran at breakneck speed up the brick path leading to Norton's front stoop. "Lesterdale!" I exclaimed in surprise.

"Eh, what do you say?" de Grandin asked.

"That's Lesterdale, the best nerve man in the city," I responded. "Wonder what brings him here?"

"Let us see," the Frenchman returned matter-of-factly. "The house is open, Let us enter."

Dr. Lesterdale had a case worthy of all his skill, we discovered almost as soon as we marched unbidden into Norton's cottage.

Betty Norton crouched in her bed, her knees drawn up, her chin resting on them, and her arms flailing the unresisting air with the fury of the grand movement stage of hysteria. As we paused at the bedroom door we caught a glimpse of her tear-smeared face as she stared wildly about the room with wide, horror-numbed eyes. "Frank," she shrieked, "oh, Frank my love, where are you?"

"Doctor," she bent a terrified look on Lesterdale, "I dreamed—I thought I was Kit Norton's wife, that I was the mother of—oh, say it isn't true, Doctor."

"*Tiens*, what is this?" de Grandin muttered. "Has she, too, emerged from a state of suspended memory?"

Lesterdale's eyes were cool with professional unconcern. Like everyone else in the city he knew the scandal of Betty's divorce and remarriage, and had he been there in any capacity other than that of physician, I could well imagine how his glance would have been blank with cold contempt as he looked at the pretty woman contorted on the bed. "Water!" he ordered shortly of the terrified nurse.

A moment later he dissolved a small white tablet in the half-filled tumbler she brought, plunged the nozzle of his hypodermic into the mixture and barked another order. "Alcohol—sponge—in the case yonder," he snapped.

The nurse got the alcohol and a cotton sponge from his kit and swabbed Betty's left arm.

The needle pierced the girl's delicate skin and I saw a blister rise as the morphia went home before the syringe-plunger's pressure.

"See the child has substitute feedings—dextro-maltose, milk and water, Wilson's formula No. 2—can't have it nurse with the mother full o' morphine. Call me if she kicks up another row." Lesterdale glanced appraisingly at Betty, noted the narcotic already stealing over her, and turned toward the door. "She ought to be quiet for the rest of the night," he added over his shoulder.

"Oh, hullo, Trowbridge," he called as he recognized me by the door. "What's up, did they rout you out, too? Devil of a note, dragging a man from the bridge table to calm a conscience-stricken female. What?"

"But do you think it's just an attack of conscience?" I countered. "Mightn't it be a case of puerperal insan—"

"No," he cut in. "Not even lactational neurosis; no symptom of it. It's hysteria, pure and simple, or"—he smiled acidly—"more simple than pure, I'd say, considering who's having it. Don't see how it happened, but something's awakened the little strumpet's conscience, and it's hurting her like the devil. Good-night," he nodded shortly as he passed down the hall without a backward glance.

"*Mordieu*, he is hard, that one; hard like a nail," de Grandin murmured. "A good neurologist he may be, Friend Trowbridge, but I think he is also a monumental fool. Let us interrogate the *garde-malade*."

The nurse recognized me with a start of surprise as we edged into the room. "Mr. Norton called at my office, and—" I began, but she cut me short.

"Oh, he did, did he?" she returned sourly. "I should think he would, after what he's done. He—"

"Slowly, *Mademoiselle*, if you please," de Grandin urged. "'Our perceptions are dull, and you go too fast. What, precisely, did Monsieur Norton do?"

The girl stared at him. "What?" she echoed. "Plenty. He came home from the office with a beautiful bouquet; then pretended he didn't know his own wife and baby, and went flying out of the house like a crazy man. He drove the poor thing to this—" she glanced compassionately at Betty. "He hadn't been gone half-an-hour when she went completely to pieces and started raving like a lunatic!"

"Ah?" de Grandin tweaked his mustache meditatively. "Now we begin to make progress. What, if you please, was the exact nature of her delusion?"

The nurse considered a moment. Years of hospital training had taught her accurate observation where symptoms were concerned, and professional habit was stronger than womanly anger. "She began crying as though her heart would break," she replied slowly; "then, when he came back the second time and stared wildly in the room before rushing off again, she seemed to change completely. I've never seen anything like it. One moment she was crying and wringing her hands, begging Mr. Norton to recognize her, the next she was like a different woman. Just for a moment she stopped crying, and a sort of dazed, surprised look came into her eyes; then she looked round the room as though she'd never seen it before—like a casualty victim coming out of the ether in the emergency ward," she finished with professional clarity.

"This dazed, bewildered condition lasted only a moment; then, like a woman recovering from a faint, she asked, 'Where am I?'

"I soothed her as best I could; told her Mr. Norton had gone out for a moment, but would be back directly, and held the baby out to her. This seemed to excite her all the more. I had to explain where she was, who she was, *and who the baby was*—can you imagine? Instead of calming her, it seemed to make her worse. She stared unbelievingly at me, and when I showed her the baby again, she fell to screaming at the top of her voice and calling for somebody named Frank. Have you any idea who it could be, Dr. Trowbridge?"

"What else happened?" I returned, evading her question.

"That's all, sir. I grew alarmed when she seemed to shrink from her own child, and called Dr. Lesterdale. He's the best nerve man in town, don't you think?"

"Quite," I agreed. "If you—"

"*Non, mon ami,*" de Grandin interrupted. "Trouble the good *mademoiselle* no more. We have already heard enough—*parbleu*, I fear we have heard more than we can conveniently piece together. Come, let us go.

"*Grand Dieu,*" he murmured as we reached the street, "it is amazing, it is astonishing, it is bewildering! Has the clock of time turned back, and are we once more in the seventeenth century?"

"Eh?" I asked.

"Is witchcraft rampant in our midst?" he returned. "*Barbe d'un bouc*, my friend, I know not whether to say we have witnessed two most extraordinary cases of mental derangement or something wholly and entirely infernal."

2

HOMER ABBOT, SON OF my old schoolmate, Judge Winslow Abbot, and one of the cleverest of the younger members of the local bar, was waiting nervously in my consulting-room next morning. "It's about Marjorie," he began, almost before we had exchanged greetings. "I'm dreadfully worried about her, Doctor!"

"What's wrong?" I asked, noting the parentheses of wrinkles which worry had etched between his brows. "Do you want me to run over and look at her?"

"No, sir; I'm afraid this business is a little out of your line," he confessed. "To tell you the truth, I've come to you more as a friend than as a physician." He paused a moment, as though debating whether to continue; then: "She's been acting queerly, recently. About a week ago she began coming down to breakfast all crocked up—circles under her eyes, no more life than a wet handkerchief, and all that sort of thing, you know. I was concerned at once, and begged her to come to you, but she just laughed at me.

"It's gone from bad to worse, since. She's irritable as the deuce—flies off the handle at nothing, scolds me like a shrew with or without reason; most of the time she seems actually trying to avoid me, makes every kind of excuse to keep from coming to the door with me in the morning, pleads a headache, or some other indisposition, to get away from me in the evening, even—"

"H'm," I smiled knowingly to myself. A happy explanation of Marjorie's sudden vagaries had occurred to me, but Homer's next words killed it.

"Three nights ago I happened to wake up about one o'clock," he hurried on. "You know that feeling of vague malaise we sometimes have for no reason at all? That's what I felt when I sat up in bed and looked round. Everything was quiet—too quiet—in the room. I switched on the night light and looked across at Marjorie's bed. It was empty.

"I waited and waited. When half an hour went by with no sign of her, I couldn't stand it any more. I looked everywhere—went through the house from cellar to attic; she wasn't anywhere. It wasn't till I'd finished my search and returned almost frantic to the bedroom that I noticed her clothing was missing from the chair where she usually puts it; when I went to the closet I found her heavy sports coat gone, too.

"I sat up waiting for her till nearly five o'clock; finally, I couldn't stick it any more, and dropped off to sleep.

"Marjorie was sleeping peacefully as a child when I woke two hours later, and when I tried to rouse her and ask where she'd been during the night, she turned from me like a fretful child, too, and mumbled something about wanting to be let alone.

"I tried my best to ask her about it that evening, but she had a couple of girl friends in to dinner and we played contract afterward, so I didn't get a word alone with her till after eleven, when the company left. Then she fairly ran upstairs to bed, complaining of a splitting headache, and each time I tried to speak to her she begged me to let her alone to suffer in peace.

"I don't think she went out that night, *but I don't know*."

"Eh?" I asked, impressed by the emphasis he laid on the last four words. "How d'ye mean?"

For answer he thrust his hand into his waistcoat pocket and extracted a tiny square of folded white paper. "What do you make of this?" he asked, handing me the packet.

I opened the paper, disclosing a dust of fine, white, crystalline powder, wet my forefinger, gathered a few grains of the substance on it, and touched it to my tongue. "Good heavens!" I ejaculated.

"Morphine, isn't it?" he asked.

"No, it is codeine," I returned. "Where—"

"On her dresser, yesterday morning," he cut in. "And there was another like it, with a few grains of the stuff still adhering to the paper, on the pantry shelf. We had coffee with our refreshments the night before, and I thought mine tasted bitter, but the others laughed at me, so I thought maybe the trouble was with me rather than the coffee. By the way, Marjorie brought the coffee in herself that night, and it wasn't till I found these powders that I recalled she brought mine in separately, the only cup on the tray—no chance for me to take the wrong one that way, you see.

"I slept like a log that night, and woke with a queer, dizzy feeling yesterday morning. Marjorie was still asleep when I was dressed and ready for breakfast, and it was just by chance I discovered the powder. You see, I thought perhaps her headache was still troubling her, and went to her dresser for some cologne. That's where I found the package I just showed you. I thought I recognized it; they gave me something of the kind in the hospital at St. Nazaire during the war."

"But see here, boy," I expostulated, "maybe we're making a mountain of a molehill. This stuff's codeine, beyond doubt, and Marjorie shouldn't be allowed to have it; but it's possible some quack gave it her for those headaches she's been complaining of—more than one woman's been made a dope fiend that way. That feeling of depression you had on waking—"

"Wasn't present this morning," he interrupted sharply. "I don't know how I came to reason it all out, but the moment I found that infernal stuff I knew she'd drugged my coffee the previous night. So I took the paper and went downstairs and fixed a dummy pack with table salt, and left it where I'd found the codeine on her dresser. It was while I was looking for salt to make the dummy I found the empty codeine paper in the pantry.

"Dr. Trowbridge," he leaned forward impressively, "last night, after dinner, my coffee was salty as brine!"

Young Homer Abbot and I faced each other a moment in solemn-eyed silence. I opened my lips to utter some banality, but he hurried on:

"I pretended to become sleepy almost immediately, and went to bed—but I didn't undress. Marjorie didn't trouble even to come upstairs to see if I had fallen asleep; I suppose she was so sure the dope had done its work. I heard the front door close before I'd been in bed half an hour, jumped up, slipped on my shoes and jacket, and ran after her. I got down just in time to see her taxi round the corner, and though I chased it like a hound hunting a rabbit, it lost me in the fog, and I had to give up.

"Marjorie came in a few minutes after five this morning," he concluded. Then, because he was still little more than a boy, and because his happy little world had tumbled to pieces before his eyes, Homer Abbot put his arm down on my desk, pillowed his face against it and cried like a heart-broken child.

"Poor chap," I sympathized. "Poor boy, it's a rotten shame, and—"

"And we had best be stirring ourselves to correct it, my friend," Jules de Grandin supplemented as he stepped noiselessly into the room.

"I must ask forgiveness for eavesdropping," he added as he paused beside me, "but I caught the beginning of the young *monsieur's* so tragic tale, and could not forbear to linger till I heard its end.

"Do not despair, my friend," he patted Homer's bowed shoulder gently. "All looks hopeless, I know, but I think there is a reason behind it all, nor is it what you think.

"Trowbridge, my friend," he added, his little eyes snapping with cold fury. "I damnation think this business of Monsieur Abbot's and that of Monsieur

Norton are bound up together somehow. Yes. Certainly there is someone, or some *thing*, in this city which stands in urgent need of eradication, and I shall supply that need—may Satan fry me in a pan with butter and parsnips if I do not so!"

Again he turned to Homer. "Think, *Monsieur*," he urged, "what happened before your so charming wife began to show this remarkable change? Consider carefully the smallest happening, the seemingly least important thing may guide us to a solution of the case. What, by example, did you do for several days before she manifested the first symptom—even the very night before her indisposition became patent?"

Young Abbot took his chin in his hand as he bent his thoughts backward. "I can't recall anything, especially, that happened about that time," he answered slowly. "Let's see, four of us went to the theater that Thursday night, and stopped at a night club afterward. U'm, yes; something rather queer *did* happen there. We had a little spat, but—?"

"Excellent!" de Grandin interjected. "This *petite querelle*, it was about what, if you please?"

"Nothing of importance," the other replied. "There was a queer, bilious-looking fellow sitting alone at a table across from us, and he kept looking at Marjorie. I didn't notice him at first, but at last he got on my nerves, and I rose to speak to him. Marjorie begged me not to make a scene, and the fellow left a few minutes afterward—damn him, I'd have wrung his neck, if I'd caught him!" he ended savagely.

"Indeed, and for why?" de Grandin asked softly.

"Just before he left the room he turned and held up a little mirror, or some small, round, bright object, and flashed a ray from it directly into Marjorie's eyes. I made a dash for him, but he'd gone before I could reach the door."

"U'm," de Grandin murmured to himself. "That is of importance, also." He nodded once or twice thoughtfully; then: "And *Madame*, your wife, she said what?" he asked.

"She fussed at me!" Homer returned in an injured voice. "Declared I'd made a disgraceful scene and humiliated her, and all that kind of thing. Next morning she slept late, and was as exhausted as though she'd just risen from a sickbed when she finally got up."

Jules de Grandin studied the end of his cigarette with slow, thoughtful care. At last, "It is fantastic," he murmured, "but I damn fear it is so, nonetheless.

"Very good, *Monsieur*," he turned again to Abbott, "you will oblige us by acting as though nothing had occurred at your house. I especially desire that do not let *Madame* suspect you have discovered her attempts to drug you. Anon, I think, we shall unravel this sorry tangle for you, but it may take time."

3

Nora McGinnis, my genial household factotum, laid a sheaf of letters beside my plate when de Grandin and I repaired to the breakfast room half an hour later.

"Hullo," I remarked, "here's one for Kit Norton. Wonder how anyone knew he's stopping here?"

"I mentioned it to the nurse before we left his house last night," de Grandin replied. "Open the letter, if you please. Monsieur Norton sleeps late this morning, I made sure he should. Meantime, the note may contain something which will prove helpful to us."

I slit the envelope and read:

> Kit:
>
> They tell me Frank divorced me because of you and Isabel divorced you on my account. They say we've been married two years and the baby's ours. I can't understand it all; and I shan't try. I'm taking the baby with me. It's best.
>
> Yours,
> Betty.

"Good heavens!" I exclaimed. "What can this mean?"

"Mean?" de Grandin was on his feet, his little eyes blazing like those of a suddenly incensed cat. "Mean? *Mort d'un rat*, it means murder; no less, my friend. Come, quick, when was that letter mailed?"

"It's postmarked 12:40," I returned. "Must have been dropped about midnight last night."

"*Hélas*—too late!" he cried. "Come, prove that my fears are all too well grounded, Friend Trowbridge!"

Grasping my hand he fairly dragged me to the study, where he motioned me to take up the telephone. Next instant he rushed to the consulting-room extension and called Main 926.

"*Allo?*" he cried when the connection was put through.

"City Mortuary," was the curt return. "Who's speaking?"

"You have there the bodies of a young woman and an infant girl—Madame Norton and her child?" de Grandin affirmed, rather than asked.

"Gawd A'mighty, how'd you know? Who is this?" came the startled reply.

"Have the goodness to answer, if you please," the Frenchman insisted.

"Yeah, we've got 'em. Th' police boat fished 'em outa th' river less'n half an hour ago. Who th' hell *is* this?"

"One who can prove she destroyed herself while of unsound mind," de Grandin returned as he hung up the receiver.

"You see?" he asked as he re-entered the study.

"No. I'm hanged if I do!" I shot back. All I understood was that Betty Norton had drowned herself and her baby.

"We shall avenge her; have no fear on that score, *mon vieux*," de Grandin promised in a low, accentless voice. "The swine responsible for this shall die, and die most unpleasantly, or may Jules de Grandin never again taste roast gosling and burgundy. I swear it!"

4

JULES DE GRANDIN TOSSED aside the copy of *l'Illustration* he had been perusing since dinner and glanced at the diminutive watch strapped to his wrist. "It is time we were going, my friend," he informed me. "Be sure to dress warmly; the March wind is sharp as a scolding woman's tongue tonight."

"Going?" I echoed. "Where—"

"To Monsieur Abbot's, of course," he returned. "I determined it this morning."

"You what?" I demanded. "Well, of all the brass-bound nerve—" I began, but Kit Norton interrupted me.

"May I come, too, sir?" he asked.

"Assuredly," the Frenchman nodded. "I think you may find interest in that which we shall undoubtlessly see tonight, young *Monsieur*."

Grumbling, but curious, I hustled into a corduroy hunting-outfit, high laced boots and a leather windbreaker. Similarly arrayed, de Grandin and Norton joined me in the hall, and, at the Frenchman's suggestion, we hailed a taxicab and rode to within a block of Abbot's house, then walked the remainder of our journey.

It was cold work, waiting in the shadow of the hedge skirting Homer's front lawn, and I was in momentary dread of being seen by a passing policeman and arrested as a suspicious character, but our vigil was at last cut short by de Grandin's soft exclamation. "*Attendez-vous, mes amis*, you recognize her?"

I peered through the wall of wind-shaken hedge in time to see a svelte figure, muffled from chin to heels in fur, glide swiftly down the steps and pause irresolutely at the curb. "Yes," I nodded, "it's Marjorie Abbot, but—"

"*Très bon*, it is enough," de Grandin cut in, turning to flash the light of his pocket electric torch toward the corner where our taxi loitered.

The vehicle drove slowly toward us, passed by and down at the curb where Marjorie stood. "Cab, lady?" hailed the chauffeur. The girl nodded, and a moment later we saw the red eye of the vehicle's tail light blink mockingly at us as it rounded the corner.

"Well," I exclaimed, "of all the treacherous tricks! That scoundrel deliberately passed us by after you'd signaled him, and—"

"And did precisely as he was instructed," de Grandin supplied with a chuckle. "Trowbridge, my friend, you are a peerless pill-dispenser, but you are sadly lacking in subtlety. Consider: Do we wish to advertise our presence to Madame Marjorie? Decidedly not. What then? If our cab remained in plain sight, Madame Marjorie could not well fail to see it, and would unquestionably think it queer if it did not apply for her patronage. Had she been forced to seek another vehicle, she would have been on her guard, and looked constantly behind to see if she were followed. In such conditions, we should have had Satan's own time to mark her destination without being discovered. As it is, our so excellent driver conveys her where she desires to go, returns for us, and makes the trip over again. *Voilà, c'est très simple, n'est-ce-pas?*"

"Umph," I admitted grudgingly. "What's next?"

"To warn Monsieur Abbot of our advent," he returned. "He awaits us; I have told him to be prepared."

We crossed the yard and rang Abbot's bell, but no response came to our summons. Despairing of making the bell heard, de Grandin hammered on the door; still no answer.

"*Eh bien*, can he have fallen asleep in good earnest?" the Frenchman fumed. "Let us go in to him."

The door was unlatched and we had no difficulty entering, but though we called repeatedly, no answer came to our hails. At length: "Upstairs, my friends," the Frenchman ordered. "Our plans seem to have miscarried, but I will not have it so."

Wrapped to the chin in blankets, but fully clothed save for shoes and jacket, Homer Abbot lay in his bed, his head tilted grotesquely to one side, his heavy respirations proclaiming the deepness of his slumber.

"Wake, my friend, rouse up, we are come!" de Grandin cried, seizing the sleeper's shoulder and giving it a vigorous shake.

Young Abbot's head rolled flaccidly from side to side, but no sign of consciousness did he give.

Once more de Grandin shook him, then, "By damn, you *will* wake, though I kill you in the process!" he declared, shoving the sleeper so fiercely that he tumbled from the bed, his limbs sprawling uncouthly, like the arms and legs of a rag-doll from which the sawdust had been drained.

"*Grand Dieu*, observe!" the little Frenchman ordered pointing dramatically to a tiny spot of red upon the upper part of Homer's shirt sleeve.

"Hypo!" I commented as I saw the telltale stain.

"*Bien oui*, drugs given by mouth failing, she had made use of injections," de Grandin agreed excitedly, "Quick, Friend Trowbridge, time is priceless; to the nearest pharmacy for strychnine and a syringe, if you please. We shall rouse him to accompany us despite all their planning!"

I hurried on my errand till my breath came pantingly, returned with the stimulant in less time than I should have thought possible, and prepared an injection. The powerful medicine acted swiftly, and Homer's lids fluttered upward almost before I could withdraw the needle.

"How now, my friend, were you caught napping?" de Grandin asked.

"Looks that way," the other answered. "I turned in as you suggested, and pretended to be sound asleep, but she must have suspected something. Shortly after I went to bed she came in, bent over me and called softly. I didn't answer, of course, but my lids must have quivered, the way they usually do when some-one looks intently at you, for she bent still closer and kissed me. Just as her lip touched mine I felt a sting in my arm, and before I could let out a yell, I was dead to the world."

"Exactly, precisely, quite so," the Frenchman agreed. "Now, let us depart. Our taxicab has returned."

"Sure, I can go there again," the chauffeur answered de Grandin's excited query. "Th' place is out th' Andover Road about five miles—deserted as hell on Sunday afternoon, too; you couldn't miss it, once you've been there."

"*Très bien; allez-vous-en!*"

"Huh?"

"Let us go, let us hasten, let us fly, my excellent one, my prince of chauf-feurs; time presses and there is five dollars extra for you if you make speed."

"Buddy, just you set back an' hold onto your hair," the driver cautioned. "Watch me earn that five-spot!"

He did. At a wholly unlawful speed we raced along the wide, smooth turn-pike, passing an occasional inter-urban bus and one or two bootleggers' cars, city-ward bound with their loads of conviviality, but encountering no other traffic.

THE HOUSE WAS RATHER small, of frame construction, and badly in need of repainting. Surrounding it was a rickety paling fence, and a yard of con-siderable extent, densely overgrown with lilac trees, dwarf cedars and a few straggling rhododendrons. Apparently no light burned inside, but de Grandin motioned us forward while he stayed to pay the chauffeur.

"Discretion is essential, my friends," he cautioned as he joined us. "Let us proceed with caution." Thereupon we dropped behind each shadowing bush and advanced by a series of short, quick dashes, like infantrymen at skirmish practice.

Slowly we circled the house, at length descried a single feeble ray of light flickering from beneath a drawn blind and tight-barred shutters. The Frenchman glued his eye to the chink whence the light emanated, then drew back with a shrug of impatience. "I can see nothing," he admitted dejectedly.

We looked at each other in helpless discomfiture, but in a moment the little man was grinning delightedly, "Messieurs Norton—Abbot," he demanded in a whisper, "can you emulate a cat?—two cats—several cats?"

"A *cat*?" the youngsters chorused in amazement.

"But certainly. A pussy-cat, a kitty," de Grandin agreed. "Can you caterwaul and meaul like a duet of tom-cats enjoying a quarrel?"

"Certainly," Abbot returned, "but—"

"There are no buts, my friend. Do you and Monsieur Norton repair to yonder lilac bush, and thereupon set up such a din as might make a dead man leave his coffin in search of peace elsewhere. Continue your concert a full two minutes, then fling a stone into a distant thicket, to simulate the crashing of departing felines through the undergrowth. Remain utterly quiet for minutes more, then join me as soundlessly as may be. You understand? Very well; be off!"

Grinning broadly, Abbot and Norton departed to a screen of lilac bushes, and in a moment there rose such a racket of howls, caterwauls and vicious hisses as might have convinced anyone that two lusty tom-cats had staged a finish-fight on the lawn.

I rocked with laughter at the exhibition, but my mirth was swallowed in admiration of de Grandin's strategy as I watched him. From under his leather jacket he drew a long, curve-bladed Senegalese knife and fell to cutting the shutter-slats away. As he worked he thrust a stick of chewing-gum between his teeth and began masticating furiously. The razor-sharp steel sheared through the rotten, worm-eaten wood almost as if it had been cheese, and in a moment an opening six inches wide by two high had been made. Cutting a slat from the other shutter barring the window, he laid the wooden cleats on the frosty lawn, then slipped the great pigeon's blood ruby from his finger and pressed it against the window-pane.

The stone cut through the glass almost as easily as the knife had hacked the wood, and in a moment a small circular opening was chopped from the pane. Just before the circle was complete, the Frenchman took the gum from his mouth, flattened it against the glass and thrust his finger-tip into it. Then, cutting the remainder of the circle with the ruby, he nonchalantly lifted out a disk of glass without a single betraying tinkle having sounded.

Shutters and window having been drilled through, he proceeded to make a small incision in the linen window blind with the tip of his knife, thereby making it possible for us to see and hear all which went on inside the lighted room.

A final burst of feline profanity and a crashing in the bushes by the fence apprised the world that one of the struggling cats had quit the field of honor hotly pursued by his victorious rival, and in another moment Abbot and Norton joined us.

With upraised finger de Grandin enjoined silence, then waved us forward to the observation-slits he had cut.

WE VIEWED THE SCENE within as though looking through the peephole of a camera obscura. An old-fashioned cannon stove, heaped almost to overflowing with glowing coal, stood in the center of the room, and from the ceiling swung an oil lamp by one of those complicated pulley arrangements once common to every rural dining-room. In a rather tattered easy-chair lounged a tall, spare man of indeterminate age, a long cord-belted dressing-gown of paisley weave covering his dinner clothes. His skin sallow with a sallowness that was more than mere pallor, there was a distinctly yellowish cast to it, like new country butter; close-cropped hair of raven blackness crowned his head as closely as a skull-cap, growing well down over his broad, low brow and seeming to lend an intensity to the burning, searching eyes which glowed like twin pools of black ink in the immobile yellow mask of his face. Slim black brows spanned his forehead and met, forming a sharp downward angle above the bridge of his thin, narrow-nostriled nose. There was neither amusement nor hate nor any other sign of emotion on his mask-like face, only intense, implacable concentration, as he bent his changeless stare on the woman standing rigid as though frozen against the wall opposite him.

"—take them off—all!" he was saying in a low, sibilant voice as we pressed our eyes to the peep-hole. Evidently we arrived in the midst of a conversation, or rather, a monolog, for the woman was mute as she was motionless.

"Marjorie!" Homer Abbot exclaimed softly as he recognized his wife rigid against the wall. Then:

"That's the man who tried to flirt with her at the supper club the—"

"And that's the man Isabel and I saw at the theater the other night—I mean before I lost my memory," Kit Norton cut in. "We were coming from the theater and I jostled him when he deliberately got in my way to peer into Isabel's face. He looked at me as though he'd have liked to murder me, but all he did was raise his hand and flash a big, bright ring before my eyes. It dazzled me for a moment, and when I reached out to grab him by the collar, he was gone. He must have—"

"Silence!" de Grandin's sharp whisper cut short his recital. The yellow-faced man was speaking again.

"At once!" he commanded in the same level, toneless voice, and I noticed that his thin lips scarcely moved as he spoke.

The woman by the wall trembled as though with a sudden chill, but her hands rose flutteringly to her throat, undid the clasp of her long fur cloak and threw it back from her shoulders. "All!" the man repeated tonelessly, inexorably.

Quickly, mechanically, she unloosed the fastenings of her costume. In a moment she was done and stood facing him, still and straight as a statue carved in ivory, arrayed only in the beauty with which generations of New Jersey forebears had endowed her.

"You are slightly rebellious," the seated man remarked. "We must cure that. Wake!"

Marjorie Abbot started as though a cup of chilled water had been dashed in her face, saw her crumpled garments on the floor at her feet, and made a wild, ineffectual clutch at the topmost wisp of silk on the pile of clothing.

"Still!" The girl straightened like a puppet stretched upright by a spring, but a tortured cry burst from her, even as she stiffened into immobility.

It was a pitiful, bleating cry which wrung my heart. Once, when I was a little boy, I spent a season on an uncle's farm and was given a lamb for pet. All summer I loved and pampered the little, woolly thing till it became tame and friendly as a house-dog. At autumn came slaughtering-time, and with the unsentimental practicality of country folk they gave my pet to the itinerant butcher who came to do the killing. Never shall I forget the startled, reproachful cry of that lamb as, his confidence and gentle friendliness betrayed, he felt the gleaming knife cross his throat. It was such a cry of helpless terror and despair Marjorie Abbot gave. But it was not repeated.

"Quiet!" commanded the yellow-faced man. "Be motionless, be speechless, but retain full consciousness. At my unspoken command you have left your silly husband and come to me; you have exposed your body to my eyes when I ordered it, though your strongest instincts forbade it. Here after you obey my slightest thought; you have neither volition nor will of your own when I command otherwise. You will know what you do, and realize that you act against your desires, but you will be powerless to explain by word or act. You will apparently willfully and wantonly drag your husband's name and your own through scandal after scandal; you will use your charm to allure; but never will you make return for what you receive; you will be pitiless, heartless, passionless, a woman taking all, giving nothing, living only to create misery and heartbreak for all with whom you come in contact. You understand?"

Only the wide, terror-stricken stare of the motionless nude girl's eyes replied, but the answer was eloquent.

"Do not think I can not do this—that your love for your husband can withstand my power," the man went on. "I caused the break between the fool Norton and his wife; it was I who made the Baintree girl desert her husband and create a scandal with Norton. But they knew nothing of what they did—I commanded their memories to sleep, and they slept. Last night I wakened Norton—how the fool must have squirmed when he saw a strange woman in his home, and learned all which had happened while I kept his memory locked in the secret chamber of my mind! Last night I released my hold upon his wife, too, so that both awakened in a strange world, separated from the mates they loved, despised by all who knew them; found themselves parents of a child whose very existence they had not suspected till I released them from my spell. I think we shall find amusement watching their efforts to adjust themselves." For the first time his thin, pale lips curved in a snarling smile.

"You wonder why I did this to them—why I do it to you?" he demanded. "Because I hate them, hate you—hate every hypocritical member of your two-faced race! In my country white men talk morality and honor, then take our women when they feel inclined; abandon them when they wish. In India I could do nothing; the English pigs prevented it. But in France I found a welcome,—they drew no color line there, but received me as a great artist. Ha—the Frenchmen proved almost as stupid as your Americans, but not quite; no nation in the world is composed of such utter fools as you! You welcomed me as a refugee from British oppression; I am free to work my will here. Your dull Western minds are malleable as wax to my superior will. I who can make multitudes believe they see me cast my rope into the sky, then climb it to the clouds, find the subjection of your wills to mine less than child's play.

"Who am I?" he broke off with sudden sharpness, staring intently at her. "Answer!"

"My lord and my master," she faltered.

"And who are you?"

"Your thing and creature, your less than slave, your chattel, to do with as you will, my lord."

"What is your wish?"

"I have no wish, no will, no desire, no mind, save to do as you command, O lord and ruler of my existence," she answered, slipping to her knees, laying her hands palm-upward on the floor, then bending forward and beating her smooth forehead softly on the rug between them.

"It is well. Resume your clothing and your duties, O monstrous uncouthness. Remember, from this time forward you know neither truth nor honor nor virtue nor fair dealing, save to make mock of them. It is understood?"

"It is understood, master." Again she struck her brow against the floor between her supplicatingly outstretched hands.

"Like hell it is!" With a maddened roar Homer Abbot smashed through the rotting shutters, crashed the window-panes to a hundred fragments and hurled himself into the superheated room. "You damned ape-faced swine," he shouted, "you might have broken Kit Norton's home and made his name a byword all over town, but you don't do it to me!"

He lunged frantically at the slender form reclining in the shabby arm-chair. Unconcerned as though there had been no interruption, his wife proceeded with the process of donning her flimsy silk undergarments.

"Ah? We have a caller, it seems," the seated man remarked pleasantly. He made no move to defend himself, but his sable, deep-set eyes narrowed to mere specks of shining black flame as he focused them on the intruder.

Homer Abbot stopped stone-still in mid-stride as though he had run into an invisible wall of steel. A dazed, half-puzzled, half-frightened look came to his face as he bent every ounce of energy toward advancing, yet remained fixed as a thing carved of stone.

"You are right, my dear sir," the yellow-faced one pursued; "I shall not make your name a scandal in the town—not in the sense you mean, at any rate. But concerning your *wife's* name—ah, that is something different. I shall kill you and command her to remain here with your body till the police arrive. She will know how you died, but she will not tell. Oh, no; she will not tell, for I shall forbid her, and you yourself have heard her acknowledge my authority."

He laughed soundlessly as he drew an automatic pistol from the pocket of his dressing-gown. It was one of those German monstrosities of murderousness, built like a miniature machine-gun, which sprays ten bullets from its muzzle at a single pressure of the trigger.

Slowly, seeming to delight in the delay, he raised the weapon till it covered Abbot's heart, then:

"Have you prayed; are you prepared to meet the White Man's God, all-conquering white man, who is so weak before the commands of my will?" he asked. "If so, I shall—"

"*Chapeau d'un cochon*, you shall do nothing, and damnably little of it!" Jules de Grandin shouted as he launched himself through the broken window.

The distance between them was quite eight feet, but the Frenchman cleared it with the lightning speed of a famished cat leaping on an unwary bird. Before the seated man could deflect his aim from Homer Abbot, de Grandin was beside him and the lamplight glittered on the wide, curved blade of his great knife as he swung it downward saberwise.

Through coat sleeve and shirt sleeve, through flesh and bone and sinew, the keen steel cut, severing the man's arm midway between carpus and elbow as nearly as a surgical operation might have done.

The hand fell to the carpeted floor with a thud, the fingers clenching in muscular spasm, and the pistol, clutched in the severed fist, sputtered a fusillade of futile shots like a bunch of firecrackers set off together.

As a spilth of ruby blood spurted from his severed radial and brachial arteries, a look of stupefaction, of incredulous wonderment, replaced the grimace of tigerish fury which had been on the yellow-skinned one's face. For a moment he regarded the bleeding stump and the small, almost femininely dainty hand lying on the floor with confounded astonishment; then his surprise seemed swallowed up in mad, unreasoning terror. In the twinkling of an eye he was changed from the calm, sinister personification of the inscrutable East to a groveling thing—a member of an inferior, dominated race trembling and defenseless before the resistless purpose of the all-conquering West. Frenziedly he clutched at his maimed arm, shrinking from de Grandin's blazing eyes and menacing steel as a beaten dog might flinch from an angry master.

He was a pitiable object as he crouched and cowered in his chair, and despite the heartless cruelties he had confessed, I felt a wave of compassion for him.

"Mercy!" he implored, shrinking still further from the Frenchman. "Have pity, *sahib*, you have conquered; be merciful!"

Jules de Grandin's little blue eyes, hot as molten lava from a volcanic crater, cold and hard as polar ice, never changed expression as he glared down upon the cringing man. "Make no mistake, *Monsieur le Serpent*," he answered in a voice one tone above a whisper. "I am come not as foeman unto foeman, but as executioner to criminal. Vile, stinking swine, your boastings to Madame Abbot were your confession, and your confession was your doom. Such mercy as you showed to the draper of Lyons, and to Madame Betty, now dead by her own hand, and to her innocent babe slain by your devilishness as surely as though your accursed hands had done the deed—such mercy as that you may expect from Jules de Grandin.

"Trowbridge, my good one," he called over his shoulder, "take them out. Lead Messieurs Norton and Abbot and Madame Marjorie, to the front gate and await me. I have one damnably pleasant duty to perform here, and can not be annoyed by your mistakenly merciful expostulations. *Allez-vous-en-tout vite!*"

We turned and left him, for there was a look of command in his face which would not be denied; but as we left I cast a single backward look, then hurried on, for in that fleeting glance I saw de Grandin seize the Hindu's neck between his slim, strong hands and force his writhing face toward the glowing barrel of the red-hot stove.

A scream of unsupportable anguish echoed through the night as we reached the gate, but I pushed my companions before me. "Don't go back," I urged. "He's getting only what he deserves, but we couldn't bear to watch it, even so."

I T WAS SOME TEN minutes later as we trudged along the turnpike toward the nearest inter-urban bus station that Marjorie Abbot, who walked stiffly as a robot beside her husband, suddenly threw her hand to her brow and burst into a fit of wild, uncontrollable weeping. "Homer—oh, Homer!" she cried. "My dear, I can tell you, now. I love you, dear; I love you—I didn't mean to do it, Homer, truly, I didn't, but he made me! Oh, my dear, dear love, I don't understand it; but I'm free; *I'm free!* My lips aren't sealed any longer!"

Jules de Grandin chuckled delightedly. "*Mais oui; mais certainement, Madame*," he laughed. "And never again shall that butter-faced son of a most unsavory and entirely immoral pig hold you, or any woman, in his thrall. No, by damn it, Jules de Grandin has made entirely certain of that. Yes, to be sure!"

A few minutes more we walked, Homer and Marjorie holding hands as frankly as country sweethearts, while they murmured soft, foolish little endearments in each other's ears. Then:

"*Tiens, Monsieur*, look not so downhearted!" de Grandin ordered Kit Norton. "Tomorrow morning you and I—yes, and the good, slow-witted Trowbridge, too—shall seek out Madame Isabel and tell her the true state of affairs. She loves you, *mon vieux*, I'll swear to it, and when she learns that what you did was not of your doing, but because of the black magic of that most damnable time-thief whom I have just sent to his proper place, I bet me your life she will understand and forgive, and you and she shall once more be happy in each other's company.

"Not here," he added after a moment's thought. "The townsfolk would never understand, and your remarriage to Madame Isabel so soonly after poor Madame Betty's tragic death—it would make fresh scandal for gossiping tongues to fondle. But there are other places, and I damn think one place is good as another, or better, when love is your companion. *N'est-ce-pas*, Friend Trowbridge?" he dug a sharp elbow into my ribs.

5

"SEE HERE, DE GRANDIN," I remarked next morning at breakfast as I scanned the headlines of my paper, "that house we visited last night burned down. Here's the story:

MAN DIES IN MYSTERY BLAZE

Fire of undetermined origin completely destroyed the old Spencer homestead, five miles from Harrisonville, late last night. The house, a frame structure, has been occupied by an East Indian gentleman, Mr. Chunda Lal, for the past several years. It contained no modern improvements, and it is thought the flames started from an overheated coal stove or an overturned oil lamp.

The blaze was first noticed by neighbors who lived a mile or more away, about one o'clock this morning, but the place was practically demolished before they could arrive on the scene. Search of the still smoking ruins today revealed a human body, charred past possibility of recognition among the debris. It is feared the unfortunate tenant perished in the fire. The loss, amounting to $4,500, was covered by insurance.

"U'm," murmured Jules de Grandin as he returned the paper, "the account is graphic, though a trifle inaccurate. Howeverly, I fear I shall not point out the errors to the excellent journalist who wrote the story. No; it would be better not."

"But it's strange the house should have burned last night," I returned. "I suppose it's one of those fortunate accidents which—?"

"*Non*, not at all; by no means!" he cut in. "It would have been strange had it been otherwise, my friend, for I took greatest pains that things should be exactly as they were. After I had impressed on this Monsieur Chunda Lal that it is extremely poor policy to trifle with other people's wives and husbands—that hot stove proved of greatest help in the process, I assure you—I carefully bound him in his chair, then arranged an alarm clock in such a way that it would spring the stove door open when one o'clock arrived. The door once open, a flood of glowing coals fell outward on the floor, which I had previously drenched with kerosene—and the inevitable process of combustion took place. However, the 'East Indian gentleman' of whom the paper speaks suffered no inconvenience thereby, since his soul had gone to the sub-cellar of hell some hours earlier.

"You remember how poor Madame Marjorie suddenly regained mastery of herself as we proceeded down the road last night?" he asked.

"Yes, of course."

"Very good. It was at that moment the rascally one departed this world for a place of everlasting torment. I had been at particular pains not to bind his wound, and—one can not bleed for long and remain alive, you know, my friend. The entirely unlamented Chunda Lal and his power over Madame Marjorie expired at the same happy instant. Yes."

"But do you mean he actually did all those things he boasted of?" I demanded. "Is it possible a man, no matter how clever he might be as a hypnotist, could so entirely change people's natures as he claimed to have done? Why, it seems incredible!"

"I agree," the Frenchman nodded, "but nevertheless, it are true. Consider: In India, where he came from, the fakirs perform certain tricks which are explicable only by hypnotism. The rope trick, by example. He declared he could perform it, and it is one of the few unexplained Eastern illusions. They apparently throw a cord into the air, make it fast to nothing at all, then climb it until they are lost to sight. No one has ever explained that. Your own Monsieur Herman, the magician, tells in his memoirs how he offered much money to anyone who would show him the technique of the illusion, but no one came forward to claim the reward. Why? Because it is a mere illusion of the eye—a piece of superhypnotism.

"Consider the evidence here: Monsieur Norton tells how, just before he apparently became a knave of the first water, he encountered this evil time-thief in a theater lobby and how the despicable one waved a bright-set ring before his eyes. That single flash was enough to center the victim's attention. Just what the relationship between the optic nerves and the brain centers of ratiocination is we do not certainly know, but all psychologists are agreed that shining objects, or swiftly whirling objects which confuse or blind the eyes, put the subject in ideal condition for quick and easy hypnosis. In any event, while Monsieur Norton's thought-guards were overwhelmed by the flashing of that ring, the brain-thief leaped in and took complete possession of his conscious-ness, captured his will and made him break the heart of the wife he loved.

"How the villain captured poor Madame Betty's mind we do not know; but we have the young Abbot's story of how his wife was overcome by the quick flash of a bright object in the night club, and we have the evidence of the complete control the miscreant established over Madame Marjorie. Certainly. It is all most unusual and instances of such hypnotism are fortunately rare, but what we have seen in this case; two lives were destroyed and the happiness of Madame Betty's first husband demolished completely. Had it not been for Jules de Grandin both Monsieur Norton and Madame Isabel, as well Monsieur and Madame Abbot, might also have been made helpless victims of the vile one's plottings.

"*Parbleu*, when I recall the evil that one wrought it makes me entirely ill. Quick, Trowbridge, my friend, assist me. My mouth is filled with a most unpleasant taste at the very thought of that never-enough-to-be-accursèd man with the yellow face. Nothing but a drink—a nobly large drink—of brandy will remove it!"

The Priestess of the Ivory Feet

Jules de Grandin replaced his Sèvres tea-cup on the tabouret and brushed the ends of his tightly waxed blond mustache with the tip of a well-manicured forefinger.

From the expression on his little, mobile face it was impossible to say whether he was nearer laughter than tears. "And the lady, *chère Madame*," he inquired solicitously, "what of her?"

"What, indeed?" echoed our hostess. Plainly, it was no laughing matter to Mrs. Mason Glendower, and I sat in a sort of horrified fascination, expecting momentarily to see the multiple-chinned, florid society dictator dissolve in tears before my eyes. A young woman's tears are appealing, an old woman's are pathetic, but a well-past-middle-aged, plump dowager's are an awful sight. Flabby, fat women quiver so when they weep.

"What, indeed?" she repeated, all three of her chins trembling ominously. "It would have been bad enough if she'd been a respectable shop-girl, or even an actress, but *this*—oh, it's too awful, Dr. de Grandin; it's terrible!"

My worst fears were realized. Mrs. Mason Glendower wept copiously and far from silently, and her chins and biceps, even her fat wrists, quivered like a pyramid of home-made quince jelly on a Thanksgiving dinner table.

"*Tch-tch*," de Grandin made a deprecating click with the tip of his tongue against his teeth. "It is deplorable, *Madame*. And the young *Monsieur*, your son, he is, then entirely smashed upon this reprehensibly attractive young woman— you can not dissuade him?"

"No!" Mrs. Mason Glendower dabbed at her reddened eyes with a wisp of absurdly inadequate cambric. "I've tried to appeal to his family pride—his pride of ancestry, I've even had Dr. Stephens in to reason with him, but it's all useless. He just smiles in a sort of sadly superior way and says Estrella has shown him the light and that he pities our blindness—our blindness, if you please, and our family pew-holders in the First Methodist Church since the congregation was organized!

"Oh, Dr. Trowbridge"—she turned imploringly to me—"can't you suggest something? You've known Raymond all his life, you know what a clean, manly, *good* boy he's always been—it's bad enough for him to be set on marrying the young person, but to have her change his religion, drag him from the faith of his fathers into this heathenish, outlandish cult—oh, it seems, sometimes, as though he's actually losing his senses! If he'd ever drunk or caroused or inclined toward wildness it would be different, but—" And her emotion overcame her, and her words were smothered beneath an avalanche of sobs.

"*Tiens*, Madame Glendower," de Grandin remarked matter-of-factly, "a man may love liquor and have his senses sometimes, but if he love a woman—*hélas*, his case is hopeless. Only marriage remains, and even that sometimes fails to cure."

For a moment he regarded the sobbing matron with a thoughtful stare, then: "It may be Dr. Trowbridge and I can reason with the young *Monsieur* to more purpose than you or the good pastor," he suggested. "In my country we have a saying, there are three sexes—men, women and clergymen. A headstrong young man, over-proud of his budding masculinity, is apt to treat advice from mother or minister alike with contemptuous impatience. The physician, on the other hand, is in a different position. He is a man of the world, a man of science, with body, parts and passions like other men, yet with a vast experience of the penalties of folly. His words may well be listened to when those of women and priests would meet only with disdain.

I sat in open-mouthed astonishment at his temerity. To his logical Gallic mind the wisdom of his advice was obvious, but though he had lived among us several years, he had not yet learned to what heights of absurdity the Mother-cult has been raised in America, nor did he understand that it is the conventional thing to regard any woman, no matter how ignorant or inexperienced, as endowed with preternatural wisdom and omniscient foresight merely because she has at some time fulfilled the biological function of race-perpetuation. And Mrs. Mason Glendower's thought-processes were, I knew, as conventional as a printed greeting card.

"You mean," the lady gasped, a sort of horrified incredulity replacing the grief in her countenance—"you mean you actually think a doctor can have more influence with a son than his pastor or his *mother?*"

"Perfectly, *Madame*," he replied imperturbably. Her scandalized astonishment was lost on him; it was as though she had asked whether in his opinion novocaine were preferable to cocaine as an anesthetic in appendectomy.

"Well—" I braced myself for the coming storm, but, amazingly, it failed to materialize. "Perhaps you're right, Dr. de Grandin," she conceded with a sudden strange meekness. "Whatever you do, you can't fail any more than Dr. Stephens and I have failed."

She smiled wanly, with a trace of embarrassment. "You'll find Raymond in his room, now," she informed us, "but I doubt he'll see you. This is the time for his 'silence,' as he calls it and—"

"*Eh bien, Madame*," the little Frenchman chuckled, "lead us to his sanctuary. We shall break this silence of his, I make no doubt. Silence is golden, as your so glorious Monsieur Shakespeare has said, but a greater than he has said there is a time for silence and a time for speech. This, I think, is that time. But yes."

A BRAZEN BOWL OF INCENSE burned in Raymond Glendower's room, its cloying, heady sweetness almost stunning us as we entered uninvited after half a dozen pleading calls and several timid knocks on the door by his mother had failed to evoke a response. Raymond perched precariously on a low, flat-topped stand similar to those used for supporting flower-pots, his legs crossed, feet folded sole upward upon his calves, his hands resting palm upward in his lap, the fingertips barely touching. His head was bowed and his eyes closed. So far as I could see, his costume consisted of a flowing white-muslin robe which might have been a folded sheet loosely belted at the waist, and a turban of the same material wound about his brow. Arms, legs, feet and breast were uncovered, for the robe hung open at the front, revealing his chest and the major portion of his torso. At first glance I was struck by the pallor of his face and the marked concavity of his cheeks; plainly the boy was suffering from primary starvation induced by a sudden diminution of diet.

"What's he been eating?" I whispered to his mother as the seated youth paid no more attention to our advent than he would have given the buzzing of a trespassing fly.

"Fruit," she whispered, back, "fruit and nuts and raisins, and very little of each. It's against the discipline of the sect to eat anything killed or cooked."

"U'm," I murmured. "How long has this been going on?"

"Ever since he met that woman—nearly two months," she returned. "My poor boy's fading away before my eyes, and—"

"S-s-sh!" I warned. Like a sleeper awakened, young Glendower had opened his eyes and wriggled from his undignified perch like a contortionist unwinding himself from a knot.

"Oh, hullo, Dr. Trowbridge," he greeted, crossing the room to take my hand cordially. If he felt any embarrassment at being caught thus he concealed it admirably. "Pleased to meet you, Dr. de Grandin," he acknowledged my introduction. "Be with you in half a sec. If you'll wait till I get some clothes on."

We retired to the drawing-room, and in a few minutes the young man, normally attired in a well-tailored blue suit, joined us. His mother excused herself almost immediately, and Raymond glanced from de Grandin to me with a humorous twist of his well-formed lips.

"All right, Dr. Trowbridge," he invited, "you may fire when ready. I suppose Mother's called you in to show me the error of my ways. She had Stephens in the other day and the reverend old fool will never know how near he came to assassination. He began by singsonging at me and ended by attacking Estrella's character. That's where I draw the line. If he hadn't been a preacher I'd have tossed him out on his neck. Just a little warning, gentlemen," he added pleasantly. "Go as far as you like in quoting Joshua, Solomon and Moses at me—I won't kick if you throw in a few passages from *Deuteronomy* for good measure, but one word against Estrella and we fight—physicians don't share clerical immunity, you know."

"By no means, *Monsieur*," de Grandin cut in quickly. "We have not had the honor of the young lady's acquaintance, and he who condemns without having seen is a fool. Also, we have no wish to scoff at your faith. Me, I am a deep student of all religions, and the practices of yoga and similar systems interest me greatly. Is it possible that we, as serious students, might be permitted to see some of the outward forms of your so interesting cult?"

The boy warmed to his request as a stray dog responds to a friendly pat upon the head. Plainly he had heard nothing but complaints and naggings since he became involved in the strange religion which he professed, and the first remarks by an outsider which did not imply criticism delighted him.

"Of course," he answered enthusiastically; "that is, I'm almost sure I can arrange it for you." He paused a moment, as though considering whether to take us further into his confidence, then:

"You see, Estrella is Exalted High Hierophant of the Church of Heavenly Gnosis, and though I am unworthy of the honor, her Sublimity has deigned to look on me with favor"—there was a reverential tremor in his voice as he pronounced the words—"and it is even possible she may receive a revelation telling her we may marry, as ordinary mortals do, though that is more than I dare hope for." Again his words trembled on his lips, and we could see he actually fought for breath as he spoke, as though his wildly beating heart had expanded in his breast and pressed his lungs for space.

"U'm?" de Grandin was all polite attention. "And will you tell us something of the society's history, young *Monsieur*?"

"Of course," Raymond answered. "The Heavenly Gnosis is the latest manifestation of the Divine All which underlies everything. For thousands of years mankind has struggled blindly through the darkness, always seeking the Divine Light, always failing in its quest. Now, through the revelations of our Supreme Hierophant, the Godhead shall be made plain. Just twenty years ago the great boon came into the world, when Estrella, the Holy Child, was born. Like

Mohammed and that other prophet whom men call Jesus, she was of humble parentage, but the Supreme Will follows Its own inscrutable designs in such matters—Buddha was a prince, Confucius was a scholar, Mohammed a camel-driver and Jesus the son of a carpenter. Estrella is the daughter of a laborer. She was born in a workman's shanty beside the tracks of the Santa Fe; her father was a section foreman and her mother a cook and washerwoman for the men; yet when the Holy Child was barely old enough to walk the cattle and horses in the fields would kneel before her and touch their noses to the earth as she toddled past.

"She was less than a year old when one of the workmen in her father's gang came upon her sitting between two great rattlesnakes while a third reptile reared on its tail before her and inclined its head in adoration. The man would have killed the snakes with his long-handled shovel, but the babe, who had never been heard to speak before, rebuked him for his impiety, reminding him that all things are God's creatures, and that he who takes life of any kind on any pretext is guilty of supreme sacrilege in usurping a function of Deity, and must expiate his sin through countless reincarnations."

"*Parbleu*, you astonish me!" said Jules de Grandin.

"Yes," Raymond continued with all the recent convert's fervor, "and from that day Estrella continued to prophesy and reveal truth after great truth. At her behest her parents gave up eating the remains of any living thing and ceased desecrating the divine element of fire by using it to cook their food. Her father abandoned his work and went to live in the desert, where day by day, in the silence of the waste places, new revelations came to the Holy Child who has condescended to cast her glorious eyes on me, the most unworthy of her worshipers."

"*Mordieu*, you amaze me!" de Grandin declared. "And then?"

"When her period of preparation was done, her mother, who had committed all the wondrous things she foretold to writing, brought her East that the teeming cities of the seaboard might hear the words of truth from her own divine lips."

"*Cordieu*, you overwhelm me!" de Grandin assured him. "And have you found many converts to the faith, *Monsieur*?"

"N-no," Raymond admitted, "but those who have affiliated with us are important individually. There was Miss Stiles, a member of one of the state's oldest and wealthiest families. She was one of the first to be converted, and distinguished herself by her great ardor and acts of piety. She also brought a number of other influential people into the light, and—"

"May one inquire where this so estimable lady may be found now?" de Grandin asked softly. "I should greatly like to discuss—"

"She has passed through her final incarnation and dwells forever in the ineffable light emanated by the Divine All," young Glendower broke in. "She was summoned from battle to victory in the very moment of performing the supreme act of adoration, and—"

"In fine, *Monsieur*," de Grandin interrupted, "one gathers she is no more— she is passed away; defunct; dead?"

"In the language of the untaught—yes," Raymond admitted, "but we who have heard the truth know that she is clothed in garments of everlasting light and resides perpetually—"

"*Mais oui*," de Grandin cut in a trifle hastily, "you are undoubtlessly right, *mon ami*. Meantime, if you will endeavor to secure us permission to meet these so fortunate ones who bask in the sunlight of *Mademoiselle's* revelations, we shall be most greatly obliged. At present we have important duties which call us elsewhere. Yes, certainly."

"WELL, WHAT ABOUT IT?" I inquired as we drove homeward. "I'm frank to admit I didn't know what he was driving at half the time, and the other half I had to sit on my hands to keep from clouting the young fool on the head."

The little Frenchman laughed delightedly. "It is the love of the *petit chien* run wild, my friend," he told me. "Some young men when smitten by it turn to poetry; some attempt great deeds of derring-do to win their ladies' favor; this one has swallowed a bolus of undigested nonsense, plagiarized by an ignorant female from half the religions of the East, up to the elbow."

"Yes, but it has a serious aspect," I reminded. "Suppose he married that charlatan, and—"

"How wealthy is the Glendower family?" he interrupted. "Is the restrained elegance in which they live a mark of good taste, or a sign of comparative poverty?"

"Why," I replied, "I don't think they're what you could call rich. Old Glendower is reputed to have left a hundred thousand or so; but that's not considered much money nowadays, and—"

"But what of Monsieur Raymond's private fortune?" he demanded. "Does he possess anything outside his expectancy upon his mother's death?"

"How the devil should I know?" I answered testily.

"*Précisément*," he agreed, in no way offended by my petulance. "If you will be good enough to drop me here, I shall seek information where it can be had reliably. Meantime, I implore you, arrange with your peerless cook to prepare a noble dinner against the time of my return. I shall be famished as a wolf."

"WHERE THE DEUCE HAVE you been?" I demanded as he entered the dining-room just as Nora McGinnis, my household factotum, was serving dessert. "We waited dinner for you till everything was nearly spoiled, and—"

"Alas, my friend, I am desolated," he assured me penitently. "But consider, is not my punishment already sufficient? Have I not endured the pangs of starvation while I bounced about in a *sacré* taxicab like an eggshell in a kettle of boiling water? But yes. They are slow of movement at the courthouse, Friend Trowbridge."

"The courthouse? You've been there? What in the world for?"

"For needed information, to be sure," he returned with a smile as he attacked his bouillon with gusto. "I learned much there which may throw light on what we heard this afternoon, *mon vieux*."

"Yes?"

"Yes, certainly; of course. I discovered, by example, that a Miss Matilda Stiles, who is undoubtlessly the same pious lady of whom the young Glendower told us, passed away a month ago, leaving several sadly disappointed relatives and a last will and testament whereby she names one Mademoiselle Estrella Hudgekins her principal legatee. Furthermore, I discovered that a certain Matilda Stiles, spinster, of this county, did devise by deed, previous to her sad demise, several parcels of excellent valuable real estate in and near the city of Harrisonville to one Timothy Hudgekins and Susanna Hudgekins, his wife, as trustees for Estrella Hudgekins. Furthermore, I found on record several bills of sale whereby numerous articles of intensely valuable personal property—diamonds, antique jewelry, and the like—were conveyed outright by the said Matilda Stiles to the aforesaid Estrella Hudgekins—*parbleu*, already I do mouth the legal jargon unconsciously, so many instruments of transference I have read this afternoon!"

"Well?" I asked.

"No, my friend, it is not well; I damn think it is exceedingly unwell." He helped himself to a generous portion of roast duckling and dressing and refilled his glass with claret. "Attend me, carefully, if you please. The young Monsieur Glendower was to receive in his own right a hundred thousand dollars from his father's estate upon attaining his majority. He passed his twenty-first birthday last month, and already the attorneys have attended to the transfer of the funds. What think you from that?"

"Why, nothing," I returned. "I'd an idea Raymond would succeed to part of the property before his mother's death. Why shouldn't he?"

"Ah, *bah!*" de Grandin replenished his plate and glass and regarded me with an expression of pained annoyance. "Can not you see, my old one? The conclusion leaps to the eye!"

"It may leap to yours," I replied with a smile, "but its visibility is zero, as far as I'm concerned."

2

"YOU TWO WILL BE the only guests outside the church tonight," Raymond Glendower warned as we drove toward the apartment hotel where the high priestess of the Church of the Heavenly Gnosis resided with her parents, "so if you'll—er—try not to notice things too much, you know I'll be awful obliged. You see—er—" he floundered miserably, but de Grandin came to his rescue with ready understanding.

"Quite so, *mon vieux*," he agreed. "It is like this: Devout members of the Catholic faith are offended when mannerless Protestants enter their churches, stare around as though they were at a museum, and fail to genuflect as they pass the altar; good Protestants take offense when ill-bred Catholics enter their churches and glance around with an air of supercilious disdain, and the Christian visitor gives offense to his Jewish brethren when he removes his hat in their synagogues, *n'est-ce-pas?*"

"That's it!" the boy agreed. "You've got the idea exactly, sir."

He leaned forward and was about to embark on another long and tiresome exposition of the excellence of his faith's tenets when the grinding of our brakes announced we had arrived at our destination.

The corridor of the Granada Apartments flashed with inharmonious colors like a kaleidoscope gone crazy, and I shook my head in foreboding. The house was not only screamingly offensive to the eye, it was patently an expensive place in which to live, and the prophetess must draw heavily on her devotees' funds in order to maintain herself in such quarters.

An ornate lift done in the ultra-modernistic manner shot us skyward, and Raymond preceded us down the passage, stopping before a brightly polished bronze door with the air of a worshiper about to enter a shrine. We entered without knocking and found ourselves in a long, narrow hall with imitation stone floor, walls and ceiling. A stone table with an alabaster glow-lamp at its center was the only piece of furniture. A huge mirror let into the wall and surrounded by bronze pegs did duty as a cloak-rack. All in all, the place was about as inviting as a corridor in the penitentiary.

The room beyond, immensely large and almost square in shape, was mellowly lighted by a brass floor-lamp with a shade of perforated metal; its floor was covered with a huge Turkey carpet; the walls were hung with Persian and Chinese rugs. Beneath the lamp, its polished case giving back subdued reflections, like quiet water at night, was a grand piano flanked by two tall Japanese vases filled to overflowing with long-stemmed red roses. Near the opened windows, where the muted roar of the city seeped upward like the crooning of distant waves, was grouped a number of chairs no two of which were mates. Several guests were already seated, talking together in hushed tones like early arrivals at a funeral service.

Oddly, though it was really a most attractive apartment, that rug-strewn room struck a sinister note. Whether it was the superheated atmosphere, the dimly diffused light or the vague reminiscence of incense which mingled with the roses' perfume I do not know, but I had a momentary feeling of panic, a wild desire to seize my companions by the arms and flee before some unseen, evil presence which seemed to brood over the place bound us fast as a spider enmeshes a luckless fly.

Near the piano, where the lamplight fell upon her, stood the high priestess of the cult, Raymond's "Holy Child," and despite my preconceived prejudices, I felt forced to admit the cub had good excuse for his infatuation.

Her extremely décolleté gown of black velvet, entirely devoid of ornamentation, clung to her magnificent figure like the drapery to the Milo Venus and set off her white arms and shoulders in startling contrast. Above the pearl-white expanse of bosom and throat, the perfectly molded shoulders and beautifully turned neck, her face was set like an ivory ikon in the golden nimbus of her hair. She was tall, beautifully made and supple as a mountain lioness. A mediæval master-painter would have joyed in her physical perfection, but assuredly he would not have painted her with a child at her breast or an aureole surrounding her golden head. No, her beauty was typical of the world, the flesh, and the franker phases of love.

Her upper lip was fluted at the corners as if used to being twisted in a petulant complaint against fate, and her long amber eyes slanting upward at the corners like an Asiatic's, were cold and hard as polished topaz; they seemed to be constantly appraising whatever they beheld. She might have been lovely, as well as beautiful, but for her eyes, but the windows of her soul looked outward only; no one could gaze into them and say what lay behind.

"Bout d'un rat mort," whispered Jules de Grandin in my ear, "this one, she is altogether too good-looking to be entirely respectable, Friend Trowbridge!"

The slow smile with which she greeted Raymond as he bowed almost double before her somehow maddened me. "You poor devil," it seemed to say, "you poor, witless, worshipping Caliban; you don't amount to much, but what there is of your body and soul that's worth having is mine—utterly mine!" Such a smile, I thought, Circe might have given the poor, fascinated man-hogs wallowing and grunting in adoring impotence about her table. As for Raymond, plain, downright adulation brought the tears to his eyes as he all but groveled before her.

As de Grandin and I were led forward for presentation I noted the figures flanking the priestess. They were a man and woman, and as unlovely a pair as one might meet in half a day's walk. The man was like a caricature, bull-necked, bullet-headed, with beetling brows and scrubby, bristle-stiff hair growing low above a forehead of bestial shallowness. Though his face was hard-shaven as an actor's or a priest's, no overlay of barber's powder could hide the wiry, beard which struggled through his skin. His evening clothes were well tailored and of the finest goods, but somehow they failed to fit properly, and I had a feeling that a suit of stripes would have been more in place on him.

The woman was like a vicious-minded comic artist's conception of a female politician, short, stocky, apparently heavy-muscled as a man and enormously strong, with a wide, hard mouth and pugnaciously protruding jaw. Her gown, an expensive creation, might have looked beautiful on a dressmaker's lay figure, but on her it seemed as out of place as though draped upon a she-gorilla.

These two, we were made to understand, were the priestess' parents.

Estrella herself spoke no word as de Grandin and I bowed before her, nor did she extend her hand. Serene, statue-still, she stood to receive our mumbled expressions of pleasure at the meeting with an aloofness which was almost contemptuous.

Only for a fleeting instant did her expression change. Something, perhaps the gleam of mockery which lurked in de Grandin's gaze, hardened her eyes for a moment, and I had a feeling that it would behoove the little Frenchman not to turn his back on her if a dagger were handy.

Raymond hovered near his divinity while de Grandin and I proceeded to the next room, where a long sideboard was loaded with silver dishes containing dried fruits, nut-kernels and raisins. The Frenchman sampled the contents of a dish, then made a wry face. "Name of the Devil," he swore, "such vileness should be prohibited by statute!"

"Well?" I asked, nodding questioningly toward the farther room.

"*Parbleu*, no; it is far from such!" he answered. "Of *Mademoiselle la Prêtreuse* I reserve decision till later, but her sire and dam—*mordieu*, were I a judge I should find them guilty of murder if they came before me on a charge of chicken-theft! Also, my friend, though their faith may preclude the use of cooked or animal food, unless Jules de Grandin's nose is a great liar, there is nothing in their discipline which forbids the use of liquor, for both of them breathe the aroma of the gin-mill most vilely."

Somewhat later the meeting assumed a slightly more sociable aspect, and we were able to hold a moment's conversation with the prophetess.

"And do you see visions of the ineffable, *Mademoiselle?*" de Grandin asked earnestly. "Do you behold the splendor of heaven in your ecstasies?"

"No," she answered coldly, "my revelations come by symbols. Since I was a little girl I've told my dreams to Mother, and she interprets them for me. So, when I dreamed a little while ago that I stood upon a mountain and felt the wind blowing about me, Mother went into her silence and divined it portended we should journey East to save the people from their sins, for the mountain was the place where we then lived and the wind of my dream was the will of the Divine All, urging me to publish His message to His people."

"And you believe this?" de Grandin asked, but with no note of incredulity in his tone.

"Of course," she answered simply. "I am the latest avatar of the Divine All. Others have come before—Buddha, Mithra, Mohammed, Confucius—but I am the greatest. By woman sin came upon mankind; only by woman can the burden be lifted again. These others, these male hierophants, showed but a part of the way; through me the whole road to everlasting happiness shall be made plain.

"Even when I was a tiny baby the beasts of the field—even the poison serpents of the desert—did reverence to the flame of divinity which burns in me!" She placed her hand proudly on her bosom as she spoke.

"You remember these occasions of adoration?" de Grandin asked in a sort of awed whisper.

"I have been told—my Mother remembers them," she returned shortly, as she turned away.

"*Grand Dieu*," de Grandin murmured, "she believes it, Friend Trowbridge; she has been fed upon this silly pap till she thinks it truth!"

All through the evening we had noticed that the guests not only treated Estrella with marked respect, but that they one and all were careful not to let themselves come in contact with her, or even with her clothes. Subconsciously I had noted this, but paid no particular attention to it till it was brought forcibly to my notice.

Among the guests was a little, homely girl, an undersized, underfed morsel of humanity who had probably never in all her life attracted a second glance from anyone. Nervous, flutteringly attentive to the lightest syllable let fall by the glorious being who headed the cult, she had kept as close to Estrella as was possible without actually touching her, and as we were preparing to take our departure she came awkwardly between Timothy Hudgekins and his daughter.

Casually, callously as he might have brushed an insect from his sleeve, the man flipped one of his great, gnarled hands outward, all but oversetting the frail girl and precipitating her violently against the prophetess.

The result was amazing. Making no effort to recover her balance, the girl slid to the floor, where she crouched at Estrella's feet in a perfect frenzy of abject terror. "Oh, your Sublimity," she cried, and her words came through blenched lips on trembling breath, "your High Sublimity, have pity! I did not mean it; I know it is forbidden to so much as touch the hem of your garment without permission, but I didn't mean it; truly, I didn't! I was pushed, I—I—" her words trailed away to soundlessness, and only the rasping of her terrified breath issued from her lips.

"Silence!" the priestess bade in a cold, toneless voice, and her great topaz eyes blazed with tigerish fury. "Silence, Sarah Couvert. Go—go and be forever accursed!"

It was as though a death-sentence had been pronounced. Utter stillness reigned in the room, broken only by the heart-broken sobs of the girl who crouched upon the floor. Every member of the cult, as though actuated by a common impulse, turned his back upon her, and weeping and alone she left the room to find her wraps.

Jules de Grandin would have held her costly evening cloak for her, but she gestured him away and left the apartment with her face buried in her handkerchief.

"SANG DU DIABLE, MY friend, look at this, *regardez-vous!*" cried de Grandin next morning at breakfast as he thrust a copy of the morning paper across the table.

COUVERT HEIRESS A SUICIDE

I read in bold-faced type:

The body of Miss Sarah Couvert, 28, heiress to the fortune of the late Herman Couvert, millionaire barrel manufacturer, who died in 1919, was found in the river near the Canal street bridge early this morning by Patrolman Aloysius P. Mahoney. The young woman was in evening dress, and it was said at her house when servants were questioned that she had attended a party last night at the apartment of Mr. and Mrs. Timothy Hudgekins in the Granada. When she failed to return from the merrymaking her housekeeper was not alarmed, she said, as Miss Couvert had been spending considerable time away from home lately.

At the Hudgekins apartment it was said Miss Couvert left shortly before eleven o'clock, apparently in the best of spirits, and her hosts were greatly shocked at learning of her rash act. No reason for her suicide can be assigned. She was definitely known to be in good health.

Then followed an extended account of the career of the genial old Alsatian cooper who had amassed a fortune in the days before national Prohibition decreased the demand for kegs and barrels. The news item ended:

Miss Couvert was the last of her family, her parents having both predeceased her and her only brother, Paul, having been killed at Belleau Wood in 1918. Unless she left a will disposing of her property, it is said the entire Couvert fortune will escheat to the state.

Reaching into his waistcoat pocket de Grandin removed one of the gold coins which, with the Frenchman's love for "hard money," he always carried.

"This bets the Couvert fortunes are never claimed by the Commonwealth of New Jersey, Friend Trowbridge." he announced, ringing the five-dollar piece on the hot-water dish cover.

He was justified in his wager. Two weeks later, Sarah Couvert's will was formally offered for probate. By it she left substantial amounts to all her servants, bequeathed the family mansion and a handsome endowment as a home for working-girls, and left the residuum of the estate, which totaled six figures, to her "dear friend, Estrella Hudgekins."

3

A N UNDERSIZED INDIVIDUAL WITH ears which stood so far from his head that they must have proved a great embarrassment on a windy day perched on the extreme forward edge of his chair and gazed pensively at the top of the brown derby clutched between his knees. "Yes, sir," he answered de Grandin's staccato questions, "me buddy an' me have had th' subject under our eye every minute since you give th case to th' chief. He wuz to his lawyer's today an' ordered a will drawn, makin' Miss Hudgekins th' sole legatee; he called her his feeancy."

"You're sure of this?" de Grandin demanded.

"Sure, I'm sure. Didn't I give th' office boy five bucks to let me look at a carbon copy o' th' rough draft o' th' will for five minutes? That sort o' information comes high, sir, an' it'll have to go in on th' expense account."

"But naturally," the Frenchman conceded. "And what of the operative at the Hotel Granada, has she forwarded a report?"

"Sure." The other delved into his inner pocket, ruffled through a sheaf of soiled papers, finally segregated a double sheet fastened with a wire clip. "Here it is. Th' Hudgekinses have been holdin' some sort o' powwow durin' th' last few days; sent th' chicken away to th' country somewhere, an' been doin' a lot o' talkin' an' plannin' behind locked doors. Number Thirty-Three couldn't git th' drift o' much o' th' argument, but just before th' young one wuz packed off she heard th' old woman tell her that her latest dream meant Raymond—by which I take it she meant th' young feller we've been shadderin'—has been elected— no, 'selected' wuz th' word—selected to perform th' act o' supreme adoration, whatever that means."

"*Morbleu*, I damn think it means no good!" de Grandin ejaculated, rising and striding restlessly across the room. "Now, have you a report from the gentleman who was to investigate Miss Stiles' case?"

"Sure. She wuz buried by Undertaker Martin, th' coroner, you know. Her maid found her dead in bed, an' rang up Dr. Replier, who'd been attendin' her for some time. He come runnin' over, looked at th' corpse, an' made out a certif'cate statin' she died o'"—he paused to consult his notebook—"o' cardiac insufficiency, whatever that is. Coroner Martin wanted a autopsy on th' case, but on account o' th' old lady's social prominence they managed to talk him out o' it."

"H'm," de Grandin commented non-committally. "Very good, my excellent one, your work is deserving of highest commendation. Should new developments arise, you will advise me at once if you please."

"Sure," the detective promised as he rose to leave.

"For heaven's sake, what's it all about?" I demanded as the door closed behind the visitor. "What's the idea of having Raymond Glendower and this girl trailed by detectives as if they were criminals?"

"Ha," he laughed shortly. "The young Glendower is a fool for want of judgment; of the young *Mademoiselle*, I do not care yet to say whether she be criminal or not. I hope the best but fear the worst, my friend."

"But why the investigation of Miss Stiles' death? If Replier said she died of cardiac insufficiency, I'm willing to accept that vague diagnosis at face value; he's able, and he's honest as the day is long. If—"

"And therefore he is as likely to be hoodwinked as your own trustful self, *mon vieux*," the little Frenchman interjected. "Consider, if you please:

"The young Glendower, anxious to impress us with the importance of the converts to this new religion of his, tells us what concerning the death of the old Mademoiselle Stiles? That she died in the very moment of performing 'the act of supreme adoration.'

"Very good. What says the evidence gathered by my men? That she died in her bed at home—at least she was found dead there by her maidservant. Somewhere there is a discrepancy, my friend, a most impressive one. What this act of adoration may be I do not know, nor do I at present very greatly care, but that the excellent deceased lady performed it in her death-bed I greatly doubt. No, my friend, I think she died elsewhere and was taken to her home that she might be found dead in her own bed, and her decease therefore considered natural. The fact that she had been ailing of a heart affection for some time, and under treatment by the good Dr. Replier, made the deception so much easier."

"But this is fantastic!" I objected. "We've not one shred of evidence on which to base this theory, and—"

"We have a great sufficiency," he contradicted, "and more will be forthcoming anon. Meantime, if only—"

A vigorous ring at the front doorbell, seconded by a shrill whistle, interrupted him. "Special delivery for Dr. de Grandin," the boy informed me as I answered the summons.

"Quickly, Friend Trowbridge, let me see!" the Frenchman cried as I took the letter from the messenger.

"Ah, *parbleu*," he glanced quickly through the document, then turned to me triumphantly, "I have them on the hip, my friend! Regard this, if you please; it is the report of the Charred Detective Agency's San Francisco branch. I entrusted them with the task of tracing our friend's antecedents. Read it, if you please."

Taking the paper, I read:

HUDGEKINS, TIMOTHY, alias Frank Hireland, alias William Faust, alias Pat Malone, alias Henry Palmer.

Description: Height 5 feet 8 inches, weight 185 pounds, inclined to stoutness, but not fat, heavily muscled and very strong. Hair, black mixed with gray, very coarse and stiff. Face broad, heavy jaw, arms exceptionally long for his height. Eyes gray.

Was once quite well known locally as a prizefighter, later as strong-arm man and bouncer in waterfront saloons. Arrested and convicted numerous times for misdemeanors, chiefly assault and battery. Twice arrested for robbery, but discharged for lack of evidence. Tried on charge of murder (1900) but acquitted for insufficient evidence.

Convicted, 1902, for badger game, in conspiracy with Susanna Hudgekins (see report below), served two years in San Quentin Prison.

Apparently reformed upon release from prison and secured job with railroad as laborer. Industrious, hard worker, well thought of by superiors there. Left job voluntarily in 1910. Not known locally since.

HUDGEKINS, SUSANNA, alias Frisco Sue, alias Annie Rooney, alias Sue Cheney, wife of above.

Description: Short, inclined to stoutness, but very strong for female. Height 5 feet 4 inches, weight about 145 pounds. Hair brown, usually dyed red or bleached. Face broad, very prominent jaw. Eyes brown.

This party was waitress and entertainer in number of music halls prior to marriage to Timothy Hudgekins (see above). Maiden name not definitely known, but believed to be Hopkins. Arrested numerous times for misdemeanors, chiefly drunkenness and disorderly conduct, several times for assault and battery. Was co-defendant in robbery and murder cases involving her husband, as noted above, Acquitted for lack of evidence.

Convicted, 1902, with Timothy Hudgekins, on charge of operating a badger game. Served 1 year in State Reformatory.

Apparently reformed upon discharge from prison. Accompanied husband on job with railroad. Disappeared with him in 1910. Not known locally since.

In 1909 this couple, showing an excellent record for industry and honesty, applied to Bidewell Home for Orphans, Los Angeles, for baby girl. They were most careful in making selection, desiring a very young child, a blond, and one of exceptionably good looks. Said since they were both so ugly, they particularly wanted a pretty child. Were finally granted permission to adopt Dorothy Ericson, 3 months old, orphan without known relatives, child of poor but highly respected Norwegian parents who died in tenement fire two months before. The child lived with her foster parents in railroad camps where they worked, and disappeared when they left the job. Nothing has been heard of her since.

"Excellent, superb; *magnifique!*" he cried exultantly as I finished reading the jerkily worded but complete report. "Behold the *dossier* of these founders of a new religion, these Messiahs of a new faith, my friend!

"Also behold the answer to the puzzle which has driven Jules de Grandin nearly frantic. A lily may grow upon a dung-heap, a rose may rise from a bed of filth, but two apes do not beget a gazelle, nor do carrion crows have doves for progeny. No, certainly not. I knew it; I was sure of it; I was certain. She could not have been their child, Friend Trowbridge; but this proves the truth of my premonition."

"But what's it all about?" I demanded. "I'm not surprised at the Hudgekins' pedigree—their appearance is certainly against them—nor does the news that the girl's not their child surprise me, but—"

"'But' be everlastingly cooked in hell's most choicely heated furnace!" he interrupted. "You ask what it means? This, *cordieu!*

"In California, that land of sunshine, alkali dust and crack-brained, fool-fostered religious thought, these two cheap criminals, these out-sweepings of the jail, in some way stumbled on a smattering of learning concerning the Eastern philosophies which have set many a Western woman's feet upon the road to madness. Perhaps they saw some monkey-faced, turbaned trickster from the Orient harvesting a crop of golden dollars from credulous old ladies of both sexes who flocked about him as country bumpkins patronize the manipulators of the three cards at county fairs. Although I should not have said they possessed so much shrewdness it appears they conceived the idea of starting a new religion—a cult of their own. The man who will demand ten signatures upon a promissory note and look askance at you if you tell him of interplanetary distances, will swallow any idle fable, no matter how absurd, if it be boldly asserted and surrounded with sufficient nonsensical mummery and labeled a religion. Very well. These two were astute enough to realize they could not hope to impose on those possessing money by themselves, for their appearance was too much against them. But ah, if they could but come upon some most attractive person—a young girl endowed with charm and beauty, by preference—and put her forward as the prophetess of their cult while they remained in the background to pull the strings which moved their pretty puppet, that would be something entirely different!

"And so they did. Appearing to reform completely, they assumed the guise of honest working-folk, adopted a baby girl with unformed mind whom they trained to work their wicked will from earliest infancy, and—*voilà*, the result we have already seen.

"Poor thing, she sincerely believes that she is not as other women, but is a being apart, sent into the world to lighten its darkness; she stated in guileless simplicity what would be blasphemy coming from knowing lips, and by her charm and beauty she snares those whose wealth has not been sufficient to fill their starved lives. Ah, my friend, youth and beauty are heaven's rarest treasures, but each time God creates a beautiful woman the Devil opens a new page in his ledger. Consider how their nefarious scheme has worked:

"Take the poor little rich Mademoiselle Couvert, by example: Endowed with riches beyond the dream of most, she still lacked every vestige of personal attractiveness, her life had been a dismal routine of emptiness and her starved, repressed soul longed for beauty as a flower longs for sunlight. When the beauteous priestess of this seventy-nine-thousand-times-damned cult deigned to notice her, even called her friend, she was ecstatic in her happiness, and it was but a matter of time till she was induced by flattery to make the priestess her heir by will. Then, deliberately, I believe, that *sale bête*, Hudgekins, pushed her against his daughter, thus forcing her unwittingly to disobey one of the cult's so stupid rules.

"Consider, my friend: We, as physicians, know to what lengths the attraction of woman for woman can go—we see it daily in schoolgirl 'crushes,' usually where a younger woman makes a veritable goddess of an older one. Again, we see it when one lacking in charm, and beauty attaches herself worshipfully to someone being endowed with both. To such starved souls the very sight of the adored one is like the touch of his sweetheart's lips to a love-sick youth. They love, they worship, they adore; not infrequently the passion's strength becomes so great as to be clearly a pathological condition. So it was in this case. When Mademoiselle Estrella mouthed the words she had been taught, and bade her worshiper depart from her side, poor Mademoiselle Couvert was overwhelmed. It was as if she had been stricken blind and never more would see the sun; there was nothing left in life for her; she destroyed herself—and her will was duly probated. Yes.

"Very well. What then? We do not know for certain how the old Mademoiselle Stiles came to her death; but I firmly believe it was criminally induced by those vile ones who had secured her signature to a will in their daughter's favor.

"But yes. What next? The young Glendower is not greatly wealthy, but his fortune of a hundred thousand dollars is not to be sneezed upon. Already we have seen how great a fool he has become for love of this beautiful girl. There is nothing he would not do to please her. We know of a certainty he has made his will naming her as sole beneficiary; perchance he would destroy himself, were she to ask it.

"Will she marry him? The hope has been held out, but I think it a vain one. These evil ones who have reaped so rich a harvest through their villainous schemes, they will not willingly permit that their little goose of the golden eggs shall become the bride of a man possessing a mere hundred thousand; besides, that money is already as good as in their pockets. No, no, my friend; the young Glendower is even now in deadly peril. Already I can see their smug-faced lawyer rising to request probate of the will which invests them with his property!

"But this 'act of supreme adoration' we keep hearing about," I asked, "what can it be?"

"*Précisément*," he agreed with a vigorous nod. "What? We do not know, but I damn fear it is bound up with the young Glendower's approaching doom, and I shall make it our business to be present when it is performed. *Pardieu*, I shall not be greatly astonished if Jules de Grandin has an act of his own to perform about that time. *Mais oui*; certainly! It might be as well, all things considered, if we were to get in touch with the excellent—"

"Detective Sergeant Costello to see Dr. de Grandin!" Nora McGinnis appeared at the drawing-room door like a cuckoo popping from its clock, and stood aside to permit six feet and several inches of Hibernian muscle, bone and good nature to enter.

"*Eh bien, mon trésor*," the Frenchman hailed, delightedly, "this is most truly a case of speaking of the angels and immediately finding a feather from their wings! In all the city there is no one I more greatly desire to see at this moment than your excellent self!"

"Thanks, Dr. de Grandin, sor," returned the big detective sergeant, smiling down at de Grandin with genuine affection. "'Tis Jerry Costello as can say th' same concernin' yerself, too. Indade, I've a case up me sleeve that won't wur-rk out no ways, so I've come to get ye to help me fit th' pieces together."

"*Avec plaisir*," the Frenchman replied. "Say on, and when you have done, I have a case for you, too, I think."

4

"WELL, SOR," THE DETECTIVE began as he eased his great bulk into an easy-chair and bit the end from the cigar I tendered him, "'tis like this: Last night somethin' after two o'clock in th' mornin', one o' th' motorcycle squad, a bright lad be th' name o' Stebbins, wuz comin' out of a coffee-pot where he'd been to git a shot o' Java to take th' frost from his bones, when he seen a big car comin' down Tunlaw Street hell-bent fer election. 'Ah ha,' says he, 'this bur-rd seems in a hurry, maybe he'd like to hurry over to th' traffic court wid a ticket,' an' wid that he tunes up his 'cycle an' sets out to see what all th' road-burnin' was about.

"'Twas a powerful car, sor, an' Stebbins had th' divil's own time keepin' it in sight, but he hung on like th' tail to a dog, drawin' closer an' closer as his gas gits to feedin' good, an' what d'ye think he seen, sor?"

"*Le bon Dieu* knows," de Grandin admitted.

"Th' limousine turns th' corner on two wheels, runnin' down Tuscarora Avenue like th' hammers o' hell, an' draws up before Mr. Marschaulk's house, pantin' like a dog that's had his lights run out. Next moment out leaps a big gorilla of a felly supportin' another man in his arms, an' makes fer th' front door.

"'What's th' main idea?' Stebbins wants to know as he draws up alongside; 'don't they have no speed laws where you come from?'

"An', 'Sure they do,' answers th' other guy, bold as brass, 'an' they has policemen that's some good to th' public, too. This here's Mr. Marschaulk, an' he's been took mighty bad. I like to burned me motor out gittin' him home, an' if ye'll run fer th' nearest, doctor, 'stead o' standin' there playin' wid that book o' summonses, I'll be thinkin' more o' ye.'

"Well, sor, Stebbins is no one's fool, an' he can see wid half an eye that Mr. Marschaulk's in a bad way, so he notes down th' car's number an' beats it down th' street till he sees a doctor's sign, then hammers on th' front door till th' sawbones—askin' yer pardon, gentlemen—comes down to see what its all about.

"They goes over to Marschaulk's in th' All America speed record, sor, an' what do they find?"

"*Dieu de Dieu*, is this a guessing-game?" de Grandin cried testily. "What did they find, *mon vieux*?"

"A corpse, sor; a dead corpse, an' nothin' else. Mr. Marschaulk's body had been dumped down in his front hall promiscuous-like, an' th' guy as brought him an' th' car he brought him in had vamoosed. Vanished into thin air, as th' felly says.

"Stebbins had th' license number, as I told ye, an' right away he locates th' owner. It were Mr. Cochran—Tobias A. Cochran, th' banker, sor; an' he'd been in his bed an' asleep fer th' last two hours. Furthermore, he told Stebbins he'd let his Filipino chauffeur go to New York th' day before, an' th' felly wuz still away. On top o' that, when they came to examine th' garage, they found unmistakable evidence it had been burglarized, in fact, th' lock wuz broke clean away."

"U'm," de Grandin murmured, "it would seem Monsieur Cochran is not implicated, then."

"No, sor; aside from his fine stand in' in th' community, his alibi's watertight as a copper kettle. But ye ain't heard nothin' yet.

"It were a coroner's case, o course, an' Mr. Martin didn't let no grass grow under his feet orderin' th' autopsy. They found Mr. Marschaulk had been dead th' better part o' two hours before Stebbins an' th' doctor found him, an' that he died o' mercuric cyanide—"

"*Bon Dieu*, the poisonest of the poisons!" de Grandin ejaculated. "Very good, my friend, what have you found? Has the man been apprehended?"

"He has not, sor, an' that's one reason I'm settin' here this minute. Stebbins wuz so taken up wid gittin' th' car's number an' runnin' fer a doctor that he didn't git a good look at th' felly. In fact, he never even seen his face, as he kept it down all th' time they wuz talkin'. That seemed natural enough at th' time, too, as he wuz supportin' Mr. Marschaulk on his shoulder, like. Th' most we know about him is he wuz heavy-set, but not fat, wid a big pair o' shoulders an' a voice like a bullfrog singin' in a clump o' reeds."

"And you can find no motive for the killing, whether it be suicide or homicide?"

"That we can't, sor. This here now Mr. Marschaulk wuz a harmless sort o' nut, sor; kind o' bugs on religion, from what I've been told. Some time ago he took up wid a new church, o' some kind an' has been runnin' wild ever since, but in a harmless way—goin' to their meetin's an' th' like o' that, ye know. It seems like he wuz out wid some o' th' church folks th' very night he died, but when we went to round up th' evidence, we drew a blank there.

"Just a little before ten o'clock he called at Mr. Hudgekins' apartment in th' Granada, but left sometime around eleven by himself. We've th' Hudgekins' word fer it, an' th' elevator boy's an' th' hallman's, too. He'd been there often enough for them to know him by sight, ye see."

"U'm, and Monsieur and Madame Hudgekins, did they remain at home?" de Grandin asked casually, but there were ominous flashes of cold lightning in his eyes as he spoke.

"As far as we can check up, they did, sor. They say they did, an' we can't find nobody who seen 'em leave, an' about a quarter after twelve Mr. Hudgekins himself called th' office an' asked fer more heat—though why he asked th' saints only know, as 'twas warm as summer last night an' them apartments is heated hot enough to roast a hog."

"*Tête du Diable*," de Grandin swore, "this spoils everything!"

"How's that, sor?"

"Tell me, my sergeant," the Frenchman demanded irrelevantly, "you interviewed Monsieur and Madame Hudgekins. What is your opinion of them?"

"Well, sor," Costello colored with embarrassment, "do ye want th' truth?"

"But certainly, however painful it may be."

"Well, then, sor, though they lives in a fine house an' wears fine clothes an' acts like a pair o' howlin' swells, if I seen 'em in different circumstances, I'd run 'em in on suspicion an' see if I couldn't make a case later. Th' man looks like a bruiser to me, like a second-rate pug that's managed to git hold of a pot o' money somewhere, an' the' woman—Lord save us, sor, I've run in many a wan lookin' far more respectable when I wuz poundin' a beat in uniform down in th' old second ward!"

"*Bien oui*," de Grandin chuckled delightedly. "I have not the pleasure of knowing your so delectable second ward, my old one, but I can well guess what sort of neighborhood it was. My sergeant, your intuitions are marvelous. Your inner judgment has the courage to call your sight a liar. Now tell me, how did Mademoiselle Hudgekins impress you?"

"I didn't see her, sor. She were out o' town, an' has been for some time. I checked that up, too."

"*Barbe d'une anguile*, this is exasperating!" de Grandin fumed. "It is 'stale-mate' at every turn, *parbleu!*"

"Oh, you're obsessed with the idea the Hudgekins are mixed up in this!" I scoffed. "It's no go, old fellow. Come, admit you're beaten, and apply yourself to trying to find what Marschaulk did and where he went after leaving the Granada last night."

"I s'pose ye're right, Dr. Trowbridge, sor," Sergeant Costello admitted sorrowfully, "but I'm wid Dr. de Grandin; I can't get it out o' me nut that that pair o' bur-rds had sumpin to do wid pore old Marschaulk's death, or at least know more about it than they're willin' to admit."

"*Hélas*, we can do nothing here," de Grandin added sadly. "Come, Friend Sergeant, let us visit the good Coroner Martin; we may find additional information. Trowbridge, *mon vieux*, I shall return when I return; more definite I can not be."

I WAS FINISHING A SOLITARY breakfast when he fairly bounced into the room, his face drawn with fatigue, but a light of elation shining in his little blue eyes. "*Triomphe*—or at least progress!" he announced as he dropped into a chair and drained a cup of coffee in three gigantic gulps. "Attend me with greatest care, my friend:

"Last night the good Costello and I repaired to Coroner Martin's and inspected the relics of the lamented Monsieur Marschaulk. Thereafter we journeyed to the Hotel Granada, where we found the same people on duty as the night before. A few questions supplied certain bits of information we had not before had. By example, we proved conclusively that those retainers of the house remembered not what they had done, but what they thought they had done. They all insisted it would have been impossible for anyone to have left the place without being seen by them, but anon it developed that just before eleven o'clock there rose a great cloud of smoke in the alley which flanks the apartment, and one and all they went to investigate its source. Something smoked most vilely in the middle of the passageway, and when they went too near they found it stung their eyes so they were practically blinded. Now, during that short interval, they finally admitted, it would have been possible for one to slip past them, through the passage on the side street and be out of sight before they realized it. Much can be accomplished in a minute, or even half a minute, by one who is fleet of foot and has his actions planned, my friend."

"Yes, that's all very well," I conceded, "but you're forgetting one thing. How could Hudgekins call up and demand more heat at twelve o'clock if he had sneaked out at eleven? Do you contend that he crept back into the house while they were looking at another smoke screen? If he did, he must have worked the trick at least four times in all, since you seem to think it was he who brought Marschaulk's body home and stole Cochran's car to do it."

He looked thoughtfully at the little disk of bubbles forming above the lump of sugar he had just dropped into his third cup of coffee. "One must think that over," he admitted. "Re-entrance to the house after two o'clock would not have been difficult, for the telephone girl quits work at half-past twelve, and at one the hallman locks the outer doors and leaves, while the lift man goes off duty at the same time and the car is thereafter operated automatically by push buttons. Each tenant has a key to the building so belated arrivals can let themselves in or out as they desire."

"But the telephone call," I insisted; "you haven't explained that yet."

"No," he agreed, "we must overcome that; but it does not destroy my theory, even though it might break down a prosecution in court.

"Consider this: After leaving the hotel, we returned to see Monsieur Martin, and I voiced my suspicions that Mademoiselle Stiles' death needed further explanation. Monsieur Martin agreed.

"Thereupon the good Costello and I resorted to a *ruse de guerre*. We told all we knew concerning Monsieur Marschaulk's death, but suppressed all mention of that *sacré* telephone call.

"My friend, we were successful. Entirely so. At our most earnest request Monsieur Martin forthwith ordered exhumation of Mademoiselle Stiles's body. In the dead of night we disentombed her and took her to his mortuary. It was hard to get Parnell, the coroner's physician, from his bed, for he is a lazy swine, but at last we succeeded in knocking him up and forced him to perform a postmortem examination. My friend, *Matilda Stiles was done to death; she was murdered!*"

"You're crazy!" I told him. "Dr. Replier's certificate stated—"

"Ah *bah*, that certificate, it is fit only to light the fire!" he cut in. "Listen: In Mademoiselle Stiles's mouth, and in her stomach, too, we did find minute, but clearly recognizable traces of $Hg(CN)$—mercuric cyanide! I repeat, Friend Trowbridge, she was murdered, and Jules de Grandin will surely lay her slayers by the heels. Yes."

"But—"

The shrill, insistent summons of the 'phone bell interrupted my protest.

The call was for de Grandin, and after a moment's low conversation he hung up, returning to the breakfast room with grimly set mouth. "*L'heure zéro* strikes tonight, Friend Trowbridge," he announced gravely. "That was the excellent detective I have had on young Glendower's trail. He reports they have just intercepted a conversation the young man had by telephone with Mademoiselle Estrella. He is to make the 'act of supreme adoration' this night."

"But what can we do?" I asked, filled with vague forebodings despite my better judgment "If—"

"*Eh bien*, first of all we can sleep; at least, *I* can," he answered with a yawn. I feel as though I could slumber round the clock—but I will thank you to have me called in time for dinner, if you please."

5

"A LLO?" DE GRANDIN SNATCHED the telephone from its hook as the bell's first warning tinkle sounded. "You say so? It is well; we come forthwith, instantly, at once!"

Turning to Costello and me he announced: "The time is come, my friends; my watcher has reported the young Glendower but now left his house en route for the Hudgekins' dwelling. Come, let us go."

Hastening into our outdoor clothes we set out for the Granada and were hailed by the undersized man with the oversized ears as we neared the hotel. "He went in ten minutes ago," the sleuth informed us, "an' unless he's got wings, he's still there."

"*Eh bien*, then we remain here," de Grandin returned, nestling deeper into the folds of the steamer rug he had wrapped about him.

Half an hour passed, an hour, two; still Raymond Glendower lingered. "I'm for going home," I suggested as a particularly sharp gust of the unseasonably cold spring wind swept down the street. "The chances are Raymond's only paying a social call anyway, and—"

"*Tiens*, if that be true, his sociability is ended," de Grandin interrupted. "Behold, he comes."

Sure enough, young Glendower emerged from the hotel, a look of such rapt inattention on his face as might be worn by a bridegroom setting out for the church.

I leaned forward to start the motor, but the Frenchman restrained me. "Wait a moment, my friend," he urged. "The young *Monsieur's* movements will be watched by sharper eyes than ours, and it is of the movements of Monsieur and Madame Hudgekins I would take note at this time."

Again we entered on a period of waiting, but this time our vigil was not so long. Less than half an hour after Raymond left the hotel a light delivery truck drove up to the Granada's service entrance and two men in overalls and jumper alighted. Within a few minutes they returned bearing between them a long wooden box upholstered in coarse denim. Apparently the thing was the base of a combination couch and clothes-chest, but from the slow care with which its bearers carried it, it might have been filled with something fragile as glass and heavy as lead.

"U'm," de Grandin twisted viciously at the tips of his tightly waxed wheat-blond mustache, "my friends, I damn think I shall try an experiment: Trowbridge, *mon ami*, do you remain here. Sergeant, will you come with me?"

They crossed the street, entered, the corner drug-store and waited something like five minutes. The Frenchman was elated, the Irishman thoughtful as they rejoined me. "Three times we did attempt to get the Hudgekins apartment by telephone," de Grandin explained with a satisfied chuckle, "and three times Mademoiselle the Central Operator informed us the line did not answer and returned our coin. Now, Friend Trowbridge, do you care to hazard a guess what the contents of that box we saw depart might have been?"

"You mean—"

"Perfectly; no less. Our friends the Hudgekins lay snugly inside that coffin-like box, undoubtlessly grinning like cats fed on cheese and thumbing their noses at the attendants in the hotel lobby. Tomorrow those innocent ones will swear upon a pile of Bibles ten meters high that neither the amiable Monsieur Hudgekins nor his equally amiable wife left the place. More, I will wager they will solemnly affirm Monsieur or Madame Hudgekins called the office by 'phone and demanded more steam in the radiators!"

"But they can't do that," I protested. "There's an inside 'phone in the house, and a call made from an instrument outside would not be taken over one of the house 'phones. They couldn't—"

My argument was cut short by the approach of a nondescript individual who touched his hat to de Grandin. "He's gone to 487 Luxor Road," this person announced, "an' Shipley just 'phoned a furniture wagon drove up an' two birds lugged a hell of a heavy box up th' stairs to th' hall.

"Oh, sure," he nodded in response to the Frenchman's admonition. "We'll call their apartment every fifteen minutes from now till you tell us to lay-off."

"*Très bien*," de Grandin snapped "Now, Friend Trowbridge, to 487 Luxor Road, if you please. Sergeant, you will come as soon as possible?"

"You betcha," Costello responded as he swung from the car and set off toward the nearest police station.

I T WAS AN UNSAVORY neighborhood through which Luxor Road ran, and the tumble-down building which was number 487 was the least respectable-appearing to be found in a thoroughly disreputable block. In days before the war the ground floor had housed a saloon, and its proprietors or their successors had evidently nourished an ambition to continue business against the form of the statute in such case made and provided, for pasted to the grimy glass of the window was a large white placard announcing that the place was closed by order of the United States District Court, and a padlock and hasp of impressive proportions decorated the principal entrance. Another sign, more difficult to decipher, hung above the doorway to the upper story, announcing that the hall above was for rent for weddings, lodges and select parties.

Up the rickety stairs leading to this dubious apartment de Grandin led the way.

The landing at the stairhead was dark as Erebus; no gleam of light seeped under the door which barred the way, but the Frenchman tiptoed across the dusty floor and tapped timidly on the panels. Silence answered his summons, but as he repeated the hail the door swung inward a few inches and a hooded figure peered through the crack. "Who comes," the porter whispered, "and why have ye not the mystic knock?"

"*Morbleu*, perhaps this knock will be more greatly to your liking?" the Frenchman answered in a low, hard whisper, as his blackjack thudded sickeningly on the warder's hooded head.

"Assist me, my friend," he ordered in a low breath, catching the man as he toppled forward and easing him to the floor. " So. Off with his robe while I make sure of his good behavior with these." The snap of handcuffs sounded, and in a moment de Grandin rose, donned the hooded mantle he had stripped from the unconscious man, and tiptoed through the door.

We felt our way across the dimly lighted anteroom beyond and parted a pair of muffling curtains to peer into a lodge hall some twenty feet wide by fifty long. Flickering candles burning in globes of red and blue glass gave the place illumination which was just one degree less than darkness. Near us was a raised platform or altar approached by three high steps carpeted with a drugget on which were worked designs of a triangle surrounding an opened eye, one of the emblems appearing on the lift of each step. Upon the altar itself stood two square columns painted a dull red and surmounted by blue candles at least two inches thick, which burned smokily, diluting, rather than dispelling, the surrounding darkness. Each column was decorated with a crudely daubed picture of a cockerel equipped with three human legs, and behind the platform was a reredos bearing the device of two interlaced triangles enclosing an opened eye and surrounded by two circles, the outer red, the inner blue. Brazen pots of incense stood upon each step, and from their perforated conical caps poured forth dense clouds of sweet, almost sickeningly perfumed smoke.

Facing the altar on two rows of backless benches sat the congregation, each so enveloped in a hooded robe that it was impossible to distinguish the face, or even the sex of various individuals.

Almost as de Grandin parted the curtains a mellow-toned gong sounded three deep, admonitory notes, and, preceded by a blue-robed figure and followed by another in robes of scarlet, Estrella Hudgekins entered the room, from the farther end. She was draped in some sort of garment of white linen embroidered in blue, red and yellow, the costume seeming to consist of a split tunic with long, wide-mouthed sleeves which reached to the wrists. The skirt, if such it could be called, depended forward from her shoulders like a clergyman's stole, and while it screened the fore part of her body, it revealed her nether limbs from hip to ankle at every shuffling step. Behind, it hung down like a loose cloak, completely veiling her from neck to heels. Upon her head was a tall cap of starched white linen shaped something like a bishop's miter and surmounted by a golden representation of the triangle enclosing the opened, all-seeing eye. Beneath the cap her golden hair had been smoothly brushed and parted, and plaited with strings of rubies and of pearls, the braids falling forward over her shoulders and reaching almost to her knees.

As she advanced into the spot of luminance cast by the altar candles we saw the reason for her sliding, shuffling walk. Her nude, white feet were shod with sandals of solid gold consisting of soles with exaggeratedly upturned toes and a single metallic instep strap, making it impossible for her to retain the rigid, metallic footgear and lift her feet even an inch from the floor.

Just before the altar her escort halted, ranging themselves on each side of her, and like a trio of mechanically controlled automata, they sank to their knees, crossed their hands upon their breasts and lowered their foreheads to the floor. At this the congregation followed suit and for a moment utter quiet reigned in the hall, as priestess and votaries lay prostrate in silent adoration.

Then up she leaped, cast off her golden shoes, and advancing to the altar's lowest step, began a stamping, whirling dance, accompanied only by the rhythmic clapping of the congregation's hands. And as she danced I saw a cloud of fine, white powder dust upward from the rug and fall, like snow on marble upon the whiteness of her feet.

"Ah?" breathed Jules de Grandin in my ear, and from his tone I knew he found the answer to something which had puzzled him.

The dance endured for possibly five minutes, then ended sharply as it had commenced, and like a queen ascending to her throne, Estrella mounted the three steps of the altar, her powder-sprinkled feet leaving a trail of whitened prints on the purple carpet as she passed.

"Come forth, O chosen of the Highest; advance, O happiest of the servants of the One," chanted one of the cowled figures who had escorted the priestess. "You who have been chosen from among the flock to make the Act of Supreme Adoration; if you have searched your soul and found no guile therein, advance and make obeisance to the Godhead's Incarnation!"

There was a fluttering of robes and a craning of hooded heads toward the rear of the hall as a new figure advanced from the shadows. He was all in spotless linen like the priestess, but as he strode resolutely forward we saw the smock-like garment which enveloped him was drawn over his everyday attire.

"*Morbleu*," de Grandin murmured, "I have it; it is easier that way! Dressing a corpse is awkward business, while stripping the robe from off a body is but an instant's work. Yes."

"Forasmuch as our brother Raymond has purified and cleansed his body by fasting and his mind and soul by meditation, and has made petition to the All-Highest for permission to perform the Act of Supreme Adoration, know ye all here assembled that it is the will of the Divine All, as manifested in a vision vouchsafed His priestess and Incarnation, that His servant be allowed to make the trial," the hooded master of ceremonies announced in a deep, sepulchral voice.

Turning to Raymond, he cautioned: "Know ye, my brother, that there is but one in all the earth deemed fitting to pass this test. The world is large, its people many; dost thou dare? Bethink you, if there be but one small taint of worldliness in your most secret thoughts, your presumption in offering yourself as life-mate to the priestess is punishable by death of body and everlasting annihilation of soul, for it has been revealed that many shall apply and only one be chosen."

To the congregation he announced: "If the candidate be a woman and pass the test, then shall the priestess cleave unto her so long as she shall live, and be forever her companion. If he be a man, he may ask her hand in marriage, and she may not refuse him. But if he fail, death shall be his portion. Is it the law?"

"It is the law!" chanted the assembly in one voice.

"And dost thou still persist in thy trial?" the hooded one demanded, turning once more to Raymond. "Remember, already two have tried and been found wanting, and the wrath of the Divine All smote and withered them even as they performed the act of adoration. Dost *thou* dare?"

"I do!" said Raymond Glendower as his eyes sought the lovely, smiling eyes of the white-robed priestess.

"It is well. Proceed, my son. Make thou the Act of Supremest Adoration, and may the favor of the Divine All accompany thee!"

IT WAS DEATHLY SILENT in the room as Raymond Glendower dropped upon his knees and crept toward the altar steps. Only the sigh of quickly indrawn breath betrayed the keyed emotion of the congregation as they leaned forward to see a man gamble with his life as forfeit.

Arms outstretched to right and left, head thrown back, body erect, the priestess stood, a lovely, cruciform figure between the flickering candles as her lover crept slowly up the altar steps.

At the topmost step he paused, kneeled erect a moment, then placed his hands palm downward each side the priestess' feet.

"Salute!" the hooded acolyte cried. "Salute with lips and tongue the feet of her who is the living shrine and temple of the Most High, the Divine All. Salute the Ivory-footed Incarnation of our God!"

Lips pursed as though to kiss a holy thing; Raymond Glendower bent his head above Estrella's ivory insteps, but:

"My hands beloved, not my feet!" she cried, dropping her arms before her and holding out her hands, palm forward, to his lips.

"*Mordieu,*" de Grandin whispered in delight, "Love conquers all, my friend, even her mistaught belief that she is God's own personal representative!"

"Sacrilege!" roared the hooded man. "It is not so written in the law! 'Tis death and worse than death for one who has not passed the test to touch the priestess' hands!"

A shaft of blinding light, gleaming as the sunlight, revealing as the glow of day, shot through the gloom and lighted up the hate-distorted features of Timothy Hudgekins beneath the monk's-hood of the robe he wore. "Sacrilege it is, *parbleu,* but it is you who make it!" de Grandin cried as he focused his flashlight upon the master of ceremonies and advanced with a slow, menacing stride across the temple's floor.

"*You?*" Hudgekins cried. "You rat, you nasty little sneak, I'll break every bone—"

He launched himself on Jules de Grandin with a bellow like an infuriated bull.

The slender Frenchman crumpled like a broken reed beneath the other's charge, then straightened like a loosed steel spring, flinging Hudgekins sprawling face downward upon the carpet where the priestess had performed her dance.

"*À moi, Sergent; à moi, les gendarmes;* I have them!" he cried, and the stamping of thick-soled boots, the impact of fist and nightstick on hooded heads, mingled with the cries, curses and lamentations of the congregation of the Church of the Heavenly Gnosis as Costello led his platoon of policemen in the raid.

"Susanna Hudgekins, alias Frisco Sue, alias Annie Rooney, alias Sue Cheney, alias only the good God alone knows what else, I charge you with conspiracy to kill and murder Raymond Glendower, and with having murdered by conspiracy Matilda Stiles and Lawson Marschaulk—look to her, Sergeant," de Grandin cried, pointing a level finger at the second hooded form which had accompanied the priestess to the altar.

"What'll we do wid th' he one an' th' gur-rl, sor?" Costello asked as he clasped a pair of handcuffs on Susanna Hudgekins' wrists.

"The man—" de Grandin began, then:

"*Grand-Dieu,* behold him!"

Timothy Hudgekins lay where he had fallen; his face buried in the deep-piled, powder-saturated carpet on which the priestess had danced. A single glance told us he was dead.

"I damn think the city mortuary would be his last abiding-place—till he fills a felon's grave," de Grandin announced callously. "He is caught in his own pitfall."

To me he explained: "When I flung the filthy beast from me his vile face did come in contact with that carpet which was saturated in cyanide of mercury. It was on that they made their poor, deluded dupe dance till her feet wore covered with the powdered poison; then he who kissed and licked them perished instantly. So died Mademoiselle Stiles and so died Monsieur Marschaulk, and, *grâce à Dieu*, the poison he spread for the young Glendower has utterly destroyed that vile reptile of the name of Hudgekins. Half stunned from his fall, he breathed the deadly powder in, it dusted on his lips and swept into his mouth. So he died. I am very pleased to see it."

"What about th' gur-rl, sor?" Costello reminded.

"Nothing," de Grandin returned shortly. "She is innocent, my friend, the dupe and tool of those wicked ones. Should you seek her for questioning anon, I think you will find her in Monsieur Glendower's custody, by all appearances."

We turned with one accord toward the altar. In the light of the guttering candles Raymond Glendower and Dorothy Ericson, whom we had known as Estrella Hudgekins, were locked in each other's arms, and kissing each other on the lips, as lovers were meant to kiss.

"CERTAINLY, MR. HUDGEKINS CALLED the office," the Granada telephone girl answered de Grandin's query. "Just a few minutes after twelve o'clock he called and asked us to send up more heat."

"Did he now?" Costello asked. "Bedad, he's some guy, that felly, isn't he, Dr. de Grandin, sor?"

"You called the Hudgekins apartment at intervals?" de Grandin asked the sleuth we'd left to watch the hotel.

"Sure," that worthy replied. "Every fifteen minutes, regular as clockwork. Always got th' same answer: 'Yer party doesn't answer,' an' by th' way, sir, all them nickels I spent to call will have to go in on th' expense account."

"But of course; cert—" de Grandin began, then. "Thief, cheat, robber, *voleur*! Would you make a monkey of me? How comes it you would charge for calls you could not make?"

The detective grinned sheepishly, and de Grandin patted his shoulder with a smile. "*Eh bien, mon petit brave*," he relented, "here is five dollars; will that perhaps cover the total of those nickels you did not spend?"

Costello leading, we entered the Hudgekins' elaborate suite. One glance about the living-room, and the Frenchman shouted with glee. "Look, behold, see, admire!" he ordered triumphantly. "Laugh at my face now, Friend Trowbridge, ask me again to explain those *sacré* 'phone calls!"

Before the telephone was an ingenious device. A mechanical arm was fastened to the receiver, while in front of the mouthpiece was a funnel-shaped horn connected with a phonograph sound-box and needle which rested on a wax cylinder. The whole was actuated by clockwork, and the lever releasing the springs was attached to the bell-clapper of a large alarm clock set for fifteen minutes after twelve.

Stooping, de Grandin turned the clock's hands back. As they reached a quarter past twelve there was a light buzzing sound, the arm lifted the receiver from its hook, and in a moment a deep, gruff voice we all recognized spoke into the mouthpiece: "Hullo, this is Mr. Hudgekins. Please have the engineer send more heat up. Our apartment is cold as ice." A pause, during which a courteous hotel official might have assured the tenant his wants would be attended to, then: "Thank you, very much. Goodnight."

"Well,"—Costello stared open-mouthed at the mechanism which would have provided an unshakable alibi in any criminal court—"well, sors, I'll be damned!"

"Undoubtlessly you will, unless you mend your ways," de Grandin agreed with a grin. "Meantime, as damnation is a hot and thirsty business, I vote we adjourn to Friend Trowbridge's and absorb a drink."

The Bride of Dewer

"I WALTER TAKE THEE ROSEMARY to be my wedded wife, to have and to hold from this day forward, for better, for worse—"

Dr. Bentley's measured, evenly modulated words, echoed by the bridegroom's somewhat tremulous repetitions, sounded through St. Philip's.

"*Eh bien*," irrepressible at church as elsewhere, Jules de Grandin whispered in my ear, "I feel myself about to weep in concert with the attenuated lady in lavender yonder, Friend Trowbridge. We may hold back the tears at a funeral, for the poor defunct one's troubles are over and done, but at a wedding—*pardieu*, who can prophesy outcome?"

"S-s-sh!" I commanded, reinforcing my scandalized frown with a sharp dig of my elbow in his ribs. "Can't you be quiet *anywhere?*"

"Under compulsion, yes," be responded, grinning elfishly at my embarrassment, "but—"

"—and have declared the same by giving and receiving a ring, and by joining hands, I now pronounce that they are man and wife"—Dr. Bentley's announcement concluded the ceremony, and the majestic strains of Mendelssohn's "Wedding March" drowned out the Frenchman' chatter.

Somewhat later, at the bride's home, de Grandin pleasantly warmed by several glasses of champagne punch, lifted Rosemary Whitney's white-gloved hand to his lips. "Madame Whitney," he assured her, and his little blue eyes swam with sudden tears, "may the happiness of this night be the smallest part of the happiness which lies in store for you; may you and Monsieur Whitney be always happy as I should have been, had not *le bon Dieu* willed otherwise!"

He was strangely silent on the way home. The propensity to chatter which kept his nimble tongue wagging most of his waking hours seemed to have deserted him entirely. Once or twice he heaved a deep, sentimental sigh; as we prepared for bed he forbore to make his usual complimentary remark about the excellence of my brandy, and even omitted to damn the instigators of the Eighteenth Amendment.

It might have been three o'clock, perhaps a bit later, when the shrewish, insistent scolding of my telephone bell woke me.

"Doctor—Dr. Trowbridge"—the voice across the wire was low and muted, as though smothered beneath a weight of sobs—"can you come over right away? Please! This is Mrs. Winnicott, and—it—it's Rosemary. Doctor, she's home, and—yes, yes," evidently she turned to someone at her elbow, "right away." Once more, to me: "Oh, Doctor, *please* hurry!"

I was out of bed and beginning to dress almost before the sharp click in my ear told me Mrs. Winnicott had hung up, but swift as I was, Jules de Grandin was quicker. The chatter of the bell had roused him, and from the doorway of my room he had heard enough to realize an urgent call had come. While I still fumbled, cursing, at the fastenings of my collar, he passed down the upper hall, fully dressed. With my medicine and instrument kits in readiness he was waiting in the lower passage as I clattered down the stairs.

"Rosemary Winnicott—Whitney, I mean," I corrected myself. "Her mother just 'phoned, and though she wasn't specific I gathered something dreadful has happened."

"*Mordie, la petite Madame la Mariee?*" he exclaimed. "*Ohé*, this is monstrous, my friend! Hurry; make haste!"

A round, red sun, precursor of a broiling June day, was slowly creeping over the horizon as we reached the Winnicott house and dashed through the front door without the formality of knocking.

In her pretty pink-and-ivory chamber Rosemary Whitney lay, pale as an image graven out of marble beneath the damask counterpane of the virginal bed she had risen from the previous morning with such sweet day-dreams as young girls know upon their wedding morns. Her eyes were quiet, though not closed, and her lips, bleached as though bereft of every drop of blood, were slightly parted. Once or twice she turned her head upon the pillow, weakly, like a fever patient, and emitted a little frightened moan. That was all.

Impotent as a mother bird which sees its fledgling helpless before a coiling serpent—and as twitteringly nervous—Mrs. Winnicott stood beside her daughter's bed, holding the little white hands that lay so listlessly on the bedspread, reaching mechanically for the phial of sal volatile which stood upon the night-table, then putting it back unopened.

"What is it? What has happened, if you please?" de Grandin cried, placing the medicine cases on a chair and fairly bounding to the bedside.

"I—I don't know—oh, I don't know!" Mrs. Winnicott wailed, wringing her hands helplessly together. "An hour ago—less, maybe—Walter and Rosemary drove up. Walter seemed stunned—almost as though he had been drugged—when he helped her from the car, and said nothing, just half-led, half-dragged her to the porch, beat upon the front door a moment, then turned and left her. I couldn't sleep, and had been sitting by the window, watching the sky lighten in the east, so I saw them come. When I reached the front door Walter had gone and my poor baby lay there, like this. She's been the same ever since. I've begged her to tell me—to answer me; but—you can see how she is for yourselves!"

"And Walter made no explanation; didn't even stay to help her up to bed?" I asked incredulously.

"No!"

"The young whelp—the scoundrel!" I gritted through my teeth. "If I could get my hands on him, I'd—"

"*Tiens*, my friend, our hands are excellently well filled right here," de Grandin reminded sharply. "Come, attend *Mademoiselle—Madame*, I mean; chastisement of the truant bridegroom may come later, when we are more at leisure."

Quick examination disclosed no physical injury of any kind. Rosemary suffered only from profound shock of some sort, though what the cause might be she was no more able to tell us than had she been a newborn babe. The Frenchman's diagnosis paralleled mine, and before I could do more than indicate my opinion he had flown to the medicine case, extracted a hypodermic syringe and a phial of tincture digitalis, then, prepared an alcohol swab for the patient's arm. With an ease and quickness that bespoke his experience in the field dressing-stations of the war, he drove the needle through the girl's white skin, and the powerful heart-regulant shot home. In a few moments her quick, light breathing became more steady, her piteous moaning less frequent, and the deathly pallor which had disfigured her features gave place to the faint suspicion of a normal color.

"*Bien—très bon!*" He regarded his handiwork complacently. "In a few moments we shall administer a sedative, *Madame*, and your daughter will sleep. From that time forth it is a matter of nursing. We shall procure a skilled attendant at once."

"Hullo, Trowbridge," greeted a familiar voice on the telephone shortly after our return from Mrs. Winnicott's, "d'ye know a fellow named Whitney—Walter Whitney? Seems to me you were his family's physician—this is Donovan talking, over at City Hospital, you know."

"Yes, I know him," I answered grimly. "What—"

"All right, you'd better come over and get him, then. A policeman picked him up a little while ago, nutty as a store full o' cuckoo clocks. Shortly before sunrise this mornin' he was drivin' his car round and round City Hall—seemed to think the Public Square was some sort o' bloomin' merry-go-round, and if the officer hadn't had more sense than most he'd be decoratin' a cell at some station house now, with a drunk an' disorderly charge against him, instead of bein' here an' keepin' more urgent cases out of a bed in H-3. Come on over and get him like a good fellow, won't you?"

"You mean—"

"I sure do, son. It's not dope an' it isn't booze—the boy's as clean as a ribbon and sound as a hound's tooth, but it's *something*, all right, and I don't mean maybe. I wish you'd come and take him off our hands. This isn't any sanitarium for the idle rich, this is a *bums'* roost, man."

"All right," I promised, turning wearily away. To de Grandin, I announced:

"It seems we'll have to revise our opinion of Walter Whitney. Evidently whatever struck poor little Rosemary hit him, too; he's over in the psychopathic ward of City Hospital, suffering from shock of some sort."

"*Morbleu*, this is tragic, no less!" the little Frenchman exclaimed as we set out to get the stricken bridegroom.

THERE WAS NO DOUBT Walter Whitney had suffered an ordeal of some kind. His face was serious, preoccupied, as though he sought to catch the lilt of faint, far-away music, or was trying desperately to recall the rime of a snatch of half-remembered verse. When we addressed him he gave back a non-comprehending, vacant-eyed stare, and if we spoke sharply he repeated our words with slow hesitancy, like a child learning to talk or an adult struggling with the intricacies of some foreign language. Once or twice his eyes brimmed with tears, as tears come sometimes at memory of some long-forgotten sorrow, and once he spoke spontaneously.

"What?" I asked, bending down to catch his mumbled answer.

"The—old tale. It's—true—after—all," he muttered slowly, unbelievingly. And when I asked him what he meant he murmured thickly: "God have mercy on us!"

2

FOR TEN LONG DAYS we labored with the bride and bridegroom. Several times a day de Grandin or I called on them, but it was the little Frenchman's indomitable will which dragged them back from the lethargy which succeeded the first onset of their strange malady to something near the normal. It was on the eleventh day, while we were visiting Rosemary, that she broke her semi-trance and spoke connectedly.

"Walter and I stole out the back door to where he'd parked his car in the alley while the guests were making merry in the front part of the house," she began with a sad, reminiscent smile, like an old woman recalling the joys of her vanished youth. "We drove to Bladenstown, where Walter had engaged a suite at the Carteret Inn by wire, and he waited in the garden while I fussed about the rooms.

"I'd slipped out of my going-away dress and put on pajamas and kimono, and had finished creaming my face and brushing my hair when—"

She paused, catching her lower lip between her milk-white teeth, like a little girl afraid of what she may say next.

"Yes, *Madame*," de Grandin prompted softly, his little blue eyes shining, "and then?"

"I heard a footstep on the stairs," she answered, a faint blush mantling her pale cheeks. "I thought it was Walter, and—" Again a little pause, then:

"I switched the lights off quickly and dropped my kimono and slippers as I ran across the room and leaped into the bed. I didn't want him to find me up, you see."

Evidently we were expected to understand, and, though neither of us did, we nodded slowly in concert.

"The steps came up the little hall leading from the stairs to our suite," she went on, "and paused before the door, then went down the hall, a little uncertainly, finally came back, and I could hear someone trying the latch tentatively.

"My heart was beating so it almost shut my breath off, and there was goose-flesh all over me; I felt a sort of feverish-chill inside, but I couldn't help but giggle. Walter was as scared as I. Somehow, one doesn't expect a man to be all cold and trembly in such circumstances, but I knew he was and—and it made me feel happier—more as if we were starting out even, you know.

"Just then the door opened a little, tiny crack, and as it did so, the moon, which had been behind the poplars growing at the lower end of the garden, sailed up into the sky and flooded the room with light. I held my breath, and put out my arms toward Walter, then—*it came in!*"

Her face went white as chalk as she pronounced the words, and we could see the tiny nodules of horripilation form on her forearms.

"It?" De Grandin wrinkled his brows in puzzlement. "What is it you say, *Madame*?"

"It came into the parlor of our suite. There was a little, tittering laugh, like the affected snicker of a wicked, senile man—an old roué listening to a nasty, scandalous story, and then I saw it. Oh!" she put her thin, pale hands to her face as though to shut away a sight too terrible for memory, and her narrow, silk-sheathed shoulders shook with sobs of revulsion.

"It wasn't like a man, and yet it was. Not more than four feet tall, very stooped and bandy-legged, with no covering except a thick, horny hide the color of toadskin, and absolutely no hair of any kind upon its body anywhere.

About the great wide grinning mouth there hung a fringe of drooping, wart-like tentacles, and another fringe of similar protuberances dangled from its chin, if it could be said to have a chin, for the head and face were more like those of a horned toad or lizard than anything I can think of. There seemed to be some sort of belt or sash about the creature's waist, and from it hung a wide-bladed short sword without a scabbard.

"It stopped just inside the room, and looked around with dreadful, shining eyes that never changed expression, then came slip-slopping on its wide, splayed feet toward the bed where I lay petrified with horror.

"I wanted to scream, to jump up and run, to fling a pillow at the awful nightmare-thing which crept closer, and closer, but all I could do was lie there and stare—I couldn't even lower the arms I'd held out to my husband when I thought I heard him at the door.

"When it was almost up to me it spoke. 'Don't 'ee try and get away, my puss,' it said, with a sort of horrible chuckle. ''Tis many and many a year since the old one had a man child to take a bride to wife, and the bargain was only for their bridenight; nothing more. Be quiet while I warm my chilled face in your bosom, my pretty, for it's been more time than you can know since I've done as much—'

"Then"—she paused a moment, fighting for breath like a winded runner finishing a race—"then it came over to me and put its arms about me—ugh! they were cold as something fished up from the river!—and kissed me—*kissed me on the mouth!*"

Her voice rose to a shrill, thin scream as she finished, and for a moment she gasped weakly, then fell back against her pillows, her slender torso retching with physical sickness induced by the dreadful memory.

I hastened to administer aromatic ammonia, and in a few minutes she regained comparative calm.

"I don't know what happened next," she whispered. "I fainted, and the next I knew I was here in bed, with Mother and the nurse beside me.

"Tell me," she added suddenly, "what's become of Walter? I've been so weak and miserable all the while that I've scarcely noticed his absence; but I haven't seen him once. Oh, Dr. Trowbridge, Dr. de Grandin, don't tell me that awful creature—that horrible monster—hurt him—killed—oh, no! That would be too cruel! Don't tell me, if it's so!"

"It is not so, *Madame*," de Grandin assured her gently. "*Monsieur* your husband has suffered severe shock also, though as yet we do not know what induced it; but we believe he will soon be himself again; then we shall bring him to you."

"Oh, thank you, thank you, sir," she answered, the first smile showing on her pale, wasted face. "Oh, I'm so glad. My Walter, my beloved, is safe!" Clean, cleansing tears, overwrought woman's best restorative, coursed down her cheeks.

"Be of good courage, *Madame*," de Grandin bade. "You have suffered much, but you have youth and love, you have each other; you also have Jules de Grandin for ally. The odds are all in your favor. But of course."

3

"WELL, WHAT D'YE MAKE of it?" I demanded as we descended the Winnicott front steps. "Sounds to me as if she fell asleep and suffered such a nightmare that it carried over into her conscious mind, and—"

"And *Monsieur* her husband, who has been no less profoundly affected—did he also suffer a realistic *cauchemar* at the same time, perhaps?" broke in the Frenchman. "*Non*, my friend, your theory is untenable. I would it were not; the explanation would provide an easy exit from our difficulties."

I set my lips grimly. "D'ye know what I think?" I answered.

"*Parbleu*, do you?" his elfin grin took the sting from the sarcasm.

"I believe the poor girl was temporarily unbalanced by some dreadfully vivid dream, and when that worthless scoundrel she married realized it, he took her home—returned her like an unprincipled woman throwing back a piece of merchandise on a shopkeeper's hands!"

"But this so strange malady he suffered—still suffers?" de Grandin protested.

"Is malingering, pure and simple, or his guilty conscience preying on his mind," I returned.

"Oh, la, la; *le bon Dieu* preserve the little patience with which heaven has endowed Jules de Grandin!" he prayed. "My good Trowbridge, my excellent, practical one, ever seeing but so much oil and pigment in a painting, but so many hundredweight of stone in a statue. *Mort d'un coq*, but you annoy me, you vex me, you anger and enrage me—me, I could twist your so stupid neck! What lies behind all this I know no more than you, but may Satan serve me fried turnip with parsley if I traverse Monsieur Robin Hood's barnyard seeking a conventional explanation for something which fairly reeks of the superphysical. No, a reason there is, there must be, but you are as far from seeing it as an Icelander is from hearing the blackbirds whistle in the horse-chestnuts of St. Cloud! Yes."

"Well, where are you going to hunt this supernatural explanation?" I demanded.

"I did not say supernatural," he answered acidly. "Everything is natural, though if we do not know, or if we misread nature's laws, we falsely call it otherwise. Consider: Fifty years ago a man beholding the radio would have called it supernatural, yet the laws of physics governing the device were known as well then as now. But their application had not yet been learned. So in this case. Who—or what—it was Madame Whitney beheld upon her bridal night we do not know, nor do we in anywise know why she should have seen it; but that it was no figment of a dream Jules de Grandin is prepared to wager his far from empty head. Certainly.

"Now, first, we shall interrogate Monsieur Whitney; perhaps he can tell us that which will put us on the proper track. Failing that, we shall make discreet inquiries at the inn where the manifestation was seen. In that way we may acquire information. In any event, we shall not cease to seek until we have found. No, Jules de Grandin is not lightly to be thrown off the trail of ghost or human evildoer, Friend Trowbridge."

"Humph!" I grunted. There seemed nothing else to say.

4

"*DES BONNES NOUVELLES, MON ami!*" de Grandin exclaimed. "But yes; certainly; assuredly we bring you great tidings of gladness: *Madame* your wife is most greatly improved, and if you show similar progress we shall take you to her within the week. Come, smile. Is it not wonderful?"

Walter Whitney raised a face which was like a death mask of joy, and the smile he essayed was sadder than any tears. "I can't see her; I shall never see her again," he answered tonelessly.

"What is it you say? But this is infamous—monstrous!" the Frenchman exploded. "Madame your wife, who has but emerged from the valley of death's shadow, desires to see you; *la pauvre, belle creature*, she expected, she deserved happiness and love and tenderness; she has had only sorrow and suffering, and you sit there, Monsieur, like a bullfrog upon the marsh-bank, and say you can not see her! It is damnable, no less, *cordieu!*" He fairly sputtered in his fury.

"I know," Whitney answered wearily. "I'm the cause of it all; she'll suffer worse, though, if I see her again."

"What, *cochon!*—you would threaten her, the wife of your bosom?" De Grandin's strong, deceptively slender fingers worked spasmodically.

For an instant faint animation showed in young Whitney's somber, brooding face. "It isn't anything I'd do to her—I'd give my heart's blood to save her an instant's suffering!—but it's through me, though without my intention, that she's suffered as she has, and any attempt on my part to join her would only renew it I can't see her, I mustn't see her again—ever. That's final."

"May Jules de Grandin stew everlastingly in hell with Judas Iscariot on his left hand and he who first invented Prohibition on his right if it be so!" the Frenchman cried.

"*Lache*, coward, wife-deserter, attend me: From her parent's arms and from her loving home you took that pure, sweet girl. Before the holy altar of your God and before all men you vowed to love and cherish her for better, for worse, in sickness and in health. Together, beneath the golden beams of the honeymoon, you set forth upon life's pathway. *Ha*, it was most pretty, was it not?" He smiled sarcastically. "Then what? This, *mordieu*: At the inn *Madame* your wife experienced a shock, she became hysterical, temporarily deranged, we will say; it is often so when young girls leave the bridal altar for their husbands' arms. And you, what of you? *Ha*, you, the man on whose lips still clung the lying words you mouthed before the altar, you saw her so piteous condition, and like the poltroon you are, you did return her to her home; yes, to her parent's house; *pardieu*, you took her back as an unprincipled woman returns a damaged gown to the shopman! Ha, you decorate your sex, *Monsieur*; I do remove my hat in your so distinguished presence!" Seizing his wide-brimmed Panama, he clapped it on his head, then swept it nearly to the floor in an elaborate parody of a ceremonious bow.

White lines showed in Walter Whitney's face, deep wrinkles of distress cut vertically, down his cheeks. "It's not so!" he cried, struggling weakly to rise. "It's a damned, infernal lie! You know it is! Damn you, you slanderous rascal, you wouldn't dare talk so if I had my strength! I tell you, I'm responsible for Rosemary's condition today, though it's no fault of mine. I said I'd give my blood to spare her—good Lord, what do you think this renunciation is costing me? I— oh, you wouldn't understand; you'd say I was crazy if I told you!"

"Your pardon, *mon petit pauvre*," de Grandin answered quickly. "I did but hurt you to be kind, as the dentist tortures for a moment with his drill that the longer agony of toothache may be avoided. You have said what I wished; I shall *not* pronounce you crazy if you tell me all; on the contrary, I shall thank you greatly. Moreover, it is the only way that I can be rendered able to help you and Madame Whitney back to happiness. Come, begin at the beginning, and tell me what you can. I am all attention."

Whitney looked at him speculatively a moment. "If you laugh at me I'll wring your neck when I get well," he threatened.

"I suppose you and Rosemary and everybody else were justified in thinking all you did of me when I took her home the other morning," he continued, "but I did it only because I knew nowhere else to go, and I knew my brain was going to snap 'most any minute, so I had to get her to a place of safety.

"I don't know whether you know it or not, Dr. Trowbridge," he added, turning to me, "but none of the men in my family that I can remember have ever married."

"Your father—" I began with a smile, but he waved the objection aside.

"I don't mean that. You've known us all; think of my uncles, my cousins, my elder brothers. See what I mean?"

I nodded. It was true. His mother's three brothers had died unmarried; had never, as far as I knew, even had sweethearts, though they were fine, sociable fellows, well provided for financially, and prime favorites with the ladies. Two of his cousins had perished in the World War, both bachelors; another was as confirmed in celibacy as I; the fourth had recently taken his vows as an Episcopal monk. His brothers, both many years his senior, were still single. No, the score was perfect. Walter was the first male of his blood to take a wife within living memory.

"Both your sisters married," I reminded him.

"That's just it; it doesn't affect the women."

"What in the world—" I began, but he turned from me to de Grandin.

"My parents were both past forty when I was born, sir," he explained. "My brothers and sisters were all old enough to have had me for a child, and both the girls were married, with families of their own before I came. I used to wonder why all our men were bachelors, but when I mentioned it, nobody seemed to care to answer. Finally, when I was just through prep school and ready to go to Amherst, my Aunt Deborah took me aside and tried to make it plain.

"Poor old girl! I can see her now, almost ninety years of age, with a chin and nose that almost met and the shrewdest, most knowing eyes I've ever seen in a human face. I used to think the man who illustrated the fairy-tale books got his idea of the witches from looking at her when I was a little tad, and later I regarded her as a harmless old nut who'd rather find the hole than the doughnut any day. Well, she's got the laugh on me from the grave, all right.

"'You must never think of marrying, Wally,' she told me. 'None of our men can, for it means only woe and calamity, usually death or madness for the wives, if they do. Look at your brothers, your uncles and your cousins; they'll never marry; neither must you.'

"Naturally, I asked why. I'd had one or two heavy love affairs during prep days, and was already thinking seriously of settling down and raising a mustache and a family as soon as I graduated from college. Her statement rather seemed to cramp my style.

"'Because it's a curse put on our family,' she answered. 'Way back, so far none of us know just how it happened, or why, one of our ancestors did something so utterly vile and wicked that his blood and his sons' blood has been cursed forever. We've traced our genealogy through the female line for generations, for two generations of the family have never lived to bear the same surname.

"'See here,'—she took me out into the hall where the old Quimper coat of arms hung framed upon the wall—'that's the crest of the ancestor who brought the curse upon us. The family—at least his direct male descendants—died out in England centuries ago and the arms were struck from the rolls of the College of Heralds for want of one to bear them, but the blood's poisoned, and you've got it in your veins. Wally, you must never, never think of marrying. It would be kinder to kill the girl outright, instead!'

"She was so earnest about it that she gave me the creeps, and laughing at her didn't better things.

"'Once, long ago, so long that I can only remember hearing my parents talk of when I was a very little girl,' she told me, 'one of our men dared the curse and married. His wife went stark, raving mad on her bridal night, and he lived to be a broken, embittered old man. That's the only instance I know of the rule being broken, but don't you break it, Wally, or you'll be sorry; you'll never forgive yourself for what you did to the girl you loved when you married her!'

"Aunt Deborah was dead and in her grave at Shadow Lawns when I came back from college, and Mother had only the vaguest notions of the curse. Like me, she was inclined to regard it as one of the old lady's crack-brained notions, and, though she never actually said so, I think she resented the influence the old girl had in keeping so many of our men single.

"Mother died two years ago, and I've lived here by myself since. Rosemary and I had known each other since the days when I used to scalp her every afternoon and hang her favorite doll in chains each morning, and while we'd never really been sweethearts in our younger days, we'd always been the best of friends and kept up the old intimacy. Last Decoration Day I was a little late getting out to Shadow Lawns, and when I reached the family plot I met Rosemary coming away. She'd been putting flowers on my parents' graves.

"That really started it. We became engaged last fall, and, as you know, were married this month.

"Oh, Lord," his face went pale and strained as though with bodily torture, "if I'd only known! *If I'd only known!*"

"*Eh bien, Monsieur*, we also desire to know," de Grandin reminded.

"We'd planned everything," Whitney continued. "The house was to be redecorated throughout, and Rosemary and I were going to spend our honeymoon away while the painters were at their work here.

"The night we married we drove to Carteret Inn and I waited in the garden while she unpacked and made her toilet for the night, The blood was pounding at my temples and my breath came so fast it almost smothered me while I strolled about that moonlit garden.

"D'ye remember how you felt sort o' weak and trembly inside the first time you went up to ring a girl's doorbell—the first time you called on your first sweetheart?" he asked, turning a wan smile in my direction.

I nodded.

"That's how I felt that night. I'd been a clean-lived chap, Dr. Trowbridge. I'm not bragging; it just happened so; but that night I thanked God from the bottom of my heart that Rosemary could give me no more than I took to her—there's consolation for all the 'good times' missed in that kind of thought, sir."

Again I nodded, thoroughly ashamed of all the suspicions I'd voiced against the lad.

"I kept looking at my watch, and it seemed to me the thing must have stopped, but at last a half-hour crawled by—it seemed more like half a century. Then I went in.

"Just as I began to mount the stairs I thought I saw a shadow in the upper hall, but when I looked a second time it was gone; so I assumed it had been one of the hotel servants passing on his duties, and paid no more attention. The latch of our door seemed stuck somehow, or perhaps my nervous fingers were clumsy; at any rate, I had some trouble getting in. Then—"

He stopped so long I thought he had repented his decision to take us into his confidence, but at length he finished:

"Then I went in. My God! What a sight! Something like a man, but green all over, like a body that has lain in the river till it's ready to drop apart was standing by the bed, holding Rosemary in its arms, and nuzzling at her bosom where her pajamas had been torn away with the most horrible, obscene mouth I've ever seen.

"I tried to rush the thing and beat it off, but my limbs were paralyzed; neither arm nor leg could I move. I couldn't even cry out to curse the foul nightmare-goblin that held my wife against its nude, slimy breast and wheezed and snuffled at her as an old, asthmatic dog might sniff and slaver at a wounded bird.

"At last the horror seemed aware of my presence. Still holding Rosemary in its arms, it lifted its misshapen head and grinned hellishly at me. Its eyes were big as silver dollars, and bright as fox-fire glowing in the marsh at night.

"'I'm come to claim my rights, Sir Guy,' it told me, though why in God's name it should address me so I've no idea. 'Tis many a year since last one of your gentle line gave in to me; they've cheated me right handsomely by staying womanless; but you've been good to me, and I thank ye right kindly for it.'

"I stood and stared, petrified with horror, weak with positive physical nausea at the very sight of the fetid thing which held my wife, and the monster seemed suddenly to notice me again. 'What, still here?' it croaked. 'Be off, ye churl! Have ye no more manners than to stand by staring while your liege lord wages his right? Be off, I say, or there ye'll stand till all is done, nor will ye lift a hand to stay me.'

"But I did lift a hand. The terror which had held me spellbound seemed to melt as I caught a glimpse of Rosemary's white face; and as the awful creature's flat, frog's claw hands ripped another shred of her nightclothes away, I yelled and charged across the room to grapple with the thing.

"With a dreadful, tittering laugh it dropped Rosemary on the bed and turned to meet my onset, drawing a sort of short, wide-bladed sword from its girdle as it did so. I never had a chance. The slimy, naked monster was shorter by a foot than I, but for all its misshapen deformity it was quick as lightning and tremendously strong. Its arms, too, were half again as long as mine, and before I could land a single blow it hit me on the head with the flat of its sword and floored me. I tried to rise, but it was on me before I could struggle to my knees, beating at my head with its blade, and down I went like a beaten prizefighter.

"How long I lay unconscious I do not know, but when I came to, the first faint streaks of morning were lighting the room, and I could see almost as plainly as by moonlight. The horrid apparition had vanished, but there was a strong, almost overpowering stench in the room—a stink like the smell of stagnant water that's clogged with drowned and rotting things.

"Rosemary lay half in, half out of bed, her lips crushed and bruised and a darkened spot upon her nose, as though she had been struck in the face. Her nightclothes were ripped to tatters, the jacket hanging to her shoulders by shreds, the trousers almost ripped away, and there were stains of blood on them.

"I got some water from the bathroom and washed her poor, bruised face and bathed her wrists and temples. Then I found some fresh pajamas in her bag. Presently she waked, but didn't seem to know me. She didn't speak, she didn't move, just lay there in a sort of waking stupor, staring, staring, and seeing nothing, and every now and then she'd moan so pitifully it wrung my heart to hear her.

"After trying vainly to revive her for a time I managed to get her clothes on somehow and lugged her downstairs to the car. Nobody was awake at that hour; nobody saw us leave, and I didn't know which way to turn. Bladenstown is strange to me, I didn't know where to look for a doctor, and there was no one to ask. If I had found one, what could I have told him? How could I explain Rosemary's condition on her wedding night? You don't suppose he'd have believed me if I'd told him the truth, do you?

"So I turned back toward Harrisonville and all the time, as I drove, something inside me seemed to say accusingly: 'It's your fault; it's your fault; this is all your doing. You wouldn't listen to Aunt Deborah; now see what you've brought on Rosemary!'

"'Your fault—your fault—your *fault!*' the humming of my motor seemed to chuckle at me as I drove.

"And it was. Too late I realized how terrible the curse on our family is, and what a dreadful ordeal I'd subjected Rosemary to. My heart was breaking when I reached her mother's house, and I couldn't find the words to tell her what had happened. I only knew I wanted to get away to crawl off somewhere like a wounded dog and die.

"Then, as I left the Winnicott house and drove toward the center of the city, something seemed to go 'snap' inside my head, and the next I knew you gentlemen had me in hand.

"So now you know why I can never see Rosemary again," he finished. "If I yield to my heart's pleadings and go to her I know I shan't be strong enough to give her up, and rather than bring that thing on her again, I'll let her—and you, and all the world—think what you will of me, and when she sues me for divorce I'll not contest the action.

"Now tell me I'm crazy!" he challenged. "Tell me this is all the result of some shock you can't explain, and that I just imagined it. I don't care what you say—I was there; I saw it, and I know."

"Assuredly you do, *mon vieux*," de Grandin conceded, "nor do I think that you are crazy, though the good God knows you have admirable excuse if you were. *Non*, I believe you firmly, but your case is not so hopeless as it seems. Remember, Jules de Grandin is with you, and it shall go hard but I shall make a monkey of this so foul thing which had no more discretion than to thrust itself into your bridal chamber. Yes, *pardieu*, I promise it!"

5

"I'M SORRY FOR WHAT I said about that boy," I confessed contritely as we left young Whitney's house. "but appearances were certainly against him, and—"

"*Zut*, no apologies, my friend!" de Grandin admonished. "I am glad you lost your temper, for your suspicions, unworthy as they were, did furnish me with the very accusations I needed to sting him from his silence and force from him the explanation which shall aid us in our task."

"Explanation?" I echoed. "I don't see we're much nearer an explanation than we were before. It's true Walter's story corroborates Rosemary's but—"

"But I damn think I see the glimmer of light ahead," the Frenchman cut in with a smile. "Consider: Did not you catch the two small clues Monsieur Walter let drop?"

"No, I can't say I did," I returned. "As far as I was concerned the whole business was an unrelated hodgepodge of horror, meaningless as the vagaries of a nightmare."

"What of the remarks made by the visitant concerning its having come to claim its rights?" he asked. "Or, by example, the odd manner in which it addressed the young Walter as Sir Guy? Does not that suggest something to you?"

"No, it doesn't."

"*Eh bien*, I should have known as much," he returned resigned. "Come, if you have time, accompany me to New York. I think our friend, Dr. Jacoby, may be able to enlighten us somewhat."

"Who is he?"

"The curator of mediaeval literature at the *Musée Metropolitaine*. *Parbleu*"— he gave a short chuckle—"that man he knows every bit of scandalous gossip in the world, provided it dates no later than the fifteenth century!"

THE LONG SUMMER TWILIGHT was deepening into darkness as we entered the walnut-paneled, book-lined office of Dr. Armand Jacoby in the big graystone building facing Fifth Avenue.

The learned doctor appeared anything but the profound savant he was, for he was excessively fat, almost entirely bald, and extremely untidy. His silk shirt, striped with alternate bands of purple and lavender, was open at the throat, his vivid green cravat was unknotted but still encircling his neck, and a thick layer of pipe-ashes besprinkled his gray-flannel trousers. "Hullo, de Grandin," he boomed in a voice as big and round as his own kettlelike abdomen, "glad to see you. What's on your mind? You must be in some sort of trouble, or you'd never have made the trip over in this infernal heat."

"*Tiens*, my friend," the Frenchman answered with a grin, "your perception is as bounteous as your hair!" Then, sobering quickly, he added: "Do you, by any happy chance, know of a mediæval legend, well-authenticated or otherwise, wherein some knight, probably an Englishman, swore fealty to some demon of the underworld, or of the ancient heathen days, giving him *le Droit du Seigneur?*"

"What was that?" I interrupted before Jacoby could reply.

The doctor looked at me as a teacher might regard a singularly backward pupil, but his innate courtesy prompted his answer.

"It was the right enjoyed by feudal lords over the persons and property of their people," he told me. "In mediæval times society was divided into three main classes, the nobility, with which the clergy might be classed, the freemen, and the serfs or villeins. The freemen were mostly inhabitants of towns, occasionally they were the yeomanry or small farmers, while the serfs or villeins were the laborers who cultivated the land. One of the peculiarities of these poor creatures' condition was they were in no circumstances allowed to move from the estate where they lived, and when the land was sold they passed with it, just like any fixture. The lord of the manor had practically unlimited power over his serfs; he might take all they possessed and he might imprison them at his pleasure, for good reason or for no reason. When they died, whatever miserable property they had been able to accumulate became his instead of passing to their children. Even the burghers and yeomen were under certain duties to their lord or *seigneur*. They had to pay him certain moneys on stated occasions, such as defraying the expenses of knighting his eldest son, marrying his eldest daughter, of bailing him out when he was captured by the enemy. These rights were properly grouped under the term *Droit du Seigneur*, but in later times the expression came to have a specialized meaning, and referred to the absolute right enjoyed by many barons of spending the first night of marriage with the bride of any of his liegemen, occupying the hymeneal chamber with the bride while the bridegroom cooled his heels outside the door. Because of this it is probable that a third of the commoners' children in mediæval Europe had gentle blood in their veins, although, of course, their social status was that of their mothers and putative fathers. The French and German peasants and burghers submitted, but the English yeomen and townsmen put one over on the nobles when they devised a law of inheritance whereby estates descended to the youngest, instead of the eldest son. You'll find it all in Blackstone's *Commentaries*, if you care to take the time."

"But—"

Dr. Jacoby waved my question aside with a waggle of his fat hand and turned directly to de Grandin. "It's an interesting question you raise," he said. "There are a dozen or more legends to that effect, and in Scotland and northern England there are several castles where the progeny of those demons who exercised their *Droit du Seigneur* are said to dwell in secret dungeons in a kind of limited immortality. There's one Scottish castle in particular where the head of the house is supposed to take the heir-apparent into his confidence upon his coming of age, tell him the story of the family scandal and give him the key to the dungeon where his half-man, half-demon relative is cooped up. No one but the head of the family and his heir are supposed to have these keys, and only they are permitted to see the monstrosity. There's a pleasant little story of the French wife of the Scottish laird who let her curiosity get the better of her, abstracted the dungeon key from her husband's dispatch case and went down to see for herself. They found her wandering about the cellar next morning, her hair snow-white and her mind a blank. She ended her days in a lunatic asylum."

"Very good," de Grandin nodded. "But have you any memoranda of such a compact being made and carried out for several generations?"

"H'm," Dr. Jacoby caressed his fat chin with the fat thumb and forefinger of his wide, white hand. "No, I can't say I have. Usually these stories are buried so deep under additional legends that it's practically impossible to get at the root-legend, but—hey, wait a minute!" His big eyes lighted with enthusiasm behind the pebbles of his thick-lensed spectacles. "There is an old tale of that kind; Queberon, or Quampaire, or some such name was the man's and the demon was called—" He paused, pondering a moment, then: "No, it's no use, I can't remember it; but if you'll give me forty-eight hours I'll dig it out for you."

"Oh, my supreme, my superb, my so magnificent Jacoby!" de Grandin answered. "Always are you to be depended on. Your offer is more than satisfactory, my old one, and I am certain you are on the right track, for the modernized style of the name I have in mind is Quimper."

"Humph, that's not so modem," Jacoby answered. "I shouldn't be surprised if it's the original patronymic."

6

TWO DAYS LATER A thick envelope arrived for de Grandin, and my excitement was almost equal to his as he slit the flap and unfolded several sheets of closely-written foolscap.

"The legend you spoke of," Jacoby wrote, "is undoubtedly that of Sir Guy de Quimper—probably pronounced 'Kam-pay' and differently spelled in the eleventh century, since there was no recognized system of orthography in those days—who was supposed to have made a bargain with a North England demon in return for his deliverance during the battle of Ascalon. I've tried to modernize a monkish account of the deal: Perhaps you'll learn what you wish from it, but I must remind you that those monks were never the ones to spoil a good story for the truth's sake, and when sufficient facts were not forthcoming, they never hesitated to call on their imaginations."

"The warning was unnecessary," de Grandin laughed, "but we shall see what *Monsieur l'Historien* has to say, none the less."

Pray ye for daughters, oh ye womenfolk of Quimper, and ask the Lord of His mercy and loving-kindness to grant ye bring no man-children into the world, for a surety there rests upon the house of Quimper, entailed on the male line, a curse the like of which was never known before, and, *priedieu*, may not be known again till the heavens be rolled up like a scroll and all the world stand mute before our God in His judgment seat.

For behold, it was a filthy act wrought by Sir Guy of Quimper, and with his words of blasphemy he bound forever the men of all his line to suffer through their womenfolk a dole and drearihead most dreadful.

It was upon the day when our good Lord Godfrey of Bouillon, most prowessed of our Christian knights, with Good Sir Tancred and their little host of true believers smote the Paynim horde upon the plains of Ascalon and scattered them like straw before the winter blast that Guy of Quimper and his men-at-arms rode forth to battle for the Holy Sepulcher. Anon the battle waxed full fierce, and though our good knights rode down the infidel as oxen tread the grain upon the threshing-floor, nathless Sir Guy and his companions were separated from the main host and one by one the Christian soldiers watered the field of battle with their blood.

And now cometh such a press of Paynim warlings that Sir Guy is fairly unseated from his charger and hurled upon the earth, whereat nigh upon a hundred of the infidel were fain to do him injury, and but that the stoutness of his armor held them off were like to have slaughtered him.

Thrice did he struggle to arise, and thrice his weight of foemen bore him down, until at last, being sore beset and fearing that his time was come, he called aloud upon St. George, saying: "Ho, good Messire St. George, thou patron of true knights of Britain, come hitherward and save thy servant who is worsted by these pestilent believers in the Antichrist!"

But our good St. George answered not his prayer, nor was there any sign from heaven.

Then my Sir Guy called right lustily upon St. Bride, St. Denis and St. Cuthbert, but the sainted ones heard not his prayer, for there were one and twenty thousand men embattled in the cause that day, and one man's plaint might soothly go unheard.

Sir Guy of Quimper lifted up his voice no more, but resigned himself to Paradise, but an infidel's steel pierced through his visor bars, and he bethought him of the pleasant land of England which he should never see again and of the gentle lady whose tears and prayers were for his safety. Then did he swear a mighty oath and cry aloud: "If so be none will hear my prayer from heaven, then I renounce and cast them off, as they have cast off me, and to the Saxon godlings of my forebears I turn. Ho, ye gods and goddesses of eld, who vanished from fair England at the coming of the Cross, hear one in whose veins courses Saxon Blood, and deliver him from his plight. Name but your boon and ye shall have it, for I am most grievously afeared my hour draweth nigh, unless ye intervene."

And forthwith came a rustling o'er the plain, and from the welkin rode a shape which eye of man had not seen for many a hoary age. All nakedly it rode upon a naked horse, and at its heels came troops of hounds which ran like little pigs behind their dam, and in its hand it bore a short sword of ancient shape, the same the Saxon serfs brandished impotently against the chivalry of our good Duke of Normandy.

"Who calls?" cried out the fearsome shape, "and what shall be the guerdon of my service?"

"'Tis Guy of Quimper calls," Sir Guy made answer, "and I am sore beset. Do but deliver me from out the heathen's hand and thy fee shall be whatsoe'er thou namest."

Then up there rose a monstrous wind as cold as bleak November's, and on the wintry blast rode Dewer. Old Dewer the ghostly huntsman of the North, all followed by his troop of little dogs, and with his good sword he smote them right and left so that heads and heads fell everywhere and scarce a Paynim stayed to do him battle.

And when the heathen host was fled Old Dewer unhorsed himself and leaned above Sir Guy and raised him up and set him on his feet. But so was his aspect and so ill-favored his face that Guy of Quimper was like to have fallen down again in a swoon at sight of it but that he thought him of his oath, and making a brave face spake forth: "Name now thy boon for by the eyes of Sainted Agnes, well and truly hast thou earned it."

Whereat Old Dewer laughed full frightfully and said: "Upon thy two knees now kneel, Sir Guy of Quimper, and claim me as thy overlord and name thyself my vassal liegeman, holding thy demesne as of fee from out my hand, upon condition that thy line shall give me seigneur's rights upon their bridal night, and this accord shall bind thee and thy heirs male forever unless such time shall rise as a woman of thy house shall stare me in the face and bid me hence from out her bower, which time I trow shall not be soon." Thereat he laughed again, and the joints of Sir Guy's limbs were loosed and scarcely could he kneel erect before Old Dewer and place his hands between the monster's at what time he spake the words of fealty.

Thus came Sir Guy's deliverance from the Turk, but at such costs of tears as might almost wash out that woeful wight his guilt. For on returning to his home Sir Guy found there a son whose name was likewise called Guy; and when his marriage banns were published some one and twenty years hence, and with singing and dancing and all glad minstrelsy the bride was put to bed, lo forth from out the empty air came Dewer. Old Dewer of the North, and claimed his right of seigneury. And forth from out her bower came the bride upon the morn, her cheeks all stained with tears and her hair unloosed, and in her eyes the light of madness. Nor did she ever speak sane word again.

And when the time was come that young Sir Guy's junior brother was to wed, Old Dewer rode forth from out the North to claim his fee, and thus for generation unto generation came he forth whenever and wherever the wedding bells did chime for one who had but one small drop of Quimper's blood within his veins. But the women molested he not, for it was not according to the compact that the female line be cursed.

But those of Sir Guy's line who knew the curse forbore to wed, and some went into Holy Church, and by their prayers and ceaseless lamentations sought surcease of the curse, and others remained virgin all their days, according to the counsel of their elders, thus cheating that old fiend whose name is Dewer, surnamed the Huntsman.

And some there were who taught their brides the words of power which should win freedom from the curse, but when the time was come they all cried craven, for where beneath the star-jeweled canopy of heaven dwells a woman with resolution to stare Old Dewer in the face and bid him hie himself away?

And so throughout the length of years Old Dewer cometh ever, and when the womenfolk would drive him from their chambers their tongues cleave to the roofs of their mouths and they are speechless while he works his evil will, and never yet has there been found a bride who can retain her senses when from his foul mouth Old Dewer presses kisses on her lips.

Pray ye, for daughters, oh ye womenfolk of Quimper, and ask the Lord of His great mercy and loving-kindness to grant that ye bring no man-children into the world, for of a surety there rests upon the men of Quimper a curse the like of which was never known before.

I may add that I consider the story entirely apocryphal. There seems no doubt that the Quimper family once existed in the north of England, and it is highly probable some representative of the house went to the Crusades, since practically every able-bodied man was drained from Europe during that prolonged period of hysteria. There are also semi-authentic data showing that one or more ladies of the house went mad, but whether their seizures dated from their wedding nights or not I can not say. The chances strongly favor the theory that the monkish chronicler seized upon the incidents of the brides' insanity to point out a moral and adorn a tale, and for lack of an authentic one, provided the story from his own imagination. There was at one time a decided movement among the English peasantry toward the worship, or at least a half-affectionate tolerance, of the old Saxon gods and goddesses, and it may well be the old monk invented the tale of Sir Guy's compact with Old Dewer in order to frighten off any who expressed an opinion that the old gods might not have been the demons the Christian priests were wont to paint them.

I might also add the Quimper arms were formally struck from the rolls two centuries or more ago because of failure of heirs in the house. Whether, as the old monk intimates, this was due to most of the men taking holy orders or remaining single in secular life, there is no way of telling. I favor the theory that one or more of the numerous plagues which swept England and the Continent in the old days, coupled with the hazards of war and the sea, may have wiped the family out.

"*Eh bien*, my friend, would you not open wide those great pop-eyes of yours, could you but know what we do?" de Grandin exclaimed as he finished the letter. "*Parbleu*, those old friars, they were great hands at dressing the truth in strange garments, but this one, I damn think has recited no more than the barest of bare facts."

"All right," I agreed, "suppose he did. While I think Dr. Jacoby is unquestionably right in his surmises, suppose we grant your premises for the sake of argument, where are we? If this mysterious goblin called Dewer actually pursues all male members of old Sir Guy's family, no matter how distantly they are related to him and frightens them and their brides into fits, what are we to do about it? Is there any way we can prevent it?"

"You ask me?" he demanded sharply. "Pains of a rheumatic bullfrog, I shall say there is! Does not the never-enough-to-be-blessed old nameless monk make plain the formula in his chronicle? Does he not tell us the proviso Old Dewer himself made, that if a bride accosted by him should look him in the face and bid him be off, off he will go, and nevermore return? Name of a little blue man, can anything be simpler?"

"It certainly can," I answered. "In the first place, Rosemary Whitney was frightened almost out of her mind by the specter, or whatever it was she saw on her wedding night. We've had a man-sized job pulling her through this illness, and a second shock like that—even the bare suggestion that she face the ordeal again—might do such serious injury to her nervous system that she'd never recover.

"In the second place, if there is such a thing as this old goblin, and if it's as horrible to look at as Rosemary and Walter say, she'd faint dead away the moment she saw it, and never be able to say her little piece. No, old man, I'm afraid things aren't as simple as you seem to think."

"*Ah bah*," he held his arm up for my inspection, "has Jules de Grandin nothing up his sleeve besides his elbow, my friend? I tell you in my bag I have a trick still left which shall make a *sacré singe* of this Monsieur Dewer and send him home a wiser and much sadder demon. Yes; I have said it."

"What do you propose doing?"

"That, my friend, I shall show when the appointed time arrives. Meanwhile, let us labor with all our strength to restore Monsieur and Madame Whitney, that they may face their ordeal with calmness. Thus far their improvement has been most gratifying. Within a week we should be ready for the great experiment."

"Suppose they fail and have another relapse?" I queried. "Remember, de Grandin, this is the health and sanity of two people with which you're gambling."

"Suppose you cease from croaking like a raven suffering with laryngitis," he countered with a grin. "My throat is parched with answering your so pig-stupid objections. A glass of brandy—not too small—if you will be so kind."

7

BEYOND THE ROW OF rustling poplars growing at the garden's lower boundary the moon sailed serenely in the zenith, gilding hedge and path and formal flowerbed with argent. Still farther off, where the river ran between lush banks of woodland, a choir of little frogs—"peepers"—sang serenades to the green-skinned ladies of their choice, and in an ancient cherry tree, so old it bore no fruit, though it still put out its blossoms in the spring, a night-bird twittered sleepily.

"Ah, you are brave, *Madame*," de Grandin affirmed, "brave like the blessed Jeanne herself, and I do most solemnly declare that you shall conquer splendidly tonight."

Rosemary lifted starry eyes to his. Preceding us to the suite in Carteret Inn—the same rooms where she and Walter had lodged so happily a month before—she had doffed her traveling-dress and put on a *robe de nuit* of pale green crepe, drawing a kimono of oyster-white embroidered with gold over it. Her face was pallid as the silk of her robe, but lines of determination such as only a woman casting dice for love and happiness can know showed about her mouth as she faced Jules de Grandin. "I'm terribly afraid," she confessed in a voice that shook with nervousness, "but I'm going to do everything you tell me to, *just* as you tell me, for it's not only me I'm fighting for, it's Walter and his happiness, and, Dr. de Grandin, I love him so!"

"*Précisément*," the little Frenchman took her hand in his and raised it to his lips, "exactly, *Madame*, quite so; and I believe that all I say is for the best. Now, if you please, compose yourself—so—that is excellent." From underneath his jacket he slipped a small silver-framed photograph of Walter Whitney and set it upright on the bureau before the seated girl. "Regard it fixedly, *Madame*," he bade; "gaze on the features of your beloved and think how much you love him—exclude all other thoughts from your mind."

It was as if he had ordered a starving man to eat, or commanded one rescued from the burning desert to drain a cup of cool water. The soft, adoring look which only women wholly slaves of love can give crept into the girl's eyes as she stared intently at the picture.

"Excellent," he murmured, "*très excellent!*" For upward of a minute he stood there as if she had been his younger sister then, very softly, he commanded:

"*Madame*, you are tired, you are fatigued, you much desire sleep. Sleep—sleep, Madame Whitney, I, Jules de Grandin, order it!"

"Sleep—sleep—" softly as a summer breeze, soothingly as a mother's lullaby, his murmured admonition was repeated again and yet again.

Rosemary took no seeming notice of his words; her shining, sweet blue eyes stayed fixed upon her husband's photograph, but slowly, almost before I realized it, her white, blue-veined lids lowered, and she leaned back in her chair.

For a minute or two de Grandin regarded her solicitously, then: "Madame Whitney!" he called softly.

No answer.

"Madame Whitney, can you hear me?"

Still no response.

"*Tres bon*; she has passed into unconsciousness," he said, and, turning to the sleeping girl:

"Anon, *Madame*, there will come one of fearful aspect, who will accost you—endeavor to do you violence. Be not afraid, *ma chère*; he can not harm you. I tell you this and you must believe. You do believe me, *Madame?*"

"I believe you," she answered sleepily.

"Good; it is well. When this one comes you will know it, though you will not see him; nor will your conscious mind realize he is here. And when he comes you will open both your eyes and say—attend me carefully, for you *must* say these words—'Dewer, enemy of my husband and of my husband's blood, depart from hence, and come not near me any more; neither near me nor any woman whom my husband's kinsmen take to wife. Dewer, go hence!'

"When first he does approach you, you shall say this, and ever you will keep your widely opened eyes upon his foul face, yet see him you will not, for I command it. And if he goes not quickly from you, you shall repeat the words of power, nor shall you show him any sign of fear. You understand?"

"I understand."

"*Tres bien.* Into your bed then, and sleep and rest all peacefully until he comes."

Mechanically the girl arose, switched off the light and crossed to the bedstead, where she removed her slippers and kimono. In another moment her light even breathing sounded through the room.

I turned to descend the stairs to join Walter where he waited in the garden, but de Grandin's light touch upon my arm stayed me. "Not yet my friend," he said; "come here, we should be near at hand in case our program goes awry." He led me toward the bathroom adjoining the suite.

It seemed an hour that we waited, though actually it must have been much less. The mournful music of the frogs, the distant hooting of a motor horn, the nearer chirping of some troubled bird were all the sounds we heard except the girl's soft breathing. Then, far away, but drawing nearer by the second, came the drumming of a horse's hoofs.

I looked out the bathroom's single little window, then drew back with an involuntary cry. Across the moon's pale face, like a drifting wisp of cloud, yet racing as no tempest-chased cloud could race, there rode the squat, sinister figure of a naked horseman upon a barebacked horse.

A moment I held my breath in acute terror, and the short hairs at the back of my neck rose stiffly and bristled against my collar. Then, more dreadful than the moon-obscuring vision, there came the sound of slipping, shuffling feet upon the floor outside the room, the door swung inward, and a light, tittering laugh which seemed all malice and no mirth sounded in the quiet room. Another instant and a fetid, nauseating stench assailed my nostrils, and I turned my head away to get a breath of pure air from the open window.

But Jules de Grandin seized my shoulder and fairly dragged me to the door. My heart stood still and all the breath in my body seemed concentrated in my throat as I looked into the moonlit chamber.

Something unspeakably obscene stood sharply outlined in a ray of silver moonlight, like an actor in some music hall of hell basking in the spotlight lit from the infernal fires. Like a toad it was, but such a toad as only lives in nightmares for it was four or more feet high, entirely covered with gray-green skin which hung in wrinkles from its twisted form, save where it stretched drum-tight across a bulging, pot-like belly.

The head was more like a lizard's than a toad's, and covered with pendulous, snake-like tentacles. A row of similar excrescences decorated its upper lip, and a fringe of dangling, worm-like things hung down beneath its chin. The goggle eyes, round and protuberant, seemed to glow with an inward light, and turned their terrifying, lidless stare in all directions at once.

The monstrous thing paused tentatively in the moonlight a moment, and once again the wicked, lecherous titter came from it. "I'm here again, my sparrow," it announced in a high, cracked voice. "Last time your booby husband—*he, he!*"—again that awful laugh!—"disturbed us at our tryst, but he'll not hamper us tonight—the beaten dog avoids his master!"

Again, seeming to struggle with some infirmity, the hideous thing lurched forward, but I had a feeling as I watched that those splayed, bandy legs could straighten instantly, and the whole flabby-looking body galvanize into frightful activity if need for action came.

Rosemary slept calmly, her head pillowed on one bent arm, and I heard de Grandin muttering mixed prayers and curses in mingled French and English as we waited her waking.

The visitant was almost at the bedside when Rosemary awakened. Rising as though in nowise terrified at the awful thing bending over her, she stared it boldly, calmly, in the face, no tremor of eyelid or twitch of lip betraying either fear or surprise.

"Dewer, enemy of my husband and of my husband's blood, depart from hence and come not near me any more; neither near me nor any woman whom my husband's kinsmen take to wife. Dewer, go hence!" she said.

The monster's webbed, clawed hands, already stretched forth to seize her, stopped short as if they had encountered an invisible wall of steel, and if such a thing were possible, its hideous face turned still more hideous. When pleased anticipation lit up its fearsome features they were terrible as the horror of a grisly dream, but when rage and unbelieving fury set on them the sight was too awful to look on. I hid my eyes behind my upraised hands.

But I did not stop my ears, so I heard it cry in a raging, squawking voice:

"Nay, nay, ye're feared o' me; ye dare not bid me hence! Look, ye soft, pink thing, 'tis Dewer stands beside ye; Old Dewer o' the North, at sight of whom men creep upon their bellies and women lose their senses. Ye dare not stare me in the face and bid me hence! Look ye, and be afraid!"

"Dewer," the soft calm words might have been addressed to a servant dismissed for pilfering from the pantry. "Dewer, enemy of my husband and of my husband's blood, depart from hence and come not near me any more!"

A skirling shriek like half-a-dozen bagpipes played out of tune at once came from the monster's mouth, and with a stamp of its wide, webbed foot, it turned and left the room. A moment later I heard the muffled beating of a horse's hoofs, and peering through the window saw a shade flit through past the moon.

"And now, my friend, let us, too, depart," de Grandin ordered as he tiptoed from the bathroom.

By Rosemary's bed he paused a moment while he whispered: "One comes soon, *ma chère*, who brings you happiness: happiness and love. Awake and greet him, and may the mellow beams of the honeymoon forever light you on your path to blissfulness. *Adieu*."

"She waits above, *mon vieux*," he called to Walter as we passed through the garden. "Be good to her, *mon fils*, her happiness is in your hands: Guard well your trust."

He was oddly silent on the homeward drive. Once or twice he heaved a sentimental sigh: As we approached my house he frankly wiped his eyes.

"What's the matter, old chap?" I asked. "Aren't you satisfied with your work?"

He seemed to waken from a revery. "Satisfied?" he murmured almost dreamily. "*Ha*—yes. I wonder if she sometimes thinks of me within the quiet of her cloister, and of the days we wandered hand in hand beside the River Loire?"

"Who—Rosemary?" I asked, amazed.

"Who?—what?—*pardieu*, I do wander in my thoughts!" he cried. "I am asleep with both eyes open, Friend Trowbridge. Come, a quarter-pint of brandy will restore me!"

Daughter of the Moonlight

T HE ANNUAL MIDSUMMER LADIES' night at the Kobbskill Country Club
proved a pretty party. The white walls of the clubhouse, reared in the severe
style of architecture affected by the early Dutch settlers, shone like an illuminated monument in the dusky blue of the July night, lights blazed at every
window, and colored bulbs decorated the overhanging roofs of the broad piaz-
zas which stretched along the front and rear of the building. The artistically
parked grounds near the house shone with Chinese lanterns which gleamed
with rose, blue, violet, gold and jade, rivaling the brilliance of the summer stars.
Jazz blared in the commodious ballroom and echoed from the big, yellow-and-
red-striped marquee set up by the first green. Brilliant as the plumage of birds
of paradise, the light silken dresses of the women made bright highlights in the
night, while the somber black and white of their escorts' costumes furnished a
pleasing contrast and made the chiaroscuro of color the more vivid. Three of
us—Jules de Grandin, our host, Colonel Patrick FitzPatrick, and I—sat on the
front veranda and rocked comfortably in wide wicker chairs, the ice in our tall
glasses tinkling pleasantly.

"*Mordieu, mes amis,*" the little Frenchman exclaimed enthusiastically, sucking appreciatively from the twin straws in his long glass. "*C'est une scène très
charmante!* It is so—how do you say?—so—ah, *mort de ma vie, les belles créa-
tures!*" His gaze rested on a pair of girls who paused momentarily beneath the
luminous drops of the crystal chandelier hanging from the porch roof at the
head of the stairs.

Limned in vivid silhouette against the background of smalt-blue sky and
black-green evergreens, the girls were oddly alike, yet curiously unlike. Both
were gowned in green, tall and slender with the modernly fleshless figure which
simulates boyishness more than femininity; both had small, clear-carved features; both wore their hair cut close at the back, rather long and prettily waved
at the front; both possessed complexions of milky whiteness, but one was

yellow-haired and violet-eyed, while the short-shorn locks of the other were red as rose-gold alloyed with copper, and her eyes, long, black-fringed and obliquing slightly downward at their outer corners, were green as moss-agate.

"*Parbleu*," the Frenchman swore delightedly, "they are like a *boutonnière*—she of the golden hair is like an *asphodèle*—a slender daffodil that sways and dances in the evening breeze; while she of the ruddy tresses, *morbleu*, she is a poppy, a glorious, glowing-red poppy to steal men's senses away, no less!"

"Humph," Colonel FitzPatrick returned, "you're nearer right than you think, old-timer. She's all of that, and then some."

"Ah, you know her?" de Grandin asked with interest.

"Ought to," FitzPatrick laughed. "The yellow-haired one's my daughter Josephine; the other's my niece, Dolores. She's lived with us since she was a kid of ten, and a queer lot she is, too."

"But certainly," the Frenchman agreed with a vigorous nod, "one with hair and eyes like hers could be no ordinary mortal. She is a *fée*, a pixy out of some story-book, a—"

"I'm not so sure of that," the other interrupted with a chuckle. "Sometimes I've thought her an imp out of quite a different place. She's been off to school—so has Josephine—for the past two years; but unless she's changed a lot, some one's in for a bad time before she goes back."

He paused a moment, drawing thoughtfully at his cigar, then: "They say Cleopatra and Helen of Troy, not to mention Helen of Tyre, had hair of that odd, metallic red; I'm inclined to credit the legends. Dolores is the sort who'd go to any lengths for a thrill. I can imagine her on the throne of an Eastern despot administering poison to her unsuspecting lovers just to see 'em squirm as they died, and having a few dozen assorted captives disemboweled to find out what made 'em tick. Pity, or even decent consideration for others' feelings just don't exist when her curiosity or convenience are concerned."

The girls seemed engaged in some sort of argument, the red-haired one striving to interest the blond in some plan, the yellow-haired girl stubbornly refusing. At length, with a shrug betraying mingled annoyance and resignation, the blond girl gave in, and they passed toward the dancing marquee arm in arm.

"There you are," FitzPatrick grumbled, "never knew it to fail; Josephine's got plenty of will of her own where I'm concerned—where anyone else is, for that matter—but Dolores can twist her round her finger any time she wishes."

We rocked, smoked and cooled ourselves with repeated orders from the club steward's stock, played several rubbers of bridge, then returned to the porch for refreshments. By two o'clock the cars began leaving the parking-lot, and by a quarter of three the home and grounds were all but deserted.

"Confound it," Colonel FitzPatrick grumbled, "where the deuce are those hare-brained girls? Don't they know I'd like to be home by daylight?"

Interrogation of several homeward-bound couples failed to elicit information concerning the girls' whereabouts, and our host had lost his temper. "Let's go round 'em up," he proposed. "I'm betting we'll find 'em lallygagging with a pair of shiny-haired sheiks in one of those fool summer-houses!"

H OWEVER WELL THE COLONEL knew his women-folk, his prediction proved a least half-way wrong before we had walked a hundred yards from the clubhouse. From a shaded bower of honeysuckle, ideally adapted for the exchange of youthful vows of undying affection, the sound of a woman sobbing piteously attracted our attention; as we approached, the green gown and yellow hair of Josephine FitzPatrick told us half our quest was over.

"Why, Jo, what's the matter?" Colonel FitzPatrick asked as he paused beside his daughter. His assumed brusqueness evaporated as he saw her abject misery, and real concern was in his voice as he continued: "Here all alone? Where's Martin? I thought I saw him here tonight."

"He was—he is—oh, I don't know where he is!" the girl returned with the inconsistency of overmastering grief. "He's somewhere with Dolores, and—oh, I wish I were dead!"

"There, daughter, there," FitzPatrick patted the girl's gleaming bare shoulder with awkward tenderness, "tell Dad about it. It can't be so very bad. Why, only last week Martin asked me for you, and—"

"That's just it" the girl interrupted with a high, half-hysterical wail. "Dolores knew he wanted me and I wanted him—she didn't want him, really; she just wanted to take him from me to show she could do it. It's always been so, Daddy. When we were little girls she always took the doll I loved the most, and broke it when she tired of it. She beat me for honors at school when she heard I was out for the history prize; I never had a beau she didn't take away from me; now she's taken Martin, and—oh, Dad, I never wanted anything in all my life as I want him. Make her give him back! She'll take him as she took my dolls, and—and she'll break him when she tires of him, too; she'll never, never give him back to me. Oh, I hate her, I *hate* her!"

"Now, Jo—" her father began awkwardly, but:

"I know what you're going to say!" she blazed. "You're going to tell me she's an orphan, hasn't anyone to love or care for her but us, and I must give in to her—give her everything I prize most, because her father and mother are dead! She got away with everything I wanted most on those grounds when we were children; but she shan't have Martin, I tell you; she *shan't!* I love him, and I want him, and I won't let her have him. I'll kill her first!"

"Go get your things," FitzPatrick interrupted authoritatively. "I'll bring Dolores in—and Martin, too." He turned away with a stern, set face and tramped purposefully toward the deeper shadow of the evergreen grove.

"Everything she says is true," he confided as we marched along. "Dolores came to us, when her parents were killed in a railway accident in Virginia. She was only ten then, and was the sole survivor of the wreck. Her father was my younger brother; her mother—humph, well, none of us knew much of her. Jim met her down South somewhere while he was heading a surveying crew. Wrote us all sorts of glowing letters about her, but I never met her—Dad absolutely forbade the match, you see, and when they were married in spite of him, refused to see either of them. Jim got it in his head I was opposed to it, too; so when Father died and cut him out of his will, he'd have nothing to do with me, wouldn't even answer my letters when I wrote and offered to share the estate half and half with him. Then he and Giatanas were killed, and I took Dolores to live with us. She's co-legatee in my will with Josephine, and I've tried to be a father to her, but—well, there have been times when I thought I'd underwritten too big an issue."

"Giatanas," de Grandin repeated softly. "An odd name for an American woman, is it not, *Monsieur*? What was her surname, if you recall?"

"She didn't have any, as far as I know," FitzPatrick returned. "That's where the difficulties arose. She wasn't an American. She was a Spanish Gipsy. The seventh daughter of the queen of the tribe, who claimed to be a seeress, and all that sort of tosh. Jim met her when his crew came on their camp, and simply went blotto over her at first glance. I don't know much about the Gipsies, but I've been told they're not Christians. At any rate, Giatanas and he were married by the tribal rite, not by a clergyman, and I suppose their marriage wasn't absolutely legal, but—"

A crashing, as of some heavy-footed animal, sounded in the undergrowth of a near-by pine copse.

"Who—what the devil's that?" Colonel FitzPatrick demanded, striding belligerently toward the disturbance, "Come out o' that, whoever you are, or I'll come in after you. Now, then, come on—good God, *look!*"

Parting the long-needled branches with blind, groping hands, a young man in evening dress stumbled and staggered into the pool of luminance shed by a Chinese lantern. His collar and tie were undone, his shirt broken loose from its studs, his clothing in utter disarray. Blood streamed over his chin in a steady spate, staining his linen and dripping on the pine needles at his feet. At first I thought his lips parted in a drunken grin, but as he reeled nearer I gave an exclamation of horror. The grimace I had thought voluntary resulted from dreadful mutilation. Where the scarf-skin and mucous membrane joined, his lips had been cut away in two semicircular sections, like a pair of parentheses laid horizontally, revealing the white, staring teeth beneath and drenching his chin and breast with a spilth of ruby blood.

"Martin, boy, whatever is the matter—how did it happen?" FitzPatrick asked in a shrill, half-unbelieving whisper.

The young man gave a slavering unintelligible answer, waving his arms wildly toward the clearing behind as his mutilated lips refused to form the words, and goggling at us with rolling, horrified eyes. His impotence and fright, his inability to speak and the wondering horror in his dazed eyes sickened me. It was like witnessing the agony of some gentle, dumb animal, tortured where it had thought to find kindness.

"Quick, Friend Trowbridge," de Grandin cried as he snatched the handkerchief from his breast pocket and deftly folded it into a pack for the boy's maimed mouth, "help me get him to the house; we must take immediate measures, for his coronary vessels are cut—his hemorrhage is dangerous. Let Monsieur Fitz-Patrick seek his niece, here is work for us!"

While we clawed through the meager supplies of the club's first-aid kit an attendant telephoned Harrisonville for an ambulance and reported that the big emergency car which Coroner Martin, in his private capacity of funeral director, kept available for service, was already on its way, for the city hospitals resolutely refused to send their cars beyond the limits of the municipality.

"*Dieu de Dieu*," the Frenchman swore feverishly, "if we could but obtain a styptic, we might make progress, but this gauze, this adhesive tape, these prepared bandages—what use are they? On the field of battle, yes; in such a case as this, where we must ever consider the coming operation which is to restore the young *monsieur's* countenance, *non*. Ah, *parbleu*, I have it! Quick, Friend Trowbridge, rush, run, hasten, fly to the so excellent chef and obtain from him some gelatin and a pan of boiling water. Yes, that will do most nobly, I apprehend."

Working quickly, he made a paste of the gelatin and water, then applied the transparent mixture to young Faber's torn lips. To my surprise it acted almost as well as collodion, and in a few minutes the entire flow of blood was staunched. We had hardly finished when Martin's ambulance drew up before the door, its powerful eight cylinder engine panting like a live thing with the strain to which it had been put in making the ten-mile run. Assisted by the genial mortician, who had dropped his other work to superintend the emergency trip, we bundled the injured man into a chair-cot and bore him to the car.

"*Mon Dieu*, my hat!" de Grandin wailed as I was about to leap into the ambulance and slam the door. "Quick, my friend, get it for me, if you please—it cost me fifty francs!"

I hustled to the check room to retrieve the missing headgear, and as I hurried out again I caught a glimpse of Josephine and Dolores FitzPatrick awaiting the colonel and his car.

Josephine, tear-scarred and tremulous, had evidently been upbraiding her cousin in no uncertain terms, but the red-haired maiden was calm beneath the reproaches.

"Martin?" I heard her exclaim in a cool, ironical voice. "Why, Jo, dear, I don't want him; you're welcome to him, I'm sure."

Something like a draft of winter air piercing through the sultry summer night seemed to chill my spine as I listened. Was it just a crack-brained fancy that made me think her thin, red lips were colored with a smear less innocent than any brand of rouge obtainable at drug stores?

THE CARELESSNESS OF A local fish-dealer in failing to provide adequate refrigeration for his finny stock occasioned a young epidemic of mild ptomaine poisonings, and I was kept busy prescribing Rochelle salt and administering hypodermic doses of morphine throughout the following day. By dinnertime I was in a state bordering on collapse, but Jules de Grandin was fresh as the newly starched linen he had donned for the evening meal.

"What have you been up to?" I asked as we enjoyed our coffee on the side veranda.

"*Eh bien*, three stories; no less," he answered with a chuckle.

"*What?*"

"Three stories, I did say," he returned. "Upon the third floor of Mercy Hospital, with the young Monsieur Faber. Jules de Grandin is clever. The wounds upon the young *monsieur's* face already make excellent progress, there is no infection, and all is prepared for me to graft flesh from his leg upon his mangled lips. When I have done, only a little, so small mustache will be needed to hide his scars from the world. Yes, it is an altogether satisfactory case."

"How the deuce did he receive that appalling hurt?" I wondered. "It looked almost as though some ferocious beast had worried him. But that's absurd, of course. There isn't any game more savage than a rabbit to be found in this section of Jersey."

"U'm," de Grandin sipped a mouthful of coffee slowly and beat a devil's tattoo on the arm of his chair with small, slender fingers. "One wonders."

"This one doesn't—not tonight, at any rate," I answered. "I'm too tired to think. It's been a hard day, and tomorrow looks like another; I'll turn in, if you don't mind."

"Happy dreams," he bade with a wave of his hand as I rose to go inside.

PERHAPS IT WAS THE salad I had eaten, perhaps the broiling heat of the July night which made me so thirsty; at any rate, I woke with patched tongue and paper-dry lips some time between midnight and dawn and reached sleepily for the carafe of chilled water on my bedside table. I upturned the chromium-plated bottle, but no cooling trickle of liquid reached my glass. "Hang it!" I muttered as I sought my slippers and started for the bathroom to replenish the exhausted water supply.

"*Dieu, non;* I shall make no treaty with such as you!" I heard de Grandin whisper as I shuffled past his door on my return trip. "Away, hell-spawn, I enter no engagements—"

I paused before his door, wondering whether it were better to waken him or let his nightmare pass, when a further sound came from beyond the panels—a queer, baffling sound, like something scratching and clawing at the stout copper screen at the window. I hesitated no longer.

"Good Lord!" I exclaimed as I entered the bedroom. Jules de Grandin lay on his bed, his limbs taut and rigid, his fingers clutching at the linen. Beyond the screen, clawing at the copper mesh with the fury of a savage beast, was the biggest owl I had ever seen. With beak and talon it fought the woven wire, and in its glowing, yellow eyes there blazed a steady glare of concentrated malignancy and hatred.

A moment I stared at the uncanny thing, completely taken aback; then, acting without conscious thought, I hurried to the window and dashed the contents of my water-bottle full in its evil face. "Be off!" I ordered sharply. The visitant's fiery eyes disappeared as though they had been two glowing coals extinguished by the flood of water, and with a scream of mingled rage and fright it flapped away in the surrounding shadows.

"*Cordieu!*" de Grandin woke with a start and sat bolt-upright. "I have had a most exceedingly evil dream, Friend Trowbridge. I dreamed a mighty owl, well-nigh as great as Uncle Sam's so glorious eagle, came clawing at the window, and bade me keep darkly secret a fact I discovered today. I refused its order, and it made at me with beak and claws, as if it were a devil-bird from hell's own subcellar!"

"H'm, the devil part of it was probably a dream," I answered, "but the owl was certainly real enough. The biggest one I ever saw was scratching at the screen like a thing possessed when I came down the hall a moment ago. I thought—"

"Ha, do you tell me? And where is it now?" he interrupted.

"Drying itself, I imagine."

"You mean—"

"I didn't know what else to do to discourage it, so I flung a quart or so of water on it."

"Oh, Trowbridge, my good, my incomparable Trowbridge!" he applauded. "You know not what you do; but always you do the right thing. Did you also address it?"

"Yes," I grinned sheepishly. "I said, 'Be off!'"

"*Mort d'un rat mort!*" he cried, leaping from the bed and flinging both arms about me. "You are priceless, my old one. You are perfection's own self, no less!"

"What the deuce—"

"You did perfectly. If it were a physical, natural bird, which I greatly doubt, the dousing you gave it was enough to discourage its ardor, beyond dispute; if it were what I damnation suspect, the baptism and your unequivocal command to take itself elsewhere were precisely what was required to rid us of its presence. Oh, my inestimable one, if I could be as sure of myself in my wisdom as you are in your ignorance, I should esteem Jules de Grandin more highly."

"Thank heaven you aren't, then," I countered with a laugh. "You're bad enough as it is; if you admired yourself any more there'd be no living with you!"

"Bête!" he cried. "I have killed for less than that; the least I should do is challenge you to mortal combat and—"

"Confound it!" I interrupted. "And at this unholy hour, too!" My bedroom telephone had commenced ringing with all the infernal insistence of which those instruments of torture are capable when we are blissfully asleep.

"Hullo, Dr. Trowbridge," came the challenge over the wire; "FitzPatrick speaking. Can you come over at once? It's Dolores—she's gone!"

"Gone?" I echoed. "Why, how do you mean? Have you notified the police—"

"Hell's fire, no! This is a case for a physician. She had some sort of seizure this afternoon and—"

"All right," I broke in, "we'll be right out."

Ten minutes later de Grandin and I were speeding toward Seven Pines, FitzPatrick's palatial country seat. [#]

The place was in a turmoil when we reached it. Lights blazed in the windows from top to bottom; the colonel, his daughter and the servants trod on each others' heels in aimless circling quests for the missing girl; everywhere was bustle, confusion and futility.

"Hanged if I know what it was," the colonel confessed as we shook hands. "Dolores had been acting queerly ever since last night when young Faber was injured. By the way, how is he, Doctor de Grandin?"

"Excellent, all things considered," the Frenchman replied. "But it is of Mademoiselle Dolores we were speaking. What of her?"

"Well, after we found Martin Faber last night I beat my way through the pines to look for her, and found her stretched out on the ground unconscious. It gave me a shock—I thought she might he dead or injured, but just as I scooped to pick her up she came round, rose without assistance, and walked to the house with me as coolly as though falling in a faint was an every-night occurrence with her."

"Tiens, and was it?" de Grandin asked.

"Not that I know," FitzPatrick answered shortly. "I asked her if she'd seen Martin, and she said she had.

"'Was he all right?' I wanted to know, and:

"'As right as usual—he's always something of an ass, isn't he, Uncle Pat?' she answered.

"'Perhaps you'd be interested if I told you he's been terribly hurt, had both lips almost torn off,' I snapped.

"'Perhaps I should, but I'm not,' she replied as cool as you please, and that's all I got from her.

"'You're inhuman!' I accused.

"'So I've been told,' she admitted.

"After that we didn't speak till we reached the clubhouse.

"I think she and Josephine had a pretty warm set-to later, for both of 'em seemed rather huffy when we drove home, and Dolores began acting queerly this morning."

"How, by example?" de Grandin asked.

"Oh, she seemed unduly depressed, even for one of her moody temperament, wouldn't eat anything, and seemed not to hear when anyone spoke to her. Just before dinner she was sitting on the porch, looking down the lawn, but not seeming to see anything, when all of a sudden I noticed her left foot was twitching and shaking like—" He paused for an adequate illustration, then: "As though a galvanic current had been applied to it.

"I looked at her, wondering what the matter was, and within a moment the spasm seemed to spread all over her. She'd shake as though with a chill, then seem to relax, go limp as a damp cloth, then tremble more violently than ever. Before I could reach her she'd slipped from her chair to the floor and lay there, twitching and trembling like a mechanical figure when the clockwork is almost run down. Her eyes were partly opened, but the eyeballs were turned up under the upper lids so the pupils were invisible. She seemed wholly unconscious when I picked her up."

"Great heavens!" I exclaimed, "that has all the earmarks of an epilep—"

"*Zut!*" de Grandin cut me short. "What happened further, if you please, Monsieur?"

"That's all. We put her to bed, and she seemed to lapse into a natural sleep. I hadn't planned on calling you until tomorrow morning; but a few minutes ago when Josephine went in to see how she was, we found she'd gone. We've searched everywhere, but she seems to have evaporated. If we'd only thought to have somebody stay with her, we might—"

"Pardon me, sir," FitzPatrick's chauffeur suggested, pausing respectfully by his employer's elbow, "I've been thinking Bruno might be able to help us here; he's a hunter, and his scent is keen, even if he hasn't been trained to track people."

"Nonsense—" the colonel began, but:

"Excellent, my old one, your idea is entirely sound," de Grandin applauded. "Obtain from Mademoiselle's wardrobe a pair of shoes, and let the dog smell them thoroughly. Then, by happy chance, if the others have not already obscured her tracks with their fruitless searchings, we may be led to her."

The dog, a long-legged, rangy hound, was brought from the stable, given the scent from a pair of Dolores' bedroom mules, and led out by the chauffeur. Slowly the man and beast walked round the house in ever-widening circles. The hound's nose was to the ground most of the time, but every now and then he would raise his muzzle and sniff the upper air as though to clear his nostrils of a confusing medley of scents. They had almost completed their twelfth circuit when the dog abruptly jerked forward against his leash, thrust his muzzle forward and gave a deep, belling bay. Next instant, dragging himself free, he set out toward a rise of ground behind FitzPatrick's grove, his gray-and-brown body extended, shoulders and hind-quarters moving rhythmically as he galloped,

"After him, Friend Trowbridge!" de Grandin cried. "He has the scent, he will assuredly take us to her."

Stumbling, scrambling over the uneven ground of the wood, we followed the dog, entered the deeper shadow of the grove, then paused irresolute, for all trace of our canine guide had vanished.

"*Sacré bleu*," de Grandin swore, "we are at fault. Here, *mon brave*, here, noble animal!" He put his fingers to his lips sounded a shrill whistle.

Answer was almost immediate. From the farther side of the wood the hound came slinking, his ears and muzzle drooping, tail tucked pitifully between his legs. Like a frightened child the beast cowered by de Grandin's legs and whimpered in abject terror.

"Huh," exclaimed the chauffeur, "th' fool dawg's lost th' scent!"

The little Frenchman slipped his finger under the animal's collar and advanced slowly toward the clearing beyond. "What lies yonder?" he asked, turning to the chauffeur.

"Th' ol' graveyard," returned the other. "Colonel FitzPatrick tried to buy it when he took over th' estate, but th' heirs wouldn't sell. Our land stops at th' boundary o' th' woods, sir."

"Eh, do you tell me?" de Grandin answered absently, patting the whimpering hound's back gently. "It may well be our good beast has found the trail only too well, and returned to us for reasons of prudence, *mon ami*. Look, what is that?" He pointed upward.

Clear-cut against the faint luminosity of the summer sky, a great, black-winged bird went sailing on outstretched, almost motionless pinions, circled slowly a moment, then swooped downward to the fenced-in close of the old, dismantled burying-ground which lay before us. Almost at once another spectral shape, and still another, followed the first in ghostly single file.

"H'm, they look like owls to me," the chauffeur returned, "but they're bigger than any owls I ever seen. Jiminy crickets, there's three of 'em! Never seen nothin' like it before."

"Let us hope you may not do so again," the little Frenchman answered. "Come, let us go."

"Not quittin', are yuh?" the chauffeur asked, half contemptuously.

The Frenchman made no reply as, the hound's collar still clutched in his hand, he strode toward the house.

Once inside the lighted hall, he swept the circle of servants with an appraising eye. "Is there a Catholic present?" he demanded.

"Sure, I'm one" volunteered the cook, on whose countenance appeared the map of County Kerry. "Wot ov it?"

"Very good. Will you be good enough to lend me your rosary, and a flask of holy water, as well, if you happen to possess it?" he returned.

"Sure, ye can have 'em, an' welcome," she answered, "but what ye're afther wantin' ov 'em is more'n I can see."

Two steps carried de Grandin to her side. "What is today, *Madame?*" he asked, staring her levelly in the eye.

"Why, sure, an' it's July thirty-first—no, 'tis August first," she answered wonderingly.

"*Précisément.* In France we call this day *la fête de Saint Pierre-ès-Liens.* You know it as the feast of Saint Peter's Chains, or—"

"Glory be to God! 'Tis Lammas!" she cried, terrified understanding shining in her face. "Wuz it fer this th' pore young gur-rl wuz stole away?"

"I would not go so far," de Grandin answered, "but a moment since the hound came whimpering and trembling to my knee after he had been to the ancient graveyard which lies beyond *Monsieur le Colonel's* woodland, and we did see three monster owls, with yellow, sulfurous eyes, fly past the moon. May I have the blessèd articles?"

"Indade ye shall!" she told him heartily. "An' it's th' brave lad ye are to venture in that haunted place. Faith, Bridget O'Flaherty wouldn't do it if th' Howly Father stood at her elbow, wid th' whole College o' Cardinals behint im! Ouch, God an' th' Howly Saints preserve this house tonight!" She signed herself reverently with the cross as she hastened to procure the rosary and blessèd water.

ONCE MORE WE FORCED our way through FitzPatrick's wood lot. Wrapped about his right wrist de Grandin wore the cook's rosary like a bracelet, in his left hand he bore a half-pint flask adorned with a label assuring the beholder that it contained "Golden Wedding Rye, 50 Years Old, Bottled in Bond," but which actually contained nothing more lawless than water from the font of St.

Joseph's church. At the Frenchman's heels I marched, a double-barreled shotgun cocked and ready, that we might be prepared to meet the foe on ghostly or terrestrial planes.

"Careful, Friend Trowbridge," he warned, "we do approach." Stepping cautiously from the shadow of the oak trees, he advanced stealthily toward the tumbledown wooden fence enclosing the disused cemetery.

Almost as we emerged from the wood there came a queer, high, piping sound, a sort of sustained whistle, so shrill as to be almost inaudible, yet so piercing in quality that it stabbed the ear as a dentist's whirling drill bites the tortured tooth. Up, wheeling blindly in ever-widening circles, then pouncing forward like birds of prey came a trio of great, sable bats, squeaking viciously as they swooped at our faces.

"Ha, evil ones, you find us not unprepared!" the little Frenchman whispered between drawn lips. "Behold this sign, ye minions of the dark—look, and be afraid!" He raised his bead-bound wrist, displaying the miniature crucifix which swung from the rosary, and at the same time thrust his left hand forward, sending a shower of holy water toward the flying things.

The bats were larger than any creatures of the kind I had ever seen; in my excitement it seemed to me they were as big as full-grown rats, with wing-spread of a yard or more, and their little, evil eyes glinted with a red and fiery malevolence as they swooped. I raised the gun and loosed both barrels at them, then broke the lock and jammed fresh cartridges feverishly into the smoking breech.

"*Holà*," de Grandin cried exultingly, "you or I, or both of us, have put them to rout, Friend Trowbridge; see they are gone!"

They were. Look as I would, I could espy no sign of the uncouth things.

"Why, I must have literally blown them to pieces," I exclaimed.

"U'm, perhaps," he conceded. "Let us see what further we may see."

Dolores FitzPatrick lay supine upon a sunken grave, her head pressed tight against the weather-gnawed tombstone, her feet toward the lower end of the sepulcher. Stretched to utmost length from her shoulders, her arms extended up and outward, while her nether limbs were thrust out stiffly at acute angles from her hips, making the design of a white St. Andrew's cross upon the mossy graveyard turf. Briars and clutching undergrowth had ripped her flimsy silken nightrobe to tatters so that scarce a shred remained to clothe her, her slippers had been shed somewhere in her flight, and stones and brambles had bruised and torn her tender feet; more than one thorn-gash scarred her slim white body, and a wisp of short, ruddy hair lay across her forehead like a bleeding wound.

"Good heavens!" I cried, dropping to my knees and taking her wrists between my fingers. "She's"—I paused, put my ear to her still breast, then looked up at the Frenchman with dawning horror in my eyes—"she's gone, de

Grandin; we're too late. The poor child must have wandered here in her delirium and fallen on this grave in a fresh seizure. See her thumbs!"

There was no mistaking the diagnostic sign; her thumbs were bent transversely her palms and the fingers clutched them with all the avid tensity of rigor mortis.

"Epilepsy, no doubt of it," I diagnosed. "The history of her case as detailed by FitzPatrick is absolutely unmistakable. The poor girl's lived beneath this shadow for years without suspecting it—that was the reason for her 'queerness and perversity' that made her hardly tolerable. She was at the dangerous age, and when the blow fell it crushed her, absolutely."

The Frenchman knelt beside her, felt her wrist and temples, and listened at her breast, then rose with what seemed to me a strangely callous indifference. "Give me the gun," he ordered as he shed his jacket and draped it over Dolores' all but nude remains. "Do you take her up and bear her to the house, my friend.

"Have you read your Bible much of late?" he asked apropos of nothing as I trudged in his wake with the lovely body in my arms.

"My Bible?"

"*Précisément.* That portion which deals with those possessed of devils?"

"No—why d'ye ask?"

"I hardly know myself," he answered almost absently, holding back a branch from my path; "it was but a thought which came to me; perhaps it is of little value, perhaps, again, it my have application here. If so, I shall explain when the time has come."

THE FIRST FAINT SIGN came as I strode up the graveled walk toward FitzPatrick's house. Just as I was about to mount the lower step of the veranda I felt a slight stirring, the faintest suggestion of fluttering motion in my burden. I took the short flight in two giant leaps, and bent to examine her countenance in the porch light's glare. There was no doubt about it. She had relaxed her clutching hold upon her thumbs, and her lower jaw, which had fallen, had once more raised itself, closing the mouth and giving to the thin, pale face a look of natural sleep. Even as I gazed incredulously into her countenance her bosom trembled and a faint sigh escaped her.

"De Grandin!" I cried. "De Grandin, she's alive!"

He nodded shortly. "I thought as much," he said; then, his manner as professionally impersonal as though he were visiting physician at a charity hospital: "See that the blankets on her bed are well warmed, and that no disturbing noises are permitted near her room. I would suggest we administer the Brown-Séquard prescription; it is often efficacious."

HOWEVER MUCH IT LACKED in sympathy, his advice was medically sound. Within a week Dolores FitzPatrick appeared quite normal. In ten days more, against my protests, she had renewed her febrile social life, driving at breakneck speed along the country roads, attending all-night dances, scattering a trail of badly damaged masculine hearts behind her, and, worst of all, indulging in the villainous poison which passed for whisky among the younger set.

The Frenchman's lack of interest in the case amazed me. Curious as a child, he was ordinarily wont to give my cases as close attention as though they were his own, and his weakness for a pretty face was a standing joke between us, yet in Dolores FitzPatrick, beautiful, heartless and fascinating as Circe's own seductive self, he seemed to take no interest.

"Well," I announced as I entered the study one scorching night some three weeks later, "perhaps you'll be interested now. She's gone. She died an hour ago with cardiac hypertrophy; I knew she'd burn herself out."

For the first time his mask of indifference slipped. "Who will have the funeral—Monsieur Martin?" he asked.

"Yes, I've already made out the death certificate for him."

He reached for the 'phone and called the coroner's number. "It is a most strange request I have to make, *Monsieur*," he confessed when the connection had been made, "but you and I have been associated before. You will understand I do not act from idle curiosity. Will you permit that I be present while you embalm Mademoiselle FitzPatrick's body? You may consider it impertinent, but—*nom d'un chou-fleur*, do you tell me? But you will not honor it, surely? *Dieu de Dieu*, you will?"

"What now?" I asked as he put back the receiver and turned a blank face to me.

"A so strange testament has been found in Mademoiselle Dolores' room," he answered. "In it she does expressly request that she be not embalmed. You attended her, my friend, you have authority; will you not prevail on Monsieur FitzPatrick to have an autopsy performed?"

"I can't," I told him. "The cause of death was perfectly obvious; I've seen it coming for days, and warned FitzPatrick of it. He'd think me crazy."

"I shall think you worse, if you refuse."

"I'm sorry," I returned. "There's no earthly excuse for a post-mortem; I wouldn't think of asking one."

And there the matter rested.

THE LAST HUMMING ECHO of the final gong-stroke spent itself in the still summer air, and like the faintest whisper of a breeze among half-dried leaves came the subdued rustle which betokened turning heads and craning necks— that gesture which even well-bred people make at such a time.

A momentary congestion at the church door while six frock-coated and perspiring gentlemen bent their backs to the unaccustomed task, then:

"I am the Resurrection and the Life, saith the Lord: he that believeth in me, though he were dead, yet shall he live. . . ."

Dr. Bentley's resonant voice sounded as he marched slowly up the aisle before the flower-decked casket. "I know that my Redeemer liveth and that He shall stand at the latter day upon the earth . . ."

The afternoon sun shone softly through the stained glass windows and glinted on the polished mahogany of the pews. Here and there it picked out spots of color, a flower, a woman's hat or a man's tie. Through a memorial panel to the right of the chancel a single beam of tinted light gleamed dully on the silver mountings of the casket. The majestic office for the burial of the dead proceeded to benediction, the choir's voices rose in "Lead, Kindly Light," drowning out the muffled boom of the traffic in the street beyond.

As the organ's final diminuendo vibrated to silence, the pallbearers rose to their appointed task and once more the solemn procession passed through the center aisle. A momentary lull came in the outside traffic as the suave mortician appeared on the church steps; then a motor purred to the curb, the hearse moved forward, and the procession was on its way.

Jules de Grandin tossed his burned-out cigarette from the window of Coroner Martin's limousine and gazed in undisguised admiration at the mortician. "You are marvelous, no less, *Monsieur*," he assured him. "In my own country, and anywhere in Europe, Mademoiselle FitzPatrick would have been consigned to the grave in four-and-twenty hours. We do not embalm there. Here, under similar conditions, you present her at the church three hot summer days after death as though she lay in natural sleep. Tell me," he leaned forward eagerly, "is it perhaps that you ignored the injunctions of her testament and embalmed her body after all?"

Martin shook his head. "Did you notice the casket?" he asked.

"It was a most beautiful piece of furniture," the Frenchman answered with non-committal politeness.

"I wasn't referring to its appearance, but to its construction," the other returned. "The outside case is mahogany, carefully glued and jointed, practically a water- and air-tight box. Inside is a shell technically known as an 'inner sealer,' a separate copper case with an hermetically sealed full-length top of plate glass. This, in turn, is lined with satin upholstery. Before we laid the young lady in this inner casket we put upward of a hundred briquettes of carbon dioxide snow—the 'dry ice' used by confectioners to keep ice cream hard for long periods—under the satin trimmings. Then we fastened down the glass top and made it airtight with rubber gaskets and liquid cement. The air space between the inner and outer caskets, and the hermetic seating of the inner case insured the carbon dioxide against rapid evaporation, the result being that the temperature in the inner casket is, and will continue for a long time to be, several degrees below freezing. You see?"

"Perfectly," de Grandin agreed with a quick nod. "You have refrigerated her—she will remain in her present condition indefinitely!"

"Well," Coroner Martin smiled deprecatingly, "I'm sure there'll be no immediate change in her condition, or—" he broke off abruptly, for we had arrived at the cemetery, and he was once more the busy official, directing an undrilled personnel in the performance of unfamiliar duties with the precision of a detachment of trained soldiers.

I kept my gaze fixed demurely on the ground, as befitted a physician whose patient was being buried, but Jules de Grandin permitted no conventions to hamper him. About the grave he strolled, taking eye-measurements of the location, noting the character of the upturned soil, examining the approaches with the practiced eye of one who had seen much military service.

"There is a new moon tonight, Friend Trowbridge," he whispered as we re-entered Martin's car for the return trip; "be so good as to make no engagements, if you please."

"A new moon?" I echoed in amazement. "What the dickens are you drooling about? What has the new moon to do with us?"

"Nothing, I hope; much, I fear," he returned seriously.

His air of suppressed excitement told me he had some enterprise afoot, but his irritating habit of keeping his plans to himself was strong as ever. To all my questions he returned no more informative answer than a shrug or a lifted eyebrow. At length he turned his shoulder squarely on me, gazed out the window and fell to humming:

> "Ma fille, pour pénitence,
> Ron et ron, petit patapon,
> Ma fille, pour pénitence,
> Nous nous embrasserons!"

The night air was heavy with dew and drenched with the perfume of honeysuckle as de Grandin and I let ourselves through the narrow door flanking the main entrance of the great Canterbury gate leading to Shadow Lawns Cemetery. Michaelson, the superintendent, was awaiting us in the office adjoining the graveyard's imposing Gothic chapel, and that he expected trouble of some sort was clearly evidenced by the heavy revolver swinging in a shoulder-holster beneath his left armpit. "Down Hindenburg—charge!" he ordered gruffly as a monstrous police dog with baleful, green eyes half rose from its station before the lifeless hearth and bared a set of awe-inspiring teeth.

"I've been on the lookout all evening," he told us as we shook hands, "but nothing's happened yet. Sure you got a straight up, Doctor de Grandin?"

The Frenchman tweaked the carefully waxed ends of his tiny blond mustache. "My informant is one I have every reason to trust," he replied. "I am not surprised you have seen nothing thus far; but it might be well if we took our stations now; we know not when something may transpire."

"All right" Michaelson agreed, slipping on a dark jacket and snapping a woven-leather leash through the dog's collar. "Let's go."

As we walked along the winding, well kept roads beneath the arching trees toward the FitzPatrick family plot, "Mighty glad you got this information in time," the superintendent said. "Shadow Lawns has been operating more than fifty years, and we've never had a grave robbery, not even in the days when medical schools had to buy stolen bodies for their work. I'd hate to have our record broken now. Wonder if there'll be a gang of 'em?"

"I doubt it," de Grandin answered. "Indeed, I think this will be scarcely what could be called a grave robbery; it is more apt to be a violation."

"H'm, I don't think I quite follow you," Michaelson confessed as we took up our position in the shadow of an imposing bronze-and-granite monument. "What makes you so sure it will be tonight?"

"The moon—the new moon," the Frenchman replied.

"The mo—well, I'll he damned!" rejoined the other.

OUR WAIT SEEMED INTERMINABLE. The low, monotonous crooning of nocturnal insects in the grass, the occasional mournful cry of a night bird, the subdued echo of the traffic of the distant city—all blended into a continuous lullaby which more than once threatened to steal my consciousness. Michaelson yawned and stretched full length on the grass, Hindenburg lay with pointed nose between his outstretched paws in canine slumber; only Jules de Grandin remained watchful and alert.

I was on the point of pillowing my head upon my arm and snatching a nap when the sudden pressure of the Frenchman's fingers on my elbow roused me. "See, my friends," he whispered. "He comes!"

Stealthily as a shadow, a figure stole between the mounded graves toward the flower-decked hummock beneath which lay the body of Dolores FitzPatrick. The man was dressed in some sort of dark clothing, without a single highlight of white linen in his costume; consequently his visibility was low against the background of the night, but from the suppleness of his movements I realized he was young, and from the furtiveness of his manner I knew he was afraid.

"How the hell did that happen?" Michaelson demanded. "The main gate's the only one open, and Johnson's on guard there with a shotgun and orders not to let even the President of the United States by without a written pass from me."

"*Ah bah*," de Grandin whispered, "there never yet was fence so high that desperate men could not swarm over it, my friend, and this one is most desperate; make no mistake concerning that."

Michaelson's hand stole toward his gun. "Shall I wing him?" he asked.

"*Mon Dieu*, no!" de Grandin forbade. "Wait till I give the word."

The great dog roused to his haunches, and opened his mouth in an almost noiseless snarl, but the Frenchman's small hand stroked his smooth head and patted his bristling neck soothingly. "Down, *mon brave*," he whispered. "Our time is not yet." Children, dogs and women loved and trusted Jules de Grandin at sight. The savage brute rested its great head against his knee and seemed actually to nod understandingly in assent.

Meantime the figure at the grave had unslung a spade and pick-ax from the pack upon its back and commenced a furious attack on the soft, untrampled earth. We watched in silence from our vantage-point, saw the parapet of defiled earth grow high and higher beside the grave, saw the digger descend lower and lower into the trench he made. From time to time the ghoul would pause, as though to measure the task yet incomplete, then renew his attack on the yielding loam with redoubled vigor.

It must have been an hour before he reached his grisly goal. We saw him cast aside his spade, bend forward in the excavation and fumble at the fastenings of the outer box which shielded the casket from the earth. Some fifteen minutes later he rose, took something from the sack which lay beside the opened grave and twisted it between his hands.

"*What* the hell?" Michaelson, murmured wonderingly.

"A sheet, if I mistake not," de Grandin answered. "Watch carefully; his technique, it is good."

He was correct in his surmise. It was a sheet the resurrectionist twisted into a rope, then knotted into a sort of running noose and dropped into the grave.

Straddling the desecrated sepulcher, one foot on each lip, the despoiler seized the loose ends of the sheet, twisted them together and hauled upward, like a man dragging a bucket from a curbless well.

Hand over hand he drew the twisted linen in; at length his task was done, and the ravished body of Dolores FitzPatrick came once more into the outer world, the linen band knotted behind her shoulders and crossing her breast transversely from underneath the arms. Her little head, crowned with its diadem of ruddy hair, hung backward limply, and her long white arms trailed listlessly behind her as the robber drew her from the rifled grave and laid her on the grass.

A sharp, metallic click sounded at my elbow. Michaelson had cocked his pistol and trained it on the ghoul, but de Grandin's quick wrestler's-grip upon his wrist arrested the shot. "*Non*, stupid one!" he bade. "Have I not said I will say when to shoot?"

From the corner of my eye I saw this by-play, but my horrified attention was riveted on the tableau at the grave. The robber had laid Dolores's body on the warm, dew-soaked turf, composed her limbs and folded her hands across her quiet bosom, then bent and rained a perfect torrent of kisses on the calm, dead face. "I'm here, dear love; I kept our compact!" he choked between ecstatic sobs. "I'll keep the promise to the end, and then you shall be mine, mine, *all mine!*" His voice rose almost to an hysterical shriek at the end, and before I realized what he did, he folded the dead form in his arms and pressed it to his breast as though it would respond to his mad caresses.

"Good heavens, a lunatic!" I whispered. "A necrophiliac; I've heard of such perverts, but—"

"*Be still!*" de Grandin's sharply whispered admonition cut me off. "Be quiet, great stupid-head, and watch what is to come!"

The madman raised the corpse in his arms as once I had borne her living body through the woods, gazed hurriedly about, then set off at a rapid pace toward the rising ground which marked the center of the cemetery.

Taking cover behind the intervening monuments, we followed, but our precautions were unnecessary, for so absorbed in his horrid task was the grave-robber that we might have walked at his heels, yet never been discovered.

A circular row of weeping willows crowned the hill toward which we moved, and in the center of the ring thus marked there stood a tall stone cross engraved with a five-word legend:

He Giveth His Beloved Sleep

To this monolith the grave-despoiler bore his prey and laid her on the close-cropped grass before the cross, then knelt beside the body and clasped the slim, cold hands in both of his; while leaning forward, he gazed into the quiet face as though he would melt death's chill by the very ardor of his glance.

"And now, my friends, I damn think we shall see what we shall see!" de Grandin whispered. "Observe, if you please; the new moon rises."

He pointed upward as he spoke. There, beyond the line of willow trees soared the crescent moon, slim as a shaving from a silversmith's lathe, sharp as a sickle from the fields of Demeter.

And even as I spied the moon I saw another thing. Clear-cut as an image in a shadowgraph against the moon's faint luminance came a great black-winged owl, another and still a third, flying straight for the morbid group beneath the cross.

"Good Lord, de Grandin, look!" I whispered, but he shook my admonition off with an impatient shrug.

"Do *you* look there, my friend, and tell me what it is you see!" he ordered.

I glanced in the direction he indicated, then shook my head as though to clear a film from before my eyes. Surely, I did but fancy it!

No, there was no mistaking. As the silver shafts of moonlight fell upon it, the body of Dolores FitzPatrick seemed to gather itself together, the long-limbed looseness of post-mortem flaccidity passed, and *the body was imbued with life*. Distinctly as I ever saw a living person rise, I saw the body of the girl which had been buried that very afternoon uprear its head, its shoulders, and rouse to a half-sitting posture. More, it turned a living, conscious face upon the man beside it, and smiled into his eyes!

A low, trembling whine, no louder than a cricket's squeak, sounded at my feet. Hindenburg, the great, fierce dog crouched and groveled on the grass, the hair upon his back raised in a bristling ruff, his bushy, wolf-like tail held closely to his hocks, every nerve in his powerful body trembling with abject fright.

"*Now* you may fire, my friend," de Grandin ordered Michaelson, and at the same time drew an automatic pistol from his pocket and sent a bullet winging on its way. But as he fired he contrived to stumble against Michaelson so that the latter's aim was deflected.

Both weapons spoke together, and there was a startled cry of pain as the echo of the shots reverberated through the graveyard.

"Quick, my friends, on him—*chargez!*" the Frenchman cried, leaping toward the man and girl who huddled in the shadow of the cross. He was a step or two before us, and I observed what Michaelson did not. As he reached his goal, he brought the barrel of his pistol crashing down, upon the robber's head, striking him unconscious.

"Did we get him?" the superintendent asked, pausing beside the prostrate man.

"I think so," de Grandin flung over his shoulder as he bent above the girl. "Examine him, if you please."

As Michaelson bent above the man, de Grandin took the woman's body in his arms.

"Great heavens—" I began, but a sharp kick from the Frenchman's boot against my shin silenced my ejaculation half uttered. Yet it was hard to restrain myself, for in the fraction of a second while he lifted her I had seen the tiny, blue-black hole drilled through the girl's left temple by the small-calibered automatic the Frenchman carried, and saw the warm, fresh blood gush from the wound! Dead she undoubtedly was, but newly dead. That bullet had crashed through living flesh and bone into a living brain!

"Say, this feller's alive!" the superintendent cried. "He's unconscious, but I can't find a wound on him, and—"

"He was most likely stunned by a glancing bullet," de Grandin cut in. "Our aim is often erratic in the dark. Tie him securely and take him to the office; Dr.

Trowbridge and I will join you as soon as we have returned this poor one to her grave."

"You're—you're sure she's dead?" Michaelson asked diffidently. "I know it sounds crazy as hell, but I'd have sworn I saw her move a moment ago, and—"

"*Tiens*, my friend, our eyes play strange tricks on us in the moonlight," the Frenchman interrupted hastily. "Come, Friend Trowbridge, let us go."

We walked a little way in silence; then, as though he were replying to my unspoken thoughts, de Grandin said: "Do not press me for an explanation now, my friend. At present let us say my aim was poor and my bullet found the wrong mark. Scandal will be avoided if we let the dead bury the dead. Anon I shall surely tell you all."

"I THINK THERE IS LITTLE to be gained by questioning him further," de Grandin counseled some two hours later when Michaelson had at last decided it was useless to press our prisoner for an explanation and was on the point of calling the police. "The families of all involved are prominent, and only ugly scandal can result from an exposé, and that would do your cemetery little good, my friend. This young man's actions are undoubtlessly caused by mental derangement; Doctor Trowbridge and I will take charge of him, and see he is looked after. Meantime, Mademoiselle FitzPatrick's body is interred and none need be the wiser. It is best so, *n'est-ce-pas?*"

"H'm, guess you're right, sir," the superintendent agreed. "We'll just hush the whole rotten business up, eh?"

The little Frenchman nodded. "Come, Friend Trowbridge," he said, "let us be gone. *Monsieur*," he bowed politely to the prisoner, "we wait on your convenience."

At HIS SUGGESTION I drove directly to the house and helped him escort the captive to the study. Once inside, de Grandin dropped his air of captor and motioned our charge to a comfortable chair. "You will smoke, perhaps?" he asked, proffering his case, then holding a match while the other set his cigarette aglow.

"And now, *petit imbécile*, it may be you will be good enough to explain the reason for this evening's lunacy to us?" he continued, seating himself across the desk from the prisoner and fixing him with a level unwinking stare.

No answer.

"*Tiens*, this is no coin in which to repay our kindness, *Monsieur*," he expostulated. "Consider how inconvenient we might have made things—may still make them, unless you choose to talk. Besides, we know so much already, you would be advised to tell us the rest."

"You don't know anything," the other answered sullenly.

"Ah, there is where you are most outrageously mistaken," de Grandin corrected. "We know, by example, that you are Robert Millington, son of Ralph Millington, cotton broker of New York and eminent church-member of Harrisonville, New Jersey. We know you were deeply—passionately to the point of insanity—in love with Mademoiselle Dolores; we know—"

"Leave her out of this!" the young man blazed. "I won't have—"

"*Mille pardons, Monsieur*," the Frenchman corrected in a cold voice, "you will have whatever we choose to give; no more, no less. Your escapade tonight has brought you to the very gate of prison, perhaps of the asylum for the insane, and you can best serve yourself by telling what we wish to know. You will speak?"

"You wouldn't believe me," the boy responded sullenly.

"You greatly underestimate our credulity, *Monsieur*. We are most trusting. We shall believe whatever you may say—provided it be the truth."

Young Millington took a deep breath, like one about to dive in icy waters. "She made me promise," he replied.

"Ah? We do make progress. What was it you promised her?"

A flush suffused the lad's cheeks, then receded, leaving them pale as death. "I loved her," he murmured, almost breathlessly. "I loved her more than anything in the world—more than family or friends, or"—he paused a moment, then, in a sort of awestruck whisper—"more than the salvation of my soul!"

"*Eh bien*, love is like that in the springtime of life," the little Frenchman nodded understandingly. He tweaked the ends of his tightly waxed mustache and nodded once again. "Have not I felt the same in the years so long buried beneath the sod of time? But certainly. Ah, *la passion délicieuse!*" He put his joined thumb and forefinger to his lips and wafted a kiss toward the ceiling. "Those moonlit evenings beside the river when we kissed and clung and shuddered in an ecstasy of exquisite torment! That matchless combination of humility and pride—that lunacy of adoration which made the adored one's heel-print in the dust more kissable than the lips of any other woman—"

"That's it—you understand!" the boy broke in hoarsely. "That's how I felt; so when she told me—"

The little Frenchman's sentimental mood vanished like the flame of a blown-out candle. "*Précisément*, when she told you—" he prompted sharply, his little round blue eyes holding the youth's gaze with an implacable, unwinking stare.

"She told me she was going to die—apparently," young Millington returned, as though the words were wrung from his unwilling lips. "She said she had an illness which only seeming death could cure, but that she wouldn't really die, and if I'd come to her grave and take her from it, and lay her where the first rays of the new moon could shine on her, she'd rise again, in perfect health, and we could go away—"

"Ah, poor besotted one!" de Grandin cried compassionately. "Truly, you would go away, for your chances of remaining in the world when once life had returned to those cruel jaws and force was once again behind those tiny, sharp teeth would have been less than that of the lamb attending a convention of famished wolves! No matter; go on. You believed her; like a silly fish you gobbled up her bait and did become her tool in this night's work. I see; I understand. Say no more, my poor foolish one. You may go, and we shall keep your secret securely in our breasts.

"Only"—he laid his hand kindly on the boy's shoulder at the door—"if you possess one single shred of gratitude, when next you go to church, thank God upon your knees that your scheme failed tonight."

"Thank God?" the boy retorted. "For what?"

"*Tiens*, for Jules de Grandin, if for nothing else," he answered. "Good night and much good luck to you, *petit Monsieur*."

"Now, PERHAPS, YOU'LL CONDESCEND to tell me something?" I asked sarcastically as the echo of young Millington's footsteps died away.

"*Exactement*," he agreed, selecting a cigar from the humidor and snipping off its end with painstaking care. "To begin: I flout my citizenship of France like a banner proudly displayed before the enemy; but I am a citizen of the world, as well, my friend. The seven seas and five continents are no strangers to me. No, I have traveled, I have seen; I have observed. In the lazarets of a hundred places I have plied this gruesome trade of patching broken bodies which we follow, good friend, and the notebooks of my memory are full of entries. By example: In a stinking trading town of Java I was once called to treat a human wreck who had loved not wisely but altogether too well. The object of his passion was a savage she-tiger, a beast-cruel Sadist. She bit his lips away in the moment of embrace. He was a most unpleasant sight, one not to be forgotten, I do assure you.

"Very good. The other evening at the country club I did behold another poor one similarly maimed. Once seen, such injuries as that are not forgotten, and I needed no second glance at the poor young Faber's lips to tell me he was even as that other one in Java.

"'Now,' I asked me, 'who have so ruthlessly destroyed this young man's looks, and for what reason?'

"Reason there was none, but very lack of reason is often the best reason of all. This Mademoiselle Dolores, she has the history of taking all which is most precious to her cousin, not because it has a value of its own, but because her cousin prizes it. Therefore, I reason, she who once broke her cousin's dolls have now ravished away her fiancé and broken him, too. She did it from pure wantonness.

"And I am right, as usual. Next day, as I prepare to recondition the poor young Faber's lips I ask him certain questions, and he replied in writing. What does he tell me? *Parbleu*, you would be astonished!

"He says he accompanied Mademoiselle Dolores to the clearing where the moon shone, for she had said she wished to tell him something. Once there she tells him of her love and begs that he will desert her cousin Josephine and go away with her. But no, he is a young man of good principle. He will not do it; he repulses her. Ha, he spoke truly who first said hell has no fury like a scorned woman! Dolores asks that young Martin will give her one little kiss in token of farewell, and all men are weak where lovely women plead thus humbly. She lifts her face to his, and all suddenly he sees the flesh melt from off her bones, and it is in the bare-skulled face of a skeleton he looks as he is about to kiss her!

"He cries out and struggles to be free, but it are useless. Her slender arms are strong as steel, and her teeth—*mon Dieu*—her teeth are like shears of white-hot metal. They fasten on his yielding lips and clip them clear away! *Voilà*, it is done, and sick with pain and horror he staggers blindly through the trees until we find him.

"So much I learn, and I think deeply. 'Who, or what, are this so strange being called Dolores?' I ask me.

"The nighttime comes, I go to bed and anon there comes a great and dreadful bird which claws at my window and makes dire threats against me if I divulge what I have learned that day. You say it are an owl. Perhaps. But does an owl talk with human words, my friend? Not ordinarily, you will concede.

"All quickly comes the call from Monsieur FitzPatrick, and to his house we go to seek the lost Dolores. The dog leads us well, but he scents something—something evil which we can not see—and turns to run away. Long since I have learned to trust the animal instinct which warns of evil and unseen things, and so I take us back to the house and ask for spiritual ammunition with which to fight the danger which awaits us in the cemetery."

"Yes, I wanted to ask you about that," I interrupted. "Wouldn't anything except a rosary and bottle of holy water serve as protection that night?"

"Many things," he agreed, "but they were handiest. The Church of Rome has no exclusive patent on fighting with and conquering the evil ones, but her methods are always efficacious—she has waged the battle so long, and so successfully."

"But why should a cross, just because it *is* a cross, be valuable in such a case?" I persisted.

He paused in thought a moment; then: "Words much repeated, with a special significance, in time acquire power," he replied. "Witchcraft is one of the world's oldest curses. Before Egypt was, the witch-cult flourished, and Babylonia and Assyria both understood the witch's awful power. Both had their charms against her, but they are gone, and their charms are gone with them. Then arose Christianity, and took up the battle with the witch-brood. Now, when a rosary is blessed and when holy water is dedicated, the priest says certain words—always the same, and always with the same intent. The formula has become invincible through centuries of repetition. Consider: You can not hear the music of your national anthem without a sudden tingling in your cheeks, a sudden contraction of the throat, a quick feeling of exaltation. Words, my friend, the power of words to conjure into sudden being a certain train of thought and a definite physical reaction. So it is with prayers oft repeated. Yes.

"Very well. With these spiritual weapons we returned to the old cemetery, and there we encounter and subdue three evil creatures which posed as bats. Perhaps they were such; perhaps, again, they were something else. At any rate, we routed them, and then we found Dolores apparently lying lifeless on a long-forgotten grave. *Morbleu*, the whole thing stank of witchery, my friend.

"Bethink you: It was the night of August first, the feast of St. Peter's Chains, or Lammas, as the English-speakers call it. That was one of the great gathering days of the witches of olden times, the others being Candlemas in February, Roodmass, or May Eve, and All Hallow Eve, or Halloween. And, my friend, in spite of all the learned fools tell us to the contrary, *witchcraft still lives!*

"Through the years and centuries it has given ground before the new religion, but in remote places it still survives. In Italy, despite repressive measures, 'the old religion' as they call it, *la vecchia religione*, still numbers many followers.

"And in other lands—in *every* land—who are better fitted to keep alive the old, unholy fires of witchcraft than the Gipsies? They are a race apart, they neither mingle nor intermarry with the people among whom they live. Their men may be thieves, but their women are open practisers of the black art. Do they not boast of second sight and 'dukkering' and charms to injure enemies or break the spells laid on by others? But yes.

"Nor have actual proven instances of acts more sinister been lacking. In Estremadura four Gipsy women were taken by the Spanish government and made to own they had killed and eaten a friar, a pilgrim and a woman of their own tribe. And remember, Dolores' mother was a woman of the Spanish Gipsies. That has much bearing on the cast.

"You will recall I asked you if you'd read your Bible lately concerning those possessed of devils? For why? Because the learned numskulls who write the 'higher criticism' have been at pains to tell us demoniacal possession was but epilepsy. Perhaps, but will the rule not work both ways? If epilepsy may simulate possession by fiends, why should not such possession mimic epilepsy?

"'Nonsense,' you say? *Ah bah*, I damn think my hypothesis was proved when her you did think dead of epilepsy came suddenly to life in your very arms that night.

"I did foresee her second death. Yes. Her body was the dwelling-place of evil, and had been racked by its tenants. The sleep and rest of death was needed, and to it she resorted. Such cases are not unknown.

"And so, when she had apparently died a 'natural' death, I besought that she be embalmed, or that you have her subjected to an autopsy, so that she might he forever rendered incapable of functioning as a living being again.

"But she was clever—almost as clever as I. She had outguessed modern mortuary science by leaving a testament expressly forbidding embalming, and you refused an autopsy.

"By Monsieur FitzPatrick's permission I went through all her correspondence. There she had been lax—she had not thought of Jules de Grandin, for he had simulated indifference in her case and had not called upon her once while his good friend Trowbridge was treating her to prevent the death she had already decided on.

"Among her papers I found but little that would guide me, but finally I came on that which I did seek, a little note from the young Millington in answer to one of hers, and in it he did renew his promise to take her from the grave, 'if she should die' (how well she had rehearsed him for his rôle!) and lay her body where the first faint rays of the new moon might rest upon it!

"That was the key, my friend. In Greece, where warlocks still make sport of science and religion, when members of the witch-cult desire to shift their scene of operations, or when discovery hovers close behind them, they take refuge in the tomb. They 'die' as this one did. But always their 'deaths' are due to some cause which leaves no outward wound upon their bodies—no injury which would prevent their future functioning. Then, if they be exhumed and placed beneath the new moon's rays, soon after burial, they rise again, as though refreshed by the nap taken in the grave—and woe betide the poor unfortunate who catches their first waking glance! With teeth and nails, like maddened brute beasts, they tear his throat away, and rip his heart from out his breast and eat it. It is their custom so to do; a most unpleasant one, I think.

"Accordingly, we watched beside her grave tonight; we saw the poor, infatuated Millington exhume her; we saw him bear her to the hilltop and lay her where the moon could shine upon her; we even saw the beginning of her return to life and wickedness. But Jules de Grandin nipped her resurrection in the bud by shooting her, and now her lovely body lies in the grave with shattered brain, and never more may evil spirits use it for their evil ends. No, she has said at last to the grave, 'Thou art my father and my mother,' and to corruption, 'Thou art my lover and my bridegroom.' Her business in this world is finished."

"But," I began, "in the philosophy of witchcraft—"

"Ho, you do remind me of another philosophy," he interrupted with a grin:

"Who loves not woman, wine and song
Remains a fool his whole life long.

"I sing most execrably; the love of woman is a gift denied me; but thanks be to kindly heaven my taste for wine is unabated. Come, let us drink and go to bed!"

The Druid's Shadow

"TEN THOUSAND LITTLE SMALL blue devils! It is annoying. I am vexed, I am harassed, I am exasperated!" Jules de Grandin felt successively in the pockets of his blue-flannel jacket, his oyster-white linen waistcoat and his pin-striped trousers, then turned such a woebegone face to me that I burst out laughing.

"Ha, *sale bête*, you laugh at my distress?" he demanded fiercely. "So. *Parbleu*, you shall pay dearly for your levity. I give you choice of three alternatives: Hand me a cigarette forthwith, convey me instantly where more can be purchased, or die by my hand within the moment. Choose!" He tweaked the tightly waxed ends of his diminutive wheat-blond mustache after the manner of the swash-buckling hero in a costume melodrama.

"I never smoked a cigarette in my life, so my first chance is gone," I grinned, "and I'm too busy to have you kill me this afternoon, so I suppose I'll have to cart you to a cigar store. There's the railway station, shall we get them at the news stand?"

I maneuvered the car across the busy street and parked beside the station entrance. "Wait a minute," I called as he leaped nimbly to the platform, "you've put bad ideas in my head. I think I'll get a cigar here. I don't usually smoke while driving, but—"

"Perfectly," he interrupted with an impish grin, "and you shall buy me a packet of cigarettes when you purchase your cigar. I impose the penalty for laughing at my misfortune a moment since."

The customary exsurgence which heralded the arrival of a train from the West was beginning as I paused beside the cigar counter. Red Caps moved leisurely toward the landing-platform, a baggage agent opened his book and drew the pencil from his cap band, one or two hotel runners showed signs of returning animation as they rose from the bench where they lounged.

I pocketed my change and turned to light my cigar as the locomotive snorted to a halt and passengers began alighting from the Pullmans, but a cheery hail brought me about as I was in the act of rejoining de Grandin. "Hullo there, Doctor Trowbridge—imagine running into you at the station— you're a sight for tired eyes! Now it *does* seem like getting home!" Burned to a crisp by the Arizona sun, lean, but by no means emaciated, and showing no trace of the decline which had driven him from our damp Eastern climate three years before, young Ransome Bartrow shouldered his way through the crowd and took my hand in a bone-crushing grip. "By George, I'm glad to see you again, sir!" he assured me, grinding my knuckles till I was ready to roar with pain.

"And I'm glad to see you, Rance," I answered. "It's hardly necessary to ask how you feel, but—"

"No buts about it," he returned with a laugh. "The doctors looked me over with a microscope—if I'd had anything from dandruff to flat feet they'd have found it—and pronounced me cured. I can live here the rest of my life, and needn't get nervous prostration every time I'm caught in a rain storm, either. Ain't that great?"

"It surely is," I congratulated. "Got your baggage? Come on, then, I want you to meet—"

"Holy smoke, that reminds me!" he burst out. "I want *you* to meet—" He turned, dragging me after him to a modishly dressed young woman who mounted guard above an imposing pile of hand-luggage. "Sylvia, dear," he announced, "this is Doctor Trowbridge. He's had the honor of knowing your lord and master since he was one second old. Doctor Trowbridge, this is my wife."

As I took the girl's hand in mine I was forced to admit Ransome had made an excellent choice, if externals were to be trusted, for she was pretty in an appealing way, with large gray eyes, soft ash-blond hair and a rather sad mouth, and from the look she gave her husband there was no need to ask whether theirs had been a love match.

"And now to meet the stern parent," young Bartrow proclaimed. "I wrote Dad I was bringing him a surprise, but I didn't tell him what it was, and I didn't tell what train I was coming on. Wanted to take him unawares, you know. I— oh, I say, Doctor Trowbridge, won't you come up to the house with us? Maybe the pater will have a stroke or something when he meets Sylvia, and it's only Christian for us to have a physician along to administer first aid and take his dying statement. Even if he doesn't go into convulsions, it'll be worth your trip to see his face when I say, 'Meet the wife.' What d'ye say?"

My commonplace reply was foreign to my thoughts, for there was more than a possibility the boy's jesting prediction might be realized.

Ransome Bartrow was his father's idol. He was his parents' first and only child, born when both were well past forty, and his advent had led to complications which took his mother's life within a year. His father had married relatively late in life, and with the passing of his adored wife had lavished all the affection of his lonely life upon his son. There was money in abundance, and nothing which could be bought had ever been denied the boy. Copybook maxims to the contrary notwithstanding, young Ransome had developed into a fine young man. He stood well in all his classes at school and excelled in most forms of athletics, rowing stroke on his varsity crew. Entering business with his father after graduation, he showed an aptitude for work which seemed to guarantee success to the newly formed firm of James Bartrow & Son, but before a year had passed the malady which strikes so many former oarsmen fastened on him, and only a hurried trip to Arizona saved his life. From the day his son departed to the West the father had counted the minutes of their separation like a rosary of sorrow, and now when his boy returned only to present a strange young woman who by the law of God and man had first claim on his affections—there might be need for digitalis when the bride was introduced.

Jules de Grandin greeted the youngsters with all the gay enthusiasm he always showed for lovers. Before we had traversed a dozen blocks toward the Bartrow mansion he was sitting with an arm about the shoulders of each, rattling off anecdote after droll anecdote, and Ransome Bartrow's deep, booming laughter mingled with the silvery laugh of his bride as they listened to the witty little Frenchman's sallies.

James Bartrow stood in the broad drawing-room of his big house, straining thoughtfully at the fireless hearth behind its fencing of polished brass fender. He was a big man, well over six feet tall, with a big head crowned with a mane of iron-gray hair and a trimly cut white beard. Something in the bigness and obvious power—physical and mental—of the man seemed to strike his son with awe, and as he tiptoed into the apartment, his bride's hand in his, de Grandin and I at his elbow, his buoyant self-assurance deserted him for the first time.

"Dad?" the appellation was pronounced with questioning diffidence. "Oh, Dad?"

Bartrow wheeled with a nervous jerk, his big, florid face in its frame of white hair lighting up at sound of his son's voice, and took a quick step forward.

"O-o-oh!" the exclamation was soft, scarcely audible, but freighted with sudden panic consternation, and the little bride cringed quickly against her husband's arm. The half-nervous, half-playful smile froze on her lips, leaving her little white teeth partially exposed, as though ready to bite. The merry light in her gray eyes blurred to a set, fixed stare of horror as a convulsive shudder of abhorrence ran through her. It was as though, expecting to meet a friend, she had been suddenly confronted by a gruesome specter—an apparition she had reason to dread and hate.

"Oh, Rance," she pleaded in a voice thick with terror. "Oh, Rance—please—" Pounding heart and laboring lungs choked her voice, but the wild, imploring glance she gave her husband pleaded for protection with an eloquence no words could equal.

Startled by the girl's unreasoning fright, I glanced at Bartrow. He had paused almost in the act of stepping; his forward foot rested lightly on the floor, scarcely touching the polished boards, and in his face had come an expression I could not fathom. Astonishment, incredulous delight, something like exultation, shone in his steel-blue eyes, and the smile which came unbidden to his bearded lips was such as a fanatic inquisitor might have worn when some long-sought and particularly virulent heretic came into his power.

The tableau lasted but an instant, and for that fleeting second the sultry September air was charged with an electric thrill of concentrated terror and delight, panic fear and savage exultation of vengeance about to be fulfilled.

Then we were once more normal twentieth century people. With words of welcome and genial thumps upon the back and chest James Bartrow greeted his son, and he was the smiling, jovial, new-found father to the bride. But I noticed that the kiss he placed upon her dutifully upturned cheek was the merest perfunctory salutation, and as his lips came near her face the girl's very flesh seemed to cringe from the contact, light as it was.

Bartrow's heavy voice boomed out an order, and a cobweb-festooned bottle in a wicker cradle was brought from the cellar by the butler. The wine was ruby-red and ruby-clear, and Jules de Grandin's small blue eyes sparkled appreciatively as they beheld the black-glass bottle. "Arcachon '89!" he murmured almost piously as he passed the glass under his nostrils, savoring the wine's aroma reverently before he drank. "*Mordieu*, it is exquisite!"

But while the rest of us drank deeply of the almost priceless vintage little Mrs. Bartrow scarcely moistened her lips, and at the bottom of her eyes when they turned toward her father-in-law was a look that made me shiver. And in her soft, low voice there came a thin, metallic rasp whenever she spoke to him which told of fear and abhorrence. By the way she sat, every nerve tense to the snapping-point, I could see she struggled mightily for self-control.

It made me ill at ease to watch this veiled, silent battle between James Bartrow and his son's wife, and at the first opportunity I murmured an excuse that I had several calls to make and hastened to the outside air.

I shot the starter to my car and turned toward home, wondering if I had not imagined it all, but:

"*Tiens*, my friend, the situation, it is interesting, *n'est-ce-pas?*" remarked de Grandin.

"The situation?" I countered. "How do you mean?"

"*Ah bah*, you do play the dummy merely for the pleasure of being stubborn! What should I mean? Does the welcomed-home bride customarily regard her hitherto unknown *beau-père* as a bird might greet a suddenly-met serpent? And does the father-in-law usually welcome home his son's wife with an expression which might have done great credit to the wicked, so hungry wolf when *la petite Chaperon Rouge* came tap-tapping at her grandmamma's cottage-door? I damn think not."

"You're crazy," I assured him testily. "It's unfortunate, I'll admit; but there's no ground for you to build one of your confounded mysteries on here."

"U'm? And what is your explanation?" he returned in a flat, accentless tone.

"Why, I can only think that Bartrow reminds his daughter-in-law irresistibly of someone she fears and hates through and through, and—"

"*Précisément*," he agreed with a vigorous nod, "and that someone she must have hated with a hate to make our estimates of hatred pale and watery. More, she must have feared him as a mediæval anchoret feared erotic dreams. Perhaps, also, since you are in explanatory mood at present, you will explain the look of recognition—of diabolic, devilish surprised recognition—which came upon Monsieur Bartrow's face as he beheld the young *Madame* for the first time?"

"*Hein?*" he prodded as I was silent.

"Oh, I don't know," I answered shortly. "It *was* queer, confoundedly queer, but—"

"But I have small doubt we shall learn more anon than we now know," he interrupted complacently. "Me, I think we have not seen the last act of this so interesting little play, my friend."

WE HAD NOT. THE sun had hardly commenced to stain the eastern sky next morning when the nagging chatter of my bedside telephone roused me and Ransome Bartrow's frightened voice implored my services. "Sylvia—it's Sylvia!" he told me breathlessly. "She's in a dreadful state!" then crashed the 'phone receiver back into its hook before I had a chance to ask him what the trouble was.

Alert as a cat, however deeply he might seem immersed in sleep, de Grandin was at my side before I finished dressing, and when I told him Ransome wanted me he dashed back to his room, donned his clothes with more speed than a fireman responding to a third alarm and joined me at the curb as I made ready to dash across town to the Bartrow home.

The chill of early morning drove the last trace of sleep from our eyes as we rushed through the quiet streets, and we were efficiently awake when Ransome Bartrow met us at the door.

"I don't know what it is—something's frightened her terribly—a burglar, perhaps—I can't get anything out of her!" he answered my preliminary questions as we trailed him up the stairs. "She's almost in collapse, Doctor. For God's sake, do something for her!"

Sylvia Bartrow was a pitiful figure as she lay in her bed. Her little, heart-shaped face seemed to have shrunk, and her big gray eyes appeared to have widened till they almost obscured her other features. Her cheeks were pale as the linen against which they lay, and her gaze was filmed with unspeakable horror. Without being told, I knew her whole being was vibrant with a desperate agony of terror, and I have never seen a glance more heartrending than the dumb, imploring look she cast on her husband as he entered.

"Shock," I pronounced after a hurried look, and turned to my medicine kit to fill a syringe with tincture digitalis. Plainly this case was too severe for aromatic ammonia or similar simple remedies.

"Shock," young Bartrow repeated stupidly.

"*Mais oui*," de Grandin explained patiently; "it is the relaxation of the controlling influence exercised by the nervous system on the vital organic functions of the body, my friend. Any extraordinary emotional stress may cause it, especially in women. What happened to affright *Madame* your wife? Surely, you were here?"

"No, I wasn't," Ransome confessed. "I couldn't sleep, and I'd gone downstairs. It's hot in Arizona, far hotter than here, but this damned damp heat is strange to me, and I couldn't bear lying in bed any longer. I'd about made up my mind to go out on the front porch and lie in a hammock when I heard Sylvia scream, and rushed up here to find her like this."

"U'm? And you heard nothing else?"

"No—er—yes; I did! As I dashed up the stairs, two at a time, I could have sworn I heard someone or something moving down the hall, but—"

"Some *thing*, *Monsieur*—can you not be more explicit?"

"Well, it sounded as though it might have been a man in stocking feet or rubber-soled shoes or—once while I was in the West a fool puma got into the upper story of the shack where I was sleeping and dashed around like a crazy thing till it found the open window and jumped out again. That's the way those footsteps—if they were footsteps—sounded. Like a great, soft-footed animal, sir."

"*Exactement*," the Frenchman nodded gravely. "And *Monsieur* your father, you did call him?"

"I did, but Dad sleeps on the floor above, and his door was locked. I could hear him snoring in his room, and I couldn't seem to get any response to my knocking, so I telephoned Doctor Trowbridge.

"Will she recover—she's not dying, Doctor?" he asked in terror, coming, to my side and looking at his wife with brimming eyes and quivering lips.

"Nonsense—of course, she's not dying!" I answered, looking up from the watch by which I timed the girl's pulse. "She's been badly frightened by something, but her heart action is getting stronger all the time. We'll give her a sedative in a little while, and she'll he practically as well as ever when she wakes up. I'd advise her to stay in bed and eat sparingly for the next day or two, though, and I'll leave some bromides to be taken every hour for the rest of today."

"Hadn't we better notify the police? It might have been a burglar she saw," Ransome suggested.

Jules de Grandin walked to the window and thrust his head out. "It is twenty feet sheer to the ground with nothing a cat might climb," he remarked after a brief survey. "Your burglar did not enter here." Then: "You were on the lower floor when _Madame_ alarmed you with her cry. Tell me, which way did the footsteps you heard seem to go?"

Ransome thought a moment, then: "It's hard to say exactly, but they seemed to go up, though—"

"A servant, perhaps?"

"No, I don't think so. The servants all sleep in the left wing on this floor, and I'm pretty sure none of 'em would have been up at that hour. But it might have been the burglar running toward the roof. Shall we look?"

We searched the third story of the house, with the exception of the chamber where James Bartrow lay in decidedly audible slumber, but nowhere did we find a trace of the intruder. At the stairway leading to the trap-door in the roof we paused, then turned away in disappointment. The door had long been secured by half a dozen twenty-penny nails driven through frame and casing. Nothing less than a battering-ram could have loosened it.

"Well, it's past me," Ransome confessed.

"You, perhaps, but not Jules de Grandin," the Frenchman answered. "I am interested, I am intrigued; my curiosity is aroused. I shall seek an explanation."

"Where?"

"Where but from Madame Sylvia? It was she who saw the intruder; who else can tell us more of him?"

"But, she's too ill—"

"Assuredly; I would not harass her with questions at this time; but when she is recovered we shall learn from her what it was that came. Me, I have already an idea, but I should like her to confirm it. Then we can take such measures as may be needed to guard against a recurrence. Yes. Certainly."

OFFICE HOURS WERE OVER and I was preparing to go upstairs and dress for dinner when James Bartrow stalked into my consulting-room. "See here,

Trowbridge," he announced in his customary brusque manner. "I feel like hell on Sunday; I want you to help me snap out of it."

"All right," I acquiesced, "I think that can be arranged. What seems to be the trouble?"

He bit the end from a cigar of man-killing proportions, set it alight with the flame from his hammered gold lighter and blew a cloud of smoke toward me across the desk. "Ever feel like kicking a cripple's crutch out from under him?" he demanded. "Ever say to yourself when you were alone in the room with someone—especially if his back were turned to you—"It would take only one blow to knock him dead. Go on, hit him?" He exhaled another smoke-wreath and regarded me through the drifting white wreaths with an intent look which was almost a challenging glare.

Despite the man's seriousness, I could not repress a grin. "Certainly, I have," I answered. "Everybody has those inexplicable impulses to do mischief. Men are only little boys grown up, you know; the principal difference is the normal adult recognizes the childishness of these impulses and dismisses them from his mind. The child gives way to them, so does the subnormal adult whose mind has retained its infantile stature after his body had developed."

"You've been working pretty hard at the office lately, haven't you?" I added, more as a peg on which to hang whatever treatment I recommended than as an actual question.

"No, I haven't," he assured me shortly. "I've been taking things devilish easy, and if you start any of that fool stuff about my needing to go away for a rest I'll clout you on the head; but—"

He paused, drew a deep inhalation from his cigar and expelled the smoke almost explosively, then:

"I might as well get it out," he exclaimed. "It's my daughter-in-law, Sylvia. Never saw anything like it. The moment I met the girl yesterday afternoon something seemed to snap like a steel trap inside my head. 'There she is,' a voice inside me seemed to say, 'you've got her at last; there she is, ready to your hand! Kill her, kill her; do it now!' Hanged if I didn't almost leap on the poor kid and strangle her where she stood, too. I know I frightened her, for I must have shown the insane impulse in my face as soon as my eyes lit on her. It was the scared look in her eyes that brought me to my senses. The impulse passed as quickly as it came, but for a moment I thought I was going to flop down in a faint; it left me weak as a cat."

"H'm," I murmured professionally. "You say this seizure came on you the moment you saw—"

"Yes, but that's not all," he interrupted. "I shouldn't be here if it were. I managed to shake off the desire to injure her—perhaps I'd better say it left of its own accord in a second—but last night I'd no sooner fallen asleep than I began dreaming of her. Lord!" He passed a handkerchief over his face, and I saw his hands were trembling. I dreamed I was walking through a great, dark wood or grove of some sort. The biggest oak trees I've ever seen were everywhere about, their branches seemed to interlace overhead and shut out every vestige of light. Suddenly I came to the biggest tree of all, and as I halted a shaft of moonlight pierced through an opening in its foliage, letting a pencil of luminance down like a spotlight in a darkened theater. Before me, in the center of that beam of light, lay Sylvia, dressed in some sort of long, loose, flowing robe of thin white cloth, with a wreath of wild roses twined in her unbound hair. She was drawn back against the gnarled roots of the tree in a half-reclining position, her wrists and ankles fastened to them with slender wicker withes. As I stopped beside her she looked up in my face with such an expression of mingled pleading and fear that it ought to have melted my heart; but it didn't. Not by a damn sight. Instead, it seemed to incense me—set me wild with a maniacal desire to kill—and I reached down, tore her dress away from her bosom and was about to plunge a knife into her breast when she screamed, and the dream winked out like an extinguished candle flame. Queer, too; I kept right on dreaming, realizing that I'd been dreaming of killing Sylvia and regretting that I hadn't been able to finish the crime. In my second dream I seemed to be deliberately wooing the return of the murder-dream, so I could take it up where I left off, like beginning a new installment of a story which had been continued at an exciting incident. Man, I tell you I never wanted anything in my life the way I wanted to kill that girl, and I've a feeling I shouldn't have stopped at mere murder if I'd been able to finish that dream!"

"*Pardonnez-moi, Messieurs*," de Grandin entered the consulting-room like an actor responding to a cue. "I was passing, I recognized Monsieur Bartrow's voice; I could not help but hear what he said.

"*Monsieur*," he directed a level, unwinking stare at the visitor, "what you dreamed last night was not altogether a dream. No, there was action, as well as vision there. This afternoon, because the good Trowbridge was overburdened with work, I took it on myself to call on Madame Sylvia. It is not the physician's province to interrogate the servants, but this is more than a mere medical case. I felt it before, now I am assured of it. Therefore, I made discreet inquiries among your domestic staff, and from the laundress I did learn that a *chemise de nuit* of Madame Sylvia had been torn longitudinally—above the breast, even as you tore her robe in your dream, *Monsieur*."

"Well?" Bartrow demanded.

"*Non*, by no means, it is not well, my friend; it is very far otherwise. You are perhaps aware that Madame Sylvia's indisposition arises from a fright she sustained, from some unknown cause—a burglar, the hypothesis has been thus far?"

"Well?" Bartrow repeated, his face hardening.

"*Monsieur*, that burglar could not be found, neither hide nor hair of him could be discovered, though Doctor Trowbridge, your son and I did search your house with a comb of the fine teeth. No. For why?" He paused, regarding Bartrow and me alternately with his alert, cat-like stare.

"All right, 'for why?'" Bartrow demanded sharply when the silence had stretched to an uncomfortable length.

"Because, *Monsieur*"—de Grandin paused impressively—"because *you were that burglar!*"

"You're mad!"

"Not at all, I was never more sane; it is you who stand upon the springboard above the pool of madness, *Monsieur*. For why you had this impulse to slay a wholly inoffensive young lady whom you had never seen before, neither you nor we can say at this time with any manner of assurance; but that you had it and that it was almost overwhelming in its strength, even at its first onset, you admit. Consider: You understand the *psychologie?*"

"I know something of the principles."

"*Bien.* You know, then, that our conscious mind—the mind of external things—acts as the governor of our actions as the little whirling balls control the engine's speed. Do you also realize that it acts as a sort of mental policeman? Good, again.

"Now, when we wish to do a little naughty thing—or a great one, for that matter—and the sound common sense of this daytime conscious mind of ours overcomes the impulse, we say we have put it from our mind. Ah ha! It is there that we most greatly delude ourselves. Certainly. We have not put it from us; far otherwise; we have *repressed* it. As the businessman would say, we have 'filed it for future reference.' Yes. Often, by good fortune, the file is lost. Occasionally, it is found, only to be repressed once more by the conscious mind.

"But when normal conscious control is overthrown, one or all of these stored-away naughty desires come bubbling to the surface. Every surgeon has seen this demonstrated when nicely brought up young ladies or religious old gentlemen are recovering from anesthesia. *Cordieu*, the language they employ would put a coal-heaver to the blush!

"Attend me, if you please: The restraint of consciousness is entirely absent when we sleep—the policeman has put away his club and uniform and gone on a vacation. Then it is we dream all manner of strange, queer things. Then it is that a repressed desire, if it be strong enough, becomes translated into action while the dreamer is in a state of somnambulism. Then it was, *Monsieur*, you walked from out your room and would have done in earnest what you perpetrated in your dream had not Madame Sylvia's scream summoned back some portion of the inhibitions of your waking self, so that you forbore to murder her, although the lingering remnant of your dream-desire stayed with you, and made you wish to do so.

The skeptical look on Bartrow's face gave way to an expression of grudging belief as the little Frenchman expanded his theory. "Well, what's to be done?" he demanded as de Grandin finished.

"I would suggest that you pack your golf clubs and go to Lake Hopatcong or the Kobbskill Club for a brief stay. There are certain matters we would attend to, and in the meantime you may recover from this so strange impulse to do your daughter-in-law an injury; I greatly fear you may do that for which you will be everlastingly sorrowful, should you remain.

"Do not mistake me," he added as Bartrow was about to form a rebellious reply, "it is no matter of exiling you from your own house, nor yet of cutting you from all communication from your son and his wife always. Quite no. We would have you absent for only a little while—no longer than is absolutely necessary—while we make arrangements. Be assured we shall write you to return at the earliest possible moment."

So it was arranged. Pleading frayed-out nerves and doctor's orders, James Bartrow left for Hopatcong that evening, leaving Ransome and his wife in possession of the house.

"Well, everything's satisfactorily arranged for a while, at least," I remarked as we returned from the station after seeing Bartrow off. "A few days of golf and laziness will probably sweep those cobwebs from his mind, and he'll he right as rain when he returns."

The little Frenchman shook his head. "We have disposed of only half the problem, and that but temporarily," he returned gloomily. "Why Monsieur Bartrow looked so strangely at his new daughter we know, though we do not know what caused the homicidal impulse which was behind the look; but why she regarded him with terror—ah, that is a far different matter, my friend, and one which needs explaining."

"Nonsense!" I scoffed. "Why shouldn't she be afraid? What girl wouldn't be terrified if she saw a man look at her like that?"

"You do forget their recognition—and revulsion—was mutual and simultaneous," he reminded.

We finished our drive in silence.

SYLVIA BARTROW LAY IN a long wicker deck-chair in the cool angle of the piazza, an orchid negligée trimmed with marabou about her slender shoulders, an eiderdown rug gathered about her feet and knees. Though her improvement had been steady since her fright a week before, she was still pale with a pallor not to be disguised by the most skillfully applied cosmetics, and the dark violet circles still showed beneath her big, melancholy gray eyes. She greeted de

Grandin and me with the faintest ghost of a smile as we mounted the porch steps.

"*Madame*, that we must trouble you thus drives us to the border of despair," the Frenchman declared as he took her pallid fingers and raised them to his lips, "but there are several questions we must ask. Believe me, it is of importance, or we should not be thus disturbing you."

The girl smiled at him with something like affection, for his uniform politeness endeared him to every woman from nine to ninety, and nodded amiably. "I'll tell you anything I can, Doctor de Grandin," she replied.

"Good. You are kind as you are beautiful, which is to say your generosity exceeds that of the good St. Nicholas," he assured her as he drew up a chair, then:

"Tell us, *Madame*, just what it was that frightened you so terribly last week. Speak with confidence; whatever you may say is spoken under the seal of medical inviolability."

She knit her brows, and her big eyes turned upward, like those of a little girl striving desperately to recall her seven-times table. "I—don't—know," she answered slowly. "I know it sounds silly—impossible, even—but I can't remember a single thing that happened that night after I fell asleep. You'd think anything which frightened anyone as much as I was frightened would be impressed on him in all its detail till his dying day; but the truth is I only remember I was terribly, horribly afraid of something which came to my room, and that's all. I can't even tell you whether it was human or animal. Maybe it was just an awful dream, and I'm just a silly child afraid of something which never was."

"U'm, perhaps," de Grandin agreed with a nod. Then: "Tell me, if you please, Madame Sylvia, were you frightened before this so unfortunate occurrence? Did anything distress you at any time, or seem to—"

"Yes!" she exclaimed. "When I first entered the drawing-room, I went nearly wild with fright. When I looked at Daddy Jim standing there by the fireplace everything seemed to go red-hot inside me from my toes to my throat; I wanted to scream, but couldn't; I wanted to run away, but didn't have the strength. And when he turned and looked at me—I thought I should die. Just imagine, and Daddy Jim's such a nice old darling, too!"

"This feeling of terror, it passed away?" de Grandin pursued seriously.

"Yes—no; not immediately. After I'd met him I realized it *couldn't* have been Daddy Jim who frightened me, really, but there was a feeling of malaise which clung to me till—"

"Yes—till?" the Frenchman prompted as she hesitated.

"Till the big fright came and drove the little one away."

"Ah, so. You had never, by any chance, known anyone whom you feared and hatred who resembled your so estimable father-in-law?"

"Why, no. I don't think I was really afraid of anyone in my life—everyone has always been kind to me, you know, and as for hating anybody, I don't think I could, really. I was just a little girl during the World War, and I used to try so hard to hate the Kaiser and von Hindenburg, but I never seemed able to do it as the other children could."

"I congratulate you," he commented non-committally. "This so strange feeling of uneasiness, you still have it?"

"No-o, I don't. I did until—" She stopped, and her pale face suffused with a faint blush.

"Yes, *ma petite*, until?" he prompted softly, leaning forward and taking her fingers lightly in his hand. "I think I know what you would say, but I do desire confirmation from your own lips."

"It's no use," she answered as tears welled in her eyes. "I've tried to down it, to say it wasn't so for Rance's sake, but it is—it is! It's Daddy Jim—I'm afraid of him—terrified. There's no earthly reason for it; he's a dear, good, kind old man, and he loves Rance to distraction and loves me for Rance's sake, but I live in constant horror of him. When he looks at me I go cold and tremble all over, and if he so much as brushes against my skirts as he passes I have to bite my lips to keep from screaming. When he kissed me that day I thought my heart would stop.

"I can't explain it, Doctor de Grandin, but the feeling's there, and I can't overcome it. Listen:

"When I was a little girl we lived on the outskirts of Flagstaff, and I had a little Maltese kitten for pet. One day I saw Muff with her back up and every hair on her tail standing straight out and her eyes fairly blazing with rage and fright as she backed slowly away from something on the ground and spit and growled with every breath. When I ran up I saw she was looking at a young rattlesnake which had come out to sun itself. That kitten had never seen a rattler or any kind of snake in all her little life, but she recognized it as something to be feared and hated—yes, *hated*—the moment she laid eyes on it. Her instinct told her. That's the way it is with me and my husband's father. Oh, Doctor de Grandin, it makes me so unhappy! I want to love him and have him love me, and I don't want to come between Rance and him, for they're all the world to each other, but—" The tears which jeweled her eyelids gushed freely now, and her narrow shoulders shook with sobs. "I try to love him," she wailed, "but I'm dreadfully afraid of him—I loathe him!"

"I knew as much already, *ma pauvre*," the Frenchman comforted, "but be of cheer, already I think I have found a way to remove this barrier which stands between you and your father-in-law. Your fear of him is grown from something deep within you, a something which none of us can as yet understand, yet which must have its roots in reason. That reason we shall endeavor to find. If you will come to Doctor Trowbridge's tonight, we shall probe the underlying causes for this feeling of revulsion which so greatly troubles you."

"You—you won't hurt me?" she faltered. Plainly terror and sustained mental tension had broken her nerve, and her only thought was to avoid pain at any cost.

"Name of a little blue man, I shall say otherwise!" he exclaimed. "You and *Monsieur* your husband shall come to dinner, and afterward we shall talk—that is all. You are not terrified of that?"

"Of course not," she replied. "That will be delightful."

"*Très bon*, until tonight, then," once more he raised her hand to his lips, then turned and left her with a smile.

"WHAT DO YOU MAKE of it?" I asked as we drove homeward. "Doesn't it strike you she's trying to evade a direct answer when she says she can't remember what frightened her?"

"Not necessarily," he returned thoughtfully. "She deceives herself, but she does so honestly, I think. Consider: She is of a decidedly neurotic type, you are agreed on that?"

I nodded.

"Very good. Like most of her kind, she is naturally very sensitive, and would suffer keenly were it not for the protective mental armor she has developed. The other night she had an experience which would have driven more matter-of-fact persons into neurasthenia, but not her. No. She said mentally to herself, 'This thing which I have seen is dreadful, it is too terrible to be true. If I remember it I go mad. *Alors*, I shall not remember it. It is not so.' And thereupon, as far as her conscious memory is concerned, it is not so. She does not realize she has given herself this mental command, nor does she know she has obeyed, but the fact remains she has. The extreme mental torture she suffered when the apparition appeared before her is buried deeply in her subconscious memory—mentally cicatrized, we might say, for she has protected her sanity by the sudden development of a sort of selective amnesia. It is better so; she might easily go mad otherwise. But tonight we shall open wide the secret storehouse of her memory, we shall see the thing which affrighted her in all its grisly reality, and we shall take it from her recollection forever. Yes. Never shall it trouble her again."

"Humph, you talk as though you were going to exorcise a demon," I commented.

He raised his shoulders and eyebrows in an eloquent shrug. "Who shall say otherwise?" he asked. "Long years ago, when the scientific patter we mouth so learnedly today had not been thought of, men called such things which troubled them by short and ugly names. She-devils which seduced the souls and bodies of men they called *succubi*; male demons which worked their will on women they denominated *incubi*. Today we talk of repressed desires, of unconscious libido, and such-like things—but have we gotten further than to change our terminology? One wonders. A tree you may denominate an oyster, and you may call an oyster a tree with equal ease, but all your new denominations to the contrary notwithstanding, the tree is still a tree, and the oyster nothing but an oyster. *N'est-ce-pas?*"

ADDED TO HIS NUMEROUS other accomplishments, Jules de Grandin possessed unquestioned talents as a chef. He was the only man Nora McGinnis, my household factotum, would permit in her kitchen for longer than five minutes at a time, for across the kitchen range they met and gossiped as fellow artists, and many were the toothsome recipes they traded. That afternoon he was long in conference with my gifted though temperamental cook, and the result was a dinner the like of which has seldom been served in Harrisonville. Shrimp gumbo preceded lobster Cardinal and *caneton à la presse* followed lobster, while a salad garnished with a sauce which surely came from fairyland accompanied the duckling. From heaven alone knew where, de Grandin procured a bottle of Mirandol '93, and this, with one of Nora's famous deep-dish apple tarts and fromage Suisse completed the perfect meal.

Coffee and cognac were served on the side veranda, and while we enjoyed the delightful sensation of the mingled processes of digestion and slow poisoning by nicotine de Grandin took possession of the conversation.

"Your estimable father." he began, addressing Ransome, "he is a connoisseur of interior decoration; his drawing-room, it is delightful. That walnut wainscot, by example, it is—"

"Good Lord, you'd better not let Dad hear you call it walnut!" Ransome broke in with a laugh. "He'd have your life. That's oak, man; he imported it especially from England, bought it standing in an old house in Kent, and it cost him almost its weight in gold to bring it over. Oak's always been the passion of Dad's life, it seems to me. He's got a hundred or more pieces of antique oak—which is twice as rare as walnut, maple or mahogany—in the house, there are nothing but oak trees growing in the grounds, and every walking-stick he owns is carved from solid oak. He has to have 'em 'specially made, for they can't be had in the shops. I've seen him pick up an acorn in the woods and fondle it as a miser might a diamond."

"Eh, do you tell me so?" de Grandin's fingers beat a quick devil's tattoo on the arm of his chair. "This is of the interest. Yes. Is it that he also collects other *objets d'art?*"

"No-o, I couldn't say that, though he has a small collection of curios in the place. There's that old stone, for instance. He brought it from a place called Pwhyll-got in Wales years ago, and has it framed in native oak and hung up on the wall of his room. I never could see much sense in it; it looks pretty much like any other bit of flat, smooth rock to me, but Dad says it once formed part of a big ring of Cromlech and—"

"*Mort d'un rat âgé*, the light; I begin to commence to see!" exclaimed the Frenchman.

"What?"

"*Mille pardons*, my friend, I did but think aloud, and all too often I think that way at random. You were saying—"

"Oh, that's all there is to his collection, really. He's got a few curious old arrowheads, and a stone knife-blade or two, but I don't suppose a real collector would give him twenty dollars for the lot."

"*Certainement*; not if he were wise," de Grandin agreed.

Deftly he turned the talk to matters of psychology, detailing several interesting cases of split personality he had witnessed in the laboratories of the Sorbonne. "I have here, by happy chance, an interesting little toy which has of late received much use in the clinics," he added, apparently as an afterthought. "Would not you care to see it?"

Prompted by a sharp kick on the shins, I declared that nothing would please me more, and Ransome and Sylvia assented, mainly for politeness' sake.

"Behold it, is it not most innocent-looking?" he asked, proudly displaying an odd-looking contraption by means of which two circular looking-glasses, slightly smaller than shaving-mirrors, were made to rotate in opposing directions by means of a miniature motor.

"*Is* it dangerous?" asked Sylvia, her woman's curiosity slightly piqued.

"Not especially," he returned, "but it gives one queer sensations if one watches it in motion. Will you try?"

Without awaiting their reply he set the machine on the study table, switched off all the lights save the central bulb which shed its beams directly on the mirrors, and pressed the switch.

A light sustained humming sounded through the room, and the mirrors began describing their opposing orbits round each other at ever-increasing speed. I watched their dazzling whirl for a moment, but turned my eyes away as de Grandin tweaked me gently by the sleeve. "Not for you, Friend Trowbridge," he whispered almost soundlessly; then:

"Behold them, my friends, how they spin and whirl, is it not a pretty sight? Look carefully, you can distinguish the different speeds at which they turn. Closer, hold your gaze intently on them for a moment. Thus you may find— sleep—sleep, my friends, You are tired, you are *fatigués*, you are exhausted. Sleep is good—very good. Sleep—sleep—sleep!"

His voice took on a low, singsong drone as he repeated the admonition to repose again and yet again, finally: "That is well. Be seated, if you please."

Like twin automata Ransome Bartrow and his bride sank into the chairs he hastily pushed forward. For a moment he regarded them thoughtfully, then snapped off the current from the motor and once more lit the lamps. Like a showman arranging his puppets, or a window-dresser disposing his figurines, he touched them lightly here and there, placing hands and feet in more restful positions, slipping cushions behind each reclining head. Then:

"Madame Sylvia, you hear me?" he asked softly.

"Yes," the reply was hardly audible as the girl breathed it lightly.

"Very good. Attend me carefully. It is the night of your arrival here. You have gone to bed. You are asleep. What transpires?"

No answer.

"*Très bon*; all is yet quiet. It is two hours later. Do you see, do you hear anything?"

Still silence.

"*Bien.* It is the moment at which the intruder entered your chamber. What is it? *Who* is it? *Whom do you see?*" His final question came with sharp, sudden emphasis.

For a moment the girl reclined quietly in her easy-chair; then a light, moaning sound escaped her. She rolled her head restlessly from side to side, like a sleeper suffering a disagreeable dream, and her breathing came more quickly.

"Speak! I demand to know what you see—whom you see!" he ordered harshly.

A quick, convulsive shudder ran through her, and with a sudden, writhing movement she slipped from her chair and lay supine on the floor. Her eyelids were slightly parted, but the eyeballs were so far rolled back that only a tiny glistening crescent of white showed between her lashes. Again she moaned softly; then the whole expression of her features changed. She thrust her head a little forward, her pale cheeks flushed red, her mouth half opened and a desirous smile lay upon her lips. She raised her hands, making little downward passes before her face, as though she stroked the cheeks of one who bent above her, and a gentle tremor ran through her as her slim bosom expanded slightly and her mouth opened and closed in a pantomime of kissing. A deep sigh of ardent ecstasy issued from between her white teeth.

"*Grand Dieu*, what have we here?" de Grandin muttered nervously. "*C'est un incube!* Behold, Friend Trowbridge, from feet to head she is a vessel that fills itself with the sweet pains of love! What does it mean?"

But even as he spoke the tableau changed. With a sudden wrench she moved to free herself from the bonds of an amorous embrace, and on her countenance, but lately beatified with passionate love, there came a look of stark and abject terror. One arm was thrown across her face, as if to ward away a blow, and her breast rose and fell in labored respiration. Her cheeks again were pale, as if every vestige of blood had left them, even her lips were grayish-blue.

She struggled to her knees, and crept writhingly away till the wall cut off her retreat, and then she groveled on the floor, her forehead lowered, hands clasped protectively upon the upturned nape of her neck, and all the while she shook and trembled like a palsied thing.

From her blenched lips came a spate of words, but strange, foreign words they were, seemingly all consonants, and in a language I could not identify.

Then, at de Grandin's sharp command she turned to English, crying: "Mercy, my Lord! Is it sin that a woman young and fair should love? Look on this form, this body and these limbs—" She rose and faced an invisible accuser, her head thrown back, her hands outspread, as one who would display her charms to best advantage. "Was not I formed for loving and for love?" she asked. "How can I ever be the cold and stony-hearted servant of your order? 'Tis love that I was made for and love which I did crave. Can a woman's soul be forfeit if she does listen to the prompting of her woman's heart?

"O-o-h!" her shrill scream rent the quiet of the room. "Not that; not that, my Lord—anything but that! See"—she sank upon her knees and looked up pleadingly while with eloquent, outflung hands she made a gesture of supreme surrender—"see me as I kneel before thee! See this body, so soft, so tender, so full of delight; it is thine—all, all thine, if only thou wilt spare me—o-o-oh—o-o-o-oh—ai-ee!" Again her frantic scream set my nerves a-tingle, and I thanked the heavenly powers that cries of pain would cause less public comment coming from a doctor's house than any other place.

She balled her fingers into diminutive fists and wrestled back and forth as though her wrists were in the vise-like grip of some grim, relentless captor.

Her eyes were open now, wide open, and filmed with horror indescribable. Her face was deathly pale, her whole body vibrant with an agony of desperate fear. In silence now she struggled, but how! She was like a madwoman, clawing, twisting, writhing. She turned her head and spat into an invisible face; she dug her feet into the rug, tried to fling herself prostrate, twined herself about her captor; once she bent swiftly and I heard the snap of her small, sharp teeth as she went through the dumb show of fleshing them in a man's arm. Her face was livid, scarcely like a living thing.

Now her struggles lessened. Her shrieks subsided to weak whimpers, and she followed pitifully, though reluctantly, in the wake of her unseen conductor like a little broken-spirited child led out for punishment. Her arms were stretched before her, hands drooping, as though her wrists were held fast in a powerful grip. Her head bent listlessly, rolled and lolled from side to side, as if extremity of terror had sapped her last shred of vitality, leaving her scarcely strong enough to stand erect.

But once again she galvanized to action. Apparently they were come to their destination, for she halted, struggled backward a moment, then held one hand out from her side as though it were being made fast to something.

And I swear I could see the marks of the invisible ligature as the cord was tightly drawn about her wrist!

Now the other hand was pinioned and now her slender ankles were crossed one upon another, and one after another we saw the furrows form, saw the silk-meshed stockings sink in on the shrinking flesh as invisible bonds were cruelly tightened.

She half leaned, half lay across a chair-arm, her body taut and rigid as a drawn bow, white and still as a lovely Andromeda carven in marble, and in her misty, tear-gemmed eyes was such a look of tragic, mute appeal as nearly broke my heart. She held her fixed, unnatural pose until my muscles ached in sympathy. "Good heavens," I exclaimed, "de Grandin, this is terrible, we must—"

"Observe, my friend, he comes, he is arrived, he is here!" the Frenchman's shout drowned out my protest as he seized me by the elbow and swung me round.

My heart all but ceased to beat as I turned. Framed in the window of the study, like a portrait of incarnate evil and malevolence executed by a master craftsman, was the face of James Bartrow.

But such a face! Gone was every vestige of the urbane man of the world I knew, and in its place there was the very distillation of savagery, wild, insane rage and lust for killing. His matted hair lay on his forehead, his beard was fairly bristling with ferocity, and on his tight-drawn lips there sat a sneering smile of mingled hate and murderous blood-lustfulness.

"So," he cried, and his voice was thin and cracked with madness, "so, I find ye, do I? Too long ye've robbed me of my vengeance, ye filth-filled vessel of pollution. The Gods cry out for sacrifice, and here am I, their servant and their priest, prepared to render them their due!"

With one gigantic heave he tore the copper screen from out the window and drew himself up to the sill. A moment he crouched there, like a great, savage cat about to spring; then with a leap he cleared the intervening space and towered over Sylvia. I started as I saw the gleam of something white in his right hand. It was a long and slender blade chipped from flint, the sort of weapon I'd seen in museums.

"I all but slew ye in the grove of Cambria," he roared, "and by the heart I would have plucked from your breast I would have made my divinations; but ye did escape me then. This time I have ye fairly. Look on me, Cwerfa, and know your hour is come, for by the stone of Cromlech's ring I brought across the seas, and by the holy mistletoe that grows upon the sacred oak, and by the mystic gem of serpents' spew, I'm here to cut the heart from out your breast as I would have long ago!

"They thought they'd packed me off and gotten rid of me—ha, ha!—but I came back, and when I found ye'd fled the house wherein I kept the Cromlech stone, I knew ye must have sought protection from the Frankish outlander as once before ye found it with the Romans, and here I am to claim your forfeit life, and none shall say me nay!" With a wild, maniacal roar he leaned across the girl and wrenched the flimsy silken drapery from her bosom.

"Your pardon, *Monsieur*, but Jules de Grandin is here, and he does most emphatically say nay!" the Frenchman interrupted and struck the towering madman a stunning blow upon the head with the carafe of chilled water which stood beside the decanter of brandy on the study table.

The bludgeoned maniac fell crashing to the floor, and almost as he fell de Grandin was on him, wrenching the stone knife from his grasp, tearing a pongee curtain from its rods and twisting it into a rope with which he pinioned Bartrow's wrists behind him and made them fast with double knots.

"And now, my friend, I would that you accompany me at once to this one's residence," he ordered, snatching down another curtain and fastening the prisoner's feet together, then dragging him to the entrance of the study and tethering him securely to one of the white pillars which flanked the doorway. "Come, it is of the greatest import!" he urged. "We have no little moment to stand here stupidly and stare."

Dazed, but goaded by his constant pleas for haste, I drove him to the Bartrow home, and waited while he clamored at the door. He had a brief parley with the servant who responded to his summons, disappeared within the house and emerged a moment later bearing a frame of ancient weathered oak in which was set an oblong of dull, grayish stone. In his left hand he swung a canvas sack like those used by banks for holding minor coins, and in it something clinked and jingled musically.

"I think I have them all," he told me. "Rush hasten, fly back to your house, my friend. There is work ahead of us!"

He led me to the cellar as soon as we returned, and in the furnace we built a roaring fire of newspapers and stray bits of wood, and when we had it blazing we heaped a few shovelfuls of coal upon it. As soon as all was glowing he tossed the oak-framed stone and the collection of flint arrowheads into the fiery crater. Last of all he flung in the stone knife he had taken from Bartrow when he struck him down.

The oak frame of the stone burned furiously, and to my great surprise the stone itself and the arrowheads and knife seemed to offer small resistance to the fire, but turned into a sort of brittle and crumbling lime. We waited fifteen minutes or so, while the fire completed its work of destruction; then the French-man seized the heavy iron poker and mashed the burned stone relics into pow-der, dumped the clinkers into the ashpit and stirred them all together till none could tell which had been Pennsylvania coal and which the old stone curios which Bartrow prized so highly. "Come, let us see what passes up above," he ordered when he had finished with the poker, and led the way to the study.

Sylvia had fallen to the floor, and de Grandin raised her and placed her comfortably in a chair, then, having rearranged the mutilated corsage of her dress, turned his attention to the still unconscious Bartrow. "I think we may release him, now," he commented, and together we undid the knots and tugged and pulled until we had him in a chair.

"Revive him, if you please," de Grandin ordered, and set the motors of his whirling mirrors going.

I dashed some water into Bartrow's' face and held a vial of ammoniated salts to his nostrils, and as his eyelids quivered de Grandin struck him lightly on the cheek. "Observe—look—see here!" he ordered.

Bartrow struggled half-way from his chair, gazed at the spinning mirrors a moment, then sat forward, his gaze riveted to the bright concentric circles they described.

Softly, carefully, forcefully, de Grandin ordered him to sleep, repeating his command until it was obeyed; then, when he had stopped the motor, he moved to the center of the room, and:

"My friends, I bid you listen to me carefully," he ordered. "You, Monsieur Ransome, know nothing of that which has transpired. It is good. Very good. Continue in your ignorance. You, Madame Sylvia, have quite forgotten every fear of olden days, and of the present; to you your father-in-law is but a kindly old gentleman who loves you and whom you love in turn.

"And you, Monsieur Bartrow the elder," he turned his piercing gaze on the older man, "whatever it was which did possess you is gone away. I have destroyed it utterly. No longer will the impulse to murder Madame Sylvia be with you. You hear me? You will—you *must* obey. She is to you the much-loved wife of your much-loved son; no more, no less, and as such you will give her your affection and make her welcome to your heart and home."

He paused a moment, then continued: "You will rise up, go to the street, and in two minutes reappear at the front door of this house, nor will you know that you have called before or why you came. Go. En *avant; allez-vous-en!*

"Awake, my friends; wake Monsieur Ransome, wake Madame Sylvia; the experiment is done and you are sleeping long!" he cried gayly, snapping his fingers at Ransome and Sylvia in turn. "*Parbleu,* I did think these little dancing mirrors would have made you sleep the clock around!" he added as they opened heavy eyes.

"Did we really fall asleep? How stupid!" Sylvia exclaimed. "I don't think it very nice of you to invite us to dinner, then put us to sleep with your horrid apparatus, Doctor de Grandin."

"Ah, *Madame*, I am desolated that it should have happened thus," he answered, "but you are doubtless rested by the nap; come, let us go upon the porch once more and smoke a cigarette."

"Good evening, everyone," James Bartrow sauntered out on the veranda, "hope I'm not intruding. I couldn't stand it out at the lake any longer, so I hopped a train and came back to town. They told me you children had gone over here, so I came along to see you were all right. Did they give you a good dinner?"

"Why, Daddy Jim, how nice of you to come!" Sylvia jumped from her chair, threw her arms about her father-in-law's neck and kissed him on both bearded cheeks. "I've been wishing you'd come back," she added.

He patted her shoulder affectionately. "Great girl, eh, Trowbridge?" he asked pridefully as he sank into a chair beside me and lighted a cigar.

We chatted inconsequentially for an hour or so; then the Bartrows, on the best of terms with us and with each other, bade us good-night.

"Now," I threatened as the echo of their laughing voices died away, "will you explain all this craziness I've seen tonight, or must I choke an explanation from you?"

He raised his shoulders in a shrug. "*Le bon Dieu* knows," he confessed. "I hardly dare to venture an opinion.

"When first we entered Monsieur Bartrow's house and saw the look of savage exultation on his face when he beheld the little bride, and the expression of stark terror with which she looked at him, I said to me, '*Parbleu*, Jules de Grandin, what are the meaning of this?' And I replied:

"'Jules de Grandin, I do not know.'

"Your West; he is like our Foreign Legion, the port of men who would be forgotten, and that young Madame Bartrow came from there I knew. Was it that in his younger days the elder Bartrow had sojourned in that country and there had formed a feud with some member of her family? And did he recognize her as a foeman's child the moment he put eyes on her? Perhaps. I could not be sure of anything, and so I waited and wondered.

"A little light came to us when he called here to consult you. He wished to kill her, he declared he had an impulse almost irresistible to do her injury, and yet he knew not why it was. Ah, but his dream—you do recall? He dreamed he trailed her through a deep, dark grove of oak trees, and there he found her, all bound and helpless, and robed in white. And white, my friend, has almost always been the color of the robe of sacrifice. What could *this* mean? I asked me. The holy angels only know.

"No, there was another one who knew, at least, in part, and Madame Sylvia was she. Held fast within the secret chamber of her mind there was a recollection of her father-in-law's visit. Undoubtlessly he spoke when he accosted her; his words would surely give some clue to why he wished her injury. 'Very well, then,' I say to me. 'If Madame Sylvia holds the answer, she shall tell us.'

"And so we did. With dinner I did bait my trap, and when she came I was prepared to make invasion of the secret kingdom of her mind. But first I asked a few small questions of her husband.

"While we were at his house I had noticed certain things concerning it. Within the lovely little park which stands about his home, I had seen nothing but oak trees, little oaks, great oaks, and oaks which were neither large nor small. That was unusual. Also I noticed much oaken furniture within the house, and the fine Tudor wainscot in the drawing-room.

"And so I asked about the wood, leading young Monsieur Ransome to correct what he thought my mistake, that he might speak more freely, and thus I learned of his father's so strange passion for oak. Also he told me of the foolish whim which made his father import and keep a Druid stone from Wales. Ah, that also was important, but just why I could not say at that time. No, I needed further information.

"So I interrogated Madame Sylvia. *Tiens*, there I was like Monsieur Robin the tailor in your so droll nursery rime, he who . . .

. . . bent his bow,
Shot at a sparrow
And killed a crow.

For where I sought only to unlatch the darkened window and let in light upon her little fear, behold, I opened wide the door upon a fearsome memory so dreadful that almost countless generations had not been long enough to bury it beneath their years. Yes."

"What do you mean?" I asked, bewildered.

He gazed at me a moment, then: "What is instinct?" he demanded.

"Why, I suppose you might call it an innate quality, apart from reason or experience, which prompts animals of the same species to react to certain definite stimuli in the same manner."

"Very good," he complimented. "The day-old chick needs no example to teach it to pick up grains of corn, the newborn infant needs not to be told to take the breast—Madame Sylvia's little kitten required none to tell him that the serpent was his deadly foe. No.

"But *why* is instinct? What makes it? It is mass memory, transmitted from our earliest forebears, and stored up in our subconscious minds for use in emergency. Nothing less.

"But we have other memories from other times. Take, by example, the common dream of falling through space. Who has not had it? For why? Because it is a racial memory. It dates from the remote day when our ancestors dwelt in trees. With them the danger of death by falling was always present. Many died thus, all at one time or other fell and were injured more or less severely. Now, any serious injury produced shock, and shock in turn produced certain definite molecular changes in the tissues of the brain. These were transmitted to the fallers' progeny. *Voilà*, we have the racial memory.

"Now, consider: Though everyone has dreamed he fell—and often wakened in an agony of terror—we never have this sense of falling while we are awake. No. Why is that? Because our waking, *modern* personality knows no such danger. Ah, then, you see? It must be another personality, distinct from that we have while waking, which dreams of falling, a personality which has a recollection of falling from a tree or over a great cliff.

"Very well. In everyday experience we meet with men who have extraordinary memories; they can remember accurately events which happened when they were but three or four years old. Such men are rare, yet they do exist.

"Very good. Why is it not then possible that there may live those who can remember the days of long ago—who can recall what happened to an ancestor of theirs as an *individual*, rather than to their whole ancestry as a group? I do not mean *consciously* remember. But no. I mean they have the memory latent, as we all have the falling-through-space memory when we are asleep.

"Place such a one as this in a state of hypnosis, where there is no interference from the conscious mind of the wake-a-day world, and that other, buried, memory might easily be resurrected. *N'est-ce-pas?*"

"But Bartrow and Sylvia seemed to recognize each other simultaneously, and they were wide awake when they did it," I objected.

"*Précisément.* You have expressed it. It is strange, it is odd, it is almost unbelievable, but it is true. Of all the millions in the world, those two, the one with strange, uncanny memory of a thwarted vengeance, the other with the dreadful recollection of a terrible ordeal, were brought together. And as steel strikes sparks from flint, so did their personalities enkindle the light of memory in each, though the memory was vague, and he knew not the reason for his hatred of her and she could not find reason for her fear of him.

"But from what we saw and heard tonight we can piece the gruesome puzzle into something like the semblance of a picture. Long, long ago, an ancestor of Bartrow's was a Druid, perhaps an Archdruid—one of those awful priests who served and worshiped nameless gods in groves of oak. Diodorus Siculus described their rites of divination by means of hearts and entrails plucked from living human sacrifices; Cæsar, in his *De Bello Gallico*, mentions the burning alive of human victims in cages made of wicker. They were a wicked, cruel, unclean hierarchy, my friend, and the noblest thing the Romans did was to destroy them, root and branch. Yes.

"Remember how Monsieur Bartrow, while in his fit of madness, swore by the gem of serpents' spew? That is surely confirmation, for on his brow the Archdruid was wont to wear a glowing jewel—probably an opal—supposed to be made from crystallized spittle of serpents. Together with the oak, the mistletoe and the yew-bough, it was regarded as a thing of peculiar holiness by them.

"*Très bon.* We have now placed Monsieur Bartrow on the stage of olden days. What of Madame Sylvia? It seems her acting of the scene of sacrifice should tell the tale.

"Undoubtlessly she was a sort of priestess of the Druids, a kind of Vestal, vowed forever to virginity, and liable to horrid death if she committed any breach of discipline. But she was, as she did say, 'formed for love,' and she did listen to the dictates of her woman's heart, only to be discovered by a Druid priest and led away to the great sacrificial oak to suffer death.

"And yet she must have lived—did not Monsieur Bartrow refer to her finding shelter with the Romans? Too, she must have had offspring, and to them given the curse of memory of the Druid's shadow which lay across her path, and of that progeny, poor Madame Sylvia was one. Yes.

"And Monsieur Bartrow—in him there lived the memory of *his* ancestor, and of his thwarted vengeance. He was peculiarly sensitive to the influence of the old ones, as is evidenced by his love of oak and his collection of Druid relics. These relics, too, although he knew it not, were constant stimulants of his unrealized thirst for vengeance. When he and Madame Sylvia did confront each other—*eh bien*, we know the rest. He was the Druid priest once more and she the victim who escaped from sacrifice. *Parbleu*, he almost balanced the account tonight, I think!"

"But see here," I asked, "isn't there still danger that he'll revert to that strange condition again? Is it safe for her to live near him?"

"I think so," he returned. "Remember, my friend, mental sores are much like those of the body. Left to themselves they mortify and fester, but if we open them—*pouf!*—they vanish. So with this strange pair. Tonight we probed beneath the surface of their conscious minds, deep into those age-old memories which plagued them, and from him we did extract the lust for vengeance long unsatisfied, and from her the gnawing fear of retribution. Also, for added safety, we have destroyed the relics of the Druids which he kept in his house and which daily gave new energy to his desire to accomplish that deed of murder in which his ancestor of ancient times did fail. No, my friend, the ghosts of the old priest who was raised this night, and of her whom he would have made his victim, have been laid forever in quiet graves of forgetfulness, and the shadow of the Druid no more will fall across the paths of Monsieur Bartrow and Madame Sylvia. It is very well."

"But suppose—"

"*Ah bah*, suppose you cease to guard that brandy bottle as a miser guards his gold," he interrupted with a smile. "My throat is desert-dry from too much explanation, and I am weary with this tiresome business of pursuing long-dead Druids and their unfaithful priestesses. Give me to drink and let me go to bed."

Stealthy Death

1. The Second Murder

"Parade—rest! Sound off!" Playing in quick time, the academy band marched the field, executed a perfect countermarch and returned to its post at the right of the ordered ranks of cadets. As the bandsmen came to a halt the trumpets of the drum corps, gay with fringed tabards, belled forth the slow, appealing notes of retreat, and: "Battalion—'tention! Present—arms!" came the adjutant's command as "The Star-Spangled Banner" sounded and the national color floated slowly from its masthead.

Jules de Grandin's white-chamois gloved right hand cupped itself before his right ear in a French army salute, his narrow, womanish shoulders squared back and his little, pointed chin thrust up and forward as the evening sun picked half a thousand answering beams from the burnished bayonets on the presented rifles. "Parfait, exquis; magnifique!" he applauded. "C'est très beau, that, my friend. You have here a fine aggregation of young men. Certainly."

I nodded absently. My thoughts were not on the stirring spectacle of the parade, nor upon the excellence of Westover Military Academy's student body. I was dreading the ordeal which lay before me when, the parade dismissed, I must tell Harold Pancoast of his father's awful death. "He'll take it better than you, Doctor Trowbridge!" the widow had whispered between tremulous lips, and:

"Poor boy, this is tragic!" the headmaster had told me deprecatingly. "Won't you wait till after parade, Doctor? Pancoast is Battalion Adjutant, and I think it would be kinder to let him complete his duties at parade before we break the news."

"Confound it!" I complained bitterly more than once; "why did they have to give me this job? The family lawyer, or—"

"Mais non, my friend," de Grandin comforted. "It is the way of life. We are born in others' pain; we perish in our own, and between beginning and end stands the physician. We help them into the world, we watch beside their sick-beds, we make their exits into immortality as painless as possible—at the last we stay to comfort those who remain. These are the obligations of our trade." He sighed. "It is, *hélas*, too true. Had kindly heaven given me a son I should have sternly forbid him to study medicine—and I should most assuredly have cracked his neck had he done otherwise!"

The last gold rays of the dying October sun were slanting through the red and russet leaves of the tree-lined avenue leading to the administration build-ing as we waited in the headmaster's office for young Pancoast. At last he came, sauntering easily along the red-brick walk, plainly in no haste to answer the official summons, laughing as only carefree youth can laugh, and looking with more than friendly regard into the face of his companion. Indeed, she was a sight to brighten any eye. A wistful, seeking look was on her features, her fine dark hair lay round her delicate, pale face like a somber nimbus, and the Chi-nese coat of quilted black satin she wore against the light evening chill was lined and collared with soft orange-pink which set off her brunette pallor to perfection. "*Parbleu*, he chooses nicely, that one," de Grandin approved as the lad bade his companion adieu with a smart military salute and turned to mount the steps to the headmaster's sanctum.

I drew a deep breath and braced myself, but I might have known the boy would take the blow like the gentleman he was. "Dead—my Dad?" he murmured slowly, unbelievingly as I concluded my evil tidings. "How? When?"

"Last night, *mon pauvre*," de Grandin took the conversation from me. "Just when, we do not know, but that he met his death by foul play there is no room for doubting. The steel of the assassin struck him from behind—a sneaking, cowardly blow, but a mighty one, *mon brave*—so that he died instantly, without pain or struggle. It is for us—you and us—to find the one responsible and give him up to justice. Yes. Certainly. You accept the chal-lenge? Good! Bravely spoken, like the soldier and the gentleman you are; I do salute you—" He drew himself to rigid attention, raising his hand with precise military courtesy.

Admiringly, I saw the Gallic subtlety with which he had addressed the lad. Had I been telling him, I should have minimized the tragic aspects of his father's death as much as possible. The Frenchman, on the contrary, had thrown them brutally before the boy, and then, with sure psychology, diverted thoughts of grief and horror by holding out the lure of vengeance.

"You're right!" the youngster answered, his chin thrust forth belligerently. "I don't know who'd want to harm my Dad—he never hurt a fly that didn't bite him first—but when we find the one who did it, we—by God, sir, we'll hang him high as Haman!"

Arrangements were quickly made. Indefinite leave was granted Harold, and I parked my car before his dormitory while he completed hurried packing for the journey to his desolated home.

"Strikes me he's taking an unconscionable time to stuff his bags," I grumbled when we had waited upward of an hour. "Perhaps he's broken down, de Grandin—I've seen sturdier lads than he collapse like deflated balloons in similar circumstances—will you excuse me while I run in and see if he's all right?"

The little Frenchman nodded and I hastened to the upper-story room young Pancoast shared with a classmate.

"Pancoast? No, sir," his roommate replied to my hurried inquiry. "He came in about an hour ago and told me his trouble, then stuffed his gear into his kit bag there"—he indicated the great pigskin valise resting in a corner of the room—"and said he had to see some one before he left for home. I thought perhaps he'd decided to go on without his grip and would send for it later. Terrible thing, his father's death, wasn't it, sir?"

"Quite," I answered. "You've no idea where he went, or why, I suppose?"

The lad colored slightly. "I—" he began, then stopped, embarrassed.

"Out with it!" I ordered curtly. "His mother's on the verge of collapse at home, and he's needed there. It's the better part of three hours' steady drive, too."

"I'm not sure, sir," the cadet answered, evidently of divided mind whether to hold fast the confidence imposed in him or break the school's unwritten law in deference to the emergency. "I'm not *certain* where he went, but—well, he's been pretty spoony on a *femme* ever since the semester started, and—maybe—he ran over to say good-bye. But it shouldn't take him this long, and—"

"All right," I broke in brusquely, "never mind the details. Where's this young woman likely to be found? We're in a hurry, son." I bent and seized the waiting kit-bag as I spoke, then paused significantly at the door.

"I haven't her address, sir," the lad replied, "Panny never mentioned it to me, but you'll be likely to find him down in Rogation Walk—that's the little lane south of the campus by the old Military Road, you know—they usually meet there between retreat and tattoo."

"Very well, I'll hunt him there," I answered. "Thanks for the information. Good-night."

Harold Pancoast lay as he had fallen, his uniform cap, top down, on the bricks of the shaded walk, the black-braided collar and gray shoulders of his blouse stained rusty red. Transversely across the back of his head, where hairline joined the neck, gaped a long incised wound from which blood, already beginning to congeal, was welling freely, and in which there showed a trace of the grayish-white of cerebro-spinal fluid. His hands were stretched above him and clenched convulsively. The blow which struck him down must have been a brutally powerful one, delivered with some sharp, heavy instrument and wielded with monstrous force, for it had hacked its way half through the atlas of his spine and, glacing upward, cut deeply in the lower occiput. No need to ask if he were dead; the guillotine could scarcely have worked with more efficiency upon the poor lad's neck.

As I gazed at him in horror another horror crept over me. Though I had not inspected his father's injuries, Parnell, the coroner's physician, had described them with the ghoulish gusto of his trade, and there before me on the son there lay the very reproduction of the wound which cost the father's life not twenty hours earlier!

"Good heavens!" I gasped, and my pounding heart-beats almost stopped my breath. "This is devilish!"

I turned and raced along the quiet, tree-rimmed walk in search of Jules de Grandin.

2. The Third Murder

"Sure, Doctor de Grandin, sor, 'tis, th' divil's own puzzle we've got here, an' no mistake," confided Detective Sergeant Jeremiah Costello as he knocked an inch of ash from his cigar and turned worried blue eyes on the diminutive Frenchman. "First off, we've got th' murther o' this here now Misther Pancoast—an' th' divil's own murther it were, too, sor—an' now we've got th' case of his kid to consider; though, th' blessèd saints be praised, *that* case is what ye might call academic, since it happened outside me jurisdiction entirely, an' catchin' o' th' scoundrel as done it is none o' me official business, unless, belike—"

Jules de Grandin nodded shortly. "It is very exceedingly belike, indeed, my friend," he interrupted. "Consider, if you please. What are the facts?" He raised his small left hand and spread the fingers fanwise, then counted on them in succession. "First we have this Monsieur Pancoast the elder, a fine and honest gentleman, if all reports be true. Very good. Night before last he leaves the dinner table for a meeting of his lodge, and drives off in his motor car. He shows no sign of worriment at the meeting; he is his usual smiling self. Very well. Precisely at eleven o'clock he leaves, for they have worked the third degree, and food is being served, but he is on a diet and can not stay to eat. That is too bad. Two fellow members see him enter his sedan and drive away toward home. What happens afterward we do not surely know; but in the morning he is found beside the door of his garage, face downward on the ground, and weltering in blood. His neck is chopped across the back, his spine is all but severed and the instrument of death has cloven through his skull and struck the *corpus dentatum* of his brain."

He nodded solemnly. "'Why has this thing been done?' I ask. To find the criminal in this case means we must find the motive, but where can it be found? We can not say. This Monsieur Pancoast is a most estimable citizen, a member of the church and of the Rotary Club, a bank director, a one-time city council-man. Yet he is dead—murdered. The case is veiled in mystery.

"*Eh bien*, if the father's case is obscure, what shall we think of the son's? A fine young man, who had harmed no one, and whom no one could reasonably wish to harm. Yet he, too, is dead—murdered—and murdered with the same strange technique as that which killed his father.

"Attend me: You, *Sergent*, have seen much killing, both in war and peace; Trowbridge, my friend, you are a surgeon and anatomist; can either of you match the wounds which slew these poor ones in all of your experience?"

I shook my head. "Not I," I answered. "I can understand how a blow might be delivered in such a way as to cut the tip of the spine, or how the base of the skull could be cut through, but these wounds are beyond me. Parnell described Pancoast's injuries to me, and it seems they were identical with Harold's. His opinion was that no such upward-slanting blow could have been struck unless the victim lay prone, and even then the weapon used would have to be curved, like a carpenter's adz, for instance, to permit the course these incisions fol-lowed."

"*Ah bah*, Parnell, he is an old woman in trousers!" de Grandin shot back. "Better would he exercise such talents as he has in a butcher shop, I think. Consider him: He says the victim must be prone. *Grand dieu des cochons!* Did we not examine the poor *petit Monsieur*? But certainly. And did we not find him stretched face downward on the earth? Yes, again. But with his tight-clenched hands above his head, as though he clutched at nothing while he fell? Of course. His attitude was one of having fallen, and he who lies upon the earth must find it impossible to fall. *Voilà*, he was killed standing; for had he lain flat upon the ground when he was struck, he must inevitably have writhed in reflex death-agony when that blow shore through his spine and skull; but standing he would have made a single wild clutch for support, then stiffened as he fell upon his face. His nerves and muscles were disposed to hold him upright, and when death comes from sudden wounding of the brain, reaction of rigidity is almost instant. You have seen it, *Sergent*; so have I. A soldier in the charge, by exam-ple, is drilled through the head by a rifle ball. He staggers on a step or two, per-haps, and then he falls, or it is better to say he topples forward, stiff and straight as though at attention, and hours afterward his poor, dead hands still grasp his musket tightly. But if that same man lies on the earth when he meets death that way, the chances are nine hundred in a thousand that he will twist and writhe, at least in one final spasm, before he stiffens. But certainly. It is for that reason that the condemned one is strapped tight to the cradle of the guillotine. If he were not, the reflex nervous action consequent upon decapitation—which is no more than a sudden injury to the spine, my friends—would surely cause him to roll sidewise on the scaffold floor, and that would rob the execution of its dignity. Yes, it is undoubtlessly so."

"Well, be gob, sor, ye're makin' th' dose harder to take than ever," Costello muttered. "First ye tell us that th' same felly kilt th' both o' them; then ye demonstrate beyant th' shadder o' a doubt that no one livin' could 'a' struck th' blows as kilt 'em. What's th' answer, if anny?"

"Hélas, as yet there is none," de Grandin returned. "Tomorrow, when the funeral has been held, I shall investigate, and probably I shall be wiser when I finish. Until that time we only know that some one for some motive as yet unguessed has done away with son and father, and from the difficult technique of both the murders, I am most confident is was the same assassin who perpetrated them. As for the motive—"

"That's just it, sor," Costello interrupted. "There ain't none."

"Précisément, mon vieux, as I was saying, this seeming absence of motive may prove most helpful to us in our researches. It is better to be lost in the midst of impenetrable night than to be witch-led by will-o'-the-wisps. So in this case. With no false leads, we commence from the beginning—start from scratch, as your athletes say. Yes, it is better so."

"Ye—ye mean to say because there's nayther hide nor hair o' motive, nor rime nor reason to these here killin's, th' case is easier?" Costello demanded.

"You have removed the words from my lips, mon brave."

"Glory be to God—'tisn't Jerry Costello who'd like to see what ye'd be aft-her callin' a har-rd case, then!" the Irishman exclaimed.

The little Frenchman grinned delightedly. "Forgive me if I seem to jerk your leg, my old one," he apologized. "Let us gather here tomorrow at this time, and we shall talk more straightly to the point, for we shall then know what we know not now."

"Be gob, 'tis meself that's hopin' so," Costello responded with none too much optimism in his tone.

A MOTORCADE OF BLACK AND shining limousines was ranked beneath the Lombardy poplars which stood before the Pancoast house. Frock-coated gentlemen and ladies in subdued attire ascended the front steps, late floral deliveries were unostentatiously shunted to the kitchen door and signed for by a black-coated, gray-gloved gentleman. The air in the big drawing-room was heavy with the scent of carnations and tuberoses.

"Good afternoon, Doctor Trowbridge; how are you, Doctor de Grandin?" Coroner Martin, officiating in his private capacity of funeral director, met us in the hall. "There are two seats over by that window," he added in an undertone.

"Take my advice and get them while you can, the air in here is thick enough to choke you."

"*Bien merci*," de Grandin murmured, treading an assortment of outstretched feet as he wove his way between the rows of folding chairs to the vacant seats beside the window. Arrived, he perched on the extreme forward rim of the chair, his silk hat held tenderly with both hands on his knees, his little, round blue eyes fixed unwinkingly upon the twin caskets of polished mahogany, as though he would drag their secrets from them by very force of will.

The funeral rites began. The clergyman, a man in early middle life who liked to think that Beecher's mantle had fallen on him, was more than generous with his words. Unrelated and entirely inapposite excerpts from Scripture were sandwiched between readings from the poets, his voice broke and quavered artistically as he spoke feelingly of "these our dear departed brethren;" when the time came for final prayer I was on the verge of sleep.

"*Capote d'une anguille*," de Grandin murmured angrily, "does he take the good God for a fool? Must he be telling him these poor ones met their deaths by murder? Does *le bon Dieu* not yet know what everyone in Harrisonville already knows by heart? Bid him say 'Amen' and cease, Friend Trowbridge; my neck is breaking; I can no longer bow my head!"

"S-s-s-sh!" I ordered in a venomous whisper, reinforcing my order with a sharp dig of my elbow in his ribs. "Be quiet; you're irreverent!"

"*Mordieu*, I am worse; I am impatient," he breathed in my ear, and raised his head to cast a look of far from friendly import on the praying divine.

"Ah?" I heard him breathe between his teeth. "A-a-ah?" Abruptly he bowed his head again, but I could see his sidelong glance was fixed on some one seated by the farther window.

When the interminable service was at length concluded and the guests had filed out, de Grandin made excuse to stay. The motor cars had left, and only one or two assistants of the mortician remained to set the funeral room in order, but still he lingered in the hall. "This cabinet, my friend," he drew me toward an elaborate piece of furniture finished in vermilion lacquer and gold-leaf, "is it not a thing of beauty? And this"—he pointed to another piece of richly inlaid brass and tortoise-shell—"surely this is a work of art."

I shrugged impatiently. "Do you think it good taste to take inventory of the furniture at such a time?" I asked acidly.

"One wonders how they came here, and when," he answered, ignoring my remark; then, as a servant hurried by with brush and dustpan, "Can you tell me whence these came?" he asked.

The maid, a woman well past middle life, gave him a look which would have withered anyone but Jules de Grandin, but he met her frown with a smile of such frank artlessness that she relented despite herself.

"Yes, sir," she returned. "Mr. Carlin—Mr. Pancoast, sir—God rest him!—brought them home with him when he returned from India. We used to have a ruck of such-like things, but he sold 'most all of 'em; these two are all that's left."

"Indeed, then Monsieur Pancoast was once a traveler?"

"Well, I don't rightly know about that, sir. I only know the talk around the house; you see, I've only been here twenty years, and he came back long before that. It's only what Mrs. Hussy—she used to cook here, and had worked for the family long before I came—it's only what she told me that I know for certain, sir, and even that's just hearsay."

"*Bien*, quite so, *exactement*," he answered thoughtfully and slipped a folded bill into her hand. "And can you by some happy chance tell one where he may find this queen among cooks, this peerless Madame Hussé?"

"Yes, sir, that I can; she's living at the Bellefield Home. She bought an an-uty and—"

"A which?" de Grandin asked.

"An an-uty—a steady income, sir. She bought it when she left service and went to live at the home. She's past eighty years old, and—"

"*Parbleu*, then we must hurry if we wish to speak with her!" de Grandin interrupted with a bow. "I thank you for the information.

"Expect me when I return, my friend," he told me as we reached the street. "I may be early or I may be late; that depends entirely upon this Madame Hussé's powers as a conversationist. At any rate, it would be wiser if you did not wait for me at dinner."

IT WAS FORTUNATE WE did not wait on him, for nine o'clock had struck and dinner was long over when he came bursting in the door, his little round blue eyes alight with excitement, a smile of satisfaction on his lips. "Has the good Costello yet arrived?" he asked as he looked hastily around the study as though he half suspected the great Irishman might be hidden beneath the couch or desk.

"Not yet," I answered, "but—" The ringing of the doorbell cut me short, and the big detective entered. A parenthesis of worry-wrinkles lay between his brows, and the look he gave de Grandin was almost one of appeal.

"Well, Doctor de Grandin, sor," he remarked, brightening as he noted the little Frenchman's expression, "what's in th' news-bag? There's sumpin' up yer sleeve beside yer elbow, I can see it be th' look o' ye."

"You have right, my friend," de Grandin answered. "Did not I tell you that the absence of a motive was a cheerful sign for us? But yes. Attend me!

"At Monsieur Pancoast's late abode this afternoon I chanced to spy two objects of *vertu* the like of which we do not ordinarily find outside of museums.

Jules de Grandin, he has traveled much, and what he knows he knows. The importation of such things is rare, for they are worth their weight in gold and—a thousand pardons if I give offense—Americans as a class are not yet educated to their beauty. Only those who have lived long in the East appreciate them, and few have brought them home. Therefore I asked a most excellently garrulous maidservant who was passing if she could tell me whence they came, and though she knew but little she gave to me the clue for which I searched, for she said first that Monsieur Pancoast brought them from India—which was not so—and that she had heard as much from a former cook, which was indubitably true.

"*Alors*, to Bellefield I did go to interview this Madame Hussé who had once been cook for Monsieur Pancoast, and she did tell me much. *Mais oui*, she told me a very great deal, indeed.

"She told me, by example, that he had studied for the ministry as a young man, and had gone to preach the Gospel in Burma. She had known him from a lad, and much surprised she was when he decided on the missioner's vocation, for he had been a—how do you say? a gay dog?—among the ladies, and such behavior as his and the minister's black coat did not seem to her in harmony.

"*Eh bien*, there is no sinner so benighted he can not see the light if he will but look toward it, and so it was with this one. Young Pancoast assumed the ministry and off he went to battle with the Evil One and teach the heathen to wear clothes.

"Now what transpired in the East she does not know; but that he returned home again and not with empty pockets, she knows full well, for great was the surprise of everyone when the erstwhile poor clergyman returned and set himself up in business. And he did prosper mightily. *Tiens*, it was the wonder of the city how everything he touched seemed transmuted into gold. Yes. And then, though well along in years for marrying, he wedded Mademoiselle Griggsby, whose father was most wealthy and whose social standing was above reproach. By her he had one son, whose name was Harold. Does not an explanation, or at least a theory, jump to your eye?"

"Because he married Griggsby's daughter an' had a son named Harold?" Costello asked with heavy sarcasm. "Well, no sor; I can't say as how me eye is troubled with any explanation jumpin' in it yet awhile."

"*Zut*, it is permissible to be stupid, but you abuse the privilege!" the little Frenchman snapped. "You know something of the East, I take it? Monsieur Kipling has nearly phrased it:

> . . . somewheres East of Suez,
> Where the best is like the worst,
> And there ain't no Ten Commandments—

"Ah? You begin to perceive? In that sun-flogged land of Burma the best *is* like the worst, or becomes so shortly after arrival. The white man's morale—and morals—break down, the saint becomes a sinner overnight. The native men are worse than despicable, the native women—*eh bien*, who suffers hunger in an orchard or dies of thirst amid running brooks, my friends? Yes, strange things happen in the East. The laws of man may be enforced, but those of God are flouted. The man who is respectable at home has no shame in betraying any woman whose skin bears the sun's kiss marks or at turning any shabby deal which lines his purse with gold and takes him home again in affluence. No. *And Pancoast quit the ministry in Burma.* A Latin or a Greek or Anglican priest may not quit his holy orders unless he is ecclesiastically unfrocked, but clergymen of the Protestant sects may lay their office down as lightly as a businessman resigning his position. Pancoast did. He said as much to Madame Hussé when once he had a bursting-out of confidence. Remember, she had known him from a little lad.

"Now, what have you to say?"

"Well, sor," Costello answered slowly, "I know ye're speakin' truth about th' East. I served me time in th' Philippines, an' seen many a man go soft in morals underneath that sun, which ain't so different from th' sun in Burma. I'm afther thinkin', but—"

"There is a friend of Monsieur Pancoast, a boyhood chum, who went in business with him after his return," de Grandin broke in. "By good chance it may be that you know him; his name is Dalky, and he was associated with Pancoast until some ten years since, when they had a quarrel and dissolved their partnership. This Monsieur Dalky, perhaps, can be of ser—"

The strident ringing of the telephone cut through his narrative.

"It's you they want" I told Costello, handing him the instrument.

"Hullo? Sure—been here fer—Howly Mither, is it so? I'll be right over!"

He clashed the monophone into its hooks and turned on us with blazing eyes.

"Gentlemen," he announced, "here's wor-rk fer us, an' no time to delay. Whilst we've been settin' here like three dam' fools, talkin' o' this an' that, there's murther bein' done. 'Tis Missis Pancoast. They got her. Th' Lord help us—they've wiped out the whole family, sors, right beneath our very noses!"

3. The Message on the Card

T HE SERVANT WE HAD talked with after the funeral met us in the hall when we reached the Pancoast home. "No, sir," she answered Costello's inquiries, "I can't tell you much about it. Mrs. Pancoast came back from the cemet'ry in a terrible state—not crying nor taking on, but sort o' all frozen up inside, you know. I didn't hear her speak a word, except once. She'd gone into her bow-duer upstairs and laid down on the couch, and along about four o'clock I thought maybe a cup o' tea might help her some, so I went up with it. She'd got up, and was standing looking at a picture o' Mr. Harold in his uniform that hung on the wall—an almost life-sized portrait it is. Just as I come into the room—I didn't knock, for I didn't want to disturb her if she was sleeping—she said, 'O, my baby; my belovèd baby boy!' Just that and nothing else, sir. No crying or anything, you understand. Then she turned and seen me standing there with the tea, and said, 'Thank you, Jane, put it on the table, please,' and went back and lay down on the couch. She was calm and collected as she always was, but I could see the heart of her was breaking inside her breast, all the same.

"She didn't come down to supper, of course, so I took some toast and eggs up to her. The tea I'd brought earlier was standing stone-cold on the table, sir; she hadn't poured a drop of it. When I went in she thanked me for the supper and had me set it on the table, and I left.

"It was something after nine o'clock, maybe, when the young woman called."

"Eh? A young woman? Do you tell me? This is of interest. Describe her, if you please," de Grandin ordered.

"I can't say as I can, sir," the woman answered. "She wasn't very tall, and she wasn't exactly what you'd call short, either. She was just medium, not tall nor short, thin nor fat. Her hair, as far as I could see, was dark, and her face was rather pale. I guess you'd call her pretty, though there was a sort o' queer, goggle-eyed expression to her that made me think—well, sir, you know how young folks are these days, what with Prohibition and cocktail parties and all—if I'd smelled anything, I'd have said she'd been drinking too much, but there wasn't any odor of alcohol about her, though she did have some kind o' strong, sweet perfume. She asked to see Mrs. Pancoast, and when I said I didn't think she could be seen, she said it was most urgent; that Mrs. Pancoast would surely see her if I'd take her card up. So she handed me a little note in an envelope—not just a visiting-card, sir—and I took it up, though I didn't feel right about doing it.

"Mrs. Pancoast didn't want to be bothered at first; told me to send the young lady away, but when she read what was written on the card her whole manner changed. She seemed all nervous and excited-like, right away, and told me to show the visitor right up.

"They stayed there talking about fifteen minutes, I should judge; then the two of 'em came down, the young lady still blear-eyed and sort o' dazed-looking and Mrs. Pancoast in an awful hurry. She was more excited than I'd ever seen her in all the twenty years I've worked here. It seemed to me like she was all trembly and twitching-like, sir. They got into the taxi, and—"

"Oh ho, there wuz a taxi, wuz there?" Costello interrupted.

"Why, yes, sir; didn't I say the young lady came in a taxi?"

"Ye did not; an' ye're neglecting to tell whether 'twas th' same one she came in that took them off, but—'

"Yes, sir, it was. She kept it waiting, sir."

"Oh, did she, now? I don't suppose ye noted its number?"

"No, sir, I didn't; but—"

"Or what kind it wuz—yellow, blue or—"

"I'm not exactly certain it *was* a taxi, sir, now I come to think of it. It was sort o' dark-colored, and—"

"An' had four wheels wid rubber tires on each o' em, I suppose? Ye're bein' mighty helpful to us, so ye are, I must say. Now git on wid it. What happened next?"

"Nothing happened, sir. They drove off and I went on about my work. First I tidied up the bow-duer and took away the supper tray—Mrs. Pancoast hadn't touched a bite—then I came downstairs and—"

"Howly St. Bridget! *Will* ye be gittin' on wid it?" Costello almost roared. "We'll admit fer th' sake o' argyment that ye done yer duties and done 'em noble, but what we're afther tryin' to find out, if ye'd please be so kind as to tell us, is when ye first found out Mrs. Pancoast had been kilt, and how ye found it out."

The woman's eyes snapped angrily. "I was coming to that," she answered tartly. "I'd come down to the basement to wash the supper things from Mrs. Pancoast's tray, when I heard a ringing at the lower front door—the tradesmen's door, you know. I went to answer it, for Cook had gone, and—oh, Mary, Mother! It was terrible!

"She lay there, gentlemen, head-foremost down the three steps that leads to the gate under the porch stairs, and blood was running all over the steps. I almost fainted, but luckily I remembered to call the coroner to come and take it—her, I mean—away. Oh, I'll never, never be able to go up those service steps again!"

"Ten thousand small and annoying active little blue devils!" de Grandin swore. "Do you tell me they took her away—removed the body before we had a chance to view it?"

"Yes, sir; of course. I knew the proper thing to do was not to touch it—her, I mean—until the coroner had come, so I 'phoned him right away and—"

"Oh, ye did, did ye?" Costello broke in. "I don't suppose ye ever heard that th' city pays policemen to catch those that commits murther? Ye called th' coroner and had him spoil what little clues we might o' found, an'—"

The goaded woman turned on him in fury. "The city may pay police to catch murderers," she blazed, "but if it does it's wasting its money on the likes o' you! Do you know who killed Mr. Carlin? No! Do you know who killed Mr. Harold? No! Will you find out who murdered poor, innocent Mrs. Pancoast? Don't make me laugh! You couldn't catch cold on a rainy day, let alone catch a sneaking murderer like the one which did these killings! You and your talk o' spoiled clues!" She tossed her head disdainfully. "Was I to leave the poor lady's remains laying by her own front door while you looked round for fingerprints and the like o' that? Not for all the police in Harrisonville would I—"

"*Tiens*, my friends, this is interesting, but not instructive. There is little to be gained from calling hard names, and time presses. Had you first notified the police, *Mademoiselle*, you would have rendered apprehension of the miscreants more certain, but as it is we must make the best of what we have to work with. No amount of weeping will restore spilled milk."

To Costello he added: "Let us inspect Madame Pancoast's boudoir. Perhaps we shall find something."

A BRIGHT FIRE BURNED BEHIND the brass fender in the cheerful apartment Maria Pancoast had quit to go to her death an hour earlier; pictures, mostly family portraits, adorned the walls, the windows were gay with bright-figured chintz. A glance at the mahogany table revealed nothing. The gayly painted wastebasket contained only a few stray wisps of crumpled notepaper; the Colonial escritoire which stood between the windows was kept with spinsterish neatness; nothing like a hastily opened note or visiting-card showed on its fresh green blotter.

"*Voilà*, my friends, I think I have it!" de Grandin cried, peering into the bed of glowing coke as he crouched on hands and knees before the fireplace. "It is burned, but—careful, very careful, my friend, a strong breath may destroy it!" He motioned Costello back, took up the brazen fire-tongs and, gently as a chemist might handle an explosive mixture, lifted a tiny curl of crackling gray-black ash from the blue flames. "*Prie Dieu* she wrote in ink!" he muttered as he bore his find to the table and laid it tenderly upon the sheet of clean white paper Costello spread before him.

The parchment shades were stripped from the lamps and at Costello's order Jane, the maid, ran to the dining-room to fetch stronger electric bulbs. Meanwhile de Grandin reached into his waistcoat pocket and took out a pair of delicate steel tweezers and a collapsible-framed jeweler's loop which he inserted in his right eye.

Carefully, almost without breathing, lest the gentle current of air from lips or nostrils destroy the carbonized cardboard, he turned the blackened relic underneath the lens of his glass.

"M—i—s—s— A—l—l," he spelled out slowly, then fell to studying the cone of blackened paper intently again. "No use, my friends, the printing is effaced by the fire beyond that part," he told us. "Now for the message on the card. If she used ink all is well, for the metallic pigment in it will have withstood the heat. If she wrote in pencil—we are luckless, I fear. Let us see."

For several minutes he turned the little cone of ash beneath the lights, then with a shrug of impatience laid it on the paper, and holding one end in a gentle, steady grip with the tweezers, dipped his fingers in a tumbler and let fall a drop of water on the charred pasteboard. The burned paper trembled like a living thing in torture as the liquid touched it, and a tiny crackling rose from it. But after a moment the moisture seemed to spread through the burned fiber, rendering it less brittle. Twice more he repeated the experiment, each time increasing the pressure of his tweezers. At length he succeeded in prying the cone of heat-contorted paper partly open.

"Ah?" he exclaimed exultantly. "It was prepared beforehand. See, she did use ink—thanks be to God!"

Again be studied the charred pasteboard and spelled out slowly: "lp—ho—ban—so—"

"Name of a name; it is plain as any flagpole!" he cried. "In vain is the evidence of crime burned, my friends. We have them, we know the bait by which they lured poor Madame Pancoast to her death! You see?" He turned bright eyes on Costello and me in turn.

"Not I," I answered.

"Nor I," the Irishman confessed.

"Mordieu, must I then teach school to you great stupid-heads?" he asked. "Consider:

"A young woman comes to see poor Madame Pancoast, scarcely four hours after she has laid away all that remained to her of son and husband. Would Madame be likely to see a stranger in such circumstances? Mademoiselle Jane, the maid, thought not, and she was undoubtlessly right. But Madame Pancoast saw this visitor. For why? Because of something written on a card. Now, what could move a woman with a shattered heart to see an unknown visitor—more, to go away with her, seemingly in a fever of impatience? The answer leaps to the eye. Certainly. It is this: Fill in the missing letters of these words, and though they make but fragments of a sentence, they speak to us in trumpet-tones. Four parts of words we have, the first of which is 'lp.' Add two letters to it, and we have 'help.' N'est-ce-pas? But certainly. Perform the same office for the other three and we have this portion of the message: 'help—who—husband—son.' What more is needed? Tonight came one who promised—in writing, grâce à Dieu—to help the stricken wife and mother bring to justice the slayer of her husband and her son! Is it to be wondered that she went with her? Pardieu, though she had known for certainty that the path led to the death she met tonight, she would have gone. Yes.

"Madame Pancoast"—he wheeled and faced a portrait of the murdered woman which hung upon the wall and brought his hand up in salute—"your sacrifice shall not be in vain. Although they know it not, these vile miscreants who lured you to your death have paved the way for Jules de Grandin to seek them out. I swear it!"

To us he ordered peremptorily: "Come, let us go!"

"Where?" Costello and I demanded in chorus.

"To Monsieur Dalky's, of course. I think that he can do us a favor. I know we can do him one, if it be not already too late. *Allez-vous-en!*"

4. The Warning

"No sir, Mr. Dalky's not in," the butler answered de Grandin's impatient inquiry. "He went out about fifteen or twenty minutes ago, and—

"Really, I couldn't say, sir," the man's manner was eloquent of outraged dignity as de Grandin demanded his employer's destination. "Mr. Dalky was not accustomed to tell me where he intended—"

"*Dix mille mousquites*, what do we care of his customs?" the Frenchman cut in. "This is of importance. We must know whither he went at once, right away—"

"I really couldn't say, sir," the butler returned imperturbably, and swung the door to.

"Listen here, young felly," Costello inserted the broad toe of his boot in the rapidly diminishing space between door and jamb and brought his broad shoulder against the panels, "d'ye see this?" He turned back the lapel of his jacket, displaying his badge. "Ye'll tell us where Dalky went, an' tell it quick, or else—"

Statement of the alternative was unnecessary. "I'll ask Mrs. Dalky, sir," the man began, but:

"Ye'll not," Costello denied. "Ye'll take us to her, an' we'll do our own askin', savvy?" The butler led us to the room where Mrs. Dalky sat beneath a reading-lamp conning the current issue of *The New Yorker*.

"A thousand pardons, *Madame*," de Grandin apologized, "but we come in greatest haste to consult Monsieur your husband. It is in relation to the so strange deaths of Monsieur Pancoast and—"

"Mr. Pancoast!" Mrs. Dalky dropped her magazine and her air of slight hauteur at once. "Why, that's what Herbert went to see about."

"Ten thousand crazy monkeys!" de Grandin swore beneath his breath, then, aloud: "When? Where, if you please? It is important!"

"We were sitting here reading," the lady replied, "when the telephone rang. Some one wanted to speak with Mr. Dalky privately, concerning the murder of Mr. Pancoast and his son. It seemed, from what I overheard, that this person had stumbled on the information accidentally and wanted to consult my husband about one or two phases of the case before they went to the police. Mr. Dalky wanted him to come here, but he said they must act at once if they were to catch the murderers, so he would meet my husband at Tunlaw and Emerson Streets in twenty minutes, then they could go directly to police headquarters, and—"

"Your pardon, *Madame*, we must go!" de Grandin almost shouted, and seizing Costello with one hand and me with the other, he fairly dragged us from the room.

"Rush, hasten, fly, my friend!" he bade me. "We have perhaps five little minutes of grace. Let us make the most of it. To those Tunlaw and Emerson Streets, with all celerity, if you please!"

The gleaming, baleful eyes of a city ambulance's red-lensed headlights bore down upon us from the opposite direction as we raced to the designated corner, and the *r-r-r-rang!* of its gong warned traffic from the road. A crowd had already begun to congregate at the curb, staring with hang-jawed wonder at something on the sidewalk.

"Jeez, Sergeant," exclaimed the patrolman who stood guard above the still figure lying on the concrete, "I never seen nothing like it. Talk about puttin' 'em on th' spot! Lookit this!" He put back the improvised shroud covering Dalky's features, and I went sick at the sight. The left side of the man's head, from brow to hair-line, was scooped away, like an apple bitten into, and from the awful, gaping wound flowed mingled blood and brain. "No need for you here, Doc," the officer added to the ambulance surgeon as the vehicle clanged to a halt and the white-jacketed intern elbowed his way through the crowd. "What this pore sucker needs is th' morgue wagon."

"How'd it happen?" Costello asked.

"Well, sir, it was all so sudden I can't rightly tell you," the patrolman answered. "I seen this here bird standin' on th' corner, kind o' lookin' round an' pullin' out his watch every once in a while, like he had a heavy date with some one, when all of a sudden a car comes rushin' round th' corner, goin' like th' hammers o' hell, an' before I knew it, it's swung up that way through Emerson Street, and this pore feller's layin' on th' sidewalk with half his face missin'." He passed a hand meditatively across his hard-shaven chin. "It musta been th' car hit 'im," he added, "though I can't see how it could 'a' cut him up that way, but I'd 'a' swore I seen sumpin sort o' jump out o' th' winder at him as th' automobile dashed past, just th' same. I suppose I'm all wet, but—"

"By no means, *mon vieux*," de Grandin interrupted. "What was it you saw flash from the passing car, if you please?"

"That's hard to say, sir," the officer responded. "I can say what it *looked* like, though."

"*Très bien*. Say on; we are all attention."

"Well, sit, don't think I'm a nut; but it *looked* like a sad-iron hitched onto a length o' clothesline. I'd 'a' swore some one inside th' car flung th' iron out th' winder, mashed th' pore chap in th' face with it, an' yanked it back—all in one motion, like. Course, it couldn't 'a' been, but—"

"What kind o' car wuz it?" demanded Costello.

"Looked like a taxi, sir. One o' them new, shiny black ones with a band o' red an' gold checkers runnin' round the tonneau, you know. It had more speed than any taxi I ever saw, an' it got clear away before I got a good look at it, for I was all taken up with this pore man, but—"

"All right, turn in your report when th' coroner's car comes for him," Costello ordered. "Annything y'ed like to ask, Doctor de Grandin?"

"I think not," the Frenchman answered. "But, if you please, I should like to have you put a guard in Mrs. Dalky's house. In no circumstances is anyone not known to the servants to be allowed to see her, and no telephone calls whatever are to be put through to her. You will do this?"

"H'm, I'll try, sor. If th' lady objects, o' course, there's nothin' we can do, for she's not accused o' crime, an' we can't isolate her that way agin her will; but I'll see what we can do.

"This burns me up," he added dismally. "Here this felly, whoever he is, goes an' pulls another murther off, right while we're lookin' at 'im, ye might say. It's monkeys he's makin' out o' us, nothin' less!"

"By no means," de Grandin denied. "True, he has accomplished his will, but for the purpose of his final apprehension, it is best that he seems to have the game entirely his own way. Our seeming inability to cope with him will make him bold, and boldness is akin to foolishness in a criminal. Consider: We were at fault concerning Monsieur Pancoast's murder; the murder of his son likewise gave us naught to go upon; almost while we watched he lured poor Madame Pancoast from her house and slew her, and as far as he can know, we know no more about the bait he used in her case than we knew of the other killings. Now comes Monsieur Dalky. The game seems all too easy; he thinks that he can kill at will and pass among us unsuspected and unmolested. Assuredly he will try the trick again, and when he does,—*parbleu*, the strongest pitcher comes to grief if it be taken to the well too often! Yes."

"What made ye think that Dalky'd be th' next to go?" Costello asked as we drove slowly through the quiet street to notify the widow.

"A little by-play which I chanced to notice at the funeral this afternoon," de Grandin answered. "It happened that I raised my head while the good clergyman was broadcasting endlessly, and as I did so I perceived a hand reach through the open window and drop a wad of paper at Monsieur Dalky's feet. He did not seem to notice it at first, and when he did he thrust it unread into his waistcoat pocket.

"There I was negligent, I grant you. I should have followed him and asked to see the contents of the note—for a note of some kind it was undoubtlessly. Why else should it have been dropped before him while he was at the funeral of his one-time partner? But I did not follow my intention. Although the incident intrigued me, I had more pressing business to attend to in searching out Monsieur Pancoast's antecedents that we might find some motive for his murder. It was not till I had interviewed Madame Hussé at the Bellefield Home that I learned of the former partnership between Pancoast and Dalky, and even then I did not greatly apprehend the danger to the latter; for though he was associated with the murdered man, he, at least, had never traveled to the East. But when the vengeful one slew Madame Pancoast, who was most surely innocent of any wrong, my fears for Monsieur Dalky were roused, and so we hastened to his house—too late, *hélas*."

We drove in silence a few moments, then: "What we have seen tonight confirms my suspicions almost certainly," he stated.

"Umph!" grunted Costello.

"Precisely, exactly, quite so. The chenay throwing-knife, do you know him?"

"Can't say I do."

"Very good. I do. On more than one occasion I had dodged him, and he requires artful dodging, I assure you. Yes. *Couteau de table du diable*—the devil's table knife—he has been called, and rightly so. Something like the bolo of your Filipinos it is, but with a curved blade, a blade not curved like a saber, but bent lengthwise, the point toward the hilt, so that the steel describes an arc. Sharpened on both edges like a razor—five inches across its widest part, weighted at the handle, it is the weapon of the devil—or of *Dakaits*, who are the foul fiend's half-brothers. They fling it with lightning speed and such force that it will sheer through iron—or one's skull. Then with a thin, tough cord of gut they pull it back again. Yes, it is true. Very well. Such a blade, Friend Trowbridge, hurled at a man's back would cut his spine and also cleave his lower skull. You apprehend me?"

"You mean it was a knife like that—"

"*Précisément.* No less. I did not at first identify it by the wound it made on the poor Pancoasts, but when I saw the so unfortunate Monsieur Dalky's cloven face, my memory bridged the gulf of years and bore me back to Burma—and the throwing-knives. With Pancoast's history in our minds, with these knife wounds to bear it out, the conclusion is obvious. The Oriental mind is flexible, but it is also conservative. Having started on a course of action, it will carry it through without the slightest deviation. I think we shall soon lay this miscreant by the heels, my friends."

"How?" Costello asked.

"Attend me carefully, and you shall see. Jules de Grandin has sworn an oath to poor, dead Madame Pancoast, and Jules de Grandin is no oath-breaker. By no means. No."

THE SHOCK WAS ALMOST more than Mrs. Dalky could bear. Both de Grandin and I were busy for upward of an hour with sedatives and soothing words. Meanwhile her condition simplified the Frenchman's program, for a police-woman who also held a nurse's license was installed beside her bed with orders to turn away all callers, and a plainclothes man was posted in the hall.

"And now, *mon vieux*," de Grandin told the butler, "you will please get me at once the formal coat and waistcoat Monsieur Dalky wore to the Pancoast funeral this afternoon. Hasten; my time is short and my temper shorter!"

Feverishly he turned the dead man's pockets out. In the lower left waistcoat was a tiny wad of crumpled rice-paper, the kind of thin, gray-white stuff which Eastern merchandise is wrapped in. Across it, roughly scrawled in red was the grotesque figure of a pointing man, a queer-looking figure in tight trousers and a conical cap, pointing with clenched fists at a row of smaller figurines. Obviously three of the smaller characters were men, their bifurcated garments proclaimed as much. Two more, judging by the crudely pictured skirts, were women. Two of the male figures had toppled over, the third and the two women stood erect.

"Ha, the implication here is plain. You see it?" de Grandin asked excitedly. "It was a warning, though the poor Dalky knew it not, apparently. Observe"— he tapped the two prone figures with his finger tip—"here lie the Pancoasts, *père et fils*. There, ready for the sacrifice is Madame Pancoast, and here is Monsieur Dalky, the sole remaining man. The last one in the group, the final woman, is who? Who but Madame Dalky, my friends? All, all are designed to die, and two are already dead, according to this drawing. Yes." He glared across the room as though in challenge to an invisible personage. "Ha, Monsieur Murderer, you may propose, but Jules de Grandin will dispose of this case and of you. I damn think I shall take you in your own trap and call your vengeance down on your own head. May Satan serve me stewed with parsley if I do not so!"

5. Allura

"SURE, IT WAS AN elegant job Coroner Martin did on Misther Dalky," Sergeant Costello commented as he stretched his feet to the fire of birch logs crackling on my study hearth and drew appreciatively at the cigar de Grandin gave him. "Were ye mindin' th' way he'd patched th' pore gentleman's face up so y'ed never notice how th' haythen murtherer done 'im in, Doctor Trow-bridge, sor?"

I nodded. "Martin's a clever man at demi-surgery," I answered. "one of the best I've ever seen, and—"

"Excuse me, sor." Nora McGinnis, who is nominally my cook and house-hold factotum, but who actually rules both my house and me with a hand of iron, appeared in the study doorway, "there's a lady in th' consultin'-room askin' to see Doctor de Grandin."

"Me?" the Frenchman asked. "You are sure? I do not practise medicine here; it must be Doctor Trowbridge whom she—"

"Th' divil a bit," Nora contradicted. "Sure, she's askin' fer th' little gentle-man wid light hair an' a waxed mustache, an' Doctor Trowbridge has nayther light nor anny kind o' hair, nor does he wax his mustache."

"You win, *ma belle*, certainly it is I," de Grandin answered with a laugh and rose to follow her.

A moment later he rejoined us, walking softly as a cat, his little round blue eyes alight with excitement. "Trowbridge, Costello, my friends," he whispered almost soundlessly, "come quietly, *comme une souris*, and see who is within. Adhere your ears to the keyhole, my friends, and likewise your eyes; I would that you should hear, as well as see!" He turned and left us and, as quietly as we could, we followed through the passage.

The writing-lamp burned on my office desk, its emerald shade picking out a spot of glowing green in the shadows of the room, and de Grandin moved it deftly so that its light fell full upon the visitor, yet left his face in dusk. At the door between the surgery and consulting-room we paused and watched the tables. Despite myself I started as my eyes rested on the face turned toward the Frenchman.

Devoid of rouge or natural coloring, save for the glowing carmine of the painted lips, the face was pale as death's own self and the texture of the fine white skin seemed more that of a Dresden blond than a brunette, although the hair beneath the modishly small hat was almost basalt-black. The nose was delicate, with slender nostrils that seemed to palpitate above the crimson lips. The face possessed a strange, compelling charm, its ivory pallor enhanced by the shadow of the long, silken lashes that lay against the cheeks, half veiling, half revealing purple eyes which slanted downward at the outer corners, giving the countenance a quaint, pathetic look. "It's she!" I murmured, forgetting that Costello could not understand, since he had never looked on her before. But I recognized her instantly. When first I saw her, she had walked with Harold Pancoast, an hour or less before he met his tragic death.

"It is my uncle, sir," she told de Grandin as we halted at the door. "He suf-fers from an obscure disease he contracted in the Orient years ago. The attacks are more violent at changes of the season—spring and autumn always affect him—and at present he's suffering acutely. We've had several doctors already, but none of them seems to understand the case. Then we heard of you." She folded her slender pale hands in her lap and looked placidly at him, and it seemed to me there was an odd expression in her gaze, like that of a person just aroused and still heavy with sleep, or one suffering from a dose of some narcotic drug.

The little Frenchman twisted the waxed tips of his diminutive blond mustache, obviously much pleased. "How was it they bade you come to me, *Mademoiselle?*" he asked.

"We heard—my uncle heard, that is—that you were a great traveler and had studied in the clinics of the East. He thought if anyone could give him relief it would be you." There was a queer, indefinable quality to her speech, her words were short, close-clipped, and seemed to stand out individually, as though each were the expression of a separate thought, and her semivowels and aspirates seemed insufficiently stressed.

For a long moment de Grandin studied her, and I thought I saw a look of wondering speculation in his face as he gazed directly into her luminous dark-blue eyes. Then: "Very well, *Mademoiselle*, I will come," he assented. "Do but wait a moment while I write out this prescription—" he took a pad of notepaper from the corner of the blotter and drew it towards him.

Crash! The atmosphere seemed shattered by the detonation and the room was plunged in sudden darkness.

I leaped forward, but a sharp, warning hiss from de Grandin stopped me in my tracks, and next instant I felt his little hand against my shoulder, pushing me insistently back to my hiding-place. Hardly had I regained the shelter of the door when the lights in the ceiling chandelier snapped on, flooding the room with brightness. Amazement almost froze me as I looked.

Calm and unmoved as a graven image the girl sat in her chair, her mild, impersonal gaze still fixed on Jules de Grandin. No charge in expression or attitude had taken place, though the desk lamp lay shattered on the floor, its shade and bulbs smashed into a thousand fragments.

"Right away, Mademoiselle," de Grandin remarked, as though he also were unaware of any untoward happening. "Come, let us go."

A long, black taxicab, its tonneau banded with squares of alternate gold and red, stood waiting at the curb before my door. The engine must have been running all the while, for de Grandin and the girl had hardly entered before it was away, traveling at a furious pace.

"Howly Moses, Trowbridge, sor, can't ye tell me what it's all about?" Costello asked as we re-entered the consulting-room and gazed upon the havoc.

"I'm afraid not," I returned, "but it looks as though a twenty-dollar lamp has been ruined, and—" I stopped, gazing at the two white spots upon my green desk-blotter. One was a woman's visiting card, engraved in neat block letters:

MISS ALLURA BATA

The other was a scribbled note from Jules de Grandin:

Friend Trowbridge:
     In vain is the net spread in the sight of any bird, and I am not caught napping by their ruse. I think the murderer suspects I am too hot upon his trail, and has decided to dispose of me; but his chances of success are small. Await me. I shall return.
     J. DE G.

"Lord knows I hope his confidence is justified," I exclaimed fervently. The thought of my little friend entering the lair of the pitiless killer appalled me.

"Wurra, if I'd 'a' known it he'd never gone off wid her unless I went along," Costello added. "He's a good little divil, Doctor Trowbridge, sor, an' if they do 'im injury, I'll—"

"*Merci*, my friend, you are most complimentary," de Grandin's laughing voice came from the doorway. "You did think I had the chance of the sparrow in the cat's mouth, *hein*? *Eh bien*, I fear this sparrow proved a highly indigestible morsel, in that event. Yes.

"If by any chance you should go to a corner, not so far away, my friend, you will find there a taxicab in a most deplorable state of disrepair. It is not healthy for the chauffeur to try conclusions with a tree, however powerful his motor may be. As for that one—" he paused, and there was something more of grimness than merriment in his smile.

"Where is he?" Costello asked. "If he tried any monkey-business—"

"*Tiens*, he surely did," de Grandin interrupted, "but with less success than a monkey would have had, I think. As for his present whereabouts"—he raised his narrow shoulders in an expressive shrug—"let us be charitable and say he is in heaven, although I fear that would be too optimistic. Perhaps I should have waited, but I had but little time to exercise my judgment, and so I acted quickly. I did not like the way he put speed to his motor the moment we had entered it, and as he was increasing the distance between you and me with each turn of his wheels, I acted on an impulse and struck him on the head. I struck him very hard, I fear, and struck him with a blackjack. It seemed to bother him considerably, for he lost control of his wheel immediately and ran into a tree. The vehicle stopped suddenly, but he continued on. The windshield intervened, but he continued on his way. Yes. He was a most unpleasant sight when last I looked at him.

"It took but half my eye," he continued, "to tell me the fellow was a foreigner, an Indian or Burmese. The trap was evidently well oiled, but so was I. *Alors*, I did escape.

"*Eh bien*, they are clever, those ones. It was a taxicab I entered, a new and pretty taxicab with lines of red and gold squares round its tonneau. The wrecked car from which I crawled a few minutes later had no such marks. No. By a device easily controlled from the driver's cab a shutter, varnished black to match the body of the car, could be instantly raised over the red and golden checkers, thus transforming what was patently a taxicab into a sumptuous private limousine. Had I not come back, you might have searched long for the taxi I was last seen in, but your search would have been in vain. It was a taxi, so the maid thought, which bore poor Madame Pancoast to her death, and it was a taxi, according to the officer, from which the death-knife was hurled at Monsieur Dalky, but neither of them could identify it accurately, and if instant chase had been given in either instance, the vehicle could have changed its identity almost while the pursuers watched, and gotten clean away. A clever scheme, *n'est-ce-pas?*"

"Well, sor, I'll be—" began Costello.

"Where's the girl?" I interrupted.

He looked at us with something like wonder in his eyes. "Do you recall how she sat stone-still, and seemed to notice not at all when I hurled your desk-lamp to the floor, and plunged the room in darkness?" he asked irrelevantly. "You saw that, for all she seemed to notice, nothing had happened, and that she took up the conversation where we left off when I turned on the lights again?"

"Yes, but where *is*—"

"*Parbleu*, you have as yet seen nothing, or at the most, but very little," he returned. "Come."

The girl sat calmly on the sofa in the study, her lovely, violet eyes staring with bovine placidity into the fire.

The little Frenchman tiptoed in and took up his position before her. "*Mademoiselle?*" he murmured questioningly.

"Doctor de Grandin?" she asked, turning her odd, almost sightless gaze on him.

"Yes, *Mademoiselle.*"

"I've come to see you about my uncle. He suffers from an obscure disease he contracted in the Orient years ago. The attacks are most violent at changes of the season—spring and autumn always affect him—and at present he is suffering acutely. We've had several doctors already, but none of them seems to understand the case. Then we heard of you."

Sergeant Costello and I looked at her, then at each other in mute astonishment. Obviously unaware that she had seen him before, the girl had stated her errand in the precise words employed in the consulting-room not half an hour earlier.

The Frenchman looked at me above her head and his lips formed a single soundless word: "Morphine."

I regarded him questioningly a moment, and he repeated the silent disyllable, holding his hand beside his leg and going through the motion of making an injection at the same time, then glancing significantly at the girl.

I nodded understandingly at last and went to fetch the drug. She seemed not to be aware of what transpired as I took a fold of skin between my thumb and finger, pinched it lightly, and thrust the needle in.

"We heard—my uncle heard, that is—that you were a great traveler and had studied in the clinics of the East," she was telling de Grandin as I shot the plunger home, and still repeating her message parrotwise, word for word as she had delivered it before, she fell asleep beneath the power of three-quarters of a grain of alkaloid of *somniferum*.

6. The Death-Dealer

"AND NOW, MY EXCELLENT one," de Grandin told Costello as he and I returned from putting the unconscious girl to bed, "I would that you telephone headquarters and have them send us two good men and a *chien de police* without delay. We shall need them, I damn think, and that without much waiting, for the spider will be restless when the fly comes not, and will undoubtlessly be seeking explanations here."

"Be dad, sor, if he comes here lookin' for flies he'll find a flock o' horseflies, an' th' kind that can't be fooled, at that!" Costello answered with a grin as he picked up the 'phone.

"NOW, MES AMIS, YOU can not be too careful," de Grandin warned the two patrolmen who answered Costello's summons. "This is a vicious one we deal with, and a clever one, as well. He thinks no more of murder than you or I consider the extermination of a bothersome gnat, and he is also quick and subtle. Yes. It is late for anyone to call. Should a visitor mount the steps, one of you inquire his business, but let the other keep well hidden and have his pistol ready. At the first hostile move you shoot, and shoot to hit. Remember, he has already killed three men and a defenseless woman. No mercy is deserved by such as he."

The officers nodded understandingly, and we disposed our forces for defense. Costello, de Grandin and I were to join the policemen alternately on the outside watch, relieving each other every hour. The two remaining in the house were to stay in the room where the girl Allura lay in drugged sleep, for the Frenchman had a theory the killer would attempt to find her if he managed to elude the guard outside. "She who was bait for us will now be bait for him," he stated as he concluded arrangements. "Let us proceed, my friends, and remember what I said, let no false notions of the preciousness of life delay your hands—he is troubled with no such scruples, I assure you."

Midnight passed and one o'clock arrived, still no indications of the visitant's approach. Costello had gone to join the outside guard, I lounged and yawned in the armchair by the bed where Allura lay, de Grandin lighted cigarette from cigarette, beat a devil's tattoo on his chair-arm and gazed impatiently at his watch from time to time.

"I'm afraid it's no use, old chap," I told him. "This fellow probably took fright when his messenger and chauffeur failed to return—he's very likely putting as much distance between himself and us as possible this very minute. If—"

Bang! the thunderous detonation drowned my voice as an explosion, almost under our window, shook the air. I leaped to my feet with a cry, but:

"Not the window, my friend—keep away, it is death!" de Grandin warned, seizing me by the arm and dragging me back. "This way—it is safest!"

As we raced downstairs the sharp, staccato discharge of a revolver sounded, followed by a mocking laugh. The Frenchman opened the front door, and dropping to his hands and knees glanced out into the night. Another pistol shot, followed by a cry of pain, sounded from the farther end of the yard; then the deep, ferocious baying of the police dog and a crashing in the rhododendron bushes told us contact of some sort had been made with the enemy.

"D'je get hit, Clancy?" called one of the policemen, charging across the lawn.

"Never mind me, git *him!*" the other cried, and his mate rushed toward the thicket where the savage dog was worrying something. A nightstick flashed twice in the rays of a street lamp, and two dull, heavy thuds told us the locust club struck flesh both times.

"Here he is, Sergeant!" the patrolman called. "Shall I bring 'im in?"

"Sure, let's have a look at him," Costello answered. "Are ye hurt bad, Clancy?"

"Not much, sir," the other answered. "He flang a knife or sumpin at me, but Ludendorff jumped 'im so quick it spoilt his aim. I could do with a bit o' bandage, though."

While Costello and the uninjured policeman dragged the infuriated dog from the unconscious man and prepared to bring him into the house, de Grandin and I assisted Clancy to the surgery. He was bleeding profusely from a long crescent-shaped incised wound in the right shoulder, but the injury was superficial, and a first-aid pack of boric and salicylic acid held in place by a fig-ure-eight bandage quickly reduced the hemorrhage.

"I'll say he's cute, sir," Clancy commented as de Grandin deftly pinned the muslin bandage into place. "We none o' us suspected he was anywheres around—he must 'a' walked on his hands, for he surely didn't make no footsteps we could hear—when all of a sudden we heard sumpin go *bang!* alongside th' house, an' a flare o' fire like a Fourth o' July rocket went up. I yanks out me gun an' fires, like you told us, an' then some one laughs at me, right behind me back, an' sumpin comes whizzin' through th' air like a little airplane an' I feels me shoulder getting numb an' blood a-runnin' down me arm.

"Lucky thing for me old Ludendorff was with me. The son-of-a-gun could make a monkey out o' me, flingin' his contact bomb past me an' drawin' me out in th' open with me back turned to 'im, so's he could fling his knife into me, but he couldn't fool th' dawg. No, sir! He smelt th' feller forty feet away an' made a bee-line for him, draggin' 'im down before you could say Jack Robinson."

The Frenchman nodded. "You were indeed most fortunate," he agreed. "In a few minutes the ambulance will come, and you may go. Meantime—you will?"

"I'm tellin' th' cock-eyed world I will!" Officer Clancy responded as de Grandin moved the brandy bottle and a glass toward him. "Say, Doc, they can cut me up every night o' th' week, if I git this kind o' medicine afterward!"

"*Mon vieux,* your comrade waits in the next room," de Grandin told the other officer. "He is wounded but happy, and I suspect you would like to join him—" he glanced invitingly through the opened door, and as the officer beheld the treatment Clancy was taking for his hurt, he nearly overset the furniture in hasty exit.

"Now, my friends—to business," the Frenchman cried as he closed the sur-gery door on the policemen and turned to eye our prisoner.

I held a bottle of sal volatile under the man's nose, and in a moment a twitching of the nostrils and fluttering of lids told us he was coming round. He clutched both chair-arms and half heaved himself upright, but:

"Slowly my friend; when your time comes to depart, you will not go alone," de Grandin ordered, digging the muzzle of his pistol into the captive's ribs. "Be seated, rest yourself, and give us information which we much desire, if you please."

"Yes, an' remember annything ye say may be used agin ye at yer trial," Costello added officially.

"Pains of a dyspeptic Billy-goat! Must you always spoil things?" de Grandin snapped, but:

"It's quite all right sir, the game seems played, and I appear to have lost," the prisoner interrupted. "What is it you would like to know?"

He was a queer figure, one of the queerest I had ever seen. A greatcoat of plum-colored cloth, collared and cuffed with kolinsky, covered him from throat to knees, and beneath the garment his massive legs, arrayed in light gray trousers, stuck forward woodenly, as though his joints were stiff. He was big, huge; wide of shoulder, deep of chest and almost obscenely gross of abdomen. His head was oversized, even for his great body, and nearly round, with out-jutting, sail-like ears. Somehow, his face reminded me of one of those old Japanese terror-masks, mahogany-colored, mustached with badger hair, and snarling malignantly. A stubble of short, gray hair covered his scalp, the fierce gray mustache above his month was stiff as bristles from a scrubbing-brush, and the smile he turned on Jules de Grandin was frozen cruelty warmed by no slightest touch of human pity, while terrible, malignant keenness lurked in his narrow, onyx-black eyes. A single glance at him convinced me that the ruthless murderer of four innocent people was before us, and that his trail of murder would be ended only with his further inability to kill. He waved a hand, loosely, wagging it from the wrist as though it were attached to his forearm by a well-oiled hinge, and I caught the gleam of a magnificent octagonal emerald—a gem worth an emperor's ransom—on his right forefinger. "What was it you wished to know?" he repeated. Then: "May I smoke?"

The Frenchman nodded assent, but kept the prisoner covered with his weapon until sure he meant to draw nothing more deadly than a silver cigarette case from his pocket.

"Begin at the beginning, if you please, Monsieur," he bade. "We know how you did slay Monsieur Pancoast and his poor son, and how you murdered his defenseless widow, also the poor Monsieur Dalky, but why, we ask to know. For why should four people you had never seen be victims of your lust for killing? Speak quickly; we have not long to wait."

The prisoner smiled, and once again I felt the chills run down my back at sight of the grimace.

"East is East and West is West,
And never the twain shall meet."

he quoted ironically. "I suppose it's no use attempting to make you share my point of view?"

"That depends on what your viewpoint is," de Grandin answered. "You killed them—why?"

"Because they deserved it richly," the other returned calmly. "Listen to this charming little story, if you can spare the time:

"I was born in Mangadone. My father was a chetty—they call them bania in India. A money-lender—usurer—in fine. You know the breed; unsavory lot they are, extracting thirty and forty per cent on loans and keeping whole generations in their debt. Yes, my father was one of them.

"He was Indian by birth, but took up trade in Burma, and flourished at it like the proverbial green bay tree. His ideas for me, though, were different from the usual Indian's. He wanted me to be a *burra sahib*—a 'somebody,' as you say. So when the time came he packed me off to England and college to study Shakespeare and the musical classes, but particularly law and finance. I came back a licensed barrister and with a master's degree in economics.

"But"—again his evil smile moved across his features—"I came back to a desolated home, as well. My father had a daughter by a second wife, a lovely little thing called Mumtaj, meaning moonflower. He cherished her, was rather more fond of her than the average benighted Indian is of his girl-children; and because of the wealth he had amassed, looked forward to a brilliant match for her.

"'Man proposes but God disposes,' it has been said, you know. In this case it was the White Man's God, through one of his accredited ministers, who disposed. In the local American mission was an earnest young *sahib* known as the Reverend Carlin Pancoast, a personable young man who wrestled mightily with Satan, and made astonishing progress at it. My father was liberal-minded; he saw much good in the ways of the *sahiblog*, believing that our ancient customs were outmoded; so it was not difficult to induce him to send my little sister Moonflower to the mission school.

"But though he was progressive, my father still adhered to some of the old ways. For instance, he kept the bulk of his wealth in precious metals and jewels, and much of it in gold and silver currency—this last was necessary in order to have ready cash for borrowers, you see. So it was not very difficult for Pancoast *Thakin* and my sister to lay hands on gold and jewels amounting to three lakhs of rupees—about a hundred thousand dollars—quite a respectable little sum, and virtually every farthing my father had.

"They fled to China, 'cross the bay,' where no one was too inquisitive and British extradition would not reach, except in the larger cities. Then they went inland and to the sea by boat. At Shanghai they parted. It was impossible for a *sahib*, especially an American preacher-*sahib*, to take a black girl home with him as wife. But it was not at all embarrassing for him to take home her father's money, which she had stolen for him, plus my sister's *purchase price*.

"What? Oh, dear me, yes. He sold her. She was 'damaged goods,' of course, but proprietors of the floating brothels that ply the China coasts and rivers aren't over-particular concerning the kind of woman-flesh they buy, provided the price is low enough. So the Reverend Pancoast *Sahib* was rid of an embarrassing incumbrance, and in a little cash to boot by the deal. Shrewd businessmen, these Yankees.

"My father was all for prosecuting in the *sahibs'* way, but I had other plans. A few odd bits of precious metals were dug up here and there—literally dug up, gentlemen, for Mother Earth is Mother India's most common safe deposit vault—and with these we began our business life all over again. I profited by what I'd learned in England, and we prospered from the start. In fifteen years we were far wealthier than when the Reverend Carlin Pancoast eloped with my father's daughter and fortune.

"But as the Chinese say, 'we had lost face'—the memory of the insult put on us by the missionary still rankled, and I began to train myself to wipe it out. From fakirs I learned the arts of hypnotism and jugglery, and from *Dakaits* whom I hired at fabulous prices I acquired perfect skill at handling the throwing-knife. Indeed, there was hardly a *budmash* in all lower Burma more expert in the murderer's trade than I when I had completed my training.

"Then I came here. Before the bloody altar of Durga—you know her as Kali, goddess of the *thags*—I took an oath that Pancoast and all his tribe should perish at my hands, and that everyone who had profited by what he stole from my father should also die.

"And—I can't expect you to appreciate this subtlety—I brought along a very useful tool in addition to my knives. I called her Allura. Not bad, eh? She certainly possesses allure, if nothing else.

"I found her in a London slum, a miserable, undernourished brat without known father and with a gin-soaked female swine for mother. I bought her for thirty shillings, and could have had her for half that, except it pleased me to make sure her dam would drink herself to death, and so I gave her more cash than she had ever seen at one time for the child.

"I almost repented of my bargain at first, for the child, though beautiful according to Western standards, was very meagerly endowed with brains, almost a half-wit, in fact. But afterward I thanked whatever gods may be that it was so.

"Her simplicity adapted her ideally to my plan, and I began to practise systematically to kill what little mind she had, substituting my own will for it. The scheme worked perfectly. Before she had reached her twelfth year she was nothing but a living robot—a mechanism with no mind at all, but perfectly responsive to my lightest wish. With only animal instinct to guide her to the simplest vital acts, she would perform any task I set her to, provided I explained in detail just what she was to do. I've sent her on a five-hundred-mile journey, had her buy a particular article in a particular shop, and return with it, as if she were an intelligent being; then, when the task was done, she lapsed once more into idiocy, for she has become a mere idiot whenever the support of my will is withdrawn.

"It was rare sport to send her to be made love to by Pancoast's cub. The silly moon-calf fell heels over head in love with her at sight, and every day I made her rehearse everything he said—she did it with the fidelity of a gramophone—and told her what to say and do at their next meeting. When I had disposed of his father I had Allura bring the son to a secluded part of the campus and—how is it you say in French, Doctor de Grandin? Ah, yes, there I administered the *coup de grâce*. It was really droll. She didn't even notice when I cut him down, just stood there, looking at the spot where he had stood, and saying, 'Poor Harold; dear Harold; I'm so sorry, dear!'

"She was useful in getting Pancoast's widow out of the house and into my reach, too.

"Dalky I handled on my own, using the telephone in approved American fashion to 'put him on the spot,' as your gangsters so quaintly phrase it.

"Your activities were becoming annoying, though, Doctor de Grandin, so I reluctantly decided to eliminate you. Tell me, how did you suspect my trap? Did Allura fail? She never did before."

"I fear you underestimated my ability to grasp the Oriental viewpoint, my friend." de Grandin answered dryly. "Besides, although it had been burned, I rescued Mademoiselle Allura's card from Madame Pancoast's fire, and read the message on it. That, and the warning we found in Monsieur Dalky's waistcoat pocket—I saw it thrown through the window to him at the Pancoast funeral—these gave me the necessary clues. Now, if you have no more to say, let us be going. The Harrisonville *gendamerie* will be delighted to provide you entertainment, I assure you."

"A final cigarette?" the prisoner asked, selecting one of the long, ivory-tipped paper tubes from his case with nice precision.

"*Mais oui*, of course," de Grandin agreed, and held his flaming lighter forward.

"I fear you *do* underestimate the Oriental mind, after all, de Grandin," the prisoner laughed, and thrust half the cigarette into his mouth, then bit it viciously.

"*Mille diables*, he has tricked us!" the Frenchman cried as a strong odor of peach kernels flooded the atmosphere and the captive lurched forward spasmodically, then fell back in his chair with gaping mouth and staring, death-glazed eyes. "He was clever, that one. All camouflaged within his cigarette he had a sac of hydrocyanic acid. Less than one grain produces almost instant death; he had a least ten times that amount ready for emergency.

"*Eh bien*, my friend," he turned to Costello with a philosophical shrug, "it will save the state the expense of a trial and of electric current to put him to death. Perhaps it is better so. Who knows?"

"What about the girl, Allura?" I asked.

He pondered a moment, then: "I hope he was mistaken," he returned. "If she could be made intelligent by hypnotism, as he said, there is a chance her seeming idiocy may be entirely cured by psychotherapy. It is worth the trial, at all events. Tomorrow we shall begin experiments.

"Meantime, I go."

"Where?" Costello and I asked together.

"Where?" he echoed, as though surprised at our stupidity. "Where but to see if those so thirsty gentlemen of the police have left one drink of brandy in the bottle for Jules de Grandin, *pardieu!*"

The Wolf of Saint Bonnot

T HE HOUSE PARTY WITH which Norval Fleetwood was celebrating the com-
pletion of Twelvetrees, his new country home, was drawing to an inauspi-
cious close. Friday and Saturday had been successful, and more than one
luckless bunny had found his way into the game-bags and thence to the pot-
pie, but with Sunday morning came a let-down that set the guests longing for
the city, the theatre, the night clubs and the comfortable crowded associations
of the workaday world. The day opened with a cold rain, by evening autumn
had capitulated and winter took possession of the world like a rowdy barbarian
sacking a captured city. The guests were weary of each other as shipwrecked
mariners might tire of their companions, and to make bad matters worse the
line that fed electric current to the house went dead. At the same instant that
the radio stopped blaring swing music every light in the house winked out.

Little spurts of flame here and there proclaimed lighted matches, a few candles were found and set alight, and by their feeble glow the host and his guests
settled down to wait a reasonable excuse to say good night to each other.

"Oh, *I* know what let's do!" Mazie Noyer, plump, forty and unbecomingly
flirtatious, cried in the high, thin voice which seems the special property of
short, fat women, "Let's have a séance! This is just the night for it; cold, dark
and spooky. Come on, everybody; I'll be the medium. I can make a dining-table
take a joke any time!"

"*Morbleu*, she states the simple truth," commented Jules de Grandin causti-
cally. "Does she not make the table the butt of her joking three times every day,
to make no mention of her *goûters* between meals? Do not join them, Friend
Trowbridge; he who puts his hands upon the table to evoke the spirits often
rises with burned fingers. Let them have their foolishness alone."

Accordingly, while Fleetwood, his young wife and seven of their guests
trailed into the dining room in the wake of Mazie's provocatively swishing

skirts, we remained before the hall fire where we could watch the dim shapes circled round the table, yet be ourselves unobserved.

The ring was quickly formed. Each member of the party placed his hands flat on the table, thumbs touching, his extended little fingers in light contact with those of his neighbors to right and left.

"I think we ought to sing," suggested Mazie. "Madame Northrop always begins her séances with a hymn. What shall it be?" For a moment there was silence, then in a quavering tremolo she began:

> "Behold the innumerable host
> Of angels clothed in light,
> Behold the spins of the just
> Whose faith is changed to sight . . ."

She ended with a drooping, pleading note, then spoke in a hushed whisper, as though she half believed her own mummery:

"Spirits of the departed, you from before whose eyes the separating veil has been lifted, we are assembled to commune with you, if any of you be present." A short pause, then, "Are there any spirits with us? If so, signify your presence by rapping once upon the table."

Another pause in which the crackling of a burning knot came almost thunderously, then: "Oh, how *nice!* Is it fine or superfine—I mean man or woman. Rap once for a man, twice for a woman, please."

Jules de Grandin's sleek blond head shot forward, every line of his face showing alert attention. Through the dim candlelit dusk we caught the echo of a single sharp incisive knock.

"A man! Who are—I mean who were you?" Mazie's thin voice shook with eagerness. "Where and when did you live? Strike once for A, twice for B, three times for C, and so on."

Another pause, and then a distinct rapping like a knuckle struck against the table. Seven strokes, then nine, then twelve, another twelve, then five, continuing until "*G-i-l-l-e-s G-a-r-n-i-e-r—St. Bonnot—in the reign of King Charles,*" had been laboriously spelled on the resounding wood.

"*Mon Dieu,* 'Gilles Garnier of St. Bonnot,' it says!" de Grandin exclaimed in a rasping whisper. "This is no longer a matter to amuse fools, Friend Trowbridge. We must intervene at once, immediately; right away." He took a step toward the dining room, but paused in midstep, his head thrown back like a dog scenting danger. I, too, felt a chill of nervous excitement—almost terror—run through me, for even as the little Frenchman paused there came from far away a long-drawn ululant howl, rising in a hopelessly prolonged crescendo, sinking to a moan, then rising once again in quavering, disconsolate despair. And as the distant howl died out amid the whistling chorus of the wind, there came an answering call from the darkened dining-room.

It started with a choking, rasping moan, as if one of the sitters at the table gasped for breath, then, as though torn from tortured flesh by torment too great to be sustained, it rose in answer to the distant cry: "Ow-o-o-o-O-O-O!" swelling with increasing stress, then sinking in a hopeless, mourning diminuendo: "OW-O-O-O-O-o-o-oo!"

Strangely, too, the half-reluctant, half-exultant cry was so quickly voiced that it was impossible to place its origin, save to say it emanated from the dining room.

"Nom d'un chat noir, who makes this business of the ape?" de Grandin challenged sharply. "I will not have it!" He burst into the dining room, eyes blazing, small mustache bristling. "Fools, bêtes, dupes, you know not what you do! To mock at them is to invite destruction of—"

He paused, choking with savage anger, and as if to punctuate his tirade the electric current came on again, flooding the big house with sudden brilliance, limning the scene in the dining room like a tableau vivant on the stage. Fleetwood and eight others sat with hands still pressed upon the table, startled, rather foolish expressions on their faces as they blinked owlishly in the sudden deluge of light. Hildegarde, his six-months' bride for whom Twelvetrees had been built, lay cheek-down on the table, her face as pale as carven ivory, her lush red lips slightly parted, as in sleep.

"Good Lord," our host exclaimed, "she's fainted! This fool joke's gone far enough." He glared about the circle at the table. "Who let out that God-awful howl?"

The little Frenchman cast an appraising look at the unconscious girl and a venomous glance at Mazie Noyer. "See to her, Friend Trowbridge, if you please," he ordered with a nod toward Hildegarde, then, to Mazie, "This is your work, Mademoiselle. I trust you are proud of it."

"I?" Miss Noyer was scandalized. "Why, I never dreamed of doing such a thing. I was as surprised as anyone when that inhuman howl started. I think you forget yourself, Dr. de Grandin. You owe me an apology."

"Mille pardons, Mademoiselle," he answered acidly, "whatever my debt is, this is no time for payment. Me, I think an evening of ennui would have been far preferable to your stupid invocation of forces of which you know nothing. We can but pray that no great harm is done." Turning on his heel he left the room without a single backward glance at Mazie, or any offer of apology for his accusation.

Am bringing Hildegarde to town for consultation.
Please see me tomorrow.
Fleetwood.

I passed the telegram to Jules de Grandin and grinned despite myself at his sober expression. "Why so serious?" I asked, helping myself to a fresh serving of griddle cakes and honey. "That sort of thing's been going on since Adam and Eve left the Garden to set up housekeeping. Norval and Hildegarde are excited, of course, but it's only a biological function, after all, and—"

"Ah *bah!*" he cut in "You annoy me, you vex me, you harass me, Friend Trowbridge. You say it is the coming of an heir to Twelvetrees that brings Monsieur and Madame Fleetwood to town. I hope that you are right, but fear you are in error. Would he telegraph if that were all? Would they have to see you right away, immediately, at once about a matter which cannot in the course of nature or respectability be nearer than three months away? I greatly doubt it."

"You're absurd," I told him.

"I hope so sincerely; but we shall eventually see who laughs in whose face, my friend."

In deference to Fleetwood's message I stayed indoors most of the following day, but dinner time came and went without further word from him. "Confound it," I grumbled, glancing irritably at my watch, "I wish they'd come. *King Lear's* playing at the Academy tonight, and I'd like to see it. If they'll only hurry we can get there before the middle of the first act, and—"

"*Eh bein*, be patient, my old one," de Grandin counseled. "Unless I am much more mistaken than I think, we shall soon see a tragedy the like of which Monsieur Shakespeare never dreamed. Indeed, I think the curtain is already rising—" He glanced at the consulting room door expectantly, and as if evoked by his words Norval Fleetwood entered.

"Hildegarde's up at the Passaic Boulevard house," he answered my inquiry as we shook hands. "It's such a wretched night I thought I'd better leave her home, and—" he paused as though the words somehow stuck in his throat, "I thought I'd better see you before you see her, sir."

"Ah?" de Grandin's barely whispered comment had a ring of triumph in it, and I favored him with a black look.

Fleetwood nodded shortly. "I'm almost wild with anxiety about her, Doctor. You remember that fool séance Mazie Noyer got up Sunday night two weeks ago—the night when the lights went out at Twelvetrees? It started right after that."

"A-a-ah?" de Grandin commented.

"What seems to be the trouble?" I asked, casting another withering glance at the small Frenchman.

"I—I'm damned if I know, sir. Hildegarde was restless as a child with fever all that night, and dull and listless as a convalescent all next day. I had to come to town and was delayed considerably getting back, and dinner should have been over an hour when I returned, but she hadn't eaten and said she had no appetite. That's strange for her, she's always been so well and healthy, you know. But"—he looked at me with the sort of serio-comic expression every man uses in such circumstances—"well, you know how they are, sir."

This time it was my turn to gloat, but I forbore to glance at de Grandin, waiting Fleetwood's next word.

"It must have been a little after eleven," he went on, "when out across the cleared land I heard the baying of a hound. Someone in the neighborhood must have a pack of the brutes and let 'em run at night, for I'd heard 'em once or twice earlier in the evening, but not so near or loud. Dr. Trowbridge—" He halted, swallowed once or twice convulsively, and drummed nervously on the edge of the desk, averting his gaze like a shamefaced schoolboy about to make a confession.

"Yes?" I prompted as the silence lengthened embarrassingly.

"You remember that horrible, inhuman howl someone let out in the dining room that Sunday night?"

I nodded.

"It was Hildegarde, sir."

"Nonsense," I objected. "Hildegarde had fainted. She couldn't—"

"Yes, it was she, sir. I know it, because next night when that devilish baying sounded almost under our window she began to roll and toss restlessly, then—then she drew back the bedclothes, rose to her knees and *answered it!*"

"A-a-ah?" de Grandin placed his fingers tip to tip, crossed his knees and regarded the toe of his patent leather evening shoe as though it were a novel sight. "And then, *Monsieur*, what next, if you please?"

"That was only the beginning, sir! I shook her and she seemed to wake, but for an hour or more she lay there fingering the bedclothes, rolling her head on the pillow and moaning piteously in her sleep. Once or twice while she lay in that odd, semiconscious state, that devilish howling sounded again, and each time she shook and trembled as if—"

"Of course," I assented. "It frightened her."

"No, it wasn't like that. It was as if she were all eagerness to get outside— fairly trembling to go, sir."

I stared at him incredulously, but his next words left me fairly breathless. "*Next night she went!*"

"What?" I almost shouted.

Again he nodded. "The howling started during dinner next evening, and Hildegarde dropped her knife and fork and almost went into hysterics. I got a gun from the den to give the beast a dose of birdshot, but when I opened the door there was nothing to be seen. I went clear round the house, and once I thought I caught a glimpse of it—a big, white shaggy brute—but it was so far out of range I didn't even try a shot.

"A little after midnight I woke up with a queer feeling of malaise, and when I looked at her bed she wasn't there. I waited nearly half an hour, then went to look for her. While I was going through the library I heard that damn dog howling again, and when I went to the window I'm hanged if I didn't see her out on the lawn—and a great white fuzzy-looking beast was fawning on her and leaping at her and licking her face! Yes, sir, there she stood in a temperature of thirty degrees with nothing but her nightdress on, fondling and playing with the beast as if it were a pet she'd known all her life!"

"What did you do?" I asked.

"Went out after her," he answered simply. "The ground was pretty hard and hurt my feet, even through my slipper-soles—and she was barefooted!—and I must have looked away once or twice as I picked my way across the lawn, though I tried to keep my eyes on her, for when I reached her the dog was gone and she was standing there with her teeth chattering with chill. I called to her, and she looked— at—me—" the words came slowly, finally halted altogether.

I patted his shoulder gently. "What is it, boy?" I asked.

"She looked at me and *snarled*. You've seen the way a vicious cur curls back its lips when you approach it? That's the way my wife looked at me, Dr. Trowbridge. And down in her throat she made a sort of savage growling noise. I was frightened, I don't mind admitting it, but I kept on, and when I got to her she seemed all right, except for the cold.

"'Dear, what're you doing here?' I asked, and she just looked at me and shook her head, as if she didn't understand a word I said. I picked her up and carried her back to the house, and she fell asleep almost the moment I put her in bed. Next morning she had no recollection of her sleep-walking, and I didn't press her. I didn't hear the dog again that night, either, though I sat up waiting for it with a shotgun till daylight."

"Later?" asked de Grandin softly.

"Yes, sir. Next night, and the next, and every night since then it's howled around the house like a banshee, but though Hildegarde tossed in her sleep and rose to answer it once or twice, she hasn't attempted to go out—not to my knowledge, at any rate."

"Now, Norval," I soothed, "this is all very distressing, but I don't think there's anything to be really alarmed about. The other night when Hildegarde fainted and I was tending her I made a discovery—has she told you?"

"You mean—"

"Just so, boy. Perhaps she isn't aware of it herself, yet, but you've a right to expect someone to be occupying a crib at Twelvetrees before next June. I'm violating no confidences when I tell you more than one patient I've had in similar conditions has been as erratic in behavior as Hildegarde. One lady could not abide the smell of fish, or even their sight. Merely seeing a bowl of goldfish made her violently sick. Another had an inordinate craving for dried herring, the saltier and smellier the better, and in several cases conditions were so bad they simulated real insanity, yet all came out right in the end, bore normal, healthy children and became normal, healthy women again. Zoöphilia—an abnormal love of animals—isn't so rare in such circumstances as you might suppose. I'm sure Hildegarde will be all right, son."

The young husband beamed on me, and to my astonishment de Grandin concurred in my opinion. "Yes, it is so," he assured Norval. "I, too, have seen strange things at times like this. No woman is accountable for anything, however strange it be, which she may do while bearing another life beneath her heart. Friend Trowbridge is undoubtedly correct. At present you have little to fear, but both of us will assist you in every manner possible. You have but to call on us, and I entreat you to do so if anything untoward appears."

"I̶T WAS DECENT OF you to back me up that way," I thanked him as the door closed on Fleetwood. "I was in a perfect sweat for fear you'd spring some sort of occult hocus-pocus on him and scare the poor lad so we'd have two of 'em to treat instead of one."

He regarded me solemnly, tapping the corner of the desk with his forefinger for emphasis. "I played the utterly unmentionable hypocrite," he answered. "No word of what I said did I believe, my friend, for I am more than sure a very evil thing has been let into the world, and that much tears—blood, too, perhaps—must be shed before we drive it back to its appointed place. All you said concerning manic-depressive insanity being present in pregnancy is true, of course, but the history of this case differentiates it from the ordinary. Normal young women may develop morbid love of animals—I have seen them derive keenest pleasure from running their fingers over the smooth backs of pussy-cats or the rugged coats of sheep dogs—but do they respond to wandering beasts' howling in kind, I ask to know? Do they run barefoot into winter weather to fondle wandering brutes; do they greet their husbands with dog-snarls? Such things make a difference, Friend Trowbridge, and as yet I fear we have but seen the prologue to the play—"

The shrilling of the office telephone cut through his disquisition.

"Dr. Trowbridge?" the tortured voice across the wire asked tremulously. "This is Norval—Norval Fleetwood. I just got home. Hildegarde's gone. Nancy, the maid, tells me a dog began to howl outside the house almost as soon as I left to see you, and Hildegarde seemed to go absolutely wild—hysterical—laughing and crying, and shouting some sort of answer to the beast. Then she let out an answering bay and rushed out into the yard. She's not come back, and Nancy's frightened almost into fits. What shall we do?"

"*Mordieu*, so soon?" de Grandin exclaimed as I retailed Norval's message to him. "Bid him wait on us, *mon vieux*, we come at once, right away, immediately!"

"TIENS, MY FRIEND, THEY fish in troubled waters who dabble in spiritualism," he remarked as we drove toward Fleetwood's. "Have I not said so before? But yes."

"Bosh!" I answered testily. "What's spiritism got to do with Hildegarde's disappearance? I suppose you're referring to the séance at Twelvetrees? When some smart Alec answered that dog's bay that night it gave the poor girl a terrific shock. That was all that was needed to set her unbalanced nervous system running wild—she probably wasn't aware of her condition and hadn't taken care of herself, so recurrent depressive insanity had resulted."

"Oh?" he asked sarcastically. "And since when has sanity or any recognized state of aberration connected with pregnancy made the patient sit up in bed and howl like a damned dog—"

"Of course," I interrupted triumphantly. "Norval gave us a typical symptom when he said she snarled at him. You know as well as I that aversion for the husband is one of the commonest incidents of this form of derangement. She's fought it hard as she could, poor child, but it's overmastered her. Now she's ran away. We may have to keep Norval out of her sight till—"

"What of the dog—as we persist in calling it—that follows her and whose howls she responds to? Do you find it convenient to ignore him, or has he slipped from your memory?"

"Rats!" I scoffed. "The country's full of night-prowling dogs, and—"

"And the city also? Dogs that howl beneath ladies' windows the moment their husbands backs are turned?"

"See here," I turned on him, "just what're you driving at? What has the dog to do with the case?"

"Little or nothing—if it is a dog," he answered slowly. "We might dismiss it as a case of Zoöphilia, as you suggested to the young Fleetwood, but—"

"But what? Out with it. What's your idea?"

"Very well. Here is my opinion: The 'dog,' as we have called it, is no dog at all, but a wolf, or rather *loup-garou*, a werewolf who has availed himself of the opportunity given by that *sacré* séance to return—"

I burst out laughing. "You *are* fantastic!"

"Let us hope so. Jules de Grandin fancies himself most excellently, but in this case nothing would please him more than to be proved a superstitious booby."

"YES, SUH," NANCY REPLIED to our questions, "Mis' Hildegarde done scairt me—out o' seven years' growth, a'most. Mistu Norval hadn't hardly turned his back when th' a'mightiest howlin' yuh ever did hear started right underneath th' winder, an' I like to fainted in mah tracks."

"What were you doing at the time?" de Grandin asked.

"Well, suh, it was this-away: We'd come in from th' country, an' Mis' Hildegarde an' me was 'most perished with th' cold. I done git me sumpin hot to drink—jes' a little gin an' lemon, suh—but she didn't want none, though she was shiverin' like a little dog that's been flung in th' river an' ain't dry yet. They—Mis' Hildegarde an' Mistu Norval—had dinner 'bout seven, an' Ah had mine at th' same time, on account o' Mis' Hildegarde wantin' me directly. Pore thing, she ain't been feelin' so pert lately. So, soon's they're finished, Ah gits up to her room an' waits there fo' her. Ah'd helped her out'n her dress and got a black-crepe neglyjay on her when all sudden-like Ah hears th' most awful hollerin' an' yellin', right under th' winder.

"'Does yuh hear that, Nancy?' Mis' Hildegarde asks me.

"'Course, Ah hears it, honey,' Ah tells her. 'Does yuh think Ah's deef?'

"Then she kinder walls up her eyes, like th' pictures of th' saints 'bout to get kilt by th' lions yuh sees, an' starts talkin' real fast-like, 'No, no; Ah won't; Ah won't, Ah tell yuh; Ah won't!' An' then she kinder breaks down an' shivers like she's taken a chill or sumpin, an' sorter turns around to me an' says, 'It's no use, Nancy. He's got me. Tell Mistu Norval Ah love—' an' with that she stops talkin' an' her lips curls back from her teeth an' her eyes goes all glassy, an' she sorter growls in her throat, an' stretches out her fingers like she was fixin' to scratch somebody, an'—jest about that time Ah gits down behind th' sofy, 'cause Ah was powerful scairt she's goin' to jump on me."

"And then?" de Grandin pressed.

"Lawd-a-massy, suh. Then th' trouble did start. She run over to th' winder an' yelled at sumpin out in th' yard, then she took out an' ran downstairs, howlin' an' carryin' on like she was a dawg her own self. 'Deed she did!"

"Can you recall what she said when she looked from the window?"

"Lawd, no suh! Ah don't speak no language 'ceptin' English."

"Think, if you please. Much depends on it. Can not you say what the words sounded like, even though they had no meaning for you?"

"Well, suh, it *sounded* like she said 'jer raven.' Not egg-zackly 'raven', suh, but that's th' nearest Ah can come to it."

"Jer raven; jer raven?" de Grandin muttered musingly. "Jer—*Barbe d'un bouc vert*, I have it! *Je reviens*—I return—I come back!"

"That's jest what she done said!" Nancy agreed. "Jest like ah told yuh, suh."

He cast a swift, triumphant glance at me. "What have you now to say, my old one?"

"Nothing, only—"

"*Très bien.* Say the 'nothing' now and let the 'only' wait. At present we must seek for Madame Hildegarde."

A hurry call was put in to police headquarters, and for upward of three hours we patrolled the cold, deserted streets, but neither sight nor information of Hildegarde could we obtain. At last, cold, discouraged and almost exhausted, we turned back, dreading Norval's tragic eyes when we reported failure.

We paused a moment at the front portico of the house while I spread my lap-robe over the engine-hood. As I turned toward the steps a feeble whimpering moan came to me from the dwarf spruce bordering the porch. A moment later we had parted the evergreens, and de Grandin flashed his pocket torch into the shadow under them.

Hildegarde crouched huddled in an angle of the wall, her flimsy black-crepe negligée in tatters, one black-satin mule hanging to her delicate unstockinged foot by its heel-strap, the other only heaven knew where. Beneath the rents in her diaphanous gown cancelli of deep, angry scratches showed, her feet were bruised and bleeding, and stained with clayey mud above the ankles, other scratches and earth-soil were on her knees and hands and arms, and the nail of every carefully-cared-for finger was grimy with fresh earth and broken to the quick. There were earth-stains on her face and hair, too, as if she might have wiped her countenance and put back the veil of her unbound tresses with muddy hands while she performed some arduous task.

"Good God!" I exclaimed, stooping to gather the all but frozen girl in my arms and bear her up the steps.

De Grandin nodded grimly. "You do the proper thing to call upon the Lord, my friend," he murmured, holding back the door for me. "We shall have need of His help before we finish—and of Jules de Grandin's help, too."

I shook my head despondently as we drove toward my house. "This case is much more serious than I'd thought at first," I confessed.

"Much," de Grandin agreed. "Very damn much, I assure you."

"MORBLEU, MY WORST FEARS are confirmed!" he exclaimed as he perused the Morning Journal next day at breakfast. "Read him, my friend," he thrust the paper at me, "read him and weep!" He pointed to an item in the upper right hand angle of the first page:

GHOULS OPEN GIRL'S GRAVE

Remove Body from Casket,
Steal Lily from Dead Hands
and Leave Remains Uncovered

Police Seek Woman in Black
Who Called at Cemetery Earlier
in Night and Frightened Sexton

Ghouls, working in the silence of St. Rose's R.C. Cemetery, on the Andover Rd. two miles north of Harrisonville, it became known early today, dug up from a freshly-made grave the body of Miss Monica Doyle, 16, daughter of Patrick Doyle, 163 Willow Ave., Harrisonville, who died last Wednesday and was buried yesterday morning.

From the slender hands crossed on the dead girl's breast, clasping a rosary and the stem of a white lily, the ghouls stole the flower and carried it away.

The corpse, with its shroud and burial clothing disordered and torn, was thrown back face down in the casket, and the lid replaced and grave left open.

The crime, with its weird settings and the added mystery of the visit to the cemetery earlier in the night of a strange black-robed woman accompanied by a monstrous white dog, who frightened the sexton, Andrew Fischer, was disclosed early this morning when Ronald Flander, 25, and Jacob Rupert, 31, grave-diggers, going to prepare a grave for an early morning funeral, noticed the fresh earth heaped up by the Doyle girl's violated grave and, going nearer, discovered the unearthed casket and corpse.

Desecration of Miss Doyle's grave forms one of the most remarkable crimes in the annals of New Jersey since the murder of Sarah Humphreys five years ago, the scene of which was the golf links of the Sedgemore Country Club which is slightly more than two miles distant from the cemetery and also abuts on the Andover Rd.

One theory advanced is that a person possessed of religious fanaticism, swayed by the superstition that a lily buried with a body will thrive on the corpse, committed the deed to remove the flower.

The police are now running down scores of clues in an effort to solve the mystery and an arrest is promised within 24 hours.

I finished the grisly account, then stared in wide-eyed horror at the Frenchman. "This *is* terrible—devilish—as you say," I admitted. "Who—"

"*Ah hah*, who asks what overturned the cream-jug when the cat emerges from the *salle à manger* with whitened whiskers?" he shot back. "Come, let us go. There is no time to lose."

"Go? Where?"

"To the cemetery of St. Rose, *parbleu*! Come, quick, make haste, my friend. The police, in pursuit of the score of clues they run down, may already have obliterated that which will be useful to us. *Nous verrons!*"

"D'ye think they'll really make an arrest?"

"God forbid," he shot back. "Come, for heaven's kindly sake, make hurrying, my old one!"

A SMALL EGG-SHAPED STOVE, CRAMMED to capacity with mixed soft coal and coke, heated the little cement-block office of St. Rose's Cemetery to mid-August temperature. Mr. Fischer, a round-faced blue-eyed man in early middle age who looked as if he would have been more at home in a white jacket behind the counter of a delicatessen, nodded us a casual greeting from behind a copy of the *Morgen Zeitung* he was perusing with interest. "From th' newspapers?" he asked. "Can't tell you nothin' more'n you already know. Can't you fellers leave me have a little peace? I'm busy this mornin'—"

"So much is obvious," de Grandin cut in with a quick smile that took the edge from his irony, "but we will take but a moment of your time. Meanwhile, since your minutes are precious, perhaps you would accept a small remuneration—" There was a flash of green and a bank note changed hands with the rapidity of a prestidigitator's card disappearing.

"Sure, what can I do for you gents?" Mr. Fischer asked amiably.

"Can you tell us of the strange lady in black whose appearance has been mentioned in the papers?"

"Sure can. It was about half-past nine or ten o'clock last night when she liked to scared a lung outer me. We close th' main gate at eight an' th' footpath gates at half-past nine, an' I'd just locked th' small gates an' got ready to hit th' sack when I heard 'em flappin' an' banging in th' wind. It was pretty bad last night, you know. I went out to see what th' matter was, an' darned if th' lock hadn't been broke. It was kinder old an' rusty anyhow, but it hadn't ought to of broken in an ordinary wind-storm. I tinkered with it for a while, but couldn't get it fixed, so I went back for a bit o' rope or wire or sumpin to tie it.

"There's a tool shed over th' other side o' the priest lines, an' I thought I'd find what I was lookin' for there. Th' men dumps everything they don't happen to be usin' in it. Well, sir, just as I was cuttin' across to th' shed, who should jump up outer nowhere but a great, long, tall woman with th' biggest, ugliest brute of a dog you ever seen standin' right alongside her. *Gott im Himmel!*"— he dropped his idiomatic American for the language of his forefathers—"was I scared!"

De Grandin flicked a bit of ash from his cigarette. "And you can describe her, perhaps?"

Mr. Fischer considered the question. "I ain't sure. It was so sudden, th' way she bobbed up outer nowhere, an' I don't mind admittin' I was more anxious to run than stand there an' took at her. She was pretty tall, a good head taller'n the average woman, I'd say, an' well, I s'pose you'd call her pretty, too. Kinder thin an' straight, with great long hair all blowin' round her face an' shoulders, dressed in some sort o' black robe with no sleeves, an'—an' kinder—I don't know just how to say it—sorter *devilish*-lookin', you might say."

"Devilish? How?"

"Well, she was smilin' like she was pleased to meet me there—an' even better pleased I was alone, if you get me. It was more like a snarl than a smile, I'd say; kinder pleased an' savage-lookin' at th' same time."

"An' that dog! *Mein Gott!* Big as a calf an' with a long, pointed snout an' great big mouth hangin' open, an' sorter funny, slantin' eyes, like a Chinaman's or sumpin' an' they was flashin' in th' dark like a cat's!"

"U'm, did they move to attack you?"

"No-o, can't say they did, actually. They just stood there, th' dog with one foot raised, like he was ready to jump me, an' th' woman standin' beside him with her hair all blowin' round her an' her hand on th' beast's back—an' *both of 'em growled at me!* So help me, th' dog growled first, an' th' woman did th' same. I din't waste no time gettin' away from *there*, I tell you!"

"And you have no idea whence they came?"

"None whatever."

"Nor where they went thereafter?"

"Not me. I got back here fast as I could, an' locked th' door an' moved th' desk against it!"

"U'm. And may one see the grave of the unfortunate *Mademoiselle* Doyle?"

Racial antipathy flared in Fischer's eyes as de Grandin used the French title, but memory of recent largess and hope of future honoraria was more potent than inherited hatred. "Sure," he agreed with markedly lessened cordiality, and slipped a stained sheepskin reefer over his shoulders. "Come on; this way."

Casket and earth had been replaced in the violated sepulchre, but the raw red earth showed like a bleeding wound against the sod.

De Grandin knelt to take a closer view of the trampled mud about the refilled grave, then rose with a nod. "Now, if you will be so good as to show us where you met the woman and her dog?" he asked.

THE CEMETERY WAS A small one and obviously catered to a far from wealthy clientele. Few graves were properly mounded, and more briars than flowers evidently grew there in summer. Bare and desolate as the better portions of the park were, however, the section set aside for indigents and those who died without the pale was infinitely worse. No turf save weed crab-grass hid the bare red clay from view, the graves were fallen in, and those which sported markers were more pathetic than those unmarked, for mere white-painted boards or stones so crudely carved that any beggar might have scorned to own one were all the monuments. "Right here it was," the superintendent halted in the rutted cinder path.

Once more the Frenchman surveyed the terrain. Sinking to his knees he looked minutely at the red and sticky clay, then rose and with a queer abbreviated stride moved toward the line of leafless Lombardy poplars which served as wind-break by the rear fence of the graveyard.

"Hey, I can't wait no longer!" Fischer called. "See me in my office if you want to ask me anything."

"*Sale caboche*," de Grandin cast a level stare of cold hatred at the sexton's retreating back. "No matter, you have served your purpose; your absence is the best gift you can give us. Quick, Friend Trowbridge, stand before me, if you please."

From his waistcoat pocket he produced a cigarette lighter and set it flaring, and from the pocket of his topcoat drew a short length of candle. "I thought we might have need of this," he explained as he proceeded to melt the grease and pour it carefully into the imprint of a slender shoe which showed in the clay.

"Whatever are you doing?" I demanded, standing before him to shield him from the wind and the glance of any curious passers-by.

He looked up, vacant-faced as a stone image, then gave me a long wink. "Perhaps I do construct a house in which to store your senseless questions, Friend Trowbridge."

As soon as the grease hardened in the footprint he wrapped it in two sheets of thick paper, then proceeded to pace across the graveyard, methodically obliterating every feminine footprint he could find.

As we drove from the cemetery, "Slowly, my friend, slowly, if you please," he bade as he scanned the scrub-pine growing by the roadway. Once or twice at his request I stopped while he made forays into the undergrowth. Finally, when we had consumed the better part of an hour traversing a mile, he returned from an investigative trip with a smile of satisfaction. "*Triomphe!*" he announced, holding his find up for inspection. It was a dainty black-satin bedroom mule, the strap designed to hold it to its wearer's foot torn loose from its stitching at one end, and the whole smeared with sticky red-clay mud.

"And now if you will put me down, I shall be very grateful," he told me as we reached the central part of town.

SOMETHING LIKE AN HOUR later he joined me in the consulting room. "Behold, my friend," he told me. "You ask for evidence; I bring you proof. This"—he carefully unwrapped a parcel and laid its contents on the desk—"is the impression of the dainty footprint I took at the cemetery. This"—from his pocket he produced the satin mule he had salvaged at the roadside—"is what we found upon our homeward trip. And this"—from another pocket he drew the first slipper's satin mate—"is Madame Hildegarde's shoe which I procured from her maid just a little while ago. It is the shoe she wore when you discovered her unconscious by her house. Now, attend me:

"The shoes are identical, save one is broken, one is whole; both are stained with red-clay mud, mud from St. Rose's Cemetery. See, each one fits the impression I took among the graves. *Enfin*, they are not only Madame Hildegarde's, they are the shoes she wore last night when she and the wolf-thing dug up the corpse of Mademoiselle Doyle. She and none other, Friend Trowbridge, was the mysterious 'woman in black,' and her companion was the revenant of Gilles Garnier, the werewolf of Saint Bonnot, which slipped into the world through the door opened by Mademoiselle Noyer at her never-to-be-enough-reprobated séance that Sunday night at Twelvetrees!

"Laugh, snicker, grin like a dog! I tell you it is so! *Plût à Dieu* it were otherwise!"

"I'm not laughing," I denied. "At first I thought that you were at your favorite game of phantom-fighting; but developments in the case have been so strange and dreadful I don't know what to say or think. But tell me—"

"Anything I can," he cut in impetuously, holding out both hands. "What would you know?"

"If Hildegarde's companion really were a werewolf why did they unearth the body of the Doyle girl? I've always heard werewolves attacked the living—"

"Also the dead, my friend. There are different grades among them; some kill dogs and sheep, but fight mankind only when attacked, some are like hyenas and prey on the dead, others—the worst—lust after living human flesh and blood, and quest and kill men, women and children. It may be that the vile Garnier chose the helpless dead as victim of their raid because—"

"*Their* raid?" I echoed. "*Their*—"

"Alas, yes. It is all too true. Poor unfortunate Madame Hildegarde has become even as her conqueror and master, Gilles Garnier. She, too, is *loup-ga-rou*. She, too, is of that multitudinous host not yet made fast in hell. Remember how she cried, 'I will not come!' last night, then told her maid, 'It is no use, he has me?' Also how she charged her *femme de chambre* with a farewell message of love to her husband ere she ran howling forth to join her ghostly master? Remember, too, how her nails were all mud-stained and broken when you found her. Assuredly she had been digging in the grave beside that other one. Yes, *hélas*, it is so."

"Then why didn't they—" I began, but the question stuck in my throat. "Why didn't they—eat—" I stopped again, nauseated.

"Because of what the dead girl's hands clasped, my old and rare. The lily they could steal away and tear to bits—I found the shreds of it embedded in the mud beside the grave, though the police had overlooked it—but the blessèd rosary and the body assoiled with prayer and holy water and incense—ha, *pardieu*, those defied them, and they could do no more then vent their futile, baffled rage upon the corpse and offer it gross insult and cast it back into its casket. No."

He snatched a cigarette from his case and set it aglow with savage energy. "You are acquainted with the so-called 'new psychology' of Freud and Jung, at least you have a working knowledge of it; from it you learn there is no such thing as true forgetfulness. Every gross desire—every hatred, every passion, every lust the conscious, waking mind experienced is indexed and pigeon-holed in the recesses of the subliminal mind. Those whose conscious recollection is free from every vestige of envy, malice, hatred or lust may go to a séance, and there liberate all the repressed—all the 'forgotten'—evil desires they have had since infancy without being anywise aware of it. We know from our study of psychology that fixed immutable laws govern mental processes. There is, by example, the law of similarity which evokes the association of ideas; there is the law of integration which splits mental images into integral fragments, and the law of reintegration which enables the subconscious mind to rearrange these split images into one completed picture of a past event or scene as one fits together the pieces of a jig-saw puzzle.

"Very well. Ten or a dozen people seat themselves in silence round a table, every condition for light hypnosis is present—lack of external distractions of the attention, darkness, a common focusing of thought upon a single objective, that of attracting spirits. In such conditions the sitters may be said to 'pool their consciousness'—the normal inhibitions of the conscious mind are relieved of duty. The sentry sleeps and the fortress gates are open. Conditions for invasion are ideal.

"*Eh bien*, my friend, do not think the enemy is slow to take advantage of his opportunity. By no means. If there be even one person at the séance whose subconscious locks up unholy thoughts—and who has been entirely free from thought-dominance of one of the Seven Deadly Sins throughout his life?—the Powers of Evil have a fifth columnist within the gates. That like attracts like is a dominant law of nature, and the law of similarity is one of the first rules of psychology. The gateway of the *psyche* is thrown open to whoever may enter in.

"Now, in such circumstances who would be the easiest one attacked? Madame Hildegarde is not strong. Her blood stream, her whole system must care for two instead of one, thereby lessening her powers of resistance.

"You ask a sign? Consider what occurred. A rapping announces a man-spirit seeking communication. His name is asked. He answers. *Eh bien*, I shall say so! He gives his great name, for there is little fear that anyone present will recognize him. 'Gilles Garnier who lived at Saint Bonnot in the reign of King Charles,' he brazenly announces himself. Do you perhaps recognize him?" He lifted his brows interrogatively.

"Why, no; never heard of him," I confessed.

"*Bien*. Neither had the others. His name, his nationality, his epoch, all sounded 'romantic' to a circle of fat-headed fools.

"But Jules de Grandin knew him! As you have studied the history of medicine and anaesthesia and the recurrent plagues which have scourged the world, so I have studied the history of those other plagues which destroyed the body or soul, sometimes both together. Listen, I will tell you of Gilles Garnier:

"In 1573 when Charles IX sat on the throne of France there dwelt at Saint Bonnot, near Dôle, a fellow named Gilles Garnier. He was an ill-favored lout, and those who knew him best knew little good of him. The country folk called him 'the hermit,' but the title carried with it no attribute of sanctity. Quite otherwise.

"Midsummer came that fateful year, and with it complaints of dogs and sheep killed, of little children torn to bits along the roadside and beneath the hedges. Three wandering minstrels—all veterans of the wars and stout swordsmen—were set upon as they rode through the wood of Saint Bonnot one night, and one of them was all but killed, though they resisted fiercely. The countryside was terrorized and even men-at-arms preferred to stay at home by night, for a *loup-garou*, or werewolf, the like of which had never been known, had claimed the land for his own from sunset to cock-crow.

"One evening in the autumn when the fields were all but nude of vegetation three laborers hurried to their homes at Chastenoy by a woodland shortcut, and heard the piteous screams of a small girl. They rushed to her aid with their billhooks and in a little clearing in the wood beheld a terrifying sight: With her back to a tree a little shepherdess defended herself as best she could with her shepherd's crook, while before her crowded a monstrous creature which never ceased its devilish baying as it leaped at her. As the rescuers rushed forward the thing fled from them and disappeared into the bracken."

He paused to light another cigarette, then: "In court when there is contrariety in testimony, supposing all witnesses had equal observation, which version would be believed?" he asked.

"Why, that supported by the greatest number of witnesses, I suppose," I answered.

"Very good. That seems logical, does it not? Consider then: Next day when the peasants laid their story before the authorities one swore the child's assailant had a man's body, though covered with hair; the other two declared it had the body of a wolf, light-grey in color, *but with the eyes of a man.*

"Perhaps you will recall that the able Monsieur Fischer told us this morning that the beast that frightened him had 'eyes like a Chinaman'?

"November 14, 1573, a little boy of eight disappeared. The child had last been seen within a cross-bow's shot of the city gates, yet he had vanished as if swallowed up. *Morbleu*, swallowed up is right! Circumstantial evidence involved this so unsaintly hermit Gilles Garnier, and a *sergent de ville* and six arquebusiers went forth to arrest him shortly after noon, November 16. His trial followed quickly.

"It is a curious circumstance, often commented on, that those involved in such crimes seldom denied guilt when put on trial. This Garnier admitted having made a pact with Satan whereby he was given power of transforming himself into a wolf at will, provided he willed it between sunset and cock-crow.

"The *trouveurs* he had attacked appeared against him, and positively identified him by his eyes. So did the little shepherdess whom he had nearly killed. The verdict, of course, was guilty, and the sentence—by the way, can you recall the date Mademoiselle Noyer convoked her séance at Twelvetrees?"

"H'm, let me see—" I made a hasty mental calculation—"why, yes, it was the twenty-sixth of November."

"*Précisément.* And it was on November 26, 1573, that Gilles Garnier, forever after to be known as the Wolf of Saint Bonnot, having been found guilty of the crime of lycanthropy, was dragged for half a mile over a rough road by ropes attached to his ankles, bound to a stake and given to the flames. That was no mere coincidence, my friend. For almost five centuries Gilles Garnier's wicked, earthbound spirit has hovered in the air, invisible and impotent, but raging to do evil. Upon the anniversary of his execution his memory is strongest, for jealousy of life and eagerness to return and raven once again are greatest then. He beats against the portals of our world like the wolf at the doors of *les trois petit cochons* of the nursery story, and where he finds a door weak enough—he *breaks through*. Yes, indubitably. It is so."

"But see here," I objected, "It's all well enough to say he's seized Hildegarde's brain—I shan't dispute that point with you—but how's he able to manifest himself physically? It might have been a vision or a ghost or spectre, whatever you wish to call it, Fischer saw in the cemetery, or that Norval saw sporting with his wife on the lawn at Twelvetrees, but it was no unsubstantial wraith that dug the little Doyle girl from her grave and tossed her poor desecrated body back into its casket. It won't do to say Hildegarde did it. Even granting she had the supernormal strength of the deranged the task would have been physically impossible for her."

"Incomparable Trowbridge!" he cried delightedly. "Always, when it looks darkest, you do show me a light in the blackness. To you Madame Hildegarde and I owe our salvation. No less!"

"There isn't any need to be sarcastic—"

"Sarcastic? *Pour l'amour d'une grenouille verte*, who speaks the sarcasm? You have resolved a most damnably complex problem into a most simple solution. You know—at least, I so inform you—that one of the common phenomena associated with spiritistic séances is the production of light. Numerous mediums have the power of attracting or emitting luminance, and even in small amateur circles where there is in all truth little enough 'light' in the psychic sense, such elemental phenomena are produced. What is this light? Some of it may be true spirit-phenomena, but mostly it is nothing but human mental energy manifested as light waves and given off by the concerted thought of the sitters at the séance.

Sometimes the essence given off is more substantial than mere vibrations capable of being recognized as light. There is unquestioned proof of true materializations at séances. Very well, what makes such materialization possible?

"A spiritual being, whether it be the ghost of one once human or otherwise, possesses passions, but neither body nor parts to make them effective. Some ghosts may show themselves, others may not, and it is the latter which visit séances in hope of materialization. Of themselves they cannot materialize any more than the most skilled bricklayer can construct a house without bricks. *Ha*, but a form of energy is radiated by the sitters at the séance, something definite as radio waves, yet not to be seen or touched or handled. This we call psychoplasm. If enough of it be present, the hovering ghost, spirit or demon can so change its vibrations, so compress it as to render it solid and ponderable. *Enfin*, he builds himself a body.

"Normally the psychoplasm returns to the bodies which gave it off, once its work is done. But suppose the spirit visitor is a larcener—one who so greatly desires once more to live and move and have his being in this world that he will not return that which furnished him a corporeal body? What then? There, my friend, lies the great danger of the séance. It may unwittingly give bodily structure to a discarnate evil entity. So it was undoubtedly in this case. Yes; of course."

"Well, where's the solution of the problem you said I'd furnished?"

"Right here, *pardieu!* I shall reassemble the sitters at the séance and make that thief Gilles Garnier give back what he stole from them. I shall most assuredly do that, and do it right away, this very night."

ALL AFTERNOON HE WAS on the telephone, tracing down the ten who had composed the circle at Twelvetrees. When all had agreed to meet at Fleetwood's town house that evening he rose warily. "Do not wait dinner for me, my friend," he told me sadly. "I would rather lose a finger than forego the little young piglet roasting in the oven, but something more important than young roast pig is involved here. I shall dine at an hotel in New York, *hélas*."

"Why, where are you going?"

"To a booking agency of the theater."

"A theatrical booking agency—"

"But yes. I have said so. Meet me at Monsieur Fleetwood's at ten tonight, if you please. *À bientôt!*"

Half-past nine was sounding on the clock in Fleetwood's drawing-room before he put in his appearance, accompanied by a tall, pale-faced man in poorly fitting evening clothes, a virtuoso's mop of long dark hair and deep-set melancholy eyes. "Prof. Morine, Dr. Trowbridge," de Grandin introduced. "Monsieur Fleetwood, Prof. Morine.

"Professor Morine is a stage hypnotist," he explained in a lower tone. "At present he is without an engagement, but the gentlemen at the theatrical agency recommended him without reserve. His fee tonight will be one hundred dollars. You agree?" He looked inquiringly at Fleetwood.

"If it'll help cure Hildegard it's cheap at twice the price."

"*Bien*. Let us say one hundred and fifty. Remember, the Professor can secure no advertisement from tonight. Moreover, he has promised to forget all which transpires in this house."

"All right, all right," Fleetwood answered petulantly, "let's get started."

"At once. Is all prepared? If you will kindly make excuse to have Madame your wife leave the room for a moment?"

Norval whispered something in Hildegarde's ear, and as they left the apartment together de Grandin addressed the company:

"*Messieurs, Mesdames*, we are assembled here tonight in an endeavor to duplicate conditions which obtained at Twelvetrees when Madame Fleetwood first became indisposed. Upon my honor I assure you no advantage will be taken of you, but it is necessary that you all submit to a state of light hypnosis. I shall stand by and personally see that all goes well. Do you agree?"

One after another of the guests reluctantly agreed until he reached Mazie Noyer. "Indeed, I won't," she answered shortly. "You just want to get me in that man's power to make a fool of me!"

"*Parbleu*, I damn think nature has forestalled us in that!" he muttered, but aloud he replied, "As you wish, *Mademoiselle*. You will excuse us while we perform our work?" With a frigid bow he turned from her and motioned the others to the next room.

All furniture had been taken from the apartment save a large round table and a dozen chairs. About the latter de Grandin traced a pentagram composed of interlaced triangles, and in each of its points he set a tall wax candle, a tiny sharp-pointed dagger with the tip outward, and a small crucifix.

Norval led in Hildegarde, and as the sitters took their places round the table Prof. Morine walked slowly from one to another, stroking each forehead and whispering soothingly. "All right, Doctor," he called softly as he completed the circuit. "What next?"

The Frenchman lighted the candles, murmuring some sort of incantation as each took flame, surveyed the dimly lit room for a moment, then turned to the Professor. "Bid them take orders from me, if you please," he answered.

While Prof. Morine repeated the command, de Grandin drew five shallow silver dishes from beneath the table, poured some thick, dark fluid into each from a prodigious hip-flask, and from another bottle poured some other liquor, dark like the first but thinner and less viscid. As he recorked the second flask I smelled the pleasant heady odor of port wine.

Each of the five dishes he placed outside the angles of the pentagram, then drew two small ecclesiastical censers from beneath the table. "Keep them in motion, my friends," he commanded as he set the powdered incense glowing and handed the Professor and me the thuribles. "Should anything appear in the darkness, swing your censers toward it without ceasing."

Turning from us to the sitters at the table he ordered, "You will concentrate with all your force upon recovering what is yours, *Messieurs, Mesdames.* You will say continuously, 'Gilles Garnier, give back that which you withhold!' Begin!"

The low, insistent monotone began—"Gilles Garnier, give back that which you withhold—Gilles Garnier, give back that which you withhold!"

The ceaseless repetition made me drowsy. I stared about the candlelit room sleepily, wondering when it would stop, and as de Grandin brushed past whispered, "Why'd you bring in this professional hypnotist? You're adept at that kind of thing, why bring in a stranger?"

"*Tiens,*" he whispered back, "there were ten of them to be subjected, counting the so odious Mademoiselle Noyer. To put them all beneath the spell would have exhausted me, and *le bon Dieu* knows I shall require all my strength and freshness. *Ha, regardez,* it comes!"

A feeling of intense cold crept into the air, and the candles flickered as if in a breeze, though the curtains at the windows hung dead-still. From one of the vessels by a star-point there came a strange soft sound, such as a cat makes when it laps milk, and the liquid in the dish showed little ripples, as if disturbed by a dabbling finger—or an invisible tongue. Lower, lower sank the liquor; the bowl was all but empty.

Softly, swiftly de Grandin moved, snatching one after another of the silver vessels, drawing them within the outline of the pentagram.

Again we waited while the mumbled refrain of the sitters dinned in our ears, "Gilles Garnier, give back that which you withhold!" In a far corner of the room a faint and ghastly phosphorescence showed.

It grew brighter and more bright, took shape, took substance—a monstrous, shaggy white wolf crouched in the angle of the wall.

The beast was bigger than a mastiff, bigger than an Irish wolfhound, almost as big as a half-grown heifer, and from its wide mouth lolled a gluttonous red tongue from which a drop of dark-red liquid dripped. But dreadful as the monster's size and aspect were, its eyes were more so. Incongruous as living orbs glaring through the eye-holes of a skull they were; fierce, fiery and malevolent, but *human.*

For a long moment the thing stared at us, then with a vicious growl it got upon its haunches, rose to all four feet, and charged full-tilt at us.

"Accursed of heaven, cast-off of hell, give back that which you withhold!" cried de Grandin, advancing to an angle of the pentagram to meet the charging fury. The Professor and I swung our censers toward the thing, and clouds of incense floated through the still air.

The great beast stopped as if in contact with a solid wall as it reached the outline of the pentagram, gave a choking, savage snarl and retreated gasping from the incense.

"Accursed of heaven, give back that which you withhold!" repeated de Grandin.

The beast eyed him questioningly, lowered itself till its belly scarcely cleared the floor, and circled slowly round the pentagram as if seeking some break in its outline.

"Accursed of heaven, give back that which you withhold!" came the inexorable command once more.

Oddly, the wolf-thing seemed losing substance. Its solidarity seemed dwindling, where a moment before it had been substantial we could now discern the outlines of the room through it, as if it were composed of vapor. It lost its red and white tones and became luminous, like a figure dimly traced in phosphorescent paint on a dark background. The head, the trunk, the limbs and tail became elongated, split off from one another, rose slowly toward the ceiling like little luminous soap bubbles, floated for a moment in midair, then settled slowly toward the group of sitters at the table.

As each luminant globe touched a sitter's head it vanished, not like a bursting bubble, but slowly, like a ponderable substance being sucked in, as milk in a goblet vanishes when imbibed through a straw.

A single tiny pear-shaped globule remained, bouncing aimlessly against the ceiling, bobbing down again, as an imprisoned wasp may make the circuit of a room into which it has inadvertently flown.

"Accursed of heaven, give back that which you withhold!" de Grandin ordered, staring fixedly at the rebounding bubble. "— give back that which—"

"Here, I've stood about enough of this—I want to know what's going on!" Mazie Noyer burst into the room. "If you're doing something mystic I want to—"

"*Pour l'amour de Dieu*, have a care!" de Grandin's appalled shout cut her short. She had walked across an angle of the pentagram, overturning and extinguishing one of the candles as she did so.

"I won't be bullied and insulted any longer, you miserable little French snip!" she announced. "I'll—"

The floating fire-ball fell to the floor as though suddenly transmuted to lead. We could hear the impact as it struck the boards. For a moment it rolled to and fro, then seemed to shrink, compress itself—and took the shape of a tiny white wolf.

Scarcely larger than a mouse it was, but a perfect replica of the great beast which had menaced us a few moments before, even to its implacable savagery.

With a howl hardly louder than a rat-squeak, yet fierce and vicious as a snake's hiss, it dashed across the room, straight at the angle of the pentagram where the candle had been overset.

"*Tenez*, we meet on something like even ground, *Monsieur le Loup-garou!*" de Grandin announced in a tone of satisfaction, seized one of the little sharp-pointed daggers from the floor and impaled the tiny monstrosity on its keen blade.

The minute, savage thing died slowly, writhing horribly. With teeth and claws it fought against the steel that pinned it to the floor, squealing dwarfish parodies of wolf-howls. At last its struggles ceased, it quivered and lay still.

"Oh, you cruel little wretch," Miss Noyer raged at him, "you killed that poor little animal as heartlessly as—"

"As I shall now kill you, *parbleu!*" he finished, grabbing up another dagger from the floor and advancing toward her. "*Sorcière*, witch-woman, ally of hell's dark powers—"

"Ee-eek!" Mazie went as white as tallow under her rouge as she rushed pell-mell from the room, and he turned grinning to me.

"I think that I am glad she fled, Friend Trowbridge," he confided. "To kill a man-wolf is a work of merit; there is neither profit nor entertainment in the killing of a woman-pig."

"Would you actually have stabbed her?" I asked aghast.

He raised his shoulders in a shrug. "Who can say? She would have been no great loss, and the temptation was strong."

"OF COURSE," HE TOLD me in my study some two hours later, "we could neglect no precautions. The pentagram has in all times been esteemed as a guard against the powers of evil; wicked spirits, even the most powerful, are balked by it. In addition I placed in each of its angles a blessèd candle from the church, a crucifix and also a dagger which had been dipped in *eau bénite*. Evil spirits of an elemental nature—those which have never been housed in human flesh—cannot face pointed steel, probably because it concentrates radiations of psychic force from the human body which are destructive to them. In addition I secured from *Monsieur le Curé* who let me have the candles the censers filled with consecrated incense. He was hard to convince, that one, but once I had convinced him that the blessèd articles were needed to combat a dread invader from the other world he went the entire pig, as your droll saying has it. Yes. Incense, you must know, is highly objectionable to wicked spirits, whether they be ghosts of long-dead evil men or ill-disposed neutrarians bent on doing mischief to mankind, whom they hate.

"*Tiens*, I thought the grease was in the fire when that never-enough-to-be-abominated Noyer woman came into the room and overset the guardian candle.

Her natural viciousness and anger made a sad disturbance, she gave the one tiny remaining bit of psychoplasm as yet not reabsorbed the very nourishment it needed to become a ravening, preying, full-sized wolf-thing once more. Had not I killed it to death with the consecrated dagger when I did it might have grown once more to its full stature—and it was already inside the protecting pentagram! *Corbleu*, I do not like to speculate on what might have happened."

"What was in those silver dishes?" I asked.

"Bait," he answered with a grin. "Blood and wine; wine and blood. The mixture of those elements is especially pleasing to the hosts of evil. In the celebration of *le messe noir*—the black Mass where Satan is invoked—the chalice is filled with mingled wine and blood from the cut throat of a sacrificed babe. Therefore, I procured fresh blood from the hospital and fresh wine from the vintner, and set my bait. The werewolf came to drink, but I would not let him lap his fill. No. When he had drank one bowlful I moved the others beyond his reach within the angles of the pentagram, lest he become too powerful for us. One does not nourish one's enemy before the encounter. Oh, no."

He looked at me expectantly, and I responded to the cue. "How'd you like a sip of wine—without blood in it?" I asked.

"Friend Trowbridge," he assured me earnestly, "the suggestion, she is superb!"

The Complete Tales of Jules de Grandin by Seabury Quinn
is collected by Night Shade Books in the following volumes:

The Horror on the Links
The Devil's Rosary
The Dark Angel
A Rival from the Grave
Black Moon